Charles John Huffam Dickens (7 February 1812 – 9 June 1870) was an English writer and social critic. He created some of the world's best-known fictional characters and is regarded by many as the greatest novelist of the Victorian era. His works enjoyed unprecedented popularity during his lifetime, and by the 20th century critics and scholars had recognised him as a literary genius. His novels and short stories are still widely read today.

Born in Portsmouth, Dickens left school to work in a factory when his father was incarcerated in a debtors' prison. Despite his lack of formal education, he edited a weekly journal for 20 years, wrote 15 novels, five novellas, hundreds of short stories and non-fiction articles, lectured and performed readings extensively, was an indefatigable letter writer, and campaigned vigorously for children's rights, education, and other social reforms.

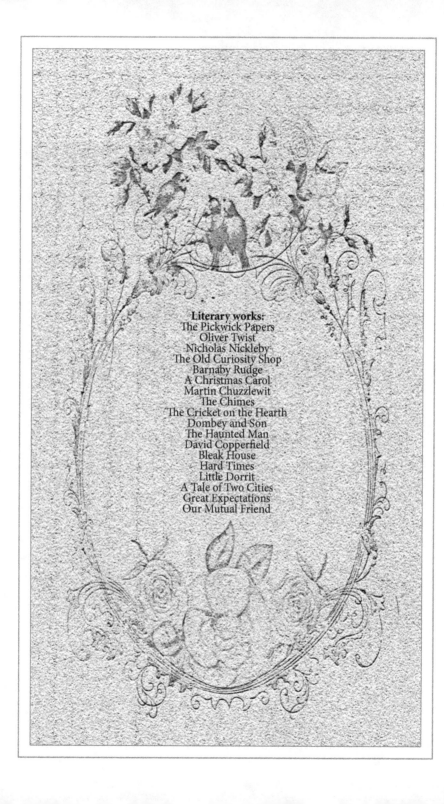

Literary works:
The Pickwick Papers
Oliver Twist
Nicholas Nickleby
The Old Curiosity Shop
Barnaby Rudge
A Christmas Carol
Martin Chuzzlewit
The Chimes
The Cricket on the Hearth
Dombey and Son
The Haunted Man
David Copperfield
Bleak House
Hard Times
Little Dorrit
A Tale of Two Cities
Great Expectations
Our Mutual Friend

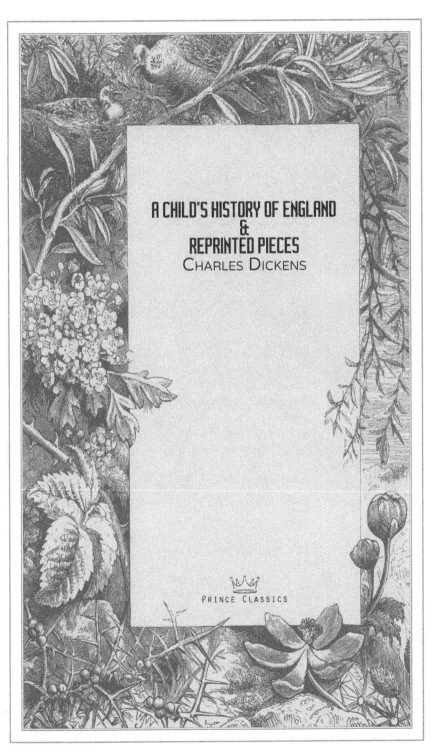

A CHILD'S HISTORY OF ENGLAND
&
REPRINTED PIECES
CHARLES DICKENS

PRINCE CLASSICS

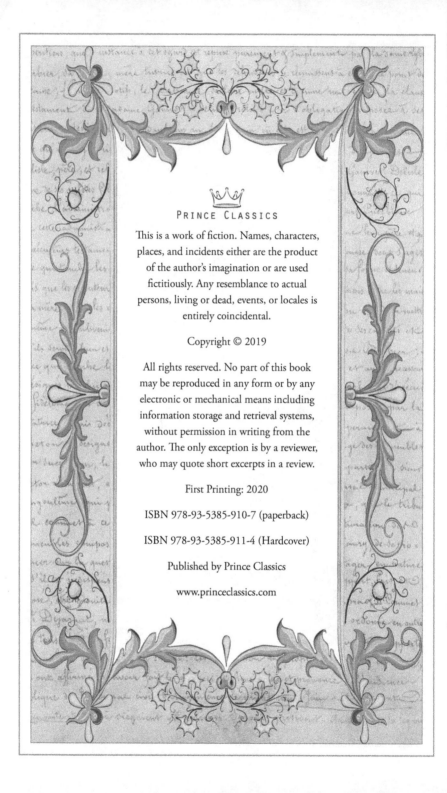

PRINCE CLASSICS

Copyright © 2019

First Printing: 2020

ISBN 978-93-5385-910-7 (paperback)

ISBN 978-93-5385-911-4 (Hardcover)

Published by Prince Classics

www.princeclassics.com

Contents

A CHILD'S HISTORY OF ENGLAND
&
REPRINTED PIECES

A CHILD'S HISTORY OF ENGLAND

CHAPTER I—ANCIENT ENGLAND AND THE ROMANS

If you look at a Map of the World, you will see, in the left-hand upper corner of the Eastern Hemisphere, two Islands lying in the sea. They are England and Scotland, and Ireland. England and Scotland form the greater part of these Islands. Ireland is the next in size. The little neighbouring islands, which are so small upon the Map as to be mere dots, are chiefly little bits of Scotland,—broken off, I dare say, in the course of a great length of time, by the power of the restless water.

In the old days, a long, long while ago, before Our Saviour was born on earth and lay asleep in a manger, these Islands were in the same place, and the stormy sea roared round them, just as it roars now. But the sea was not alive, then, with great ships and brave sailors, sailing to and from all parts of the world. It was very lonely. The Islands lay solitary, in the great expanse of water. The foaming waves dashed against their cliffs, and the bleak winds blew over their forests; but the winds and waves brought no adventurers to land upon the Islands, and the savage Islanders knew nothing of the rest of the world, and the rest of the world knew nothing of them.

It is supposed that the Phœnicians, who were an ancient people, famous for carrying on trade, came in ships to these Islands, and found that they produced tin and lead; both very useful things, as you know, and both produced to this very hour upon the sea-coast. The most celebrated tin mines in Cornwall are, still, close to the sea. One of them, which I have seen, is so close to it that it is hollowed out underneath the ocean; and the miners say, that in stormy weather, when they are at work down in that deep place, they can hear the noise of the waves thundering above their heads. So, the Phœnicians, coasting about the Islands, would come, without much difficulty, to where the tin and lead were.

The Phœnicians traded with the Islanders for these metals, and gave the Islanders some other useful things in exchange. The Islanders were, at first, poor savages, going almost naked, or only dressed in the rough skins of beasts, and staining their bodies, as other savages do, with coloured earths and the juices of plants. But the Phœnicians, sailing over to the opposite coasts of France and Belgium, and saying to the people there, 'We have been to those white cliffs across the water, which you can see in fine weather, and from that country, which is called Britain, we bring this tin and lead,' tempted some of the French and Belgians to come over also. These people settled themselves on the south coast of England, which is now called Kent; and, although they were a rough people too, they taught the savage Britons some useful arts, and improved that part of the Islands. It is probable that other people came over from Spain to Ireland, and settled there.

Thus, by little and little, strangers became mixed with the Islanders, and the savage Britons grew into a wild, bold people; almost savage, still, especially in the interior of the country away from the sea where the foreign settlers seldom went; but hardy, brave, and strong.

The whole country was covered with forests, and swamps. The greater part of it was very misty and cold. There were no roads, no bridges, no streets, no houses that you would think deserving of the name. A town was nothing but a collection of straw-covered huts, hidden in a thick wood, with a ditch all round, and a low wall, made of mud, or the trunks of trees placed one upon another. The people planted little or no corn, but lived upon the flesh of their flocks and cattle. They made no coins, but used metal rings for money. They were clever in basket-work, as savage people often are; and they could make a coarse kind of cloth, and some very bad earthenware. But in building fortresses they were much more clever.

They made boats of basket-work, covered with the skins of animals, but seldom, if ever, ventured far from the shore. They made swords, of copper mixed with tin; but, these swords were of an awkward shape, and so soft that a heavy blow would bend one. They made light shields, short pointed daggers, and spears—which they jerked back after they had thrown them at an enemy, by a long strip of leather fastened to the stem. The butt-end was a rattle, to frighten an enemy's horse. The ancient Britons, being divided into as many as thirty or forty tribes, each commanded by its own little king, were constantly fighting with one another, as savage people usually do; and they always fought with these weapons.

They were very fond of horses. The standard of Kent was the picture of a white horse. They could break them in and manage them wonderfully well. Indeed, the horses (of which they had an abundance, though they were rather small) were so well taught in those days, that they can scarcely be said to have improved since; though the men are so much wiser. They understood, and obeyed, every word of command; and would stand still by themselves, in all the din and noise of battle, while their masters went to fight on foot. The Britons could not have succeeded in their most remarkable art, without the aid of these sensible and trusty animals. The art I mean, is the construction and management of war-chariots or cars, for which they have ever been celebrated in history. Each of the best sort of these chariots, not quite breast high in front, and open at the back, contained one man to drive, and two or three others to fight—all standing up. The horses who drew them were so well trained, that they would tear, at full gallop, over the most stony ways, and even through the woods; dashing down their masters' enemies beneath their hoofs, and cutting them to pieces with the blades of swords, or scythes, which were fastened to the wheels, and stretched out beyond the car on each side, for that cruel purpose. In a moment, while at full speed, the horses would stop, at the driver's command. The men within would leap out, deal blows about them with their swords like hail, leap on the horses, on the pole, spring back into the chariots anyhow; and, as soon as they were safe, the horses tore away again.

The Britons had a strange and terrible religion, called the Religion of the Druids. It seems to have been brought over, in very early times indeed, from the opposite country of France, anciently called Gaul, and to have mixed up the worship of the Serpent, and of the Sun and Moon, with the worship of some of the Heathen Gods and Goddesses. Most of its ceremonies were kept secret by the priests, the Druids, who pretended to be enchanters, and who carried magicians' wands, and wore, each of them, about his neck, what he told the ignorant people was a Serpent's egg in a golden case. But it is certain

13

that the Druidical ceremonies included the sacrifice of human victims, the torture of some suspected criminals, and, on particular occasions, even the burning alive, in immense wicker cages, of a number of men and animals together. The Druid Priests had some kind of veneration for the Oak, and for the mistletoe—the same plant that we hang up in houses at Christmas Time now—when its white berries grew upon the Oak. They met together in dark woods, which they called Sacred Groves; and there they instructed, in their mysterious arts, young men who came to them as pupils, and who sometimes stayed with them as long as twenty years.

These Druids built great Temples and altars, open to the sky, fragments of some of which are yet remaining. Stonehenge, on Salisbury Plain, in Wiltshire, is the most extraordinary of these. Three curious stones, called Kits Coty House, on Bluebell Hill, near Maidstone, in Kent, form another. We know, from examination of the great blocks of which such buildings are made, that they could not have been raised without the aid of some ingenious machines, which are common now, but which the ancient Britons certainly did not use in making their own uncomfortable houses. I should not wonder if the Druids, and their pupils who stayed with them twenty years, knowing more than the rest of the Britons, kept the people out of sight while they made these buildings, and then pretended that they built them by magic. Perhaps they had a hand in the fortresses too; at all events, as they were very powerful, and very much believed in, and as they made and executed the laws, and paid no taxes, I don't wonder that they liked their trade. And, as they persuaded the people the more Druids there were, the better off the people would be, I don't wonder that there were a good many of them. But it is pleasant to think that there are no Druids, now, who go on in that way, and pretend to carry Enchanters' Wands and Serpents' Eggs—and of course there is nothing of the kind, anywhere.

Such was the improved condition of the ancient Britons, fifty-five years before the birth of Our Saviour, when the Romans, under their great General, Julius Cæsar, were masters of all the rest of the known world. Julius Cæsar had then just conquered Gaul; and hearing, in Gaul, a good deal about the opposite Island with the white cliffs, and about the bravery of the Britons who inhabited it—some of whom had been fetched over to help the Gauls in the war against him—he resolved, as he was so near, to come and conquer Britain next.

So, Julius Cæsar came sailing over to this Island of ours, with eighty vessels and twelve thousand men. And he came from the French coast between Calais and Boulogne, 'because thence was the shortest passage into Britain;' just for the same reason as our steam-boats now take the same track, every day. He expected to conquer Britain easily: but it was not such easy work as he supposed—for the bold Britons fought most bravely; and, what with not having his horse-soldiers with him (for they had been driven back by a storm), and what with having some of his vessels dashed to pieces by a high tide after they were drawn ashore, he ran great risk of being totally defeated. However, for once that the bold Britons beat him, he beat them twice; though not so soundly but that he was very glad to accept their proposals of peace, and go away.

But, in the spring of the next year, he came back; this time, with eight hundred vessels and thirty thousand men. The British tribes chose, as their general-in-chief, a Briton, whom the Romans in their Latin language called Cassivellaunus, but whose British name is supposed to have been Caswallon. A brave general he was, and well he and his soldiers fought the Roman army! So well, that whenever in that war the Roman soldiers saw a great cloud of dust, and heard the rattle of the rapid British chariots, they trembled in their hearts. Besides a number of smaller battles, there was a battle fought near Canterbury, in Kent; there was a battle fought near Chertsey, in Surrey; there was a battle fought near a marshy little town in a wood, the capital of that part of Britain which belonged to Cassivellaunus, and which was probably near what is now Saint Albans, in Hertfordshire. However, brave Cassivellaunus had the worst of it, on the whole; though he and his men always fought like lions. As the other British chiefs were jealous of him, and were always quarrelling with him, and with one another, he gave up, and proposed peace. Julius Cæsar was very glad to grant peace easily, and to go away again with all his remaining ships and men. He had expected to find pearls in Britain, and he may have found a few for anything I know; but, at all events, he found delicious oysters, and I am sure he found tough Britons—of whom, I dare say, he made the same complaint as Napoleon Bonaparte the great French

General did, eighteen hundred years afterwards, when he said they were such unreasonable fellows that they never knew when they were beaten. They never did know, I believe, and never will.

Nearly a hundred years passed on, and all that time, there was peace in Britain. The Britons improved their towns and mode of life: became more civilised, travelled, and learnt a great deal from the Gauls and Romans. At last, the Roman Emperor, Claudius, sent Aulus Plautius, a skilful general, with a mighty force, to subdue the Island, and shortly afterwards arrived himself. They did little; and Ostorius Scapula, another general, came. Some of the British Chiefs of Tribes submitted. Others resolved to fight to the death. Of these brave men, the bravest was Caractacus, or Caradoc, who gave battle to the Romans, with his army, among the mountains of North Wales. 'This day,' said he to his soldiers, 'decides the fate of Britain! Your liberty, or your eternal slavery, dates from this hour. Remember your brave ancestors, who drove the great Cæsar himself across the sea!' On hearing these words, his men, with a great shout, rushed upon the Romans. But the strong Roman swords and armour were too much for the weaker British weapons in close conflict. The Britons lost the day. The wife and daughter of the brave Caractacus were taken prisoners; his brothers delivered themselves up; he himself was betrayed into the hands of the Romans by his false and base stepmother: and they carried him, and all his family, in triumph to Rome.

But a great man will be great in misfortune, great in prison, great in chains. His noble air, and dignified endurance of distress, so touched the Roman people who thronged the streets to see him, that he and his family were restored to freedom. No one knows whether his great heart broke, and he died in Rome, or whether he ever returned to his own dear country. English oaks have grown up from acorns, and withered away, when they were hundreds of years old—and other oaks have sprung up in their places, and died too, very aged—since the rest of the history of the brave Caractacus was forgotten.

Still, the Britons would not yield. They rose again and again, and died by thousands, sword in hand. They rose, on every possible occasion. Suetonius, another Roman general, came, and stormed the Island of Anglesey (then called Mona), which was supposed to be sacred, and he burnt the Druids in their own wicker cages, by their own fires. But, even while he was in Britain, with his victorious troops, the Britons rose. Because Boadicea, a British queen, the widow of the King of the Norfolk and Suffolk people, resisted the plundering of her property by the Romans who were settled in England, she was scourged, by order of Catus a Roman officer; and her two daughters were shamefully insulted in her presence, and her husband's relations were made slaves. To avenge this injury, the Britons rose, with all their might and rage. They drove Catus into Gaul; they laid the Roman possessions waste; they forced the Romans out of London, then a poor little town, but a trading place; they hanged, burnt, crucified, and slew by the sword, seventy thousand Romans in a few days. Suetonius strengthened his army, and advanced to give them battle. They strengthened their army, and desperately attacked his, on the field where it was strongly posted. Before the first charge of the Britons was made, Boadicea, in a war-chariot, with her fair hair streaming in the wind, and her injured daughters lying at her feet, drove among the troops, and cried to them for vengeance on their oppressors, the licentious Romans. The Britons fought to the last; but they were vanquished with great slaughter, and the unhappy queen took poison.

Still, the spirit of the Britons was not broken. When Suetonius left the country, they fell upon his troops, and retook the Island of Anglesey. Agricola came, fifteen or twenty years afterwards, and retook it once more, and devoted seven years to subduing the country, especially that part of it which is now called Scotland; but, its people, the Caledonians, resisted him at every inch of ground. They fought the bloodiest battles with him; they killed their very wives and children, to prevent his making prisoners of them; they fell, fighting, in such great numbers that certain hills in Scotland are yet supposed to be vast heaps of stones piled up above their graves. Hadrian came, thirty years afterwards, and still they resisted him. Severus came, nearly a hundred years afterwards, and they worried his great army like dogs, and rejoiced to see them die, by thousands, in the bogs and swamps. Caracalla, the son and successor of Severus, did the most to conquer them, for a time; but not by force of arms. He knew how little that would do. He yielded up a quantity of land to the Caledonians, and gave the Britons the same privileges as the

Romans possessed. There was peace, after this, for seventy years.

Then new enemies arose. They were the Saxons, a fierce, sea-faring people from the countries to the North of the Rhine, the great river of Germany on the banks of which the best grapes grow to make the German wine. They began to come, in pirate ships, to the sea-coast of Gaul and Britain, and to plunder them. They were repulsed by Carausius, a native either of Belgium or of Britain, who was appointed by the Romans to the command, and under whom the Britons first began to fight upon the sea. But, after this time, they renewed their ravages. A few years more, and the Scots (which was then the name for the people of Ireland), and the Picts, a northern people, began to make frequent plundering incursions into the South of Britain. All these attacks were repeated, at intervals, during two hundred years, and through a long succession of Roman Emperors and chiefs; during all which length of time, the Britons rose against the Romans, over and over again. At last, in the days of the Roman Honorius, when the Roman power all over the world was fast declining, and when Rome wanted all her soldiers at home, the Romans abandoned all hope of conquering Britain, and went away. And still, at last, as at first, the Britons rose against them, in their old brave manner; for, a very little while before, they had turned away the Roman magistrates, and declared themselves an independent people.

Five hundred years had passed, since Julius Cæsar's first invasion of the Island, when the Romans departed from it for ever. In the course of that time, although they had been the cause of terrible fighting and bloodshed, they had done much to improve the condition of the Britons. They had made great military roads; they had built forts; they had taught them how to dress, and arm themselves, much better than they had ever known how to do before; they had refined the whole British way of living. Agricola had built a great wall of earth, more than seventy miles long, extending from Newcastle to beyond Carlisle, for the purpose of keeping out the Picts and Scots; Hadrian had strengthened it; Severus, finding it much in want of repair, had built it afresh of stone.

Above all, it was in the Roman time, and by means of Roman ships, that the Christian Religion was first brought into Britain, and its people first taught the great lesson that, to be good in the sight of God, they must love their neighbours as themselves, and do unto others as they would be done by. The Druids declared that it was very wicked to believe in any such thing, and cursed all the people who did believe it, very heartily. But, when the people found that they were none the better for the blessings of the Druids, and none the worse for the curses of the Druids, but, that the sun shone and the rain fell without consulting the Druids at all, they just began to think that the Druids were mere men, and that it signified very little whether they cursed or blessed. After which, the pupils of the Druids fell off greatly in numbers, and the Druids took to other trades.

Thus I have come to the end of the Roman time in England. It is but little that is known of those five hundred years; but some remains of them are still found. Often, when labourers are digging up the ground, to make foundations for houses or churches, they light on rusty money that once belonged to the Romans. Fragments of plates from which they ate, of goblets from which they drank, and of pavement on which they trod, are discovered among the earth that is broken by the plough, or the dust that is crumbled by the gardener's spade. Wells that the Romans sunk, still yield water; roads that the Romans made, form part of our highways. In some old battle-fields, British spear-heads and Roman armour have been found, mingled together in decay, as they fell in the thick pressure of the fight. Traces of Roman camps overgrown with grass, and of mounds that are the burial-places of heaps of Britons, are to be seen in almost all parts of the country. Across the bleak moors of Northumberland, the wall of Severus, overrun with moss and weeds, still stretches, a strong ruin; and the shepherds and their dogs lie sleeping on it in the summer weather. On Salisbury Plain, Stonehenge yet stands: a monument of the earlier time when the Roman name was unknown in Britain, and when the Druids, with their best magic wands, could not have written it in the sands of the wild sea-shore.

CHAPTER II—ANCIENT ENGLAND UNDER THE EARLY SAXONS

The Romans had scarcely gone away from Britain, when the Britons began to wish they had never left it. For, the Romans being gone, and the Britons being much reduced in numbers by their long wars, the Picts and Scots came pouring in, over the broken and unguarded wall of Severus, in swarms. They plundered the richest towns, and killed the people; and came back so often for more booty and more slaughter, that the unfortunate Britons lived a life of terror. As if the Picts and Scots were not bad enough on land, the Saxons attacked the islanders by sea; and, as if something more were still wanting to make them miserable, they quarrelled bitterly among themselves as to what prayers they ought to say, and how they ought to say them. The priests, being very angry with one another on these questions, cursed one another in the heartiest manner; and (uncommonly like the old Druids) cursed all the people whom they could not persuade. So, altogether, the Britons were very badly off, you may believe.

They were in such distress, in short, that they sent a letter to Rome entreating help—which they called the Groans of the Britons; and in which they said, 'The barbarians chase us into the sea, the sea throws us back upon the barbarians, and we have only the hard choice left us of perishing by the sword, or perishing by the waves.' But, the Romans could not help them, even if they were so inclined; for they had enough to do to defend themselves against their own enemies, who were then very fierce and strong. At last, the Britons, unable to bear their hard condition any longer, resolved to make peace with the Saxons, and to invite the Saxons to come into their country, and help them to keep out the Picts and Scots.

It was a British Prince named Vortigern who took this resolution, and who made a treaty of friendship with Hengist and Horsa, two Saxon chiefs. Both of these names, in the old Saxon language, signify Horse; for the Saxons, like many other nations in a rough state, were fond of giving men the names of animals, as Horse, Wolf, Bear, Hound. The Indians of North America,—a very inferior people to the Saxons, though—do the same to this day.

Hengist and Horsa drove out the Picts and Scots; and Vortigern, being grateful to them for that service, made no opposition to their settling themselves in that part of England which is called the Isle of Thanet, or to their inviting over more of their countrymen to join them. But Hengist had a beautiful daughter named Rowena; and when, at a feast, she filled a golden goblet to the brim with wine, and gave it to Vortigern, saying in a sweet voice, 'Dear King, thy health!' the King fell in love with her. My opinion is, that the cunning Hengist meant him to do so, in order that the Saxons might have greater influence with him; and that the fair Rowena came to that feast, golden goblet and all, on purpose.

At any rate, they were married; and, long afterwards, whenever the King was angry with the Saxons, or jealous of their encroachments, Rowena would put her beautiful arms round his neck, and softly say, 'Dear King, they are my people! Be favourable to them, as you loved that Saxon girl who gave you the golden goblet of wine at the feast!' And, really, I don't see how the King could help himself.

Ah! We must all die! In the course of years, Vortigern died—he was dethroned, and put in prison, first, I am afraid; and Rowena died; and generations of Saxons and Britons died; and events that happened during a long, long time, would have been quite forgotten but for the tales and songs of the old Bards, who used to go about from feast to feast, with their white beards, recounting the deeds of their forefathers. Among the histories of which they sang and talked, there was a famous one, concerning the bravery and virtues of King Arthur, supposed to have been a British Prince in those old times. But, whether such a person really lived, or whether there were several persons whose histories came to be confused together under that one name, or whether all about him was invention, no one knows.

I will tell you, shortly, what is most interesting in the early Saxon times, as they are described in these songs and stories of the Bards.

In, and long after, the days of Vortigern, fresh bodies of Saxons, under various chiefs, came pouring into Britain. One body, conquering the Britons in the East, and settling there, called their kingdom Essex; another body settled in the West, and called their kingdom Wessex; the Northfolk, or Norfolk people, established themselves in one place; the Southfolk, or Suffolk people, established themselves in another; and gradually seven kingdoms or states arose in England, which were called the Saxon Heptarchy. The poor Britons, falling back before these crowds of fighting men whom they had innocently invited over as friends, retired into Wales and the adjacent country; into Devonshire, and into Cornwall. Those parts of England long remained unconquered. And in Cornwall now—where the sea-coast is very gloomy, steep, and rugged—where, in the dark winter-time, ships have often been wrecked close to the land, and every soul on board has perished—where the winds and waves howl drearily and split the solid rocks into arches and caverns—there are very ancient ruins, which the people call the ruins of King Arthur's Castle.

Kent is the most famous of the seven Saxon kingdoms, because the Christian religion was preached to the Saxons there (who domineered over the Britons too much, to care for what they said about their religion, or anything else) by Augustine, a monk from Rome. King Ethelbert, of Kent, was soon converted; and the moment he said he was a Christian, his courtiers all said they were Christians; after which, ten thousand of his subjects said they were Christians too. Augustine built a little church, close to this King's palace, on the ground now occupied by the beautiful cathedral of Canterbury. Sebert, the King's nephew, built on a muddy marshy place near London, where there had been a temple to Apollo, a church dedicated to Saint Peter, which is now Westminster Abbey. And, in London itself, on the foundation of a temple to Diana, he built another little church which has risen up, since that old time, to be Saint Paul's.

After the death of Ethelbert, Edwin, King of Northumbria, who was such a good king that it was said a woman or child might openly carry a purse of gold, in his reign, without fear, allowed his child to be baptised, and held a great council to consider whether he and his people should all be Christians or not. It was decided that they should be. Coifi, the chief priest of the old religion, made a great speech on the occasion. In this discourse, he told the people that he had found out the old gods to be impostors. 'I am quite satisfied of it,' he said. 'Look at me! I have been serving them all my life, and they have done nothing for me; whereas, if they had been really powerful, they could not have decently done less, in return for all I have done for them, than make my fortune. As they have never made my fortune, I am quite convinced they are impostors!' When this singular priest had finished speaking, he hastily armed himself with sword and lance, mounted a war-horse, rode at a furious gallop in sight of all the people to the temple, and flung his lance against it as an insult. From that time, the Christian religion spread itself among the Saxons, and became their faith.

The next very famous prince was Egbert. He lived about a hundred and fifty years afterwards, and claimed to have a better right to the throne of Wessex than Beortric, another Saxon prince who was at the head of that kingdom, and who married Edburga, the daughter of Offa, king of another of the seven kingdoms. This Queen Edburga was a handsome murderess, who poisoned people when they offended her. One day, she mixed a cup of poison for a certain noble belonging to the court; but her husband drank of it too, by mistake, and died. Upon this, the people revolted, in great crowds; and running to the palace, and thundering at the gates, cried, 'Down with the wicked queen, who poisons men!' They drove her out of the country, and abolished the title she had disgraced. When years had passed away, some travellers came home from Italy, and said that in the town of Pavia they had seen a ragged beggar-woman, who had once been handsome, but was then shrivelled, bent, and yellow, wandering about the streets, crying for bread; and that this beggar-woman was the poisoning English queen. It was, indeed, Edburga; and so she died, without a shelter for her wretched head.

Egbert, not considering himself safe in England, in consequence of his having claimed the crown of Wessex (for he thought his rival might take him prisoner and put him to death), sought refuge at the court of Charlemagne, King of France. On the death of Beortric, so unhappily poisoned by mistake, Egbert came back to Britain; succeeded to the throne of Wessex; conquered some of the other monarchs of the seven kingdoms; added their territories to his own; and, for the first time, called the country over which he ruled,

England.

And now, new enemies arose, who, for a long time, troubled England sorely. These were the Northmen, the people of Denmark and Norway, whom the English called the Danes. They were a warlike people, quite at home upon the sea; not Christians; very daring and cruel. They came over in ships, and plundered and burned wheresoever they landed. Once, they beat Egbert in battle. Once, Egbert beat them. But, they cared no more for being beaten than the English themselves. In the four following short reigns, of Ethelwulf, and his sons, Ethelbald, Ethelbert, and Ethelred, they came back, over and over again, burning and plundering, and laying England waste. In the last-mentioned reign, they seized Edmund, King of East England, and bound him to a tree. Then, they proposed to him that he should change his religion; but he, being a good Christian, steadily refused. Upon that, they beat him, made cowardly jests upon him, all defenceless as he was, shot arrows at him, and, finally, struck off his head. It is impossible to say whose head they might have struck off next, but for the death of King Ethelred from a wound he had received in fighting against them, and the succession to his throne of the best and wisest king that ever lived in England.

CHAPTER III—ENGLAND UNDER THE GOOD SAXON, ALFRED

Alfred the Great was a young man, three-and-twenty years of age, when he became king. Twice in his childhood, he had been taken to Rome, where the Saxon nobles were in the habit of going on journeys which they supposed to be religious; and, once, he had stayed for some time in Paris. Learning, however, was so little cared for, then, that at twelve years old he had not been taught to read; although, of the sons of King Ethelwulf, he, the youngest, was the favourite. But he had—as most men who grow up to be great and good are generally found to have had—an excellent mother; and, one day, this lady, whose name was Osburga, happened, as she was sitting among her sons, to read a book of Saxon poetry. The art of printing was not known until long and long after that period, and the book, which was written, was what is called 'illuminated,' with beautiful bright letters, richly painted. The brothers admiring it very much, their mother said, 'I will give it to that one of you four princes who first learns to read.' Alfred sought out a tutor that very day, applied himself to learn with great diligence, and soon won the book. He was proud of it, all his life.

This great king, in the first year of his reign, fought nine battles with the Danes. He made some treaties with them too, by which the false Danes swore they would quit the country. They pretended to consider that they had taken a very solemn oath, in swearing this upon the holy bracelets that they wore, and which were always buried with them when they died; but they cared little for it, for they thought nothing of breaking oaths and treaties too, as soon as it suited their purpose, and coming back again to fight, plunder, and burn, as usual. One fatal winter, in the fourth year of King Alfred's reign, they spread themselves in great numbers over the whole of England; and so dispersed and routed the King's soldiers that the King was left alone, and was obliged to disguise himself as a common peasant, and to take refuge in the cottage of one of his cowherds who did not know his face.

Here, King Alfred, while the Danes sought him far and near, was left alone one day, by the cowherd's wife, to watch some cakes which she put to bake upon the hearth. But, being at work upon his bow and arrows, with which he hoped to punish the false Danes when a brighter time should come, and thinking deeply of his poor unhappy subjects whom the Danes chased through the land, his noble mind forgot the cakes, and they were burnt. 'What!' said the cowherd's wife, who scolded him well when she came back, and little thought she was scolding the King, 'you will be ready enough to eat them by-and-by, and yet you cannot watch them, idle dog?'

At length, the Devonshire men made head against a new host of Danes who landed on their coast; killed their chief, and captured their flag; on which was represented the likeness of a Raven—a very fit bird for a thievish army like that, I think. The loss of their standard troubled the Danes greatly, for they believed it to be enchanted—woven by the three daughters of one father in a single afternoon—and they had a story among themselves that when they were victorious in battle, the Raven stretched his wings and seemed to fly; and that when they were defeated, he would droop. He had good reason to droop, now, if he could have done anything half so sensible; for, King Alfred joined the Devonshire men; made a camp with them on a piece of firm ground in the midst of a bog in Somersetshire; and prepared for a great attempt for vengeance on the Danes, and the deliverance of his oppressed people.

But, first, as it was important to know how numerous those pestilent Danes were, and how they were fortified, King Alfred, being a good musician, disguised himself as a glee-man or minstrel, and went, with his harp, to the Danish camp. He played and sang in the very tent of Guthrum the Danish leader, and entertained the Danes as they caroused. While he seemed to think of nothing but his music, he was watchful of their tents, their arms, their discipline, everything that he desired to know. And right soon did this great king entertain them to a different tune; for, summoning all his true followers to meet him at an appointed place, where they received him with joyful shouts and tears, as the monarch whom many of them had given up for lost or dead, he put himself at their head, marched on the Danish camp, defeated the Danes with great slaughter, and besieged them for fourteen days to prevent their escape. But, being as merciful as he was good and brave, he then, instead of killing them, proposed peace: on condition that they should altogether depart from that Western part of England, and settle in the East; and that Guthrum should become a Christian, in remembrance of the Divine religion which now taught his conqueror, the noble Alfred, to forgive the enemy who had so often injured him. This, Guthrum did. At his baptism, King Alfred was his godfather. And Guthrum was an honourable chief who well deserved that clemency; for, ever afterwards he was loyal and faithful to the king. The Danes under him were faithful too. They plundered and burned no more, but worked like honest men. They ploughed, and sowed, and reaped, and led good honest English lives. And I hope the children of those Danes played, many a time, with Saxon children in the sunny fields; and that Danish young men fell in love with Saxon girls, and married them; and that English travellers, benighted at the doors of Danish cottages, often went in for shelter until morning; and that Danes and Saxons sat by the red fire, friends, talking of King Alfred the Great.

All the Danes were not like these under Guthrum; for, after some years, more of them came over, in the old plundering and burning way—among them a fierce pirate of the name of Hastings, who had the boldness to sail up the Thames to Gravesend, with eighty ships. For three years, there was a war with these Danes; and there was a famine in the country, too, and a plague, both upon human creatures and beasts. But King Alfred, whose mighty heart never failed him, built large ships nevertheless, with which to pursue the pirates on the sea; and he encouraged his soldiers, by his brave example, to fight valiantly against them on the shore. At last, he drove them all away; and then there was repose in England.

As great and good in peace, as he was great and good in war, King Alfred never rested from his labours to improve his people. He loved to talk with clever men, and with travellers from foreign countries, and to write down what they told him, for his people to read. He had studied Latin after learning to read English, and now another of his labours was, to translate Latin books into the English-Saxon tongue, that his people might be interested, and improved by their contents. He made just laws, that they

27

might live more happily and freely; he turned away all partial judges, that no wrong might be done them; he was so careful of their property, and punished robbers so severely, that it was a common thing to say that under the great King Alfred, garlands of golden chains and jewels might have hung across the streets, and no man would have touched one. He founded schools; he patiently heard causes himself in his Court of Justice; the great desires of his heart were, to do right to all his subjects, and to leave England better, wiser, happier in all ways, than he found it. His industry in these efforts was quite astonishing. Every day he divided into certain portions, and in each portion devoted himself to a certain pursuit. That he might divide his time exactly, he had wax torches or candles made, which were all of the same size, were notched across at regular distances, and were always kept burning. Thus, as the candles burnt down, he divided the day into notches, almost as accurately as we now divide it into hours upon the clock. But when the candles were first invented, it was found that the wind and draughts of air, blowing into the palace through the doors and windows, and through the chinks in the walls, caused them to gutter and burn unequally. To prevent this, the King had them put into cases formed of wood and white horn. And these were the first lanthorns ever made in England.

All this time, he was afflicted with a terrible unknown disease, which caused him violent and frequent pain that nothing could relieve. He bore it, as he had borne all the troubles of his life, like a brave good man, until he was fifty-three years old; and then, having reigned thirty years, he died. He died in the year nine hundred and one; but, long ago as that is, his fame, and the love and gratitude with which his subjects regarded him, are freshly remembered to the present hour.

In the next reign, which was the reign of Edward, surnamed The Elder, who was chosen in council to succeed, a nephew of King Alfred troubled the country by trying to obtain the throne. The Danes in the East of England took part with this usurper (perhaps because they had honoured his uncle so much, and honoured him for his uncle's sake), and there was hard fighting; but, the King, with the assistance of his sister, gained the day, and reigned in peace for four and twenty years. He gradually extended his power over the whole of England, and so the Seven Kingdoms were united into one.

When England thus became one kingdom, ruled over by one Saxon king, the Saxons had been settled in the country more than four hundred and fifty years. Great changes had taken place in its customs during that time. The Saxons were still greedy eaters and great drinkers, and their feasts were often of a noisy and drunken kind; but many new comforts and even elegances had become known, and were fast increasing. Hangings for the walls of rooms, where, in these modern days, we paste up paper, are known to have been sometimes made of silk, ornamented with birds and flowers in needlework. Tables and chairs were curiously carved in different woods; were sometimes decorated with gold or silver; sometimes even made of those precious metals. Knives and spoons were used at table; golden ornaments were worn—with silk and cloth, and golden tissues and embroideries; dishes were made of gold and silver, brass and bone. There were varieties of drinking-horns, bedsteads, musical instruments. A harp was passed round, at a feast, like the drinking-bowl, from guest to guest; and each one usually sang or played when his turn came. The weapons of the Saxons were stoutly made, and among them was a terrible iron hammer that gave deadly blows, and was long remembered. The Saxons themselves were a handsome people. The men were proud of their long fair hair, parted on the forehead; their ample beards, their fresh complexions, and clear eyes. The beauty of the Saxon women filled all England with a new delight and grace.

I have more to tell of the Saxons yet, but I stop to say this now, because under the Great Alfred, all the best points of the English-Saxon character were first encouraged, and in him first shown. It has been the greatest character among the nations of the earth. Wherever the descendants of the Saxon race have gone, have sailed, or otherwise made their way, even to the remotest regions of the world, they have been patient, persevering, never to be broken in spirit, never to be turned aside from enterprises on which they have resolved. In Europe, Asia, Africa, America, the whole world over; in the desert, in the forest, on the sea; scorched by a burning sun, or frozen by ice that never melts; the Saxon blood remains unchanged. Wheresoever that race goes, there, law, and industry, and safety for life and property, and all the great results of steady perseverance, are certain to arise.

I pause to think with admiration, of the noble king who, in his single person, possessed all the Saxon virtues. Whom misfortune could not subdue, whom prosperity could not spoil, whose perseverance nothing could shake. Who was hopeful in defeat, and generous in success. Who loved justice, freedom, truth, and knowledge. Who, in his care to instruct his people, probably did more to preserve the beautiful old Saxon language, than I can imagine. Without whom, the English tongue in which I tell this story might have wanted half its meaning. As it is said that his spirit still inspires some of our best English laws, so, let you and I pray that it may animate our English hearts, at least to this—to resolve, when we see any of our fellow-creatures left in ignorance, that we will do our best, while life is in us, to have them taught; and to tell those rulers whose duty it is to teach them, and who neglect their duty, that they have profited very little by all the years that have rolled away since the year nine hundred and one, and that they are far behind the bright example of King Alfred the Great.

CHAPTER IV—ENGLAND UNDER ATHELSTAN AND THE SIX BOY-KINGS

Athelstan, the son of Edward the Elder, succeeded that king. He reigned only fifteen years; but he remembered the glory of his grandfather, the great Alfred, and governed England well. He reduced the turbulent people of Wales, and obliged them to pay him a tribute in money, and in cattle, and to send him their best hawks and hounds. He was victorious over the Cornish men, who were not yet quite under the Saxon government. He restored such of the old laws as were good, and had fallen into disuse; made some wise new laws, and took care of the poor and weak. A strong alliance, made against him by Anlaf a Danish prince, Constantine King of the Scots, and the people of North Wales, he broke and defeated in one great battle, long famous for the vast numbers slain in it. After that, he had a quiet reign; the lords and ladies about him had leisure to become polite and agreeable; and foreign princes were glad (as they have sometimes been since) to come to England on visits to the English court.

When Athelstan died, at forty-seven years old, his brother Edmund, who was only eighteen, became king. He was the first of six boy-kings, as you will presently know.

They called him the Magnificent, because he showed a taste for improvement and refinement. But he was beset by the Danes, and had a short and troubled reign, which came to a troubled end. One night, when he was feasting in his hall, and had eaten much and drunk deep, he saw, among the company, a noted robber named Leof, who had been banished from England. Made very angry by the boldness of this man, the King turned to his cup-bearer, and said, 'There is a robber sitting at the table yonder, who, for his crimes, is an outlaw in the land—a hunted wolf, whose life any man may take, at any time. Command that robber to depart!' 'I will not depart!' said Leof. 'No?' cried the King. 'No, by the Lord!' said Leof. Upon that the King rose from his seat, and, making passionately at the robber, and seizing him by his long hair, tried to throw him down. But the robber had a dagger underneath his cloak, and, in the scuffle, stabbed the King to death. That done, he set his back against the wall, and fought so desperately, that although he was soon cut to pieces by the King's armed men, and the wall and pavement were splashed with his blood, yet it was not before he had killed and wounded many of them. You may imagine what rough lives the kings of those times led, when one of them could struggle, half drunk, with a public robber in his own dining-hall, and be stabbed in presence of the company who ate and drank with him.

Then succeeded the boy-king Edred, who was weak and sickly in body, but of a strong mind. And his armies fought the Northmen, the Danes, and Norwegians, or the Sea-Kings, as they were called, and beat them for the time. And, in nine years, Edred died, and passed away.

Then came the boy-king Edwy, fifteen years of age; but the real king, who had the real power, was a monk named Dunstan—a clever priest, a little mad, and not a little proud and cruel.

Dunstan was then Abbot of Glastonbury Abbey, whither the body of King Edmund the Magnificent was carried, to be buried. While yet a boy, he had got out of his bed one night (being then in a fever), and walked about Glastonbury Church when it was under repair; and, because he did not tumble off some scaffolds that were there, and break his neck, it was reported that he had been shown over the building by an angel. He had also made a harp that was said to play of itself—which it very likely did, as Æolian Harps, which are played by the wind, and are understood now, always do. For these wonders he had been once denounced by his enemies, who were jealous of his favour with the late King Athelstan, as a magician; and he had been waylaid, bound hand and foot, and thrown into a marsh. But he got out again, somehow, to cause a great deal of trouble yet.

The priests of those days were, generally, the only scholars. They were learned in many things. Having to make their own convents and monasteries on uncultivated grounds that were granted to them by the Crown, it was necessary that they should be good farmers and good gardeners, or their lands would have been too poor to support them. For the decoration of the chapels where they prayed, and for the comfort of the refectories where they ate and drank, it was necessary that there should be good carpenters, good smiths, good painters, among them. For their greater safety in sickness and accident, living alone by themselves in solitary places, it was necessary that they should study the virtues of plants and herbs, and should know how to dress cuts, burns, scalds, and bruises, and how to set broken limbs. Accordingly, they taught themselves, and one another, a great variety of useful arts; and became skilful in agriculture, medicine, surgery, and handicraft. And when they wanted the aid of any little piece of machinery, which would be simple enough now, but was marvellous then, to impose a trick upon the poor peasants, they knew very well how to make it; and did make it many a time and often, I have no doubt.

Dunstan, Abbot of Glastonbury Abbey, was one of the most sagacious of these monks. He was an ingenious smith, and worked at a forge in a little cell. This cell was made too short to admit of his lying at full length when he went to sleep—as if that did any good to anybody!—and he used to tell the most extraordinary lies about demons and spirits, who, he said, came there to persecute him. For instance, he related that one day when he was at work, the devil looked in at the little window, and tried to tempt him to lead a life of idle pleasure; whereupon, having his pincers in the fire, red hot, he seized the devil by the nose, and put him to such pain, that his bellowings were heard for miles and miles. Some people are inclined to think this nonsense a part of Dunstan's madness (for his head never quite recovered the fever), but I think not. I observe that it induced the ignorant people to consider him a holy man, and that it made him very powerful. Which was exactly what he always wanted.

On the day of the coronation of the handsome boy-king Edwy, it was remarked by Odo, Archbishop of Canterbury (who was a Dane by birth), that the King quietly left the coronation feast, while all the company were there. Odo, much displeased, sent his friend Dunstan to seek him. Dunstan finding him in the company of his beautiful young wife Elgiva, and her mother Ethelgiva, a good and virtuous lady, not only grossly abused them, but dragged the young King back into the feasting-hall by force. Some, again, think Dunstan did this because the young King's fair wife was his own cousin, and the monks objected to people marrying their own cousins; but I believe he did it, because he was an imperious, audacious, ill-conditioned priest, who, having loved a young lady himself before he became a sour monk, hated all love now, and everything belonging to it.

The young King was quite old enough to feel this insult. Dunstan had been Treasurer in the last reign, and he soon charged Dunstan with having taken some of the last king's money. The Glastonbury Abbot fled to Belgium (very narrowly escaping some pursuers who were sent to put out his eyes, as you will wish they had, when you read what follows), and his abbey was given to priests who were married; whom he always, both before and afterwards, opposed. But he quickly conspired with his friend, Odo the Dane, to set up the King's young brother, Edgar, as his rival for the throne; and, not content with this revenge, he caused the beautiful queen Elgiva, though a lovely girl of only seventeen or eighteen, to be stolen from one of the Royal Palaces, branded in the cheek with a red-hot iron, and sold into slavery in Ireland. But the Irish people pitied and befriended her; and they said, 'Let us restore the girl-queen to the boy-king, and make the young lovers happy!' and they cured her of her cruel wound, and sent her home as beautiful as before. But the villain Dunstan, and that other villain, Odo, caused her to be waylaid at Gloucester as she was joyfully hurrying to join her husband, and to be hacked and hewn with swords, and to be barbarously maimed and lamed, and left to die. When Edwy the Fair (his people called him so, because he was so young and handsome) heard of her dreadful fate, he died of a broken heart; and so the pitiful story of the poor young wife and husband ends! Ah! Better to be two cottagers in these better times, than king and queen of England in those bad days, though never so fair!

Then came the boy-king, Edgar, called the Peaceful, fifteen years old. Dunstan, being still the real king, drove all married priests out of the monasteries and abbeys, and replaced them by solitary monks like himself, of the rigid order called the Benedictines. He made himself Archbishop of Canterbury, for his greater glory; and exercised such power over the neighbouring British princes, and so collected them about the King, that once, when the King held his court at Chester, and went on the river Dee to visit the monastery of St. John, the eight oars of his boat were pulled (as the people used to delight in relating in stories and songs) by eight crowned kings, and steered by the King of England. As Edgar was very obedient to Dunstan and the monks, they took great pains to represent him as the best of kings. But he was really profligate, debauched, and vicious. He once forcibly carried off a young lady from the convent at Wilton; and Dunstan, pretending to be very much shocked, condemned him not to wear his crown upon his head for seven years—no great punishment, I dare say, as it can hardly have been a more comfortable ornament to wear, than a stewpan without a handle. His marriage with his second wife, Elfrida, is one of the worst events of his reign. Hearing of the beauty of this lady, he despatched his favourite courtier, Athelwold, to her father's castle in Devonshire, to see if she were really as charming as fame reported. Now, she was so exceedingly beautiful that Athelwold fell in love with her himself, and married her; but he told the King that she was only rich—not handsome. The King, suspecting the truth when they came home, resolved to pay the newly-married couple a visit; and, suddenly, told Athelwold to prepare for his immediate coming. Athelwold, terrified, confessed to his young wife what he had said and done, and implored her to disguise her beauty by some ugly dress or silly manner, that he might be safe from the King's anger. She promised that she would; but she was a proud woman, who would far rather have been a queen than the wife of a courtier. She dressed herself in her best dress, and adorned herself with her richest jewels; and when the King came, presently, he discovered the cheat. So, he caused his false friend, Athelwold, to be murdered in a wood, and married his widow, this bad Elfrida. Six or seven years afterwards, he died; and was buried, as if he had been all that the monks said he was, in the abbey of Glastonbury, which he—or Dunstan for him—had much enriched.

England, in one part of this reign, was so troubled by wolves, which, driven out of the open country, hid themselves in the mountains of Wales when they were not attacking travellers and animals, that the tribute payable by the Welsh people was forgiven them, on condition of their producing, every year, three hundred wolves' heads. And the Welshmen were so sharp upon the wolves, to save their money, that in four years there was not a wolf left.

Then came the boy-king, Edward, called the Martyr, from the manner of his death. Elfrida had a son, named Ethelred, for whom she claimed the throne; but Dunstan did not choose to favour him, and he made Edward king. The boy was hunting, one day, down in Dorsetshire, when he rode near to Corfe Castle, where Elfrida and Ethelred lived. Wishing to see them kindly, he rode away from his attendants and galloped to the castle gate, where he arrived at twilight, and blew his hunting-horn. 'You are welcome, dear King,' said Elfrida, coming out, with her brightest smiles. 'Pray you dismount and enter.' 'Not so, dear madam,' said the King. 'My company will miss me, and fear that I have met with some harm. Please you to give me a cup of wine, that I may drink here, in the saddle, to you and to my little brother, and so ride away with the good speed I have made in riding here.' Elfrida, going in to bring the wine, whispered an armed servant, one of her attendants, who stole out of the darkening gateway, and crept round behind the King's horse. As the King raised the cup to his lips, saying, 'Health!' to the wicked woman who was smiling on him, and to his innocent brother whose hand she held in hers, and who was only ten years old, this armed man made a spring and stabbed him in the back. He dropped the cup and spurred his horse away; but, soon fainting with loss of blood, dropped from the saddle, and, in his fall, entangled one of his feet in the stirrup. The frightened horse dashed on; trailing his rider's curls upon the ground; dragging his smooth young face through ruts, and stones, and briers, and fallen leaves, and mud; until the hunters, tracking the animal's course by the King's blood, caught his bridle, and released the disfigured body.

Then came the sixth and last of the boy-kings, Ethelred, whom Elfrida, when he cried out at the sight of his murdered brother riding away from the castle gate, unmercifully beat with a torch which she snatched from one of the attendants. The people so disliked this boy, on account of his cruel mother and the murder she had done to promote him, that Dunstan would not have had him for king, but would have made Edgitha, the daughter of the dead King Edgar, and of the lady whom he stole out of the convent at Wilton, Queen of England, if she would have consented. But she knew the stories of the youthful kings too well, and would not be persuaded from the convent where she lived in peace; so, Dunstan put Ethelred on the throne, having no one else to put there, and gave him the nickname of The Unready—knowing that he wanted resolution and firmness.

At first, Elfrida possessed great influence over the young King, but, as he grew older and came of age, her influence declined. The infamous woman, not having it in her power to do any more evil, then retired from court, and, according, to the fashion of the time, built churches and monasteries, to expiate her guilt. As if a church, with a steeple reaching to the very stars, would have been any sign of true repentance for the blood of the poor boy, whose murdered form was trailed at his horse's heels! As if she could have buried her wickedness beneath the senseless stones of the whole world, piled up one upon another, for the monks to live in!

About the ninth or tenth year of this reign, Dunstan died. He was growing old then, but was as stern and artful as ever. Two circumstances that happened in connexion with him, in this reign of Ethelred, made a great noise. Once, he was present at a meeting of the Church, when the question was discussed whether priests should have permission to marry; and, as he sat with his head hung down, apparently thinking about it, a voice seemed to come out of a crucifix in the room, and warn the meeting to be of his opinion. This was some juggling of Dunstan's, and was probably his own voice disguised. But he played off a worse juggle than that, soon afterwards; for, another meeting being held on the same subject, and he and his supporters being seated on one side of a great room, and their opponents on the other, he rose and said, 'To Christ himself, as judge, do I commit this cause!' Immediately on these words being spoken, the floor where the opposite party sat gave way, and some were killed and many wounded. You may be pretty sure that it had been weakened under Dunstan's direction, and that it fell at Dunstan's signal. His part of the floor did not go down. No, no. He was too good a workman for that.

When he died, the monks settled that he was a Saint, and called him Saint Dunstan ever afterwards. They might just as well have settled that he was a coach-horse, and could just as easily have called him one.

Ethelred the Unready was glad enough, I dare say, to be rid of this holy saint; but, left to himself, he was a poor weak king, and his reign was a reign of defeat and shame. The restless Danes, led by Sweyn, a son of the King of Denmark who had quarrelled with his father and had been banished from home, again came into England, and, year after year, attacked and despoiled large towns. To coax these sea-kings away, the weak Ethelred paid them money; but, the more money he paid, the more money the Danes wanted. At first, he gave them ten thousand pounds; on their next invasion, sixteen thousand pounds; on their next invasion, four and twenty thousand pounds: to pay which large sums, the unfortunate English people were heavily taxed. But, as the Danes still came back and wanted more, he thought it would be a good plan to marry into some powerful foreign family that would help him with soldiers. So, in the year one thousand and two, he courted and married Emma, the sister of Richard Duke of Normandy; a lady who was called the Flower of Normandy.

And now, a terrible deed was done in England, the like of which was never done on English ground before or since. On the thirteenth of November, in pursuance of secret instructions sent by the King over the whole country, the inhabitants of every town and city armed, and murdered all the Danes who were their neighbours.

Young and old, babies and soldiers, men and women, every Dane was killed. No doubt there were among them many ferocious men who had done the English great wrong, and whose pride and insolence, in swaggering in the houses of the English and insulting their wives and daughters, had become unbearable; but no doubt there were also among them many peaceful Christian Danes who had married English women and become like English men. They were all slain, even to Gunhilda, the sister of the King of Denmark, married to an English lord; who was first obliged to see the murder of her husband and her child, and then was killed herself.

When the King of the sea-kings heard of this deed of blood, he swore that he would have a great revenge. He raised an army, and a mightier fleet of ships than ever yet had sailed to England; and in all his army there was not a slave or an old man, but every soldier was a free man, and the son of a free man, and in the prime of life, and sworn to be revenged upon the English nation, for the massacre of that dread thirteenth of November, when his countrymen and countrywomen, and the little children whom they loved, were killed with fire and sword. And so, the sea-kings came to England in many great ships, each bearing the flag of its own commander. Golden eagles, ravens, dragons, dolphins, beasts of prey, threatened England from the prows of those ships, as they came onward through the water; and were reflected in the shining shields that hung upon their sides. The ship that bore the standard of the King of the sea-kings was carved and painted like a mighty serpent; and the King in his anger prayed that the Gods in whom he trusted might all desert him, if his serpent did not strike its fangs into England's heart.

And indeed it did. For, the great army landing from the great fleet, near Exeter, went forward, laying England waste, and striking their lances in the earth as they advanced, or throwing them into rivers, in token of their making all the island theirs. In remembrance of the black November night when the Danes were murdered, wheresoever the invaders came, they made the Saxons prepare and spread for them great feasts; and when they had eaten those feasts, and had drunk a curse to England with wild rejoicings, they drew their swords, and killed their Saxon entertainers, and marched on. For six long years they carried on this war: burning the crops, farmhouses, barns, mills, granaries; killing the labourers in the fields; preventing the seed from being sown in the ground; causing famine and starvation; leaving only heaps of ruin and smoking ashes, where they had found rich towns. To crown this misery, English officers and men deserted, and even the favourites of Ethelred the Unready, becoming traitors, seized many of the English ships, turned pirates against their own country, and aided by a storm occasioned the loss of nearly the whole English navy.

There was but one man of note, at this miserable pass, who was true to his country and the feeble King. He was a priest, and a brave one. For twenty days, the Archbishop of Canterbury defended that city against its Danish besiegers; and when a traitor in the town threw the gates open and admitted them, he said, in chains, 'I will not buy my life with money that must be extorted from the suffering people. Do with me what you please!'

Again and again, he steadily refused to purchase his release with gold wrung from the poor.

At last, the Danes being tired of this, and being assembled at a drunken merry-making, had him brought into the feasting-hall.

'Now, bishop,' they said, 'we want gold!'

He looked round on the crowd of angry faces; from the shaggy beards close to him, to the shaggy beards against the walls, where men were mounted on tables and forms to see him over the heads of others: and he knew that his time was come.

'I have no gold,' he said.

'Get it, bishop!' they all thundered.

'That, I have often told you I will not,' said he.

They gathered closer round him, threatening, but he stood unmoved. Then, one man struck him; then, another; then a cursing soldier picked up from a heap in a corner of the hall, where fragments had been rudely thrown at dinner, a great ox-bone, and cast it at his face, from which the blood came spurting forth; then, others ran to the same heap, and knocked him down with other bones, and bruised and battered him; until one soldier whom he had baptised (willing, as I hope for the sake of that soldier's soul, to shorten the sufferings of the good man) struck him dead with his battle-axe.

If Ethelred had had the heart to emulate the courage of this noble archbishop, he might have done something yet. But he paid the Danes forty-eight thousand pounds, instead, and gained so little by the cowardly act, that Sweyn soon afterwards came over to subdue all England. So broken was the attachment of the English people, by this time, to their incapable King and their forlorn country which could not protect them, that they welcomed Sweyn on all sides, as a deliverer. London faithfully stood out, as long as the King was within its walls; but, when he sneaked away, it also welcomed the Dane. Then, all was over; and the King took refuge abroad with the Duke of Normandy, who had already given shelter to the King's wife, once the Flower of that country, and to her children.

Still, the English people, in spite of their sad sufferings, could not quite forget the great King Alfred and the Saxon race. When Sweyn died suddenly, in little more than a month after he had been proclaimed King of England, they generously sent to Ethelred, to say that they would have him for their King again, 'if he would only govern them better than he had governed them before.' The Unready, instead of coming himself, sent Edward, one of his sons, to make promises for him. At last, he followed, and the English declared him King. The Danes declared Canute, the son of Sweyn, King. Thus, direful war began again, and lasted for three years, when the Unready died. And I know of nothing better that he did, in all his reign of eight and thirty years.

Was Canute to be King now? Not over the Saxons, they said; they must have Edmund, one of the sons of the Unready, who was surnamed Ironside, because of his strength and stature. Edmund and Canute thereupon fell to, and fought five battles—O unhappy England, what a fighting-ground it was!—and then Ironside, who was a big man, proposed to Canute, who was a little man, that they two should fight it out in single combat. If Canute had been the big man, he would probably have said yes, but, being the little man, he decidedly said no. However, he declared that he was willing to divide the kingdom—to take all that lay north of Watling Street, as the old Roman military road from Dover to Chester was called, and to give Ironside all that lay south of it. Most men being weary of so much bloodshed, this was done. But Canute soon became sole King of England; for Ironside died suddenly within two months. Some think that he was killed, and killed by Canute's orders. No one knows.

CHAPTER V—ENGLAND UNDER CANUTE THE DANE

Canute reigned eighteen years. He was a merciless King at first. After he had clasped the hands of the Saxon chiefs, in token of the sincerity with which he swore to be just and good to them in return for their acknowledging him, he denounced and slew many of them, as well as many relations of the late King. 'He who brings me the head of one of my enemies,' he used to say, 'shall be dearer to me than a brother.' And he was so severe in hunting down his enemies, that he must have got together a pretty large family of these dear brothers. He was strongly inclined to kill Edmund and Edward, two children, sons of poor Ironside; but, being afraid to do so in England, he sent them over to the King of Sweden, with a request that the King would be so good as 'dispose of them.' If the King of Sweden had been like many, many other men of that day, he would have had their innocent throats cut; but he was a kind man, and brought them up tenderly.

Normandy ran much in Canute's mind. In Normandy were the two children of the late king—Edward and Alfred by name; and their uncle the Duke might one day claim the crown for them. But the Duke showed so little inclination to do so now, that he proposed to Canute to marry his sister, the widow of The Unready; who, being but a showy flower, and caring for nothing so much as becoming a queen again, left her children and was wedded to him.

Successful and triumphant, assisted by the valour of the English in his foreign wars, and with little strife to trouble him at home, Canute had a prosperous reign, and made many improvements. He was a poet and a musician. He grew sorry, as he grew older, for the blood he had shed at first; and went to Rome in a Pilgrim's dress, by way of washing it out. He gave a great deal of money to foreigners on his journey; but he took it from the English before he started. On the whole, however, he certainly became a far better man when he had no opposition to contend with, and was as great a King as England had known for some time.

The old writers of history relate how that Canute was one day disgusted with his courtiers for their flattery, and how he caused his chair to be set on the sea-shore, and feigned to command the tide as it came up not to wet the edge of his robe, for the land was his; how the tide came up, of course, without regarding him; and how he then turned to his flatterers, and rebuked them, saying, what was the might of any earthly king, to the might of the Creator, who could say unto the sea, 'Thus far shalt thou go, and no farther!' We may learn from this, I think, that a little sense will go a long way in a king; and that courtiers are not easily cured of flattery, nor kings of a liking for it. If the courtiers of Canute had not known, long before, that the King was fond of flattery, they would have known better than to offer it in such large doses. And if they had not known that he was vain of this speech (anything but a wonderful speech it seems to me, if a good child had made it), they would not have been at such great pains to repeat it. I fancy I see them all on the sea-shore together; the King's chair sinking in the sand; the King in a mighty good humour with his own wisdom; and the courtiers pretending to be quite stunned by it!

It is not the sea alone that is bidden to go 'thus far, and no farther.' The great command goes forth to all the kings upon the earth, and went to Canute in the year one thousand and thirty-five, and stretched him dead upon his bed. Beside it, stood his Norman wife. Perhaps, as the King looked his last upon her, he, who had so often thought distrustfully of Normandy, long ago, thought once more of the two exiled Princes in their uncle's court, and of the little favour they could feel for either Danes or Saxons, and of a rising cloud in Normandy that slowly moved towards England.

CHAPTER VI—ENGLAND UNDER HAROLD HAREFOOT, HARDICANUTE, AND EDWARD THE CONFESSOR

Canute left three sons, by name Sweyn, Harold, and Hardicanute; but his Queen, Emma, once the Flower of Normandy, was the mother of only Hardicanute. Canute had wished his dominions to be divided between the three, and had wished Harold to have England; but the Saxon people in the South of England, headed by a nobleman with great possessions, called the powerful Earl Godwin (who is said to have been originally a poor cow-boy), opposed this, and desired to have, instead, either Hardicanute, or one of the two exiled Princes who were over in Normandy. It seemed so certain that there would be more bloodshed to settle this dispute, that many people left their homes, and took refuge in the woods and swamps. Happily, however, it was agreed to refer the whole question to a great meeting at Oxford, which decided that Harold should have all the country north of the Thames, with London for his capital city, and that Hardicanute should have all the south. The quarrel was so arranged; and, as Hardicanute was in Denmark troubling himself very little about anything but eating and getting drunk, his mother and Earl Godwin governed the south for him.

They had hardly begun to do so, and the trembling people who had hidden themselves were scarcely at home again, when Edward, the elder of the two exiled Princes, came over from Normandy with a few followers, to claim the English Crown. His mother Emma, however, who only cared for her last son Hardicanute, instead of assisting him, as he expected, opposed him so strongly with all her influence that he was very soon glad to get safely back. His brother Alfred was not so fortunate. Believing in an affectionate letter, written some time afterwards to him and his brother, in his mother's name (but whether really with or without his mother's knowledge is now uncertain), he allowed himself to be tempted over to England, with a good force of soldiers, and landing on the Kentish coast, and being met and welcomed by Earl Godwin, proceeded into Surrey, as far as the town of Guildford. Here, he and his men halted in the evening to rest, having still the Earl in their company; who had ordered lodgings and good cheer for them. But, in the dead of the night, when they were off their guard, being divided into small parties sleeping soundly after a long march and a plentiful supper in different houses, they were set upon by the King's troops, and taken prisoners. Next morning they were drawn out in a line, to the number of six hundred men, and were barbarously tortured and killed; with the exception of every tenth man, who was sold into slavery. As to the wretched Prince Alfred, he was stripped naked, tied to a horse and sent away into the Isle of Ely, where his eyes were torn out of his head, and where in a few days he miserably died. I am not sure that the Earl had wilfully entrapped him, but I suspect it strongly.

Harold was now King all over England, though it is doubtful whether the Archbishop of Canterbury (the greater part of the priests were Saxons, and not friendly to the Danes) ever consented to crown him. Crowned or uncrowned, with the Archbishop's leave or without it, he was King for four years: after which short reign he died, and was buried; having never done much in life but go a hunting. He was such a fast runner at this, his favourite sport, that the people called him Harold Harefoot.

Hardicanute was then at Bruges, in Flanders, plotting, with his mother (who had gone over there after the cruel murder of Prince Alfred), for the invasion of England. The Danes and Saxons, finding themselves without a King, and dreading new disputes, made common cause, and joined in inviting him to occupy the Throne. He consented, and soon troubled them enough; for he brought over numbers of Danes, and taxed the people so insupportably to enrich those greedy favourites that there were many insurrections, especially one at Worcester, where the citizens rose and killed his tax-collectors; in revenge for which he burned their city. He was a brutal King, whose first public act was to order the dead body of poor Harold Harefoot to be dug up, beheaded, and thrown into the river. His end was worthy of such a beginning. He fell down drunk, with a goblet of wine in his hand, at a wedding-feast at Lambeth, given in honour of the marriage of his standard-bearer, a Dane named Towed the Proud. And he never spoke again.

Edward, afterwards called by the monks The Confessor, succeeded; and his first act was to oblige his mother Emma, who had favoured him so little, to retire into the country; where she died some ten years afterwards. He was the exiled prince whose brother Alfred had been so foully killed. He had been invited over from Normandy by Hardicanute, in the course of his short reign of two years, and had been handsomely treated at court. His cause was now favoured by the powerful Earl Godwin, and he was soon made King. This Earl had been suspected by the people, ever since Prince Alfred's cruel death; he had even been tried in the last reign for the Prince's murder, but had been pronounced not guilty; chiefly, as it was supposed, because of a present he had made to the swinish King, of a gilded ship with a figure-head of solid gold, and a crew of eighty splendidly armed men. It was his interest to help the new King with his power, if the new King would help him against the popular distrust and hatred. So they made a bargain. Edward the Confessor got the Throne. The Earl got more power and more land, and his daughter Editha was made queen; for it was a part of their compact that the King should take her for his wife.

But, although she was a gentle lady, in all things worthy to be beloved—good, beautiful, sensible, and kind—the King from the first neglected her. Her father and her six proud brothers, resenting this cold treatment, harassed the King greatly by exerting all their power to make him unpopular. Having lived so long in Normandy, he preferred the Normans to the English. He made a Norman Archbishop, and Norman Bishops; his great officers and favourites were all Normans; he introduced the Norman fashions and the Norman language; in imitation of the state custom of Normandy, he attached a great seal to his state documents, instead of merely marking them, as the Saxon Kings had done, with the sign of the cross—just as poor people who have never been taught to write, now make the same mark for their names. All this, the powerful Earl Godwin and his six proud sons represented to the people as disfavour shown towards the English; and thus they daily increased their own power, and daily diminished the power of the King.

They were greatly helped by an event that occurred when he had reigned eight years. Eustace, Earl of Bologne, who had married the King's sister, came to England on a visit. After staying at the court some time, he set forth, with his numerous train of attendants, to return home. They were to embark at Dover. Entering that peaceful town in armour, they took possession of the best houses, and noisily demanded to be lodged and entertained without payment. One of the bold men of Dover, who would not endure to have these domineering strangers jingling their heavy swords and iron corselets up and down his house, eating his meat and drinking his strong liquor, stood in his doorway and refused admission to the first armed man who came there. The armed man drew, and wounded him. The man of Dover struck the armed man dead. Intelligence of what he had done, spreading through the streets to where the Count Eustace and his men were standing by their horses, bridle in hand, they passionately mounted, galloped to the house, surrounded it, forced their way in (the doors and windows being closed when they came up), and killed the man of Dover at his own fireside. They then clattered through the streets, cutting down and riding over men, women, and children. This did not last long, you may believe. The men of Dover set upon them with great fury, killed nineteen of the foreigners, wounded many more, and, blockading the road to the port so that they should not embark, beat them out of the town by the way they had come. Hereupon, Count Eustace rides as hard as man can ride to Gloucester, where Edward is, surrounded by Norman monks and Norman lords. 'Justice!' cries the Count, 'upon the men of Dover, who have set upon and slain my people!' The King sends immediately for the powerful Earl Godwin, who happens to be near; reminds him that Dover is under his government; and orders him to repair to Dover and do military execution on the inhabitants. 'It does not become you,' says the proud Earl in reply, 'to condemn without a hearing those whom you have sworn to protect. I will not do it.'

The King, therefore, summoned the Earl, on pain of banishment and loss of his titles and property, to appear before the court to answer this disobedience. The Earl refused to appear. He, his eldest son Harold, and his second son Sweyn, hastily raised as many fighting men as their utmost power could collect, and demanded to have Count Eustace and his followers surrendered to the justice of the country. The King, in his turn, refused to give them up, and raised a strong force. After some treaty and delay, the troops of the great Earl and his sons began to fall off. The Earl, with a part of his family and abundance of treasure, sailed to Flanders; Harold escaped to Ireland; and the power of the great family was for that time gone in England. But, the people did not forget them.

Then, Edward the Confessor, with the true meanness of a mean spirit, visited his dislike of the once powerful father and sons upon the helpless daughter and sister, his unoffending wife, whom all who saw her (her husband and his monks excepted) loved. He seized rapaciously upon her fortune and her jewels, and allowing her only one attendant, confined her in a gloomy convent, of which a sister of his—no doubt an unpleasant lady after his own heart—was abbess or jailer.

Having got Earl Godwin and his six sons well out of his way, the King favoured the Normans more than ever. He invited over William, Duke Of Normandy, the son of that Duke who had received him and his murdered brother long ago, and of a peasant girl, a tanner's daughter, with whom that Duke had fallen in love for her beauty as he saw her washing clothes in a brook. William, who was a great warrior, with a passion for fine horses, dogs, and arms, accepted the invitation; and the Normans in England, finding themselves more numerous than ever when he arrived with his retinue, and held in still greater honour at court than before, became more and more haughty towards the people, and were more and more disliked by them.

The old Earl Godwin, though he was abroad, knew well how the people felt; for, with part of the treasure he had carried away with him, he kept spies and agents in his pay all over England.

Accordingly, he thought the time was come for fitting out a great expedition against the Norman-loving King. With it, he sailed to the Isle of Wight, where he was joined by his son Harold, the most gallant and brave of all his family. And so the father and son came sailing up the Thames to Southwark; great numbers of the people declaring for them, and shouting for the English Earl and the English Harold, against the Norman favourites!

The King was at first as blind and stubborn as kings usually have been whensoever they have been in the hands of monks. But the people rallied so thickly round the old Earl and his son, and the old Earl was so steady in demanding without bloodshed the restoration of himself and his family to their rights, that at last the court took the alarm. The Norman Archbishop of Canterbury, and the Norman Bishop of London, surrounded by their retainers, fought their way out of London, and escaped from Essex to France in a fishing-boat. The other Norman favourites dispersed in all directions. The old Earl and his sons (except Sweyn, who had committed crimes against the law) were restored to their possessions and dignities. Editha, the virtuous and lovely Queen of the insensible King, was triumphantly released from her prison, the convent, and once more sat in her chair of state, arrayed in the jewels of which, when she had no champion to support her rights, her cold-blooded husband had deprived her.

The old Earl Godwin did not long enjoy his restored fortune. He fell down in a fit at the King's table, and died upon the third day afterwards. Harold succeeded to his power, and to a far higher place in the attachment of the people than his father had ever held. By his valour he subdued the King's enemies in many bloody fights. He was vigorous against rebels in Scotland—this was the time when Macbeth slew Duncan, upon which event our English Shakespeare, hundreds of years afterwards, wrote his great tragedy; and he killed the restless Welsh King Griffith, and brought his head to England.

What Harold was doing at sea, when he was driven on the French coast by a tempest, is not at all certain; nor does it at all matter. That his ship was forced by a storm on that shore, and that he was taken prisoner, there is no doubt. In those barbarous days, all shipwrecked strangers were taken prisoners, and obliged to pay ransom. So, a certain Count Guy, who was the Lord of Ponthieu where Harold's disaster happened, seized him, instead of relieving him like a hospitable and Christian lord as he ought to have done, and expected to make a very good thing of it.

But Harold sent off immediately to Duke William of Normandy, complaining of this treatment; and the Duke no sooner heard of it than he ordered Harold to be escorted to the ancient town of Rouen, where he then was, and where he received him as an honoured guest. Now, some writers tell us that Edward the Confessor, who was by this time old and had no children, had made a will, appointing Duke William of Normandy his successor, and had informed the Duke of his having done so. There is no doubt that he was anxious about his successor; because he had even invited over, from abroad, Edward the Outlaw, a son of Ironside, who had come to England with his wife and three children, but whom the King had strangely refused to see when he did come, and who had died in London suddenly (princes were terribly liable to sudden death in those days), and had been buried in St. Paul's Cathedral. The King might possibly have made such a will; or, having always been fond of the Normans, he might have encouraged Norman William to aspire to the English crown, by something that he said to him when he was staying at the English court. But, certainly William did now aspire to it; and knowing that Harold would be a powerful rival, he called together a great assembly of his nobles, offered Harold his daughter Adele in marriage, informed him that he meant on King Edward's death to claim the English crown as his own inheritance, and required Harold then and there to swear to aid him. Harold, being in the Duke's power, took this oath upon the Missal, or Prayer-book. It is a good example of the superstitions of the monks, that this Missal, instead of being placed upon a table, was placed upon a tub; which, when Harold had sworn, was uncovered, and shown to be full of dead men's bones—bones, as the monks pretended, of saints. This was supposed to make Harold's oath a great deal more impressive and binding. As if the great name of the Creator of Heaven and earth could be made more solemn by a knuckle-bone, or a double-tooth, or a finger-nail, of Dunstan!

Within a week or two after Harold's return to England, the dreary old Confessor was found to be dying. After wandering in his mind like a very weak old man, he died. As he had put himself entirely in the hands of the monks when he was alive, they praised him lustily when he was dead. They had gone so far, already, as to persuade him that he could work miracles; and had brought people afflicted with a bad disorder of the skin, to him, to be touched and cured. This was called 'touching for the King's Evil,' which afterwards became a royal custom. You know, however, Who really touched the sick, and healed them; and you know His sacred name is not among the dusty line of human kings.

CHAPTER VII—ENGLAND UNDER HAROLD THE SECOND, AND CONQUERED BY THE NORMANS

Harold was crowned King of England on the very day of the maudlin Confessor's funeral. He had good need to be quick about it. When the news reached Norman William, hunting in his park at Rouen, he dropped his bow, returned to his palace, called his nobles to council, and presently sent ambassadors to Harold, calling on him to keep his oath and resign the Crown. Harold would do no such thing. The barons of France leagued together round Duke William for the invasion of England. Duke William promised freely to distribute English wealth and English lands among them. The Pope sent to Normandy a consecrated banner, and a ring containing a hair which he warranted to have grown on the head of Saint Peter. He blessed the enterprise; and cursed Harold; and requested that the Normans would pay 'Peter's Pence'—or a tax to himself of a penny a year on every house—a little more regularly in future, if they could make it convenient.

King Harold had a rebel brother in Flanders, who was a vassal of Harold Hardrada, King of Norway. This brother, and this Norwegian King, joining their forces against England, with Duke William's help, won a fight in which the English were commanded by two nobles; and then besieged York. Harold, who was waiting for the Normans on the coast at Hastings, with his army, marched to Stamford Bridge upon the river Derwent to give them instant battle.

He found them drawn up in a hollow circle, marked out by their shining spears. Riding round this circle at a distance, to survey it, he saw a brave figure on horseback, in a blue mantle and a bright helmet, whose horse suddenly stumbled and threw him.

'Who is that man who has fallen?' Harold asked of one of his captains.

'The King of Norway,' he replied.

'He is a tall and stately king,' said Harold, 'but his end is near.'

He added, in a little while, 'Go yonder to my brother, and tell him, if he withdraw his troops, he shall be Earl of Northumberland, and rich and powerful in England.'

The captain rode away and gave the message.

'What will he give to my friend the King of Norway?' asked the brother.

'Seven feet of earth for a grave,' replied the captain.

'No more?' returned the brother, with a smile.

'The King of Norway being a tall man, perhaps a little more,' replied the captain.

'Ride back!' said the brother, 'and tell King Harold to make ready for the fight!'

He did so, very soon. And such a fight King Harold led against that force, that his brother, and the Norwegian King, and every chief of note in all their host, except the Norwegian King's son, Olave, to whom he gave honourable dismissal, were left dead upon the field. The victorious army marched to York. As King Harold sat there at the feast, in the midst of all his company, a stir was heard at the doors; and messengers all covered with mire from riding far and fast through broken ground came hurrying in, to report that the Normans had landed in England.

The intelligence was true. They had been tossed about by contrary winds, and some of their ships had been wrecked. A part of their own shore, to which they had been driven back, was strewn with Norman bodies. But they had once more made sail, led by the Duke's own galley, a present from his wife, upon the prow whereof the figure of a golden boy stood pointing towards England. By day, the banner of the three Lions of Normandy, the diverse coloured sails, the gilded vans, the many decorations of this gorgeous ship, had glittered in the sun and sunny water; by night, a light had sparkled like a star at her mast-head. And now, encamped near Hastings, with their leader lying in the old Roman castle of Pevensey, the English retiring in all directions, the land for miles around scorched and smoking, fired and pillaged, was the whole Norman power, hopeful and strong on English ground.

Harold broke up the feast and hurried to London. Within a week, his army was ready. He sent out spies to ascertain the Norman strength. William took them, caused them to be led through his whole camp, and then dismissed. 'The Normans,' said these spies to Harold, 'are not bearded on the upper lip as we English are, but are shorn. They are priests.' 'My men,' replied Harold, with a laugh, 'will find those priests good soldiers!'

'The Saxons,' reported Duke William's outposts of Norman soldiers, who were instructed to retire as King Harold's army advanced, 'rush on us through their pillaged country with the fury of madmen.'

'Let them come, and come soon!' said Duke William.

Some proposals for a reconciliation were made, but were soon abandoned. In the middle of the month of October, in the year one thousand and sixty-six, the Normans and the English came front to front. All night the armies lay encamped before each other, in a part of the country then called Senlac, now called (in remembrance of them) Battle. With the first dawn of day, they arose. There, in the faint light, were the English on a hill; a wood behind them; in their midst, the Royal banner, representing a fighting warrior, woven in gold thread, adorned with precious stones; beneath the banner, as it rustled in the wind, stood King Harold on foot, with two of his remaining brothers by his side; around them, still and silent as the dead, clustered the whole English army—every soldier covered by his shield, and bearing in his hand his dreaded English battle-axe.

On an opposite hill, in three lines, archers, foot-soldiers, horsemen, was the Norman force. Of a sudden, a great battle-cry, 'God help us!' burst from the Norman lines. The English answered with their own battle-cry, 'God's Rood! Holy Rood!' The Normans then came sweeping down the hill to attack the English.

There was one tall Norman Knight who rode before the Norman army on a prancing horse, throwing up his heavy sword and catching it, and singing of the bravery of his countrymen. An English Knight, who rode out from the

English force to meet him, fell by this Knight's hand. Another English Knight rode out, and he fell too. But then a third rode out, and killed the Norman. This was in the first beginning of the fight. It soon raged everywhere.

The English, keeping side by side in a great mass, cared no more for the showers of Norman arrows than if they had been showers of Norman rain. When the Norman horsemen rode against them, with their battle-axes they cut men and horses down. The Normans gave way. The English pressed forward. A cry went forth among the Norman troops that Duke William was killed. Duke William took off his helmet, in order that his face might be distinctly seen, and rode along the line before his men. This gave them courage. As they turned again to face the English, some of their Norman horse divided the pursuing body of the English from the rest, and thus all that foremost portion of the English army fell, fighting bravely. The main body still remaining firm, heedless of the Norman arrows, and with their battle-axes cutting down the crowds of horsemen when they rode up, like forests of young trees, Duke William pretended to retreat. The eager English followed. The Norman army closed again, and fell upon them with great slaughter.

'Still,' said Duke William, 'there are thousands of the English, firms as rocks around their King. Shoot upward, Norman archers, that your arrows may fall down upon their faces!'

The sun rose high, and sank, and the battle still raged. Through all the wild October day, the clash and din resounded in the air. In the red sunset, and in the white moonlight, heaps upon heaps of dead men lay strewn, a dreadful spectacle, all over the ground.

King Harold, wounded with an arrow in the eye, was nearly blind. His brothers were already killed. Twenty Norman Knights, whose battered armour had flashed fiery and golden in the sunshine all day long, and now looked silvery in the moonlight, dashed forward to seize the Royal banner from the English Knights and soldiers, still faithfully collected round their blinded King. The King received a mortal wound, and dropped. The English broke and fled. The Normans rallied, and the day was lost.

O what a sight beneath the moon and stars, when lights were shining in the tent of the victorious Duke William, which was pitched near the spot where Harold fell—and he and his knights were carousing, within—and soldiers with torches, going slowly to and fro, without, sought for the corpse of Harold among piles of dead—and the Warrior, worked in golden thread and precious stones, lay low, all torn and soiled with blood—and the three Norman Lions kept watch over the field!

CHAPTER VIII—ENGLAND UNDER WILLIAM THE FIRST, THE NORMAN CONQUEROR

Upon the ground where the brave Harold fell, William the Norman afterwards founded an abbey, which, under the name of Battle Abbey, was a rich and splendid place through many a troubled year, though now it is a grey ruin overgrown with ivy. But the first work he had to do, was to conquer the English thoroughly; and that, as you know by this time, was hard work for any man.

He ravaged several counties; he burned and plundered many towns; he laid waste scores upon scores of miles of pleasant country; he destroyed innumerable lives. At length Stigand, Archbishop of Canterbury, with other representatives of the clergy and the people, went to his camp, and submitted to him. Edgar, the insignificant son of Edmund Ironside, was proclaimed King by others, but nothing came of it. He fled to Scotland afterwards, where his sister, who was young and beautiful, married the Scottish King. Edgar himself was not important enough for anybody to care much about him.

On Christmas Day, William was crowned in Westminster Abbey, under the title of William the First; but he is best known as William the Conqueror. It was a strange coronation. One of the bishops who performed the ceremony asked the Normans, in French, if they would have Duke William for their king? They answered Yes. Another of the bishops put the same question to the Saxons, in English. They too answered Yes, with a loud shout. The noise being heard by a guard of Norman horse-soldiers outside, was mistaken for resistance on the part of the English. The guard instantly set fire to the neighbouring houses, and a tumult ensued; in the midst of which the King, being left alone in the Abbey, with a few priests (and they all being in a terrible fright together), was hurriedly crowned. When the crown was placed upon his head, he swore to govern the English as well as the best of their own monarchs. I dare say you think, as I do, that if we except the Great Alfred, he might pretty easily have done that.

Numbers of the English nobles had been killed in the last disastrous battle. Their estates, and the estates of all the nobles who had fought against him there, King William seized upon, and gave to his own Norman knights and nobles. Many great English families of the present time acquired their English lands in this way, and are very proud of it.

But what is got by force must be maintained by force. These nobles were obliged to build castles all over England, to defend their new property; and, do what he would, the King could neither soothe nor quell the nation as he wished. He gradually introduced the Norman language and the Norman customs; yet, for a long time the great body of the English remained sullen and revengeful. On his going over to Normandy, to visit his subjects there, the oppressions of his half-brother Odo, whom he left in charge of his English kingdom, drove the people mad. The men of Kent even invited over, to take possession of Dover, their old enemy Count Eustace of Boulogne, who had led the fray when the Dover man was slain at his own fireside. The men of Hereford, aided by the Welsh, and commanded by a chief named Edric the Wild, drove the Normans out of their country. Some of those who had been dispossessed of their lands, banded together in the North of England; some, in Scotland; some, in the thick woods and marshes; and whensoever they could fall upon the Normans, or upon the English who had submitted to the Normans, they fought, despoiled, and murdered, like the desperate outlaws that they were. Conspiracies were set on foot for a general massacre of the Normans, like the old massacre of the Danes. In short, the English were in a murderous mood all through the kingdom.

King William, fearing he might lose his conquest, came back, and tried to pacify the London people by soft words. He then set forth to repress the country people by stern deeds. Among the towns which he besieged, and where he killed and maimed the inhabitants without any distinction, sparing none, young or old, armed or unarmed, were Oxford, Warwick, Leicester, Nottingham, Derby, Lincoln, York. In all these places, and in many others, fire and sword worked their utmost horrors, and made the land dreadful to behold. The streams and rivers were discoloured with blood; the sky was blackened with smoke; the fields were wastes of ashes; the waysides were heaped up with dead. Such are the fatal results of conquest and ambition! Although William was a harsh and angry man, I do not suppose that he deliberately meant to work this shocking ruin, when he invaded England. But what he had got by the strong hand, he could only keep by the strong hand, and in so doing he made England a great grave.

Two sons of Harold, by name Edmund and Godwin, came over from Ireland, with some ships, against the Normans, but were defeated. This was scarcely done, when the outlaws in the woods so harassed York, that the Governor sent to the King for help. The King despatched a general and a large force to occupy the town of Durham. The Bishop of that place met the general outside the town, and warned him not to enter, as he would be in danger there. The general cared nothing for the warning, and went in with all his men. That night, on every hill within sight of Durham, signal fires were seen to blaze. When the morning dawned, the English, who had assembled in great strength, forced the gates, rushed into the town, and slew the Normans every one. The English afterwards besought the Danes to come and help them. The Danes came, with two hundred and forty ships. The outlawed nobles joined them; they captured York, and drove the Normans out of that city. Then, William bribed the Danes to go away; and took such vengeance on the English, that all the former fire and sword, smoke and ashes, death and ruin, were nothing compared with it. In melancholy songs, and doleful stories, it was still sung and told by cottage fires on winter evenings, a hundred years afterwards, how, in those dreadful days of the Normans, there was not, from the River Humber to the River Tyne, one inhabited village left, nor one cultivated field—how there was nothing but a dismal ruin, where the human creatures and the beasts lay dead together.

The outlaws had, at this time, what they called a Camp of Refuge, in the midst of the fens of Cambridgeshire. Protected by those marshy grounds which were difficult of approach, they lay among the reeds and rushes, and were hidden by the mists that rose up from the watery earth. Now, there also was, at that time, over the sea in Flanders, an Englishman named Hereward, whose father had died in his absence, and whose property had been given to a Norman. When he heard of this wrong that had been done him (from such of the exiled English as chanced to wander into that country), he longed for revenge; and joining the outlaws in their camp of refuge, became their commander. He was so good a soldier, that the Normans supposed him to be aided by enchantment. William, even after he had made a road three miles in length across the Cambridgeshire marshes, on purpose to attack this supposed enchanter, thought it necessary to engage an old lady, who pretended to be a sorceress, to come and do a little enchantment in the royal cause. For this purpose she was pushed on before the troops in a wooden tower; but Hereward very soon disposed of this unfortunate sorceress, by burning her, tower and all. The monks of the convent of Ely near at hand, however, who were fond of good living, and who found it very uncomfortable to have the country blockaded and their supplies of meat and drink cut off, showed the King a secret way of surprising the camp. So Hereward was soon defeated. Whether he afterwards died quietly, or whether he was killed after killing sixteen of the men who attacked him (as some old rhymes relate that he did), I cannot say. His defeat put an end to the Camp of Refuge; and, very soon afterwards, the King, victorious both in Scotland and in England, quelled the last rebellious English noble. He then surrounded himself with Norman lords, enriched by the property of English nobles; had a great survey made of all the land in England, which was entered as the property of its new owners, on a roll called Doomsday Book; obliged the people to put out their fires and candles at a certain hour every night, on the ringing of a bell which was called The Curfew; introduced the Norman dresses and manners; made the Normans masters everywhere, and the English, servants; turned out the English bishops, and put Normans in their places; and showed himself to be the Conqueror indeed.

But, even with his own Normans, he had a restless life. They were always hungering and thirsting for the riches of the English; and the more he gave, the more they wanted. His priests were as greedy as his soldiers. We know of only one Norman who plainly told his master, the King, that he had come with him to England to do his duty as a faithful servant, and that property taken by force from other men had no charms for him. His name was Guilbert. We should not forget his name, for it is good to remember and to honour honest men.

Besides all these troubles, William the Conqueror was troubled by quarrels among his sons. He had three living. Robert, called Curthose, because of his short legs; William, called Rufus or the Red, from the colour of his hair; and Henry, fond of learning, and called, in the Norman language, Beauclerc, or Fine-Scholar. When Robert grew up, he asked of his father the government of Normandy, which he had nominally possessed, as a child, under his mother, Matilda. The King refusing to grant it, Robert became jealous and discontented; and happening one day, while in this temper, to be ridiculed by his brothers, who threw water on him from a balcony as he was walking before the door, he drew his sword, rushed up-stairs, and was only prevented by the King himself from putting them to death. That same night, he hotly departed with some followers from his father's court, and endeavoured to take the Castle of Rouen by surprise. Failing in this, he shut himself up in another Castle in Normandy, which the King besieged, and where Robert one day unhorsed and nearly killed him without knowing who he was. His submission when he discovered his father, and the intercession of the queen and others, reconciled them; but not soundly; for Robert soon strayed abroad, and went from court to court with his complaints. He was a gay, careless, thoughtless fellow, spending all he got on musicians and dancers; but his mother loved him, and often, against the King's command, supplied him with money through a messenger named Samson. At length the incensed King swore he would tear out Samson's eyes; and Samson, thinking that his only hope of safety was in becoming a monk, became one, went on such errands no more, and kept his eyes in his head.

All this time, from the turbulent day of his strange coronation, the Conqueror had been struggling, you see, at any cost of cruelty and bloodshed, to maintain what he had seized. All his reign, he struggled still, with the same object ever before him. He was a stern, bold man, and he succeeded in it.

He loved money, and was particular in his eating, but he had only leisure to indulge one other passion, and that was his love of hunting. He carried it to such a height that he ordered whole villages and towns to be swept away to make forests for the deer. Not satisfied with sixty-eight Royal

Forests, he laid waste an immense district, to form another in Hampshire, called the New Forest. The many thousands of miserable peasants who saw their little houses pulled down, and themselves and children turned into the open country without a shelter, detested him for his merciless addition to their many sufferings; and when, in the twenty-first year of his reign (which proved to be the last), he went over to Rouen, England was as full of hatred against him, as if every leaf on every tree in all his Royal Forests had been a curse upon his head. In the New Forest, his son Richard (for he had four sons) had been gored to death by a Stag; and the people said that this so cruelly-made Forest would yet be fatal to others of the Conqueror's race.

He was engaged in a dispute with the King of France about some territory. While he stayed at Rouen, negotiating with that King, he kept his bed and took medicines: being advised by his physicians to do so, on account of having grown to an unwieldy size. Word being brought to him that the King of France made light of this, and joked about it, he swore in a great rage that he should rue his jests. He assembled his army, marched into the disputed territory, burnt—his old way!—the vines, the crops, and fruit, and set the town of Mantes on fire. But, in an evil hour; for, as he rode over the hot ruins, his horse, setting his hoofs upon some burning embers, started, threw him forward against the pommel of the saddle, and gave him a mortal hurt. For six weeks he lay dying in a monastery near Rouen, and then made his will, giving England to William, Normandy to Robert, and five thousand pounds to Henry. And now, his violent deeds lay heavy on his mind. He ordered money to be given to many English churches and monasteries, and—which was much better repentance—released his prisoners of state, some of whom had been confined in his dungeons twenty years.

It was a September morning, and the sun was rising, when the King was awakened from slumber by the sound of a church bell. 'What bell is that?' he faintly asked. They told him it was the bell of the chapel of Saint Mary. 'I commend my soul,' said he, 'to Mary!' and died.

Think of his name, The Conqueror, and then consider how he lay in death! The moment he was dead, his physicians, priests, and nobles, not knowing what contest for the throne might now take place, or what might happen in it, hastened away, each man for himself and his own property; the mercenary servants of the court began to rob and plunder; the body of the King, in the indecent strife, was rolled from the bed, and lay alone, for hours, upon the ground. O Conqueror, of whom so many great names are proud now, of whom so many great names thought nothing then, it were better to have conquered one true heart, than England!

By-and-by, the priests came creeping in with prayers and candles; and a good knight, named Herluin, undertook (which no one else would do) to convey the body to Caen, in Normandy, in order that it might be buried in St. Stephen's church there, which the Conqueror had founded. But fire, of which he had made such bad use in his life, seemed to follow him of itself in death. A great conflagration broke out in the town when the body was placed in the church; and those present running out to extinguish the flames, it was once again left alone.

It was not even buried in peace. It was about to be let down, in its Royal robes, into a tomb near the high altar, in presence of a great concourse of people, when a loud voice in the crowd cried out, 'This ground is mine! Upon it, stood my father's house. This King despoiled me of both ground and house to build this church. In the great name of God, I here forbid his body to be covered with the earth that is my right!' The priests and bishops present, knowing the speaker's right, and knowing that the King had often denied him justice, paid him down sixty shillings for the grave. Even then, the corpse was not at rest. The tomb was too small, and they tried to force it in. It broke, a dreadful smell arose, the people hurried out into the air, and, for the third time, it was left alone.

Where were the Conqueror's three sons, that they were not at their father's burial? Robert was lounging among minstrels, dancers, and gamesters, in France or Germany. Henry was carrying his five thousand pounds safely away in a convenient chest he had got made. William the Red was hurrying to England, to lay hands upon the Royal treasure and the crown.

CHAPTER IX—ENGLAND UNDER WILLIAM THE SECOND, CALLED RUFUS

William the Red, in breathless haste, secured the three great forts of Dover, Pevensey, and Hastings, and made with hot speed for Winchester, where the Royal treasure was kept. The treasurer delivering him the keys, he found that it amounted to sixty thousand pounds in silver, besides gold and jewels. Possessed of this wealth, he soon persuaded the Archbishop of Canterbury to crown him, and became William the Second, King of England.

Rufus was no sooner on the throne, than he ordered into prison again the unhappy state captives whom his father had set free, and directed a goldsmith to ornament his father's tomb profusely with gold and silver. It would have been more dutiful in him to have attended the sick Conqueror when he was dying; but England itself, like this Red King, who once governed it, has sometimes made expensive tombs for dead men whom it treated shabbily when they were alive.

The King's brother, Robert of Normandy, seeming quite content to be only Duke of that country; and the King's other brother, Fine-Scholar, being quiet enough with his five thousand pounds in a chest; the King flattered himself, we may suppose, with the hope of an easy reign. But easy reigns were difficult to have in those days. The turbulent Bishop Odo (who had blessed the Norman army at the Battle of Hastings, and who, I dare say, took all the credit of the victory to himself) soon began, in concert with some powerful Norman nobles, to trouble the Red King.

The truth seems to be that this bishop and his friends, who had lands in England and lands in Normandy, wished to hold both under one Sovereign; and greatly preferred a thoughtless good-natured person, such as Robert was, to Rufus; who, though far from being an amiable man in any respect, was keen, and not to be imposed upon. They declared in Robert's favour, and retired to their castles (those castles were very troublesome to kings) in a sullen humour. The Red King, seeing the Normans thus falling from him, revenged himself upon them by appealing to the English; to whom he made a variety of promises, which he never meant to perform—in particular, promises to soften the cruelty of the Forest Laws; and who, in return, so aided him with their valour, that Odo was besieged in the Castle of Rochester, and forced to abandon it, and to depart from England for ever: whereupon the other rebellious Norman nobles were soon reduced and scattered.

Then, the Red King went over to Normandy, where the people suffered greatly under the loose rule of Duke Robert. The King's object was to seize upon the Duke's dominions. This, the Duke, of course, prepared to resist; and miserable war between the two brothers seemed inevitable, when the powerful nobles on both sides, who had seen so much of war, interfered to prevent it. A treaty was made. Each of the two brothers agreed to give up something of his claims, and that the longer-liver of the two should inherit all the dominions of the other. When they had come to this loving understanding, they embraced and joined their forces against Fine-Scholar; who had bought some territory of Robert with a part of his five thousand pounds, and was considered a dangerous individual in consequence.

St. Michael's Mount, in Normandy (there is another St. Michael's Mount, in Cornwall, wonderfully like it), was then, as it is now, a strong place perched upon the top of a high rock, around which, when the tide is in, the sea flows, leaving no road to the mainland. In this place, Fine-Scholar shut himself up with his soldiers, and here he was closely besieged by his two brothers. At one time, when he was reduced to great distress for want of water, the generous Robert not only permitted his men to get water, but sent Fine-Scholar wine from his own table; and, on being remonstrated with by the Red King, said 'What! shall we let our own brother die of thirst? Where shall we get another, when he is gone?' At another time, the Red King riding alone on the shore of the bay, looking up at the Castle, was taken by two of Fine-Scholar's men, one of whom was about to kill him, when he cried out, 'Hold, knave! I am the King of England!' The story says that the soldier raised him from the ground respectfully and humbly, and that the King took him into his service. The story may or may not be true; but at any rate it is true that Fine-Scholar could not hold out against his united brothers, and that he abandoned Mount St. Michael, and wandered about—as poor and forlorn as other scholars have been sometimes known to be.

The Scotch became unquiet in the Red King's time, and were twice defeated—the second time, with the loss of their King, Malcolm, and his son. The Welsh became unquiet too. Against them, Rufus was less successful; for they fought among their native mountains, and did great execution on the King's troops. Robert of Normandy became unquiet too; and, complaining that his brother the King did not faithfully perform his part of their agreement, took up arms, and obtained assistance from the King of France, whom Rufus, in the end, bought off with vast sums of money. England became unquiet too. Lord Mowbray, the powerful Earl of Northumberland, headed a great conspiracy to depose the King, and to place upon the throne, Stephen, the Conqueror's near relative. The plot was discovered; all the chief conspirators were seized; some were fined, some were put in prison, some were put to death. The Earl of Northumberland himself was shut up in a dungeon beneath Windsor Castle, where he died, an old man, thirty long years afterwards. The Priests in England were more unquiet than any other class or power; for the Red King treated them with such small ceremony that he refused to appoint new bishops or archbishops when the old ones died, but kept all the wealth belonging to those offices in his own hands. In return for this, the Priests wrote his life when he was dead, and abused him well. I am inclined to think, myself, that there was little to choose between the Priests and the Red King; that both sides were greedy and designing; and that they were fairly matched.

The Red King was false of heart, selfish, covetous, and mean. He had a worthy minister in his favourite, Ralph, nicknamed—for almost every famous person had a nickname in those rough days—Flambard, or the Firebrand. Once, the King being ill, became penitent, and made Anselm, a foreign priest and a good man, Archbishop of Canterbury. But he no sooner got well again than he repented of his repentance, and persisted in wrongfully keeping to himself some of the wealth belonging to the archbishopric. This led to violent disputes, which were aggravated by there being in Rome at that time two rival Popes; each of whom declared he was the only real original infallible Pope, who couldn't make a mistake. At last, Anselm, knowing the

Red King's character, and not feeling himself safe in England, asked leave to return abroad. The Red King gladly gave it; for he knew that as soon as Anselm was gone, he could begin to store up all the Canterbury money again, for his own use.

By such means, and by taxing and oppressing the English people in every possible way, the Red King became very rich. When he wanted money for any purpose, he raised it by some means or other, and cared nothing for the injustice he did, or the misery he caused. Having the opportunity of buying from Robert the whole duchy of Normandy for five years, he taxed the English people more than ever, and made the very convents sell their plate and valuables to supply him with the means to make the purchase. But he was as quick and eager in putting down revolt as he was in raising money; for, a part of the Norman people objecting—very naturally, I think—to being sold in this way, he headed an army against them with all the speed and energy of his father. He was so impatient, that he embarked for Normandy in a great gale of wind. And when the sailors told him it was dangerous to go to sea in such angry weather, he replied, 'Hoist sail and away! Did you ever hear of a king who was drowned?'

You will wonder how it was that even the careless Robert came to sell his dominions. It happened thus. It had long been the custom for many English people to make journeys to Jerusalem, which were called pilgrimages, in order that they might pray beside the tomb of Our Saviour there. Jerusalem belonging to the Turks, and the Turks hating Christianity, these Christian travellers were often insulted and ill used. The Pilgrims bore it patiently for some time, but at length a remarkable man, of great earnestness and eloquence, called Peter the Hermit, began to preach in various places against the Turks, and to declare that it was the duty of good Christians to drive away those unbelievers from the tomb of Our Saviour, and to take possession of it, and protect it. An excitement such as the world had never known before was created. Thousands and thousands of men of all ranks and conditions departed for Jerusalem to make war against the Turks. The war is called in history the first Crusade, and every Crusader wore a cross marked on his right shoulder.

All the Crusaders were not zealous Christians. Among them were vast numbers of the restless, idle, profligate, and adventurous spirit of the time. Some became Crusaders for the love of change; some, in the hope of plunder; some, because they had nothing to do at home; some, because they did what the priests told them; some, because they liked to see foreign countries; some, because they were fond of knocking men about, and would as soon knock a Turk about as a Christian. Robert of Normandy may have been influenced by all these motives; and by a kind desire, besides, to save the Christian Pilgrims from bad treatment in future. He wanted to raise a number of armed men, and to go to the Crusade. He could not do so without money. He had no money; and he sold his dominions to his brother, the Red King, for five years. With the large sum he thus obtained, he fitted out his Crusaders gallantly, and went away to Jerusalem in martial state. The Red King, who made money out of everything, stayed at home, busily squeezing more money out of Normans and English.

After three years of great hardship and suffering—from shipwreck at sea; from travel in strange lands; from hunger, thirst, and fever, upon the burning sands of the desert; and from the fury of the Turks—the valiant Crusaders got possession of Our Saviour's tomb. The Turks were still resisting and fighting bravely, but this success increased the general desire in Europe to join the Crusade. Another great French Duke was proposing to sell his dominions for a term to the rich Red King, when the Red King's reign came to a sudden and violent end.

You have not forgotten the New Forest which the Conqueror made, and which the miserable people whose homes he had laid waste, so hated. The cruelty of the Forest Laws, and the torture and death they brought upon the peasantry, increased this hatred. The poor persecuted country people believed that the New Forest was enchanted. They said that in thunder-storms, and on dark nights, demons appeared, moving beneath the branches of the gloomy trees. They said that a terrible spectre had foretold to Norman hunters that the Red King should be punished there. And now, in the pleasant season of May, when the Red King had reigned almost thirteen years; and a second Prince of the Conqueror's blood—another Richard, the son of Duke

67

Robert—was killed by an arrow in this dreaded Forest; the people said that the second time was not the last, and that there was another death to come.

It was a lonely forest, accursed in the people's hearts for the wicked deeds that had been done to make it; and no man save the King and his Courtiers and Huntsmen, liked to stray there. But, in reality, it was like any other forest. In the spring, the green leaves broke out of the buds; in the summer, flourished heartily, and made deep shades; in the winter, shrivelled and blew down, and lay in brown heaps on the moss. Some trees were stately, and grew high and strong; some had fallen of themselves; some were felled by the forester's axe; some were hollow, and the rabbits burrowed at their roots; some few were struck by lightning, and stood white and bare. There were hill-sides covered with rich fern, on which the morning dew so beautifully sparkled; there were brooks, where the deer went down to drink, or over which the whole herd bounded, flying from the arrows of the huntsmen; there were sunny glades, and solemn places where but little light came through the rustling leaves. The songs of the birds in the New Forest were pleasanter to hear than the shouts of fighting men outside; and even when the Red King and his Court came hunting through its solitudes, cursing loud and riding hard, with a jingling of stirrups and bridles and knives and daggers, they did much less harm there than among the English or Normans, and the stags died (as they lived) far easier than the people.

Upon a day in August, the Red King, now reconciled to his brother, Fine-Scholar, came with a great train to hunt in the New Forest. Fine-Scholar was of the party. They were a merry party, and had lain all night at Malwood-Keep, a hunting-lodge in the forest, where they had made good cheer, both at supper and breakfast, and had drunk a deal of wine. The party dispersed in various directions, as the custom of hunters then was. The King took with him only Sir Walter Tyrrel, who was a famous sportsman, and to whom he had given, before they mounted horse that morning, two fine arrows.

The last time the King was ever seen alive, he was riding with Sir Walter Tyrrel, and their dogs were hunting together.

It was almost night, when a poor charcoal-burner, passing through the forest with his cart, came upon the solitary body of a dead man, shot with an arrow in the breast, and still bleeding. He got it into his cart. It was the body of the King. Shaken and tumbled, with its red beard all whitened with lime and clotted with blood, it was driven in the cart by the charcoal-burner next day to Winchester Cathedral, where it was received and buried.

Sir Walter Tyrrel, who escaped to Normandy, and claimed the protection of the King of France, swore in France that the Red King was suddenly shot dead by an arrow from an unseen hand, while they were hunting together; that he was fearful of being suspected as the King's murderer; and that he instantly set spurs to his horse, and fled to the sea-shore. Others declared that the King and Sir Walter Tyrrel were hunting in company, a little before sunset, standing in bushes opposite one another, when a stag came between them. That the King drew his bow and took aim, but the string broke. That the King then cried, 'Shoot, Walter, in the Devil's name!' That Sir Walter shot. That the arrow glanced against a tree, was turned aside from the stag, and struck the King from his horse, dead.

By whose hand the Red King really fell, and whether that hand despatched the arrow to his breast by accident or by design, is only known to God. Some think his brother may have caused him to be killed; but the Red King had made so many enemies, both among priests and people, that suspicion may reasonably rest upon a less unnatural murderer. Men know no more than that he was found dead in the New Forest, which the suffering people had regarded as a doomed ground for his race.

CHAPTER X—ENGLAND UNDER HENRY THE FIRST, CALLED FINE-SCHOLAR

Fine-scholar, on hearing of the Red King's death, hurried to Winchester with as much speed as Rufus himself had made, to seize the Royal treasure. But the keeper of the treasure who had been one of the hunting-party in the Forest, made haste to Winchester too, and, arriving there at about the same time, refused to yield it up. Upon this, Fine-Scholar drew his sword, and threatened to kill the treasurer; who might have paid for his fidelity with his life, but that he knew longer resistance to be useless when he found the Prince supported by a company of powerful barons, who declared they were determined to make him King. The treasurer, therefore, gave up the money and jewels of the Crown: and on the third day after the death of the Red King, being a Sunday, Fine-Scholar stood before the high altar in Westminster Abbey, and made a solemn declaration that he would resign the Church property which his brother had seized; that he would do no wrong to the nobles; and that he would restore to the people the laws of Edward the Confessor, with all the improvements of William the Conqueror. So began the reign of King Henry the First.

The people were attached to their new King, both because he had known distresses, and because he was an Englishman by birth and not a Norman. To strengthen this last hold upon them, the King wished to marry an English lady; and could think of no other wife than Maud the Good, the daughter of the King of Scotland. Although this good Princess did not love the King, she was so affected by the representations the nobles made to her of the great charity it would be in her to unite the Norman and Saxon races, and prevent hatred and bloodshed between them for the future, that she consented to become his wife. After some disputing among the priests, who said that as she had been in a convent in her youth, and had worn the veil of a nun, she could not lawfully be married—against which the Princess stated that her aunt, with whom she had lived in her youth, had indeed sometimes thrown a piece of black stuff over her, but for no other reason than because the nun's veil was the only dress the conquering Normans respected in girl or woman, and not because she had taken the vows of a nun, which she never had—she was declared free to marry, and was made King Henry's Queen. A good Queen she was; beautiful, kind-hearted, and worthy of a better husband than the King.

For he was a cunning and unscrupulous man, though firm and clever. He cared very little for his word, and took any means to gain his ends. All this is shown in his treatment of his brother Robert—Robert, who had suffered him to be refreshed with water, and who had sent him the wine from his own table, when he was shut up, with the crows flying below him, parched with thirst, in the castle on the top of St. Michael's Mount, where his Red brother would have let him die.

Before the King began to deal with Robert, he removed and disgraced all the favourites of the late King; who were for the most part base characters, much detested by the people. Flambard, or Firebrand, whom the late King had made Bishop of Durham, of all things in the world, Henry imprisoned in the Tower; but Firebrand was a great joker and a jolly companion, and made himself so popular with his guards that they pretended to know nothing about a long rope that was sent into his prison at the bottom of a deep flagon of wine. The guards took the wine, and Firebrand took the rope; with which, when they were fast asleep, he let himself down from a window in the night, and so got cleverly aboard ship and away to Normandy.

Now Robert, when his brother Fine-Scholar came to the throne, was still absent in the Holy Land. Henry pretended that Robert had been made Sovereign of that country; and he had been away so long, that the ignorant people believed it. But, behold, when Henry had been some time King of England, Robert came home to Normandy; having leisurely returned from Jerusalem through Italy, in which beautiful country he had enjoyed himself very much, and had married a lady as beautiful as itself! In Normandy, he found Firebrand waiting to urge him to assert his claim to the English crown, and declare war against King Henry. This, after great loss of time in feasting and dancing with his beautiful Italian wife among his Norman friends, he at last did.

The English in general were on King Henry's side, though many of the Normans were on Robert's. But the English sailors deserted the King, and took a great part of the English fleet over to Normandy; so that Robert came to invade this country in no foreign vessels, but in English ships. The virtuous Anselm, however, whom Henry had invited back from abroad, and made Archbishop of Canterbury, was steadfast in the King's cause; and it was so well supported that the two armies, instead of fighting, made a peace. Poor Robert, who trusted anybody and everybody, readily trusted his brother, the King; and agreed to go home and receive a pension from England, on condition that all his followers were fully pardoned. This the King very faithfully promised, but Robert was no sooner gone than he began to punish them.

Among them was the Earl of Shrewsbury, who, on being summoned by the King to answer to five-and-forty accusations, rode away to one of his strong castles, shut himself up therein, called around him his tenants and vassals, and fought for his liberty, but was defeated and banished. Robert, with all his faults, was so true to his word, that when he first heard of this nobleman having risen against his brother, he laid waste the Earl of Shrewsbury's estates in Normandy, to show the King that he would favour no breach of their treaty. Finding, on better information, afterwards, that the Earl's only crime was having been his friend, he came over to England, in his old thoughtless, warm-hearted way, to intercede with the King, and remind him of the solemn promise to pardon all his followers.

This confidence might have put the false King to the blush, but it did not. Pretending to be very friendly, he so surrounded his brother with spies and traps, that Robert, who was quite in his power, had nothing for it but to renounce his pension and escape while he could. Getting home to Normandy, and understanding the King better now, he naturally allied himself with his old friend the Earl of Shrewsbury, who had still thirty castles in that country. This was exactly what Henry wanted. He immediately declared that Robert had broken the treaty, and next year invaded Normandy.

He pretended that he came to deliver the Normans, at their own request, from his brother's misrule. There is reason to fear that his misrule was bad enough; for his beautiful wife had died, leaving him with an infant son, and his court was again so careless, dissipated, and ill-regulated, that it was said he sometimes lay in bed of a day for want of clothes to put on—his attendants having stolen all his dresses. But he headed his army like a brave prince and a gallant soldier, though he had the misfortune to be taken prisoner by King Henry, with four hundred of his Knights. Among them was poor harmless Edgar Atheling, who loved Robert well. Edgar was not important enough to be severe with. The King afterwards gave him a small pension, which he lived upon and died upon, in peace, among the quiet woods and fields of England.

And Robert—poor, kind, generous, wasteful, heedless Robert, with so many faults, and yet with virtues that might have made a better and a happier man—what was the end of him? If the King had had the magnanimity to say with a kind air, 'Brother, tell me, before these noblemen, that from this time you will be my faithful follower and friend, and never raise your hand against me or my forces more!' he might have trusted Robert to the death. But the King was not a magnanimous man. He sentenced his brother to be confined for life in one of the Royal Castles. In the beginning of his imprisonment, he was allowed to ride out, guarded; but he one day broke away from his guard and galloped of. He had the evil fortune to ride into a swamp, where his horse stuck fast and he was taken. When the King heard of it he ordered him to be blinded, which was done by putting a red-hot metal basin on his eyes.

And so, in darkness and in prison, many years, he thought of all his past life, of the time he had wasted, of the treasure he had squandered, of the opportunities he had lost, of the youth he had thrown away, of the talents he had neglected. Sometimes, on fine autumn mornings, he would sit and think of the old hunting parties in the free Forest, where he had been the foremost and the gayest. Sometimes, in the still nights, he would wake, and mourn for the many nights that had stolen past him at the gaming-table; sometimes, would seem to hear, upon the melancholy wind, the old songs of the minstrels; sometimes, would dream, in his blindness, of the light and glitter of the Norman Court. Many and many a time, he groped back, in his fancy, to Jerusalem, where he had fought so well; or, at the head of his brave companions, bowed his feathered helmet to the shouts of welcome greeting him in Italy, and seemed again to walk among the sunny vineyards, or on the shore of the blue sea, with his lovely wife. And then, thinking of her grave, and of his fatherless boy, he would stretch out his solitary arms and weep.

At length, one day, there lay in prison, dead, with cruel and disfiguring scars upon his eyelids, bandaged from his jailer's sight, but on which the eternal Heavens looked down, a worn old man of eighty. He had once been Robert of Normandy. Pity him!

At the time when Robert of Normandy was taken prisoner by his brother, Robert's little son was only five years old. This child was taken, too, and carried before the King, sobbing and crying; for, young as he was, he knew he had good reason to be afraid of his Royal uncle. The King was not much accustomed to pity those who were in his power, but his cold heart seemed for the moment to soften towards the boy. He was observed to make a great effort, as if to prevent himself from being cruel, and ordered the child to be taken away; whereupon a certain Baron, who had married a daughter of Duke Robert's (by name, Helie of Saint Saen), took charge of him, tenderly. The King's gentleness did not last long. Before two years were over, he sent messengers to this lord's Castle to seize the child and bring him away. The Baron was not there at the time, but his servants were faithful, and carried the boy off in his sleep and hid him. When the Baron came home, and was told what the King had done, he took the child abroad, and, leading him by the hand, went from King to King and from Court to Court, relating how the child had a claim to the throne of England, and how his uncle the King, knowing that he had that claim, would have murdered him, perhaps, but for his escape.

The youth and innocence of the pretty little William Fitz-Robert (for that was his name) made him many friends at that time. When he became a young man, the King of France, uniting with the French Counts of Anjou and Flanders, supported his cause against the King of England, and took many of the King's towns and castles in Normandy. But, King Henry, artful and cunning always, bribed some of William's friends with money, some with promises, some with power. He bought off the Count of Anjou, by promising to marry his eldest son, also named William, to the Count's daughter; and indeed the whole trust of this King's life was in such bargains, and he believed (as many another King has done since, and as one King did in France a very little time ago) that every man's truth and honour can be bought at some price. For all this, he was so afraid of William Fitz-Robert and his friends, that, for a long time, he believed his life to be in danger; and never lay down to sleep, even in his palace surrounded by his guards, without having a sword and buckler at his bedside.

To strengthen his power, the King with great ceremony betrothed his eldest daughter Matilda, then a child only eight years old, to be the wife of Henry the Fifth, the Emperor of Germany. To raise her marriage-portion, he taxed the English people in a most oppressive manner; then treated them to a great procession, to restore their good humour; and sent Matilda away, in fine state, with the German ambassadors, to be educated in the country of her future husband.

And now his Queen, Maud the Good, unhappily died. It was a sad thought for that gentle lady, that the only hope with which she had married a man whom she had never loved—the hope of reconciling the Norman and English races—had failed. At the very time of her death, Normandy and all France was in arms against England; for, so soon as his last danger was over, King Henry had been false to all the French powers he had promised, bribed, and bought, and they had naturally united against him. After some fighting, however, in which few suffered but the unhappy common people (who always suffered, whatsoever was the matter), he began to promise, bribe, and buy again; and by those means, and by the help of the Pope, who exerted himself to save more bloodshed, and by solemnly declaring, over and over again, that he really was in earnest this time, and would keep his word, the King made peace.

One of the first consequences of this peace was, that the King went over to Normandy with his son Prince William and a great retinue, to have the Prince acknowledged as his successor by the Norman Nobles, and to contract the promised marriage (this was one of the many promises the King had broken) between him and the daughter of the Count of Anjou. Both these things were triumphantly done, with great show and rejoicing; and on the twenty-fifth of November, in the year one thousand one hundred and twenty, the whole retinue prepared to embark at the Port of Barfleur, for the voyage home.

On that day, and at that place, there came to the King, Fitz-Stephen, a sea-captain, and said:

'My liege, my father served your father all his life, upon the sea. He steered the ship with the golden boy upon the prow, in which your father sailed to conquer England. I beseech you to grant me the same office. I have a fair vessel in the harbour here, called The White Ship, manned by fifty sailors of renown. I pray you, Sire, to let your servant have the honour of steering you in The White Ship to England!'

'I am sorry, friend,' replied the King, 'that my vessel is already chosen, and that I cannot (therefore) sail with the son of the man who served my father. But the Prince and all his company shall go along with you, in the fair White Ship, manned by the fifty sailors of renown.'

An hour or two afterwards, the King set sail in the vessel he had chosen, accompanied by other vessels, and, sailing all night with a fair and gentle wind, arrived upon the coast of England in the morning. While it was yet night, the people in some of those ships heard a faint wild cry come over the sea, and wondered what it was.

Now, the Prince was a dissolute, debauched young man of eighteen, who bore no love to the English, and had declared that when he came to the throne he would yoke them to the plough like oxen. He went aboard The White Ship, with one hundred and forty youthful Nobles like himself, among whom were eighteen noble ladies of the highest rank. All this gay company, with their servants and the fifty sailors, made three hundred souls aboard the fair White Ship.

'Give three casks of wine, Fitz-Stephen,' said the Prince, 'to the fifty sailors of renown! My father the King has sailed out of the harbour. What time is there to make merry here, and yet reach England with the rest?'

'Prince!' said Fitz-Stephen, 'before morning, my fifty and The White

Ship shall overtake the swiftest vessel in attendance on your father the King, if we sail at midnight!'

Then the Prince commanded to make merry; and the sailors drank out the three casks of wine; and the Prince and all the noble company danced in the moonlight on the deck of The White Ship.

When, at last, she shot out of the harbour of Barfleur, there was not a sober seaman on board. But the sails were all set, and the oars all going merrily. Fitz-Stephen had the helm. The gay young nobles and the beautiful ladies, wrapped in mantles of various bright colours to protect them from the cold, talked, laughed, and sang. The Prince encouraged the fifty sailors to row harder yet, for the honour of The White Ship.

Crash! A terrific cry broke from three hundred hearts. It was the cry the people in the distant vessels of the King heard faintly on the water. The White Ship had struck upon a rock—was filling—going down!

Fitz-Stephen hurried the Prince into a boat, with some few Nobles. 'Push off,' he whispered; 'and row to land. It is not far, and the sea is smooth. The rest of us must die.'

But, as they rowed away, fast, from the sinking ship, the Prince heard the voice of his sister Marie, the Countess of Perche, calling for help. He never in his life had been so good as he was then. He cried in an agony, 'Row back at any risk! I cannot bear to leave her!'

They rowed back. As the Prince held out his arms to catch his sister, such numbers leaped in, that the boat was overset. And in the same instant The White Ship went down.

Only two men floated. They both clung to the main yard of the ship, which had broken from the mast, and now supported them. One asked the other who he was? He said, 'I am a nobleman, Godfrey by name, the son of Gilbert de l'Aigle. And you?' said he. 'I am Berold, a poor butcher of Rouen,' was the answer. Then, they said together, 'Lord be merciful to us both!' and tried to encourage one another, as they drifted in the cold benumbing sea on that unfortunate November night.

By-and-by, another man came swimming towards them, whom they knew, when he pushed aside his long wet hair, to be Fitz-Stephen. 'Where is the Prince?' said he. 'Gone! Gone!' the two cried together. 'Neither he, nor his brother, nor his sister, nor the King's niece, nor her brother, nor any one of all the brave three hundred, noble or commoner, except we three, has risen above the water!' Fitz-Stephen, with a ghastly face, cried, 'Woe! woe, to me!' and sunk to the bottom.

The other two clung to the yard for some hours. At length the young noble said faintly, 'I am exhausted, and chilled with the cold, and can hold no longer. Farewell, good friend! God preserve you!' So, he dropped and sunk; and of all the brilliant crowd, the poor Butcher of Rouen alone was saved. In the morning, some fishermen saw him floating in his sheep-skin coat, and got him into their boat—the sole relater of the dismal tale.

For three days, no one dared to carry the intelligence to the King. At length, they sent into his presence a little boy, who, weeping bitterly, and kneeling at his feet, told him that The White Ship was lost with all on board. The King fell to the ground like a dead man, and never, never afterwards, was seen to smile.

But he plotted again, and promised again, and bribed and bought again, in his old deceitful way. Having no son to succeed him, after all his pains ('The Prince will never yoke us to the plough, now!' said the English people), he took a second wife—Adelais or Alice, a duke's daughter, and the Pope's niece. Having no more children, however, he proposed to the Barons to swear that they would recognise as his successor, his daughter Matilda, whom, as she was now a widow, he married to the eldest son of the Count of Anjou, Geoffrey, surnamed Plantagenet, from a custom he had of wearing a sprig of flowering broom (called Genêt in French) in his cap for a feather. As one false man usually makes many, and as a false King, in particular, is pretty certain to make a false Court, the Barons took the oath about the succession of Matilda (and her children after her), twice over, without in the least intending to keep it. The King was now relieved from any remaining fears of William Fitz-Robert, by his death in the Monastery of St. Omer, in France, at twenty-six years old, of a pike-wound in the hand. And as Matilda gave birth to three sons, he thought the succession to the throne secure.

He spent most of the latter part of his life, which was troubled by family quarrels, in Normandy, to be near Matilda. When he had reigned upward of thirty-five years, and was sixty-seven years old, he died of an indigestion and fever, brought on by eating, when he was far from well, of a fish called Lamprey, against which he had often been cautioned by his physicians. His remains were brought over to Reading Abbey to be buried.

You may perhaps hear the cunning and promise-breaking of King Henry the First, called 'policy' by some people, and 'diplomacy' by others. Neither of these fine words will in the least mean that it was true; and nothing that is not true can possibly be good.

His greatest merit, that I know of, was his love of learning—I should have given him greater credit even for that, if it had been strong enough to induce him to spare the eyes of a certain poet he once took prisoner, who was a knight besides. But he ordered the poet's eyes to be torn from his head, because he had laughed at him in his verses; and the poet, in the pain of that torture, dashed out his own brains against his prison wall. King Henry the First was avaricious, revengeful, and so false, that I suppose a man never lived whose word was less to be relied upon.

CHAPTER XI—ENGLAND UNDER MATILDA AND STEPHEN

The King was no sooner dead than all the plans and schemes he had laboured at so long, and lied so much for, crumbled away like a hollow heap of sand. Stephen, whom he had never mistrusted or suspected, started up to claim the throne.

Stephen was the son of Adela, the Conqueror's daughter, married to the Count of Blois. To Stephen, and to his brother Henry, the late King had been liberal; making Henry Bishop of Winchester, and finding a good marriage for Stephen, and much enriching him. This did not prevent Stephen from hastily producing a false witness, a servant of the late King, to swear that the King had named him for his heir upon his death-bed. On this evidence the Archbishop of Canterbury crowned him. The new King, so suddenly made, lost not a moment in seizing the Royal treasure, and hiring foreign soldiers with some of it to protect his throne.

If the dead King had even done as the false witness said, he would have had small right to will away the English people, like so many sheep or oxen, without their consent. But he had, in fact, bequeathed all his territory to Matilda; who, supported by Robert, Earl of Gloucester, soon began to dispute the crown. Some of the powerful barons and priests took her side; some took Stephen's; all fortified their castles; and again the miserable English people were involved in war, from which they could never derive advantage whosoever was victorious, and in which all parties plundered, tortured, starved, and ruined them.

Five years had passed since the death of Henry the First—and during those five years there had been two terrible invasions by the people of Scotland under their King, David, who was at last defeated with all his army—when Matilda, attended by her brother Robert and a large force, appeared in England to maintain her claim. A battle was fought between her troops and King Stephen's at Lincoln; in which the King himself was taken prisoner, after bravely fighting until his battle-axe and sword were broken, and was carried into strict confinement at Gloucester. Matilda then submitted herself to the Priests, and the Priests crowned her Queen of England.

She did not long enjoy this dignity. The people of London had a great affection for Stephen; many of the Barons considered it degrading to be ruled by a woman; and the Queen's temper was so haughty that she made innumerable enemies. The people of London revolted; and, in alliance with the troops of Stephen, besieged her at Winchester, where they took her brother Robert prisoner, whom, as her best soldier and chief general, she was glad to exchange for Stephen himself, who thus regained his liberty. Then, the long war went on afresh. Once, she was pressed so hard in the Castle of Oxford, in the winter weather when the snow lay thick upon the ground, that her only chance of escape was to dress herself all in white, and, accompanied by no more than three faithful Knights, dressed in like manner that their figures might not be seen from Stephen's camp as they passed over the snow, to steal away on foot, cross the frozen Thames, walk a long distance, and at last gallop away on horseback. All this she did, but to no great purpose then; for her brother dying while the struggle was yet going on, she at last withdrew to Normandy.

In two or three years after her withdrawal her cause appeared in England, afresh, in the person of her son Henry, young Plantagenet, who, at only eighteen years of age, was very powerful: not only on account of his mother having resigned all Normandy to him, but also from his having married Eleanor, the divorced wife of the French King, a bad woman, who had great possessions in France. Louis, the French King, not relishing this arrangement, helped Eustace, King Stephen's son, to invade Normandy: but Henry drove their united forces out of that country, and then returned here, to assist his partisans, whom the King was then besieging at Wallingford upon the Thames. Here, for two days, divided only by the river, the two armies lay encamped opposite to one another—on the eve, as it seemed to all men, of another desperate fight, when the Earl of Arundel took heart and said 'that it was not reasonable to prolong the unspeakable miseries of two kingdoms to minister to the ambition of two princes.'

Many other noblemen repeating and supporting this when it was once uttered, Stephen and young Plantagenet went down, each to his own bank of the river, and held a conversation across it, in which they arranged a truce; very much to the dissatisfaction of Eustace, who swaggered away with some followers, and laid violent hands on the Abbey of St. Edmund's-Bury, where he presently died mad. The truce led to a solemn council at Winchester, in which it was agreed that Stephen should retain the crown, on condition of his declaring Henry his successor; that William, another son of the King's, should inherit his father's rightful possessions; and that all the Crown lands which Stephen had given away should be recalled, and all the Castles he had permitted to be built demolished. Thus terminated the bitter war, which had now lasted fifteen years, and had again laid England waste. In the next year Stephen died, after a troubled reign of nineteen years.

Although King Stephen was, for the time in which he lived, a humane and moderate man, with many excellent qualities; and although nothing worse is known of him than his usurpation of the Crown, which he probably excused to himself by the consideration that King Henry the First was a usurper too—which was no excuse at all; the people of England suffered more in these dread nineteen years, than at any former period even of their suffering history. In the division of the nobility between the two rival claimants of the Crown, and in the growth of what is called the Feudal System (which made the peasants the born vassals and mere slaves of the Barons), every Noble had his strong Castle, where he reigned the cruel king of all the neighbouring people. Accordingly, he perpetrated whatever cruelties he chose. And never were worse cruelties committed upon earth than in wretched England in those nineteen years.

The writers who were living then describe them fearfully. They say that the castles were filled with devils rather than with men; that the peasants, men and women, were put into dungeons for their gold and silver, were tortured with fire and smoke, were hung up by the thumbs, were hung up by the heels with great weights to their heads, were torn with jagged irons, killed with hunger, broken to death in narrow chests filled with sharp-pointed stones, murdered in countless fiendish ways. In England there was no corn, no meat, no cheese, no butter, there were no tilled lands, no harvests. Ashes of burnt towns, and dreary wastes, were all that the traveller, fearful of the robbers who prowled abroad at all hours, would see in a long day's journey; and from sunrise until night, he would not come upon a home.

The clergy sometimes suffered, and heavily too, from pillage, but many of them had castles of their own, and fought in helmet and armour like the barons, and drew lots with other fighting men for their share of booty. The Pope (or Bishop of Rome), on King Stephen's resisting his ambition, laid England under an Interdict at one period of this reign; which means that he allowed no service to be performed in the churches, no couples to be married, no bells to be rung, no dead bodies to be buried. Any man having the power to refuse these things, no matter whether he were called a Pope or a Poulterer, would, of course, have the power of afflicting numbers of innocent people. That nothing might be wanting to the miseries of King Stephen's time, the Pope threw in this contribution to the public store—not very like the widow's contribution, as I think, when Our Saviour sat in Jerusalem over-against the Treasury, 'and she threw in two mites, which make a farthing.'

CHAPTER XII—ENGLAND UNDER HENRY THE SECOND

PART THE FIRST

Henry Plantagenet, when he was but twenty-one years old, quietly succeeded to the throne of England, according to his agreement made with the late King at Winchester. Six weeks after Stephen's death, he and his Queen, Eleanor, were crowned in that city; into which they rode on horseback in great state, side by side, amidst much shouting and rejoicing, and clashing of music, and strewing of flowers.

The reign of King Henry the Second began well. The King had great possessions, and (what with his own rights, and what with those of his wife) was lord of one-third part of France. He was a young man of vigour, ability, and resolution, and immediately applied himself to remove some of the evils which had arisen in the last unhappy reign. He revoked all the grants of land that had been hastily made, on either side, during the late struggles; he obliged numbers of disorderly soldiers to depart from England; he reclaimed all the castles belonging to the Crown; and he forced the wicked nobles to pull down their own castles, to the number of eleven hundred, in which such dismal cruelties had been inflicted on the people. The King's brother, Geoffrey, rose against him in France, while he was so well employed, and rendered it necessary for him to repair to that country; where, after he had subdued and made a friendly arrangement with his brother (who did not live long), his ambition to increase his possessions involved him in a war with the French King, Louis, with whom he had been on such friendly terms just before, that to the French King's infant daughter, then a baby in the cradle, he had promised one of his little sons in marriage, who was a child of five years old. However, the war came to nothing at last, and the Pope made the two Kings friends again.

Now, the clergy, in the troubles of the last reign, had gone on very ill indeed. There were all kinds of criminals among them—murderers, thieves, and vagabonds; and the worst of the matter was, that the good priests would not give up the bad priests to justice, when they committed crimes, but persisted in sheltering and defending them. The King, well knowing that there could be no peace or rest in England while such things lasted, resolved to reduce the power of the clergy; and, when he had reigned seven years, found (as he considered) a good opportunity for doing so, in the death of the Archbishop of Canterbury. 'I will have for the new Archbishop,' thought the King, 'a friend in whom I can trust, who will help me to humble these rebellious priests, and to have them dealt with, when they do wrong, as other men who do wrong are dealt with.' So, he resolved to make his favourite, the new Archbishop; and this favourite was so extraordinary a man, and his story is so curious, that I must tell you all about him.

Once upon a time, a worthy merchant of London, named Gilbert à Becket, made a pilgrimage to the Holy Land, and was taken prisoner by a Saracen lord. This lord, who treated him kindly and not like a slave, had one fair daughter, who fell in love with the merchant; and who told him that she wanted to become a Christian, and was willing to marry him if they could fly to a Christian country. The merchant returned her love, until he found an opportunity to escape, when he did not trouble himself about the Saracen lady, but escaped with his servant Richard, who had been taken prisoner along with him, and arrived in England and forgot her. The Saracen lady, who was more loving than the merchant, left her father's house in disguise to follow him, and made her way, under many hardships, to the sea-shore. The merchant had taught her only two English words (for I suppose he must have learnt the Saracen tongue himself, and made love in that language), of which London was one, and his own name, Gilbert, the other. She went among the ships, saying, 'London! London!' over and over again, until the sailors understood that she wanted to find an English vessel that would carry her there; so they showed her such a ship, and she paid for her passage with some of her jewels, and sailed away. Well! The merchant was sitting in his counting-house in London one day, when he heard a great noise in the street; and presently Richard came running in from the warehouse, with his eyes wide open and his breath almost gone, saying, 'Master, master, here is the Saracen lady!' The merchant thought Richard was mad; but Richard said, 'No, master! As I live, the Saracen lady is going up and down the city, calling

Gilbert! Gilbert!' Then, he took the merchant by the sleeve, and pointed out of window; and there they saw her among the gables and water-spouts of the dark, dirty street, in her foreign dress, so forlorn, surrounded by a wondering crowd, and passing slowly along, calling Gilbert, Gilbert! When the merchant saw her, and thought of the tenderness she had shown him in his captivity, and of her constancy, his heart was moved, and he ran down into the street; and she saw him coming, and with a great cry fainted in his arms. They were married without loss of time, and Richard (who was an excellent man) danced with joy the whole day of the wedding; and they all lived happy ever afterwards.

This merchant and this Saracen lady had one son, Thomas à Becket. He it was who became the Favourite of King Henry the Second.

He had become Chancellor, when the King thought of making him Archbishop. He was clever, gay, well educated, brave; had fought in several battles in France; had defeated a French knight in single combat, and brought his horse away as a token of the victory. He lived in a noble palace, he was the tutor of the young Prince Henry, he was served by one hundred and forty knights, his riches were immense. The King once sent him as his ambassador to France; and the French people, beholding in what state he travelled, cried out in the streets, 'How splendid must the King of England be, when this is only the Chancellor!' They had good reason to wonder at the magnificence of Thomas à Becket, for, when he entered a French town, his procession was headed by two hundred and fifty singing boys; then, came his hounds in couples; then, eight waggons, each drawn by five horses driven by five drivers: two of the waggons filled with strong ale to be given away to the people; four, with his gold and silver plate and stately clothes; two, with the dresses of his numerous servants. Then, came twelve horses, each with a monkey on his back; then, a train of people bearing shields and leading fine war-horses splendidly equipped; then, falconers with hawks upon their wrists; then, a host of knights, and gentlemen and priests; then, the Chancellor with his brilliant garments flashing in the sun, and all the people capering and shouting with delight.

The King was well pleased with all this, thinking that it only made himself the more magnificent to have so magnificent a favourite; but he sometimes jested with the Chancellor upon his splendour too. Once, when they were riding together through the streets of London in hard winter weather, they saw a shivering old man in rags. 'Look at the poor object!' said the King. 'Would it not be a charitable act to give that aged man a comfortable warm cloak?' 'Undoubtedly it would,' said Thomas à Becket, 'and you do well, Sir, to think of such Christian duties.' 'Come!' cried the King, 'then give him your cloak!' It was made of rich crimson trimmed with ermine. The King tried to pull it off, the Chancellor tried to keep it on, both were near rolling from their saddles in the mud, when the Chancellor submitted, and the King gave the cloak to the old beggar: much to the beggar's astonishment, and much to the merriment of all the courtiers in attendance. For, courtiers are not only eager to laugh when the King laughs, but they really do enjoy a laugh against a Favourite.

'I will make,' thought King Henry the second, 'this Chancellor of mine, Thomas à Becket, Archbishop of Canterbury. He will then be the head of the Church, and, being devoted to me, will help me to correct the Church. He has always upheld my power against the power of the clergy, and once publicly told some bishops (I remember), that men of the Church were equally bound to me, with men of the sword. Thomas à Becket is the man, of all other men in England, to help me in my great design.' So the King, regardless of all objection, either that he was a fighting man, or a lavish man, or a courtly man, or a man of pleasure, or anything but a likely man for the office, made him Archbishop accordingly.

Now, Thomas à Becket was proud and loved to be famous. He was already famous for the pomp of his life, for his riches, his gold and silver plate, his waggons, horses, and attendants. He could do no more in that way than he had done; and being tired of that kind of fame (which is a very poor one), he longed to have his name celebrated for something else. Nothing, he knew, would render him so famous in the world, as the setting of his utmost power and ability against the utmost power and ability of the King. He resolved with the whole strength of his mind to do it.

He may have had some secret grudge against the King besides. The King may have offended his proud humour at some time or other, for anything I know. I think it likely, because it is a common thing for Kings, Princes, and other great people, to try the tempers of their favourites rather severely. Even the little affair of the crimson cloak must have been anything but a pleasant one to a haughty man. Thomas à Becket knew better than any one in England what the King expected of him. In all his sumptuous life, he had never yet been in a position to disappoint the King. He could take up that proud stand now, as head of the Church; and he determined that it should be written in history, either that he subdued the King, or that the King subdued him.

So, of a sudden, he completely altered the whole manner of his life. He turned off all his brilliant followers, ate coarse food, drank bitter water, wore next his skin sackcloth covered with dirt and vermin (for it was then thought very religious to be very dirty), flogged his back to punish himself, lived chiefly in a little cell, washed the feet of thirteen poor people every day, and looked as miserable as he possibly could. If he had put twelve hundred monkeys on horseback instead of twelve, and had gone in procession with eight thousand waggons instead of eight, he could not have half astonished the people so much as by this great change. It soon caused him to be more talked about as an Archbishop than he had been as a Chancellor.

The King was very angry; and was made still more so, when the new Archbishop, claiming various estates from the nobles as being rightfully Church property, required the King himself, for the same reason, to give up Rochester Castle, and Rochester City too. Not satisfied with this, he declared that no power but himself should appoint a priest to any Church in the part of England over which he was Archbishop; and when a certain gentleman of Kent made such an appointment, as he claimed to have the right to do, Thomas à Becket excommunicated him.

Excommunication was, next to the Interdict I told you of at the close of the last chapter, the great weapon of the clergy. It consisted in declaring the person who was excommunicated, an outcast from the Church and from all religious offices; and in cursing him all over, from the top of his head to the sole of his foot, whether he was standing up, lying down, sitting, kneeling, walking, running, hopping, jumping, gaping, coughing, sneezing, or whatever else he was doing. This unchristian nonsense would of course have made no sort of difference to the person cursed—who could say his prayers at home if he were shut out of church, and whom none but God could judge—but for the fears and superstitions of the people, who avoided excommunicated persons, and made their lives unhappy. So, the King said to the New Archbishop, 'Take off this Excommunication from this gentleman of Kent.' To which the Archbishop replied, 'I shall do no such thing.'

The quarrel went on. A priest in Worcestershire committed a most dreadful murder, that aroused the horror of the whole nation. The King demanded to have this wretch delivered up, to be tried in the same court and in the same way as any other murderer. The Archbishop refused, and kept him in the Bishop's prison. The King, holding a solemn assembly in Westminster Hall, demanded that in future all priests found guilty before their Bishops of crimes against the law of the land should be considered priests no longer, and should be delivered over to the law of the land for punishment. The Archbishop again refused. The King required to know whether the clergy would obey the ancient customs of the country? Every priest there, but one, said, after Thomas à Becket, 'Saving my order.' This really meant that they would only obey those customs when they did not interfere with their own claims; and the King went out of the Hall in great wrath.

Some of the clergy began to be afraid, now, that they were going too far. Though Thomas à Becket was otherwise as unmoved as Westminster Hall, they prevailed upon him, for the sake of their fears, to go to the King at Woodstock, and promise to observe the ancient customs of the country, without saying anything about his order. The King received this submission favourably, and summoned a great council of the clergy to meet at the Castle of Clarendon, by Salisbury. But when the council met, the Archbishop again insisted on the words 'saying my order;' and he still insisted, though lords entreated him, and priests wept before him and knelt to him, and an adjoining room was thrown open, filled with armed soldiers of the King, to threaten him. At length he gave way, for that time, and the ancient customs (which included what the King had demanded in vain) were stated in writing, and were signed and sealed by the chief of the clergy, and were called the Constitutions of Clarendon.

The quarrel went on, for all that. The Archbishop tried to see the King. The King would not see him. The Archbishop tried to escape from England. The sailors on the coast would launch no boat to take him away. Then, he again resolved to do his worst in opposition to the King, and began openly to set the ancient customs at defiance.

The King summoned him before a great council at Northampton, where he accused him of high treason, and made a claim against him, which was not a just one, for an enormous sum of money. Thomas à Becket was alone against the whole assembly, and the very Bishops advised him to resign his office and abandon his contest with the King. His great anxiety and agitation stretched him on a sick-bed for two days, but he was still undaunted. He went to the adjourned council, carrying a great cross in his right hand, and sat down holding it erect before him. The King angrily retired into an inner room. The whole assembly angrily retired and left him there. But there he sat. The Bishops came out again in a body, and renounced him as a traitor. He only said, 'I hear!' and sat there still. They retired again into the inner room, and his trial proceeded without him. By-and-by, the Earl of Leicester, heading the barons, came out to read his sentence. He refused to hear it, denied the power of the court, and said he would refer his cause to the Pope. As he walked out of the hall, with the cross in his hand, some of those present picked up rushes—rushes were strewn upon the floors in those days by way of carpet—and threw them at him. He proudly turned his head, and said that were he not Archbishop, he would chastise those cowards with the sword he had known how to use in bygone days. He then mounted his horse, and rode away, cheered and surrounded by the common people, to whom he threw open his house that night and gave a supper, supping with them himself. That same night he secretly departed from the town; and so, travelling by night and hiding by day, and calling himself 'Brother Dearman,' got away, not without difficulty, to Flanders.

The struggle still went on. The angry King took possession of the revenues of the archbishopric, and banished all the relations and servants of Thomas à Becket, to the number of four hundred. The Pope and the French King both protected him, and an abbey was assigned for his residence. Stimulated by this support, Thomas à Becket, on a great festival day, formally proceeded to a great church crowded with people, and going up into the pulpit publicly cursed and excommunicated all who had supported the Constitutions of Clarendon: mentioning many English noblemen by name, and not distantly hinting at the King of England himself.

When intelligence of this new affront was carried to the King in his chamber, his passion was so furious that he tore his clothes, and rolled like a madman on his bed of straw and rushes. But he was soon up and doing. He ordered all the ports and coasts of England to be narrowly watched, that no letters of Interdict might be brought into the kingdom; and sent messengers and bribes to the Pope's palace at Rome. Meanwhile, Thomas à Becket, for his part, was not idle at Rome, but constantly employed his utmost arts in his own behalf. Thus the contest stood, until there was peace between France and England (which had been for some time at war), and until the two children of the two Kings were married in celebration of it. Then, the French King brought about a meeting between Henry and his old favourite, so long his enemy.

Even then, though Thomas à Becket knelt before the King, he was obstinate and immovable as to those words about his order. King Louis of France was weak enough in his veneration for Thomas à Becket and such men, but this was a little too much for him. He said that à Becket 'wanted to be greater than the saints and better than St. Peter,' and rode away from him with the King of England. His poor French Majesty asked à Becket's pardon for so doing, however, soon afterwards, and cut a very pitiful figure.

At last, and after a world of trouble, it came to this. There was another meeting on French ground between King Henry and Thomas à Becket, and it was agreed that Thomas à Becket should be Archbishop of Canterbury, according to the customs of former Archbishops, and that the King should put him in possession of the revenues of that post. And now, indeed, you might suppose the struggle at an end, and Thomas à Becket at rest. No, not even yet. For Thomas à Becket hearing, by some means, that King Henry, when he was in dread of his kingdom being placed under an interdict, had had his eldest son Prince Henry secretly crowned, not only persuaded the Pope to suspend the Archbishop of York who had performed that ceremony, and to excommunicate the Bishops who had assisted at it, but sent a messenger of his own into England, in spite of all the King's precautions along the coast, who delivered the letters of excommunication into the Bishops' own hands. Thomas à Becket then came over to England himself, after an absence of seven years. He was privately warned that it was dangerous to come, and that an ireful knight, named Ranulf de Broc, had threatened that he should not live to eat a loaf of bread in England; but he came.

The common people received him well, and marched about with him in a soldierly way, armed with such rustic weapons as they could get. He tried to see the young prince who had once been his pupil, but was prevented. He hoped for some little support among the nobles and priests, but found none. He made the most of the peasants who attended him, and feasted them, and went from Canterbury to Harrow-on-the-Hill, and from Harrow-on-the-Hill back to Canterbury, and on Christmas Day preached in the Cathedral there, and told the people in his sermon that he had come to die among them, and that it was likely he would be murdered. He had no fear, however—or, if he had any, he had much more obstinacy—for he, then and there, excommunicated three of his enemies, of whom Ranulf de Broc, the ireful knight, was one.

As men in general had no fancy for being cursed, in their sitting and walking, and gaping and sneezing, and all the rest of it, it was very natural in the persons so freely excommunicated to complain to the King. It was equally natural in the King, who had hoped that this troublesome opponent was at last quieted, to fall into a mighty rage when he heard of these new affronts; and, on the Archbishop of York telling him that he never could hope for rest while Thomas à Becket lived, to cry out hastily before his court, 'Have I no one here who will deliver me from this man?' There were four knights present, who, hearing the King's words, looked at one another, and went out.

The names of these knights were Reginald Fitzurse, William Tracy, Hugh de Morville, and Richard Brito; three of whom had been in the train of Thomas à Becket in the old days of his splendour. They rode away on horseback, in a very secret manner, and on the third day after Christmas Day arrived at Saltwood House, not far from Canterbury, which belonged to the family of Ranulf de Broc. They quietly collected some followers here, in case they should need any; and proceeding to Canterbury, suddenly appeared (the four knights and twelve men) before the Archbishop, in his own house, at two o'clock in the afternoon. They neither bowed nor spoke, but sat down on the floor in silence, staring at the Archbishop.

Thomas à Becket said, at length, 'What do you want?'

'We want,' said Reginald Fitzurse, 'the excommunication taken from the Bishops, and you to answer for your offences to the King.' Thomas à Becket defiantly replied, that the power of the clergy was above the power of the King. That it was not for such men as they were, to threaten him. That if he were threatened by all the swords in England, he would never yield.

'Then we will do more than threaten!' said the knights. And they went out with the twelve men, and put on their armour, and drew their shining swords, and came back.

His servants, in the meantime, had shut up and barred the great gate of the palace. At first, the knights tried to shatter it with their battle-axes; but, being shown a window by which they could enter, they let the gate alone, and climbed in that way. While they were battering at the door, the attendants of Thomas à Becket had implored him to take refuge in the Cathedral; in which, as a sanctuary or sacred place, they thought the knights would dare to do no violent deed. He told them, again and again, that he would not stir. Hearing the distant voices of the monks singing the evening service, however, he said it was now his duty to attend, and therefore, and for no other reason, he would go.

There was a near way between his Palace and the Cathedral, by some beautiful old cloisters which you may yet see. He went into the Cathedral, without any hurry, and having the Cross carried before him as usual. When he was safely there, his servants would have fastened the door, but he said No! it was the house of God and not a fortress.

As he spoke, the shadow of Reginald Fitzurse appeared in the Cathedral doorway, darkening the little light there was outside, on the dark winter evening. This knight said, in a strong voice, 'Follow me, loyal servants of the King!' The rattle of the armour of the other knights echoed through the Cathedral, as they came clashing in.

It was so dark, in the lofty aisles and among the stately pillars of the church, and there were so many hiding-places in the crypt below and in the narrow passages above, that Thomas à Becket might even at that pass have saved himself if he would. But he would not. He told the monks resolutely that he would not. And though they all dispersed and left him there with no other follower than Edward Gryme, his faithful cross-bearer, he was as firm then, as ever he had been in his life.

The knights came on, through the darkness, making a terrible noise with their armed tread upon the stone pavement of the church. 'Where is the traitor?' they cried out. He made no answer. But when they cried, 'Where is the Archbishop?' he said proudly, 'I am here!' and came out of the shade and stood before them.

The knights had no desire to kill him, if they could rid the King and themselves of him by any other means. They told him he must either fly or go with them. He said he would do neither; and he threw William Tracy off with such force when he took hold of his sleeve, that Tracy reeled again. By his reproaches and his steadiness, he so incensed them, and exasperated their fierce humour, that Reginald Fitzurse, whom he called by an ill name, said, 'Then die!' and struck at his head. But the faithful Edward Gryme put out his arm, and there received the main force of the blow, so that it only made his master bleed. Another voice from among the knights again called to Thomas à Becket to fly; but, with his blood running down his face, and his hands clasped, and his head bent, he commanded himself to God, and stood firm. Then they cruelly killed him close to the altar of St. Bennet; and his body fell upon the pavement, which was dirtied with his blood and brains.

It is an awful thing to think of the murdered mortal, who had so showered his curses about, lying, all disfigured, in the church, where a few lamps here and there were but red specks on a pall of darkness; and to think of the guilty knights riding away on horseback, looking over their shoulders at the dim Cathedral, and remembering what they had left inside.

PART THE SECOND

When the King heard how Thomas à Becket had lost his life in Canterbury Cathedral, through the ferocity of the four Knights, he was filled with dismay. Some have supposed that when the King spoke those hasty words, 'Have I no one here who will deliver me from this man?' he wished, and meant à Becket to be slain. But few things are more unlikely; for, besides that the King was not naturally cruel (though very passionate), he was wise, and must have known full well what any stupid man in his dominions must have known, namely, that such a murder would rouse the Pope and the whole Church against him.

He sent respectful messengers to the Pope, to represent his innocence (except in having uttered the hasty words); and he swore solemnly and publicly to his innocence, and contrived in time to make his peace. As to the four guilty Knights, who fled into Yorkshire, and never again dared to show themselves at Court, the Pope excommunicated them; and they lived miserably for some time, shunned by all their countrymen. At last, they went humbly to Jerusalem as a penance, and there died and were buried.

It happened, fortunately for the pacifying of the Pope, that an opportunity arose very soon after the murder of à Becket, for the King to declare his power in Ireland—which was an acceptable undertaking to the Pope, as the Irish, who had been converted to Christianity by one Patricius (otherwise Saint Patrick) long ago, before any Pope existed, considered that the Pope had nothing at all to do with them, or they with the Pope, and accordingly refused to pay him Peter's Pence, or that tax of a penny a house which I have elsewhere mentioned. The King's opportunity arose in this way.

The Irish were, at that time, as barbarous a people as you can well imagine. They were continually quarrelling and fighting, cutting one another's throats, slicing one another's noses, burning one another's houses, carrying away one another's wives, and committing all sorts of violence. The country was divided into five kingdoms—Desmond, Thomond, Connaught, Ulster, and Leinster—each governed by a separate King, of whom one claimed to be the chief of the rest. Now, one of these Kings, named Dermond Mac Murrough (a wild kind of name, spelt in more than one wild kind of way), had carried off the wife of a friend of his, and concealed her on an island in a bog. The friend resenting this (though it was quite the custom of the country), complained to the chief King, and, with the chief King's help, drove Dermond Mac Murrough out of his dominions. Dermond came over to England for revenge; and offered to hold his realm as a vassal of King Henry, if King Henry would help him to regain it. The King consented to these terms; but only assisted him, then, with what were called Letters Patent, authorising any English subjects who were so disposed, to enter into his service, and aid his cause.

There was, at Bristol, a certain Earl Richard de Clare, called Strongbow; of no very good character; needy and desperate, and ready for anything that offered him a chance of improving his fortunes. There were, in South Wales, two other broken knights of the same good-for-nothing sort, called Robert Fitz-Stephen, and Maurice Fitz-Gerald. These three, each with a small band of followers, took up Dermond's cause; and it was agreed that if it proved successful, Strongbow should marry Dermond's daughter Eva, and be declared his heir.

The trained English followers of these knights were so superior in all the discipline of battle to the Irish, that they beat them against immense superiority of numbers. In one fight, early in the war, they cut off three hundred heads, and laid them before Mac Murrough; who turned them every one up with his hands, rejoicing, and, coming to one which was the head of a man whom he had much disliked, grasped it by the hair and ears, and tore off the nose and lips with his teeth. You may judge from this, what kind of a gentleman an Irish King in those times was. The captives, all through this war, were horribly treated; the victorious party making nothing of breaking their limbs, and casting them into the sea from the tops of high rocks. It was in the midst of the miseries and cruelties attendant on the taking of Waterford, where the dead lay piled in the streets, and the filthy gutters ran with blood, that Strongbow married Eva. An odious marriage-company those mounds of corpse's must have made, I think, and one quite worthy of the young lady's father.

He died, after Waterford and Dublin had been taken, and various successes achieved; and Strongbow became King of Leinster. Now came King Henry's opportunity. To restrain the growing power of Strongbow, he himself repaired to Dublin, as Strongbow's Royal Master, and deprived him of his kingdom, but confirmed him in the enjoyment of great possessions. The King, then, holding state in Dublin, received the homage of nearly all the Irish Kings and Chiefs, and so came home again with a great addition to his reputation as Lord of Ireland, and with a new claim on the favour of the Pope. And now, their reconciliation was completed—more easily and mildly by the Pope, than the King might have expected, I think.

At this period of his reign, when his troubles seemed so few and his prospects so bright, those domestic miseries began which gradually made the King the most unhappy of men, reduced his great spirit, wore away his health, and broke his heart.

He had four sons. Henry, now aged eighteen—his secret crowning of whom had given such offence to Thomas à Becket. Richard, aged sixteen; Geoffrey, fifteen; and John, his favourite, a young boy whom the courtiers named Lackland, because he had no inheritance, but to whom the King meant to give the Lordship of Ireland. All these misguided boys, in their turn, were unnatural sons to him, and unnatural brothers to each other. Prince Henry, stimulated by the French King, and by his bad mother, Queen Eleanor, began the undutiful history,

First, he demanded that his young wife, Margaret, the French King's daughter, should be crowned as well as he. His father, the King, consented, and it was done. It was no sooner done, than he demanded to have a part of his father's dominions, during his father's life. This being refused, he made off from his father in the night, with his bad heart full of bitterness, and took refuge at the French King's Court. Within a day or two, his brothers Richard and Geoffrey followed. Their mother tried to join them—escaping in man's clothes—but she was seized by King Henry's men, and immured in prison, where she lay, deservedly, for sixteen years. Every day, however, some grasping English noblemen, to whom the King's protection of his people from their avarice and oppression had given offence, deserted him and joined the Princes. Every day he heard some fresh intelligence of the Princes levying armies against him; of Prince Henry's wearing a crown before his own ambassadors at the French Court, and being called the Junior King of England; of all the Princes swearing never to make peace with him, their father, without the consent and approval of the Barons of France. But, with his fortitude and energy unshaken, King Henry met the shock of these disasters with a resolved and cheerful face. He called upon all Royal fathers who had sons, to help him, for his cause was theirs; he hired, out of his riches, twenty thousand men to fight the false French King, who stirred his own blood against him; and he carried on the war with such vigour, that Louis soon proposed a conference to treat for peace.

The conference was held beneath an old wide-spreading green elm-tree, upon a plain in France. It led to nothing. The war recommenced. Prince Richard began his fighting career, by leading an army against his father; but his father beat him and his army back; and thousands of his men would have rued the day in which they fought in such a wicked cause, had not the King received news of an invasion of England by the Scots, and promptly come home through a great storm to repress it. And whether he really began to fear that he suffered these troubles because à Becket had been murdered; or whether he wished to rise in the favour of the Pope, who had now declared à Becket to be a saint, or in the favour of his own people, of whom many believed that even à Becket's senseless tomb could work miracles, I don't know: but the King no sooner landed in England than he went straight to Canterbury; and when he came within sight of the distant Cathedral, he dismounted from his horse, took off his shoes, and walked with bare and bleeding feet to à Becket's grave. There, he lay down on the ground, lamenting, in the presence of many people; and by-and-by he went into the Chapter House, and, removing his clothes from his back and shoulders, submitted himself to be beaten with knotted cords (not beaten very hard, I dare say though) by eighty Priests, one after another. It chanced that on the very day when the King made this curious exhibition of himself, a complete victory was obtained over the Scots; which very much delighted the Priests, who said that it was won because of his great example of repentance. For the Priests in general had found out, since à Becket's death, that they admired him of all things—though they had hated him very cordially when he was alive.

The Earl of Flanders, who was at the head of the base conspiracy of the King's undutiful sons and their foreign friends, took the opportunity of the King being thus employed at home, to lay siege to Rouen, the capital of Normandy. But the King, who was extraordinarily quick and active in all his movements, was at Rouen, too, before it was supposed possible that he could have left England; and there he so defeated the said Earl of Flanders, that the conspirators proposed peace, and his bad sons Henry and Geoffrey submitted. Richard resisted for six weeks; but, being beaten out of castle after castle, he at last submitted too, and his father forgave him.

To forgive these unworthy princes was only to afford them breathing-time for new faithlessness. They were so false, disloyal, and dishonourable, that they were no more to be trusted than common thieves. In the very next year, Prince Henry rebelled again, and was again forgiven. In eight years more, Prince Richard rebelled against his elder brother; and Prince Geoffrey infamously said that the brothers could never agree well together, unless they were united against their father. In the very next year after their reconciliation by the King, Prince Henry again rebelled against his father; and again submitted, swearing to be true; and was again forgiven; and again rebelled with Geoffrey.

But the end of this perfidious Prince was come. He fell sick at a French town; and his conscience terribly reproaching him with his baseness, he sent messengers to the King his father, imploring him to come and see him, and to forgive him for the last time on his bed of death. The generous King, who had a royal and forgiving mind towards his children always, would have gone; but this Prince had been so unnatural, that the noblemen about the King suspected treachery, and represented to him that he could not safely trust his life with such a traitor, though his own eldest son. Therefore the King sent him a ring from off his finger as a token of forgiveness; and when the Prince had kissed it, with much grief and many tears, and had confessed to those around him how bad, and wicked, and undutiful a son he had been; he said to the attendant Priests: 'O, tie a rope about my body, and draw me out of bed, and lay me down upon a bed of ashes, that I may die with prayers to God in a repentant manner!' And so he died, at twenty-seven years old.

Three years afterwards, Prince Geoffrey, being unhorsed at a tournament, had his brains trampled out by a crowd of horses passing over him. So, there only remained Prince Richard, and Prince John—who had grown to be a young man now, and had solemnly sworn to be faithful to his father. Richard soon rebelled again, encouraged by his friend the French King, Philip the Second (son of Louis, who was dead); and soon submitted and was again forgiven, swearing on the New Testament never to rebel again; and in another year or so, rebelled again; and, in the presence of his father, knelt down on his knee before the King of France; and did the French King homage: and declared that with his aid he would possess himself, by force, of all his father's French dominions.

And yet this Richard called himself a soldier of Our Saviour! And yet this Richard wore the Cross, which the Kings of France and England had both taken, in the previous year, at a brotherly meeting underneath the old wide-spreading elm-tree on the plain, when they had sworn (like him) to devote themselves to a new Crusade, for the love and honour of the Truth!

Sick at heart, wearied out by the falsehood of his sons, and almost ready to lie down and die, the unhappy King who had so long stood firm, began to fail. But the Pope, to his honour, supported him; and obliged the French King and Richard, though successful in fight, to treat for peace. Richard wanted to be Crowned King of England, and pretended that he wanted to be married (which he really did not) to the French King's sister, his promised wife, whom King Henry detained in England. King Henry wanted, on the other hand, that the French King's sister should be married to his favourite son, John: the only one of his sons (he said) who had never rebelled against him. At last King Henry, deserted by his nobles one by one, distressed, exhausted, broken-hearted, consented to establish peace.

One final heavy sorrow was reserved for him, even yet. When they brought him the proposed treaty of peace, in writing, as he lay very ill in bed, they brought him also the list of the deserters from their allegiance, whom he was required to pardon. The first name upon this list was John, his favourite son, in whom he had trusted to the last.

'O John! child of my heart!' exclaimed the King, in a great agony of mind. 'O John, whom I have loved the best! O John, for whom I have contended through these many troubles! Have you betrayed me too!' And then he lay down with a heavy groan, and said, 'Now let the world go as it will. I care for nothing more!'

After a time, he told his attendants to take him to the French town of Chinon—a town he had been fond of, during many years. But he was fond of no place now; it was too true that he could care for nothing more upon this earth. He wildly cursed the hour when he was born, and cursed the children whom he left behind him; and expired.

As, one hundred years before, the servile followers of the Court had abandoned the Conqueror in the hour of his death, so they now abandoned his descendant. The very body was stripped, in the plunder of the Royal chamber; and it was not easy to find the means of carrying it for burial to the abbey church of Fontevraud.

Richard was said in after years, by way of flattery, to have the heart of a Lion. It would have been far better, I think, to have had the heart of a Man. His heart, whatever it was, had cause to beat remorsefully within his breast, when he came—as he did—into the solemn abbey, and looked on his dead father's uncovered face. His heart, whatever it was, had been a black and perjured heart, in all its dealings with the deceased King, and more deficient in a single touch of tenderness than any wild beast's in the forest.

There is a pretty story told of this Reign, called the story of Fair Rosamond. It relates how the King doted on Fair Rosamond, who was the loveliest girl in all the world; and how he had a beautiful Bower built for her in a Park at Woodstock; and how it was erected in a labyrinth, and could only be found by a clue of silk. How the bad Queen Eleanor, becoming jealous of Fair Rosamond, found out the secret of the clue, and one day, appeared

101

before her, with a dagger and a cup of poison, and left her to the choice between those deaths. How Fair Rosamond, after shedding many piteous tears and offering many useless prayers to the cruel Queen, took the poison, and fell dead in the midst of the beautiful bower, while the unconscious birds sang gaily all around her.

Now, there was a fair Rosamond, and she was (I dare say) the loveliest girl in all the world, and the King was certainly very fond of her, and the bad Queen Eleanor was certainly made jealous. But I am afraid—I say afraid, because I like the story so much—that there was no bower, no labyrinth, no silken clue, no dagger, no poison. I am afraid fair Rosamond retired to a nunnery near Oxford, and died there, peaceably; her sister-nuns hanging a silken drapery over her tomb, and often dressing it with flowers, in remembrance of the youth and beauty that had enchanted the King when he too was young, and when his life lay fair before him.

It was dark and ended now; faded and gone. Henry Plantagenet lay quiet in the abbey church of Fontevraud, in the fifty-seventh year of his age—never to be completed—after governing England well, for nearly thirty-five years.

CHAPTER XIII—ENGLAND UNDER RICHARD THE FIRST, CALLED THE LION-HEART

In the year of our Lord one thousand one hundred and eighty-nine, Richard of the Lion Heart succeeded to the throne of King Henry the Second, whose paternal heart he had done so much to break. He had been, as we have seen, a rebel from his boyhood; but, the moment he became a king against whom others might rebel, he found out that rebellion was a great wickedness. In the heat of this pious discovery, he punished all the leading people who had befriended him against his father. He could scarcely have done anything that would have been a better instance of his real nature, or a better warning to fawners and parasites not to trust in lion-hearted princes.

He likewise put his late father's treasurer in chains, and locked him up in a dungeon from which he was not set free until he had relinquished, not only all the Crown treasure, but all his own money too. So, Richard certainly got the Lion's share of the wealth of this wretched treasurer, whether he had a Lion's heart or not.

He was crowned King of England, with great pomp, at Westminster: walking to the Cathedral under a silken canopy stretched on the tops of four lances, each carried by a great lord. On the day of his coronation, a dreadful murdering of the Jews took place, which seems to have given great delight to numbers of savage persons calling themselves Christians. The King had issued a proclamation forbidding the Jews (who were generally hated, though they were the most useful merchants in England) to appear at the ceremony; but as they had assembled in London from all parts, bringing presents to show their respect for the new Sovereign, some of them ventured down to Westminster Hall with their gifts; which were very readily accepted. It is supposed, now, that some noisy fellow in the crowd, pretending to be a very delicate Christian, set up a howl at this, and struck a Jew who was trying to get in at the Hall door with his present. A riot arose. The Jews who had got into the Hall, were driven forth; and some of the rabble cried out that the new

King had commanded the unbelieving race to be put to death. Thereupon the crowd rushed through the narrow streets of the city, slaughtering all the Jews they met; and when they could find no more out of doors (on account of their having fled to their houses, and fastened themselves in), they ran madly about, breaking open all the houses where the Jews lived, rushing in and stabbing or spearing them, sometimes even flinging old people and children out of window into blazing fires they had lighted up below. This great cruelty lasted four-and-twenty hours, and only three men were punished for it. Even they forfeited their lives not for murdering and robbing the Jews, but for burning the houses of some Christians.

King Richard, who was a strong, restless, burly man, with one idea always in his head, and that the very troublesome idea of breaking the heads of other men, was mightily impatient to go on a Crusade to the Holy Land, with a great army. As great armies could not be raised to go, even to the Holy Land, without a great deal of money, he sold the Crown domains, and even the high offices of State; recklessly appointing noblemen to rule over his English subjects, not because they were fit to govern, but because they could pay high for the privilege. In this way, and by selling pardons at a dear rate and by varieties of avarice and oppression, he scraped together a large treasure. He then appointed two Bishops to take care of his kingdom in his absence, and gave great powers and possessions to his brother John, to secure his friendship. John would rather have been made Regent of England; but he was a sly man, and friendly to the expedition; saying to himself, no doubt, 'The more fighting, the more chance of my brother being killed; and when he is killed, then I become King John!'

Before the newly levied army departed from England, the recruits and the general populace distinguished themselves by astonishing cruelties on the unfortunate Jews: whom, in many large towns, they murdered by hundreds in the most horrible manner.

At York, a large body of Jews took refuge in the Castle, in the absence of its Governor, after the wives and children of many of them had been slain before their eyes. Presently came the Governor, and demanded admission. 'How can we give it thee, O Governor!' said the Jews upon the walls, 'when, if we open the gate by so much as the width of a foot, the roaring crowd behind thee will press in and kill us?'

Upon this, the unjust Governor became angry, and told the people that he approved of their killing those Jews; and a mischievous maniac of a friar, dressed all in white, put himself at the head of the assault, and they assaulted the Castle for three days.

Then said Jocen, the head-Jew (who was a Rabbi or Priest), to the rest, 'Brethren, there is no hope for us with the Christians who are hammering at the gates and walls, and who must soon break in. As we and our wives and children must die, either by Christian hands, or by our own, let it be by our own. Let us destroy by fire what jewels and other treasure we have here, then fire the castle, and then perish!'

A few could not resolve to do this, but the greater part complied. They made a blazing heap of all their valuables, and, when those were consumed, set the castle in flames. While the flames roared and crackled around them, and shooting up into the sky, turned it blood-red, Jocen cut the throat of his beloved wife, and stabbed himself. All the others who had wives or children, did the like dreadful deed. When the populace broke in, they found (except the trembling few, cowering in corners, whom they soon killed) only heaps of greasy cinders, with here and there something like part of the blackened trunk of a burnt tree, but which had lately been a human creature, formed by the beneficent hand of the Creator as they were.

After this bad beginning, Richard and his troops went on, in no very good manner, with the Holy Crusade. It was undertaken jointly by the King of England and his old friend Philip of France. They commenced the business by reviewing their forces, to the number of one hundred thousand men. Afterwards, they severally embarked their troops for Messina, in Sicily, which was appointed as the next place of meeting.

King Richard's sister had married the King of this place, but he was dead: and his uncle Tancred had usurped the crown, cast the Royal Widow into prison, and possessed himself of her estates. Richard fiercely demanded his sister's release, the restoration of her lands, and (according to the Royal custom of the Island) that she should have a golden chair, a golden table, four-and-twenty silver cups, and four-and-twenty silver dishes. As he was too powerful to be successfully resisted, Tancred yielded to his demands; and then the French King grew jealous, and complained that the English King wanted to be absolute in the Island of Messina and everywhere else. Richard, however, cared little or nothing for this complaint; and in consideration of a present of twenty thousand pieces of gold, promised his pretty little nephew Arthur, then a child of two years old, in marriage to Tancred's daughter. We shall hear again of pretty little Arthur by-and-by.

This Sicilian affair arranged without anybody's brains being knocked out (which must have rather disappointed him), King Richard took his sister away, and also a fair lady named Berengaria, with whom he had fallen in love in France, and whom his mother, Queen Eleanor (so long in prison, you remember, but released by Richard on his coming to the Throne), had brought out there to be his wife; and sailed with them for Cyprus.

He soon had the pleasure of fighting the King of the Island of Cyprus, for allowing his subjects to pillage some of the English troops who were shipwrecked on the shore; and easily conquering this poor monarch, he seized his only daughter, to be a companion to the lady Berengaria, and put the King himself into silver fetters. He then sailed away again with his mother, sister, wife, and the captive princess; and soon arrived before the town of Acre, which the French King with his fleet was besieging from the sea. But the French King was in no triumphant condition, for his army had been thinned by the swords of the Saracens, and wasted by the plague; and Saladin, the brave Sultan of the Turks, at the head of a numerous army, was at that time gallantly defending the place from the hills that rise above it.

Wherever the united army of Crusaders went, they agreed in few points except in gaming, drinking, and quarrelling, in a most unholy manner; in debauching the people among whom they tarried, whether they were friends or foes; and in carrying disturbance and ruin into quiet places. The French King was jealous of the English King, and the English King was jealous of the French King, and the disorderly and violent soldiers of the two nations were jealous of one another; consequently, the two Kings could not at first agree, even upon a joint assault on Acre; but when they did make up their quarrel for that purpose, the Saracens promised to yield the town, to give up to the Christians the wood of the Holy Cross, to set at liberty all their Christian captives, and to pay two hundred thousand pieces of gold. All this was to be done within forty days; but, not being done, King Richard ordered some three thousand Saracen prisoners to be brought out in the front of his camp, and there, in full view of their own countrymen, to be butchered.

The French King had no part in this crime; for he was by that time travelling homeward with the greater part of his men; being offended by the overbearing conduct of the English King; being anxious to look after his own dominions; and being ill, besides, from the unwholesome air of that hot and sandy country. King Richard carried on the war without him; and remained in the East, meeting with a variety of adventures, nearly a year and a half. Every night when his army was on the march, and came to a halt, the heralds cried out three times, to remind all the soldiers of the cause in which they were engaged, 'Save the Holy Sepulchre!' and then all the soldiers knelt and said 'Amen!' Marching or encamping, the army had continually to strive with the hot air of the glaring desert, or with the Saracen soldiers animated and directed by the brave Saladin, or with both together. Sickness and death, battle and wounds, were always among them; but through every difficulty King Richard fought like a giant, and worked like a common labourer. Long and long after he was quiet in his grave, his terrible battle-axe, with twenty English pounds of English steel in its mighty head, was a legend among the Saracens; and when all the Saracen and Christian hosts had been dust for many a year, if a Saracen horse started at any object by the wayside, his rider would exclaim, 'What dost thou fear, Fool? Dost thou think King Richard is behind it?'

No one admired this King's renown for bravery more than Saladin himself, who was a generous and gallant enemy. When Richard lay ill of a fever, Saladin sent him fresh fruits from Damascus, and snow from the mountain-tops. Courtly messages and compliments were frequently exchanged between them—and then King Richard would mount his horse and kill as many Saracens as he could; and Saladin would mount his, and kill as many Christians as he could. In this way King Richard fought to his heart's content at Arsoof and at Jaffa; and finding himself with nothing exciting to do at Ascalon, except to rebuild, for his own defence, some fortifications there which the Saracens had destroyed, he kicked his ally the Duke of Austria, for being too proud to work at them.

The army at last came within sight of the Holy City of Jerusalem; but, being then a mere nest of jealousy, and quarrelling and fighting, soon retired, and agreed with the Saracens upon a truce for three years, three months, three days, and three hours. Then, the English Christians, protected by the noble Saladin from Saracen revenge, visited Our Saviour's tomb; and then King Richard embarked with a small force at Acre to return home.

But he was shipwrecked in the Adriatic Sea, and was fain to pass through Germany, under an assumed name. Now, there were many people in Germany who had served in the Holy Land under that proud Duke of Austria who had been kicked; and some of them, easily recognising a man so remarkable as King Richard, carried their intelligence to the kicked Duke, who straightway took him prisoner at a little inn near Vienna.

The Duke's master the Emperor of Germany, and the King of France, were equally delighted to have so troublesome a monarch in safe keeping. Friendships which are founded on a partnership in doing wrong, are never true; and the King of France was now quite as heartily King Richard's foe, as he had ever been his friend in his unnatural conduct to his father. He monstrously pretended that King Richard had designed to poison him in the East; he charged him with having murdered, there, a man whom he had in truth befriended; he bribed the Emperor of Germany to keep him close prisoner; and, finally, through the plotting of these two princes, Richard was brought before the German legislature, charged with the foregoing crimes, and many others. But he defended himself so well, that many of the assembly were moved to tears by his eloquence and earnestness. It was decided that he should be treated, during the rest of his captivity, in a manner more becoming his dignity than he had been, and that he should be set free on the payment of a heavy ransom. This ransom the English people willingly raised. When Queen Eleanor took it over to Germany, it was at first evaded and refused.

But she appealed to the honour of all the princes of the German Empire in behalf of her son, and appealed so well that it was accepted, and the King released. Thereupon, the King of France wrote to Prince John—'Take care of thyself. The devil is unchained!'

Prince John had reason to fear his brother, for he had been a traitor to him in his captivity. He had secretly joined the French King; had vowed to the English nobles and people that his brother was dead; and had vainly tried to seize the crown. He was now in France, at a place called Evreux. Being the meanest and basest of men, he contrived a mean and base expedient for making himself acceptable to his brother. He invited the French officers of the garrison in that town to dinner, murdered them all, and then took the fortress. With this recommendation to the good will of a lion-hearted monarch, he hastened to King Richard, fell on his knees before him, and obtained the intercession of Queen Eleanor. 'I forgive him,' said the King, 'and I hope I may forget the injury he has done me, as easily as I know he will forget my pardon.'

While King Richard was in Sicily, there had been trouble in his dominions at home: one of the bishops whom he had left in charge thereof, arresting the other; and making, in his pride and ambition, as great a show as if he were King himself. But the King hearing of it at Messina, and appointing a new Regency, this Longchamp (for that was his name) had fled to France in a woman's dress, and had there been encouraged and supported by the French King. With all these causes of offence against Philip in his mind, King Richard had no sooner been welcomed home by his enthusiastic subjects with great display and splendour, and had no sooner been crowned afresh at Winchester, than he resolved to show the French King that the Devil was unchained indeed, and made war against him with great fury.

There was fresh trouble at home about this time, arising out of the discontents of the poor people, who complained that they were far more heavily taxed than the rich, and who found a spirited champion in William Fitz-Osbert, called Longbeard. He became the leader of a secret society, comprising fifty thousand men; he was seized by surprise; he stabbed the citizen who first laid hands upon him; and retreated, bravely fighting, to a church, which he maintained four days, until he was dislodged by fire, and run through the body as he came out. He was not killed, though; for he was dragged, half dead, at the tail of a horse to Smithfield, and there hanged. Death was long a favourite remedy for silencing the people's advocates; but as we go on with this history, I fancy we shall find them difficult to make an end of, for all that.

The French war, delayed occasionally by a truce, was still in progress when a certain Lord named Vidomar, Viscount of Limoges, chanced to find in his ground a treasure of ancient coins. As the King's vassal, he sent the King half of it; but the King claimed the whole. The lord refused to yield the whole. The King besieged the lord in his castle, swore that he would take the castle by storm, and hang every man of its defenders on the battlements.

There was a strange old song in that part of the country, to the effect that in Limoges an arrow would be made by which King Richard would die. It may be that Bertrand de Gourdon, a young man who was one of the defenders of the castle, had often sung it or heard it sung of a winter night, and remembered it when he saw, from his post upon the ramparts, the King attended only by his chief officer riding below the walls surveying the place. He drew an arrow to the head, took steady aim, said between his teeth, 'Now I pray God speed thee well, arrow!' discharged it, and struck the King in the left shoulder.

Although the wound was not at first considered dangerous, it was severe enough to cause the King to retire to his tent, and direct the assault to be made without him. The castle was taken; and every man of its defenders was hanged, as the King had sworn all should be, except Bertrand de Gourdon, who was reserved until the royal pleasure respecting him should be known.

By that time unskilful treatment had made the wound mortal and the King knew that he was dying. He directed Bertrand to be brought into his tent. The young man was brought there, heavily chained, King Richard looked at him steadily. He looked, as steadily, at the King.

'Knave!' said King Richard. 'What have I done to thee that thou shouldest take my life?'

110

'What hast thou done to me?' replied the young man. 'With thine own hands thou hast killed my father and my two brothers. Myself thou wouldest have hanged. Let me die now, by any torture that thou wilt. My comfort is, that no torture can save Thee. Thou too must die; and, through me, the world is quit of thee!'

Again the King looked at the young man steadily. Again the young man looked steadily at him. Perhaps some remembrance of his generous enemy Saladin, who was not a Christian, came into the mind of the dying King.

'Youth!' he said, 'I forgive thee. Go unhurt!' Then, turning to the chief officer who had been riding in his company when he received the wound, King Richard said:

'Take off his chains, give him a hundred shillings, and let him depart.'

He sunk down on his couch, and a dark mist seemed in his weakened eyes to fill the tent wherein he had so often rested, and he died. His age was forty-two; he had reigned ten years. His last command was not obeyed; for the chief officer flayed Bertrand de Gourdon alive, and hanged him.

There is an old tune yet known—a sorrowful air will sometimes outlive many generations of strong men, and even last longer than battle-axes with twenty pounds of steel in the head—by which this King is said to have been discovered in his captivity. Blondel, a favourite Minstrel of King Richard, as the story relates, faithfully seeking his Royal master, went singing it outside the gloomy walls of many foreign fortresses and prisons; until at last he heard it echoed from within a dungeon, and knew the voice, and cried out in ecstasy, 'O Richard, O my King!' You may believe it, if you like; it would be easy to believe worse things. Richard was himself a Minstrel and a Poet. If he had not been a Prince too, he might have been a better man perhaps, and might have gone out of the world with less bloodshed and waste of life to answer for.

CHAPTER XIV—ENGLAND UNDER KING JOHN, CALLED LACKLAND

At two-and-thirty years of age, John became King of England. His pretty little nephew Arthur had the best claim to the throne; but John seized the treasure, and made fine promises to the nobility, and got himself crowned at Westminster within a few weeks after his brother Richard's death. I doubt whether the crown could possibly have been put upon the head of a meaner coward, or a more detestable villain, if England had been searched from end to end to find him out.

The French King, Philip, refused to acknowledge the right of John to his new dignity, and declared in favour of Arthur. You must not suppose that he had any generosity of feeling for the fatherless boy; it merely suited his ambitious schemes to oppose the King of England. So John and the French King went to war about Arthur.

He was a handsome boy, at that time only twelve years old. He was not born when his father, Geoffrey, had his brains trampled out at the tournament; and, besides the misfortune of never having known a father's guidance and protection, he had the additional misfortune to have a foolish mother (Constance by name), lately married to her third husband. She took Arthur, upon John's accession, to the French King, who pretended to be very much his friend, and who made him a Knight, and promised him his daughter in marriage; but, who cared so little about him in reality, that finding it his interest to make peace with King John for a time, he did so without the least consideration for the poor little Prince, and heartlessly sacrificed all his interests.

Young Arthur, for two years afterwards, lived quietly; and in the course of that time his mother died. But, the French King then finding it his interest to quarrel with King John again, again made Arthur his pretence, and invited the orphan boy to court. 'You know your rights, Prince,' said the French King, 'and you would like to be a King. Is it not so?' 'Truly,' said Prince Arthur, 'I should greatly like to be a King!' 'Then,' said Philip, 'you shall have two hundred gentlemen who are Knights of mine, and with them you shall go to win back the provinces belonging to you, of which your uncle, the usurping King of England, has taken possession. I myself, meanwhile, will head a force against him in Normandy.' Poor Arthur was so flattered and so grateful that he signed a treaty with the crafty French King, agreeing to consider him his superior Lord, and that the French King should keep for himself whatever he could take from King John.

Now, King John was so bad in all ways, and King Philip was so perfidious, that Arthur, between the two, might as well have been a lamb between a fox and a wolf. But, being so young, he was ardent and flushed with hope; and, when the people of Brittany (which was his inheritance) sent him five hundred more knights and five thousand foot soldiers, he believed his fortune was made. The people of Brittany had been fond of him from his birth, and had requested that he might be called Arthur, in remembrance of that dimly-famous English Arthur, of whom I told you early in this book, whom they believed to have been the brave friend and companion of an old King of their own. They had tales among them about a prophet called Merlin (of the same old time), who had foretold that their own King should be restored to them after hundreds of years; and they believed that the prophecy would be fulfilled in Arthur; that the time would come when he would rule them with a crown of Brittany upon his head; and when neither King of France nor King of England would have any power over them. When Arthur found himself riding in a glittering suit of armour on a richly caparisoned horse, at the head of his train of knights and soldiers, he began to believe this too, and to consider old Merlin a very superior prophet.

He did not know—how could he, being so innocent and inexperienced?—that his little army was a mere nothing against the power of the King of England. The French King knew it; but the poor boy's fate was little to him, so that the King of England was worried and distressed. Therefore, King Philip went his way into Normandy and Prince Arthur went his way towards Mirebeau, a French town near Poictiers, both very well pleased.

Prince Arthur went to attack the town of Mirebeau, because his grandmother Eleanor, who has so often made her appearance in this history (and who had always been his mother's enemy), was living there, and because his Knights said, 'Prince, if you can take her prisoner, you will be able to bring the King your uncle to terms!' But she was not to be easily taken. She was old enough by this time—eighty—but she was as full of stratagem as she was full of years and wickedness. Receiving intelligence of young Arthur's approach, she shut herself up in a high tower, and encouraged her soldiers to defend it like men. Prince Arthur with his little army besieged the high tower. King John, hearing how matters stood, came up to the rescue, with his army. So here was a strange family-party! The boy-Prince besieging his grandmother, and his uncle besieging him!

This position of affairs did not last long. One summer night King John, by treachery, got his men into the town, surprised Prince Arthur's force, took two hundred of his knights, and seized the Prince himself in his bed. The Knights were put in heavy irons, and driven away in open carts drawn by bullocks, to various dungeons where they were most inhumanly treated, and where some of them were starved to death. Prince Arthur was sent to the castle of Falaise.

One day, while he was in prison at that castle, mournfully thinking it strange that one so young should be in so much trouble, and looking out of the small window in the deep dark wall, at the summer sky and the birds, the door was softly opened, and he saw his uncle the King standing in the shadow of the archway, looking very grim.

'Arthur,' said the King, with his wicked eyes more on the stone floor than on his nephew, 'will you not trust to the gentleness, the friendship, and the truthfulness of your loving uncle?'

'I will tell my loving uncle that,' replied the boy, 'when he does me right. Let him restore to me my kingdom of England, and then come to me and ask the question.'

The King looked at him and went out. 'Keep that boy close prisoner,' said he to the warden of the castle.

Then, the King took secret counsel with the worst of his nobles how the Prince was to be got rid of. Some said, 'Put out his eyes and keep him in prison, as Robort of Normandy was kept.' Others said, 'Have him stabbed.' Others, 'Have him hanged.' Others, 'Have him poisoned.'

King John, feeling that in any case, whatever was done afterwards, it would be a satisfaction to his mind to have those handsome eyes burnt out that had looked at him so proudly while his own royal eyes were blinking at the stone floor, sent certain ruffians to Falaise to blind the boy with red-hot irons. But Arthur so pathetically entreated them, and shed such piteous tears, and so appealed to Hubert de Bourg (or Burgh), the warden of the castle, who had a love for him, and was an honourable, tender man, that Hubert could not bear it. To his eternal honour he prevented the torture from being performed, and, at his own risk, sent the savages away.

The chafed and disappointed King bethought himself of the stabbing suggestion next, and, with his shuffling manner and his cruel face, proposed it to one William de Bray. 'I am a gentleman and not an executioner,' said William de Bray, and left the presence with disdain.

But it was not difficult for a King to hire a murderer in those days. King John found one for his money, and sent him down to the castle of Falaise. 'On what errand dost thou come?' said Hubert to this fellow. 'To despatch young Arthur,' he returned. 'Go back to him who sent thee,' answered Hubert, 'and say that I will do it!'

King John very well knowing that Hubert would never do it, but that he courageously sent this reply to save the Prince or gain time, despatched messengers to convey the young prisoner to the castle of Rouen.

Arthur was soon forced from the good Hubert—of whom he had never stood in greater need than then—carried away by night, and lodged in his new prison: where, through his grated window, he could hear the deep waters of the river Seine, rippling against the stone wall below.

One dark night, as he lay sleeping, dreaming perhaps of rescue by those unfortunate gentlemen who were obscurely suffering and dying in his cause, he was roused, and bidden by his jailer to come down the staircase to the foot of the tower. He hurriedly dressed himself and obeyed. When they came to the bottom of the winding stairs, and the night air from the river blew upon their faces, the jailer trod upon his torch and put it out. Then, Arthur, in the darkness, was hurriedly drawn into a solitary boat. And in that boat, he found his uncle and one other man.

He knelt to them, and prayed them not to murder him. Deaf to his entreaties, they stabbed him and sunk his body in the river with heavy stones. When the spring-morning broke, the tower-door was closed, the boat was gone, the river sparkled on its way, and never more was any trace of the poor boy beheld by mortal eyes.

The news of this atrocious murder being spread in England, awakened a hatred of the King (already odious for his many vices, and for his having stolen away and married a noble lady while his own wife was living) that never slept again through his whole reign. In Brittany, the indignation was intense. Arthur's own sister Eleanor was in the power of John and shut up in a convent at Bristol, but his half-sister Alice was in Brittany. The people chose her, and the murdered prince's father-in-law, the last husband of Constance, to represent them; and carried their fiery complaints to King Philip. King Philip summoned King John (as the holder of territory in France) to come before him and defend himself. King John refusing to appear, King Philip declared him false, perjured, and guilty; and again made war. In a little time, by conquering the greater part of his French territory, King Philip deprived him of one-third of his dominions. And, through all the fighting that took place, King John was always found, either to be eating and drinking, like a gluttonous fool, when the danger was at a distance, or to be running away, like a beaten cur, when it was near.

You might suppose that when he was losing his dominions at this rate, and when his own nobles cared so little for him or his cause that they plainly refused to follow his banner out of England, he had enemies enough. But he made another enemy of the Pope, which he did in this way.

The Archbishop of Canterbury dying, and the junior monks of that place wishing to get the start of the senior monks in the appointment of his successor, met together at midnight, secretly elected a certain Reginald, and sent him off to Rome to get the Pope's approval. The senior monks and the King soon finding this out, and being very angry about it, the junior monks gave way, and all the monks together elected the Bishop of Norwich, who was the King's favourite. The Pope, hearing the whole story, declared that neither election would do for him, and that he elected Stephen Langton. The monks submitting to the Pope, the King turned them all out bodily, and banished them as traitors. The Pope sent three bishops to the King, to threaten him with an Interdict. The King told the bishops that if any Interdict were laid upon his kingdom, he would tear out the eyes and cut off the noses of all the monks he could lay hold of, and send them over to Rome in that undecorated state as a present for their master. The bishops, nevertheless, soon published the Interdict, and fled.

After it had lasted a year, the Pope proceeded to his next step; which was Excommunication. King John was declared excommunicated, with all the usual ceremonies. The King was so incensed at this, and was made so desperate by the disaffection of his Barons and the hatred of his people, that it is said he even privately sent ambassadors to the Turks in Spain, offering to renounce his religion and hold his kingdom of them if they would help him. It is related that the ambassadors were admitted to the presence of the Turkish Emir through long lines of Moorish guards, and that they found the Emir with his eyes seriously fixed on the pages of a large book, from which he never once looked up. That they gave him a letter from the King containing his proposals, and were gravely dismissed. That presently the Emir sent for one of them, and conjured him, by his faith in his religion, to say what kind of man the King of England truly was? That the ambassador, thus pressed, replied that the King of England was a false tyrant, against whom his own subjects would soon rise. And that this was quite enough for the Emir.

Money being, in his position, the next best thing to men, King John spared no means of getting it. He set on foot another oppressing and torturing of the unhappy Jews (which was quite in his way), and invented a new punishment for one wealthy Jew of Bristol. Until such time as that Jew should produce a certain large sum of money, the King sentenced him to be imprisoned, and, every day, to have one tooth violently wrenched out of his head—beginning with the double teeth. For seven days, the oppressed man bore the daily pain and lost the daily tooth; but, on the eighth, he paid the money. With the treasure raised in such ways, the King made an expedition into Ireland, where some English nobles had revolted. It was one of the very few places from which he did not run away; because no resistance was shown. He made another expedition into Wales—whence he did run away in the end: but not before he had got from the Welsh people, as hostages, twenty-seven young men of the best families; every one of whom he caused to be slain in the following year.

To Interdict and Excommunication, the Pope now added his last sentence; Deposition. He proclaimed John no longer King, absolved all his subjects from their allegiance, and sent Stephen Langton and others to the King of France to tell him that, if he would invade England, he should be forgiven all his sins—at least, should be forgiven them by the Pope, if that would do.

As there was nothing that King Philip desired more than to invade England, he collected a great army at Rouen, and a fleet of seventeen hundred ships to bring them over. But the English people, however bitterly they hated the King, were not a people to suffer invasion quietly. They flocked to Dover, where the English standard was, in such great numbers to enrol themselves as defenders of their native land, that there were not provisions for them, and the King could only select and retain sixty thousand. But, at this crisis, the Pope, who had his own reasons for objecting to either King John or King Philip being too powerful, interfered. He entrusted a legate, whose name was Pandolf, with the easy task of frightening King John. He sent him to the English Camp, from France, to terrify him with exaggerations of King Philip's power, and his own weakness in the discontent of the English Barons and people. Pandolf discharged his commission so well, that King John, in a wretched panic, consented to acknowledge Stephen Langton; to resign his kingdom 'to God, Saint Peter, and Saint Paul'—which meant the Pope; and to hold it, ever afterwards, by the Pope's leave, on payment of an annual sum of money. To this shameful contract he publicly bound himself in the church of the Knights Templars at Dover: where he laid at the legate's feet a part of the tribute, which the legate haughtily trampled upon. But they do say, that this was merely a genteel flourish, and that he was afterwards seen to pick it up and pocket it.

There was an unfortunate prophet, the name of Peter, who had greatly increased King John's terrors by predicting that he would be unknighted (which the King supposed to signify that he would die) before the Feast of the Ascension should be past. That was the day after this humiliation. When the next morning came, and the King, who had been trembling all night, found himself alive and safe, he ordered the prophet—and his son too—to be dragged through the streets at the tails of horses, and then hanged, for having frightened him.

As King John had now submitted, the Pope, to King Philip's great astonishment, took him under his protection, and informed King Philip that he found he could not give him leave to invade England. The angry Philip resolved to do it without his leave but he gained nothing and lost much; for, the English, commanded by the Earl of Salisbury, went over, in five hundred ships, to the French coast, before the French fleet had sailed away from it, and utterly defeated the whole.

The Pope then took off his three sentences, one after another, and empowered Stephen Langton publicly to receive King John into the favour of the Church again, and to ask him to dinner. The King, who hated Langton with all his might and main—and with reason too, for he was a great and a good man, with whom such a King could have no sympathy—pretended to cry and to be very grateful. There was a little difficulty about settling how much the King should pay as a recompense to the clergy for the losses he had caused them; but, the end of it was, that the superior clergy got a good deal, and the inferior clergy got little or nothing—which has also happened since King John's time, I believe.

When all these matters were arranged, the King in his triumph became more fierce, and false, and insolent to all around him than he had ever been. An alliance of sovereigns against King Philip, gave him an opportunity of landing an army in France; with which he even took a town! But, on the French King's gaining a great victory, he ran away, of course, and made a truce for five years.

And now the time approached when he was to be still further humbled, and made to feel, if he could feel anything, what a wretched creature he was. Of all men in the world, Stephen Langton seemed raised up by Heaven to oppose and subdue him. When he ruthlessly burnt and destroyed the property of his own subjects, because their Lords, the Barons, would not serve him abroad, Stephen Langton fearlessly reproved and threatened him. When he swore to restore the laws of King Edward, or the laws of King Henry the First, Stephen Langton knew his falsehood, and pursued him through all his evasions. When the Barons met at the abbey of Saint Edmund's-Bury, to consider their wrongs and the King's oppressions, Stephen Langton roused them by his fervid words to demand a solemn charter of rights and liberties from their perjured master, and to swear, one by one, on the High Altar, that they would have it, or would wage war against him to the death. When the King hid himself in London from the Barons, and was at last obliged to receive them, they told him roundly they would not believe him unless Stephen Langton became a surety that he would keep his word. When he took the Cross to invest himself with some interest, and belong to something that was received with favour, Stephen Langton was still immovable. When he appealed to the Pope, and the Pope wrote to Stephen Langton in behalf of his new favourite, Stephen Langton was deaf, even to the Pope himself, and saw before him nothing but the welfare of England and the crimes of the English King.

At Easter-time, the Barons assembled at Stamford, in Lincolnshire, in proud array, and, marching near to Oxford where the King was, delivered into the hands of Stephen Langton and two others, a list of grievances. 'And these,' they said, 'he must redress, or we will do it for ourselves!' When Stephen Langton told the King as much, and read the list to him, he went half mad with rage. But that did him no more good than his afterwards trying to pacify the Barons with lies. They called themselves and their followers, 'The army of God and the Holy Church.' Marching through the country, with the people thronging to them everywhere (except at Northampton, where they failed in an attack upon the castle), they at last triumphantly set up their banner in London itself, whither the whole land, tired of the tyrant, seemed to flock to join them. Seven knights alone, of all the knights in England, remained with the King; who, reduced to this strait, at last sent the Earl of Pembroke to the Barons to say that he approved of everything, and would meet them to sign their charter when they would. 'Then,' said the Barons, 'let the day be the fifteenth of June, and the place, Runny-Mead.'

On Monday, the fifteenth of June, one thousand two hundred and fourteen, the King came from Windsor Castle, and the Barons came from the town of Staines, and they met on Runny-Mead, which is still a pleasant meadow by the Thames, where rushes grow in the clear water of the winding river, and its banks are green with grass and trees. On the side of the Barons, came the General of their army, Robert Fitz-Walter, and a great concourse of the nobility of England. With the King, came, in all, some four-and-twenty persons of any note, most of whom despised him, and were merely his advisers in form. On that great day, and in that great company, the King signed Magna Charta—the great charter of England—by which he pledged himself to maintain the Church in its rights; to relieve the Barons of oppressive obligations as vassals of the Crown—of which the Barons, in their turn, pledged themselves to relieve their vassals, the people; to respect the liberties of London and all other cities and boroughs; to protect foreign merchants who came to England; to imprison no man without a fair trial; and to sell, delay, or deny justice to none. As the Barons knew his falsehood well, they further required, as their securities, that he should send out of his kingdom all his foreign troops; that for two months they should hold possession of the city of London, and Stephen Langton of the Tower; and that five-and-twenty of their body, chosen by themselves, should be a lawful committee to watch the keeping of the charter, and to make war upon him if he broke it.

All this he was obliged to yield. He signed the charter with a smile, and, if he could have looked agreeable, would have done so, as he departed from the splendid assembly. When he got home to Windsor Castle, he was quite a madman in his helpless fury. And he broke the charter immediately

121

afterwards.

He sent abroad for foreign soldiers, and sent to the Pope for help, and plotted to take London by surprise, while the Barons should be holding a great tournament at Stamford, which they had agreed to hold there as a celebration of the charter. The Barons, however, found him out and put it off. Then, when the Barons desired to see him and tax him with his treachery, he made numbers of appointments with them, and kept none, and shifted from place to place, and was constantly sneaking and skulking about. At last he appeared at Dover, to join his foreign soldiers, of whom numbers came into his pay; and with them he besieged and took Rochester Castle, which was occupied by knights and soldiers of the Barons. He would have hanged them every one; but the leader of the foreign soldiers, fearful of what the English people might afterwards do to him, interfered to save the knights; therefore the King was fain to satisfy his vengeance with the death of all the common men. Then, he sent the Earl of Salisbury, with one portion of his army, to ravage the eastern part of his own dominions, while he carried fire and slaughter into the northern part; torturing, plundering, killing, and inflicting every possible cruelty upon the people; and, every morning, setting a worthy example to his men by setting fire, with his own monster-hands, to the house where he had slept last night. Nor was this all; for the Pope, coming to the aid of his precious friend, laid the kingdom under an Interdict again, because the people took part with the Barons. It did not much matter, for the people had grown so used to it now, that they had begun to think nothing about it. It occurred to them—perhaps to Stephen Langton too— that they could keep their churches open, and ring their bells, without the Pope's permission as well as with it. So, they tried the experiment—and found that it succeeded perfectly.

It being now impossible to bear the country, as a wilderness of cruelty, or longer to hold any terms with such a forsworn outlaw of a King, the Barons sent to Louis, son of the French monarch, to offer him the English crown. Caring as little for the Pope's excommunication of him if he accepted the offer, as it is possible his father may have cared for the Pope's forgiveness of his sins, he landed at Sandwich (King John immediately running away from

Dover, where he happened to be), and went on to London. The Scottish King, with whom many of the Northern English Lords had taken refuge; numbers of the foreign soldiers, numbers of the Barons, and numbers of the people went over to him every day;—King John, the while, continually running away in all directions.

The career of Louis was checked however, by the suspicions of the Barons, founded on the dying declaration of a French Lord, that when the kingdom was conquered he was sworn to banish them as traitors, and to give their estates to some of his own Nobles. Rather than suffer this, some of the Barons hesitated: others even went over to King John.

It seemed to be the turning-point of King John's fortunes, for, in his savage and murderous course, he had now taken some towns and met with some successes. But, happily for England and humanity, his death was near. Crossing a dangerous quicksand, called the Wash, not very far from Wisbeach, the tide came up and nearly drowned his army. He and his soldiers escaped; but, looking back from the shore when he was safe, he saw the roaring water sweep down in a torrent, overturn the waggons, horses, and men, that carried his treasure, and engulf them in a raging whirlpool from which nothing could be delivered.

Cursing, and swearing, and gnawing his fingers, he went on to Swinestead Abbey, where the monks set before him quantities of pears, and peaches, and new cider—some say poison too, but there is very little reason to suppose so—of which he ate and drank in an immoderate and beastly way. All night he lay ill of a burning fever, and haunted with horrible fears. Next day, they put him in a horse-litter, and carried him to Sleaford Castle, where he passed another night of pain and horror. Next day, they carried him, with greater difficulty than on the day before, to the castle of Newark upon Trent; and there, on the eighteenth of October, in the forty-ninth year of his age, and the seventeenth of his vile reign, was an end of this miserable brute.

CHAPTER XV—ENGLAND UNDER HENRY THE THIRD, CALLED, OF WINCHESTER

If any of the English Barons remembered the murdered Arthur's sister, Eleanor the fair maid of Brittany, shut up in her convent at Bristol, none among them spoke of her now, or maintained her right to the Crown. The dead Usurper's eldest boy, Henry by name, was taken by the Earl of Pembroke, the Marshal of England, to the city of Gloucester, and there crowned in great haste when he was only ten years old. As the Crown itself had been lost with the King's treasure in the raging water, and as there was no time to make another, they put a circle of plain gold upon his head instead. 'We have been the enemies of this child's father,' said Lord Pembroke, a good and true gentleman, to the few Lords who were present, 'and he merited our ill-will; but the child himself is innocent, and his youth demands our friendship and protection.' Those Lords felt tenderly towards the little boy, remembering their own young children; and they bowed their heads, and said, 'Long live King Henry the Third!'

Next, a great council met at Bristol, revised Magna Charta, and made Lord Pembroke Regent or Protector of England, as the King was too young to reign alone. The next thing to be done, was to get rid of Prince Louis of France, and to win over those English Barons who were still ranged under his banner. He was strong in many parts of England, and in London itself; and he held, among other places, a certain Castle called the Castle of Mount Sorel, in Leicestershire. To this fortress, after some skirmishing and truce-making, Lord Pembroke laid siege. Louis despatched an army of six hundred knights and twenty thousand soldiers to relieve it. Lord Pembroke, who was not strong enough for such a force, retired with all his men. The army of the French Prince, which had marched there with fire and plunder, marched away with fire and plunder, and came, in a boastful swaggering manner, to Lincoln. The town submitted; but the Castle in the town, held by a brave widow lady, named Nichola de Camville (whose property it was), made such a sturdy resistance, that the French Count in command of the army of the

French Prince found it necessary to besiege this Castle. While he was thus engaged, word was brought to him that Lord Pembroke, with four hundred knights, two hundred and fifty men with cross-bows, and a stout force both of horse and foot, was marching towards him. 'What care I?' said the French Count. 'The Englishman is not so mad as to attack me and my great army in a walled town!' But the Englishman did it for all that, and did it—not so madly but so wisely, that he decoyed the great army into the narrow, ill-paved lanes and byways of Lincoln, where its horse-soldiers could not ride in any strong body; and there he made such havoc with them, that the whole force surrendered themselves prisoners, except the Count; who said that he would never yield to any English traitor alive, and accordingly got killed. The end of this victory, which the English called, for a joke, the Fair of Lincoln, was the usual one in those times—the common men were slain without any mercy, and the knights and gentlemen paid ransom and went home.

The wife of Louis, the fair Blanche of Castile, dutifully equipped a fleet of eighty good ships, and sent it over from France to her husband's aid. An English fleet of forty ships, some good and some bad, gallantly met them near the mouth of the Thames, and took or sunk sixty-five in one fight. This great loss put an end to the French Prince's hopes. A treaty was made at Lambeth, in virtue of which the English Barons who had remained attached to his cause returned to their allegiance, and it was engaged on both sides that the Prince and all his troops should retire peacefully to France. It was time to go; for war had made him so poor that he was obliged to borrow money from the citizens of London to pay his expenses home.

Lord Pembroke afterwards applied himself to governing the country justly, and to healing the quarrels and disturbances that had arisen among men in the days of the bad King John. He caused Magna Charta to be still more improved, and so amended the Forest Laws that a Peasant was no longer put to death for killing a stag in a Royal Forest, but was only imprisoned. It would have been well for England if it could have had so good a Protector many years longer, but that was not to be. Within three years after the young King's Coronation, Lord Pembroke died; and you may see his tomb, at this day, in the old Temple Church in London.

The Protectorship was now divided. Peter de Roches, whom King John had made Bishop of Winchester, was entrusted with the care of the person of the young sovereign; and the exercise of the Royal authority was confided to Earl Hubert de Burgh. These two personages had from the first no liking for each other, and soon became enemies. When the young King was declared of age, Peter de Roches, finding that Hubert increased in power and favour, retired discontentedly, and went abroad. For nearly ten years afterwards Hubert had full sway alone.

But ten years is a long time to hold the favour of a King. This King, too, as he grew up, showed a strong resemblance to his father, in feebleness, inconsistency, and irresolution. The best that can be said of him is that he was not cruel. De Roches coming home again, after ten years, and being a novelty, the King began to favour him and to look coldly on Hubert. Wanting money besides, and having made Hubert rich, he began to dislike Hubert. At last he was made to believe, or pretended to believe, that Hubert had misappropriated some of the Royal treasure; and ordered him to furnish an account of all he had done in his administration. Besides which, the foolish charge was brought against Hubert that he had made himself the King's favourite by magic. Hubert very well knowing that he could never defend himself against such nonsense, and that his old enemy must be determined on his ruin, instead of answering the charges fled to Merton Abbey. Then the King, in a violent passion, sent for the Mayor of London, and said to the Mayor, 'Take twenty thousand citizens, and drag me Hubert de Burgh out of that abbey, and bring him here.' The Mayor posted off to do it, but the Archbishop of Dublin (who was a friend of Hubert's) warning the King that an abbey was a sacred place, and that if he committed any violence there, he must answer for it to the Church, the King changed his mind and called the Mayor back, and declared that Hubert should have four months to prepare his defence, and should be safe and free during that time.

Hubert, who relied upon the King's word, though I think he was old enough to have known better, came out of Merton Abbey upon these conditions, and journeyed away to see his wife: a Scottish Princess who was then at St. Edmund's-Bury.

Almost as soon as he had departed from the Sanctuary, his enemies persuaded the weak King to send out one Sir Godfrey de Crancumb, who commanded three hundred vagabonds called the Black Band, with orders to seize him. They came up with him at a little town in Essex, called Brentwood, when he was in bed. He leaped out of bed, got out of the house, fled to the church, ran up to the altar, and laid his hand upon the cross. Sir Godfrey and the Black Band, caring neither for church, altar, nor cross, dragged him forth to the church door, with their drawn swords flashing round his head, and sent for a Smith to rivet a set of chains upon him. When the Smith (I wish I knew his name!) was brought, all dark and swarthy with the smoke of his forge, and panting with the speed he had made; and the Black Band, falling aside to show him the Prisoner, cried with a loud uproar, 'Make the fetters heavy! make them strong!' the Smith dropped upon his knee—but not to the Black Band—and said, 'This is the brave Earl Hubert de Burgh, who fought at Dover Castle, and destroyed the French fleet, and has done his country much good service. You may kill me, if you like, but I will never make a chain for Earl Hubert de Burgh!'

The Black Band never blushed, or they might have blushed at this. They knocked the Smith about from one to another, and swore at him, and tied the Earl on horseback, undressed as he was, and carried him off to the Tower of London. The Bishops, however, were so indignant at the violation of the Sanctuary of the Church, that the frightened King soon ordered the Black Band to take him back again; at the same time commanding the Sheriff of Essex to prevent his escaping out of Brentwood Church. Well! the Sheriff dug a deep trench all round the church, and erected a high fence, and watched the church night and day; the Black Band and their Captain watched it too, like three hundred and one black wolves. For thirty-nine days, Hubert de Burgh remained within. At length, upon the fortieth day, cold and hunger were too much for him, and he gave himself up to the Black Band, who carried him off, for the second time, to the Tower. When his trial came on, he refused to plead; but at last it was arranged that he should give up all the royal lands which had been bestowed upon him, and should be kept at the Castle of Devizes, in what was called 'free prison,' in charge of four knights appointed by four lords. There, he remained almost a year, until, learning that a follower of his old enemy the Bishop was made Keeper of the Castle, and fearing that he might be killed by treachery, he climbed the ramparts one dark night, dropped from the top of the high Castle wall into the moat, and coming safely to the ground, took refuge in another church. From this place he was delivered by a party of horse despatched to his help by some nobles, who were by this time in revolt against the King, and assembled in Wales. He was finally pardoned and restored to his estates, but he lived privately, and never more aspired to a high post in the realm, or to a high place in the King's favour. And thus end—more happily than the stories of many favourites of Kings—the adventures of Earl Hubert de Burgh.

The nobles, who had risen in revolt, were stirred up to rebellion by the overbearing conduct of the Bishop of Winchester, who, finding that the King secretly hated the Great Charter which had been forced from his father, did his utmost to confirm him in that dislike, and in the preference he showed to foreigners over the English. Of this, and of his even publicly declaring that the Barons of England were inferior to those of France, the English Lords complained with such bitterness, that the King, finding them well supported by the clergy, became frightened for his throne, and sent away the Bishop and all his foreign associates. On his marriage, however, with Eleanor, a French lady, the daughter of the Count of Provence, he openly favoured the foreigners again; and so many of his wife's relations came over, and made such an immense family-party at court, and got so many good things, and pocketed so much money, and were so high with the English whose money they pocketed, that the bolder English Barons murmured openly about a clause there was in the Great Charter, which provided for the banishment of unreasonable favourites. But, the foreigners only laughed disdainfully, and said, 'What are your English laws to us?'

King Philip of France had died, and had been succeeded by Prince Louis, who had also died after a short reign of three years, and had been succeeded by his son of the same name—so moderate and just a man that he was not the least in the world like a King, as Kings went. Isabella, King Henry's mother, wished very much (for a certain spite she had) that England should make war against this King; and, as King Henry was a mere puppet in anybody's hands who knew how to manage his feebleness, she easily carried her point with him. But, the Parliament were determined to give him no money for such a war. So, to defy the Parliament, he packed up thirty large casks of silver—I don't know how he got so much; I dare say he screwed it out of the miserable Jews—and put them aboard ship, and went away himself to carry war into France: accompanied by his mother and his brother Richard, Earl of Cornwall, who was rich and clever. But he only got well beaten, and came home.

The good-humour of the Parliament was not restored by this. They reproached the King with wasting the public money to make greedy foreigners rich, and were so stern with him, and so determined not to let him have more of it to waste if they could help it, that he was at his wit's end for some, and tried so shamelessly to get all he could from his subjects, by excuses or by force, that the people used to say the King was the sturdiest beggar in England. He took the Cross, thinking to get some money by that means; but, as it was very well known that he never meant to go on a crusade, he got none. In all this contention, the Londoners were particularly keen against the King, and the King hated them warmly in return. Hating or loving, however, made no difference; he continued in the same condition for nine or ten years, when at last the Barons said that if he would solemnly confirm their liberties afresh, the Parliament would vote him a large sum.

As he readily consented, there was a great meeting held in Westminster Hall, one pleasant day in May, when all the clergy, dressed in their robes and holding every one of them a burning candle in his hand, stood up (the Barons being also there) while the Archbishop of Canterbury read the sentence of excommunication against any man, and all men, who should henceforth, in any way, infringe the Great Charter of the Kingdom. When he had done, they all put out their burning candles with a curse upon the soul of any one, and every one, who should merit that sentence. The King concluded with an oath to keep the Charter, 'As I am a man, as I am a Christian, as I am a Knight, as I am a King!'

It was easy to make oaths, and easy to break them; and the King did both, as his father had done before him. He took to his old courses again when he

129

was supplied with money, and soon cured of their weakness the few who had ever really trusted him. When his money was gone, and he was once more borrowing and begging everywhere with a meanness worthy of his nature, he got into a difficulty with the Pope respecting the Crown of Sicily, which the Pope said he had a right to give away, and which he offered to King Henry for his second son, Prince Edmund. But, if you or I give away what we have not got, and what belongs to somebody else, it is likely that the person to whom we give it, will have some trouble in taking it. It was exactly so in this case. It was necessary to conquer the Sicilian Crown before it could be put upon young Edmund's head. It could not be conquered without money. The Pope ordered the clergy to raise money. The clergy, however, were not so obedient to him as usual; they had been disputing with him for some time about his unjust preference of Italian Priests in England; and they had begun to doubt whether the King's chaplain, whom he allowed to be paid for preaching in seven hundred churches, could possibly be, even by the Pope's favour, in seven hundred places at once. 'The Pope and the King together,' said the Bishop of London, 'may take the mitre off my head; but, if they do, they will find that I shall put on a soldier's helmet. I pay nothing.' The Bishop of Worcester was as bold as the Bishop of London, and would pay nothing either. Such sums as the more timid or more helpless of the clergy did raise were squandered away, without doing any good to the King, or bringing the Sicilian Crown an inch nearer to Prince Edmund's head. The end of the business was, that the Pope gave the Crown to the brother of the King of France (who conquered it for himself), and sent the King of England in, a bill of one hundred thousand pounds for the expenses of not having won it.

The King was now so much distressed that we might almost pity him, if it were possible to pity a King so shabby and ridiculous. His clever brother, Richard, had bought the title of King of the Romans from the German people, and was no longer near him, to help him with advice. The clergy, resisting the very Pope, were in alliance with the Barons. The Barons were headed by Simon de Montfort, Earl of Leicester, married to King Henry's sister, and, though a foreigner himself, the most popular man in England against the foreign favourites. When the King next met his Parliament, the Barons, led by this Earl, came before him, armed from head to foot, and cased in armour.

When the Parliament again assembled, in a month's time, at Oxford, this Earl was at their head, and the King was obliged to consent, on oath, to what was called a Committee of Government: consisting of twenty-four members: twelve chosen by the Barons, and twelve chosen by himself.

But, at a good time for him, his brother Richard came back. Richard's first act (the Barons would not admit him into England on other terms) was to swear to be faithful to the Committee of Government—which he immediately began to oppose with all his might. Then, the Barons began to quarrel among themselves; especially the proud Earl of Gloucester with the Earl of Leicester, who went abroad in disgust. Then, the people began to be dissatisfied with the Barons, because they did not do enough for them. The King's chances seemed so good again at length, that he took heart enough— or caught it from his brother—to tell the Committee of Government that he abolished them—as to his oath, never mind that, the Pope said!—and to seize all the money in the Mint, and to shut himself up in the Tower of London. Here he was joined by his eldest son, Prince Edward; and, from the Tower, he made public a letter of the Pope's to the world in general, informing all men that he had been an excellent and just King for five-and-forty years.

As everybody knew he had been nothing of the sort, nobody cared much for this document. It so chanced that the proud Earl of Gloucester dying, was succeeded by his son; and that his son, instead of being the enemy of the Earl of Leicester, was (for the time) his friend. It fell out, therefore, that these two Earls joined their forces, took several of the Royal Castles in the country, and advanced as hard as they could on London. The London people, always opposed to the King, declared for them with great joy. The King himself remained shut up, not at all gloriously, in the Tower. Prince Edward made the best of his way to Windsor Castle. His mother, the Queen, attempted to follow him by water; but, the people seeing her barge rowing up the river, and hating her with all their hearts, ran to London Bridge, got together a quantity of stones and mud, and pelted the barge as it came through, crying furiously, 'Drown the Witch! Drown her!' They were so near doing it, that the Mayor took the old lady under his protection, and shut her up in St. Paul's until the danger was past.

It would require a great deal of writing on my part, and a great deal of reading on yours, to follow the King through his disputes with the Barons, and to follow the Barons through their disputes with one another—so I will make short work of it for both of us, and only relate the chief events that arose out of these quarrels. The good King of France was asked to decide between them. He gave it as his opinion that the King must maintain the Great Charter, and that the Barons must give up the Committee of Government, and all the rest that had been done by the Parliament at Oxford: which the Royalists, or King's party, scornfully called the Mad Parliament. The Barons declared that these were not fair terms, and they would not accept them. Then they caused the great bell of St. Paul's to be tolled, for the purpose of rousing up the London people, who armed themselves at the dismal sound and formed quite an army in the streets. I am sorry to say, however, that instead of falling upon the King's party with whom their quarrel was, they fell upon the miserable Jews, and killed at least five hundred of them. They pretended that some of these Jews were on the King's side, and that they kept hidden in their houses, for the destruction of the people, a certain terrible composition called Greek Fire, which could not be put out with water, but only burnt the fiercer for it. What they really did keep in their houses was money; and this their cruel enemies wanted, and this their cruel enemies took, like robbers and murderers.

The Earl of Leicester put himself at the head of these Londoners and other forces, and followed the King to Lewes in Sussex, where he lay encamped with his army. Before giving the King's forces battle here, the Earl addressed his soldiers, and said that King Henry the Third had broken so many oaths, that he had become the enemy of God, and therefore they would wear white crosses on their breasts, as if they were arrayed, not against a fellow-Christian, but against a Turk. White-crossed accordingly, they rushed into the fight. They would have lost the day—the King having on his side all the foreigners in England: and, from Scotland, John Comyn, John Baliol, and Robert Bruce, with all their men—but for the impatience of Prince Edward, who, in his hot desire to have vengeance on the people of London, threw the whole of his father's army into confusion. He was taken Prisoner; so was the King; so was the King's brother the King of the Romans; and five thousand

Englishmen were left dead upon the bloody grass.

For this success, the Pope excommunicated the Earl of Leicester: which neither the Earl nor the people cared at all about. The people loved him and supported him, and he became the real King; having all the power of the government in his own hands, though he was outwardly respectful to King Henry the Third, whom he took with him wherever he went, like a poor old limp court-card. He summoned a Parliament (in the year one thousand two hundred and sixty-five) which was the first Parliament in England that the people had any real share in electing; and he grew more and more in favour with the people every day, and they stood by him in whatever he did.

Many of the other Barons, and particularly the Earl of Gloucester, who had become by this time as proud as his father, grew jealous of this powerful and popular Earl, who was proud too, and began to conspire against him. Since the battle of Lewes, Prince Edward had been kept as a hostage, and, though he was otherwise treated like a Prince, had never been allowed to go out without attendants appointed by the Earl of Leicester, who watched him. The conspiring Lords found means to propose to him, in secret, that they should assist him to escape, and should make him their leader; to which he very heartily consented.

So, on a day that was agreed upon, he said to his attendants after dinner (being then at Hereford), 'I should like to ride on horseback, this fine afternoon, a little way into the country.' As they, too, thought it would be very pleasant to have a canter in the sunshine, they all rode out of the town together in a gay little troop. When they came to a fine level piece of turf, the Prince fell to comparing their horses one with another, and offering bets that one was faster than another; and the attendants, suspecting no harm, rode galloping matches until their horses were quite tired. The Prince rode no matches himself, but looked on from his saddle, and staked his money. Thus they passed the whole merry afternoon. Now, the sun was setting, and they were all going slowly up a hill, the Prince's horse very fresh and all the other horses very weary, when a strange rider mounted on a grey steed appeared at the top of the hill, and waved his hat. 'What does the fellow mean?' said the attendants one to another. The Prince answered on the instant by setting spurs to his horse, dashing away at his utmost speed, joining the man, riding into the midst of a little crowd of horsemen who were then seen waiting under some trees, and who closed around him; and so he departed in a cloud of dust, leaving the road empty of all but the baffled attendants, who sat looking at one another, while their horses drooped their ears and panted.

The Prince joined the Earl of Gloucester at Ludlow. The Earl of Leicester, with a part of the army and the stupid old King, was at Hereford. One of the Earl of Leicester's sons, Simon de Montfort, with another part of the army, was in Sussex. To prevent these two parts from uniting was the Prince's first object. He attacked Simon de Montfort by night, defeated him, seized his banners and treasure, and forced him into Kenilworth Castle in Warwickshire, which belonged to his family.

His father, the Earl of Leicester, in the meanwhile, not knowing what had happened, marched out of Hereford, with his part of the army and the King, to meet him. He came, on a bright morning in August, to Evesham, which is watered by the pleasant river Avon. Looking rather anxiously across the prospect towards Kenilworth, he saw his own banners advancing; and his face brightened with joy. But, it clouded darkly when he presently perceived that the banners were captured, and in the enemy's hands; and he said, 'It is over. The Lord have mercy on our souls, for our bodies are Prince Edward's!'

He fought like a true Knight, nevertheless. When his horse was killed under him, he fought on foot. It was a fierce battle, and the dead lay in heaps everywhere. The old King, stuck up in a suit of armour on a big war-horse, which didn't mind him at all, and which carried him into all sorts of places where he didn't want to go, got into everybody's way, and very nearly got knocked on the head by one of his son's men. But he managed to pipe out, 'I am Harry of Winchester!' and the Prince, who heard him, seized his bridle, and took him out of peril. The Earl of Leicester still fought bravely, until his best son Henry was killed, and the bodies of his best friends choked his path; and then he fell, still fighting, sword in hand. They mangled his body, and sent it as a present to a noble lady—but a very unpleasant lady, I should think—who was the wife of his worst enemy. They could not mangle his memory in the minds of the faithful people, though. Many years afterwards, they loved him more than ever, and regarded him as a Saint, and always spoke of him as 'Sir Simon the Righteous.'

And even though he was dead, the cause for which he had fought still lived, and was strong, and forced itself upon the King in the very hour of victory. Henry found himself obliged to respect the Great Charter, however much he hated it, and to make laws similar to the laws of the Great Earl of Leicester, and to be moderate and forgiving towards the people at last— even towards the people of London, who had so long opposed him. There were more risings before all this was done, but they were set at rest by these means, and Prince Edward did his best in all things to restore peace. One Sir Adam de Gourdon was the last dissatisfied knight in arms; but, the Prince vanquished him in single combat, in a wood, and nobly gave him his life, and became his friend, instead of slaying him. Sir Adam was not ungrateful. He ever afterwards remained devoted to his generous conqueror.

When the troubles of the Kingdom were thus calmed, Prince Edward and his cousin Henry took the Cross, and went away to the Holy Land, with many English Lords and Knights. Four years afterwards the King of the Romans died, and, next year (one thousand two hundred and seventy-two), his brother the weak King of England died. He was sixty-eight years old then, and had reigned fifty-six years. He was as much of a King in death, as he had ever been in life. He was the mere pale shadow of a King at all times.

CHAPTER XVI—ENGLAND UNDER EDWARD THE FIRST, CALLED LONGSHANKS

It was now the year of our Lord one thousand two hundred and seventy-two; and Prince Edward, the heir to the throne, being away in the Holy Land, knew nothing of his father's death. The Barons, however, proclaimed him King, immediately after the Royal funeral; and the people very willingly consented, since most men knew too well by this time what the horrors of a contest for the crown were. So King Edward the First, called, in a not very complimentary manner, Longshanks, because of the slenderness of his legs, was peacefully accepted by the English Nation.

His legs had need to be strong, however long and thin they were; for they had to support him through many difficulties on the fiery sands of Asia, where his small force of soldiers fainted, died, deserted, and seemed to melt away. But his prowess made light of it, and he said, 'I will go on, if I go on with no other follower than my groom!'

A Prince of this spirit gave the Turks a deal of trouble. He stormed Nazareth, at which place, of all places on earth, I am sorry to relate, he made a frightful slaughter of innocent people; and then he went to Acre, where he got a truce of ten years from the Sultan. He had very nearly lost his life in Acre, through the treachery of a Saracen Noble, called the Emir of Jaffa, who, making the pretence that he had some idea of turning Christian and wanted to know all about that religion, sent a trusty messenger to Edward very often—with a dagger in his sleeve. At last, one Friday in Whitsun week, when it was very hot, and all the sandy prospect lay beneath the blazing sun, burnt up like a great overdone biscuit, and Edward was lying on a couch, dressed for coolness in only a loose robe, the messenger, with his chocolate-coloured face and his bright dark eyes and white teeth, came creeping in with a letter, and kneeled down like a tame tiger. But, the moment Edward stretched out his hand to take the letter, the tiger made a spring at his heart. He was quick, but Edward was quick too. He seized the traitor by his chocolate throat, threw him to the ground, and slew him with the very dagger he had drawn. The weapon had struck Edward in the arm, and although the wound itself was slight, it threatened to be mortal, for the blade of the dagger had been smeared with poison. Thanks, however, to a better surgeon than was often to be found in those times, and to some wholesome herbs, and above all, to his faithful wife, Eleanor, who devotedly nursed him, and is said by some to have sucked the poison from the wound with her own red lips (which I am very willing to believe), Edward soon recovered and was sound again.

As the King his father had sent entreaties to him to return home, he now began the journey. He had got as far as Italy, when he met messengers who brought him intelligence of the King's death. Hearing that all was quiet at home, he made no haste to return to his own dominions, but paid a visit to the Pope, and went in state through various Italian Towns, where he was welcomed with acclamations as a mighty champion of the Cross from the Holy Land, and where he received presents of purple mantles and prancing horses, and went along in great triumph. The shouting people little knew that he was the last English monarch who would ever embark in a crusade, or that within twenty years every conquest which the Christians had made in the Holy Land at the cost of so much blood, would be won back by the Turks. But all this came to pass.

There was, and there is, an old town standing in a plain in France, called Châlons. When the King was coming towards this place on his way to England, a wily French Lord, called the Count of Châlons, sent him a polite challenge to come with his knights and hold a fair tournament with the Count and his knights, and make a day of it with sword and lance. It was represented to the King that the Count of Châlons was not to be trusted, and that, instead of a holiday fight for mere show and in good humour, he secretly meant a real battle, in which the English should be defeated by superior force.

The King, however, nothing afraid, went to the appointed place on the appointed day with a thousand followers. When the Count came with two thousand and attacked the English in earnest, the English rushed at them with such valour that the Count's men and the Count's horses soon began to be tumbled down all over the field. The Count himself seized the King

137

round the neck, but the King tumbled him out of his saddle in return for the compliment, and, jumping from his own horse, and standing over him, beat away at his iron armour like a blacksmith hammering on his anvil. Even when the Count owned himself defeated and offered his sword, the King would not do him the honour to take it, but made him yield it up to a common soldier. There had been such fury shown in this fight, that it was afterwards called the little Battle of Châlons.

The English were very well disposed to be proud of their King after these adventures; so, when he landed at Dover in the year one thousand two hundred and seventy-four (being then thirty-six years old), and went on to Westminster where he and his good Queen were crowned with great magnificence, splendid rejoicings took place. For the coronation-feast there were provided, among other eatables, four hundred oxen, four hundred sheep, four hundred and fifty pigs, eighteen wild boars, three hundred flitches of bacon, and twenty thousand fowls. The fountains and conduits in the street flowed with red and white wine instead of water; the rich citizens hung silks and cloths of the brightest colours out of their windows to increase the beauty of the show, and threw out gold and silver by whole handfuls to make scrambles for the crowd. In short, there was such eating and drinking, such music and capering, such a ringing of bells and tossing of caps, such a shouting, and singing, and revelling, as the narrow overhanging streets of old London City had not witnessed for many a long day. All the people were merry except the poor Jews, who, trembling within their houses, and scarcely daring to peep out, began to foresee that they would have to find the money for this joviality sooner or later.

To dismiss this sad subject of the Jews for the present, I am sorry to add that in this reign they were most unmercifully pillaged. They were hanged in great numbers, on accusations of having clipped the King's coin—which all kinds of people had done. They were heavily taxed; they were disgracefully badged; they were, on one day, thirteen years after the coronation, taken up with their wives and children and thrown into beastly prisons, until they purchased their release by paying to the King twelve thousand pounds. Finally, every kind of property belonging to them was seized by the King, except so little as would defray the charge of their taking themselves away into foreign countries. Many years elapsed before the hope of gain induced any of their race to return to England, where they had been treated so heartlessly and had suffered so much.

If King Edward the First had been as bad a king to Christians as he was to Jews, he would have been bad indeed. But he was, in general, a wise and great monarch, under whom the country much improved. He had no love for the Great Charter—few Kings had, through many, many years—but he had high qualities. The first bold object which he conceived when he came home, was, to unite under one Sovereign England, Scotland, and Wales; the two last of which countries had each a little king of its own, about whom the people were always quarrelling and fighting, and making a prodigious disturbance—a great deal more than he was worth. In the course of King Edward's reign he was engaged, besides, in a war with France. To make these quarrels clearer, we will separate their histories and take them thus. Wales, first. France, second. Scotland, third.

* * * * *

Llewellyn was the Prince of Wales. He had been on the side of the Barons in the reign of the stupid old King, but had afterwards sworn allegiance to him. When King Edward came to the throne, Llewellyn was required to swear allegiance to him also; which he refused to do. The King, being crowned and in his own dominions, three times more required Llewellyn to come and do homage; and three times more Llewellyn said he would rather not. He was going to be married to Eleanor de Montfort, a young lady of the family mentioned in the last reign; and it chanced that this young lady, coming from France with her youngest brother, Emeric, was taken by an English ship, and was ordered by the English King to be detained. Upon this, the quarrel came to a head. The King went, with his fleet, to the coast of Wales, where, so encompassing Llewellyn, that he could only take refuge in the bleak mountain region of Snowdon in which no provisions could reach him, he was soon starved into an apology, and into a treaty of peace, and into paying the expenses of the war. The King, however, forgave him some of the hardest conditions of the treaty, and consented to his marriage. And he now thought he had reduced Wales to obedience.

But the Welsh, although they were naturally a gentle, quiet, pleasant people, who liked to receive strangers in their cottages among the mountains, and to set before them with free hospitality whatever they had to eat and drink, and to play to them on their harps, and sing their native ballads to them, were a people of great spirit when their blood was up. Englishmen, after this affair, began to be insolent in Wales, and to assume the air of masters; and the Welsh pride could not bear it. Moreover, they believed in that unlucky old Merlin, some of whose unlucky old prophecies somebody always seemed doomed to remember when there was a chance of its doing harm; and just at this time some blind old gentleman with a harp and a long white beard, who was an excellent person, but had become of an unknown age and tedious, burst out with a declaration that Merlin had predicted that when English money had become round, a Prince of Wales would be crowned in London. Now, King Edward had recently forbidden the English penny to be cut into halves and quarters for halfpence and farthings, and had actually introduced a round coin; therefore, the Welsh people said this was the time Merlin meant, and rose accordingly.

King Edward had bought over Prince David, Llewellyn's brother, by heaping favours upon him; but he was the first to revolt, being perhaps troubled in his conscience. One stormy night, he surprised the Castle of Hawarden, in possession of which an English nobleman had been left; killed the whole garrison, and carried off the nobleman a prisoner to Snowdon. Upon this, the Welsh people rose like one man. King Edward, with his army, marching from Worcester to the Menai Strait, crossed it—near to where the wonderful tubular iron bridge now, in days so different, makes a passage for railway trains—by a bridge of boats that enabled forty men to march abreast. He subdued the Island of Anglesea, and sent his men forward to observe the enemy. The sudden appearance of the Welsh created a panic among them, and they fell back to the bridge. The tide had in the meantime risen and separated the boats; the Welsh pursuing them, they were driven into the sea, and there they sunk, in their heavy iron armour, by thousands. After this victory Llewellyn, helped by the severe winter-weather of Wales, gained another battle; but the King ordering a portion of his English army to advance through South Wales, and catch him between two foes, and Llewellyn bravely turning to meet this new enemy, he was surprised and killed—very meanly, for he was unarmed and defenceless. His head was struck off and sent to London, where it was fixed upon the Tower, encircled with a wreath, some say of ivy, some say of willow, some say of silver, to make it look like a ghastly coin in ridicule of the prediction.

David, however, still held out for six months, though eagerly sought after by the King, and hunted by his own countrymen. One of them finally betrayed him with his wife and children. He was sentenced to be hanged, drawn, and quartered; and from that time this became the established punishment of Traitors in England—a punishment wholly without excuse, as being revolting, vile, and cruel, after its object is dead; and which has no sense in it, as its only real degradation (and that nothing can blot out) is to the country that permits on any consideration such abominable barbarity.

Wales was now subdued. The Queen giving birth to a young prince in the Castle of Carnarvon, the King showed him to the Welsh people as their countryman, and called him Prince of Wales; a title that has ever since been borne by the heir-apparent to the English throne—which that little Prince soon became, by the death of his elder brother. The King did better things for the Welsh than that, by improving their laws and encouraging their trade. Disturbances still took place, chiefly occasioned by the avarice and pride of the English Lords, on whom Welsh lands and castles had been bestowed; but they were subdued, and the country never rose again. There is a legend that to prevent the people from being incited to rebellion by the songs of their bards and harpers, Edward had them all put to death. Some of them may have fallen among other men who held out against the King; but this general slaughter is, I think, a fancy of the harpers themselves, who, I dare say, made a song about it many years afterwards, and sang it by the Welsh firesides until it came to be believed.

The foreign war of the reign of Edward the First arose in this way. The crews of two vessels, one a Norman ship, and the other an English ship, happened to go to the same place in their boats to fill their casks with fresh

water. Being rough angry fellows, they began to quarrel, and then to fight—
the English with their fists; the Normans with their knives—and, in the fight,
a Norman was killed. The Norman crew, instead of revenging themselves
upon those English sailors with whom they had quarrelled (who were too
strong for them, I suspect), took to their ship again in a great rage, attacked
the first English ship they met, laid hold of an unoffending merchant who
happened to be on board, and brutally hanged him in the rigging of their
own vessel with a dog at his feet. This so enraged the English sailors that
there was no restraining them; and whenever, and wherever, English sailors
met Norman sailors, they fell upon each other tooth and nail. The Irish and
Dutch sailors took part with the English; the French and Genoese sailors
helped the Normans; and thus the greater part of the mariners sailing over
the sea became, in their way, as violent and raging as the sea itself when it is
disturbed.

King Edward's fame had been so high abroad that he had been chosen
to decide a difference between France and another foreign power, and had
lived upon the Continent three years. At first, neither he nor the French
King Philip (the good Louis had been dead some time) interfered in these
quarrels; but when a fleet of eighty English ships engaged and utterly defeated
a Norman fleet of two hundred, in a pitched battle fought round a ship at
anchor, in which no quarter was given, the matter became too serious to be
passed over. King Edward, as Duke of Guienne, was summoned to present
himself before the King of France, at Paris, and answer for the damage
done by his sailor subjects. At first, he sent the Bishop of London as his
representative, and then his brother Edmund, who was married to the French
Queen's mother. I am afraid Edmund was an easy man, and allowed himself
to be talked over by his charming relations, the French court ladies; at all
events, he was induced to give up his brother's dukedom for forty days—as a
mere form, the French King said, to satisfy his honour—and he was so very
much astonished, when the time was out, to find that the French King had no
idea of giving it up again, that I should not wonder if it hastened his death:
which soon took place.

King Edward was a King to win his foreign dukedom back again, if it could be won by energy and valour. He raised a large army, renounced his allegiance as Duke of Guienne, and crossed the sea to carry war into France. Before any important battle was fought, however, a truce was agreed upon for two years; and in the course of that time, the Pope effected a reconciliation. King Edward, who was now a widower, having lost his affectionate and good wife, Eleanor, married the French King's sister, Margaret; and the Prince of Wales was contracted to the French King's daughter Isabella.

Out of bad things, good things sometimes arise. Out of this hanging of the innocent merchant, and the bloodshed and strife it caused, there came to be established one of the greatest powers that the English people now possess. The preparations for the war being very expensive, and King Edward greatly wanting money, and being very arbitrary in his ways of raising it, some of the Barons began firmly to oppose him. Two of them, in particular, Humphrey Bohun, Earl of Hereford, and Roger Bigod, Earl of Norfolk, were so stout against him, that they maintained he had no right to command them to head his forces in Guienne, and flatly refused to go there. 'By Heaven, Sir Earl,' said the King to the Earl of Hereford, in a great passion, 'you shall either go or be hanged!' 'By Heaven, Sir King,' replied the Earl, 'I will neither go nor yet will I be hanged!' and both he and the other Earl sturdily left the court, attended by many Lords. The King tried every means of raising money. He taxed the clergy, in spite of all the Pope said to the contrary; and when they refused to pay, reduced them to submission, by saying Very well, then they had no claim upon the government for protection, and any man might plunder them who would—which a good many men were very ready to do, and very readily did, and which the clergy found too losing a game to be played at long. He seized all the wool and leather in the hands of the merchants, promising to pay for it some fine day; and he set a tax upon the exportation of wool, which was so unpopular among the traders that it was called 'The evil toll.' But all would not do. The Barons, led by those two great Earls, declared any taxes imposed without the consent of Parliament, unlawful; and the Parliament refused to impose taxes, until the King should confirm afresh the two Great Charters, and should solemnly declare in writing, that there was no power in the country to raise money from the people, evermore, but the power of Parliament representing all ranks of the people. The King was

143

very unwilling to diminish his own power by allowing this great privilege in the Parliament; but there was no help for it, and he at last complied. We shall come to another King by-and-by, who might have saved his head from rolling off, if he had profited by this example.

The people gained other benefits in Parliament from the good sense and wisdom of this King. Many of the laws were much improved; provision was made for the greater safety of travellers, and the apprehension of thieves and murderers; the priests were prevented from holding too much land, and so becoming too powerful; and Justices of the Peace were first appointed (though not at first under that name) in various parts of the country.

* * * * *

And now we come to Scotland, which was the great and lasting trouble of the reign of King Edward the First.

About thirteen years after King Edward's coronation, Alexander the Third, the King of Scotland, died of a fall from his horse. He had been married to Margaret, King Edward's sister. All their children being dead, the Scottish crown became the right of a young Princess only eight years old, the daughter of Eric, King of Norway, who had married a daughter of the deceased sovereign. King Edward proposed, that the Maiden of Norway, as this Princess was called, should be engaged to be married to his eldest son; but, unfortunately, as she was coming over to England she fell sick, and landing on one of the Orkney Islands, died there. A great commotion immediately began in Scotland, where as many as thirteen noisy claimants to the vacant throne started up and made a general confusion.

King Edward being much renowned for his sagacity and justice, it seems to have been agreed to refer the dispute to him. He accepted the trust, and went, with an army, to the Border-land where England and Scotland joined. There, he called upon the Scottish gentlemen to meet him at the Castle of Norham, on the English side of the river Tweed; and to that Castle they came. But, before he would take any step in the business, he required those Scottish gentlemen, one and all, to do homage to him as their superior Lord; and when they hesitated, he said, 'By holy Edward, whose crown I wear, I will have my rights, or I will die in maintaining them!' The Scottish gentlemen, who had not expected this, were disconcerted, and asked for three weeks to think about it.

At the end of the three weeks, another meeting took place, on a green plain on the Scottish side of the river. Of all the competitors for the Scottish throne, there were only two who had any real claim, in right of their near kindred to the Royal Family. These were John Baliol and Robert Bruce: and the right was, I have no doubt, on the side of John Baliol. At this particular meeting John Baliol was not present, but Robert Bruce was; and on Robert Bruce being formally asked whether he acknowledged the King of England for his superior lord, he answered, plainly and distinctly, Yes, he did. Next day, John Baliol appeared, and said the same. This point settled, some arrangements were made for inquiring into their titles.

The inquiry occupied a pretty long time—more than a year. While it was going on, King Edward took the opportunity of making a journey through Scotland, and calling upon the Scottish people of all degrees to acknowledge themselves his vassals, or be imprisoned until they did. In the meanwhile, Commissioners were appointed to conduct the inquiry, a Parliament was held at Berwick about it, the two claimants were heard at full length, and there was a vast amount of talking. At last, in the great hall of the Castle of Berwick, the King gave judgment in favour of John Baliol: who, consenting to receive his crown by the King of England's favour and permission, was crowned at Scone, in an old stone chair which had been used for ages in the abbey there, at the coronations of Scottish Kings. Then, King Edward caused the great seal of Scotland, used since the late King's death, to be broken in four pieces, and placed in the English Treasury; and considered that he now had Scotland (according to the common saying) under his thumb.

Scotland had a strong will of its own yet, however. King Edward, determined that the Scottish King should not forget he was his vassal, summoned him repeatedly to come and defend himself and his judges before the English Parliament when appeals from the decisions of Scottish courts of justice were being heard. At length, John Baliol, who had no great heart of his own, had so much heart put into him by the brave spirit of the

145

Scottish people, who took this as a national insult, that he refused to come any more. Thereupon, the King further required him to help him in his war abroad (which was then in progress), and to give up, as security for his good behaviour in future, the three strong Scottish Castles of Jedburgh, Roxburgh, and Berwick. Nothing of this being done; on the contrary, the Scottish people concealing their King among their mountains in the Highlands and showing a determination to resist; Edward marched to Berwick with an army of thirty thousand foot, and four thousand horse; took the Castle, and slew its whole garrison, and the inhabitants of the town as well—men, women, and children. Lord Warrenne, Earl of Surrey, then went on to the Castle of Dunbar, before which a battle was fought, and the whole Scottish army defeated with great slaughter. The victory being complete, the Earl of Surrey was left as guardian of Scotland; the principal offices in that kingdom were given to Englishmen; the more powerful Scottish Nobles were obliged to come and live in England; the Scottish crown and sceptre were brought away; and even the old stone chair was carried off and placed in Westminster Abbey, where you may see it now. Baliol had the Tower of London lent him for a residence, with permission to range about within a circle of twenty miles. Three years afterwards he was allowed to go to Normandy, where he had estates, and where he passed the remaining six years of his life: far more happily, I dare say, than he had lived for a long while in angry Scotland.

Now, there was, in the West of Scotland, a gentleman of small fortune, named William Wallace, the second son of a Scottish knight. He was a man of great size and great strength; he was very brave and daring; when he spoke to a body of his countrymen, he could rouse them in a wonderful manner by the power of his burning words; he loved Scotland dearly, and he hated England with his utmost might. The domineering conduct of the English who now held the places of trust in Scotland made them as intolerable to the proud Scottish people as they had been, under similar circumstances, to the Welsh; and no man in all Scotland regarded them with so much smothered rage as William Wallace. One day, an Englishman in office, little knowing what he was, affronted him. Wallace instantly struck him dead, and taking refuge among the rocks and hills, and there joining with his countryman, Sir William Douglas, who was also in arms against King Edward, became

146

the most resolute and undaunted champion of a people struggling for their independence that ever lived upon the earth.

The English Guardian of the Kingdom fled before him, and, thus encouraged, the Scottish people revolted everywhere, and fell upon the English without mercy. The Earl of Surrey, by the King's commands, raised all the power of the Border-counties, and two English armies poured into Scotland. Only one Chief, in the face of those armies, stood by Wallace, who, with a force of forty thousand men, awaited the invaders at a place on the river Forth, within two miles of Stirling. Across the river there was only one poor wooden bridge, called the bridge of Kildean—so narrow, that but two men could cross it abreast. With his eyes upon this bridge, Wallace posted the greater part of his men among some rising grounds, and waited calmly. When the English army came up on the opposite bank of the river, messengers were sent forward to offer terms. Wallace sent them back with a defiance, in the name of the freedom of Scotland. Some of the officers of the Earl of Surrey in command of the English, with their eyes also on the bridge, advised him to be discreet and not hasty. He, however, urged to immediate battle by some other officers, and particularly by Cressingham, King Edward's treasurer, and a rash man, gave the word of command to advance. One thousand English crossed the bridge, two abreast; the Scottish troops were as motionless as stone images. Two thousand English crossed; three thousand, four thousand, five. Not a feather, all this time, had been seen to stir among the Scottish bonnets. Now, they all fluttered. 'Forward, one party, to the foot of the Bridge!' cried Wallace, 'and let no more English cross! The rest, down with me on the five thousand who have come over, and cut them all to pieces!' It was done, in the sight of the whole remainder of the English army, who could give no help. Cressingham himself was killed, and the Scotch made whips for their horses of his skin.

King Edward was abroad at this time, and during the successes on the Scottish side which followed, and which enabled bold Wallace to win the whole country back again, and even to ravage the English borders. But, after a few winter months, the King returned, and took the field with more than his usual energy. One night, when a kick from his horse as they both lay on the ground together broke two of his ribs, and a cry arose that he was killed, he leaped into his saddle, regardless of the pain he suffered, and rode through the camp. Day then appearing, he gave the word (still, of course, in that bruised and aching state) Forward! and led his army on to near Falkirk, where the Scottish forces were seen drawn up on some stony ground, behind a morass. Here, he defeated Wallace, and killed fifteen thousand of his men. With the shattered remainder, Wallace drew back to Stirling; but, being pursued, set fire to the town that it might give no help to the English, and escaped. The inhabitants of Perth afterwards set fire to their houses for the same reason, and the King, unable to find provisions, was forced to withdraw his army.

Another Robert Bruce, the grandson of him who had disputed the Scottish crown with Baliol, was now in arms against the King (that elder Bruce being dead), and also John Comyn, Baliol's nephew. These two young men might agree in opposing Edward, but could agree in nothing else, as they were rivals for the throne of Scotland. Probably it was because they knew this, and knew what troubles must arise even if they could hope to get the better of the great English King, that the principal Scottish people applied to the Pope for his interference. The Pope, on the principle of losing nothing for want of trying to get it, very coolly claimed that Scotland belonged to him; but this was a little too much, and the Parliament in a friendly manner told him so.

In the spring time of the year one thousand three hundred and three, the King sent Sir John Segrave, whom he made Governor of Scotland, with twenty thousand men, to reduce the rebels. Sir John was not as careful as he should have been, but encamped at Rosslyn, near Edinburgh, with his army divided into three parts. The Scottish forces saw their advantage; fell on each part separately; defeated each; and killed all the prisoners. Then, came the King himself once more, as soon as a great army could be raised; he passed through the whole north of Scotland, laying waste whatsoever came in his way; and he took up his winter quarters at Dunfermline. The Scottish cause now looked so hopeless, that Comyn and the other nobles made submission and received their pardons. Wallace alone stood out. He was invited to surrender, though on no distinct pledge that his life should be spared; but he still defied the ireful King, and lived among the steep crags of the Highland glens, where the eagles made their nests, and where the mountain torrents roared, and the white snow was deep, and the bitter winds blew round his unsheltered head, as he lay through many a pitch-dark night wrapped up in his plaid. Nothing could break his spirit; nothing could lower his courage; nothing could induce him to forget or to forgive his country's wrongs. Even when the Castle of Stirling, which had long held out, was besieged by the King with every kind of military engine then in use; even when the lead upon cathedral roofs was taken down to help to make them; even when the King, though an old man, commanded in the siege as if he were a youth, being so resolved to conquer; even when the brave garrison (then found with amazement to be not two hundred people, including several ladies) were starved and beaten out and were made to submit on their knees, and with every form of disgrace that could aggravate their sufferings; even then, when there was not a ray of hope in Scotland, William Wallace was as proud and firm as if he had beheld the powerful and relentless Edward lying dead at his feet.

Who betrayed William Wallace in the end, is not quite certain. That he was betrayed—probably by an attendant—is too true. He was taken to the Castle of Dumbarton, under Sir John Menteith, and thence to London, where the great fame of his bravery and resolution attracted immense concourses of people to behold him. He was tried in Westminster Hall, with a crown of laurel on his head—it is supposed because he was reported to have said that he ought to wear, or that he would wear, a crown there and was found guilty as a robber, a murderer, and a traitor. What they called a robber (he said to those who tried him) he was, because he had taken spoil from the King's men. What they called a murderer, he was, because he had slain an insolent Englishman. What they called a traitor, he was not, for he had never sworn allegiance to the King, and had ever scorned to do it. He was dragged at the tails of horses to West Smithfield, and there hanged on a high gallows, torn open before he was dead, beheaded, and quartered. His head was set upon a pole on London Bridge, his right arm was sent to Newcastle, his left arm to Berwick, his legs to Perth and Aberdeen. But, if King Edward had had his body cut into inches, and had sent every separate inch into a separate town, he could not have dispersed it half so far and wide as his fame. Wallace will be remembered in songs and stories, while there are songs and stories in the English tongue, and Scotland will hold him dear while her lakes and mountains last.

Released from this dreaded enemy, the King made a fairer plan of Government for Scotland, divided the offices of honour among Scottish gentlemen and English gentlemen, forgave past offences, and thought, in his old age, that his work was done.

But he deceived himself. Comyn and Bruce conspired, and made an appointment to meet at Dumfries, in the church of the Minorites. There is a story that Comyn was false to Bruce, and had informed against him to the King; that Bruce was warned of his danger and the necessity of flight, by receiving, one night as he sat at supper, from his friend the Earl of Gloucester, twelve pennies and a pair of spurs; that as he was riding angrily to keep his appointment (through a snow-storm, with his horse's shoes reversed that he might not be tracked), he met an evil-looking serving man, a messenger of Comyn, whom he killed, and concealed in whose dress he found letters that proved Comyn's treachery. However this may be, they were likely enough to quarrel in any case, being hot-headed rivals; and, whatever they quarrelled about, they certainly did quarrel in the church where they met, and Bruce drew his dagger and stabbed Comyn, who fell upon the pavement. When Bruce came out, pale and disturbed, the friends who were waiting for him asked what was the matter? 'I think I have killed Comyn,' said he. 'You only think so?' returned one of them; 'I will make sure!' and going into the church, and finding him alive, stabbed him again and again. Knowing that the King would never forgive this new deed of violence, the party then declared Bruce King of Scotland: got him crowned at Scone—without the chair; and set up the rebellious standard once again.

When the King heard of it he kindled with fiercer anger than he had ever shown yet. He caused the Prince of Wales and two hundred and seventy of the young nobility to be knighted—the trees in the Temple Gardens were cut down to make room for their tents, and they watched their armour all night, according to the old usage: some in the Temple Church: some in Westminster Abbey—and at the public Feast which then took place, he swore, by Heaven, and by two swans covered with gold network which his minstrels placed upon the table, that he would avenge the death of Comyn, and would punish the false Bruce. And before all the company, he charged the Prince his son, in case that he should die before accomplishing his vow, not to bury him until it was fulfilled. Next morning the Prince and the rest of the young Knights rode away to the Border-country to join the English army; and the King, now weak and sick, followed in a horse-litter.

Bruce, after losing a battle and undergoing many dangers and much misery, fled to Ireland, where he lay concealed through the winter. That winter, Edward passed in hunting down and executing Bruce's relations and adherents, sparing neither youth nor age, and showing no touch of pity or sign of mercy. In the following spring, Bruce reappeared and gained some victories. In these frays, both sides were grievously cruel. For instance— Bruce's two brothers, being taken captives desperately wounded, were ordered by the King to instant execution. Bruce's friend Sir John Douglas, taking his own Castle of Douglas out of the hands of an English Lord, roasted the dead bodies of the slaughtered garrison in a great fire made of every movable within it; which dreadful cookery his men called the Douglas Larder. Bruce, still successful, however, drove the Earl of Pembroke and the Earl of Gloucester into the Castle of Ayr and laid siege to it.

The King, who had been laid up all the winter, but had directed the army from his sick-bed, now advanced to Carlisle, and there, causing the litter in which he had travelled to be placed in the Cathedral as an offering to Heaven, mounted his horse once more, and for the last time. He was now sixty-nine years old, and had reigned thirty-five years. He was so ill, that in four days he could go no more than six miles; still, even at that pace, he went on and resolutely kept his face towards the Border. At length, he lay down at the village of Burgh-upon-Sands; and there, telling those around him to impress upon the Prince that he was to remember his father's vow, and was never to rest until he had thoroughly subdued Scotland, he yielded up his last breath.

CHAPTER XVII—ENGLAND UNDER EDWARD THE SECOND

King Edward the Second, the first Prince of Wales, was twenty-three years old when his father died. There was a certain favourite of his, a young man from Gascony, named Piers Gaveston, of whom his father had so much disapproved that he had ordered him out of England, and had made his son swear by the side of his sick-bed, never to bring him back. But, the Prince no sooner found himself King, than he broke his oath, as so many other Princes and Kings did (they were far too ready to take oaths), and sent for his dear friend immediately.

Now, this same Gaveston was handsome enough, but was a reckless, insolent, audacious fellow. He was detested by the proud English Lords: not only because he had such power over the King, and made the Court such a dissipated place, but, also, because he could ride better than they at tournaments, and was used, in his impudence, to cut very bad jokes on them; calling one, the old hog; another, the stage-player; another, the Jew; another, the black dog of Ardenne. This was as poor wit as need be, but it made those Lords very wroth; and the surly Earl of Warwick, who was the black dog, swore that the time should come when Piers Gaveston should feel the black dog's teeth.

It was not come yet, however, nor did it seem to be coming. The King made him Earl of Cornwall, and gave him vast riches; and, when the King went over to France to marry the French Princess, Isabella, daughter of Philip le Bel: who was said to be the most beautiful woman in the world: he made Gaveston, Regent of the Kingdom. His splendid marriage-ceremony in the Church of Our Lady at Boulogne, where there were four Kings and three Queens present (quite a pack of Court Cards, for I dare say the Knaves were not wanting), being over, he seemed to care little or nothing for his beautiful wife; but was wild with impatience to meet Gaveston again.

When he landed at home, he paid no attention to anybody else, but ran into the favourite's arms before a great concourse of people, and hugged him, and kissed him, and called him his brother. At the coronation which soon followed, Gaveston was the richest and brightest of all the glittering company there, and had the honour of carrying the crown. This made the proud Lords fiercer than ever; the people, too, despised the favourite, and would never call him Earl of Cornwall, however much he complained to the King and asked him to punish them for not doing so, but persisted in styling him plain Piers Gaveston.

The Barons were so unceremonious with the King in giving him to understand that they would not bear this favourite, that the King was obliged to send him out of the country. The favourite himself was made to take an oath (more oaths!) that he would never come back, and the Barons supposed him to be banished in disgrace, until they heard that he was appointed Governor of Ireland. Even this was not enough for the besotted King, who brought him home again in a year's time, and not only disgusted the Court and the people by his doting folly, but offended his beautiful wife too, who never liked him afterwards.

He had now the old Royal want—of money—and the Barons had the new power of positively refusing to let him raise any. He summoned a Parliament at York; the Barons refused to make one, while the favourite was near him. He summoned another Parliament at Westminster, and sent Gaveston away. Then, the Barons came, completely armed, and appointed a committee of themselves to correct abuses in the state and in the King's household. He got some money on these conditions, and directly set off with Gaveston to the Border-country, where they spent it in idling away the time, and feasting, while Bruce made ready to drive the English out of Scotland. For, though the old King had even made this poor weak son of his swear (as some say) that he would not bury his bones, but would have them boiled clean in a caldron, and carried before the English army until Scotland was entirely subdued, the second Edward was so unlike the first that Bruce gained strength and power every day.

The committee of Nobles, after some months of deliberation, ordained that the King should henceforth call a Parliament together, once every year, and even twice if necessary, instead of summoning it only when he chose.

Further, that Gaveston should once more be banished, and, this time, on pain of death if he ever came back. The King's tears were of no avail; he was obliged to send his favourite to Flanders. As soon as he had done so, however, he dissolved the Parliament, with the low cunning of a mere fool, and set off to the North of England, thinking to get an army about him to oppose the Nobles. And once again he brought Gaveston home, and heaped upon him all the riches and titles of which the Barons had deprived him.

The Lords saw, now, that there was nothing for it but to put the favourite to death. They could have done so, legally, according to the terms of his banishment; but they did so, I am sorry to say, in a shabby manner. Led by the Earl of Lancaster, the King's cousin, they first of all attacked the King and Gaveston at Newcastle. They had time to escape by sea, and the mean King, having his precious Gaveston with him, was quite content to leave his lovely wife behind. When they were comparatively safe, they separated; the King went to York to collect a force of soldiers; and the favourite shut himself up, in the meantime, in Scarborough Castle overlooking the sea. This was what the Barons wanted. They knew that the Castle could not hold out; they attacked it, and made Gaveston surrender. He delivered himself up to the Earl of Pembroke—that Lord whom he had called the Jew—on the Earl's pledging his faith and knightly word, that no harm should happen to him and no violence be done him.

Now, it was agreed with Gaveston that he should be taken to the Castle of Wallingford, and there kept in honourable custody. They travelled as far as Dedington, near Banbury, where, in the Castle of that place, they stopped for a night to rest. Whether the Earl of Pembroke left his prisoner there, knowing what would happen, or really left him thinking no harm, and only going (as he pretended) to visit his wife, the Countess, who was in the neighbourhood, is no great matter now; in any case, he was bound as an honourable gentleman to protect his prisoner, and he did not do it. In the morning, while the favourite was yet in bed, he was required to dress himself and come down into the court-yard. He did so without any mistrust, but started and turned pale when he found it full of strange armed men. 'I think you know me?' said their leader, also armed from head to foot. 'I am the black dog of Ardenne!' The time was come when Piers Gaveston was to feel the black dog's teeth indeed. They set him on a mule, and carried him, in mock state and with military music, to the black dog's kennel—Warwick Castle—where a hasty council, composed of some great noblemen, considered what should be done with him. Some were for sparing him, but one loud voice—it was the black dog's bark, I dare say—sounded through the Castle Hall, uttering these words: 'You have the fox in your power. Let him go now, and you must hunt him again.'

They sentenced him to death. He threw himself at the feet of the Earl of Lancaster—the old hog—but the old hog was as savage as the dog. He was taken out upon the pleasant road, leading from Warwick to Coventry, where the beautiful river Avon, by which, long afterwards, William Shakespeare was born and now lies buried, sparkled in the bright landscape of the beautiful May-day; and there they struck off his wretched head, and stained the dust with his blood.

When the King heard of this black deed, in his grief and rage he denounced relentless war against his Barons, and both sides were in arms for half a year. But, it then became necessary for them to join their forces against Bruce, who had used the time well while they were divided, and had now a great power in Scotland.

Intelligence was brought that Bruce was then besieging Stirling Castle, and that the Governor had been obliged to pledge himself to surrender it, unless he should be relieved before a certain day. Hereupon, the King ordered the nobles and their fighting-men to meet him at Berwick; but, the nobles cared so little for the King, and so neglected the summons, and lost time, that only on the day before that appointed for the surrender, did the King find himself at Stirling, and even then with a smaller force than he had expected. However, he had, altogether, a hundred thousand men, and Bruce had not more than forty thousand; but, Bruce's army was strongly posted in three square columns, on the ground lying between the Burn or Brook of Bannock and the walls of Stirling Castle.

On the very evening, when the King came up, Bruce did a brave act that encouraged his men. He was seen by a certain Henry de Bohun, an English Knight, riding about before his army on a little horse, with a light battle-axe in his hand, and a crown of gold on his head. This English Knight, who was mounted on a strong war-horse, cased in steel, strongly armed, and able (as he thought) to overthrow Bruce by crushing him with his mere weight, set spurs to his great charger, rode on him, and made a thrust at him with his heavy spear. Bruce parried the thrust, and with one blow of his battle-axe split his skull.

The Scottish men did not forget this, next day when the battle raged. Randolph, Bruce's valiant Nephew, rode, with the small body of men he commanded, into such a host of the English, all shining in polished armour in the sunlight, that they seemed to be swallowed up and lost, as if they had plunged into the sea. But, they fought so well, and did such dreadful execution, that the English staggered. Then came Bruce himself upon them, with all the rest of his army. While they were thus hard pressed and amazed, there appeared upon the hills what they supposed to be a new Scottish army, but what were really only the camp followers, in number fifteen thousand: whom Bruce had taught to show themselves at that place and time. The Earl of Gloucester, commanding the English horse, made a last rush to change the fortune of the day; but Bruce (like Jack the Giant-killer in the story) had had pits dug in the ground, and covered over with turfs and stakes. Into these, as they gave way beneath the weight of the horses, riders and horses rolled by hundreds. The English were completely routed; all their treasure, stores, and engines, were taken by the Scottish men; so many waggons and other wheeled vehicles were seized, that it is related that they would have reached, if they had been drawn out in a line, one hundred and eighty miles. The fortunes of Scotland were, for the time, completely changed; and never was a battle won, more famous upon Scottish ground, than this great battle of Bannockburn.

Plague and famine succeeded in England; and still the powerless King and his disdainful Lords were always in contention. Some of the turbulent chiefs of Ireland made proposals to Bruce, to accept the rule of that country. He sent his brother Edward to them, who was crowned King of Ireland. He afterwards went himself to help his brother in his Irish wars, but his brother was defeated in the end and killed. Robert Bruce, returning to Scotland, still increased his strength there.

As the King's ruin had begun in a favourite, so it seemed likely to end in one. He was too poor a creature to rely at all upon himself; and his new favourite was one Hugh le Despenser, the son of a gentleman of ancient family. Hugh was handsome and brave, but he was the favourite of a weak King, whom no man cared a rush for, and that was a dangerous place to hold. The Nobles leagued against him, because the King liked him; and they lay in wait, both for his ruin and his father's. Now, the King had married him to the daughter of the late Earl of Gloucester, and had given both him and his father great possessions in Wales. In their endeavours to extend these, they gave violent offence to an angry Welsh gentleman, named John de Mowbray, and to divers other angry Welsh gentlemen, who resorted to arms, took their castles, and seized their estates. The Earl of Lancaster had first placed the favourite (who was a poor relation of his own) at Court, and he considered his own dignity offended by the preference he received and the honours he acquired; so he, and the Barons who were his friends, joined the Welshmen, marched on London, and sent a message to the King demanding to have the favourite and his father banished. At first, the King unaccountably took it into his head to be spirited, and to send them a bold reply; but when they quartered themselves around Holborn and Clerkenwell, and went down, armed, to the Parliament at Westminster, he gave way, and complied with their demands.

His turn of triumph came sooner than he expected. It arose out of an accidental circumstance. The beautiful Queen happening to be travelling, came one night to one of the royal castles, and demanded to be lodged and entertained there until morning. The governor of this castle, who was one of the enraged lords, was away, and in his absence, his wife refused admission to the Queen; a scuffle took place among the common men on either side, and some of the royal attendants were killed. The people, who cared nothing for the King, were very angry that their beautiful Queen should be thus rudely treated in her own dominions; and the King, taking advantage of this feeling, besieged the castle, took it, and then called the two Despensers home. Upon this, the confederate lords and the Welshmen went over to Bruce. The King encountered them at Boroughbridge, gained the victory, and took a number of distinguished prisoners; among them, the Earl of Lancaster, now an old man, upon whose destruction he was resolved. This Earl was taken to his own castle of Pontefract, and there tried and found guilty by an unfair court appointed for the purpose; he was not even allowed to speak in his own defence. He was insulted, pelted, mounted on a starved pony without saddle or bridle, carried out, and beheaded. Eight-and-twenty knights were hanged, drawn, and quartered. When the King had despatched this bloody work, and had made a fresh and a long truce with Bruce, he took the Despensers into greater favour than ever, and made the father Earl of Winchester.

One prisoner, and an important one, who was taken at Boroughbridge, made his escape, however, and turned the tide against the King. This was Roger Mortimer, always resolutely opposed to him, who was sentenced to death, and placed for safe custody in the Tower of London. He treated his guards to a quantity of wine into which he had put a sleeping potion; and, when they were insensible, broke out of his dungeon, got into a kitchen, climbed up the chimney, let himself down from the roof of the building with a rope-ladder, passed the sentries, got down to the river, and made away in a boat to where servants and horses were waiting for him. He finally escaped to France, where Charles le Bel, the brother of the beautiful Queen, was King. Charles sought to quarrel with the King of England, on pretence of his not having come to do him homage at his coronation. It was proposed that the beautiful Queen should go over to arrange the dispute; she went, and wrote home to the King, that as he was sick and could not come to France himself, perhaps it would be better to send over the young Prince, their son, who was only twelve years old, who could do homage to her brother in his stead, and in whose company she would immediately return. The King sent him: but, both he and the Queen remained at the French Court, and Roger Mortimer became the Queen's lover.

When the King wrote, again and again, to the Queen to come home, she did not reply that she despised him too much to live with him any more (which was the truth), but said she was afraid of the two Despensers. In short, her design was to overthrow the favourites' power, and the King's power, such as it was, and invade England. Having obtained a French force of two thousand men, and being joined by all the English exiles then in France, she landed, within a year, at Orewell, in Suffolk, where she was immediately joined by the Earls of Kent and Norfolk, the King's two brothers; by other powerful noblemen; and lastly, by the first English general who was despatched to check her: who went over to her with all his men. The people of London, receiving these tidings, would do nothing for the King, but broke open the Tower, let out all his prisoners, and threw up their caps and hurrahed for the beautiful Queen.

The King, with his two favourites, fled to Bristol, where he left old Despenser in charge of the town and castle, while he went on with the son to Wales. The Bristol men being opposed to the King, and it being impossible to hold the town with enemies everywhere within the walls, Despenser yielded it up on the third day, and was instantly brought to trial for having traitorously influenced what was called 'the King's mind'—though I doubt if the King ever had any. He was a venerable old man, upwards of ninety years of age, but his age gained no respect or mercy. He was hanged, torn open while he was yet alive, cut up into pieces, and thrown to the dogs. His son was soon taken, tried at Hereford before the same judge on a long series of foolish charges, found guilty, and hanged upon a gallows fifty feet high, with a chaplet of nettles round his head. His poor old father and he were innocent enough of any worse crimes than the crime of having been friends of a King, on whom, as a mere man, they would never have deigned to cast a favourable look. It is a bad crime, I know, and leads to worse; but, many lords and gentlemen—I even think some ladies, too, if I recollect right—have committed it in England, who have neither been given to the dogs, nor hanged up fifty feet high.

The wretched King was running here and there, all this time, and never getting anywhere in particular, until he gave himself up, and was taken off to Kenilworth Castle. When he was safely lodged there, the Queen went to London and met the Parliament. And the Bishop of Hereford, who was the most skilful of her friends, said, What was to be done now? Here was an imbecile, indolent, miserable King upon the throne; wouldn't it be better to take him off, and put his son there instead? I don't know whether the Queen really pitied him at this pass, but she began to cry; so, the Bishop said, Well, my Lords and Gentlemen, what do you think, upon the whole, of sending down to Kenilworth, and seeing if His Majesty (God bless him, and forbid we should depose him!) won't resign?

My Lords and Gentlemen thought it a good notion, so a deputation of them went down to Kenilworth; and there the King came into the great hall of the Castle, commonly dressed in a poor black gown; and when he saw a certain bishop among them, fell down, poor feeble-headed man, and made a wretched spectacle of himself. Somebody lifted him up, and then Sir William Trussel, the Speaker of the House of Commons, almost frightened him to death by making him a tremendous speech to the effect that he was no longer a King, and that everybody renounced allegiance to him. After which, Sir Thomas Blount, the Steward of the Household, nearly finished him, by coming forward and breaking his white wand—which was a ceremony only performed at a King's death. Being asked in this pressing manner what he thought of resigning, the King said he thought it was the best thing he could do. So, he did it, and they proclaimed his son next day.

I wish I could close his history by saying that he lived a harmless life in the Castle and the Castle gardens at Kenilworth, many years—that he had a favourite, and plenty to eat and drink—and, having that, wanted nothing. But he was shamefully humiliated. He was outraged, and slighted, and had dirty water from ditches given him to shave with, and wept and said he would have clean warm water, and was altogether very miserable. He was moved from this castle to that castle, and from that castle to the other castle, because this lord or that lord, or the other lord, was too kind to him: until at last he came to Berkeley Castle, near the River Severn, where (the Lord Berkeley being then ill and absent) he fell into the hands of two black ruffians, called Thomas Gournay and William Ogle.

One night—it was the night of September the twenty-first, one thousand three hundred and twenty-seven—dreadful screams were heard, by the startled people in the neighbouring town, ringing through the thick walls of the Castle, and the dark, deep night; and they said, as they were thus horribly awakened from their sleep, 'May Heaven be merciful to the King; for those cries forbode that no good is being done to him in his dismal prison!' Next morning he was dead—not bruised, or stabbed, or marked upon the body, but much distorted in the face; and it was whispered afterwards, that those two villains, Gournay and Ogle, had burnt up his inside with a red-hot iron.

If you ever come near Gloucester, and see the centre tower of its beautiful Cathedral, with its four rich pinnacles, rising lightly in the air; you may remember that the wretched Edward the Second was buried in the old abbey of that ancient city, at forty-three years old, after being for nineteen years and a half a perfectly incapable King.

CHAPTER XVIII—ENGLAND UNDER EDWARD THE THIRD

Roger Mortimer, the Queen's lover (who escaped to France in the last chapter), was far from profiting by the examples he had had of the fate of favourites. Having, through the Queen's influence, come into possession of the estates of the two Despensers, he became extremely proud and ambitious, and sought to be the real ruler of England. The young King, who was crowned at fourteen years of age with all the usual solemnities, resolved not to bear this, and soon pursued Mortimer to his ruin.

The people themselves were not fond of Mortimer—first, because he was a Royal favourite; secondly, because he was supposed to have helped to make a peace with Scotland which now took place, and in virtue of which the young King's sister Joan, only seven years old, was promised in marriage to David, the son and heir of Robert Bruce, who was only five years old. The nobles hated Mortimer because of his pride, riches, and power. They went so far as to take up arms against him; but were obliged to submit. The Earl of Kent, one of those who did so, but who afterwards went over to Mortimer and the Queen, was made an example of in the following cruel manner:

He seems to have been anything but a wise old earl; and he was persuaded by the agents of the favourite and the Queen, that poor King Edward the Second was not really dead; and thus was betrayed into writing letters favouring his rightful claim to the throne. This was made out to be high treason, and he was tried, found guilty, and sentenced to be executed. They took the poor old lord outside the town of Winchester, and there kept him waiting some three or four hours until they could find somebody to cut off his head. At last, a convict said he would do it, if the government would pardon him in return; and they gave him the pardon; and at one blow he put the Earl of Kent out of his last suspense.

While the Queen was in France, she had found a lovely and good young lady, named Philippa, who she thought would make an excellent wife for her son. The young King married this lady, soon after he came to the throne; and her first child, Edward, Prince of Wales, afterwards became celebrated, as we shall presently see, under the famous title of Edward the Black Prince.

The young King, thinking the time ripe for the downfall of Mortimer, took counsel with Lord Montacute how he should proceed. A Parliament was going to be held at Nottingham, and that lord recommended that the favourite should be seized by night in Nottingham Castle, where he was sure to be. Now, this, like many other things, was more easily said than done; because, to guard against treachery, the great gates of the Castle were locked every night, and the great keys were carried up-stairs to the Queen, who laid them under her own pillow. But the Castle had a governor, and the governor being Lord Montacute's friend, confided to him how he knew of a secret passage underground, hidden from observation by the weeds and brambles with which it was overgrown; and how, through that passage, the conspirators might enter in the dead of the night, and go straight to Mortimer's room. Accordingly, upon a certain dark night, at midnight, they made their way through this dismal place: startling the rats, and frightening the owls and bats: and came safely to the bottom of the main tower of the Castle, where the King met them, and took them up a profoundly-dark staircase in a deep silence. They soon heard the voice of Mortimer in council with some friends; and bursting into the room with a sudden noise, took him prisoner. The Queen cried out from her bed-chamber, 'Oh, my sweet son, my dear son, spare my gentle Mortimer!' They carried him off, however; and, before the next Parliament, accused him of having made differences between the young King and his mother, and of having brought about the death of the Earl of Kent, and even of the late King; for, as you know by this time, when they wanted to get rid of a man in those old days, they were not very particular of what they accused him. Mortimer was found guilty of all this, and was sentenced to be hanged at Tyburn. The King shut his mother up in genteel confinement, where she passed the rest of her life; and now he became King in earnest.

The first effort he made was to conquer Scotland. The English lords who had lands in Scotland, finding that their rights were not respected under the late peace, made war on their own account: choosing for their general,

Edward, the son of John Baliol, who made such a vigorous fight, that in less than two months he won the whole Scottish Kingdom. He was joined, when thus triumphant, by the King and Parliament; and he and the King in person besieged the Scottish forces in Berwick. The whole Scottish army coming to the assistance of their countrymen, such a furious battle ensued, that thirty thousand men are said to have been killed in it. Baliol was then crowned King of Scotland, doing homage to the King of England; but little came of his successes after all, for the Scottish men rose against him, within no very long time, and David Bruce came back within ten years and took his kingdom.

France was a far richer country than Scotland, and the King had a much greater mind to conquer it. So, he let Scotland alone, and pretended that he had a claim to the French throne in right of his mother. He had, in reality, no claim at all; but that mattered little in those times. He brought over to his cause many little princes and sovereigns, and even courted the alliance of the people of Flanders—a busy, working community, who had very small respect for kings, and whose head man was a brewer. With such forces as he raised by these means, Edward invaded France; but he did little by that, except run into debt in carrying on the war to the extent of three hundred thousand pounds. The next year he did better; gaining a great sea-fight in the harbour of Sluys. This success, however, was very shortlived, for the Flemings took fright at the siege of Saint Omer and ran away, leaving their weapons and baggage behind them. Philip, the French King, coming up with his army, and Edward being very anxious to decide the war, proposed to settle the difference by single combat with him, or by a fight of one hundred knights on each side. The French King said, he thanked him; but being very well as he was, he would rather not. So, after some skirmishing and talking, a short peace was made.

It was soon broken by King Edward's favouring the cause of John, Earl of Montford; a French nobleman, who asserted a claim of his own against the French King, and offered to do homage to England for the Crown of France, if he could obtain it through England's help. This French lord, himself, was soon defeated by the French King's son, and shut up in a tower in Paris; but his wife, a courageous and beautiful woman, who is said to have had the courage of a man, and the heart of a lion, assembled the people of Brittany, where she then was; and, showing them her infant son, made many pathetic entreaties to them not to desert her and their young Lord. They took fire at this appeal, and rallied round her in the strong castle of Hennebon. Here she was not only besieged without by the French under Charles de Blois, but was endangered within by a dreary old bishop, who was always representing to the people what horrors they must undergo if they were faithful—first from famine, and afterwards from fire and sword. But this noble lady, whose heart never failed her, encouraged her soldiers by her own example; went from post to post like a great general; even mounted on horseback fully armed, and, issuing from the castle by a by-path, fell upon the French camp, set fire to the tents, and threw the whole force into disorder. This done, she got safely back to Hennebon again, and was received with loud shouts of joy by the defenders of the castle, who had given her up for lost. As they were now very short of provisions, however, and as they could not dine off enthusiasm, and as the old bishop was always saying, 'I told you what it would come to!' they began to lose heart, and to talk of yielding the castle up. The brave Countess retiring to an upper room and looking with great grief out to sea, where she expected relief from England, saw, at this very time, the English ships in the distance, and was relieved and rescued! Sir Walter Manning, the English commander, so admired her courage, that, being come into the castle with the English knights, and having made a feast there, he assaulted the French by way of dessert, and beat them off triumphantly. Then he and the knights came back to the castle with great joy; and the Countess who had watched them from a high tower, thanked them with all her heart, and kissed them every one.

This noble lady distinguished herself afterwards in a sea-fight with the French off Guernsey, when she was on her way to England to ask for more troops. Her great spirit roused another lady, the wife of another French lord (whom the French King very barbarously murdered), to distinguish herself scarcely less. The time was fast coming, however, when Edward, Prince of Wales, was to be the great star of this French and English war.

It was in the month of July, in the year one thousand three hundred and forty-six, when the King embarked at Southampton for France, with an army of about thirty thousand men in all, attended by the Prince of Wales and by several of the chief nobles. He landed at La Hogue in Normandy; and, burning and destroying as he went, according to custom, advanced up the left bank of the River Seine, and fired the small towns even close to Paris; but, being watched from the right bank of the river by the French King and all his army, it came to this at last, that Edward found himself, on Saturday the twenty-sixth of August, one thousand three hundred and forty-six, on a rising ground behind the little French village of Crecy, face to face with the French King's force. And, although the French King had an enormous army—in number more than eight times his—he there resolved to beat him or be beaten.

The young Prince, assisted by the Earl of Oxford and the Earl of Warwick, led the first division of the English army; two other great Earls led the second; and the King, the third. When the morning dawned, the King received the sacrament, and heard prayers, and then, mounted on horseback with a white wand in his hand, rode from company to company, and rank to rank, cheering and encouraging both officers and men. Then the whole army breakfasted, each man sitting on the ground where he had stood; and then they remained quietly on the ground with their weapons ready.

Up came the French King with all his great force. It was dark and angry weather; there was an eclipse of the sun; there was a thunder-storm, accompanied with tremendous rain; the frightened birds flew screaming above the soldiers' heads. A certain captain in the French army advised the French King, who was by no means cheerful, not to begin the battle until the morrow. The King, taking this advice, gave the word to halt. But, those behind not understanding it, or desiring to be foremost with the rest, came pressing on. The roads for a great distance were covered with this immense army, and with the common people from the villages, who were flourishing their rude weapons, and making a great noise. Owing to these circumstances, the French army advanced in the greatest confusion; every French lord doing what he liked with his own men, and putting out the men of every other French lord.

166

Now, their King relied strongly upon a great body of cross-bowmen from Genoa; and these he ordered to the front to begin the battle, on finding that he could not stop it. They shouted once, they shouted twice, they shouted three times, to alarm the English archers; but, the English would have heard them shout three thousand times and would have never moved. At last the cross-bowmen went forward a little, and began to discharge their bolts; upon which, the English let fly such a hail of arrows, that the Genoese speedily made off—for their cross-bows, besides being heavy to carry, required to be wound up with a handle, and consequently took time to re-load; the English, on the other hand, could discharge their arrows almost as fast as the arrows could fly.

When the French King saw the Genoese turning, he cried out to his men to kill those scoundrels, who were doing harm instead of service. This increased the confusion. Meanwhile the English archers, continuing to shoot as fast as ever, shot down great numbers of the French soldiers and knights; whom certain sly Cornish-men and Welshmen, from the English army, creeping along the ground, despatched with great knives.

The Prince and his division were at this time so hard-pressed, that the Earl of Warwick sent a message to the King, who was overlooking the battle from a windmill, beseeching him to send more aid.

'Is my son killed?' said the King.

'No, sire, please God,' returned the messenger.

'Is he wounded?' said the King.

'No, sire.'

'Is he thrown to the ground?' said the King.

'No, sire, not so; but, he is very hard-pressed.'

'Then,' said the King, 'go back to those who sent you, and tell them I shall send no aid; because I set my heart upon my son proving himself this day a brave knight, and because I am resolved, please God, that the honour of a great victory shall be his!'

167

These bold words, being reported to the Prince and his division, so raised their spirits, that they fought better than ever. The King of France charged gallantly with his men many times; but it was of no use. Night closing in, his horse was killed under him by an English arrow, and the knights and nobles who had clustered thick about him early in the day, were now completely scattered. At last, some of his few remaining followers led him off the field by force since he would not retire of himself, and they journeyed away to Amiens. The victorious English, lighting their watch-fires, made merry on the field, and the King, riding to meet his gallant son, took him in his arms, kissed him, and told him that he had acted nobly, and proved himself worthy of the day and of the crown. While it was yet night, King Edward was hardly aware of the great victory he had gained; but, next day, it was discovered that eleven princes, twelve hundred knights, and thirty thousand common men lay dead upon the French side. Among these was the King of Bohemia, an old blind man; who, having been told that his son was wounded in the battle, and that no force could stand against the Black Prince, called to him two knights, put himself on horse-back between them, fastened the three bridles together, and dashed in among the English, where he was presently slain. He bore as his crest three white ostrich feathers, with the motto Ich dien, signifying in English 'I serve.' This crest and motto were taken by the Prince of Wales in remembrance of that famous day, and have been borne by the Prince of Wales ever since.

Five days after this great battle, the King laid siege to Calais. This siege—ever afterwards memorable—lasted nearly a year. In order to starve the inhabitants out, King Edward built so many wooden houses for the lodgings of his troops, that it is said their quarters looked like a second Calais suddenly sprung around the first. Early in the siege, the governor of the town drove out what he called the useless mouths, to the number of seventeen hundred persons, men and women, young and old. King Edward allowed them to pass through his lines, and even fed them, and dismissed them with money; but, later in the siege, he was not so merciful—five hundred more, who were afterwards driven out, dying of starvation and misery. The garrison were so hard-pressed at last, that they sent a letter to King Philip, telling him that they had eaten all the horses, all the dogs, and all the rats and mice that could be found in the place; and, that if he did not relieve them, they must either surrender to the English, or eat one another. Philip made one effort to give them relief; but they were so hemmed in by the English power, that he could not succeed, and was fain to leave the place. Upon this they hoisted the English flag, and surrendered to King Edward. 'Tell your general,' said he to the humble messengers who came out of the town, 'that I require to have sent here, six of the most distinguished citizens, bare-legged, and in their shirts, with ropes about their necks; and let those six men bring with them the keys of the castle and the town.'

When the Governor of Calais related this to the people in the Market-place, there was great weeping and distress; in the midst of which, one worthy citizen, named Eustace de Saint Pierre, rose up and said, that if the six men required were not sacrificed, the whole population would be; therefore, he offered himself as the first. Encouraged by this bright example, five other worthy citizens rose up one after another, and offered themselves to save the rest. The Governor, who was too badly wounded to be able to walk, mounted a poor old horse that had not been eaten, and conducted these good men to the gate, while all the people cried and mourned.

Edward received them wrathfully, and ordered the heads of the whole six to be struck off. However, the good Queen fell upon her knees, and besought the King to give them up to her. The King replied, 'I wish you had been somewhere else; but I cannot refuse you.' So she had them properly dressed, made a feast for them, and sent them back with a handsome present, to the great rejoicing of the whole camp. I hope the people of Calais loved the daughter to whom she gave birth soon afterwards, for her gentle mother's sake.

Now came that terrible disease, the Plague, into Europe, hurrying from the heart of China; and killed the wretched people—especially the poor—in such enormous numbers, that one-half of the inhabitants of England are related to have died of it. It killed the cattle, in great numbers, too; and so few working men remained alive, that there were not enough left to till the ground.

After eight years of differing and quarrelling, the Prince of Wales again invaded France with an army of sixty thousand men. He went through the south of the country, burning and plundering wheresoever he went; while his father, who had still the Scottish war upon his hands, did the like in Scotland, but was harassed and worried in his retreat from that country by the Scottish men, who repaid his cruelties with interest.

The French King, Philip, was now dead, and was succeeded by his son John. The Black Prince, called by that name from the colour of the armour he wore to set off his fair complexion, continuing to burn and destroy in France, roused John into determined opposition; and so cruel had the Black Prince been in his campaign, and so severely had the French peasants suffered, that he could not find one who, for love, or money, or the fear of death, would tell him what the French King was doing, or where he was. Thus it happened that he came upon the French King's forces, all of a sudden, near the town of Poitiers, and found that the whole neighbouring country was occupied by a vast French army. 'God help us!' said the Black Prince, 'we must make the best of it.'

So, on a Sunday morning, the eighteenth of September, the Prince whose army was now reduced to ten thousand men in all—prepared to give battle to the French King, who had sixty thousand horse alone. While he was so engaged, there came riding from the French camp, a Cardinal, who had persuaded John to let him offer terms, and try to save the shedding of Christian blood. 'Save my honour,' said the Prince to this good priest, 'and save the honour of my army, and I will make any reasonable terms.' He offered to give up all the towns, castles, and prisoners, he had taken, and to swear to make no war in France for seven years; but, as John would hear of nothing but his surrender, with a hundred of his chief knights, the treaty was broken off, and the Prince said quietly—'God defend the right; we shall fight to-morrow.'

Therefore, on the Monday morning, at break of day, the two armies prepared for battle. The English were posted in a strong place, which could only be approached by one narrow lane, skirted by hedges on both sides. The French attacked them by this lane; but were so galled and slain by English arrows from behind the hedges, that they were forced to retreat. Then went six hundred English bowmen round about, and, coming upon the rear of the French army, rained arrows on them thick and fast. The French knights, thrown into confusion, quitted their banners and dispersed in all directions. Said Sir John Chandos to the Prince, 'Ride forward, noble Prince, and the day is yours. The King of France is so valiant a gentleman, that I know he will never fly, and may be taken prisoner.' Said the Prince to this, 'Advance, English banners, in the name of God and St. George!' and on they pressed until they came up with the French King, fighting fiercely with his battle-axe, and, when all his nobles had forsaken him, attended faithfully to the last by his youngest son Philip, only sixteen years of age. Father and son fought well, and the King had already two wounds in his face, and had been beaten down, when he at last delivered himself to a banished French knight, and gave him his right-hand glove in token that he had done so.

The Black Prince was generous as well as brave, and he invited his royal prisoner to supper in his tent, and waited upon him at table, and, when they afterwards rode into London in a gorgeous procession, mounted the French King on a fine cream-coloured horse, and rode at his side on a little pony. This was all very kind, but I think it was, perhaps, a little theatrical too, and has been made more meritorious than it deserved to be; especially as I am inclined to think that the greatest kindness to the King of France would have been not to have shown him to the people at all. However, it must be said, for these acts of politeness, that, in course of time, they did much to soften the horrors of war and the passions of conquerors. It was a long, long time before the common soldiers began to have the benefit of such courtly deeds; but they did at last; and thus it is possible that a poor soldier who asked for quarter at the battle of Waterloo, or any other such great fight, may have owed his life indirectly to Edward the Black Prince.

At this time there stood in the Strand, in London, a palace called the Savoy, which was given up to the captive King of France and his son for their residence. As the King of Scotland had now been King Edward's captive for eleven years too, his success was, at this time, tolerably complete. The Scottish business was settled by the prisoner being released under the title of Sir David, King of Scotland, and by his engaging to pay a large ransom. The state of France encouraged England to propose harder terms to that country, where the people rose against the unspeakable cruelty and barbarity of its nobles; where the nobles rose in turn against the people; where the most frightful outrages were committed on all sides; and where the insurrection of the peasants, called the insurrection of the Jacquerie, from Jacques, a common Christian name among the country people of France, awakened terrors and hatreds that have scarcely yet passed away. A treaty called the Great Peace, was at last signed, under which King Edward agreed to give up the greater part of his conquests, and King John to pay, within six years, a ransom of three million crowns of gold. He was so beset by his own nobles and courtiers for having yielded to these conditions—though they could help him to no better—that he came back of his own will to his old palace-prison of the Savoy, and there died.

There was a Sovereign of Castile at that time, called Pedro the Cruel, who deserved the name remarkably well: having committed, among other cruelties, a variety of murders. This amiable monarch being driven from his throne for his crimes, went to the province of Bordeaux, where the Black Prince—now married to his cousin Joan, a pretty widow—was residing, and besought his help. The Prince, who took to him much more kindly than a prince of such fame ought to have taken to such a ruffian, readily listened to his fair promises, and agreeing to help him, sent secret orders to some troublesome disbanded soldiers of his and his father's, who called themselves the Free Companions, and who had been a pest to the French people, for some time, to aid this Pedro. The Prince, himself, going into Spain to head the army of relief, soon set Pedro on his throne again—where he no sooner found himself, than, of course, he behaved like the villain he was, broke his word without the least shame, and abandoned all the promises he had made to the Black Prince.

Now, it had cost the Prince a good deal of money to pay soldiers to support this murderous King; and finding himself, when he came back disgusted to Bordeaux, not only in bad health, but deeply in debt, he began to tax his French subjects to pay his creditors. They appealed to the French King, Charles; war again broke out; and the French town of Limoges, which the Prince had greatly benefited, went over to the French King. Upon this he ravaged the province of which it was the capital; burnt, and plundered, and killed in the old sickening way; and refused mercy to the prisoners, men, women, and children taken in the offending town, though he was so ill and so much in need of pity himself from Heaven, that he was carried in a litter. He lived to come home and make himself popular with the people and Parliament, and he died on Trinity Sunday, the eighth of June, one thousand three hundred and seventy-six, at forty-six years old.

The whole nation mourned for him as one of the most renowned and beloved princes it had ever had; and he was buried with great lamentations in Canterbury Cathedral. Near to the tomb of Edward the Confessor, his monument, with his figure, carved in stone, and represented in the old black armour, lying on its back, may be seen at this day, with an ancient coat of mail, a helmet, and a pair of gauntlets hanging from a beam above it, which most people like to believe were once worn by the Black Prince.

King Edward did not outlive his renowned son, long. He was old, and one Alice Perrers, a beautiful lady, had contrived to make him so fond of her in his old age, that he could refuse her nothing, and made himself ridiculous. She little deserved his love, or—what I dare say she valued a great deal more—the jewels of the late Queen, which he gave her among other rich presents. She took the very ring from his finger on the morning of the day when he died, and left him to be pillaged by his faithless servants. Only one good priest was true to him, and attended him to the last.

Besides being famous for the great victories I have related, the reign of King Edward the Third was rendered memorable in better ways, by the growth of architecture and the erection of Windsor Castle. In better ways still, by the rising up of Wickliffe, originally a poor parish priest: who devoted himself to exposing, with wonderful power and success, the ambition and corruption of the Pope, and of the whole church of which he was the head.

Some of those Flemings were induced to come to England in this reign too, and to settle in Norfolk, where they made better woollen cloths than the English had ever had before. The Order of the Garter (a very fine thing in its

173

way, but hardly so important as good clothes for the nation) also dates from this period. The King is said to have picked 'up a lady's garter at a ball, and to have said, Honi soit qui mal y pense—in English, 'Evil be to him who evil thinks of it.' The courtiers were usually glad to imitate what the King said or did, and hence from a slight incident the Order of the Garter was instituted, and became a great dignity. So the story goes.

CHAPTER XIX—ENGLAND UNDER RICHARD THE SECOND

Richard, son of the Black Prince, a boy eleven years of age, succeeded to the Crown under the title of King Richard the Second. The whole English nation were ready to admire him for the sake of his brave father. As to the lords and ladies about the Court, they declared him to be the most beautiful, the wisest, and the best—even of princes—whom the lords and ladies about the Court, generally declare to be the most beautiful, the wisest, and the best of mankind. To flatter a poor boy in this base manner was not a very likely way to develop whatever good was in him; and it brought him to anything but a good or happy end.

The Duke of Lancaster, the young King's uncle—commonly called John of Gaunt, from having been born at Ghent, which the common people so pronounced—was supposed to have some thoughts of the throne himself; but, as he was not popular, and the memory of the Black Prince was, he submitted to his nephew.

The war with France being still unsettled, the Government of England wanted money to provide for the expenses that might arise out of it; accordingly a certain tax, called the Poll-tax, which had originated in the last reign, was ordered to be levied on the people. This was a tax on every person in the kingdom, male and female, above the age of fourteen, of three groats (or three four-penny pieces) a year; clergymen were charged more, and only beggars were exempt.

I have no need to repeat that the common people of England had long been suffering under great oppression. They were still the mere slaves of the lords of the land on which they lived, and were on most occasions harshly and unjustly treated. But, they had begun by this time to think very seriously of not bearing quite so much; and, probably, were emboldened by that French insurrection I mentioned in the last chapter.

The people of Essex rose against the Poll-tax, and being severely handled by the government officers, killed some of them. At this very time one of the tax-collectors, going his rounds from house to house, at Dartford in Kent came to the cottage of one Wat, a tiler by trade, and claimed the tax upon his daughter. Her mother, who was at home, declared that she was under the age of fourteen; upon that, the collector (as other collectors had already done in different parts of England) behaved in a savage way, and brutally insulted Wat Tyler's daughter. The daughter screamed, the mother screamed. Wat the Tiler, who was at work not far off, ran to the spot, and did what any honest father under such provocation might have done—struck the collector dead at a blow.

Instantly the people of that town uprose as one man. They made Wat Tyler their leader; they joined with the people of Essex, who were in arms under a priest called Jack Straw; they took out of prison another priest named John Ball; and gathering in numbers as they went along, advanced, in a great confused army of poor men, to Blackheath. It is said that they wanted to abolish all property, and to declare all men equal. I do not think this very likely; because they stopped the travellers on the roads and made them swear to be true to King Richard and the people. Nor were they at all disposed to injure those who had done them no harm, merely because they were of high station; for, the King's mother, who had to pass through their camp at Blackheath, on her way to her young son, lying for safety in the Tower of London, had merely to kiss a few dirty-faced rough-bearded men who were noisily fond of royalty, and so got away in perfect safety. Next day the whole mass marched on to London Bridge.

There was a drawbridge in the middle, which William Walworth the Mayor caused to be raised to prevent their coming into the city; but they soon terrified the citizens into lowering it again, and spread themselves, with great uproar, over the streets. They broke open the prisons; they burned the papers in Lambeth Palace; they destroyed the Duke of Lancaster's Palace, the Savoy, in the Strand, said to be the most beautiful and splendid in England; they set fire to the books and documents in the Temple; and made a great riot. Many of these outrages were committed in drunkenness; since those citizens, who had well-filled cellars, were only too glad to throw them open to save the rest of their property; but even the drunken rioters were very careful to steal nothing. They were so angry with one man, who was seen to take a silver cup at the Savoy Palace, and put it in his breast, that they drowned him in the river, cup and all.

The young King had been taken out to treat with them before they committed these excesses; but, he and the people about him were so frightened by the riotous shouts, that they got back to the Tower in the best way they could. This made the insurgents bolder; so they went on rioting away, striking off the heads of those who did not, at a moment's notice, declare for King Richard and the people; and killing as many of the unpopular persons whom they supposed to be their enemies as they could by any means lay hold of. In this manner they passed one very violent day, and then proclamation was made that the King would meet them at Mile-end, and grant their requests.

The rioters went to Mile-end to the number of sixty thousand, and the King met them there, and to the King the rioters peaceably proposed four conditions. First, that neither they, nor their children, nor any coming after them, should be made slaves any more. Secondly, that the rent of land should be fixed at a certain price in money, instead of being paid in service. Thirdly, that they should have liberty to buy and sell in all markets and public places, like other free men. Fourthly, that they should be pardoned for past offences. Heaven knows, there was nothing very unreasonable in these proposals! The young King deceitfully pretended to think so, and kept thirty clerks up, all night, writing out a charter accordingly.

Now, Wat Tyler himself wanted more than this. He wanted the entire abolition of the forest laws. He was not at Mile-end with the rest, but, while that meeting was being held, broke into the Tower of London and slew the archbishop and the treasurer, for whose heads the people had cried out loudly the day before. He and his men even thrust their swords into the bed of the Princess of Wales while the Princess was in it, to make certain that none of their enemies were concealed there.

So, Wat and his men still continued armed, and rode about the city. Next morning, the King with a small train of some sixty gentlemen—among whom was Walworth the Mayor—rode into Smithfield, and saw Wat and his people at a little distance. Says Wat to his men, 'There is the King. I will go speak with him, and tell him what we want.'

Straightway Wat rode up to him, and began to talk. 'King,' says Wat, 'dost thou see all my men there?'

'Ah,' says the King. 'Why?'

'Because,' says Wat, 'they are all at my command, and have sworn to do whatever I bid them.'

Some declared afterwards that as Wat said this, he laid his hand on the King's bridle. Others declared that he was seen to play with his own dagger. I think, myself, that he just spoke to the King like a rough, angry man as he was, and did nothing more. At any rate he was expecting no attack, and preparing for no resistance, when Walworth the Mayor did the not very valiant deed of drawing a short sword and stabbing him in the throat. He dropped from his horse, and one of the King's people speedily finished him. So fell Wat Tyler. Fawners and flatterers made a mighty triumph of it, and set up a cry which will occasionally find an echo to this day. But Wat was a hard-working man, who had suffered much, and had been foully outraged; and it is probable that he was a man of a much higher nature and a much braver spirit than any of the parasites who exulted then, or have exulted since, over his defeat.

Seeing Wat down, his men immediately bent their bows to avenge his fall. If the young King had not had presence of mind at that dangerous moment, both he and the Mayor to boot, might have followed Tyler pretty fast. But the King riding up to the crowd, cried out that Tyler was a traitor, and that he would be their leader. They were so taken by surprise, that they set up a great shouting, and followed the boy until he was met at Islington by a large body of soldiers.

The end of this rising was the then usual end. As soon as the King found himself safe, he unsaid all he had said, and undid all he had done; some fifteen hundred of the rioters were tried (mostly in Essex) with great rigour, and executed with great cruelty. Many of them were hanged on gibbets, and left there as a terror to the country people; and, because their miserable friends took some of the bodies down to bury, the King ordered the rest to be chained up—which was the beginning of the barbarous custom of hanging in chains. The King's falsehood in this business makes such a pitiful figure, that I think Wat Tyler appears in history as beyond comparison the truer and more respectable man of the two.

Richard was now sixteen years of age, and married Anne of Bohemia, an excellent princess, who was called 'the good Queen Anne.' She deserved a better husband; for the King had been fawned and flattered into a treacherous, wasteful, dissolute, bad young man.

There were two Popes at this time (as if one were not enough!), and their quarrels involved Europe in a great deal of trouble. Scotland was still troublesome too; and at home there was much jealousy and distrust, and plotting and counter-plotting, because the King feared the ambition of his relations, and particularly of his uncle, the Duke of Lancaster, and the duke had his party against the King, and the King had his party against the duke. Nor were these home troubles lessened when the duke went to Castile to urge his claim to the crown of that kingdom; for then the Duke of Gloucester, another of Richard's uncles, opposed him, and influenced the Parliament to demand the dismissal of the King's favourite ministers. The King said in reply, that he would not for such men dismiss the meanest servant in his kitchen. But, it had begun to signify little what a King said when a Parliament was determined; so Richard was at last obliged to give way, and to agree to another Government of the kingdom, under a commission of fourteen nobles, for a year. His uncle of Gloucester was at the head of this commission, and, in fact, appointed everybody composing it.

Having done all this, the King declared as soon as he saw an opportunity that he had never meant to do it, and that it was all illegal; and he got the judges secretly to sign a declaration to that effect. The secret oozed out directly, and was carried to the Duke of Gloucester. The Duke of Gloucester, at the head of forty thousand men, met the King on his entering into London to enforce his authority; the King was helpless against him; his favourites and ministers were impeached and were mercilessly executed. Among them were two men whom the people regarded with very different feelings; one, Robert Tresilian, Chief Justice, who was hated for having made what was called 'the bloody circuit' to try the rioters; the other, Sir Simon Burley, an honourable knight, who had been the dear friend of the Black Prince, and the governor and guardian of the King. For this gentleman's life the good Queen even begged of Gloucester on her knees; but Gloucester (with or without reason) feared and hated him, and replied, that if she valued her husband's crown, she had better beg no more. All this was done under what was called by some the wonderful—and by others, with better reason, the merciless—Parliament.

But Gloucester's power was not to last for ever. He held it for only a year longer; in which year the famous battle of Otterbourne, sung in the old ballad of Chevy Chase, was fought. When the year was out, the King, turning suddenly to Gloucester, in the midst of a great council said, 'Uncle, how old am I?' 'Your highness,' returned the Duke, 'is in your twenty-second year.' 'Am I so much?' said the King; 'then I will manage my own affairs! I am much obliged to you, my good lords, for your past services, but I need them no more.' He followed this up, by appointing a new Chancellor and a new Treasurer, and announced to the people that he had resumed the Government. He held it for eight years without opposition. Through all that time, he kept his determination to revenge himself some day upon his uncle Gloucester, in his own breast.

At last the good Queen died, and then the King, desiring to take a second wife, proposed to his council that he should marry Isabella, of France, the daughter of Charles the Sixth: who, the French courtiers said (as the English courtiers had said of Richard), was a marvel of beauty and wit, and quite a phenomenon—of seven years old. The council were divided about this marriage, but it took place. It secured peace between England and France for a quarter of a century; but it was strongly opposed to the prejudices of the English people. The Duke of Gloucester, who was anxious to take the occasion of making himself popular, declaimed against it loudly, and this at length decided the King to execute the vengeance he had been nursing so long.

He went with a gay company to the Duke of Gloucester's house, Pleshey

Castle, in Essex, where the Duke, suspecting nothing, came out into the court-yard to receive his royal visitor. While the King conversed in a friendly manner with the Duchess, the Duke was quietly seized, hurried away, shipped for Calais, and lodged in the castle there. His friends, the Earls of Arundel and Warwick, were taken in the same treacherous manner, and confined to their castles. A few days after, at Nottingham, they were impeached of high treason. The Earl of Arundel was condemned and beheaded, and the Earl of Warwick was banished. Then, a writ was sent by a messenger to the Governor of Calais, requiring him to send the Duke of Gloucester over to be tried. In three days he returned an answer that he could not do that, because the Duke of Gloucester had died in prison. The Duke was declared a traitor, his property was confiscated to the King, a real or pretended confession he had made in prison to one of the Justices of the Common Pleas was produced against him, and there was an end of the matter. How the unfortunate duke died, very few cared to know. Whether he really died naturally; whether he killed himself; whether, by the King's order, he was strangled, or smothered between two beds (as a serving-man of the Governor's named Hall, did afterwards declare), cannot be discovered. There is not much doubt that he was killed, somehow or other, by his nephew's orders. Among the most active nobles in these proceedings were the King's cousin, Henry Bolingbroke, whom the King had made Duke of Hereford to smooth down the old family quarrels, and some others: who had in the family-plotting times done just such acts themselves as they now condemned in the duke. They seem to have been a corrupt set of men; but such men were easily found about the court in such days.

The people murmured at all this, and were still very sore about the French marriage. The nobles saw how little the King cared for law, and how crafty he was, and began to be somewhat afraid for themselves. The King's life was a life of continued feasting and excess; his retinue, down to the meanest servants, were dressed in the most costly manner, and caroused at his tables, it is related, to the number of ten thousand persons every day. He himself, surrounded by a body of ten thousand archers, and enriched by a duty on wool which the Commons had granted him for life, saw no danger of ever being otherwise than powerful and absolute, and was as fierce and haughty as a King could be.

181

He had two of his old enemies left, in the persons of the Dukes of Hereford and Norfolk. Sparing these no more than the others, he tampered with the Duke of Hereford until he got him to declare before the Council that the Duke of Norfolk had lately held some treasonable talk with him, as he was riding near Brentford; and that he had told him, among other things, that he could not believe the King's oath—which nobody could, I should think. For this treachery he obtained a pardon, and the Duke of Norfolk was summoned to appear and defend himself. As he denied the charge and said his accuser was a liar and a traitor, both noblemen, according to the manner of those times, were held in custody, and the truth was ordered to be decided by wager of battle at Coventry. This wager of battle meant that whosoever won the combat was to be considered in the right; which nonsense meant in effect, that no strong man could ever be wrong. A great holiday was made; a great crowd assembled, with much parade and show; and the two combatants were about to rush at each other with their lances, when the King, sitting in a pavilion to see fair, threw down the truncheon he carried in his hand, and forbade the battle. The Duke of Hereford was to be banished for ten years, and the Duke of Norfolk was to be banished for life. So said the King. The Duke of Hereford went to France, and went no farther. The Duke of Norfolk made a pilgrimage to the Holy Land, and afterwards died at Venice of a broken heart.

Faster and fiercer, after this, the King went on in his career. The Duke of Lancaster, who was the father of the Duke of Hereford, died soon after the departure of his son; and, the King, although he had solemnly granted to that son leave to inherit his father's property, if it should come to him during his banishment, immediately seized it all, like a robber. The judges were so afraid of him, that they disgraced themselves by declaring this theft to be just and lawful. His avarice knew no bounds. He outlawed seventeen counties at once, on a frivolous pretence, merely to raise money by way of fines for misconduct. In short, he did as many dishonest things as he could; and cared so little for the discontent of his subjects—though even the spaniel favourites began to whisper to him that there was such a thing as discontent afloat—that he took that time, of all others, for leaving England and making an expedition against the Irish.

He was scarcely gone, leaving the Duke of York Regent in his absence, when his cousin, Henry of Hereford, came over from France to claim the rights of which he had been so monstrously deprived. He was immediately joined by the two great Earls of Northumberland and Westmoreland; and his uncle, the Regent, finding the King's cause unpopular, and the disinclination of the army to act against Henry, very strong, withdrew with the Royal forces towards Bristol. Henry, at the head of an army, came from Yorkshire (where he had landed) to London and followed him. They joined their forces— how they brought that about, is not distinctly understood—and proceeded to Bristol Castle, whither three noblemen had taken the young Queen. The castle surrendering, they presently put those three noblemen to death. The Regent then remained there, and Henry went on to Chester.

All this time, the boisterous weather had prevented the King from receiving intelligence of what had occurred. At length it was conveyed to him in Ireland, and he sent over the Earl of Salisbury, who, landing at Conway, rallied the Welshmen, and waited for the King a whole fortnight; at the end of that time the Welshmen, who were perhaps not very warm for him in the beginning, quite cooled down and went home. When the King did land on the coast at last, he came with a pretty good power, but his men cared nothing for him, and quickly deserted. Supposing the Welshmen to be still at Conway, he disguised himself as a priest, and made for that place in company with his two brothers and some few of their adherents. But, there were no Welshmen left—only Salisbury and a hundred soldiers. In this distress, the King's two brothers, Exeter and Surrey, offered to go to Henry to learn what his intentions were. Surrey, who was true to Richard, was put into prison. Exeter, who was false, took the royal badge, which was a hart, off his shield, and assumed the rose, the badge of Henry. After this, it was pretty plain to the King what Henry's intentions were, without sending any more messengers to ask.

The fallen King, thus deserted—hemmed in on all sides, and pressed with hunger—rode here and rode there, and went to this castle, and went to that castle, endeavouring to obtain some provisions, but could find none. He rode wretchedly back to Conway, and there surrendered himself to the Earl of Northumberland, who came from Henry, in reality to take him prisoner, but in appearance to offer terms; and whose men were hidden not far off. By this earl he was conducted to the castle of Flint, where his cousin Henry met him, and dropped on his knee as if he were still respectful to his sovereign.

'Fair cousin of Lancaster,' said the King, 'you are very welcome' (very welcome, no doubt; but he would have been more so, in chains or without a head).

'My lord,' replied Henry, 'I am come a little before my time; but, with your good pleasure, I will show you the reason. Your people complain with some bitterness, that you have ruled them rigorously for two-and-twenty years. Now, if it please God, I will help you to govern them better in future.'

'Fair cousin,' replied the abject King, 'since it pleaseth you, it pleaseth me mightily.'

After this, the trumpets sounded, and the King was stuck on a wretched horse, and carried prisoner to Chester, where he was made to issue a proclamation, calling a Parliament. From Chester he was taken on towards London. At Lichfield he tried to escape by getting out of a window and letting himself down into a garden; it was all in vain, however, and he was carried on and shut up in the Tower, where no one pitied him, and where the whole people, whose patience he had quite tired out, reproached him without mercy. Before he got there, it is related, that his very dog left him and departed from his side to lick the hand of Henry.

The day before the Parliament met, a deputation went to this wrecked King, and told him that he had promised the Earl of Northumberland at Conway Castle to resign the crown. He said he was quite ready to do it, and signed a paper in which he renounced his authority and absolved his people from their allegiance to him. He had so little spirit left that he gave his royal ring to his triumphant cousin Henry with his own hand, and said, that if he could have had leave to appoint a successor, that same Henry was the man of all others whom he would have named. Next day, the Parliament assembled in Westminster Hall, where Henry sat at the side of the throne, which was empty and covered with a cloth of gold. The paper just signed by the King was read to the multitude amid shouts of joy, which were echoed through all the streets; when some of the noise had died away, the King was formally deposed. Then Henry arose, and, making the sign of the cross on his forehead and breast, challenged the realm of England as his right; the archbishops of Canterbury and York seated him on the throne.

The multitude shouted again, and the shouts re-echoed throughout all the streets. No one remembered, now, that Richard the Second had ever been the most beautiful, the wisest, and the best of princes; and he now made living (to my thinking) a far more sorry spectacle in the Tower of London, than Wat Tyler had made, lying dead, among the hoofs of the royal horses in Smithfield.

The Poll-tax died with Wat. The Smiths to the King and Royal Family, could make no chains in which the King could hang the people's recollection of him; so the Poll-tax was never collected.

CHAPTER XX—ENGLAND UNDER HENRY THE FOURTH, CALLED BOLINGBROKE

During the last reign, the preaching of Wickliffe against the pride and cunning of the Pope and all his men, had made a great noise in England. Whether the new King wished to be in favour with the priests, or whether he hoped, by pretending to be very religious, to cheat Heaven itself into the belief that he was not a usurper, I don't know. Both suppositions are likely enough. It is certain that he began his reign by making a strong show against the followers of Wickliffe, who were called Lollards, or heretics—although his father, John of Gaunt, had been of that way of thinking, as he himself had been more than suspected of being. It is no less certain that he first established in England the detestable and atrocious custom, brought from abroad, of burning those people as a punishment for their opinions. It was the importation into England of one of the practices of what was called the Holy Inquisition: which was the most unholy and the most infamous tribunal that ever disgraced mankind, and made men more like demons than followers of Our Saviour.

No real right to the crown, as you know, was in this King. Edward Mortimer, the young Earl of March—who was only eight or nine years old, and who was descended from the Duke of Clarence, the elder brother of Henry's father—was, by succession, the real heir to the throne. However, the King got his son declared Prince of Wales; and, obtaining possession of the young Earl of March and his little brother, kept them in confinement (but not severely) in Windsor Castle. He then required the Parliament to decide what was to be done with the deposed King, who was quiet enough, and who only said that he hoped his cousin Henry would be 'a good lord' to him. The Parliament replied that they would recommend his being kept in some secret place where the people could not resort, and where his friends could not be admitted to see him. Henry accordingly passed this sentence upon him, and it now began to be pretty clear to the nation that Richard the Second would not live very long.

It was a noisy Parliament, as it was an unprincipled one, and the Lords quarrelled so violently among themselves as to which of them had been loyal and which disloyal, and which consistent and which inconsistent, that forty gauntlets are said to have been thrown upon the floor at one time as challenges to as many battles: the truth being that they were all false and base together, and had been, at one time with the old King, and at another time with the new one, and seldom true for any length of time to any one. They soon began to plot again. A conspiracy was formed to invite the King to a tournament at Oxford, and then to take him by surprise and kill him. This murderous enterprise, which was agreed upon at secret meetings in the house of the Abbot of Westminster, was betrayed by the Earl of Rutland—one of the conspirators. The King, instead of going to the tournament or staying at Windsor (where the conspirators suddenly went, on finding themselves discovered, with the hope of seizing him), retired to London, proclaimed them all traitors, and advanced upon them with a great force. They retired into the west of England, proclaiming Richard King; but, the people rose against them, and they were all slain. Their treason hastened the death of the deposed monarch. Whether he was killed by hired assassins, or whether he was starved to death, or whether he refused food on hearing of his brothers being killed (who were in that plot), is very doubtful. He met his death somehow; and his body was publicly shown at St. Paul's Cathedral with only the lower part of the face uncovered. I can scarcely doubt that he was killed by the King's orders.

The French wife of the miserable Richard was now only ten years old; and, when her father, Charles of France, heard of her misfortunes and of her lonely condition in England, he went mad: as he had several times done before, during the last five or six years. The French Dukes of Burgundy and Bourbon took up the poor girl's cause, without caring much about it, but on the chance of getting something out of England. The people of Bordeaux, who had a sort of superstitious attachment to the memory of Richard, because he was born there, swore by the Lord that he had been the best man in all his kingdom—which was going rather far—and promised to do great things against the English. Nevertheless, when they came to consider that they, and the whole people of France, were ruined by their own nobles, and that the English rule was much the better of the two, they cooled down again; and the two dukes, although they were very great men, could do nothing without them. Then, began negotiations between France and England for the sending home to Paris of the poor little Queen with all her jewels and her fortune of two hundred thousand francs in gold. The King was quite willing to restore the young lady, and even the jewels; but he said he really could not part with the money. So, at last she was safely deposited at Paris without her fortune, and then the Duke of Burgundy (who was cousin to the French King) began to quarrel with the Duke of Orleans (who was brother to the French King) about the whole matter; and those two dukes made France even more wretched than ever.

As the idea of conquering Scotland was still popular at home, the King marched to the river Tyne and demanded homage of the King of that country. This being refused, he advanced to Edinburgh, but did little there; for, his army being in want of provisions, and the Scotch being very careful to hold him in check without giving battle, he was obliged to retire. It is to his immortal honour that in this sally he burnt no villages and slaughtered no people, but was particularly careful that his army should be merciful and harmless. It was a great example in those ruthless times.

A war among the border people of England and Scotland went on for twelve months, and then the Earl of Northumberland, the nobleman who had helped Henry to the crown, began to rebel against him—probably because nothing that Henry could do for him would satisfy his extravagant expectations. There was a certain Welsh gentleman, named Owen Glendower, who had been a student in one of the Inns of Court, and had afterwards been in the service of the late King, whose Welsh property was taken from him by a powerful lord related to the present King, who was his neighbour. Appealing for redress, and getting none, he took up arms, was made an outlaw, and declared himself sovereign of Wales. He pretended to be a magician; and not only were the Welsh people stupid enough to believe him, but, even Henry believed him too; for, making three expeditions into Wales, and being three times driven back by the wildness of the country, the bad weather, and the skill of Glendower, he thought he was defeated by the Welshman's magic arts. However, he took Lord Grey and Sir Edmund Mortimer, prisoners, and allowed the relatives of Lord Grey to ransom him, but would not extend such favour to Sir Edmund Mortimer. Now, Henry Percy, called Hotspur, son of the Earl of Northumberland, who was married to Mortimer's sister, is supposed to have taken offence at this; and, therefore, in conjunction with his father and some others, to have joined Owen Glendower, and risen against Henry. It is by no means clear that this was the real cause of the conspiracy; but perhaps it was made the pretext. It was formed, and was very powerful; including Scroop, Archbishop of York, and the Earl of Douglas, a powerful and brave Scottish nobleman. The King was prompt and active, and the two armies met at Shrewsbury.

There were about fourteen thousand men in each. The old Earl of Northumberland being sick, the rebel forces were led by his son. The King wore plain armour to deceive the enemy; and four noblemen, with the same object, wore the royal arms. The rebel charge was so furious, that every one of those gentlemen was killed, the royal standard was beaten down, and the young Prince of Wales was severely wounded in the face. But he was one of the bravest and best soldiers that ever lived, and he fought so well, and the King's troops were so encouraged by his bold example, that they rallied immediately, and cut the enemy's forces all to pieces. Hotspur was killed by an arrow in the brain, and the rout was so complete that the whole rebellion was struck down by this one blow. The Earl of Northumberland surrendered himself soon after hearing of the death of his son, and received a pardon for all his offences.

There were some lingerings of rebellion yet: Owen Glendower being retired to Wales, and a preposterous story being spread among the ignorant people that King Richard was still alive. How they could have believed such nonsense it is difficult to imagine; but they certainly did suppose that the Court fool of the late King, who was something like him, was he, himself; so that it seemed as if, after giving so much trouble to the country in his life, he was still to trouble it after his death. This was not the worst. The young Earl of March and his brother were stolen out of Windsor Castle. Being retaken, and being found to have been spirited away by one Lady Spencer, she accused her own brother, that Earl of Rutland who was in the former conspiracy and was now Duke of York, of being in the plot. For this he was ruined in fortune, though not put to death; and then another plot arose among the old Earl of Northumberland, some other lords, and that same Scroop, Archbishop of York, who was with the rebels before. These conspirators caused a writing to be posted on the church doors, accusing the King of a variety of crimes; but, the King being eager and vigilant to oppose them, they were all taken, and the Archbishop was executed. This was the first time that a great churchman had been slain by the law in England; but the King was resolved that it should be done, and done it was.

The next most remarkable event of this time was the seizure, by Henry, of the heir to the Scottish throne—James, a boy of nine years old. He had been put aboard-ship by his father, the Scottish King Robert, to save him from the designs of his uncle, when, on his way to France, he was accidentally taken by some English cruisers. He remained a prisoner in England for nineteen years, and became in his prison a student and a famous poet.

With the exception of occasional troubles with the Welsh and with the French, the rest of King Henry's reign was quiet enough. But, the King was far from happy, and probably was troubled in his conscience by knowing that he had usurped the crown, and had occasioned the death of his miserable cousin. The Prince of Wales, though brave and generous, is said to have been wild and dissipated, and even to have drawn his sword on Gascoigne, the Chief Justice of the King's Bench, because he was firm in dealing impartially with one of his dissolute companions. Upon this the Chief Justice is said to have ordered him immediately to prison; the Prince of Wales is said to have submitted with a good grace; and the King is said to have exclaimed, 'Happy is the monarch who has so just a judge, and a son so willing to obey the laws.' This is all very doubtful, and so is another story (of which Shakespeare has made beautiful use), that the Prince once took the crown out of his father's chamber as he was sleeping, and tried it on his own head.

The King's health sank more and more, and he became subject to violent eruptions on the face and to bad epileptic fits, and his spirits sank every day. At last, as he was praying before the shrine of St. Edward at Westminster

Abbey, he was seized with a terrible fit, and was carried into the Abbot's chamber, where he presently died. It had been foretold that he would die at Jerusalem, which certainly is not, and never was, Westminster. But, as the Abbot's room had long been called the Jerusalem chamber, people said it was all the same thing, and were quite satisfied with the prediction.

The King died on the 20th of March, 1413, in the forty-seventh year of his age, and the fourteenth of his reign. He was buried in Canterbury Cathedral. He had been twice married, and had, by his first wife, a family of four sons and two daughters. Considering his duplicity before he came to the throne, his unjust seizure of it, and above all, his making that monstrous law for the burning of what the priests called heretics, he was a reasonably good king, as kings went.

CHAPTER XXI—ENGLAND UNDER HENRY THE FIFTH

FIRST PART

The Prince of Wales began his reign like a generous and honest man. He set the young Earl of March free; he restored their estates and their honours to the Percy family, who had lost them by their rebellion against his father; he ordered the imbecile and unfortunate Richard to be honourably buried among the Kings of England; and he dismissed all his wild companions, with assurances that they should not want, if they would resolve to be steady, faithful, and true.

It is much easier to burn men than to burn their opinions; and those of the Lollards were spreading every day. The Lollards were represented by the priests—probably falsely for the most part—to entertain treasonable designs against the new King; and Henry, suffering himself to be worked upon by these representations, sacrificed his friend Sir John Oldcastle, the Lord Cobham, to them, after trying in vain to convert him by arguments. He was declared guilty, as the head of the sect, and sentenced to the flames; but he escaped from the Tower before the day of execution (postponed for fifty days by the King himself), and summoned the Lollards to meet him near London on a certain day. So the priests told the King, at least. I doubt whether there was any conspiracy beyond such as was got up by their agents. On the day appointed, instead of five-and-twenty thousand men, under the command of Sir John Oldcastle, in the meadows of St. Giles, the King found only eighty men, and no Sir John at all. There was, in another place, an addle-headed brewer, who had gold trappings to his horses, and a pair of gilt spurs in his breast—expecting to be made a knight next day by Sir John, and so to gain the right to wear them—but there was no Sir John, nor did anybody give information respecting him, though the King offered great rewards for such intelligence. Thirty of these unfortunate Lollards were hanged and drawn immediately, and were then burnt, gallows and all; and the various prisons in and around London were crammed full of others. Some of these unfortunate men made various confessions of treasonable designs; but, such confessions were easily got, under torture and the fear of fire, and are very little to be trusted. To finish the sad story of Sir John Oldcastle at once, I may mention that he escaped into Wales, and remained there safely, for four years. When discovered by Lord Powis, it is very doubtful if he would have been taken alive—so great was the old soldier's bravery—if a miserable old woman had not come behind him and broken his legs with a stool. He was carried to London in a horse-litter, was fastened by an iron chain to a gibbet, and so roasted to death.

To make the state of France as plain as I can in a few words, I should tell you that the Duke of Orleans, and the Duke of Burgundy, commonly called 'John without fear,' had had a grand reconciliation of their quarrel in the last reign, and had appeared to be quite in a heavenly state of mind. Immediately after which, on a Sunday, in the public streets of Paris, the Duke of Orleans was murdered by a party of twenty men, set on by the Duke of Burgundy—according to his own deliberate confession. The widow of King Richard had been married in France to the eldest son of the Duke of Orleans. The poor mad King was quite powerless to help her, and the Duke of Burgundy became the real master of France. Isabella dying, her husband (Duke of Orleans since the death of his father) married the daughter of the Count of Armagnac, who, being a much abler man than his young son-in-law, headed his party; thence called after him Armagnacs. Thus, France was now in this terrible condition, that it had in it the party of the King's son, the Dauphin Louis; the party of the Duke of Burgundy, who was the father of the Dauphin's ill-used wife; and the party of the Armagnacs; all hating each other; all fighting together; all composed of the most depraved nobles that the earth has ever known; and all tearing unhappy France to pieces.

The late King had watched these dissensions from England, sensible (like the French people) that no enemy of France could injure her more than her own nobility. The present King now advanced a claim to the French throne. His demand being, of course, refused, he reduced his proposal to a certain large amount of French territory, and to demanding the French princess, Catherine, in marriage, with a fortune of two millions of golden crowns. He was offered less territory and fewer crowns, and no princess; but he called his ambassadors home and prepared for war. Then, he proposed to take the princess with one million of crowns. The French Court replied that he should have the princess with two hundred thousand crowns less; he said this would not do (he had never seen the princess in his life), and assembled his army at Southampton. There was a short plot at home just at that time, for deposing him, and making the Earl of March king; but the conspirators were all speedily condemned and executed, and the King embarked for France.

It is dreadful to observe how long a bad example will be followed; but, it is encouraging to know that a good example is never thrown away. The King's first act on disembarking at the mouth of the river Seine, three miles from Harfleur, was to imitate his father, and to proclaim his solemn orders that the lives and property of the peaceable inhabitants should be respected on pain of death. It is agreed by French writers, to his lasting renown, that even while his soldiers were suffering the greatest distress from want of food, these commands were rigidly obeyed.

With an army in all of thirty thousand men, he besieged the town of Harfleur both by sea and land for five weeks; at the end of which time the town surrendered, and the inhabitants were allowed to depart with only fivepence each, and a part of their clothes. All the rest of their possessions was divided amongst the English army. But, that army suffered so much, in spite of its successes, from disease and privation, that it was already reduced one half. Still, the King was determined not to retire until he had struck a greater blow. Therefore, against the advice of all his counsellors, he moved on with his little force towards Calais. When he came up to the river Somme he was unable to cross, in consequence of the fort being fortified; and, as the English moved up the left bank of the river looking for a crossing, the French, who had broken all the bridges, moved up the right bank, watching them, and waiting to attack them when they should try to pass it. At last the English found a crossing and got safely over. The French held a council of war at Rouen, resolved to give the English battle, and sent heralds to King Henry to know by which road he was going. 'By the road that will take me straight to Calais!' said the King, and sent them away with a present of a hundred crowns.

The English moved on, until they beheld the French, and then the King gave orders to form in line of battle. The French not coming on, the army broke up after remaining in battle array till night, and got good rest and refreshment at a neighbouring village. The French were now all lying in another village, through which they knew the English must pass. They were resolved that the English should begin the battle. The English had no means of retreat, if their King had any such intention; and so the two armies passed the night, close together.

To understand these armies well, you must bear in mind that the immense French army had, among its notable persons, almost the whole of that wicked nobility, whose debauchery had made France a desert; and so besotted were they by pride, and by contempt for the common people, that they had scarcely any bowmen (if indeed they had any at all) in their whole enormous number: which, compared with the English army, was at least as six to one. For these proud fools had said that the bow was not a fit weapon for knightly hands, and that France must be defended by gentlemen only. We shall see, presently, what hand the gentlemen made of it.

Now, on the English side, among the little force, there was a good proportion of men who were not gentlemen by any means, but who were good stout archers for all that. Among them, in the morning—having slept little at night, while the French were carousing and making sure of victory—the King rode, on a grey horse; wearing on his head a helmet of shining steel, surmounted by a crown of gold, sparkling with precious stones; and bearing over his armour, embroidered together, the arms of England and the arms of France. The archers looked at the shining helmet and the crown of gold and the sparkling jewels, and admired them all; but, what they admired most was the King's cheerful face, and his bright blue eye, as he told them that, for himself, he had made up his mind to conquer there or to die there, and that England should never have a ransom to pay for him. There was one brave knight who chanced to say that he wished some of the many gallant gentlemen and good soldiers, who were then idle at home in England, were there to increase their numbers. But the King told him that, for his part, he did not wish for one more man. 'The fewer we have,' said he, 'the greater will be the honour we shall win!' His men, being now all in good heart, were refreshed with bread and wine, and heard prayers, and waited quietly for the French. The King waited for the French, because they were drawn up thirty deep (the little English force was only three deep), on very difficult and heavy ground; and he knew that when they moved, there must be confusion among them.

As they did not move, he sent off two parties:—one to lie concealed in a wood on the left of the French: the other, to set fire to some houses behind the French after the battle should be begun. This was scarcely done, when three of the proud French gentlemen, who were to defend their country without any help from the base peasants, came riding out, calling upon the English to surrender. The King warned those gentlemen himself to retire with all speed if they cared for their lives, and ordered the English banners to advance. Upon that, Sir Thomas Erpingham, a great English general, who commanded the archers, threw his truncheon into the air, joyfully, and all the English men, kneeling down upon the ground and biting it as if they took possession of the country, rose up with a great shout and fell upon the French.

Every archer was furnished with a great stake tipped with iron; and his orders were, to thrust this stake into the ground, to discharge his arrow, and then to fall back, when the French horsemen came on. As the haughty French gentlemen, who were to break the English archers and utterly destroy them with their knightly lances, came riding up, they were received with such a blinding storm of arrows, that they broke and turned. Horses and men rolled over one another, and the confusion was terrific. Those who rallied and charged the archers got among the stakes on slippery and boggy ground, and were so bewildered that the English archers—who wore no armour, and even took off their leathern coats to be more active—cut them to pieces, root and branch. Only three French horsemen got within the stakes, and those were instantly despatched. All this time the dense French army, being in armour, were sinking knee-deep into the mire; while the light English archers, half-naked, were as fresh and active as if they were fighting on a marble floor.

But now, the second division of the French coming to the relief of the first, closed up in a firm mass; the English, headed by the King, attacked them; and the deadliest part of the battle began. The King's brother, the Duke of Clarence, was struck down, and numbers of the French surrounded him; but, King Henry, standing over the body, fought like a lion until they were beaten off.

Presently, came up a band of eighteen French knights, bearing the banner of a certain French lord, who had sworn to kill or take the English King. One of them struck him such a blow with a battle-axe that he reeled and fell upon his knees; but, his faithful men, immediately closing round him, killed every one of those eighteen knights, and so that French lord never kept his oath.

The French Duke of Alençon, seeing this, made a desperate charge, and cut his way close up to the Royal Standard of England. He beat down the Duke of York, who was standing near it; and, when the King came to his rescue, struck off a piece of the crown he wore. But, he never struck another blow in this world; for, even as he was in the act of saying who he was, and that he surrendered to the King; and even as the King stretched out his hand to give him a safe and honourable acceptance of the offer; he fell dead, pierced by innumerable wounds.

The death of this nobleman decided the battle. The third division of the French army, which had never struck a blow yet, and which was, in itself, more than double the whole English power, broke and fled. At this time of the fight, the English, who as yet had made no prisoners, began to take them in immense numbers, and were still occupied in doing so, or in killing those who would not surrender, when a great noise arose in the rear of the French— their flying banners were seen to stop—and King Henry, supposing a great reinforcement to have arrived, gave orders that all the prisoners should be put to death. As soon, however, as it was found that the noise was only occasioned by a body of plundering peasants, the terrible massacre was stopped.

Then King Henry called to him the French herald, and asked him to whom the victory belonged.

The herald replied, 'To the King of England.'

'We have not made this havoc and slaughter,' said the King. 'It is the wrath of Heaven on the sins of France. What is the name of that castle yonder?'

The herald answered him, 'My lord, it is the castle of Azincourt.' Said the King, 'From henceforth this battle shall be known to posterity, by the name of the battle of Azincourt.'

Our English historians have made it Agincourt; but, under that name, it will ever be famous in English annals.

The loss upon the French side was enormous. Three Dukes were killed, two more were taken prisoners, seven Counts were killed, three more were taken prisoners, and ten thousand knights and gentlemen were slain upon the field. The English loss amounted to sixteen hundred men, among whom were the Duke of York and the Earl of Suffolk.

War is a dreadful thing; and it is appalling to know how the English were obliged, next morning, to kill those prisoners mortally wounded, who yet writhed in agony upon the ground; how the dead upon the French side were stripped by their own countrymen and countrywomen, and afterwards buried in great pits; how the dead upon the English side were piled up in a great barn, and how their bodies and the barn were all burned together. It is in such things, and in many more much too horrible to relate, that the real desolation and wickedness of war consist. Nothing can make war otherwise than horrible. But the dark side of it was little thought of and soon forgotten; and it cast no shade of trouble on the English people, except on those who had lost friends or relations in the fight. They welcomed their King home with shouts of rejoicing, and plunged into the water to bear him ashore on their shoulders, and flocked out in crowds to welcome him in every town through which he passed, and hung rich carpets and tapestries out of the windows, and strewed the streets with flowers, and made the fountains run with wine, as the great field of Agincourt had run with blood.

SECOND PART

That proud and wicked French nobility who dragged their country to destruction, and who were every day and every year regarded with deeper hatred and detestation in the hearts of the French people, learnt nothing, even from the defeat of Agincourt. So far from uniting against the common enemy, they became, among themselves, more violent, more bloody, and more false—if that were possible—than they had been before. The Count of Armagnac persuaded the French king to plunder of her treasures Queen Isabella of Bavaria, and to make her a prisoner. She, who had hitherto been the bitter enemy of the Duke of Burgundy, proposed to join him, in revenge. He carried her off to Troyes, where she proclaimed herself Regent of France, and made him her lieutenant. The Armagnac party were at that time possessed of Paris; but, one of the gates of the city being secretly opened on a certain night to a party of the duke's men, they got into Paris, threw into the prisons all the Armagnacs upon whom they could lay their hands, and, a few nights afterwards, with the aid of a furious mob of sixty thousand people, broke the prisons open, and killed them all. The former Dauphin was now dead, and the King's third son bore the title. Him, in the height of this murderous scene, a French knight hurried out of bed, wrapped in a sheet, and bore away to Poitiers. So, when the revengeful Isabella and the Duke of Burgundy entered Paris in triumph after the slaughter of their enemies, the Dauphin was proclaimed at Poitiers as the real Regent.

King Henry had not been idle since his victory of Agincourt, but had repulsed a brave attempt of the French to recover Harfleur; had gradually conquered a great part of Normandy; and, at this crisis of affairs, took the important town of Rouen, after a siege of half a year. This great loss so alarmed the French, that the Duke of Burgundy proposed that a meeting to treat of peace should be held between the French and the English kings in a plain by the river Seine. On the appointed day, King Henry appeared there, with his two brothers, Clarence and Gloucester, and a thousand men. The unfortunate French King, being more mad than usual that day, could not come; but the Queen came, and with her the Princess Catherine: who was a very lovely creature, and who made a real impression on King Henry, now that he saw her for the first time. This was the most important circumstance that arose out of the meeting.

As if it were impossible for a French nobleman of that time to be true to his word of honour in anything, Henry discovered that the Duke of Burgundy

199

was, at that very moment, in secret treaty with the Dauphin; and he therefore abandoned the negotiation.

The Duke of Burgundy and the Dauphin, each of whom with the best reason distrusted the other as a noble ruffian surrounded by a party of noble ruffians, were rather at a loss how to proceed after this; but, at length they agreed to meet, on a bridge over the river Yonne, where it was arranged that there should be two strong gates put up, with an empty space between them; and that the Duke of Burgundy should come into that space by one gate, with ten men only; and that the Dauphin should come into that space by the other gate, also with ten men, and no more.

So far the Dauphin kept his word, but no farther. When the Duke of Burgundy was on his knee before him in the act of speaking, one of the Dauphin's noble ruffians cut the said duke down with a small axe, and others speedily finished him.

It was in vain for the Dauphin to pretend that this base murder was not done with his consent; it was too bad, even for France, and caused a general horror. The duke's heir hastened to make a treaty with King Henry, and the French Queen engaged that her husband should consent to it, whatever it was. Henry made peace, on condition of receiving the Princess Catherine in marriage, and being made Regent of France during the rest of the King's lifetime, and succeeding to the French crown at his death. He was soon married to the beautiful Princess, and took her proudly home to England, where she was crowned with great honour and glory.

This peace was called the Perpetual Peace; we shall soon see how long it lasted. It gave great satisfaction to the French people, although they were so poor and miserable, that, at the time of the celebration of the Royal marriage, numbers of them were dying with starvation, on the dunghills in the streets of Paris. There was some resistance on the part of the Dauphin in some few parts of France, but King Henry beat it all down.

And now, with his great possessions in France secured, and his beautiful wife to cheer him, and a son born to give him greater happiness, all appeared bright before him. But, in the fulness of his triumph and the height of his power, Death came upon him, and his day was done. When he fell ill at Vincennes, and found that he could not recover, he was very calm and quiet, and spoke serenely to those who wept around his bed. His wife and child, he said, he left to the loving care of his brother the Duke of Bedford, and his other faithful nobles. He gave them his advice that England should establish a friendship with the new Duke of Burgundy, and offer him the regency of France; that it should not set free the royal princes who had been taken at Agincourt; and that, whatever quarrel might arise with France, England should never make peace without holding Normandy. Then, he laid down his head, and asked the attendant priests to chant the penitential psalms. Amid which solemn sounds, on the thirty-first of August, one thousand four hundred and twenty-two, in only the thirty-fourth year of his age and the tenth of his reign, King Henry the Fifth passed away.

Slowly and mournfully they carried his embalmed body in a procession of great state to Paris, and thence to Rouen where his Queen was: from whom the sad intelligence of his death was concealed until he had been dead some days. Thence, lying on a bed of crimson and gold, with a golden crown upon the head, and a golden ball and sceptre lying in the nerveless hands, they carried it to Calais, with such a great retinue as seemed to dye the road black. The King of Scotland acted as chief mourner, all the Royal Household followed, the knights wore black armour and black plumes of feathers, crowds of men bore torches, making the night as light as day; and the widowed Princess followed last of all. At Calais there was a fleet of ships to bring the funeral host to Dover. And so, by way of London Bridge, where the service for the dead was chanted as it passed along, they brought the body to Westminster Abbey, and there buried it with great respect.

CHAPTER XXII—ENGLAND UNDER HENRY THE SIXTH

PART THE FIRST

It had been the wish of the late King, that while his infant son King Henry the Sixth, at this time only nine months old, was under age, the Duke of Gloucester should be appointed Regent. The English Parliament, however, preferred to appoint a Council of Regency, with the Duke of Bedford at its head: to be represented, in his absence only, by the Duke of Gloucester. The Parliament would seem to have been wise in this, for Gloucester soon showed himself to be ambitious and troublesome, and, in the gratification of his own personal schemes, gave dangerous offence to the Duke of Burgundy, which was with difficulty adjusted.

As that duke declined the Regency of France, it was bestowed by the poor French King upon the Duke of Bedford. But, the French King dying within two months, the Dauphin instantly asserted his claim to the French throne, and was actually crowned under the title of Charles the Seventh. The Duke of Bedford, to be a match for him, entered into a friendly league with the Dukes of Burgundy and Brittany, and gave them his two sisters in marriage. War with France was immediately renewed, and the Perpetual Peace came to an untimely end.

In the first campaign, the English, aided by this alliance, were speedily successful. As Scotland, however, had sent the French five thousand men, and might send more, or attack the North of England while England was busy with France, it was considered that it would be a good thing to offer the Scottish King, James, who had been so long imprisoned, his liberty, on his paying forty thousand pounds for his board and lodging during nineteen years, and engaging to forbid his subjects from serving under the flag of France. It is pleasant to know, not only that the amiable captive at last regained his freedom upon these terms, but, that he married a noble English lady, with whom he had been long in love, and became an excellent King. I am afraid we have met with some Kings in this history, and shall meet with some more, who would have been very much the better, and would have left the world much happier, if they had been imprisoned nineteen years too.

In the second campaign, the English gained a considerable victory at Verneuil, in a battle which was chiefly remarkable, otherwise, for their resorting to the odd expedient of tying their baggage-horses together by the heads and tails, and jumbling them up with the baggage, so as to convert them into a sort of live fortification—which was found useful to the troops, but which I should think was not agreeable to the horses. For three years afterwards very little was done, owing to both sides being too poor for war, which is a very expensive entertainment; but, a council was then held in Paris, in which it was decided to lay siege to the town of Orleans, which was a place of great importance to the Dauphin's cause. An English army of ten thousand men was despatched on this service, under the command of the Earl of Salisbury, a general of fame. He being unfortunately killed early in the siege, the Earl of Suffolk took his place; under whom (reinforced by Sir John Falstaff, who brought up four hundred waggons laden with salt herrings and other provisions for the troops, and, beating off the French who tried to intercept him, came victorious out of a hot skirmish, which was afterwards called in jest the Battle of the Herrings) the town of Orleans was so completely hemmed in, that the besieged proposed to yield it up to their countryman the Duke of Burgundy. The English general, however, replied that his English men had won it, so far, by their blood and valour, and that his English men must have it. There seemed to be no hope for the town, or for the Dauphin, who was so dismayed that he even thought of flying to Scotland or to Spain—when a peasant girl rose up and changed the whole state of affairs.

The story of this peasant girl I have now to tell.

PART THE SECOND: THE STORY OF JOAN OF ARC

In a remote village among some wild hills in the province of Lorraine, there lived a countryman whose name was Jacques d'Arc. He had a daughter, Joan of Arc, who was at this time in her twentieth year. She had been a solitary girl from her childhood; she had often tended sheep and cattle for whole days where no human figure was seen or human voice heard; and she had often knelt, for hours together, in the gloomy, empty, little village chapel, looking up at the altar and at the dim lamp burning before it, until she fancied that she saw shadowy figures standing there, and even that she heard them speak to her. The people in that part of France were very ignorant and superstitious, and they had many ghostly tales to tell about what they had dreamed, and what they saw among the lonely hills when the clouds and the mists were resting on them. So, they easily believed that Joan saw strange sights, and they whispered among themselves that angels and spirits talked to her.

At last, Joan told her father that she had one day been surprised by a great unearthly light, and had afterwards heard a solemn voice, which said it was Saint Michael's voice, telling her that she was to go and help the Dauphin. Soon after this (she said), Saint Catherine and Saint Margaret had appeared to her with sparkling crowns upon their heads, and had encouraged her to be virtuous and resolute. These visions had returned sometimes; but the Voices very often; and the voices always said, 'Joan, thou art appointed by Heaven to go and help the Dauphin!' She almost always heard them while the chapel bells were ringing.

There is no doubt, now, that Joan believed she saw and heard these things. It is very well known that such delusions are a disease which is not by any means uncommon. It is probable enough that there were figures of Saint Michael, and Saint Catherine, and Saint Margaret, in the little chapel (where they would be very likely to have shining crowns upon their heads), and that they first gave Joan the idea of those three personages. She had long been a moping, fanciful girl, and, though she was a very good girl, I dare say she was a little vain, and wishful for notoriety.

Her father, something wiser than his neighbours, said, 'I tell thee, Joan, it is thy fancy. Thou hadst better have a kind husband to take care of thee, girl, and work to employ thy mind!' But Joan told him in reply, that she had taken a vow never to have a husband, and that she must go as Heaven directed her, to help the Dauphin.

It happened, unfortunately for her father's persuasions, and most unfortunately for the poor girl, too, that a party of the Dauphin's enemies found their way into the village while Joan's disorder was at this point, and burnt the chapel, and drove out the inhabitants. The cruelties she saw committed, touched Joan's heart and made her worse. She said that the voices and the figures were now continually with her; that they told her she was the girl who, according to an old prophecy, was to deliver France; and she must go and help the Dauphin, and must remain with him until he should be crowned at Rheims: and that she must travel a long way to a certain lord named Baudricourt, who could and would, bring her into the Dauphin's presence.

As her father still said, 'I tell thee, Joan, it is thy fancy,' she set off to find out this lord, accompanied by an uncle, a poor village wheelwright and cartmaker, who believed in the reality of her visions. They travelled a long way and went on and on, over a rough country, full of the Duke of Burgundy's men, and of all kinds of robbers and marauders, until they came to where this lord was.

When his servants told him that there was a poor peasant girl named Joan of Arc, accompanied by nobody but an old village wheelwright and cart-maker, who wished to see him because she was commanded to help the Dauphin and save France, Baudricourt burst out a-laughing, and bade them send the girl away. But, he soon heard so much about her lingering in the town, and praying in the churches, and seeing visions, and doing harm to no one, that he sent for her, and questioned her. As she said the same things after she had been well sprinkled with holy water as she had said before the sprinkling, Baudricourt began to think there might be something in it. At all events, he thought it worth while to send her on to the town of Chinon, where the Dauphin was. So, he bought her a horse, and a sword, and gave her two squires to conduct her. As the Voices had told Joan that she was to wear a man's dress, now, she put one on, and girded her sword to her side, and bound spurs to her heels, and mounted her horse and rode away with her two squires. As to her uncle the wheelwright, he stood staring at his niece in wonder until she was out of sight—as well he might—and then went home again. The best place, too.

Joan and her two squires rode on and on, until they came to Chinon, where she was, after some doubt, admitted into the Dauphin's presence. Picking him out immediately from all his court, she told him that she came commanded by Heaven to subdue his enemies and conduct him to his coronation at Rheims. She also told him (or he pretended so afterwards, to make the greater impression upon his soldiers) a number of his secrets known only to himself, and, furthermore, she said there was an old, old sword in the cathedral of Saint Catherine at Fierbois, marked with five old crosses on the blade, which Saint Catherine had ordered her to wear.

Now, nobody knew anything about this old, old sword, but when the cathedral came to be examined—which was immediately done—there, sure enough, the sword was found! The Dauphin then required a number of grave priests and bishops to give him their opinion whether the girl derived her power from good spirits or from evil spirits, which they held prodigiously long debates about, in the course of which several learned men fell fast asleep and snored loudly. At last, when one gruff old gentleman had said to Joan, 'What language do your Voices speak?' and when Joan had replied to the gruff old gentleman, 'A pleasanter language than yours,' they agreed that it was all correct, and that Joan of Arc was inspired from Heaven. This wonderful circumstance put new heart into the Dauphin's soldiers when they heard of it, and dispirited the English army, who took Joan for a witch.

So Joan mounted horse again, and again rode on and on, until she came to Orleans. But she rode now, as never peasant girl had ridden yet. She rode upon a white war-horse, in a suit of glittering armour; with the old, old sword from the cathedral, newly burnished, in her belt; with a white flag carried before her, upon which were a picture of God, and the words Jesus Maria. In this splendid state, at the head of a great body of troops escorting provisions of all kinds for the starving inhabitants of Orleans, she appeared before that beleaguered city.

When the people on the walls beheld her, they cried out 'The Maid is come! The Maid of the Prophecy is come to deliver us!' And this, and the sight of the Maid fighting at the head of their men, made the French so bold, and made the English so fearful, that the English line of forts was soon broken, the troops and provisions were got into the town, and Orleans was saved.

Joan, henceforth called The Maid of Orleans, remained within the walls for a few days, and caused letters to be thrown over, ordering Lord Suffolk and his Englishmen to depart from before the town according to the will of Heaven. As the English general very positively declined to believe that Joan knew anything about the will of Heaven (which did not mend the matter with his soldiers, for they stupidly said if she were not inspired she was a witch, and it was of no use to fight against a witch), she mounted her white war-horse again, and ordered her white banner to advance.

The besiegers held the bridge, and some strong towers upon the bridge; and here the Maid of Orleans attacked them. The fight was fourteen hours long. She planted a scaling ladder with her own hands, and mounted a tower wall, but was struck by an English arrow in the neck, and fell into the trench. She was carried away and the arrow was taken out, during which operation she screamed and cried with the pain, as any other girl might have done; but presently she said that the Voices were speaking to her and soothing her to rest. After a while, she got up, and was again foremost in the fight. When the English who had seen her fall and supposed her dead, saw this, they were troubled with the strangest fears, and some of them cried out that they beheld Saint Michael on a white horse (probably Joan herself) fighting for the French. They lost the bridge, and lost the towers, and next day set their chain of forts on fire, and left the place.

But as Lord Suffolk himself retired no farther than the town of Jargeau, which was only a few miles off, the Maid of Orleans besieged him there, and he was taken prisoner. As the white banner scaled the wall, she was struck upon the head with a stone, and was again tumbled down into the ditch; but, she only cried all the more, as she lay there, 'On, on, my countrymen! And fear nothing, for the Lord hath delivered them into our hands!' After this new success of the Maid's, several other fortresses and places which had previously held out against the Dauphin were delivered up without a battle; and at Patay she defeated the remainder of the English army, and set up her victorious white banner on a field where twelve hundred Englishmen lay dead.

She now urged the Dauphin (who always kept out of the way when

207

there was any fighting) to proceed to Rheims, as the first part of her mission was accomplished; and to complete the whole by being crowned there. The Dauphin was in no particular hurry to do this, as Rheims was a long way off, and the English and the Duke of Burgundy were still strong in the country through which the road lay. However, they set forth, with ten thousand men, and again the Maid of Orleans rode on and on, upon her white war-horse, and in her shining armour. Whenever they came to a town which yielded readily, the soldiers believed in her; but, whenever they came to a town which gave them any trouble, they began to murmur that she was an impostor. The latter was particularly the case at Troyes, which finally yielded, however, through the persuasion of one Richard, a friar of the place. Friar Richard was in the old doubt about the Maid of Orleans, until he had sprinkled her well with holy water, and had also well sprinkled the threshold of the gate by which she came into the city. Finding that it made no change in her or the gate, he said, as the other grave old gentlemen had said, that it was all right, and became her great ally.

So, at last, by dint of riding on and on, the Maid of Orleans, and the Dauphin, and the ten thousand sometimes believing and sometimes unbelieving men, came to Rheims. And in the great cathedral of Rheims, the Dauphin actually was crowned Charles the Seventh in a great assembly of the people. Then, the Maid, who with her white banner stood beside the King in that hour of his triumph, kneeled down upon the pavement at his feet, and said, with tears, that what she had been inspired to do, was done, and that the only recompense she asked for, was, that she should now have leave to go back to her distant home, and her sturdily incredulous father, and her first simple escort the village wheelwright and cart-maker. But the King said 'No!' and made her and her family as noble as a King could, and settled upon her the income of a Count.

Ah! happy had it been for the Maid of Orleans, if she had resumed her rustic dress that day, and had gone home to the little chapel and the wild hills, and had forgotten all these things, and had been a good man's wife, and had heard no stranger voices than the voices of little children!

It was not to be, and she continued helping the King (she did a world for him, in alliance with Friar Richard), and trying to improve the lives of the coarse soldiers, and leading a religious, an unselfish, and a modest life, herself, beyond any doubt. Still, many times she prayed the King to let her go home; and once she even took off her bright armour and hung it up in a church, meaning never to wear it more. But, the King always won her back again—while she was of any use to him—and so she went on and on and on, to her doom.

When the Duke of Bedford, who was a very able man, began to be active for England, and, by bringing the war back into France and by holding the Duke of Burgundy to his faith, to distress and disturb Charles very much, Charles sometimes asked the Maid of Orleans what the Voices said about it? But, the Voices had become (very like ordinary voices in perplexed times) contradictory and confused, so that now they said one thing, and now said another, and the Maid lost credit every day. Charles marched on Paris, which was opposed to him, and attacked the suburb of Saint Honoré. In this fight, being again struck down into the ditch, she was abandoned by the whole army. She lay unaided among a heap of dead, and crawled out how she could. Then, some of her believers went over to an opposition Maid, Catherine of La Rochelle, who said she was inspired to tell where there were treasures of buried money—though she never did—and then Joan accidentally broke the old, old sword, and others said that her power was broken with it. Finally, at the siege of Compiègne, held by the Duke of Burgundy, where she did valiant service, she was basely left alone in a retreat, though facing about and fighting to the last; and an archer pulled her off her horse.

O the uproar that was made, and the thanksgivings that were sung, about the capture of this one poor country-girl! O the way in which she was demanded to be tried for sorcery and heresy, and anything else you like, by the Inquisitor-General of France, and by this great man, and by that great man, until it is wearisome to think of! She was bought at last by the Bishop of Beauvais for ten thousand francs, and was shut up in her narrow prison: plain Joan of Arc again, and Maid of Orleans no more.

I should never have done if I were to tell you how they had Joan out to examine her, and cross-examine her, and re-examine her, and worry her into saying anything and everything; and how all sorts of scholars and doctors bestowed their utmost tediousness upon her. Sixteen times she was brought out and shut up again, and worried, and entrapped, and argued with, until she was heart-sick of the dreary business. On the last occasion of this kind she was brought into a burial-place at Rouen, dismally decorated with a scaffold, and a stake and faggots, and the executioner, and a pulpit with a friar therein, and an awful sermon ready. It is very affecting to know that even at that pass the poor girl honoured the mean vermin of a King, who had so used her for his purposes and so abandoned her; and, that while she had been regardless of reproaches heaped upon herself, she spoke out courageously for him.

It was natural in one so young to hold to life. To save her life, she signed a declaration prepared for her—signed it with a cross, for she couldn't write—that all her visions and Voices had come from the Devil. Upon her recanting the past, and protesting that she would never wear a man's dress in future, she was condemned to imprisonment for life, 'on the bread of sorrow and the water of affliction.'

But, on the bread of sorrow and the water of affliction, the visions and the Voices soon returned. It was quite natural that they should do so, for that kind of disease is much aggravated by fasting, loneliness, and anxiety of mind. It was not only got out of Joan that she considered herself inspired again, but, she was taken in a man's dress, which had been left—to entrap her—in her prison, and which she put on, in her solitude; perhaps, in remembrance of her past glories, perhaps, because the imaginary Voices told her. For this relapse into the sorcery and heresy and anything else you like, she was sentenced to be burnt to death. And, in the market-place of Rouen, in the hideous dress which the monks had invented for such spectacles; with priests and bishops sitting in a gallery looking on, though some had the Christian grace to go away, unable to endure the infamous scene; this shrieking girl—last seen amidst the smoke and fire, holding a crucifix between her hands; last heard, calling upon Christ—was burnt to ashes. They threw her ashes into the river Seine; but they will rise against her murderers on the last day.

From the moment of her capture, neither the French King nor one single man in all his court raised a finger to save her. It is no defence of them that they may have never really believed in her, or that they may have won her victories by their skill and bravery. The more they pretended to believe in her, the more they had caused her to believe in herself; and she had ever been true to them, ever brave, ever nobly devoted. But, it is no wonder, that they, who were in all things false to themselves, false to one another, false to their country, false to Heaven, false to Earth, should be monsters of ingratitude and treachery to a helpless peasant girl.

In the picturesque old town of Rouen, where weeds and grass grow high on the cathedral towers, and the venerable Norman streets are still warm in the blessed sunlight though the monkish fires that once gleamed horribly upon them have long grown cold, there is a statue of Joan of Arc, in the scene of her last agony, the square to which she has given its present name. I know some statues of modern times—even in the World's metropolis, I think—which commemorate less constancy, less earnestness, smaller claims upon the world's attention, and much greater impostors.

PART THE THIRD

Bad deeds seldom prosper, happily for mankind; and the English cause gained no advantage from the cruel death of Joan of Arc. For a long time, the war went heavily on. The Duke of Bedford died; the alliance with the Duke of Burgundy was broken; and Lord Talbot became a great general on the English side in France. But, two of the consequences of wars are, Famine— because the people cannot peacefully cultivate the ground—and Pestilence, which comes of want, misery, and suffering. Both these horrors broke out in both countries, and lasted for two wretched years. Then, the war went on again, and came by slow degrees to be so badly conducted by the English government, that, within twenty years from the execution of the Maid of Orleans, of all the great French conquests, the town of Calais alone remained in English hands.

While these victories and defeats were taking place in the course of time, many strange things happened at home. The young King, as he grew up, proved to be very unlike his great father, and showed himself a miserable puny creature. There was no harm in him—he had a great aversion to shedding blood: which was something—but, he was a weak, silly, helpless young man, and a mere shuttlecock to the great lordly battledores about the Court.

Of these battledores, Cardinal Beaufort, a relation of the King, and the Duke of Gloucester, were at first the most powerful. The Duke of Gloucester had a wife, who was nonsensically accused of practising witchcraft to cause the King's death and lead to her husband's coming to the throne, he being the next heir. She was charged with having, by the help of a ridiculous old woman named Margery (who was called a witch), made a little waxen doll in the King's likeness, and put it before a slow fire that it might gradually melt away. It was supposed, in such cases, that the death of the person whom the doll was made to represent, was sure to happen. Whether the duchess was as ignorant as the rest of them, and really did make such a doll with such an intention, I don't know; but, you and I know very well that she might have made a thousand dolls, if she had been stupid enough, and might have melted them all, without hurting the King or anybody else. However, she was tried for it, and so was old Margery, and so was one of the duke's chaplains, who was charged with having assisted them. Both he and Margery were put to death, and the duchess, after being taken on foot and bearing a lighted candle, three times round the City, as a penance, was imprisoned for life. The duke, himself, took all this pretty quietly, and made as little stir about the matter as if he were rather glad to be rid of the duchess.

But, he was not destined to keep himself out of trouble long. The royal shuttlecock being three-and-twenty, the battledores were very anxious to get him married. The Duke of Gloucester wanted him to marry a daughter of the Count of Armagnac; but, the Cardinal and the Earl of Suffolk were all for Margaret, the daughter of the King of Sicily, who they knew was a resolute, ambitious woman and would govern the King as she chose. To make friends with this lady, the Earl of Suffolk, who went over to arrange the match, consented to accept her for the King's wife without any fortune, and even to give up the two most valuable possessions England then had in France. So, the marriage was arranged, on terms very advantageous to the lady; and Lord Suffolk brought her to England, and she was married at Westminster. On what pretence this queen and her party charged the Duke of Gloucester with high treason within a couple of years, it is impossible to make out, the matter is so confused; but, they pretended that the King's life was in danger, and they took the duke prisoner. A fortnight afterwards, he was found dead in bed (they said), and his body was shown to the people, and Lord Suffolk came in for the best part of his estates. You know by this time how strangely liable state prisoners were to sudden death.

If Cardinal Beaufort had any hand in this matter, it did him no good, for he died within six weeks; thinking it very hard and curious—at eighty years old!—that he could not live to be Pope.

This was the time when England had completed her loss of all her great French conquests. The people charged the loss principally upon the Earl of Suffolk, now a duke, who had made those easy terms about the Royal Marriage, and who, they believed, had even been bought by France. So he was impeached as a traitor, on a great number of charges, but chiefly on accusations of having aided the French King, and of designing to make his own son King of England. The Commons and the people being violent against him, the King was made (by his friends) to interpose to save him, by banishing him for five years, and proroguing the Parliament. The duke had much ado to escape from a London mob, two thousand strong, who lay in wait for him in St. Giles's fields; but, he got down to his own estates in Suffolk, and sailed away from Ipswich. Sailing across the Channel, he sent into Calais to know if he might land there; but, they kept his boat and men in the harbour, until an English ship, carrying a hundred and fifty men and called the Nicholas of the Tower, came alongside his little vessel, and ordered him on board. 'Welcome, traitor, as men say,' was the captain's grim and not very respectful salutation. He was kept on board, a prisoner, for eight-and-forty hours, and then a small boat appeared rowing toward the ship. As this boat came nearer, it was seen to have in it a block, a rusty sword, and an executioner in a black mask. The duke was handed down into it, and there his head was cut off with six strokes of the rusty sword. Then, the little boat rowed away to Dover beach, where the body was cast out, and left until the duchess claimed it. By whom, high in authority, this murder was committed, has never appeared. No one was ever punished for it.

There now arose in Kent an Irishman, who gave himself the name of

Mortimer, but whose real name was Jack Cade. Jack, in imitation of Wat Tyler, though he was a very different and inferior sort of man, addressed the Kentish men upon their wrongs, occasioned by the bad government of England, among so many battledores and such a poor shuttlecock; and the Kentish men rose up to the number of twenty thousand. Their place of assembly was Blackheath, where, headed by Jack, they put forth two papers, which they called 'The Complaint of the Commons of Kent,' and 'The Requests of the Captain of the Great Assembly in Kent.' They then retired to Sevenoaks. The royal army coming up with them here, they beat it and killed their general. Then, Jack dressed himself in the dead general's armour, and led his men to London.

Jack passed into the City from Southwark, over the bridge, and entered it in triumph, giving the strictest orders to his men not to plunder. Having made a show of his forces there, while the citizens looked on quietly, he went back into Southwark in good order, and passed the night. Next day, he came back again, having got hold in the meantime of Lord Say, an unpopular nobleman. Says Jack to the Lord Mayor and judges: 'Will you be so good as to make a tribunal in Guildhall, and try me this nobleman?' The court being hastily made, he was found guilty, and Jack and his men cut his head off on Cornhill. They also cut off the head of his son-in-law, and then went back in good order to Southwark again.

But, although the citizens could bear the beheading of an unpopular lord, they could not bear to have their houses pillaged. And it did so happen that Jack, after dinner—perhaps he had drunk a little too much—began to plunder the house where he lodged; upon which, of course, his men began to imitate him. Wherefore, the Londoners took counsel with Lord Scales, who had a thousand soldiers in the Tower; and defended London Bridge, and kept Jack and his people out. This advantage gained, it was resolved by divers great men to divide Jack's army in the old way, by making a great many promises on behalf of the state, that were never intended to be performed. This did divide them; some of Jack's men saying that they ought to take the conditions which were offered, and others saying that they ought not, for they were only a snare; some going home at once; others staying where they were; and all doubting and quarrelling among themselves.

Jack, who was in two minds about fighting or accepting a pardon, and who indeed did both, saw at last that there was nothing to expect from his men, and that it was very likely some of them would deliver him up and get a reward of a thousand marks, which was offered for his apprehension. So, after they had travelled and quarrelled all the way from Southwark to Blackheath, and from Blackheath to Rochester, he mounted a good horse and galloped away into Sussex. But, there galloped after him, on a better horse, one Alexander Iden, who came up with him, had a hard fight with him, and killed him. Jack's head was set aloft on London Bridge, with the face looking towards Blackheath, where he had raised his flag; and Alexander Iden got the thousand marks.

It is supposed by some, that the Duke of York, who had been removed from a high post abroad through the Queen's influence, and sent out of the way, to govern Ireland, was at the bottom of this rising of Jack and his men, because he wanted to trouble the government. He claimed (though not yet publicly) to have a better right to the throne than Henry of Lancaster, as one of the family of the Earl of March, whom Henry the Fourth had set aside. Touching this claim, which, being through female relationship, was not according to the usual descent, it is enough to say that Henry the Fourth was the free choice of the people and the Parliament, and that his family had now reigned undisputed for sixty years. The memory of Henry the Fifth was so famous, and the English people loved it so much, that the Duke of York's claim would, perhaps, never have been thought of (it would have been so hopeless) but for the unfortunate circumstance of the present King's being by this time quite an idiot, and the country very ill governed. These two circumstances gave the Duke of York a power he could not otherwise have had.

Whether the Duke knew anything of Jack Cade, or not, he came over from Ireland while Jack's head was on London Bridge; being secretly advised that the Queen was setting up his enemy, the Duke of Somerset, against him. He went to Westminster, at the head of four thousand men, and on his knees before the King, represented to him the bad state of the country, and petitioned him to summon a Parliament to consider it. This the King promised. When the Parliament was summoned, the Duke of York accused the Duke of Somerset, and the Duke of Somerset accused the Duke of York; and, both in and out of Parliament, the followers of each party were full of violence and hatred towards the other. At length the Duke of York put himself at the head of a large force of his tenants, and, in arms, demanded the reformation of the Government. Being shut out of London, he encamped at Dartford, and the royal army encamped at Blackheath. According as either side triumphed, the Duke of York was arrested, or the Duke of Somerset was arrested. The trouble ended, for the moment, in the Duke of York renewing his oath of allegiance, and going in peace to one of his own castles.

Half a year afterwards the Queen gave birth to a son, who was very ill received by the people, and not believed to be the son of the King. It shows the Duke of York to have been a moderate man, unwilling to involve England in new troubles, that he did not take advantage of the general discontent at this time, but really acted for the public good. He was made a member of the cabinet, and the King being now so much worse that he could not be carried about and shown to the people with any decency, the duke was made Lord Protector of the kingdom, until the King should recover, or the Prince should come of age. At the same time the Duke of Somerset was committed to the Tower. So, now the Duke of Somerset was down, and the Duke of York was up. By the end of the year, however, the King recovered his memory and some spark of sense; upon which the Queen used her power—which recovered with him—to get the Protector disgraced, and her favourite released. So now the Duke of York was down, and the Duke of Somerset was up.

These ducal ups and downs gradually separated the whole nation into the two parties of York and Lancaster, and led to those terrible civil wars long known as the Wars of the Red and White Roses, because the red rose was the badge of the House of Lancaster, and the white rose was the badge of the House of York.

The Duke of York, joined by some other powerful noblemen of the White Rose party, and leading a small army, met the King with another small army at St. Alban's, and demanded that the Duke of Somerset should be given up. The poor King, being made to say in answer that he would sooner die, was instantly attacked. The Duke of Somerset was killed, and the King himself was wounded in the neck, and took refuge in the house of a poor tanner. Whereupon, the Duke of York went to him, led him with great submission to the Abbey, and said he was very sorry for what had happened. Having now the King in his possession, he got a Parliament summoned and himself once more made Protector, but, only for a few months; for, on the King getting a little better again, the Queen and her party got him into their possession, and disgraced the Duke once more. So, now the Duke of York was down again.

Some of the best men in power, seeing the danger of these constant changes, tried even then to prevent the Red and the White Rose Wars. They brought about a great council in London between the two parties. The White Roses assembled in Blackfriars, the Red Roses in Whitefriars; and some good priests communicated between them, and made the proceedings known at evening to the King and the judges. They ended in a peaceful agreement that there should be no more quarrelling; and there was a great royal procession to St. Paul's, in which the Queen walked arm-in-arm with her old enemy, the Duke of York, to show the people how comfortable they all were. This state of peace lasted half a year, when a dispute between the Earl of Warwick (one of the Duke's powerful friends) and some of the King's servants at Court, led to an attack upon that Earl—who was a White Rose—and to a sudden breaking out of all old animosities. So, here were greater ups and downs than ever.

There were even greater ups and downs than these, soon after. After various battles, the Duke of York fled to Ireland, and his son the Earl of March to Calais, with their friends the Earls of Salisbury and Warwick; and a Parliament was held declaring them all traitors. Little the worse for this, the Earl of Warwick presently came back, landed in Kent, was joined by the Archbishop of Canterbury and other powerful noblemen and gentlemen, engaged the King's forces at Northampton, signally defeated them, and took the King himself prisoner, who was found in his tent. Warwick would have been glad, I dare say, to have taken the Queen and Prince too, but they escaped into Wales and thence into Scotland.

The King was carried by the victorious force straight to London, and made to call a new Parliament, which immediately declared that the Duke of York and those other noblemen were not traitors, but excellent subjects. Then, back comes the Duke from Ireland at the head of five hundred horsemen, rides from London to Westminster, and enters the House of Lords. There, he laid his hand upon the cloth of gold which covered the empty throne, as if he had half a mind to sit down in it—but he did not. On the Archbishop of Canterbury, asking him if he would visit the King, who was in his palace close by, he replied, 'I know no one in this country, my lord, who ought not to visit me.' None of the lords present spoke a single word; so, the duke went out as he had come in, established himself royally in the King's palace, and, six days afterwards, sent in to the Lords a formal statement of his claim to the throne. The lords went to the King on this momentous subject, and after a great deal of discussion, in which the judges and the other law officers were afraid to give an opinion on either side, the question was compromised. It was agreed that the present King should retain the crown for his life, and that it should then pass to the Duke of York and his heirs.

But, the resolute Queen, determined on asserting her son's right, would hear of no such thing. She came from Scotland to the north of England, where several powerful lords armed in her cause. The Duke of York, for his part, set off with some five thousand men, a little time before Christmas Day, one thousand four hundred and sixty, to give her battle. He lodged at Sandal Castle, near Wakefield, and the Red Roses defied him to come out on Wakefield Green, and fight them then and there. His generals said, he had best wait until his gallant son, the Earl of March, came up with his power; but, he was determined to accept the challenge. He did so, in an evil hour. He was hotly pressed on all sides, two thousand of his men lay dead on Wakefield Green, and he himself was taken prisoner. They set him down in mock state on an ant-hill, and twisted grass about his head, and pretended to pay court to him on their knees, saying, 'O King, without a kingdom, and Prince without a people, we hope your gracious Majesty is very well and happy!' They did worse than this; they cut his head off, and handed it on a pole to the Queen, who laughed with delight when she saw it (you recollect their walking so religiously and comfortably to St. Paul's!), and had it fixed, with a paper crown upon its head, on the walls of York. The Earl of Salisbury lost his head, too; and the Duke of York's second son, a handsome boy who was flying with his tutor over Wakefield Bridge, was stabbed in the heart by a murderous, lord—Lord Clifford by name—whose father had been killed by the White Roses in the fight at St. Alban's. There was awful sacrifice of life in this battle, for no quarter was given, and the Queen was wild for revenge. When men unnaturally fight against their own countrymen, they are always observed to be more unnaturally cruel and filled with rage than they are against any other enemy.

But, Lord Clifford had stabbed the second son of the Duke of York—not the first. The eldest son, Edward Earl of March, was at Gloucester; and, vowing vengeance for the death of his father, his brother, and their faithful friends, he began to march against the Queen. He had to turn and fight a great body of Welsh and Irish first, who worried his advance. These he defeated in a great fight at Mortimer's Cross, near Hereford, where he beheaded a number of the Red Roses taken in battle, in retaliation for the beheading of the White Roses at Wakefield. The Queen had the next turn of beheading. Having moved towards London, and falling in, between St. Alban's and Barnet, with the Earl of Warwick and the Duke of Norfolk, White Roses both, who were there with an army to oppose her, and had got the King with them; she defeated them with great loss, and struck off the heads of two prisoners of note, who were in the King's tent with him, and to whom the King had promised his protection. Her triumph, however, was very short. She had no treasure, and her army subsisted by plunder. This caused them to be hated and dreaded by the people, and particularly by the London people, who were wealthy. As soon as the Londoners heard that Edward, Earl of March, united with the Earl of Warwick, was advancing towards the city, they refused to send the Queen supplies, and made a great rejoicing.

The Queen and her men retreated with all speed, and Edward and Warwick came on, greeted with loud acclamations on every side. The courage, beauty, and virtues of young Edward could not be sufficiently praised by the whole people. He rode into London like a conqueror, and met with an enthusiastic welcome. A few days afterwards, Lord Falconbridge and the

Bishop of Exeter assembled the citizens in St. John's Field, Clerkenwell, and asked them if they would have Henry of Lancaster for their King? To this they all roared, 'No, no, no!' and 'King Edward! King Edward!' Then, said those noblemen, would they love and serve young Edward? To this they all cried, 'Yes, yes!' and threw up their caps and clapped their hands, and cheered tremendously.

Therefore, it was declared that by joining the Queen and not protecting those two prisoners of note, Henry of Lancaster had forfeited the crown; and Edward of York was proclaimed King. He made a great speech to the applauding people at Westminster, and sat down as sovereign of England on that throne, on the golden covering of which his father—worthy of a better fate than the bloody axe which cut the thread of so many lives in England, through so many years—had laid his hand.

CHAPTER XXIII—ENGLAND UNDER EDWARD THE FOURTH

King Edward the Fourth was not quite twenty-one years of age when he took that unquiet seat upon the throne of England. The Lancaster party, the Red Roses, were then assembling in great numbers near York, and it was necessary to give them battle instantly. But, the stout Earl of Warwick leading for the young King, and the young King himself closely following him, and the English people crowding round the Royal standard, the White and the Red Roses met, on a wild March day when the snow was falling heavily, at Towton; and there such a furious battle raged between them, that the total loss amounted to forty thousand men—all Englishmen, fighting, upon English ground, against one another. The young King gained the day, took down the heads of his father and brother from the walls of York, and put up the heads of some of the most famous noblemen engaged in the battle on the other side. Then, he went to London and was crowned with great splendour.

A new Parliament met. No fewer than one hundred and fifty of the principal noblemen and gentlemen on the Lancaster side were declared traitors, and the King—who had very little humanity, though he was handsome in person and agreeable in manners—resolved to do all he could, to pluck up the Red Rose root and branch.

Queen Margaret, however, was still active for her young son. She obtained help from Scotland and from Normandy, and took several important English castles. But, Warwick soon retook them; the Queen lost all her treasure on board ship in a great storm; and both she and her son suffered great misfortunes. Once, in the winter weather, as they were riding through a forest, they were attacked and plundered by a party of robbers; and, when they had escaped from these men and were passing alone and on foot through a thick dark part of the wood, they came, all at once, upon another robber. So the Queen, with a stout heart, took the little Prince by the hand, and going straight up to that robber, said to him, 'My friend, this is the young son of your lawful King! I confide him to your care.' The robber was surprised, but took the boy in his arms, and faithfully restored him and his mother to their friends. In the end, the Queen's soldiers being beaten and dispersed, she went abroad again, and kept quiet for the present.

Now, all this time, the deposed King Henry was concealed by a Welsh knight, who kept him close in his castle. But, next year, the Lancaster party recovering their spirits, raised a large body of men, and called him out of his retirement, to put him at their head. They were joined by some powerful noblemen who had sworn fidelity to the new King, but who were ready, as usual, to break their oaths, whenever they thought there was anything to be got by it. One of the worst things in the history of the war of the Red and White Roses, is the ease with which these noblemen, who should have set an example of honour to the people, left either side as they took slight offence, or were disappointed in their greedy expectations, and joined the other. Well! Warwick's brother soon beat the Lancastrians, and the false noblemen, being taken, were beheaded without a moment's loss of time. The deposed King had a narrow escape; three of his servants were taken, and one of them bore his cap of estate, which was set with pearls and embroidered with two golden crowns. However, the head to which the cap belonged, got safely into Lancashire, and lay pretty quietly there (the people in the secret being very true) for more than a year. At length, an old monk gave such intelligence as led to Henry's being taken while he was sitting at dinner in a place called Waddington Hall. He was immediately sent to London, and met at Islington by the Earl of Warwick, by whose directions he was put upon a horse, with his legs tied under it, and paraded three times round the pillory. Then, he was carried off to the Tower, where they treated him well enough.

The White Rose being so triumphant, the young King abandoned himself entirely to pleasure, and led a jovial life. But, thorns were springing up under his bed of roses, as he soon found out. For, having been privately married to Elizabeth Woodville, a young widow lady, very beautiful and very captivating; and at last resolving to make his secret known, and to declare her his Queen; he gave some offence to the Earl of Warwick, who was usually called the King-Maker, because of his power and influence, and because of his having lent such great help to placing Edward on the throne. This offence was not lessened by the jealousy with which the Nevil family (the Earl of Warwick's) regarded the promotion of the Woodville family. For, the young Queen was so bent on providing for her relations, that she made her father an earl and a great officer of state; married her five sisters to young noblemen of the highest rank; and provided for her younger brother, a young man of twenty, by marrying him to an immensely rich old duchess of eighty. The Earl of Warwick took all this pretty graciously for a man of his proud temper, until the question arose to whom the King's sister, Margaret, should be married. The Earl of Warwick said, 'To one of the French King's sons,' and was allowed to go over to the French King to make friendly proposals for that purpose, and to hold all manner of friendly interviews with him. But, while he was so engaged, the Woodville party married the young lady to the Duke of Burgundy! Upon this he came back in great rage and scorn, and shut himself up discontented, in his Castle of Middleham.

A reconciliation, though not a very sincere one, was patched up between the Earl of Warwick and the King, and lasted until the Earl married his daughter, against the King's wishes, to the Duke of Clarence. While the marriage was being celebrated at Calais, the people in the north of England, where the influence of the Nevil family was strongest, broke out into rebellion; their complaint was, that England was oppressed and plundered by the Woodville family, whom they demanded to have removed from power. As they were joined by great numbers of people, and as they openly declared that they were supported by the Earl of Warwick, the King did not know what to do. At last, as he wrote to the earl beseeching his aid, he and his new son-in-law came over to England, and began to arrange the business by shutting the King up in Middleham Castle in the safe keeping of the Archbishop of York; so England was not only in the strange position of having two kings at once, but they were both prisoners at the same time.

Even as yet, however, the King-Maker was so far true to the King, that he dispersed a new rising of the Lancastrians, took their leader prisoner, and brought him to the King, who ordered him to be immediately executed. He presently allowed the King to return to London, and there innumerable pledges of forgiveness and friendship were exchanged between them, and between the Nevils and the Woodvilles; the King's eldest daughter was promised in marriage to the heir of the Nevil family; and more friendly oaths were sworn, and more friendly promises made, than this book would hold.

They lasted about three months. At the end of that time, the Archbishop of York made a feast for the King, the Earl of Warwick, and the Duke of Clarence, at his house, the Moor, in Hertfordshire. The King was washing his hands before supper, when some one whispered him that a body of a hundred men were lying in ambush outside the house. Whether this were true or untrue, the King took fright, mounted his horse, and rode through the dark night to Windsor Castle. Another reconciliation was patched up between him and the King-Maker, but it was a short one, and it was the last. A new rising took place in Lincolnshire, and the King marched to repress it. Having done so, he proclaimed that both the Earl of Warwick and the Duke of Clarence were traitors, who had secretly assisted it, and who had been prepared publicly to join it on the following day. In these dangerous circumstances they both took ship and sailed away to the French court.

And here a meeting took place between the Earl of Warwick and his old enemy, the Dowager Queen Margaret, through whom his father had had his head struck off, and to whom he had been a bitter foe. But, now, when he said that he had done with the ungrateful and perfidious Edward of York, and that henceforth he devoted himself to the restoration of the House of Lancaster, either in the person of her husband or of her little son, she embraced him as if he had ever been her dearest friend. She did more than that; she married her son to his second daughter, the Lady Anne. However agreeable this marriage was to the new friends, it was very disagreeable to the Duke of Clarence, who perceived that his father-in-law, the King-Maker, would never make him King, now. So, being but a weak-minded young traitor, possessed of very little worth or sense, he readily listened to an artful court lady sent over for the purpose, and promised to turn traitor once more, and go over to his brother, King Edward, when a fitting opportunity should come.

The Earl of Warwick, knowing nothing of this, soon redeemed his promise to the Dowager Queen Margaret, by invading England and landing at Plymouth, where he instantly proclaimed King Henry, and summoned all

Englishmen between the ages of sixteen and sixty, to join his banner. Then, with his army increasing as he marched along, he went northward, and came so near King Edward, who was in that part of the country, that Edward had to ride hard for it to the coast of Norfolk, and thence to get away in such ships as he could find, to Holland. Thereupon, the triumphant King-Maker and his false son-in-law, the Duke of Clarence, went to London, took the old King out of the Tower, and walked him in a great procession to Saint Paul's Cathedral with the crown upon his head. This did not improve the temper of the Duke of Clarence, who saw himself farther off from being King than ever; but he kept his secret, and said nothing. The Nevil family were restored to all their honours and glories, and the Woodvilles and the rest were disgraced. The King-Maker, less sanguinary than the King, shed no blood except that of the Earl of Worcester, who had been so cruel to the people as to have gained the title of the Butcher. Him they caught hidden in a tree, and him they tried and executed. No other death stained the King-Maker's triumph.

To dispute this triumph, back came King Edward again, next year, landing at Ravenspur, coming on to York, causing all his men to cry 'Long live King Henry!' and swearing on the altar, without a blush, that he came to lay no claim to the crown. Now was the time for the Duke of Clarence, who ordered his men to assume the White Rose, and declare for his brother. The Marquis of Montague, though the Earl of Warwick's brother, also declining to fight against King Edward, he went on successfully to London, where the Archbishop of York let him into the City, and where the people made great demonstrations in his favour. For this they had four reasons. Firstly, there were great numbers of the King's adherents hiding in the City and ready to break out; secondly, the King owed them a great deal of money, which they could never hope to get if he were unsuccessful; thirdly, there was a young prince to inherit the crown; and fourthly, the King was gay and handsome, and more popular than a better man might have been with the City ladies. After a stay of only two days with these worthy supporters, the King marched out to Barnet Common, to give the Earl of Warwick battle. And now it was to be seen, for the last time, whether the King or the King-Maker was to carry the day.

While the battle was yet pending, the fainthearted Duke of Clarence began to repent, and sent over secret messages to his father-in-law, offering his services in mediation with the King. But, the Earl of Warwick disdainfully rejected them, and replied that Clarence was false and perjured, and that he would settle the quarrel by the sword. The battle began at four o'clock in the morning and lasted until ten, and during the greater part of the time it was fought in a thick mist—absurdly supposed to be raised by a magician. The loss of life was very great, for the hatred was strong on both sides. The King-Maker was defeated, and the King triumphed. Both the Earl of Warwick and his brother were slain, and their bodies lay in St. Paul's, for some days, as a spectacle to the people.

Margaret's spirit was not broken even by this great blow. Within five days she was in arms again, and raised her standard in Bath, whence she set off with her army, to try and join Lord Pembroke, who had a force in Wales. But, the King, coming up with her outside the town of Tewkesbury, and ordering his brother, the Duke of Gloucester, who was a brave soldier, to attack her men, she sustained an entire defeat, and was taken prisoner, together with her son, now only eighteen years of age. The conduct of the King to this poor youth was worthy of his cruel character. He ordered him to be led into his tent. 'And what,' said he, 'brought you to England?' 'I came to England,' replied the prisoner, with a spirit which a man of spirit might have admired in a captive, 'to recover my father's kingdom, which descended to him as his right, and from him descends to me, as mine.' The King, drawing off his iron gauntlet, struck him with it in the face; and the Duke of Clarence and some other lords, who were there, drew their noble swords, and killed him.

His mother survived him, a prisoner, for five years; after her ransom by the King of France, she survived for six years more. Within three weeks of this murder, Henry died one of those convenient sudden deaths which were so common in the Tower; in plainer words, he was murdered by the King's order.

Having no particular excitement on his hands after this great defeat of the Lancaster party, and being perhaps desirous to get rid of some of his fat (for he was now getting too corpulent to be handsome), the King thought of making war on France. As he wanted more money for this purpose than the

Parliament could give him, though they were usually ready enough for war, he invented a new way of raising it, by sending for the principal citizens of London, and telling them, with a grave face, that he was very much in want of cash, and would take it very kind in them if they would lend him some. It being impossible for them safely to refuse, they complied, and the moneys thus forced from them were called—no doubt to the great amusement of the King and the Court—as if they were free gifts, 'Benevolences.' What with grants from Parliament, and what with Benevolences, the King raised an army and passed over to Calais. As nobody wanted war, however, the French King made proposals of peace, which were accepted, and a truce was concluded for seven long years. The proceedings between the Kings of France and England on this occasion, were very friendly, very splendid, and very distrustful. They finished with a meeting between the two Kings, on a temporary bridge over the river Somme, where they embraced through two holes in a strong wooden grating like a lion's cage, and made several bows and fine speeches to one another.

It was time, now, that the Duke of Clarence should be punished for his treacheries; and Fate had his punishment in store. He was, probably, not trusted by the King—for who could trust him who knew him!—and he had certainly a powerful opponent in his brother Richard, Duke of Gloucester, who, being avaricious and ambitious, wanted to marry that widowed daughter of the Earl of Warwick's who had been espoused to the deceased young Prince, at Calais. Clarence, who wanted all the family wealth for himself, secreted this lady, whom Richard found disguised as a servant in the City of London, and whom he married; arbitrators appointed by the King, then divided the property between the brothers. This led to ill-will and mistrust between them. Clarence's wife dying, and he wishing to make another marriage, which was obnoxious to the King, his ruin was hurried by that means, too. At first, the Court struck at his retainers and dependents, and accused some of them of magic and witchcraft, and similar nonsense. Successful against this small game, it then mounted to the Duke himself, who was impeached by his brother the King, in person, on a variety of such charges. He was found guilty, and sentenced to be publicly executed. He never was publicly executed, but he met his death somehow, in the Tower, and, no doubt, through some agency of the King or his brother Gloucester, or both. It was supposed at the time that he was told to choose the manner of his death, and that he chose to be drowned in a butt of Malmsey wine. I hope the story may be true, for it would have been a becoming death for such a miserable creature.

The King survived him some five years. He died in the forty-second year of his life, and the twenty-third of his reign. He had a very good capacity and some good points, but he was selfish, careless, sensual, and cruel. He was a favourite with the people for his showy manners; and the people were a good example to him in the constancy of their attachment. He was penitent on his death-bed for his 'benevolences,' and other extortions, and ordered restitution to be made to the people who had suffered from them. He also called about his bed the enriched members of the Woodville family, and the proud lords whose honours were of older date, and endeavoured to reconcile them, for the sake of the peaceful succession of his son and the tranquillity of England.

CHAPTER XXIV—ENGLAND UNDER EDWARD THE FIFTH

The late King's eldest son, the Prince of Wales, called Edward after him, was only thirteen years of age at his father's death. He was at Ludlow Castle with his uncle, the Earl of Rivers. The prince's brother, the Duke of York, only eleven years of age, was in London with his mother. The boldest, most crafty, and most dreaded nobleman in England at that time was their uncle Richard, Duke of Gloucester, and everybody wondered how the two poor boys would fare with such an uncle for a friend or a foe.

The Queen, their mother, being exceedingly uneasy about this, was anxious that instructions should be sent to Lord Rivers to raise an army to escort the young King safely to London. But, Lord Hastings, who was of the Court party opposed to the Woodvilles, and who disliked the thought of giving them that power, argued against the proposal, and obliged the Queen to be satisfied with an escort of two thousand horse. The Duke of Gloucester did nothing, at first, to justify suspicion. He came from Scotland (where he was commanding an army) to York, and was there the first to swear allegiance to his nephew. He then wrote a condoling letter to the Queen-Mother, and set off to be present at the coronation in London.

Now, the young King, journeying towards London too, with Lord Rivers and Lord Gray, came to Stony Stratford, as his uncle came to Northampton, about ten miles distant; and when those two lords heard that the Duke of Gloucester was so near, they proposed to the young King that they should go back and greet him in his name. The boy being very willing that they should do so, they rode off and were received with great friendliness, and asked by the Duke of Gloucester to stay and dine with him. In the evening, while they were merry together, up came the Duke of Buckingham with three hundred horsemen; and next morning the two lords and the two dukes, and the three hundred horsemen, rode away together to rejoin the King. Just as they were entering Stony Stratford, the Duke of Gloucester, checking his horse, turned suddenly on the two lords, charged them with alienating from him the affections of his sweet nephew, and caused them to be arrested by the three hundred horsemen and taken back. Then, he and the Duke of Buckingham went straight to the King (whom they had now in their power), to whom they made a show of kneeling down, and offering great love and submission; and then they ordered his attendants to disperse, and took him, alone with them, to Northampton.

A few days afterwards they conducted him to London, and lodged him in the Bishop's Palace. But, he did not remain there long; for, the Duke of Buckingham with a tender face made a speech expressing how anxious he was for the Royal boy's safety, and how much safer he would be in the Tower until his coronation, than he could be anywhere else. So, to the Tower he was taken, very carefully, and the Duke of Gloucester was named Protector of the State.

Although Gloucester had proceeded thus far with a very smooth countenance—and although he was a clever man, fair of speech, and not ill-looking, in spite of one of his shoulders being something higher than the other—and although he had come into the City riding bare-headed at the King's side, and looking very fond of him—he had made the King's mother more uneasy yet; and when the Royal boy was taken to the Tower, she became so alarmed that she took sanctuary in Westminster with her five daughters.

Nor did she do this without reason, for, the Duke of Gloucester, finding that the lords who were opposed to the Woodville family were faithful to the young King nevertheless, quickly resolved to strike a blow for himself. Accordingly, while those lords met in council at the Tower, he and those who were in his interest met in separate council at his own residence, Crosby Palace, in Bishopsgate Street. Being at last quite prepared, he one day appeared unexpectedly at the council in the Tower, and appeared to be very jocular and merry. He was particularly gay with the Bishop of Ely: praising the strawberries that grew in his garden on Holborn Hill, and asking him to have some gathered that he might eat them at dinner. The Bishop, quite proud of the honour, sent one of his men to fetch some; and the Duke, still very jocular and gay, went out; and the council all said what a very agreeable duke he was! In a little time, however, he came back quite altered—not at all jocular—frowning and fierce—and suddenly said,—

'What do those persons deserve who have compassed my destruction; I being the King's lawful, as well as natural, protector?'

To this strange question, Lord Hastings replied, that they deserved death, whosoever they were.

'Then,' said the Duke, 'I tell you that they are that sorceress my brother's wife;' meaning the Queen: 'and that other sorceress, Jane Shore. Who, by witchcraft, have withered my body, and caused my arm to shrink as I now show you.'

He then pulled up his sleeve and showed them his arm, which was shrunken, it is true, but which had been so, as they all very well knew, from the hour of his birth.

Jane Shore, being then the lover of Lord Hastings, as she had formerly been of the late King, that lord knew that he himself was attacked. So, he said, in some confusion, 'Certainly, my Lord, if they have done this, they be worthy of punishment.'

'If?' said the Duke of Gloucester; 'do you talk to me of ifs? I tell you that they have so done, and I will make it good upon thy body, thou traitor!'

With that, he struck the table a great blow with his fist. This was a signal to some of his people outside to cry 'Treason!' They immediately did so, and there was a rush into the chamber of so many armed men that it was filled in a moment.

'First,' said the Duke of Gloucester to Lord Hastings, 'I arrest thee, traitor! And let him,' he added to the armed men who took him, 'have a priest at once, for by St. Paul I will not dine until I have seen his head off!'

Lord Hastings was hurried to the green by the Tower chapel, and there beheaded on a log of wood that happened to be lying on the ground. Then, the Duke dined with a good appetite, and after dinner summoning the principal citizens to attend him, told them that Lord Hastings and the rest had designed to murder both himself and the Duke if Buckingham, who stood by his side, if he had not providentially discovered their design. He requested them to be so obliging as to inform their fellow-citizens of the truth of what he said, and issued a proclamation (prepared and neatly copied out beforehand) to the same effect.

On the same day that the Duke did these things in the Tower, Sir Richard Ratcliffe, the boldest and most undaunted of his men, went down to Pontefract; arrested Lord Rivers, Lord Gray, and two other gentlemen; and publicly executed them on the scaffold, without any trial, for having intended the Duke's death. Three days afterwards the Duke, not to lose time, went down the river to Westminster in his barge, attended by divers bishops, lords, and soldiers, and demanded that the Queen should deliver her second son, the Duke of York, into his safe keeping. The Queen, being obliged to comply, resigned the child after she had wept over him; and Richard of Gloucester placed him with his brother in the Tower. Then, he seized Jane Shore, and, because she had been the lover of the late King, confiscated her property, and got her sentenced to do public penance in the streets by walking in a scanty dress, with bare feet, and carrying a lighted candle, to St. Paul's Cathedral, through the most crowded part of the City.

Having now all things ready for his own advancement, he caused a friar to preach a sermon at the cross which stood in front of St. Paul's Cathedral, in which he dwelt upon the profligate manners of the late King, and upon the late shame of Jane Shore, and hinted that the princes were not his children. 'Whereas, good people,' said the friar, whose name was Shaw, 'my Lord the Protector, the noble Duke of Gloucester, that sweet prince, the pattern of all the noblest virtues, is the perfect image and express likeness of his father.' There had been a little plot between the Duke and the friar, that the Duke should appear in the crowd at this moment, when it was expected that the people would cry 'Long live King Richard!' But, either through the friar saying the words too soon, or through the Duke's coming too late, the Duke and the words did not come together, and the people only laughed, and the friar sneaked off ashamed.

The Duke of Buckingham was a better hand at such business than the friar, so he went to the Guildhall the next day, and addressed the citizens

232

in the Lord Protector's behalf. A few dirty men, who had been hired and stationed there for the purpose, crying when he had done, 'God save King Richard!' he made them a great bow, and thanked them with all his heart. Next day, to make an end of it, he went with the mayor and some lords and citizens to Bayard Castle, by the river, where Richard then was, and read an address, humbly entreating him to accept the Crown of England. Richard, who looked down upon them out of a window and pretended to be in great uneasiness and alarm, assured them there was nothing he desired less, and that his deep affection for his nephews forbade him to think of it. To this the Duke of Buckingham replied, with pretended warmth, that the free people of England would never submit to his nephew's rule, and that if Richard, who was the lawful heir, refused the Crown, why then they must find some one else to wear it. The Duke of Gloucester returned, that since he used that strong language, it became his painful duty to think no more of himself, and to accept the Crown.

Upon that, the people cheered and dispersed; and the Duke of Gloucester and the Duke of Buckingham passed a pleasant evening, talking over the play they had just acted with so much success, and every word of which they had prepared together.

CHAPTER XXV—ENGLAND UNDER RICHARD THE THIRD

King Richard the Third was up betimes in the morning, and went to Westminster Hall. In the Hall was a marble seat, upon which he sat himself down between two great noblemen, and told the people that he began the new reign in that place, because the first duty of a sovereign was to administer the laws equally to all, and to maintain justice. He then mounted his horse and rode back to the City, where he was received by the clergy and the crowd as if he really had a right to the throne, and really were a just man. The clergy and the crowd must have been rather ashamed of themselves in secret, I think, for being such poor-spirited knaves.

The new King and his Queen were soon crowned with a great deal of show and noise, which the people liked very much; and then the King set forth on a royal progress through his dominions. He was crowned a second time at York, in order that the people might have show and noise enough; and wherever he went was received with shouts of rejoicing—from a good many people of strong lungs, who were paid to strain their throats in crying, 'God save King Richard!' The plan was so successful that I am told it has been imitated since, by other usurpers, in other progresses through other dominions.

While he was on this journey, King Richard stayed a week at Warwick. And from Warwick he sent instructions home for one of the wickedest murders that ever was done—the murder of the two young princes, his nephews, who were shut up in the Tower of London.

Sir Robert Brackenbury was at that time Governor of the Tower. To him, by the hands of a messenger named John Green, did King Richard send a letter, ordering him by some means to put the two young princes to death. But Sir Robert—I hope because he had children of his own, and loved them—sent John Green back again, riding and spurring along the dusty roads, with the answer that he could not do so horrible a piece of work. The King, having frowningly considered a little, called to him Sir James Tyrrel, his master of the horse, and to him gave authority to take command of the Tower, whenever he would, for twenty-four hours, and to keep all the keys of the Tower during that space of time. Tyrrel, well knowing what was wanted, looked about him for two hardened ruffians, and chose John Dighton, one of his own grooms, and Miles Forest, who was a murderer by trade. Having secured these two assistants, he went, upon a day in August, to the Tower, showed his authority from the King, took the command for four-and-twenty hours, and obtained possession of the keys. And when the black night came he went creeping, creeping, like a guilty villain as he was, up the dark, stone winding stairs, and along the dark stone passages, until he came to the door of the room where the two young princes, having said their prayers, lay fast asleep, clasped in each other's arms. And while he watched and listened at the door, he sent in those evil demons, John Dighton and Miles Forest, who smothered the two princes with the bed and pillows, and carried their bodies down the stairs, and buried them under a great heap of stones at the staircase foot. And when the day came, he gave up the command of the Tower, and restored the keys, and hurried away without once looking behind him; and Sir Robert Brackenbury went with fear and sadness to the princes' room, and found the princes gone for ever.

You know, through all this history, how true it is that traitors are never true, and you will not be surprised to learn that the Duke of Buckingham soon turned against King Richard, and joined a great conspiracy that was formed to dethrone him, and to place the crown upon its rightful owner's head. Richard had meant to keep the murder secret; but when he heard through his spies that this conspiracy existed, and that many lords and gentlemen drank in secret to the healths of the two young princes in the Tower, he made it known that they were dead. The conspirators, though thwarted for a moment, soon resolved to set up for the crown against the murderous Richard, Henry Earl of Richmond, grandson of Catherine: that widow of Henry the Fifth who married Owen Tudor. And as Henry was of the house of Lancaster, they proposed that he should marry the Princess Elizabeth, the eldest daughter of the late King, now the heiress of the house of York, and thus by uniting the rival families put an end to the fatal wars of the Red and White Roses. All being settled, a time was appointed for Henry to come over from Brittany, and for a great rising against Richard to take place in several parts of England at the same hour. On a certain day, therefore, in October, the revolt took place; but unsuccessfully. Richard was prepared, Henry was driven back at sea by a storm, his followers in England were dispersed, and the Duke of Buckingham was taken, and at once beheaded in the market-place at Salisbury.

The time of his success was a good time, Richard thought, for summoning a Parliament and getting some money. So, a Parliament was called, and it flattered and fawned upon him as much as he could possibly desire, and declared him to be the rightful King of England, and his only son Edward, then eleven years of age, the next heir to the throne.

Richard knew full well that, let the Parliament say what it would, the Princess Elizabeth was remembered by people as the heiress of the house of York; and having accurate information besides, of its being designed by the conspirators to marry her to Henry of Richmond, he felt that it would much strengthen him and weaken them, to be beforehand with them, and marry her to his son. With this view he went to the Sanctuary at Westminster, where the late King's widow and her daughter still were, and besought them to come to Court: where (he swore by anything and everything) they should be safely and honourably entertained. They came, accordingly, but had scarcely been at Court a month when his son died suddenly—or was poisoned—and his plan was crushed to pieces.

In this extremity, King Richard, always active, thought, 'I must make another plan.' And he made the plan of marrying the Princess Elizabeth himself, although she was his niece. There was one difficulty in the way: his wife, the Queen Anne, was alive. But, he knew (remembering his nephews) how to remove that obstacle, and he made love to the Princess Elizabeth, telling her he felt perfectly confident that the Queen would die in February. The Princess was not a very scrupulous young lady, for, instead of rejecting the murderer of her brothers with scorn and hatred, she openly declared she loved him dearly; and, when February came and the Queen did not die, she expressed her impatient opinion that she was too long about it. However, King Richard was not so far out in his prediction, but, that she died in March—he took good care of that—and then this precious pair hoped to

236

be married. But they were disappointed, for the idea of such a marriage was so unpopular in the country, that the King's chief counsellors, Ratcliffe and Catesby, would by no means undertake to propose it, and the King was even obliged to declare in public that he had never thought of such a thing.

He was, by this time, dreaded and hated by all classes of his subjects. His nobles deserted every day to Henry's side; he dared not call another Parliament, lest his crimes should be denounced there; and for want of money, he was obliged to get Benevolences from the citizens, which exasperated them all against him. It was said too, that, being stricken by his conscience, he dreamed frightful dreams, and started up in the night-time, wild with terror and remorse. Active to the last, through all this, he issued vigorous proclamations against Henry of Richmond and all his followers, when he heard that they were coming against him with a Fleet from France; and took the field as fierce and savage as a wild boar—the animal represented on his shield.

Henry of Richmond landed with six thousand men at Milford Haven, and came on against King Richard, then encamped at Leicester with an army twice as great, through North Wales. On Bosworth Field the two armies met; and Richard, looking along Henry's ranks, and seeing them crowded with the English nobles who had abandoned him, turned pale when he beheld the powerful Lord Stanley and his son (whom he had tried hard to retain) among them. But, he was as brave as he was wicked, and plunged into the thickest of the fight. He was riding hither and thither, laying about him in all directions, when he observed the Earl of Northumberland—one of his few great allies—to stand inactive, and the main body of his troops to hesitate. At the same moment, his desperate glance caught Henry of Richmond among a little group of his knights. Riding hard at him, and crying 'Treason!' he killed his standard-bearer, fiercely unhorsed another gentleman, and aimed a powerful stroke at Henry himself, to cut him down. But, Sir William Stanley parried it as it fell, and before Richard could raise his arm again, he was borne down in a press of numbers, unhorsed, and killed. Lord Stanley picked up the crown, all bruised and trampled, and stained with blood, and put it upon Richmond's head, amid loud and rejoicing cries of 'Long live King Henry!'

That night, a horse was led up to the church of the Grey Friars at Leicester; across whose back was tied, like some worthless sack, a naked body brought there for burial. It was the body of the last of the Plantagenet line, King Richard the Third, usurper and murderer, slain at the battle of Bosworth Field in the thirty-second year of his age, after a reign of two years.

CHAPTER XXVI—ENGLAND UNDER HENRY THE SEVENTH

King Henry the Seventh did not turn out to be as fine a fellow as the nobility and people hoped, in the first joy of their deliverance from Richard the Third. He was very cold, crafty, and calculating, and would do almost anything for money. He possessed considerable ability, but his chief merit appears to have been that he was not cruel when there was nothing to be got by it.

The new King had promised the nobles who had espoused his cause that he would marry the Princess Elizabeth. The first thing he did, was, to direct her to be removed from the castle of Sheriff Hutton in Yorkshire, where Richard had placed her, and restored to the care of her mother in London. The young Earl of Warwick, Edward Plantagenet, son and heir of the late Duke of Clarence, had been kept a prisoner in the same old Yorkshire Castle with her. This boy, who was now fifteen, the new King placed in the Tower for safety. Then he came to London in great state, and gratified the people with a fine procession; on which kind of show he often very much relied for keeping them in good humour. The sports and feasts which took place were followed by a terrible fever, called the Sweating Sickness; of which great numbers of people died. Lord Mayors and Aldermen are thought to have suffered most from it; whether, because they were in the habit of over-eating themselves, or because they were very jealous of preserving filth and nuisances in the City (as they have been since), I don't know.

The King's coronation was postponed on account of the general ill-health, and he afterwards deferred his marriage, as if he were not very anxious that it should take place: and, even after that, deferred the Queen's coronation so long that he gave offence to the York party. However, he set these things right in the end, by hanging some men and seizing on the rich possessions of others; by granting more popular pardons to the followers of the late King than could, at first, be got from him; and, by employing about his Court, some very scrupulous persons who had been employed in the previous reign.

As this reign was principally remarkable for two very curious impostures which have become famous in history, we will make those two stories its principal feature.

There was a priest at Oxford of the name of Simons, who had for a pupil a handsome boy named Lambert Simnel, the son of a baker. Partly to gratify his own ambitious ends, and partly to carry out the designs of a secret party formed against the King, this priest declared that his pupil, the boy, was no other than the young Earl of Warwick; who (as everybody might have known) was safely locked up in the Tower of London. The priest and the boy went over to Ireland; and, at Dublin, enlisted in their cause all ranks of the people: who seem to have been generous enough, but exceedingly irrational. The Earl of Kildare, the governor of Ireland, declared that he believed the boy to be what the priest represented; and the boy, who had been well tutored by the priest, told them such things of his childhood, and gave them so many descriptions of the Royal Family, that they were perpetually shouting and hurrahing, and drinking his health, and making all kinds of noisy and thirsty demonstrations, to express their belief in him. Nor was this feeling confined to Ireland alone, for the Earl of Lincoln—whom the late usurper had named as his successor—went over to the young Pretender; and, after holding a secret correspondence with the Dowager Duchess of Burgundy—the sister of Edward the Fourth, who detested the present King and all his race—sailed to Dublin with two thousand German soldiers of her providing. In this promising state of the boy's fortunes, he was crowned there, with a crown taken off the head of a statue of the Virgin Mary; and was then, according to the Irish custom of those days, carried home on the shoulders of a big chieftain possessing a great deal more strength than sense. Father Simons, you may be sure, was mighty busy at the coronation.

Ten days afterwards, the Germans, and the Irish, and the priest, and the boy, and the Earl of Lincoln, all landed in Lancashire to invade England. The King, who had good intelligence of their movements, set up his standard at Nottingham, where vast numbers resorted to him every day; while the Earl of Lincoln could gain but very few. With his small force he tried to make for the town of Newark; but the King's army getting between him and that place, he had no choice but to risk a battle at Stoke. It soon ended in the complete destruction of the Pretender's forces, one half of whom were killed; among them, the Earl himself. The priest and the baker's boy were taken prisoners. The priest, after confessing the trick, was shut up in prison, where he afterwards died—suddenly perhaps. The boy was taken into the King's kitchen and made a turnspit. He was afterwards raised to the station of one of the King's falconers; and so ended this strange imposition.

There seems reason to suspect that the Dowager Queen—always a restless and busy woman—had had some share in tutoring the baker's son. The King was very angry with her, whether or no. He seized upon her property, and shut her up in a convent at Bermondsey.

One might suppose that the end of this story would have put the Irish people on their guard; but they were quite ready to receive a second impostor, as they had received the first, and that same troublesome Duchess of Burgundy soon gave them the opportunity. All of a sudden there appeared at Cork, in a vessel arriving from Portugal, a young man of excellent abilities, of very handsome appearance and most winning manners, who declared himself to be Richard, Duke of York, the second son of King Edward the Fourth. 'O,' said some, even of those ready Irish believers, 'but surely that young Prince was murdered by his uncle in the Tower!'—'It is supposed so,' said the engaging young man; 'and my brother was killed in that gloomy prison; but I escaped—it don't matter how, at present—and have been wandering about the world for seven long years.' This explanation being quite satisfactory to numbers of the Irish people, they began again to shout and to hurrah, and to drink his health, and to make the noisy and thirsty demonstrations all over again. And the big chieftain in Dublin began to look out for another coronation, and another young King to be carried home on his back.

Now, King Henry being then on bad terms with France, the French King, Charles the Eighth, saw that, by pretending to believe in the handsome young man, he could trouble his enemy sorely. So, he invited him over to the French Court, and appointed him a body-guard, and treated him in all respects as if he really were the Duke of York. Peace, however, being soon concluded between the two Kings, the pretended Duke was turned adrift, and wandered for protection to the Duchess of Burgundy. She, after feigning to inquire into the reality of his claims, declared him to be the very picture of her dear departed brother; gave him a body-guard at her Court, of thirty halberdiers; and called him by the sounding name of the White Rose of England.

The leading members of the White Rose party in England sent over an agent, named Sir Robert Clifford, to ascertain whether the White Rose's claims were good: the King also sent over his agents to inquire into the Rose's history. The White Roses declared the young man to be really the Duke of York; the King declared him to be Perkin Warbeck, the son of a merchant of the city of Tournay, who had acquired his knowledge of England, its language and manners, from the English merchants who traded in Flanders; it was also stated by the Royal agents that he had been in the service of Lady Brompton, the wife of an exiled English nobleman, and that the Duchess of Burgundy had caused him to be trained and taught, expressly for this deception. The King then required the Archduke Philip—who was the sovereign of Burgundy—to banish this new Pretender, or to deliver him up; but, as the Archduke replied that he could not control the Duchess in her own land, the King, in revenge, took the market of English cloth away from Antwerp, and prevented all commercial intercourse between the two countries.

He also, by arts and bribes, prevailed on Sir Robert Clifford to betray his employers; and he denouncing several famous English noblemen as being secretly the friends of Perkin Warbeck, the King had three of the foremost executed at once. Whether he pardoned the remainder because they were poor, I do not know; but it is only too probable that he refused to pardon one famous nobleman against whom the same Clifford soon afterwards informed separately, because he was rich. This was no other than Sir William Stanley, who had saved the King's life at the battle of Bosworth Field. It is very doubtful whether his treason amounted to much more than his having said, that if he were sure the young man was the Duke of York, he would not take arms against him. Whatever he had done he admitted, like an honourable spirit; and he lost his head for it, and the covetous King gained all his wealth.

Perkin Warbeck kept quiet for three years; but, as the Flemings began to complain heavily of the loss of their trade by the stoppage of the Antwerp market on his account, and as it was not unlikely that they might even go so far as to take his life, or give him up, he found it necessary to do something. Accordingly he made a desperate sally, and landed, with only a few hundred men, on the coast of Deal. But he was soon glad to get back to the place from whence he came; for the country people rose against his followers, killed a great many, and took a hundred and fifty prisoners: who were all driven to London, tied together with ropes, like a team of cattle. Every one of them was hanged on some part or other of the sea-shore; in order, that if any more men should come over with Perkin Warbeck, they might see the bodies as a warning before they landed.

Then the wary King, by making a treaty of commerce with the Flemings, drove Perkin Warbeck out of that country; and, by completely gaining over the Irish to his side, deprived him of that asylum too. He wandered away to Scotland, and told his story at that Court. King James the Fourth of Scotland, who was no friend to King Henry, and had no reason to be (for King Henry had bribed his Scotch lords to betray him more than once; but had never succeeded in his plots), gave him a great reception, called him his cousin, and gave him in marriage the Lady Catherine Gordon, a beautiful and charming creature related to the royal house of Stuart.

Alarmed by this successful reappearance of the Pretender, the King still undermined, and bought, and bribed, and kept his doings and Perkin Warbeck's story in the dark, when he might, one would imagine, have rendered the matter clear to all England. But, for all this bribing of the Scotch lords at the Scotch King's Court, he could not procure the Pretender to be delivered up to him. James, though not very particular in many respects, would not betray him; and the ever-busy Duchess of Burgundy so provided him with arms, and good soldiers, and with money besides, that he had soon a little army of fifteen hundred men of various nations. With these, and aided by the Scottish King in person, he crossed the border into England, and made a proclamation to the people, in which he called the King 'Henry Tudor;' offered large rewards to any who should take or distress him; and announced himself as King Richard the Fourth come to receive the homage of his faithful subjects. His faithful subjects, however, cared nothing for him, and hated his faithful troops: who, being of different nations, quarrelled also among themselves. Worse than this, if worse were possible, they began to plunder the country; upon which the White Rose said, that he would rather lose his rights, than gain them through the miseries of the English people. The Scottish King made a jest of his scruples; but they and their whole force went back again without fighting a battle.

The worst consequence of this attempt was, that a rising took place among the people of Cornwall, who considered themselves too heavily taxed to meet the charges of the expected war. Stimulated by Flammock, a lawyer, and Joseph, a blacksmith, and joined by Lord Audley and some other country gentlemen, they marched on all the way to Deptford Bridge, where they fought a battle with the King's army. They were defeated—though the Cornish men fought with great bravery—and the lord was beheaded, and the lawyer and the blacksmith were hanged, drawn, and quartered. The rest were pardoned. The King, who believed every man to be as avaricious as himself, and thought that money could settle anything, allowed them to make bargains for their liberty with the soldiers who had taken them.

Perkin Warbeck, doomed to wander up and down, and never to find rest anywhere—a sad fate: almost a sufficient punishment for an imposture, which he seems in time to have half believed himself—lost his Scottish refuge through a truce being made between the two Kings; and found himself, once more, without a country before him in which he could lay his head. But James (always honourable and true to him, alike when he melted down his plate, and even the great gold chain he had been used to wear, to pay soldiers in his cause; and now, when that cause was lost and hopeless) did not conclude the treaty, until he had safely departed out of the Scottish dominions. He, and his beautiful wife, who was faithful to him under all reverses, and left her state and home to follow his poor fortunes, were put aboard ship with everything necessary for their comfort and protection, and sailed for Ireland.

But, the Irish people had had enough of counterfeit Earls of Warwick and Dukes of York, for one while; and would give the White Rose no aid. So, the White Rose—encircled by thorns indeed—resolved to go with his beautiful wife to Cornwall as a forlorn resource, and see what might be made of the Cornish men, who had risen so valiantly a little while before, and who had fought so bravely at Deptford Bridge.

To Whitsand Bay, in Cornwall, accordingly, came Perkin Warbeck and his wife; and the lovely lady he shut up for safety in the Castle of St. Michael's Mount, and then marched into Devonshire at the head of three thousand Cornishmen. These were increased to six thousand by the time of his arrival in Exeter; but, there the people made a stout resistance, and he went on to Taunton, where he came in sight of the King's army. The stout Cornish men, although they were few in number, and badly armed, were so bold, that they never thought of retreating; but bravely looked forward to a battle on the morrow. Unhappily for them, the man who was possessed of so many engaging qualities, and who attracted so many people to his side when he had nothing else with which to tempt them, was not as brave as they. In the night, when the two armies lay opposite to each other, he mounted a swift horse and fled. When morning dawned, the poor confiding Cornish men, discovering that they had no leader, surrendered to the King's power. Some of them were hanged, and the rest were pardoned and went miserably home.

Before the King pursued Perkin Warbeck to the sanctuary of Beaulieu in the New Forest, where it was soon known that he had taken refuge, he sent a body of horsemen to St. Michael's Mount, to seize his wife. She was soon taken and brought as a captive before the King. But she was so beautiful, and so good, and so devoted to the man in whom she believed, that the King regarded her with compassion, treated her with great respect, and placed her at Court, near the Queen's person. And many years after Perkin Warbeck was no more, and when his strange story had become like a nursery tale, she was called the White Rose, by the people, in remembrance of her beauty.

The sanctuary at Beaulieu was soon surrounded by the King's men; and the King, pursuing his usual dark, artful ways, sent pretended friends to Perkin Warbeck to persuade him to come out and surrender himself. This he soon did; the King having taken a good look at the man of whom he had heard so much—from behind a screen—directed him to be well mounted, and to ride behind him at a little distance, guarded, but not bound in any way. So they entered London with the King's favourite show—a procession; and some of the people hooted as the Pretender rode slowly through the streets to the Tower; but the greater part were quiet, and very curious to see him. From the Tower, he was taken to the Palace at Westminster, and there lodged like a gentleman, though closely watched. He was examined every now and then as to his imposture; but the King was so secret in all he did, that even then he gave it a consequence, which it cannot be supposed to have in itself deserved.

At last Perkin Warbeck ran away, and took refuge in another sanctuary near Richmond in Surrey. From this he was again persuaded to deliver himself up; and, being conveyed to London, he stood in the stocks for a whole day, outside Westminster Hall, and there read a paper purporting to be his full confession, and relating his history as the King's agents had originally described it. He was then shut up in the Tower again, in the company of the Earl of Warwick, who had now been there for fourteen years: ever since his removal out of Yorkshire, except when the King had had him at Court, and had shown him to the people, to prove the imposture of the Baker's boy. It is but too probable, when we consider the crafty character of Henry the Seventh, that these two were brought together for a cruel purpose. A plot was soon discovered between them and the keepers, to murder the Governor, get possession of the keys, and proclaim Perkin Warbeck as King Richard the Fourth. That there was some such plot, is likely; that they were tempted into it, is at least as likely; that the unfortunate Earl of Warwick—last male of the Plantagenet line—was too unused to the world, and too ignorant and simple to know much about it, whatever it was, is perfectly certain; and that it was the King's interest to get rid of him, is no less so. He was beheaded on Tower Hill, and Perkin Warbeck was hanged at Tyburn.

Such was the end of the pretended Duke of York, whose shadowy history was made more shadowy—and ever will be—by the mystery and craft of the King. If he had turned his great natural advantages to a more honest account, he might have lived a happy and respected life, even in those days. But he died upon a gallows at Tyburn, leaving the Scottish lady, who had loved him so well, kindly protected at the Queen's Court. After some time she forgot her old loves and troubles, as many people do with Time's merciful assistance, and married a Welsh gentleman. Her second husband, Sir Matthew Cradoc, more honest and more happy than her first, lies beside her in a tomb in the old church of Swansea.

The ill-blood between France and England in this reign, arose out of the continued plotting of the Duchess of Burgundy, and disputes respecting the affairs of Brittany. The King feigned to be very patriotic, indignant, and warlike; but he always contrived so as never to make war in reality, and always to make money. His taxation of the people, on pretence of war with France, involved, at one time, a very dangerous insurrection, headed by Sir John Egremont, and a common man called John à Chambre. But it was subdued by the royal forces, under the command of the Earl of Surrey. The knighted John escaped to the Duchess of Burgundy, who was ever ready to receive any one who gave the King trouble; and the plain John was hanged at York, in the midst of a number of his men, but on a much higher gibbet, as being a greater traitor. Hung high or hung low, however, hanging is much the same to the person hung.

Within a year after her marriage, the Queen had given birth to a son, who was called Prince Arthur, in remembrance of the old British prince of romance and story; and who, when all these events had happened, being then in his fifteenth year, was married to Catherine, the daughter of the Spanish monarch, with great rejoicings and bright prospects; but in a very few months he sickened and died. As soon as the King had recovered from his grief, he thought it a pity that the fortune of the Spanish Princess, amounting to two hundred thousand crowns, should go out of the family; and therefore arranged that the young widow should marry his second son Henry, then twelve years of age, when he too should be fifteen. There were objections to this marriage on the part of the clergy; but, as the infallible Pope was gained over, and, as he must be right, that settled the business for the time. The King's eldest daughter was provided for, and a long course of disturbance was considered to be set at rest, by her being married to the Scottish King.

And now the Queen died. When the King had got over that grief too, his mind once more reverted to his darling money for consolation, and he thought of marrying the Dowager Queen of Naples, who was immensely rich: but, as it turned out not to be practicable to gain the money however practicable it might have been to gain the lady, he gave up the idea. He was not so fond of her but that he soon proposed to marry the Dowager Duchess of Savoy; and, soon afterwards, the widow of the King of Castile, who was raving mad. But he made a money-bargain instead, and married neither.

The Duchess of Burgundy, among the other discontented people to whom she had given refuge, had sheltered Edmund de la Pole (younger brother of that Earl of Lincoln who was killed at Stoke), now Earl of Suffolk. The King had prevailed upon him to return to the marriage of Prince Arthur; but, he soon afterwards went away again; and then the King, suspecting a conspiracy, resorted to his favourite plan of sending him some treacherous friends, and buying of those scoundrels the secrets they disclosed or invented. Some arrests and executions took place in consequence. In the end, the King, on a promise of not taking his life, obtained possession of the person of Edmund de la Pole, and shut him up in the Tower.

This was his last enemy. If he had lived much longer he would have made many more among the people, by the grinding exaction to which he constantly exposed them, and by the tyrannical acts of his two prime favourites in all money-raising matters, Edmund Dudley and Richard Empson. But Death—the enemy who is not to be bought off or deceived, and on whom no money, and no treachery has any effect—presented himself at this juncture, and ended the King's reign. He died of the gout, on the twenty-second of April, one thousand five hundred and nine, and in the fifty-third year of his age, after reigning twenty-four years; he was buried in the beautiful Chapel of Westminster Abbey, which he had himself founded, and which still bears his name.

It was in this reign that the great Christopher Columbus, on behalf of Spain, discovered what was then called The New World. Great wonder, interest, and hope of wealth being awakened in England thereby, the King and the merchants of London and Bristol fitted out an English expedition for further discoveries in the New World, and entrusted it to Sebastian Cabot, of Bristol, the son of a Venetian pilot there. He was very successful in his voyage, and gained high reputation, both for himself and England.

CHAPTER XXVII—ENGLAND UNDER HENRY THE EIGHTH, CALLED BLUFF KING HAL AND BURLY KING HARRY

PART THE FIRST

We now come to King Henry the Eighth, whom it has been too much the fashion to call 'Bluff King Hal,' and 'Burly King Harry,' and other fine names; but whom I shall take the liberty to call, plainly, one of the most detestable villains that ever drew breath. You will be able to judge, long before we come to the end of his life, whether he deserves the character.

He was just eighteen years of age when he came to the throne. People said he was handsome then; but I don't believe it. He was a big, burly, noisy, small-eyed, large-faced, double-chinned, swinish-looking fellow in later life (as we know from the likenesses of him, painted by the famous Hans Holbein), and it is not easy to believe that so bad a character can ever have been veiled under a prepossessing appearance.

He was anxious to make himself popular; and the people, who had long disliked the late King, were very willing to believe that he deserved to be so. He was extremely fond of show and display, and so were they. Therefore there was great rejoicing when he married the Princess Catherine, and when they were both crowned. And the King fought at tournaments and always came off victorious—for the courtiers took care of that—and there was a general outcry that he was a wonderful man. Empson, Dudley, and their supporters were accused of a variety of crimes they had never committed, instead of the offences of which they really had been guilty; and they were pilloried, and set upon horses with their faces to the tails, and knocked about and beheaded, to the satisfaction of the people, and the enrichment of the King.

The Pope, so indefatigable in getting the world into trouble, had mixed himself up in a war on the continent of Europe, occasioned by the reigning Princes of little quarrelling states in Italy having at various times married into other Royal families, and so led to their claiming a share in those petty

Governments. The King, who discovered that he was very fond of the Pope, sent a herald to the King of France, to say that he must not make war upon that holy personage, because he was the father of all Christians. As the French King did not mind this relationship in the least, and also refused to admit a claim King Henry made to certain lands in France, war was declared between the two countries. Not to perplex this story with an account of the tricks and designs of all the sovereigns who were engaged in it, it is enough to say that England made a blundering alliance with Spain, and got stupidly taken in by that country; which made its own terms with France when it could and left England in the lurch. Sir Edward Howard, a bold admiral, son of the Earl of Surrey, distinguished himself by his bravery against the French in this business; but, unfortunately, he was more brave than wise, for, skimming into the French harbour of Brest with only a few row-boats, he attempted (in revenge for the defeat and death of Sir Thomas Knyvett, another bold English admiral) to take some strong French ships, well defended with batteries of cannon. The upshot was, that he was left on board of one of them (in consequence of its shooting away from his own boat), with not more than about a dozen men, and was thrown into the sea and drowned: though not until he had taken from his breast his gold chain and gold whistle, which were the signs of his office, and had cast them into the sea to prevent their being made a boast of by the enemy. After this defeat—which was a great one, for Sir Edward Howard was a man of valour and fame—the King took it into his head to invade France in person; first executing that dangerous Earl of Suffolk whom his father had left in the Tower, and appointing Queen Catherine to the charge of his kingdom in his absence. He sailed to Calais, where he was joined by Maximilian, Emperor of Germany, who pretended to be his soldier, and who took pay in his service: with a good deal of nonsense of that sort, flattering enough to the vanity of a vain blusterer. The King might be successful enough in sham fights; but his idea of real battles chiefly consisted in pitching silken tents of bright colours that were ignominiously blown down by the wind, and in making a vast display of gaudy flags and golden curtains. Fortune, however, favoured him better than he deserved; for, after much waste of time in tent pitching, flag flying, gold curtaining, and other such masquerading, he gave the French battle at a place called Guinegate:

where they took such an unaccountable panic, and fled with such swiftness, that it was ever afterwards called by the English the Battle of Spurs. Instead of following up his advantage, the King, finding that he had had enough of real fighting, came home again.

The Scottish King, though nearly related to Henry by marriage, had taken part against him in this war. The Earl of Surrey, as the English general, advanced to meet him when he came out of his own dominions and crossed the river Tweed. The two armies came up with one another when the Scottish King had also crossed the river Till, and was encamped upon the last of the Cheviot Hills, called the Hill of Flodden. Along the plain below it, the English, when the hour of battle came, advanced. The Scottish army, which had been drawn up in five great bodies, then came steadily down in perfect silence. So they, in their turn, advanced to meet the English army, which came on in one long line; and they attacked it with a body of spearmen, under Lord Home. At first they had the best of it; but the English recovered themselves so bravely, and fought with such valour, that, when the Scottish King had almost made his way up to the Royal Standard, he was slain, and the whole Scottish power routed. Ten thousand Scottish men lay dead that day on Flodden Field; and among them, numbers of the nobility and gentry. For a long time afterwards, the Scottish peasantry used to believe that their King had not been really killed in this battle, because no Englishman had found an iron belt he wore about his body as a penance for having been an unnatural and undutiful son. But, whatever became of his belt, the English had his sword and dagger, and the ring from his finger, and his body too, covered with wounds. There is no doubt of it; for it was seen and recognised by English gentlemen who had known the Scottish King well.

When King Henry was making ready to renew the war in France, the French King was contemplating peace. His queen, dying at this time, he proposed, though he was upwards of fifty years old, to marry King Henry's sister, the Princess Mary, who, besides being only sixteen, was betrothed to the Duke of Suffolk. As the inclinations of young Princesses were not much considered in such matters, the marriage was concluded, and the poor girl was escorted to France, where she was immediately left as the French King's bride, with only one of all her English attendants. That one was a pretty young girl named Anne Boleyn, niece of the Earl of Surrey, who had been made Duke of Norfolk, after the victory of Flodden Field. Anne Boleyn's is a name to be remembered, as you will presently find.

And now the French King, who was very proud of his young wife, was preparing for many years of happiness, and she was looking forward, I dare say, to many years of misery, when he died within three months, and left her a young widow. The new French monarch, Francis the First, seeing how important it was to his interests that she should take for her second husband no one but an Englishman, advised her first lover, the Duke of Suffolk, when King Henry sent him over to France to fetch her home, to marry her. The Princess being herself so fond of that Duke, as to tell him that he must either do so then, or for ever lose her, they were wedded; and Henry afterwards forgave them. In making interest with the King, the Duke of Suffolk had addressed his most powerful favourite and adviser, Thomas Wolsey—a name very famous in history for its rise and downfall.

Wolsey was the son of a respectable butcher at Ipswich, in Suffolk and received so excellent an education that he became a tutor to the family of the Marquis of Dorset, who afterwards got him appointed one of the late King's chaplains. On the accession of Henry the Eighth, he was promoted and taken into great favour. He was now Archbishop of York; the Pope had made him a Cardinal besides; and whoever wanted influence in England or favour with the King—whether he were a foreign monarch or an English nobleman—was obliged to make a friend of the great Cardinal Wolsey.

He was a gay man, who could dance and jest, and sing and drink; and those were the roads to so much, or rather so little, of a heart as King Henry had. He was wonderfully fond of pomp and glitter, and so was the King. He knew a good deal of the Church learning of that time; much of which consisted in finding artful excuses and pretences for almost any wrong thing, and in arguing that black was white, or any other colour. This kind of learning pleased the King too. For many such reasons, the Cardinal was high in estimation with the King; and, being a man of far greater ability, knew as well how to manage him, as a clever keeper may know how to manage a wolf

252

or a tiger, or any other cruel and uncertain beast, that may turn upon him and tear him any day. Never had there been seen in England such state as my Lord Cardinal kept. His wealth was enormous; equal, it was reckoned, to the riches of the Crown. His palaces were as splendid as the King's, and his retinue was eight hundred strong. He held his Court, dressed out from top to toe in flaming scarlet; and his very shoes were golden, set with precious stones. His followers rode on blood horses; while he, with a wonderful affectation of humility in the midst of his great splendour, ambled on a mule with a red velvet saddle and bridle and golden stirrups.

Through the influence of this stately priest, a grand meeting was arranged to take place between the French and English Kings in France; but on ground belonging to England. A prodigious show of friendship and rejoicing was to be made on the occasion; and heralds were sent to proclaim with brazen trumpets through all the principal cities of Europe, that, on a certain day, the Kings of France and England, as companions and brothers in arms, each attended by eighteen followers, would hold a tournament against all knights who might choose to come.

Charles, the new Emperor of Germany (the old one being dead), wanted to prevent too cordial an alliance between these sovereigns, and came over to England before the King could repair to the place of meeting; and, besides making an agreeable impression upon him, secured Wolsey's interest by promising that his influence should make him Pope when the next vacancy occurred. On the day when the Emperor left England, the King and all the Court went over to Calais, and thence to the place of meeting, between Ardres and Guisnes, commonly called the Field of the Cloth of Gold. Here, all manner of expense and prodigality was lavished on the decorations of the show; many of the knights and gentlemen being so superbly dressed that it was said they carried their whole estates upon their shoulders.

There were sham castles, temporary chapels, fountains running wine, great cellars full of wine free as water to all comers, silk tents, gold lace and foil, gilt lions, and such things without end; and, in the midst of all, the rich Cardinal out-shone and out-glittered all the noblemen and gentlemen assembled. After a treaty made between the two Kings with as much solemnity

253

as if they had intended to keep it, the lists—nine hundred feet long, and three hundred and twenty broad—were opened for the tournament; the Queens of France and England looking on with great array of lords and ladies. Then, for ten days, the two sovereigns fought five combats every day, and always beat their polite adversaries; though they do write that the King of England, being thrown in a wrestle one day by the King of France, lost his kingly temper with his brother-in-arms, and wanted to make a quarrel of it. Then, there is a great story belonging to this Field of the Cloth of Gold, showing how the English were distrustful of the French, and the French of the English, until Francis rode alone one morning to Henry's tent; and, going in before he was out of bed, told him in joke that he was his prisoner; and how Henry jumped out of bed and embraced Francis; and how Francis helped Henry to dress, and warmed his linen for him; and how Henry gave Francis a splendid jewelled collar, and how Francis gave Henry, in return, a costly bracelet. All this and a great deal more was so written about, and sung about, and talked about at that time (and, indeed, since that time too), that the world has had good cause to be sick of it, for ever.

Of course, nothing came of all these fine doings but a speedy renewal of the war between England and France, in which the two Royal companions and brothers in arms longed very earnestly to damage one another. But, before it broke out again, the Duke of Buckingham was shamefully executed on Tower Hill, on the evidence of a discharged servant—really for nothing, except the folly of having believed in a friar of the name of Hopkins, who had pretended to be a prophet, and who had mumbled and jumbled out some nonsense about the Duke's son being destined to be very great in the land. It was believed that the unfortunate Duke had given offence to the great Cardinal by expressing his mind freely about the expense and absurdity of the whole business of the Field of the Cloth of Gold. At any rate, he was beheaded, as I have said, for nothing. And the people who saw it done were very angry, and cried out that it was the work of 'the butcher's son!'

The new war was a short one, though the Earl of Surrey invaded France again, and did some injury to that country. It ended in another treaty of peace between the two kingdoms, and in the discovery that the Emperor of

Germany was not such a good friend to England in reality, as he pretended to be. Neither did he keep his promise to Wolsey to make him Pope, though the King urged him. Two Popes died in pretty quick succession; but the foreign priests were too much for the Cardinal, and kept him out of the post. So the Cardinal and King together found out that the Emperor of Germany was not a man to keep faith with; broke off a projected marriage between the King's daughter Mary, Princess of Wales, and that sovereign; and began to consider whether it might not be well to marry the young lady, either to Francis himself, or to his eldest son.

There now arose at Wittemberg, in Germany, the great leader of the mighty change in England which is called The Reformation, and which set the people free from their slavery to the priests. This was a learned Doctor, named Martin Luther, who knew all about them, for he had been a priest, and even a monk, himself. The preaching and writing of Wickliffe had set a number of men thinking on this subject; and Luther, finding one day to his great surprise, that there really was a book called the New Testament which the priests did not allow to be read, and which contained truths that they suppressed, began to be very vigorous against the whole body, from the Pope downward. It happened, while he was yet only beginning his vast work of awakening the nation, that an impudent fellow named Tetzel, a friar of very bad character, came into his neighbourhood selling what were called Indulgences, by wholesale, to raise money for beautifying the great Cathedral of St. Peter's, at Rome. Whoever bought an Indulgence of the Pope was supposed to buy himself off from the punishment of Heaven for his offences. Luther told the people that these Indulgences were worthless bits of paper, before God, and that Tetzel and his masters were a crew of impostors in selling them.

The King and the Cardinal were mightily indignant at this presumption; and the King (with the help of Sir Thomas More, a wise man, whom he afterwards repaid by striking off his head) even wrote a book about it, with which the Pope was so well pleased that he gave the King the title of Defender of the Faith. The King and the Cardinal also issued flaming warnings to the people not to read Luther's books, on pain of excommunication. But they did read them for all that; and the rumour of what was in them spread far and wide.

When this great change was thus going on, the King began to show himself in his truest and worst colours. Anne Boleyn, the pretty little girl who had gone abroad to France with his sister, was by this time grown up to be very beautiful, and was one of the ladies in attendance on Queen Catherine. Now, Queen Catherine was no longer young or handsome, and it is likely that she was not particularly good-tempered; having been always rather melancholy, and having been made more so by the deaths of four of her children when they were very young. So, the King fell in love with the fair Anne Boleyn, and said to himself, 'How can I be best rid of my own troublesome wife whom I am tired of, and marry Anne?'

You recollect that Queen Catherine had been the wife of Henry's brother. What does the King do, after thinking it over, but calls his favourite priests about him, and says, O! his mind is in such a dreadful state, and he is so frightfully uneasy, because he is afraid it was not lawful for him to marry the Queen! Not one of those priests had the courage to hint that it was rather curious he had never thought of that before, and that his mind seemed to have been in a tolerably jolly condition during a great many years, in which he certainly had not fretted himself thin; but, they all said, Ah! that was very true, and it was a serious business; and perhaps the best way to make it right, would be for his Majesty to be divorced! The King replied, Yes, he thought that would be the best way, certainly; so they all went to work.

If I were to relate to you the intrigues and plots that took place in the endeavour to get this divorce, you would think the History of England the most tiresome book in the world. So I shall say no more, than that after a vast deal of negotiation and evasion, the Pope issued a commission to Cardinal Wolsey and Cardinal Campeggio (whom he sent over from Italy for the purpose), to try the whole case in England. It is supposed—and I think with reason—that Wolsey was the Queen's enemy, because she had reproved him for his proud and gorgeous manner of life. But, he did not at first know that the King wanted to marry Anne Boleyn; and when he did know it, he even went down on his knees, in the endeavour to dissuade him.

The Cardinals opened their court in the Convent of the Black Friars, near to where the bridge of that name in London now stands; and the King and Queen, that they might be near it, took up their lodgings at the adjoining palace of Bridewell, of which nothing now remains but a bad prison. On the opening of the court, when the King and Queen were called on to appear, that poor ill-used lady, with a dignity and firmness and yet with a womanly affection worthy to be always admired, went and kneeled at the King's feet, and said that she had come, a stranger, to his dominions; that she had been a good and true wife to him for twenty years; and that she could acknowledge no power in those Cardinals to try whether she should be considered his wife after all that time, or should be put away. With that, she got up and left the court, and would never afterwards come back to it.

The King pretended to be very much overcome, and said, O! my lords and gentlemen, what a good woman she was to be sure, and how delighted he would be to live with her unto death, but for that terrible uneasiness in his mind which was quite wearing him away! So, the case went on, and there was nothing but talk for two months. Then Cardinal Campeggio, who, on behalf of the Pope, wanted nothing so much as delay, adjourned it for two more months; and before that time was elapsed, the Pope himself adjourned it indefinitely, by requiring the King and Queen to come to Rome and have it tried there. But by good luck for the King, word was brought to him by some of his people, that they had happened to meet at supper, Thomas Cranmer, a learned Doctor of Cambridge, who had proposed to urge the Pope on, by referring the case to all the learned doctors and bishops, here and there and everywhere, and getting their opinions that the King's marriage was unlawful. The King, who was now in a hurry to marry Anne Boleyn, thought this such a good idea, that he sent for Cranmer, post haste, and said to Lord Rochfort, Anne Boleyn's father, 'Take this learned Doctor down to your country-house, and there let him have a good room for a study, and no end of books out of which to prove that I may marry your daughter.' Lord Rochfort, not at all reluctant, made the learned Doctor as comfortable as he could; and the learned Doctor went to work to prove his case. All this time, the King and Anne Boleyn were writing letters to one another almost daily, full of impatience to have the case settled; and Anne Boleyn was showing herself (as

257

I think) very worthy of the fate which afterwards befel her.

It was bad for Cardinal Wolsey that he had left Cranmer to render this help. It was worse for him that he had tried to dissuade the King from marrying Anne Boleyn. Such a servant as he, to such a master as Henry, would probably have fallen in any case; but, between the hatred of the party of the Queen that was, and the hatred of the party of the Queen that was to be, he fell suddenly and heavily. Going down one day to the Court of Chancery, where he now presided, he was waited upon by the Dukes of Norfolk and Suffolk, who told him that they brought an order to him to resign that office, and to withdraw quietly to a house he had at Esher, in Surrey. The Cardinal refusing, they rode off to the King; and next day came back with a letter from him, on reading which, the Cardinal submitted. An inventory was made out of all the riches in his palace at York Place (now Whitehall), and he went sorrowfully up the river, in his barge, to Putney. An abject man he was, in spite of his pride; for being overtaken, riding out of that place towards Esher, by one of the King's chamberlains who brought him a kind message and a ring, he alighted from his mule, took off his cap, and kneeled down in the dirt. His poor Fool, whom in his prosperous days he had always kept in his palace to entertain him, cut a far better figure than he; for, when the Cardinal said to the chamberlain that he had nothing to send to his lord the King as a present, but that jester who was a most excellent one, it took six strong yeomen to remove the faithful fool from his master.

The once proud Cardinal was soon further disgraced, and wrote the most abject letters to his vile sovereign; who humbled him one day and encouraged him the next, according to his humour, until he was at last ordered to go and reside in his diocese of York. He said he was too poor; but I don't know how he made that out, for he took a hundred and sixty servants with him, and seventy-two cart-loads of furniture, food, and wine. He remained in that part of the country for the best part of a year, and showed himself so improved by his misfortunes, and was so mild and so conciliating, that he won all hearts. And indeed, even in his proud days, he had done some magnificent things for learning and education. At last, he was arrested for high treason; and, coming slowly on his journey towards London, got as far as Leicester. Arriving at

Leicester Abbey after dark, and very ill, he said—when the monks came out at the gate with lighted torches to receive him—that he had come to lay his bones among them. He had indeed; for he was taken to a bed, from which he never rose again. His last words were, 'Had I but served God as diligently as I have served the King, He would not have given me over, in my grey hairs. Howbeit, this is my just reward for my pains and diligence, not regarding my service to God, but only my duty to my prince.' The news of his death was quickly carried to the King, who was amusing himself with archery in the garden of the magnificent Palace at Hampton Court, which that very Wolsey had presented to him. The greatest emotion his royal mind displayed at the loss of a servant so faithful and so ruined, was a particular desire to lay hold of fifteen hundred pounds which the Cardinal was reported to have hidden somewhere.

The opinions concerning the divorce, of the learned doctors and bishops and others, being at last collected, and being generally in the King's favour, were forwarded to the Pope, with an entreaty that he would now grant it. The unfortunate Pope, who was a timid man, was half distracted between his fear of his authority being set aside in England if he did not do as he was asked, and his dread of offending the Emperor of Germany, who was Queen Catherine's nephew. In this state of mind he still evaded and did nothing. Then, Thomas Cromwell, who had been one of Wolsey's faithful attendants, and had remained so even in his decline, advised the King to take the matter into his own hands, and make himself the head of the whole Church. This, the King by various artful means, began to do; but he recompensed the clergy by allowing them to burn as many people as they pleased, for holding Luther's opinions. You must understand that Sir Thomas More, the wise man who had helped the King with his book, had been made Chancellor in Wolsey's place. But, as he was truly attached to the Church as it was even in its abuses, he, in this state of things, resigned.

Being now quite resolved to get rid of Queen Catherine, and to marry Anne Boleyn without more ado, the King made Cranmer Archbishop of Canterbury, and directed Queen Catherine to leave the Court. She obeyed; but replied that wherever she went, she was Queen of England still, and would remain so, to the last. The King then married Anne Boleyn privately; and the new Archbishop of Canterbury, within half a year, declared his marriage with Queen Catherine void, and crowned Anne Boleyn Queen.

She might have known that no good could ever come from such wrong, and that the corpulent brute who had been so faithless and so cruel to his first wife, could be more faithless and more cruel to his second. She might have known that, even when he was in love with her, he had been a mean and selfish coward, running away, like a frightened cur, from her society and her house, when a dangerous sickness broke out in it, and when she might easily have taken it and died, as several of the household did. But, Anne Boleyn arrived at all this knowledge too late, and bought it at a dear price. Her bad marriage with a worse man came to its natural end. Its natural end was not, as we shall too soon see, a natural death for her.

CHAPTER XXVIII—ENGLAND UNDER HENRY THE EIGHTH

PART THE SECOND

The Pope was thrown into a very angry state of mind when he heard of the King's marriage, and fumed exceedingly. Many of the English monks and friars, seeing that their order was in danger, did the same; some even declaimed against the King in church before his face, and were not to be stopped until he himself roared out 'Silence!' The King, not much the worse for this, took it pretty quietly; and was very glad when his Queen gave birth to a daughter, who was christened Elizabeth, and declared Princess of Wales as her sister Mary had already been.

One of the most atrocious features of this reign was that Henry the Eighth was always trimming between the reformed religion and the unreformed one; so that the more he quarrelled with the Pope, the more of his own subjects he roasted alive for not holding the Pope's opinions. Thus, an unfortunate student named John Frith, and a poor simple tailor named Andrew Hewet who loved him very much, and said that whatever John Frith believed he believed, were burnt in Smithfield—to show what a capital Christian the King was.

But, these were speedily followed by two much greater victims, Sir Thomas More, and John Fisher, the Bishop of Rochester. The latter, who was a good and amiable old man, had committed no greater offence than believing in Elizabeth Barton, called the Maid of Kent—another of those ridiculous women who pretended to be inspired, and to make all sorts of heavenly revelations, though they indeed uttered nothing but evil nonsense. For this offence—as it was pretended, but really for denying the King to be the supreme Head of the Church—he got into trouble, and was put in prison; but, even then, he might have been suffered to die naturally (short work having been made of executing the Kentish Maid and her principal followers), but that the Pope, to spite the King, resolved to make him a cardinal. Upon that the King made a ferocious joke to the effect that the

Pope might send Fisher a red hat—which is the way they make a cardinal—but he should have no head on which to wear it; and he was tried with all unfairness and injustice, and sentenced to death. He died like a noble and virtuous old man, and left a worthy name behind him. The King supposed, I dare say, that Sir Thomas More would be frightened by this example; but, as he was not to be easily terrified, and, thoroughly believing in the Pope, had made up his mind that the King was not the rightful Head of the Church, he positively refused to say that he was. For this crime he too was tried and sentenced, after having been in prison a whole year. When he was doomed to death, and came away from his trial with the edge of the executioner's axe turned towards him—as was always done in those times when a state prisoner came to that hopeless pass—he bore it quite serenely, and gave his blessing to his son, who pressed through the crowd in Westminster Hall and kneeled down to receive it. But, when he got to the Tower Wharf on his way back to his prison, and his favourite daughter, Margaret Roper, a very good woman, rushed through the guards again and again, to kiss him and to weep upon his neck, he was overcome at last. He soon recovered, and never more showed any feeling but cheerfulness and courage. When he was going up the steps of the scaffold to his death, he said jokingly to the Lieutenant of the Tower, observing that they were weak and shook beneath his tread, 'I pray you, master Lieutenant, see me safe up; and, for my coming down, I can shift for myself.' Also he said to the executioner, after he had laid his head upon the block, 'Let me put my beard out of the way; for that, at least, has never committed any treason.' Then his head was struck off at a blow. These two executions were worthy of King Henry the Eighth. Sir Thomas More was one of the most virtuous men in his dominions, and the Bishop was one of his oldest and truest friends. But to be a friend of that fellow was almost as dangerous as to be his wife.

When the news of these two murders got to Rome, the Pope raged against the murderer more than ever Pope raged since the world began, and prepared a Bull, ordering his subjects to take arms against him and dethrone him. The King took all possible precautions to keep that document out of his dominions, and set to work in return to suppress a great number of the English monasteries and abbeys.

This destruction was begun by a body of commissioners, of whom Cromwell (whom the King had taken into great favour) was the head; and was carried on through some few years to its entire completion. There is no doubt that many of these religious establishments were religious in nothing but in name, and were crammed with lazy, indolent, and sensual monks. There is no doubt that they imposed upon the people in every possible way; that they had images moved by wires, which they pretended were miraculously moved by Heaven; that they had among them a whole tun measure full of teeth, all purporting to have come out of the head of one saint, who must indeed have been a very extraordinary person with that enormous allowance of grinders; that they had bits of coal which they said had fried Saint Lawrence, and bits of toe-nails which they said belonged to other famous saints; penknives, and boots, and girdles, which they said belonged to others; and that all these bits of rubbish were called Relics, and adored by the ignorant people. But, on the other hand, there is no doubt either, that the King's officers and men punished the good monks with the bad; did great injustice; demolished many beautiful things and many valuable libraries; destroyed numbers of paintings, stained glass windows, fine pavements, and carvings; and that the whole court were ravenously greedy and rapacious for the division of this great spoil among them. The King seems to have grown almost mad in the ardour of this pursuit; for he declared Thomas à Becket a traitor, though he had been dead so many years, and had his body dug up out of his grave. He must have been as miraculous as the monks pretended, if they had told the truth, for he was found with one head on his shoulders, and they had shown another as his undoubted and genuine head ever since his death; it had brought them vast sums of money, too. The gold and jewels on his shrine filled two great chests, and eight men tottered as they carried them away. How rich the monasteries were you may infer from the fact that, when they were all suppressed, one hundred and thirty thousand pounds a year—in those days an immense sum—came to the Crown.

These things were not done without causing great discontent among the people. The monks had been good landlords and hospitable entertainers of all travellers, and had been accustomed to give away a great deal of corn, and fruit, and meat, and other things. In those days it was difficult to change goods into money, in consequence of the roads being very few and very bad, and the carts, and waggons of the worst description; and they must either have given away some of the good things they possessed in enormous quantities, or have suffered them to spoil and moulder. So, many of the people missed what it was more agreeable to get idly than to work for; and the monks who were driven out of their homes and wandered about encouraged their discontent; and there were, consequently, great risings in Lincolnshire and Yorkshire. These were put down by terrific executions, from which the monks themselves did not escape, and the King went on grunting and growling in his own fat way, like a Royal pig.

I have told all this story of the religious houses at one time, to make it plainer, and to get back to the King's domestic affairs.

The unfortunate Queen Catherine was by this time dead; and the King was by this time as tired of his second Queen as he had been of his first. As he had fallen in love with Anne when she was in the service of Catherine, so he now fell in love with another lady in the service of Anne. See how wicked deeds are punished, and how bitterly and self-reproachfully the Queen must now have thought of her own rise to the throne! The new fancy was a Lady Jane Seymour; and the King no sooner set his mind on her, than he resolved to have Anne Boleyn's head. So, he brought a number of charges against Anne, accusing her of dreadful crimes which she had never committed, and implicating in them her own brother and certain gentlemen in her service: among whom one Norris, and Mark Smeaton a musician, are best remembered. As the lords and councillors were as afraid of the King and as subservient to him as the meanest peasant in England was, they brought in Anne Boleyn guilty, and the other unfortunate persons accused with her, guilty too. Those gentlemen died like men, with the exception of Smeaton, who had been tempted by the King into telling lies, which he called confessions, and who had expected to be pardoned; but who, I am very glad to say, was not. There was then only the Queen to dispose of. She had been surrounded in the Tower with women spies; had been monstrously persecuted and foully slandered; and had received no justice. But her spirit rose with her afflictions; and, after having in vain tried to soften the King by writing an affecting letter to him which still exists, 'from her doleful prison in the Tower,' she resigned herself to death. She said to those about her, very cheerfully, that she had heard say the executioner was a good one, and that she had a little neck (she laughed and clasped it with her hands as she said that), and would soon be out of her pain. And she was soon out of her pain, poor creature, on the Green inside the Tower, and her body was flung into an old box and put away in the ground under the chapel.

There is a story that the King sat in his palace listening very anxiously for the sound of the cannon which was to announce this new murder; and that, when he heard it come booming on the air, he rose up in great spirits and ordered out his dogs to go a-hunting. He was bad enough to do it; but whether he did it or not, it is certain that he married Jane Seymour the very next day.

I have not much pleasure in recording that she lived just long enough to give birth to a son who was christened Edward, and then to die of a fever: for, I cannot but think that any woman who married such a ruffian, and knew what innocent blood was on his hands, deserved the axe that would assuredly have fallen on the neck of Jane Seymour, if she had lived much longer.

Cranmer had done what he could to save some of the Church property for purposes of religion and education; but, the great families had been so hungry to get hold of it, that very little could be rescued for such objects. Even Miles Coverdale, who did the people the inestimable service of translating the Bible into English (which the unreformed religion never permitted to be done), was left in poverty while the great families clutched the Church lands and money. The people had been told that when the Crown came into possession of these funds, it would not be necessary to tax them; but they were taxed afresh directly afterwards. It was fortunate for them, indeed, that so many nobles were so greedy for this wealth; since, if it had remained with the Crown, there might have been no end to tyranny for hundreds of years. One of the most active writers on the Church's side against the King was a member of his own family—a sort of distant cousin, Reginald Pole by name—who attacked him in the most violent manner (though he received a pension from him all the time), and fought for the Church with his pen, day and night. As he was beyond the King's reach—being in Italy—the King politely invited him over to discuss the subject; but he, knowing better than to come, and wisely staying where he was, the King's rage fell upon his brother Lord Montague, the Marquis of Exeter, and some other gentlemen: who were tried for high treason in corresponding with him and aiding him—which they probably did—and were all executed. The Pope made Reginald Pole a cardinal; but, so much against his will, that it is thought he even aspired in his own mind to the vacant throne of England, and had hopes of marrying the Princess Mary. His being made a high priest, however, put an end to all that. His mother, the venerable Countess of Salisbury—who was, unfortunately for herself, within the tyrant's reach—was the last of his relatives on whom his wrath fell. When she was told to lay her grey head upon the block, she answered the executioner, 'No! My head never committed treason, and if you want it, you shall seize it.' So, she ran round and round the scaffold with the executioner striking at her, and her grey hair bedabbled with blood; and even when they held her down upon the block she moved her head about to the last, resolved to be no party to her own barbarous murder. All this the people bore, as they had borne everything else.

Indeed they bore much more; for the slow fires of Smithfield were continually burning, and people were constantly being roasted to death— still to show what a good Christian the King was. He defied the Pope and his Bull, which was now issued, and had come into England; but he burned innumerable people whose only offence was that they differed from the Pope's religious opinions. There was a wretched man named Lambert, among others, who was tried for this before the King, and with whom six bishops argued one after another. When he was quite exhausted (as well he might be, after six bishops), he threw himself on the King's mercy; but the King blustered out that he had no mercy for heretics. So, he too fed the fire.

All this the people bore, and more than all this yet. The national spirit seems to have been banished from the kingdom at this time. The very people who were executed for treason, the very wives and friends of the 'bluff' King, spoke of him on the scaffold as a good prince, and a gentle prince—just as serfs in similar circumstances have been known to do, under the Sultan and Bashaws of the East, or under the fierce old tyrants of Russia, who poured boiling and freezing water on them alternately, until they died. The Parliament were as bad as the rest, and gave the King whatever he wanted; among other vile accommodations, they gave him new powers of murdering, at his will and pleasure, any one whom he might choose to call a traitor. But the worst measure they passed was an Act of Six Articles, commonly called at the time 'the whip with six strings;' which punished offences against the Pope's opinions, without mercy, and enforced the very worst parts of the monkish religion. Cranmer would have modified it, if he could; but, being overborne by the Romish party, had not the power. As one of the articles declared that priests should not marry, and as he was married himself, he sent his wife and children into Germany, and began to tremble at his danger; none the less because he was, and had long been, the King's friend. This whip of six strings was made under the King's own eye. It should never be forgotten of him how cruelly he supported the worst of the Popish doctrines when there was nothing to be got by opposing them.

This amiable monarch now thought of taking another wife. He proposed to the French King to have some of the ladies of the French Court exhibited before him, that he might make his Royal choice; but the French King answered that he would rather not have his ladies trotted out to be shown like horses at a fair. He proposed to the Dowager Duchess of Milan, who replied that she might have thought of such a match if she had had two heads; but, that only owning one, she must beg to keep it safe. At last Cromwell represented that there was a Protestant Princess in Germany— those who held the reformed religion were called Protestants, because their leaders had Protested against the abuses and impositions of the unreformed Church—named Anne of Cleves, who was beautiful, and would answer the purpose admirably. The King said was she a large woman, because he must have a fat wife? 'O yes,' said Cromwell; 'she was very large, just the thing.' On hearing this the King sent over his famous painter, Hans Holbein, to take her portrait. Hans made her out to be so good-looking that the King was satisfied, and the marriage was arranged. But, whether anybody had paid Hans to touch up the picture; or whether Hans, like one or two other painters, flattered a princess in the ordinary way of business, I cannot say:

all I know is, that when Anne came over and the King went to Rochester to meet her, and first saw her without her seeing him, he swore she was 'a great Flanders mare,' and said he would never marry her. Being obliged to do it now matters had gone so far, he would not give her the presents he had prepared, and would never notice her. He never forgave Cromwell his part in the affair. His downfall dates from that time.

It was quickened by his enemies, in the interests of the unreformed religion, putting in the King's way, at a state dinner, a niece of the Duke of Norfolk, Catherine Howard, a young lady of fascinating manners, though small in stature and not particularly beautiful. Falling in love with her on the spot, the King soon divorced Anne of Cleves after making her the subject of much brutal talk, on pretence that she had been previously betrothed to some one else—which would never do for one of his dignity—and married Catherine. It is probable that on his wedding day, of all days in the year, he sent his faithful Cromwell to the scaffold, and had his head struck off. He further celebrated the occasion by burning at one time, and causing to be drawn to the fire on the same hurdles, some Protestant prisoners for denying the Pope's doctrines, and some Roman Catholic prisoners for denying his own supremacy. Still the people bore it, and not a gentleman in England raised his hand.

But, by a just retribution, it soon came out that Catherine Howard, before her marriage, had been really guilty of such crimes as the King had falsely attributed to his second wife Anne Boleyn; so, again the dreadful axe made the King a widower, and this Queen passed away as so many in that reign had passed away before her. As an appropriate pursuit under the circumstances, Henry then applied himself to superintending the composition of a religious book called 'A necessary doctrine for any Christian Man.' He must have been a little confused in his mind, I think, at about this period; for he was so false to himself as to be true to some one: that some one being Cranmer, whom the Duke of Norfolk and others of his enemies tried to ruin; but to whom the King was steadfast, and to whom he one night gave his ring, charging him when he should find himself, next day, accused of treason, to show it to the council board. This Cranmer did to the confusion of his enemies. I suppose the King thought he might want him a little longer.

He married yet once more. Yes, strange to say, he found in England another woman who would become his wife, and she was Catherine Parr, widow of Lord Latimer. She leaned towards the reformed religion; and it is some comfort to know, that she tormented the King considerably by arguing a variety of doctrinal points with him on all possible occasions. She had very nearly done this to her own destruction. After one of these conversations the King in a very black mood actually instructed Gardiner, one of his Bishops who favoured the Popish opinions, to draw a bill of accusation against her, which would have inevitably brought her to the scaffold where her predecessors had died, but that one of her friends picked up the paper of instructions which had been dropped in the palace, and gave her timely notice. She fell ill with terror; but managed the King so well when he came to entrap her into further statements—by saying that she had only spoken on such points to divert his mind and to get some information from his extraordinary wisdom—that he gave her a kiss and called her his sweetheart. And, when the Chancellor came next day actually to take her to the Tower, the King sent him about his business, and honoured him with the epithets of a beast, a knave, and a fool. So near was Catherine Parr to the block, and so narrow was her escape!

There was war with Scotland in this reign, and a short clumsy war with France for favouring Scotland; but, the events at home were so dreadful, and leave such an enduring stain on the country, that I need say no more of what happened abroad.

A few more horrors, and this reign is over. There was a lady, Anne Askew, in Lincolnshire, who inclined to the Protestant opinions, and whose husband being a fierce Catholic, turned her out of his house. She came to London, and was considered as offending against the six articles, and was taken to the Tower, and put upon the rack—probably because it was hoped that she might, in her agony, criminate some obnoxious persons; if falsely, so much the better. She was tortured without uttering a cry, until the Lieutenant of the Tower would suffer his men to torture her no more; and then two priests who were present actually pulled off their robes, and turned the wheels of the rack with their own hands, so rending and twisting and breaking her that she was afterwards carried to the fire in a chair. She was burned with three others, a gentleman, a clergyman, and a tailor; and so the world went on.

Either the King became afraid of the power of the Duke of Norfolk, and his son the Earl of Surrey, or they gave him some offence, but he resolved to pull them down, to follow all the rest who were gone. The son was tried first—of course for nothing—and defended himself bravely; but of course he was found guilty, and of course he was executed. Then his father was laid hold of, and left for death too.

But the King himself was left for death by a Greater King, and the earth was to be rid of him at last. He was now a swollen, hideous spectacle, with a great hole in his leg, and so odious to every sense that it was dreadful to approach him. When he was found to be dying, Cranmer was sent for from his palace at Croydon, and came with all speed, but found him speechless. Happily, in that hour he perished. He was in the fifty-sixth year of his age, and the thirty-eighth of his reign.

Henry the Eighth has been favoured by some Protestant writers, because the Reformation was achieved in his time. But the mighty merit of it lies with other men and not with him; and it can be rendered none the worse by this monster's crimes, and none the better by any defence of them. The plain truth is, that he was a most intolerable ruffian, a disgrace to human nature, and a blot of blood and grease upon the History of England.

CHAPTER XXIX—ENGLAND UNDER EDWARD THE SIXTH

Henry the Eighth had made a will, appointing a council of sixteen to govern the kingdom for his son while he was under age (he was now only ten years old), and another council of twelve to help them. The most powerful of the first council was the Earl of Hertford, the young King's uncle, who lost no time in bringing his nephew with great state up to Enfield, and thence to the Tower. It was considered at the time a striking proof of virtue in the young King that he was sorry for his father's death; but, as common subjects have that virtue too, sometimes, we will say no more about it.

There was a curious part of the late King's will, requiring his executors to fulfil whatever promises he had made. Some of the court wondering what these might be, the Earl of Hertford and the other noblemen interested, said that they were promises to advance and enrich them. So, the Earl of Hertford made himself Duke of Somerset, and made his brother Edward Seymour a baron; and there were various similar promotions, all very agreeable to the parties concerned, and very dutiful, no doubt, to the late King's memory. To be more dutiful still, they made themselves rich out of the Church lands, and were very comfortable. The new Duke of Somerset caused himself to be declared Protector of the kingdom, and was, indeed, the King.

As young Edward the Sixth had been brought up in the principles of the Protestant religion, everybody knew that they would be maintained. But Cranmer, to whom they were chiefly entrusted, advanced them steadily and temperately. Many superstitious and ridiculous practices were stopped; but practices which were harmless were not interfered with.

The Duke of Somerset, the Protector, was anxious to have the young King engaged in marriage to the young Queen of Scotland, in order to prevent that princess from making an alliance with any foreign power; but, as a large party in Scotland were unfavourable to this plan, he invaded that country. His excuse for doing so was, that the Border men—that is, the Scotch who lived in that part of the country where England and Scotland joined—troubled the English very much. But there were two sides to this question; for the English Border men troubled the Scotch too; and, through many long years, there were perpetual border quarrels which gave rise to numbers of old tales and songs. However, the Protector invaded Scotland; and Arran, the Scottish Regent, with an army twice as large as his, advanced to meet him. They encountered on the banks of the river Esk, within a few miles of Edinburgh; and there, after a little skirmish, the Protector made such moderate proposals, in offering to retire if the Scotch would only engage not to marry their princess to any foreign prince, that the Regent thought the English were afraid. But in this he made a horrible mistake; for the English soldiers on land, and the English sailors on the water, so set upon the Scotch, that they broke and fled, and more than ten thousand of them were killed. It was a dreadful battle, for the fugitives were slain without mercy. The ground for four miles, all the way to Edinburgh, was strewn with dead men, and with arms, and legs, and heads. Some hid themselves in streams and were drowned; some threw away their armour and were killed running, almost naked; but in this battle of Pinkey the English lost only two or three hundred men. They were much better clothed than the Scotch; at the poverty of whose appearance and country they were exceedingly astonished.

A Parliament was called when Somerset came back, and it repealed the whip with six strings, and did one or two other good things; though it unhappily retained the punishment of burning for those people who did not make believe to believe, in all religious matters, what the Government had declared that they must and should believe. It also made a foolish law (meant to put down beggars), that any man who lived idly and loitered about for three days together, should be burned with a hot iron, made a slave, and wear an iron fetter. But this savage absurdity soon came to an end, and went the way of a great many other foolish laws.

The Protector was now so proud that he sat in Parliament before all the nobles, on the right hand of the throne. Many other noblemen, who only wanted to be as proud if they could get a chance, became his enemies of course; and it is supposed that he came back suddenly from Scotland because he had received news that his brother, Lord Seymour, was becoming dangerous to him. This lord was now High Admiral of England; a very handsome man, and a great favourite with the Court ladies—even with the young Princess Elizabeth, who romped with him a little more than young princesses in these times do with any one. He had married Catherine Parr, the late King's widow, who was now dead; and, to strengthen his power, he secretly supplied the young King with money. He may even have engaged with some of his brother's enemies in a plot to carry the boy off. On these and other accusations, at any rate, he was confined in the Tower, impeached, and found guilty; his own brother's name being—unnatural and sad to tell—the first signed to the warrant of his execution. He was executed on Tower Hill, and died denying his treason. One of his last proceedings in this world was to write two letters, one to the Princess Elizabeth, and one to the Princess Mary, which a servant of his took charge of, and concealed in his shoe. These letters are supposed to have urged them against his brother, and to revenge his death. What they truly contained is not known; but there is no doubt that he had, at one time, obtained great influence over the Princess Elizabeth.

All this while, the Protestant religion was making progress. The images which the people had gradually come to worship, were removed from the churches; the people were informed that they need not confess themselves to priests unless they chose; a common prayer-book was drawn up in the English language, which all could understand, and many other improvements were made; still moderately. For Cranmer was a very moderate man, and even restrained the Protestant clergy from violently abusing the unreformed religion—as they very often did, and which was not a good example. But the people were at this time in great distress. The rapacious nobility who had come into possession of the Church lands, were very bad landlords. They enclosed great quantities of ground for the feeding of sheep, which was then more profitable than the growing of crops; and this increased the general distress. So the people, who still understood little of what was going on about them, and still readily believed what the homeless monks told them—many of whom had been their good friends in their better days—took it into their heads that all this was owing to the reformed religion, and therefore rose, in many parts of the country.

The most powerful risings were in Devonshire and Norfolk. In

Devonshire, the rebellion was so strong that ten thousand men united within a few days, and even laid siege to Exeter. But Lord Russell, coming to the assistance of the citizens who defended that town, defeated the rebels; and, not only hanged the Mayor of one place, but hanged the vicar of another from his own church steeple. What with hanging and killing by the sword, four thousand of the rebels are supposed to have fallen in that one county. In Norfolk (where the rising was more against the enclosure of open lands than against the reformed religion), the popular leader was a man named Robert Ket, a tanner of Wymondham. The mob were, in the first instance, excited against the tanner by one John Flowerdew, a gentleman who owed him a grudge: but the tanner was more than a match for the gentleman, since he soon got the people on his side, and established himself near Norwich with quite an army. There was a large oak-tree in that place, on a spot called Moushold Hill, which Ket named the Tree of Reformation; and under its green boughs, he and his men sat, in the midsummer weather, holding courts of justice, and debating affairs of state. They were even impartial enough to allow some rather tiresome public speakers to get up into this Tree of Reformation, and point out their errors to them, in long discourses, while they lay listening (not always without some grumbling and growling) in the shade below. At last, one sunny July day, a herald appeared below the tree, and proclaimed Ket and all his men traitors, unless from that moment they dispersed and went home: in which case they were to receive a pardon. But, Ket and his men made light of the herald and became stronger than ever, until the Earl of Warwick went after them with a sufficient force, and cut them all to pieces. A few were hanged, drawn, and quartered, as traitors, and their limbs were sent into various country places to be a terror to the people. Nine of them were hanged upon nine green branches of the Oak of Reformation; and so, for the time, that tree may be said to have withered away.

The Protector, though a haughty man, had compassion for the real distresses of the common people, and a sincere desire to help them. But he was too proud and too high in degree to hold even their favour steadily; and many of the nobles always envied and hated him, because they were as proud and not as high as he. He was at this time building a great Palace in the Strand: to get the stone for which he blew up church steeples with gunpowder, and pulled down bishops' houses: thus making himself still more disliked. At length, his principal enemy, the Earl of Warwick—Dudley by name, and the son of that Dudley who had made himself so odious with Empson, in the reign of Henry the Seventh—joined with seven other members of the Council against him, formed a separate Council; and, becoming stronger in a few days, sent him to the Tower under twenty-nine articles of accusation. After being sentenced by the Council to the forfeiture of all his offices and lands, he was liberated and pardoned, on making a very humble submission. He was even taken back into the Council again, after having suffered this fall, and married his daughter, Lady Anne Seymour, to Warwick's eldest son. But such a reconciliation was little likely to last, and did not outlive a year. Warwick, having got himself made Duke of Northumberland, and having advanced the more important of his friends, then finished the history by causing the Duke of Somerset and his friend Lord Grey, and others, to be arrested for treason, in having conspired to seize and dethrone the King. They were also accused of having intended to seize the new Duke of Northumberland, with his friends Lord Northampton and Lord Pembroke; to murder them if they found need; and to raise the City to revolt. All this the fallen Protector positively denied; except that he confessed to having spoken of the murder of those three noblemen, but having never designed it. He was acquitted of the charge of treason, and found guilty of the other charges; so when the people—who remembered his having been their friend, now that he was disgraced and in danger, saw him come out from his trial with the axe turned from him—they thought he was altogether acquitted, and sent up a loud shout of joy.

But the Duke of Somerset was ordered to be beheaded on Tower Hill, at eight o'clock in the morning, and proclamations were issued bidding the citizens keep at home until after ten. They filled the streets, however, and crowded the place of execution as soon as it was light; and, with sad faces and sad hearts, saw the once powerful Protector ascend the scaffold to lay his head upon the dreadful block. While he was yet saying his last words to them with manly courage, and telling them, in particular, how it comforted him, at that pass, to have assisted in reforming the national religion, a member of the Council was seen riding up on horseback. They again thought that the Duke was saved by his bringing a reprieve, and again shouted for joy. But the

Duke himself told them they were mistaken, and laid down his head and had it struck off at a blow.

Many of the bystanders rushed forward and steeped their handkerchiefs in his blood, as a mark of their affection. He had, indeed, been capable of many good acts, and one of them was discovered after he was no more. The Bishop of Durham, a very good man, had been informed against to the Council, when the Duke was in power, as having answered a treacherous letter proposing a rebellion against the reformed religion. As the answer could not be found, he could not be declared guilty; but it was now discovered, hidden by the Duke himself among some private papers, in his regard for that good man. The Bishop lost his office, and was deprived of his possessions.

It is not very pleasant to know that while his uncle lay in prison under sentence of death, the young King was being vastly entertained by plays, and dances, and sham fights: but there is no doubt of it, for he kept a journal himself. It is pleasanter to know that not a single Roman Catholic was burnt in this reign for holding that religion; though two wretched victims suffered for heresy. One, a woman named Joan Bocher, for professing some opinions that even she could only explain in unintelligible jargon. The other, a Dutchman, named Von Paris, who practised as a surgeon in London. Edward was, to his credit, exceedingly unwilling to sign the warrant for the woman's execution: shedding tears before he did so, and telling Cranmer, who urged him to do it (though Cranmer really would have spared the woman at first, but for her own determined obstinacy), that the guilt was not his, but that of the man who so strongly urged the dreadful act. We shall see, too soon, whether the time ever came when Cranmer is likely to have remembered this with sorrow and remorse.

Cranmer and Ridley (at first Bishop of Rochester, and afterwards Bishop of London) were the most powerful of the clergy of this reign. Others were imprisoned and deprived of their property for still adhering to the unreformed religion; the most important among whom were Gardiner Bishop of Winchester, Heath Bishop of Worcester, Day Bishop of Chichester, and Bonner that Bishop of London who was superseded by Ridley. The Princess Mary, who inherited her mother's gloomy temper, and hated the reformed religion as connected with her mother's wrongs and sorrows—she knew nothing else about it, always refusing to read a single book in which it was truly described—held by the unreformed religion too, and was the only person in the kingdom for whom the old Mass was allowed to be performed; nor would the young King have made that exception even in her favour, but for the strong persuasions of Cranmer and Ridley. He always viewed it with horror; and when he fell into a sickly condition, after having been very ill, first of the measles and then of the small-pox, he was greatly troubled in mind to think that if he died, and she, the next heir to the throne, succeeded, the Roman Catholic religion would be set up again.

This uneasiness, the Duke of Northumberland was not slow to encourage: for, if the Princess Mary came to the throne, he, who had taken part with the Protestants, was sure to be disgraced. Now, the Duchess of Suffolk was descended from King Henry the Seventh; and, if she resigned what little or no right she had, in favour of her daughter Lady Jane Grey, that would be the succession to promote the Duke's greatness; because Lord Guilford Dudley, one of his sons, was, at this very time, newly married to her. So, he worked upon the King's fears, and persuaded him to set aside both the Princess Mary and the Princess Elizabeth, and assert his right to appoint his successor. Accordingly the young King handed to the Crown lawyers a writing signed half a dozen times over by himself, appointing Lady Jane Grey to succeed to the Crown, and requiring them to have his will made out according to law. They were much against it at first, and told the King so; but the Duke of Northumberland—being so violent about it that the lawyers even expected him to beat them, and hotly declaring that, stripped to his shirt, he would fight any man in such a quarrel—they yielded. Cranmer, also, at first hesitated; pleading that he had sworn to maintain the succession of the Crown to the Princess Mary; but, he was a weak man in his resolutions, and afterwards signed the document with the rest of the council.

It was completed none too soon; for Edward was now sinking in a rapid decline; and, by way of making him better, they handed him over to a woman-doctor who pretended to be able to cure it. He speedily got worse. On the sixth of July, in the year one thousand five hundred and fifty-three, he died, very peaceably and piously, praying God, with his last breath, to protect the reformed religion.

This King died in the sixteenth year of his age, and in the seventh of his reign. It is difficult to judge what the character of one so young might afterwards have become among so many bad, ambitious, quarrelling nobles. But, he was an amiable boy, of very good abilities, and had nothing coarse or cruel or brutal in his disposition—which in the son of such a father is rather surprising.

CHAPTER XXX—ENGLAND UNDER MARY

The Duke of Northumberland was very anxious to keep the young King's death a secret, in order that he might get the two Princesses into his power. But, the Princess Mary, being informed of that event as she was on her way to London to see her sick brother, turned her horse's head, and rode away into Norfolk. The Earl of Arundel was her friend, and it was he who sent her warning of what had happened.

As the secret could not be kept, the Duke of Northumberland and the council sent for the Lord Mayor of London and some of the aldermen, and made a merit of telling it to them. Then, they made it known to the people, and set off to inform Lady Jane Grey that she was to be Queen.

She was a pretty girl of only sixteen, and was amiable, learned, and clever. When the lords who came to her, fell on their knees before her, and told her what tidings they brought, she was so astonished that she fainted. On recovering, she expressed her sorrow for the young King's death, and said that she knew she was unfit to govern the kingdom; but that if she must be Queen, she prayed God to direct her. She was then at Sion House, near Brentford; and the lords took her down the river in state to the Tower, that she might remain there (as the custom was) until she was crowned. But the people were not at all favourable to Lady Jane, considering that the right to be Queen was Mary's, and greatly disliking the Duke of Northumberland. They were not put into a better humour by the Duke's causing a vintner's servant, one Gabriel Pot, to be taken up for expressing his dissatisfaction among the crowd, and to have his ears nailed to the pillory, and cut off. Some powerful men among the nobility declared on Mary's side. They raised troops to support her cause, had her proclaimed Queen at Norwich, and gathered around her at the castle of Framlingham, which belonged to the Duke of Norfolk. For, she was not considered so safe as yet, but that it was best to keep her in a castle on the sea-coast, from whence she might be sent abroad, if necessary.

The Council would have despatched Lady Jane's father, the Duke of Suffolk, as the general of the army against this force; but, as Lady Jane implored that her father might remain with her, and as he was known to be but a weak man, they told the Duke of Northumberland that he must take the command himself. He was not very ready to do so, as he mistrusted the Council much; but there was no help for it, and he set forth with a heavy heart, observing to a lord who rode beside him through Shoreditch at the head of the troops, that, although the people pressed in great numbers to look at them, they were terribly silent.

And his fears for himself turned out to be well founded. While he was waiting at Cambridge for further help from the Council, the Council took it into their heads to turn their backs on Lady Jane's cause, and to take up the Princess Mary's. This was chiefly owing to the before-mentioned Earl of Arundel, who represented to the Lord Mayor and aldermen, in a second interview with those sagacious persons, that, as for himself, he did not perceive the Reformed religion to be in much danger—which Lord Pembroke backed by flourishing his sword as another kind of persuasion. The Lord Mayor and aldermen, thus enlightened, said there could be no doubt that the Princess Mary ought to be Queen. So, she was proclaimed at the Cross by St. Paul's, and barrels of wine were given to the people, and they got very drunk, and danced round blazing bonfires—little thinking, poor wretches, what other bonfires would soon be blazing in Queen Mary's name.

After a ten days' dream of royalty, Lady Jane Grey resigned the Crown with great willingness, saying that she had only accepted it in obedience to her father and mother; and went gladly back to her pleasant house by the river, and her books. Mary then came on towards London; and at Wanstead in Essex, was joined by her half-sister, the Princess Elizabeth. They passed through the streets of London to the Tower, and there the new Queen met some eminent prisoners then confined in it, kissed them, and gave them their liberty. Among these was that Gardiner, Bishop of Winchester, who had been imprisoned in the last reign for holding to the unreformed religion. Him she soon made chancellor.

The Duke of Northumberland had been taken prisoner, and, together with his son and five others, was quickly brought before the Council. He, not unnaturally, asked that Council, in his defence, whether it was treason to obey orders that had been issued under the great seal; and, if it were, whether they, who had obeyed them too, ought to be his judges? But they made light of these points; and, being resolved to have him out of the way, soon sentenced him to death. He had risen into power upon the death of another man, and made but a poor show (as might be expected) when he himself lay low. He entreated Gardiner to let him live, if it were only in a mouse's hole; and, when he ascended the scaffold to be beheaded on Tower Hill, addressed the people in a miserable way, saying that he had been incited by others, and exhorting them to return to the unreformed religion, which he told them was his faith. There seems reason to suppose that he expected a pardon even then, in return for this confession; but it matters little whether he did or not. His head was struck off.

Mary was now crowned Queen. She was thirty-seven years of age, short and thin, wrinkled in the face, and very unhealthy. But she had a great liking for show and for bright colours, and all the ladies of her Court were magnificently dressed. She had a great liking too for old customs, without much sense in them; and she was oiled in the oldest way, and blessed in the oldest way, and done all manner of things to in the oldest way, at her coronation. I hope they did her good.

She soon began to show her desire to put down the Reformed religion, and put up the unreformed one: though it was dangerous work as yet, the people being something wiser than they used to be. They even cast a shower of stones—and among them a dagger—at one of the royal chaplains who attacked the Reformed religion in a public sermon. But the Queen and her priests went steadily on. Ridley, the powerful bishop of the last reign, was seized and sent to the Tower. Latimer, also celebrated among the Clergy of the last reign, was likewise sent to the Tower, and Cranmer speedily followed. Latimer was an aged man; and, as his guards took him through Smithfield, he looked round it, and said, 'This is a place that hath long groaned for me.' For he knew well, what kind of bonfires would soon be burning. Nor was the knowledge confined to him. The prisons were fast filled with the chief Protestants, who were there left rotting in darkness, hunger, dirt, and separation from their friends; many, who had time left them for escape, fled from the kingdom; and the dullest of the people began, now, to see what was coming.

It came on fast. A Parliament was got together; not without strong suspicion of unfairness; and they annulled the divorce, formerly pronounced by Cranmer between the Queen's mother and King Henry the Eighth, and unmade all the laws on the subject of religion that had been made in the last King Edward's reign. They began their proceedings, in violation of the law, by having the old mass said before them in Latin, and by turning out a bishop who would not kneel down. They also declared guilty of treason, Lady Jane Grey for aspiring to the Crown; her husband, for being her husband; and Cranmer, for not believing in the mass aforesaid. They then prayed the Queen graciously to choose a husband for herself, as soon as might be.

Now, the question who should be the Queen's husband had given rise to a great deal of discussion, and to several contending parties. Some said Cardinal Pole was the man—but the Queen was of opinion that he was not the man, he being too old and too much of a student. Others said that the gallant young Courtenay, whom the Queen had made Earl of Devonshire, was the man—and the Queen thought so too, for a while; but she changed her mind. At last it appeared that Philip, Prince of Spain, was certainly the man—though certainly not the people's man; for they detested the idea of such a marriage from the beginning to the end, and murmured that the Spaniard would establish in England, by the aid of foreign soldiers, the worst abuses of the Popish religion, and even the terrible Inquisition itself.

These discontents gave rise to a conspiracy for marrying young Courtenay to the Princess Elizabeth, and setting them up, with popular tumults all over the kingdom, against the Queen. This was discovered in time by Gardiner; but in Kent, the old bold county, the people rose in their old bold way. Sir Thomas Wyat, a man of great daring, was their leader. He raised his standard at Maidstone, marched on to Rochester, established himself in the old castle there, and prepared to hold out against the Duke of Norfolk, who came against him with a party of the Queen's guards, and a body of five hundred London men. The London men, however, were all for Elizabeth, and not at all for Mary. They declared, under the castle walls, for Wyat; the Duke retreated; and Wyat came on to Deptford, at the head of fifteen thousand men.

But these, in their turn, fell away. When he came to Southwark, there were only two thousand left. Not dismayed by finding the London citizens in arms, and the guns at the Tower ready to oppose his crossing the river there, Wyat led them off to Kingston-upon-Thames, intending to cross the bridge that he knew to be in that place, and so to work his way round to Ludgate, one of the old gates of the City. He found the bridge broken down, but mended it, came across, and bravely fought his way up Fleet Street to Ludgate Hill. Finding the gate closed against him, he fought his way back again, sword in hand, to Temple Bar. Here, being overpowered, he surrendered himself, and three or four hundred of his men were taken, besides a hundred killed. Wyat, in a moment of weakness (and perhaps of torture) was afterwards made to accuse the Princess Elizabeth as his accomplice to some very small extent. But his manhood soon returned to him, and he refused to save his life by making any more false confessions. He was quartered and distributed in the usual brutal way, and from fifty to a hundred of his followers were hanged. The rest were led out, with halters round their necks, to be pardoned, and to make a parade of crying out, 'God save Queen Mary!'

In the danger of this rebellion, the Queen showed herself to be a woman of courage and spirit. She disdained to retreat to any place of safety, and went down to the Guildhall, sceptre in hand, and made a gallant speech to the Lord Mayor and citizens. But on the day after Wyat's defeat, she did the most cruel act, even of her cruel reign, in signing the warrant for the execution of Lady Jane Grey.

They tried to persuade Lady Jane to accept the unreformed religion; but she steadily refused. On the morning when she was to die, she saw from her window the bleeding and headless body of her husband brought back in a cart from the scaffold on Tower Hill where he had laid down his life. But, as she had declined to see him before his execution, lest she should be overpowered and not make a good end, so, she even now showed a constancy and calmness that will never be forgotten. She came up to the scaffold with a firm step and a quiet face, and addressed the bystanders in a steady voice. They were not numerous; for she was too young, too innocent and fair, to be murdered before the people on Tower Hill, as her husband had just been; so, the place of her execution was within the Tower itself. She said that she had done an unlawful act in taking what was Queen Mary's right; but that she had done so with no bad intent, and that she died a humble Christian. She begged the executioner to despatch her quickly, and she asked him, 'Will you take my head off before I lay me down?' He answered, 'No, Madam,' and then she was very quiet while they bandaged her eyes. Being blinded, and unable to see the block on which she was to lay her young head, she was seen to feel about for it with her hands, and was heard to say, confused, 'O what shall I do! Where is it?' Then they guided her to the right place, and the executioner struck off her head. You know too well, now, what dreadful deeds the executioner did in England, through many, many years, and how his axe descended on the hateful block through the necks of some of the bravest, wisest, and best in the land. But it never struck so cruel and so vile a blow as this.

The father of Lady Jane soon followed, but was little pitied. Queen Mary's next object was to lay hold of Elizabeth, and this was pursued with great eagerness. Five hundred men were sent to her retired house at Ashridge, by Berkhampstead, with orders to bring her up, alive or dead. They got there at ten at night, when she was sick in bed. But, their leaders followed her lady into her bedchamber, whence she was brought out betimes next morning, and put into a litter to be conveyed to London. She was so weak and ill, that she was five days on the road; still, she was so resolved to be seen by the people that she had the curtains of the litter opened; and so, very pale and sickly, passed through the streets. She wrote to her sister, saying she was innocent of any crime, and asking why she was made a prisoner; but she got no answer, and was ordered to the Tower. They took her in by the Traitor's Gate, to which she objected, but in vain. One of the lords who conveyed her offered to cover her with his cloak, as it was raining, but she put it away from her, proudly and scornfully, and passed into the Tower, and sat down in a court-yard on a stone. They besought her to come in out of the wet; but she answered that it was better sitting there, than in a worse place. At length she went to her apartment, where she was kept a prisoner, though not so close a prisoner as at Woodstock, whither she was afterwards removed, and where she is said to have one day envied a milkmaid whom she heard singing in the sunshine as she went through the green fields. Gardiner, than whom there were not many worse men among the fierce and sullen priests, cared little to keep secret his stern desire for her death: being used to say that it was of little service to shake off the leaves, and lop the branches of the tree of heresy, if its root, the hope of heretics, were left. He failed, however, in his benevolent design. Elizabeth was, at length, released; and Hatfield House was assigned to her as a residence, under the care of one Sir Thomas Pope.

It would seem that Philip, the Prince of Spain, was a main cause of this change in Elizabeth's fortunes. He was not an amiable man, being, on the contrary, proud, overbearing, and gloomy; but he and the Spanish lords who came over with him, assuredly did discountenance the idea of doing any violence to the Princess. It may have been mere prudence, but we will hope it was manhood and honour. The Queen had been expecting her husband with great impatience, and at length he came, to her great joy, though he never cared much for her. They were married by Gardiner, at Winchester, and there was more holiday-making among the people; but they had their old distrust of this Spanish marriage, in which even the Parliament shared. Though the members of that Parliament were far from honest, and were strongly suspected to have been bought with Spanish money, they would pass no bill to enable the Queen to set aside the Princess Elizabeth and appoint her own successor.

Although Gardiner failed in this object, as well as in the darker one of bringing the Princess to the scaffold, he went on at a great pace in the revival of the unreformed religion. A new Parliament was packed, in which there were no Protestants. Preparations were made to receive Cardinal Pole in England as the Pope's messenger, bringing his holy declaration that all the nobility who had acquired Church property, should keep it—which was done to enlist their selfish interest on the Pope's side. Then a great scene was enacted, which was the triumph of the Queen's plans. Cardinal Pole arrived in great splendour and dignity, and was received with great pomp.

The Parliament joined in a petition expressive of their sorrow at the change in the national religion, and praying him to receive the country again into the Popish Church. With the Queen sitting on her throne, and the King on one side of her, and the Cardinal on the other, and the Parliament present, Gardiner read the petition aloud. The Cardinal then made a great speech, and was so obliging as to say that all was forgotten and forgiven, and that the kingdom was solemnly made Roman Catholic again.

Everything was now ready for the lighting of the terrible bonfires. The Queen having declared to the Council, in writing, that she would wish none of her subjects to be burnt without some of the Council being present, and that she would particularly wish there to be good sermons at all burnings, the Council knew pretty well what was to be done next. So, after the Cardinal had blessed all the bishops as a preface to the burnings, the Chancellor Gardiner opened a High Court at Saint Mary Overy, on the Southwark side of London Bridge, for the trial of heretics. Here, two of the late Protestant clergymen, Hooper, Bishop of Gloucester, and Rogers, a Prebendary of St. Paul's, were brought to be tried. Hooper was tried first for being married, though a priest, and for not believing in the mass. He admitted both of these accusations, and said that the mass was a wicked imposition. Then they tried Rogers, who said the same. Next morning the two were brought up to be sentenced; and then Rogers said that his poor wife, being a German woman and a stranger in the land, he hoped might be allowed to come to speak to him before he died. To this the inhuman Gardiner replied, that she was not his wife. 'Yea, but she is, my lord,' said Rogers, 'and she hath been my wife these eighteen years.' His request was still refused, and they were both sent to Newgate; all those who stood in the streets to sell things, being ordered to put out their lights that the people might not see them. But, the people stood at their doors with candles in their hands, and prayed for them as they went by. Soon afterwards, Rogers was taken out of jail to be burnt in Smithfield; and, in the crowd as he went along, he saw his poor wife and his ten children, of whom the youngest was a little baby. And so he was burnt to death.

The next day, Hooper, who was to be burnt at Gloucester, was brought out to take his last journey, and was made to wear a hood over his face that he might not be known by the people. But, they did know him for all that, down in his own part of the country; and, when he came near Gloucester, they lined the road, making prayers and lamentations. His guards took him to a lodging, where he slept soundly all night. At nine o'clock next morning, he was brought forth leaning on a staff; for he had taken cold in prison, and was infirm. The iron stake, and the iron chain which was to bind him to it, were fixed up near a great elm-tree in a pleasant open place before the cathedral, where, on peaceful Sundays, he had been accustomed to preach and to pray, when he was bishop of Gloucester. This tree, which had no leaves then, it being February, was filled with people; and the priests of Gloucester College were looking complacently on from a window, and there was a great concourse of spectators in every spot from which a glimpse of the dreadful sight could be beheld. When the old man kneeled down on the small platform at the foot of the stake, and prayed aloud, the nearest people were observed to be so attentive to his prayers that they were ordered to stand farther back; for it did not suit the Romish Church to have those Protestant words heard. His prayers concluded, he went up to the stake and was stripped to his shirt, and chained ready for the fire. One of his guards had such compassion on him that, to shorten his agonies, he tied some packets of gunpowder about him. Then they heaped up wood and straw and reeds, and set them all alight. But, unhappily, the wood was green and damp, and there was a wind blowing that blew what flame there was, away. Thus, through three-quarters of an hour, the good old man was scorched and roasted and smoked, as the fire rose and sank; and all that time they saw him, as he burned, moving his lips in prayer, and beating his breast with one hand, even after the other was burnt away and had fallen off.

Cranmer, Ridley, and Latimer, were taken to Oxford to dispute with a commission of priests and doctors about the mass. They were shamefully treated; and it is recorded that the Oxford scholars hissed and howled and groaned, and misconducted themselves in an anything but a scholarly way. The prisoners were taken back to jail, and afterwards tried in St. Mary's Church. They were all found guilty. On the sixteenth of the month of October, Ridley and Latimer were brought out, to make another of the dreadful bonfires.

The scene of the suffering of these two good Protestant men was in the

City ditch, near Baliol College. On coming to the dreadful spot, they kissed the stakes, and then embraced each other. And then a learned doctor got up into a pulpit which was placed there, and preached a sermon from the text, 'Though I give my body to be burned, and have not charity, it profiteth me nothing.' When you think of the charity of burning men alive, you may imagine that this learned doctor had a rather brazen face. Ridley would have answered his sermon when it came to an end, but was not allowed. When Latimer was stripped, it appeared that he had dressed himself under his other clothes, in a new shroud; and, as he stood in it before all the people, it was noted of him, and long remembered, that, whereas he had been stooping and feeble but a few minutes before, he now stood upright and handsome, in the knowledge that he was dying for a just and a great cause. Ridley's brother-in-law was there with bags of gunpowder; and when they were both chained up, he tied them round their bodies. Then, a light was thrown upon the pile to fire it. 'Be of good comfort, Master Ridley,' said Latimer, at that awful moment, 'and play the man! We shall this day light such a candle, by God's grace, in England, as I trust shall never be put out.' And then he was seen to make motions with his hands as if he were washing them in the flames, and to stroke his aged face with them, and was heard to cry, 'Father of Heaven, receive my soul!' He died quickly, but the fire, after having burned the legs of Ridley, sunk. There he lingered, chained to the iron post, and crying, 'O! I cannot burn! O! for Christ's sake let the fire come unto me!' And still, when his brother-in-law had heaped on more wood, he was heard through the blinding smoke, still dismally crying, 'O! I cannot burn, I cannot burn!' At last, the gunpowder caught fire, and ended his miseries.

Five days after this fearful scene, Gardiner went to his tremendous account before God, for the cruelties he had so much assisted in committing.

Cranmer remained still alive and in prison. He was brought out again in February, for more examining and trying, by Bonner, Bishop of London: another man of blood, who had succeeded to Gardiner's work, even in his lifetime, when Gardiner was tired of it. Cranmer was now degraded as a priest, and left for death; but, if the Queen hated any one on earth, she hated him, and it was resolved that he should be ruined and disgraced to the utmost.

There is no doubt that the Queen and her husband personally urged on these deeds, because they wrote to the Council, urging them to be active in the kindling of the fearful fires. As Cranmer was known not to be a firm man, a plan was laid for surrounding him with artful people, and inducing him to recant to the unreformed religion. Deans and friars visited him, played at bowls with him, showed him various attentions, talked persuasively with him, gave him money for his prison comforts, and induced him to sign, I fear, as many as six recantations. But when, after all, he was taken out to be burnt, he was nobly true to his better self, and made a glorious end.

After prayers and a sermon, Dr. Cole, the preacher of the day (who had been one of the artful priests about Cranmer in prison), required him to make a public confession of his faith before the people. This, Cole did, expecting that he would declare himself a Roman Catholic. 'I will make a profession of my faith,' said Cranmer, 'and with a good will too.'

Then, he arose before them all, and took from the sleeve of his robe a written prayer and read it aloud. That done, he kneeled and said the Lord's Prayer, all the people joining; and then he arose again and told them that he believed in the Bible, and that in what he had lately written, he had written what was not the truth, and that, because his right hand had signed those papers, he would burn his right hand first when he came to the fire. As for the Pope, he did refuse him and denounce him as the enemy of Heaven. Hereupon the pious Dr. Cole cried out to the guards to stop that heretic's mouth and take him away.

So they took him away, and chained him to the stake, where he hastily took off his own clothes to make ready for the flames. And he stood before the people with a bald head and a white and flowing beard. He was so firm now when the worst was come, that he again declared against his recantation, and was so impressive and so undismayed, that a certain lord, who was one of the directors of the execution, called out to the men to make haste! When the fire was lighted, Cranmer, true to his latest word, stretched out his right hand, and crying out, 'This hand hath offended!' held it among the flames, until it blazed and burned away. His heart was found entire among his ashes, and he left at last a memorable name in English history. Cardinal Pole celebrated

289

the day by saying his first mass, and next day he was made Archbishop of Canterbury in Cranmer's place.

The Queen's husband, who was now mostly abroad in his own dominions, and generally made a coarse jest of her to his more familiar courtiers, was at war with France, and came over to seek the assistance of England. England was very unwilling to engage in a French war for his sake; but it happened that the King of France, at this very time, aided a descent upon the English coast. Hence, war was declared, greatly to Philip's satisfaction; and the Queen raised a sum of money with which to carry it on, by every unjustifiable means in her power. It met with no profitable return, for the French Duke of Guise surprised Calais, and the English sustained a complete defeat. The losses they met with in France greatly mortified the national pride, and the Queen never recovered the blow.

There was a bad fever raging in England at this time, and I am glad to write that the Queen took it, and the hour of her death came. 'When I am dead and my body is opened,' she said to those around those around her, 'ye shall find Calais written on my heart.' I should have thought, if anything were written on it, they would have found the words—Jane Grey, Hooper, Rogers, Ridley, Latimer, Cranmer, and three hundred people burnt alive within four years of my wicked reign, including sixty women and forty little children. But it is enough that their deaths were written in Heaven.

The Queen died on the seventeenth of November, fifteen hundred and fifty-eight, after reigning not quite five years and a half, and in the forty-fourth year of her age. Cardinal Pole died of the same fever next day.

As Bloody Queen Mary, this woman has become famous, and as Bloody Queen Mary, she will ever be justly remembered with horror and detestation in Great Britain. Her memory has been held in such abhorrence that some writers have arisen in later years to take her part, and to show that she was, upon the whole, quite an amiable and cheerful sovereign! 'By their fruits ye shall know them,' said Our Saviour. The stake and the fire were the fruits of this reign, and you will judge this Queen by nothing else.

CHAPTER XXXI—ENGLAND UNDER ELIZABETH

There was great rejoicing all over the land when the Lords of the Council went down to Hatfield, to hail the Princess Elizabeth as the new Queen of England. Weary of the barbarities of Mary's reign, the people looked with hope and gladness to the new Sovereign. The nation seemed to wake from a horrible dream; and Heaven, so long hidden by the smoke of the fires that roasted men and women to death, appeared to brighten once more.

Queen Elizabeth was five-and-twenty years of age when she rode through the streets of London, from the Tower to Westminster Abbey, to be crowned. Her countenance was strongly marked, but on the whole, commanding and dignified; her hair was red, and her nose something too long and sharp for a woman's. She was not the beautiful creature her courtiers made out; but she was well enough, and no doubt looked all the better for coming after the dark and gloomy Mary. She was well educated, but a roundabout writer, and rather a hard swearer and coarse talker. She was clever, but cunning and deceitful, and inherited much of her father's violent temper. I mention this now, because she has been so over-praised by one party, and so over-abused by another, that it is hardly possible to understand the greater part of her reign without first understanding what kind of woman she really was.

She began her reign with the great advantage of having a very wise and careful Minister, Sir William Cecil, whom she afterwards made Lord Burleigh. Altogether, the people had greater reason for rejoicing than they usually had, when there were processions in the streets; and they were happy with some reason. All kinds of shows and images were set up; Gog and Magog were hoisted to the top of Temple Bar, and (which was more to the purpose) the Corporation dutifully presented the young Queen with the sum of a thousand marks in gold—so heavy a present, that she was obliged to take it into her carriage with both hands. The coronation was a great success; and, on the next day, one of the courtiers presented a petition to the new Queen, praying that as it was the custom to release some prisoners on such occasions, she would have the goodness to release the four Evangelists, Matthew, Mark, Luke, and John, and also the Apostle Saint Paul, who had been for some time shut up in a strange language so that the people could not get at them.

To this, the Queen replied that it would be better first to inquire of themselves whether they desired to be released or not; and, as a means of finding out, a great public discussion—a sort of religious tournament—was appointed to take place between certain champions of the two religions, in Westminster Abbey. You may suppose that it was soon made pretty clear to common sense, that for people to benefit by what they repeat or read, it is rather necessary they should understand something about it. Accordingly, a Church Service in plain English was settled, and other laws and regulations were made, completely establishing the great work of the Reformation. The Romish bishops and champions were not harshly dealt with, all things considered; and the Queen's Ministers were both prudent and merciful.

The one great trouble of this reign, and the unfortunate cause of the greater part of such turmoil and bloodshed as occurred in it, was Mary Stuart, Queen of Scots. We will try to understand, in as few words as possible, who Mary was, what she was, and how she came to be a thorn in the royal pillow of Elizabeth.

She was the daughter of the Queen Regent of Scotland, Mary of Guise. She had been married, when a mere child, to the Dauphin, the son and heir of the King of France. The Pope, who pretended that no one could rightfully wear the crown of England without his gracious permission, was strongly opposed to Elizabeth, who had not asked for the said gracious permission. And as Mary Queen of Scots would have inherited the English crown in right of her birth, supposing the English Parliament not to have altered the succession, the Pope himself, and most of the discontented who were followers of his, maintained that Mary was the rightful Queen of England, and Elizabeth the wrongful Queen. Mary being so closely connected with France, and France being jealous of England, there was far greater danger in this than there would have been if she had had no alliance with that great power. And when her young husband, on the death of his father, became Francis the Second, King of France, the matter grew very serious. For, the young couple styled themselves King and Queen of England, and the Pope was disposed to help them by doing all the mischief he could.

Now, the reformed religion, under the guidance of a stern and powerful preacher, named John Knox, and other such men, had been making fierce progress in Scotland. It was still a half savage country, where there was a great deal of murdering and rioting continually going on; and the Reformers, instead of reforming those evils as they should have done, went to work in the ferocious old Scottish spirit, laying churches and chapels waste, pulling down pictures and altars, and knocking about the Grey Friars, and the Black Friars, and the White Friars, and the friars of all sorts of colours, in all directions. This obdurate and harsh spirit of the Scottish Reformers (the Scotch have always been rather a sullen and frowning people in religious matters) put up the blood of the Romish French court, and caused France to send troops over to Scotland, with the hope of setting the friars of all sorts of colours on their legs again; of conquering that country first, and England afterwards; and so crushing the Reformation all to pieces. The Scottish Reformers, who had formed a great league which they called The Congregation of the Lord, secretly represented to Elizabeth that, if the reformed religion got the worst of it with them, it would be likely to get the worst of it in England too; and thus, Elizabeth, though she had a high notion of the rights of Kings and Queens to do anything they liked, sent an army to Scotland to support the Reformers, who were in arms against their sovereign. All these proceedings led to a treaty of peace at Edinburgh, under which the French consented to depart from the kingdom. By a separate treaty, Mary and her young husband engaged to renounce their assumed title of King and Queen of England. But this treaty they never fulfilled.

It happened, soon after matters had got to this state, that the young French King died, leaving Mary a young widow. She was then invited by her Scottish subjects to return home and reign over them; and as she was not now happy where she was, she, after a little time, complied.

Elizabeth had been Queen three years, when Mary Queen of Scots embarked at Calais for her own rough, quarrelling country. As she came out of the harbour, a vessel was lost before her eyes, and she said, 'O! good

293

God! what an omen this is for such a voyage!' She was very fond of France, and sat on the deck, looking back at it and weeping, until it was quite dark. When she went to bed, she directed to be called at daybreak, if the French coast were still visible, that she might behold it for the last time. As it proved to be a clear morning, this was done, and she again wept for the country she was leaving, and said many times, 'Farewell, France! Farewell, France! I shall never see thee again!' All this was long remembered afterwards, as sorrowful and interesting in a fair young princess of nineteen. Indeed, I am afraid it gradually came, together with her other distresses, to surround her with greater sympathy than she deserved.

When she came to Scotland, and took up her abode at the palace of Holyrood in Edinburgh, she found herself among uncouth strangers and wild uncomfortable customs very different from her experiences in the court of France. The very people who were disposed to love her, made her head ache when she was tired out by her voyage, with a serenade of discordant music—a fearful concert of bagpipes, I suppose—and brought her and her train home to her palace on miserable little Scotch horses that appeared to be half starved. Among the people who were not disposed to love her, she found the powerful leaders of the Reformed Church, who were bitter upon her amusements, however innocent, and denounced music and dancing as works of the devil. John Knox himself often lectured her, violently and angrily, and did much to make her life unhappy. All these reasons confirmed her old attachment to the Romish religion, and caused her, there is no doubt, most imprudently and dangerously both for herself and for England too, to give a solemn pledge to the heads of the Romish Church that if she ever succeeded to the English crown, she would set up that religion again. In reading her unhappy history, you must always remember this; and also that during her whole life she was constantly put forward against the Queen, in some form or other, by the Romish party.

That Elizabeth, on the other hand, was not inclined to like her, is pretty certain. Elizabeth was very vain and jealous, and had an extraordinary dislike to people being married. She treated Lady Catherine Grey, sister of the beheaded Lady Jane, with such shameful severity, for no other reason than her being secretly married, that she died and her husband was ruined; so, when a second marriage for Mary began to be talked about, probably Elizabeth disliked her more. Not that Elizabeth wanted suitors of her own, for they started up from Spain, Austria, Sweden, and England. Her English lover at this time, and one whom she much favoured too, was Lord Robert Dudley, Earl of Leicester—himself secretly married to Amy Robsart, the daughter of an English gentleman, whom he was strongly suspected of causing to be murdered, down at his country seat, Cumnor Hall in Berkshire, that he might be free to marry the Queen. Upon this story, the great writer, Sir Walter Scott, has founded one of his best romances. But if Elizabeth knew how to lead her handsome favourite on, for her own vanity and pleasure, she knew how to stop him for her own pride; and his love, and all the other proposals, came to nothing. The Queen always declared in good set speeches, that she would never be married at all, but would live and die a Maiden Queen. It was a very pleasant and meritorious declaration, I suppose; but it has been puffed and trumpeted so much, that I am rather tired of it myself.

Divers princes proposed to marry Mary, but the English court had reasons for being jealous of them all, and even proposed as a matter of policy that she should marry that very Earl of Leicester who had aspired to be the husband of Elizabeth. At last, Lord Darnley, son of the Earl of Lennox, and himself descended from the Royal Family of Scotland, went over with Elizabeth's consent to try his fortune at Holyrood. He was a tall simpleton; and could dance and play the guitar; but I know of nothing else he could do, unless it were to get very drunk, and eat gluttonously, and make a contemptible spectacle of himself in many mean and vain ways. However, he gained Mary's heart, not disdaining in the pursuit of his object to ally himself with one of her secretaries, David Rizzio, who had great influence with her. He soon married the Queen. This marriage does not say much for her, but what followed will presently say less.

Mary's brother, the Earl of Murray, and head of the Protestant party in Scotland, had opposed this marriage, partly on religious grounds, and partly perhaps from personal dislike of the very contemptible bridegroom. When it had taken place, through Mary's gaining over to it the more powerful of the lords about her, she banished Murray for his pains; and, when he and some other nobles rose in arms to support the reformed religion, she herself, within a month of her wedding day, rode against them in armour with loaded pistols in her saddle. Driven out of Scotland, they presented themselves before Elizabeth—who called them traitors in public, and assisted them in private, according to her crafty nature.

Mary had been married but a little while, when she began to hate her husband, who, in his turn, began to hate that David Rizzio, with whom he had leagued to gain her favour, and whom he now believed to be her lover. He hated Rizzio to that extent, that he made a compact with Lord Ruthven and three other lords to get rid of him by murder. This wicked agreement they made in solemn secrecy upon the first of March, fifteen hundred and sixty-six, and on the night of Saturday the ninth, the conspirators were brought by Darnley up a private staircase, dark and steep, into a range of rooms where they knew that Mary was sitting at supper with her sister, Lady Argyle, and this doomed man. When they went into the room, Darnley took the Queen round the waist, and Lord Ruthven, who had risen from a bed of sickness to do this murder, came in, gaunt and ghastly, leaning on two men. Rizzio ran behind the Queen for shelter and protection. 'Let him come out of the room,' said Ruthven. 'He shall not leave the room,' replied the Queen; 'I read his danger in your face, and it is my will that he remain here.' They then set upon him, struggled with him, overturned the table, dragged him out, and killed him with fifty-six stabs. When the Queen heard that he was dead, she said, 'No more tears. I will think now of revenge!'

Within a day or two, she gained her husband over, and prevailed on the tall idiot to abandon the conspirators and fly with her to Dunbar. There, he issued a proclamation, audaciously and falsely denying that he had any knowledge of the late bloody business; and there they were joined by the Earl Bothwell and some other nobles. With their help, they raised eight thousand men; returned to Edinburgh, and drove the assassins into England. Mary soon afterwards gave birth to a son—still thinking of revenge.

That she should have had a greater scorn for her husband after his late cowardice and treachery than she had had before, was natural enough. There is little doubt that she now began to love Bothwell instead, and to plan with him means of getting rid of Darnley. Bothwell had such power over her that he induced her even to pardon the assassins of Rizzio. The arrangements for the Christening of the young Prince were entrusted to him, and he was one of the most important people at the ceremony, where the child was named James: Elizabeth being his godmother, though not present on the occasion. A week afterwards, Darnley, who had left Mary and gone to his father's house at Glasgow, being taken ill with the small-pox, she sent her own physician to attend him. But there is reason to apprehend that this was merely a show and a pretence, and that she knew what was doing, when Bothwell within another month proposed to one of the late conspirators against Rizzio, to murder Darnley, 'for that it was the Queen's mind that he should be taken away.' It is certain that on that very day she wrote to her ambassador in France, complaining of him, and yet went immediately to Glasgow, feigning to be very anxious about him, and to love him very much. If she wanted to get him in her power, she succeeded to her heart's content; for she induced him to go back with her to Edinburgh, and to occupy, instead of the palace, a lone house outside the city called the Kirk of Field. Here, he lived for about a week. One Sunday night, she remained with him until ten o'clock, and then left him, to go to Holyrood to be present at an entertainment given in celebration of the marriage of one of her favourite servants. At two o'clock in the morning the city was shaken by a great explosion, and the Kirk of Field was blown to atoms.

Darnley's body was found next day lying under a tree at some distance. How it came there, undisfigured and unscorched by gunpowder, and how this crime came to be so clumsily and strangely committed, it is impossible to discover. The deceitful character of Mary, and the deceitful character of Elizabeth, have rendered almost every part of their joint history uncertain and obscure. But, I fear that Mary was unquestionably a party to her husband's murder, and that this was the revenge she had threatened. The Scotch people universally believed it. Voices cried out in the streets of Edinburgh in the dead of the night, for justice on the murderess. Placards were posted by unknown hands in the public places denouncing Bothwell as the murderer, and the Queen as his accomplice; and, when he afterwards married her (though himself already married), previously making a show of taking her prisoner by force, the indignation of the people knew no bounds. The women particularly are described as having been quite frantic against the Queen, and to have hooted and cried after her in the streets with terrific vehemence.

Such guilty unions seldom prosper. This husband and wife had lived together but a month, when they were separated for ever by the successes of a band of Scotch nobles who associated against them for the protection of the young Prince: whom Bothwell had vainly endeavoured to lay hold of, and whom he would certainly have murdered, if the Earl of Mar, in whose hands the boy was, had not been firmly and honourably faithful to his trust. Before this angry power, Bothwell fled abroad, where he died, a prisoner and mad, nine miserable years afterwards. Mary being found by the associated lords to deceive them at every turn, was sent a prisoner to Lochleven Castle; which, as it stood in the midst of a lake, could only be approached by boat. Here, one Lord Lindsay, who was so much of a brute that the nobles would have done better if they had chosen a mere gentleman for their messenger, made her sign her abdication, and appoint Murray, Regent of Scotland. Here, too, Murray saw her in a sorrowing and humbled state.

She had better have remained in the castle of Lochleven, dull prison as it was, with the rippling of the lake against it, and the moving shadows of the water on the room walls; but she could not rest there, and more than once tried to escape. The first time she had nearly succeeded, dressed in the clothes of her own washer-woman, but, putting up her hand to prevent one of the boatmen from lifting her veil, the men suspected her, seeing how white it was, and rowed her back again. A short time afterwards, her fascinating manners enlisted in her cause a boy in the Castle, called the little Douglas, who, while the family were at supper, stole the keys of the great gate, went softly out with the Queen, locked the gate on the outside, and rowed her away across the lake, sinking the keys as they went along. On the opposite shore she was met by another Douglas, and some few lords; and, so accompanied, rode away on horseback to Hamilton, where they raised three thousand men. Here, she issued a proclamation declaring that the abdication she had signed in her prison was illegal, and requiring the Regent to yield to his lawful Queen.

Being a steady soldier, and in no way discomposed although he was without an army, Murray pretended to treat with her, until he had collected a force about half equal to her own, and then he gave her battle. In one quarter of an hour he cut down all her hopes. She had another weary ride on horse-back of sixty long Scotch miles, and took shelter at Dundrennan Abbey, whence she fled for safety to Elizabeth's dominions.

Mary Queen of Scots came to England—to her own ruin, the trouble of the kingdom, and the misery and death of many—in the year one thousand five hundred and sixty-eight. How she left it and the world, nineteen years afterwards, we have now to see.

SECOND PART

When Mary Queen of Scots arrived in England, without money and even without any other clothes than those she wore, she wrote to Elizabeth, representing herself as an innocent and injured piece of Royalty, and entreating her assistance to oblige her Scottish subjects to take her back again and obey her. But, as her character was already known in England to be a very different one from what she made it out to be, she was told in answer that she must first clear herself. Made uneasy by this condition, Mary, rather than stay in England, would have gone to Spain, or to France, or would even have gone back to Scotland. But, as her doing either would have been likely to trouble England afresh, it was decided that she should be detained here. She first came to Carlisle, and, after that, was moved about from castle to castle, as was considered necessary; but England she never left again.

After trying very hard to get rid of the necessity of clearing herself, Mary, advised by Lord Herries, her best friend in England, agreed to answer the charges against her, if the Scottish noblemen who made them would attend to maintain them before such English noblemen as Elizabeth might appoint for that purpose. Accordingly, such an assembly, under the name of a conference, met, first at York, and afterwards at Hampton Court. In its presence Lord Lennox, Darnley's father, openly charged Mary with the murder of his son; and whatever Mary's friends may now say or write in her behalf, there is no doubt that, when her brother Murray produced against her a casket containing certain guilty letters and verses which he stated to have passed between her and Bothwell, she withdrew from the inquiry. Consequently, it is to be supposed that she was then considered guilty by those who had the best opportunities of judging of the truth, and that the feeling which afterwards arose in her behalf was a very generous but not a very reasonable one.

However, the Duke of Norfolk, an honourable but rather weak nobleman, partly because Mary was captivating, partly because he was ambitious, partly because he was over-persuaded by artful plotters against Elizabeth, conceived a strong idea that he would like to marry the Queen of Scots—though he was a little frightened, too, by the letters in the casket. This idea being secretly encouraged by some of the noblemen of Elizabeth's court, and even by the favourite Earl of Leicester (because it was objected to by other favourites who were his rivals), Mary expressed her approval of it, and the King of France and the King of Spain are supposed to have done the same. It was not so quietly planned, though, but that it came to Elizabeth's ears, who warned the Duke 'to be careful what sort of pillow he was going to lay his head upon.' He made a humble reply at the time; but turned sulky soon afterwards, and, being considered dangerous, was sent to the Tower.

Thus, from the moment of Mary's coming to England she began to be the centre of plots and miseries.

A rise of the Catholics in the north was the next of these, and it was only checked by many executions and much bloodshed. It was followed by a great conspiracy of the Pope and some of the Catholic sovereigns of Europe to depose Elizabeth, place Mary on the throne, and restore the unreformed religion. It is almost impossible to doubt that Mary knew and approved of this; and the Pope himself was so hot in the matter that he issued a bull, in which he openly called Elizabeth the 'pretended Queen' of England, excommunicated her, and excommunicated all her subjects who should continue to obey her. A copy of this miserable paper got into London, and was found one morning publicly posted on the Bishop of London's gate. A great hue and cry being raised, another copy was found in the chamber of a student of Lincoln's Inn, who confessed, being put upon the rack, that he had received it from one John Felton, a rich gentleman who lived across the Thames, near Southwark.

This John Felton, being put upon the rack too, confessed that he had posted the placard on the Bishop's gate. For this offence he was, within four days, taken to St. Paul's Churchyard, and there hanged and quartered. As to the Pope's bull, the people by the reformation having thrown off the Pope, did not care much, you may suppose, for the Pope's throwing off them. It was a mere dirty piece of paper, and not half so powerful as a street ballad.

On the very day when Felton was brought to his trial, the poor Duke of Norfolk was released. It would have been well for him if he had kept away from the Tower evermore, and from the snares that had taken him there. But, even while he was in that dismal place he corresponded with Mary, and as soon as he was out of it, he began to plot again. Being discovered in correspondence with the Pope, with a view to a rising in England which should force Elizabeth to consent to his marriage with Mary and to repeal the laws against the Catholics, he was re-committed to the Tower and brought to trial. He was found guilty by the unanimous verdict of the Lords who tried him, and was sentenced to the block.

It is very difficult to make out, at this distance of time, and between opposite accounts, whether Elizabeth really was a humane woman, or desired to appear so, or was fearful of shedding the blood of people of great name who were popular in the country. Twice she commanded and countermanded the execution of this Duke, and it did not take place until five months after his trial. The scaffold was erected on Tower Hill, and there he died like a brave man. He refused to have his eyes bandaged, saying that he was not at all afraid of death; and he admitted the justice of his sentence, and was much regretted by the people.

Although Mary had shrunk at the most important time from disproving her guilt, she was very careful never to do anything that would admit it. All such proposals as were made to her by Elizabeth for her release, required that admission in some form or other, and therefore came to nothing. Moreover, both women being artful and treacherous, and neither ever trusting the other, it was not likely that they could ever make an agreement. So, the Parliament, aggravated by what the Pope had done, made new and strong laws against the spreading of the Catholic religion in England, and declared it treason in any one to say that the Queen and her successors were not the lawful sovereigns of England. It would have done more than this, but for Elizabeth's moderation.

Since the Reformation, there had come to be three great sects of religious people—or people who called themselves so—in England; that is to say, those who belonged to the Reformed Church, those who belonged to the Unreformed Church, and those who were called the Puritans, because they said that they wanted to have everything very pure and plain in all the Church service. These last were for the most part an uncomfortable people, who thought it highly meritorious to dress in a hideous manner, talk through their noses, and oppose all harmless enjoyments. But they were powerful too, and very much in earnest, and they were one and all the determined enemies of the Queen of Scots. The Protestant feeling in England was further strengthened by the tremendous cruelties to which Protestants were exposed in France and in the Netherlands. Scores of thousands of them were put to death in those countries with every cruelty that can be imagined, and at last, in the autumn of the year one thousand five hundred and seventy-two, one of the greatest barbarities ever committed in the world took place at Paris.

It is called in history, The Massacre of Saint Bartholomew, because it took place on Saint Bartholomew's Eve. The day fell on Saturday the twenty-third of August. On that day all the great leaders of the Protestants (who were there called Huguenots) were assembled together, for the purpose, as was represented to them, of doing honour to the marriage of their chief, the young King of Navarre, with the sister of Charles the Ninth: a miserable young King who then occupied the French throne. This dull creature was made to believe by his mother and other fierce Catholics about him that the Huguenots meant to take his life; and he was persuaded to give secret orders that, on the tolling of a great bell, they should be fallen upon by an overpowering force of armed men, and slaughtered wherever they could be found. When the appointed hour was close at hand, the stupid wretch, trembling from head to foot, was taken into a balcony by his mother to see the atrocious work begun. The moment the bell tolled, the murderers broke forth. During all that night and the two next days, they broke into the houses, fired the houses, shot and stabbed the Protestants, men, women, and children, and flung their bodies into the streets. They were shot at in the streets as they passed along, and their blood ran down the gutters. Upwards of ten thousand Protestants were killed in Paris alone; in all France four or five times that number. To return thanks to Heaven for these diabolical murders, the Pope and his train actually went in public procession at Rome, and as if this were not shame enough for them, they had a medal struck to commemorate the event. But, however comfortable the wholesale murders were to these high authorities, they had not that soothing effect upon the doll-King. I am happy to state that he never knew a moment's peace afterwards; that he was continually crying out that he saw the Huguenots covered with blood and wounds falling dead before him; and that he died within a year, shrieking and yelling and raving to that degree, that if all the Popes who had ever lived had been rolled into one, they would not have afforded His guilty Majesty the slightest consolation.

When the terrible news of the massacre arrived in England, it made a powerful impression indeed upon the people. If they began to run a little wild against the Catholics at about this time, this fearful reason for it, coming so soon after the days of bloody Queen Mary, must be remembered in their excuse. The Court was not quite so honest as the people—but perhaps it sometimes is not. It received the French ambassador, with all the lords and ladies dressed in deep mourning, and keeping a profound silence. Nevertheless, a proposal of marriage which he had made to Elizabeth only two days before the eve of Saint Bartholomew, on behalf of the Duke of Alençon, the French King's brother, a boy of seventeen, still went on; while on the other hand, in her usual crafty way, the Queen secretly supplied the Huguenots with money and weapons.

I must say that for a Queen who made all those fine speeches, of which I have confessed myself to be rather tired, about living and dying a Maiden Queen, Elizabeth was 'going' to be married pretty often. Besides always having some English favourite or other whom she by turns encouraged and swore at and knocked about—for the maiden Queen was very free with her fists—she held this French Duke off and on through several years. When he at last came over to England, the marriage articles were actually drawn up, and it was settled that the wedding should take place in six weeks. The Queen was then so bent upon it, that she prosecuted a poor Puritan named Stubbs, and a poor bookseller named Page, for writing and publishing a pamphlet against it. Their right hands were chopped off for this crime; and poor Stubbs—more loyal than I should have been myself under the circumstances—immediately pulled off his hat with his left hand, and cried, 'God save the Queen!' Stubbs was cruelly treated; for the marriage never took place after all, though the Queen pledged herself to the Duke with a ring from her own finger. He went away, no better than he came, when the courtship had lasted some ten years altogether; and he died a couple of years afterwards, mourned by Elizabeth, who appears to have been really fond of him. It is not much to her credit, for he was a bad enough member of a bad family.

To return to the Catholics. There arose two orders of priests, who were very busy in England, and who were much dreaded. These were the Jesuits (who were everywhere in all sorts of disguises), and the Seminary Priests. The people had a great horror of the first, because they were known to have taught that murder was lawful if it were done with an object of which they approved; and they had a great horror of the second, because they came to teach the old religion, and to be the successors of 'Queen Mary's priests,' as those yet lingering in England were called, when they should die out. The severest laws were made against them, and were most unmercifully executed. Those who sheltered them in their houses often suffered heavily for what was an act of humanity; and the rack, that cruel torture which tore men's limbs asunder, was constantly kept going. What these unhappy men confessed, or what was ever confessed by any one under that agony, must always be received with great doubt, as it is certain that people have frequently owned to the most absurd and impossible crimes to escape such dreadful suffering. But I cannot doubt it to have been proved by papers, that there were many plots, both among the Jesuits, and with France, and with Scotland, and with Spain, for the destruction of Queen Elizabeth, for the placing of Mary on the throne, and for the revival of the old religion.

If the English people were too ready to believe in plots, there were, as I have said, good reasons for it. When the massacre of Saint Bartholomew was yet fresh in their recollection, a great Protestant Dutch hero, the Prince of Orange, was shot by an assassin, who confessed that he had been kept and trained for the purpose in a college of Jesuits. The Dutch, in this surprise and distress, offered to make Elizabeth their sovereign, but she declined the honour, and sent them a small army instead, under the command of the Earl of Leicester, who, although a capital Court favourite, was not much of a general. He did so little in Holland, that his campaign there would probably have been forgotten, but for its occasioning the death of one of the best writers, the best knights, and the best gentlemen, of that or any age. This was Sir Philip Sidney, who was wounded by a musket ball in the thigh as he mounted a fresh horse, after having had his own killed under him. He had to ride back wounded, a long distance, and was very faint with fatigue and loss of blood, when some water, for which he had eagerly asked, was handed to him. But he was so good and gentle even then, that seeing a poor badly wounded common soldier lying on the ground, looking at the water with longing eyes, he said, 'Thy necessity is greater than mine,' and gave it up to him. This touching action of a noble heart is perhaps as well known as any incident in history—is as famous far and wide as the blood-stained Tower of London, with its axe, and block, and murders out of number. So delightful is an act of true humanity, and so glad are mankind to remember it.

At home, intelligence of plots began to thicken every day. I suppose the people never did live under such continual terrors as those by which they were possessed now, of Catholic risings, and burnings, and poisonings, and I don't know what. Still, we must always remember that they lived near and close to awful realities of that kind, and that with their experience it was not difficult to believe in any enormity. The government had the same fear, and did not take the best means of discovering the truth—for, besides torturing the suspected, it employed paid spies, who will always lie for their own profit. It even made some of the conspiracies it brought to light, by sending false letters to disaffected people, inviting them to join in pretended plots, which they too readily did.

But, one great real plot was at length discovered, and it ended the career of Mary, Queen of Scots. A seminary priest named Ballard, and a Spanish soldier named Savage, set on and encouraged by certain French priests, imparted a design to one Antony Babington—a gentleman of fortune in Derbyshire, who had been for some time a secret agent of Mary's—for murdering the Queen. Babington then confided the scheme to some other Catholic gentlemen who were his friends, and they joined in it heartily. They were vain, weak-headed young men, ridiculously confident, and preposterously proud of their plan; for they got a gimcrack painting made, of the six choice spirits who were to murder Elizabeth, with Babington in an attitude for the centre figure. Two of their number, however, one of whom was a priest, kept Elizabeth's wisest minister, Sir Francis Walsingham, acquainted with the whole project from the first. The conspirators were completely deceived to the final point, when Babington gave Savage, because he was shabby, a ring from his finger, and some money from his purse, wherewith to buy himself new clothes in which to kill the Queen. Walsingham, having then full evidence against the whole band, and two letters of Mary's besides, resolved to seize them. Suspecting something wrong, they stole out of the city, one by one, and hid themselves in St. John's Wood, and other places which really were hiding places then; but they were all taken, and all executed. When they were seized, a gentleman was sent from Court to inform Mary of the fact, and of her being involved in the discovery. Her friends have complained that she was kept in very hard and severe custody. It does not appear very likely, for she was going out a hunting that very morning.

Queen Elizabeth had been warned long ago, by one in France who had good information of what was secretly doing, that in holding Mary alive, she held 'the wolf who would devour her.' The Bishop of London had, more lately, given the Queen's favourite minister the advice in writing, 'forthwith to cut off the Scottish Queen's head.' The question now was, what to do with her? The Earl of Leicester wrote a little note home from Holland, recommending that she should be quietly poisoned; that noble favourite having accustomed his mind, it is possible, to remedies of that nature. His black advice, however, was disregarded, and she was brought to trial at Fotheringay Castle in Northamptonshire, before a tribunal of forty, composed of both religions. There, and in the Star Chamber at Westminster, the trial lasted a fortnight. She defended herself with great ability, but could only deny the confessions that had been made by Babington and others; could only call her own letters, produced against her by her own secretaries, forgeries; and, in short, could only deny everything. She was found guilty, and declared to have incurred the penalty of death. The Parliament met, approved the sentence, and prayed the Queen to have it executed. The Queen replied that she requested them to consider whether no means could be found of saving Mary's life without endangering her own. The Parliament rejoined, No; and the citizens illuminated their houses and lighted bonfires, in token of their joy that all these plots and troubles were to be ended by the death of the Queen of Scots.

She, feeling sure that her time was now come, wrote a letter to the Queen of England, making three entreaties; first, that she might be buried in France; secondly, that she might not be executed in secret, but before her servants and some others; thirdly, that after her death, her servants should not be molested, but should be suffered to go home with the legacies she left them. It was an affecting letter, and Elizabeth shed tears over it, but sent no answer. Then came a special ambassador from France, and another from Scotland, to intercede for Mary's life; and then the nation began to clamour, more and more, for her death.

What the real feelings or intentions of Elizabeth were, can never be known now; but I strongly suspect her of only wishing one thing more than Mary's death, and that was to keep free of the blame of it. On the first of February, one thousand five hundred and eighty-seven, Lord Burleigh having drawn out the warrant for the execution, the Queen sent to the secretary Davison to bring it to her, that she might sign it: which she did. Next day, when Davison told her it was sealed, she angrily asked him why such haste was necessary? Next day but one, she joked about it, and swore a little. Again, next day but one, she seemed to complain that it was not yet done, but still she would not be plain with those about her. So, on the seventh, the Earls of Kent and Shrewsbury, with the Sheriff of Northamptonshire, came with the warrant to Fotheringay, to tell the Queen of Scots to prepare for death.

When those messengers of ill omen were gone, Mary made a frugal supper, drank to her servants, read over her will, went to bed, slept for some hours, and then arose and passed the remainder of the night saying prayers. In the morning she dressed herself in her best clothes; and, at eight o'clock when the sheriff came for her to her chapel, took leave of her servants who were there assembled praying with her, and went down-stairs, carrying a Bible in one hand and a crucifix in the other. Two of her women and four of her men were allowed to be present in the hall; where a low scaffold, only two feet from the ground, was erected and covered with black; and where the executioner from the Tower, and his assistant, stood, dressed in black velvet. The hall was full of people. While the sentence was being read she sat upon a stool; and, when it was finished, she again denied her guilt, as she had done before. The Earl of Kent and the Dean of Peterborough, in their Protestant zeal, made some very unnecessary speeches to her; to which she replied that she died in the Catholic religion, and they need not trouble themselves about that matter. When her head and neck were uncovered by the executioners, she said that she had not been used to be undressed by such hands, or before so much company. Finally, one of her women fastened a cloth over her face, and she laid her neck upon the block, and repeated more than once in Latin, 'Into thy hands, O Lord, I commend my spirit!' Some say her head was struck off in two blows, some say in three. However that be, when it was held up, streaming with blood, the real hair beneath the false hair she had long worn was seen to be as grey as that of a woman of seventy, though she was at that time only in her forty-sixth year. All her beauty was gone.

But she was beautiful enough to her little dog, who cowered under her dress, frightened, when she went upon the scaffold, and who lay down beside her headless body when all her earthly sorrows were over.

THIRD PART

On its being formally made known to Elizabeth that the sentence had been executed on the Queen of Scots, she showed the utmost grief and rage, drove her favourites from her with violent indignation, and sent Davison to the Tower; from which place he was only released in the end by paying an immense fine which completely ruined him. Elizabeth not only over-acted her part in making these pretences, but most basely reduced to poverty one of her faithful servants for no other fault than obeying her commands.

James, King of Scotland, Mary's son, made a show likewise of being very angry on the occasion; but he was a pensioner of England to the amount of five thousand pounds a year, and he had known very little of his mother, and he possibly regarded her as the murderer of his father, and he soon took it quietly.

Philip, King of Spain, however, threatened to do greater things than ever had been done yet, to set up the Catholic religion and punish Protestant England. Elizabeth, hearing that he and the Prince of Parma were making great preparations for this purpose, in order to be beforehand with them sent out Admiral Drake (a famous navigator, who had sailed about the world, and had already brought great plunder from Spain) to the port of Cadiz, where he burnt a hundred vessels full of stores. This great loss obliged the Spaniards to put off the invasion for a year; but it was none the less formidable for that, amounting to one hundred and thirty ships, nineteen thousand soldiers, eight thousand sailors, two thousand slaves, and between two and three thousand great guns. England was not idle in making ready to resist this great force. All the men between sixteen years old and sixty, were trained and drilled; the national fleet of ships (in number only thirty-four at first) was enlarged by public contributions and by private ships, fitted out by noblemen; the city of London, of its own accord, furnished double the number of ships and men that it was required to provide; and, if ever the national spirit was up in England, it was up all through the country to resist the Spaniards. Some of the Queen's advisers were for seizing the principal English Catholics, and putting them to death; but the Queen—who, to her honour, used to say, that she would never believe any ill of her subjects, which a parent would not believe of her own children—rejected the advice, and only confined a few of those who were the most suspected, in the fens in Lincolnshire. The great body of Catholics deserved this confidence; for they behaved most loyally, nobly, and bravely.

So, with all England firing up like one strong, angry man, and with both sides of the Thames fortified, and with the soldiers under arms, and with the sailors in their ships, the country waited for the coming of the proud Spanish fleet, which was called The Invincible Armada. The Queen herself, riding in armour on a white horse, and the Earl of Essex and the Earl of Leicester holding her bridal rein, made a brave speech to the troops at Tilbury Fort opposite

Gravesend, which was received with such enthusiasm as is seldom known. Then came the Spanish Armada into the English Channel, sailing along in the form of a half moon, of such great size that it was seven miles broad. But the English were quickly upon it, and woe then to all the Spanish ships that dropped a little out of the half moon, for the English took them instantly! And it soon appeared that the great Armada was anything but invincible, for on a summer night, bold Drake sent eight blazing fire-ships right into the midst of it. In terrible consternation the Spaniards tried to get out to sea, and so became dispersed; the English pursued them at a great advantage; a storm came on, and drove the Spaniards among rocks and shoals; and the swift end of the Invincible fleet was, that it lost thirty great ships and ten thousand men, and, defeated and disgraced, sailed home again. Being afraid to go by the English Channel, it sailed all round Scotland and Ireland; some of the ships getting cast away on the latter coast in bad weather, the Irish, who were a kind of savages, plundered those vessels and killed their crews. So ended this great attempt to invade and conquer England. And I think it will be a long time before any other invincible fleet coming to England with the same object, will fare much better than the Spanish Armada.

Though the Spanish king had had this bitter taste of English bravery, he was so little the wiser for it, as still to entertain his old designs, and even to conceive the absurd idea of placing his daughter on the English throne. But the Earl of Essex, Sir Walter Raleigh, Sir Thomas Howard, and some other distinguished leaders, put to sea from Plymouth, entered the port of Cadiz once more, obtained a complete victory over the shipping assembled there, and got possession of the town. In obedience to the Queen's express instructions, they behaved with great humanity; and the principal loss of the Spaniards was a vast sum of money which they had to pay for ransom. This was one of many gallant achievements on the sea, effected in this reign. Sir Walter Raleigh himself, after marrying a maid of honour and giving offence to the Maiden Queen thereby, had already sailed to South America in search of gold.

The Earl of Leicester was now dead, and so was Sir Thomas Walsingham, whom Lord Burleigh was soon to follow. The principal favourite was the Earl of Essex, a spirited and handsome man, a favourite with the people too as well as with the Queen, and possessed of many admirable qualities. It was much debated at Court whether there should be peace with Spain or no, and he was very urgent for war. He also tried hard to have his own way in the appointment of a deputy to govern in Ireland. One day, while this question was in dispute, he hastily took offence, and turned his back upon the Queen; as a gentle reminder of which impropriety, the Queen gave him a tremendous box on the ear, and told him to go to the devil. He went home instead, and did not reappear at Court for half a year or so, when he and the Queen were reconciled, though never (as some suppose) thoroughly.

From this time the fate of the Earl of Essex and that of the Queen seemed to be blended together. The Irish were still perpetually quarrelling and fighting among themselves, and he went over to Ireland as Lord Lieutenant, to the great joy of his enemies (Sir Walter Raleigh among the rest), who were glad to have so dangerous a rival far off. Not being by any means successful there, and knowing that his enemies would take advantage of that circumstance to injure him with the Queen, he came home again, though against her orders. The Queen being taken by surprise when he appeared before her, gave him her hand to kiss, and he was overjoyed—though it was not a very lovely hand by this time—but in the course of the same day she ordered him to confine himself to his room, and two or three days afterwards had him taken into custody. With the same sort of caprice—and as capricious an old woman she now was, as ever wore a crown or a head either—she sent him broth from her own table on his falling ill from anxiety, and cried about him.

He was a man who could find comfort and occupation in his books, and he did so for a time; not the least happy time, I dare say, of his life. But it happened unfortunately for him, that he held a monopoly in sweet wines: which means that nobody could sell them without purchasing his permission. This right, which was only for a term, expiring, he applied to have it renewed. The Queen refused, with the rather strong observation—but she did make strong observations—that an unruly beast must be stinted in his food. Upon this, the angry Earl, who had been already deprived of many offices, thought himself in danger of complete ruin, and turned against the Queen, whom he called a vain old woman who had grown as crooked in her mind as she had in her figure. These uncomplimentary expressions the ladies of the Court immediately snapped up and carried to the Queen, whom they did not put in a better tempter, you may believe. The same Court ladies, when they had beautiful dark hair of their own, used to wear false red hair, to be like the Queen. So they were not very high-spirited ladies, however high in rank.

The worst object of the Earl of Essex, and some friends of his who used to meet at Lord Southampton's house, was to obtain possession of the Queen, and oblige her by force to dismiss her ministers and change her favourites. On Saturday the seventh of February, one thousand six hundred and one, the council suspecting this, summoned the Earl to come before them. He, pretending to be ill, declined; it was then settled among his friends, that as the next day would be Sunday, when many of the citizens usually assembled at the Cross by St. Paul's Cathedral, he should make one bold effort to induce them to rise and follow him to the Palace.

So, on the Sunday morning, he and a small body of adherents started out of his house—Essex House by the Strand, with steps to the river—having first shut up in it, as prisoners, some members of the council who came to examine him—and hurried into the City with the Earl at their head crying out 'For the Queen! For the Queen! A plot is laid for my life!' No one heeded them, however, and when they came to St. Paul's there were no citizens there. In the meantime the prisoners at Essex House had been released by one of the Earl's own friends; he had been promptly proclaimed a traitor in the City itself; and the streets were barricaded with carts and guarded by soldiers. The Earl got back to his house by water, with difficulty, and after an attempt to defend his house against the troops and cannon by which it was soon surrounded, gave himself up that night. He was brought to trial on the nineteenth, and found guilty; on the twenty-fifth, he was executed on Tower Hill, where he died, at thirty-four years old, both courageously and penitently. His step-father suffered with him. His enemy, Sir Walter Raleigh, stood near the scaffold all the time—but not so near it as we shall see him stand, before we finish his history.

In this case, as in the cases of the Duke of Norfolk and Mary Queen of Scots, the Queen had commanded, and countermanded, and again commanded, the execution. It is probable that the death of her young and gallant favourite in the prime of his good qualities, was never off her mind afterwards, but she held out, the same vain, obstinate and capricious woman, for another year. Then she danced before her Court on a state occasion—and cut, I should think, a mighty ridiculous figure, doing so in an immense ruff, stomacher and wig, at seventy years old. For another year still, she held out, but, without any more dancing, and as a moody, sorrowful, broken creature. At last, on the tenth of March, one thousand six hundred and three, having been ill of a very bad cold, and made worse by the death of the Countess of Nottingham who was her intimate friend, she fell into a stupor and was supposed to be dead. She recovered her consciousness, however, and then nothing would induce her to go to bed; for she said that she knew that if she did, she should never get up again. There she lay for ten days, on cushions on the floor, without any food, until the Lord Admiral got her into bed at last, partly by persuasions and partly by main force. When they asked her who should succeed her, she replied that her seat had been the seat of Kings, and that she would have for her successor, 'No rascal's son, but a King's.' Upon this, the lords present stared at one another, and took the liberty of asking whom she meant; to which she replied, 'Whom should I mean, but our cousin of Scotland!' This was on the twenty-third of March. They asked her once again that day, after she was speechless, whether she was still in the same mind? She struggled up in bed, and joined her hands over her head in the form of a crown, as the only reply she could make. At three o'clock next morning, she very quietly died, in the forty-fifth year of her reign.

That reign had been a glorious one, and is made for ever memorable by the distinguished men who flourished in it. Apart from the great voyagers, statesmen, and scholars, whom it produced, the names of Bacon, Spenser, and Shakespeare, will always be remembered with pride and veneration by the civilised world, and will always impart (though with no great reason, perhaps) some portion of their lustre to the name of Elizabeth herself. It was a great reign for discovery, for commerce, and for English enterprise and spirit in general. It was a great reign for the Protestant religion and for the Reformation which made England free. The Queen was very popular, and in her progresses, or journeys about her dominions, was everywhere received with the liveliest joy. I think the truth is, that she was not half so good as she has been made out, and not half so bad as she has been made out. She had her fine qualities, but she was coarse, capricious, and treacherous, and had all the faults of an excessively vain young woman long after she was an old one. On the whole, she had a great deal too much of her father in her, to please me.

Many improvements and luxuries were introduced in the course of these five-and-forty years in the general manner of living; but cock-fighting, bull-baiting, and bear-baiting, were still the national amusements; and a coach was so rarely seen, and was such an ugly and cumbersome affair when it was seen, that even the Queen herself, on many high occasions, rode on horseback on a pillion behind the Lord Chancellor.

CHAPTER XXXII—ENGLAND UNDER JAMES THE FIRST

'Our cousin of Scotland' was ugly, awkward, and shuffling both in mind and person. His tongue was much too large for his mouth, his legs were much too weak for his body, and his dull goggle-eyes stared and rolled like an idiot's. He was cunning, covetous, wasteful, idle, drunken, greedy, dirty, cowardly, a great swearer, and the most conceited man on earth. His figure—what is commonly called rickety from his birth—presented a most ridiculous appearance, dressed in thick padded clothes, as a safeguard against being stabbed (of which he lived in continual fear), of a grass-green colour from head to foot, with a hunting-horn dangling at his side instead of a sword, and his hat and feather sticking over one eye, or hanging on the back of his head, as he happened to toss it on. He used to loll on the necks of his favourite courtiers, and slobber their faces, and kiss and pinch their cheeks; and the greatest favourite he ever had, used to sign himself in his letters to his royal master, His Majesty's 'dog and slave,' and used to address his majesty as 'his Sowship.' His majesty was the worst rider ever seen, and thought himself the best. He was one of the most impertinent talkers (in the broadest Scotch) ever heard, and boasted of being unanswerable in all manner of argument. He wrote some of the most wearisome treatises ever read—among others, a book upon witchcraft, in which he was a devout believer—and thought himself a prodigy of authorship. He thought, and wrote, and said, that a king had a right to make and unmake what laws he pleased, and ought to be accountable to nobody on earth. This is the plain, true character of the personage whom the greatest men about the court praised and flattered to that degree, that I doubt if there be anything much more shameful in the annals of human nature.

He came to the English throne with great ease. The miseries of a disputed succession had been felt so long, and so dreadfully, that he was proclaimed within a few hours of Elizabeth's death, and was accepted by the nation, even without being asked to give any pledge that he would govern well, or that he would redress crying grievances. He took a month to come from Edinburgh to London; and, by way of exercising his new power, hanged a pickpocket on the journey without any trial, and knighted everybody he could lay hold of. He made two hundred knights before he got to his palace in London, and seven hundred before he had been in it three months. He also shovelled sixty-two new peers into the House of Lords—and there was a pretty large sprinkling of Scotchmen among them, you may believe.

His Sowship's prime Minister, Cecil (for I cannot do better than call his majesty what his favourite called him), was the enemy of Sir Walter Raleigh, and also of Sir Walter's political friend, Lord Cobham; and his Sowship's first trouble was a plot originated by these two, and entered into by some others, with the old object of seizing the King and keeping him in imprisonment until he should change his ministers. There were Catholic priests in the plot, and there were Puritan noblemen too; for, although the Catholics and Puritans were strongly opposed to each other, they united at this time against his Sowship, because they knew that he had a design against both, after pretending to be friendly to each; this design being to have only one high and convenient form of the Protestant religion, which everybody should be bound to belong to, whether they liked it or not. This plot was mixed up with another, which may or may not have had some reference to placing on the throne, at some time, the Lady Arabella Stuart; whose misfortune it was, to be the daughter of the younger brother of his Sowship's father, but who was quite innocent of any part in the scheme. Sir Walter Raleigh was accused on the confession of Lord Cobham—a miserable creature, who said one thing at one time, and another thing at another time, and could be relied upon in nothing. The trial of Sir Walter Raleigh lasted from eight in the morning until nearly midnight; he defended himself with such eloquence, genius, and spirit against all accusations, and against the insults of Coke, the Attorney-General—who, according to the custom of the time, foully abused him—that those who went there detesting the prisoner, came away admiring him, and declaring that anything so wonderful and so captivating was never heard. He was found guilty, nevertheless, and sentenced to death. Execution was deferred, and he was taken to the Tower. The two Catholic priests, less fortunate, were executed with the usual atrocity; and Lord Cobham and two others were pardoned on the scaffold. His Sowship thought it wonderfully knowing in him to surprise the people by pardoning these three at the very block; but, blundering, and bungling, as usual, he had very nearly overreached himself. For, the messenger on horseback who brought the pardon, came so late, that he was pushed to the outside of the crowd, and was obliged to shout and roar out what he came for. The miserable Cobham did not gain much by being spared that day. He lived, both as a prisoner and a beggar, utterly despised, and miserably poor, for thirteen years, and then died in an old outhouse belonging to one of his former servants.

This plot got rid of, and Sir Walter Raleigh safely shut up in the Tower, his Sowship held a great dispute with the Puritans on their presenting a petition to him, and had it all his own way—not so very wonderful, as he would talk continually, and would not hear anybody else—and filled the Bishops with admiration. It was comfortably settled that there was to be only one form of religion, and that all men were to think exactly alike. But, although this was arranged two centuries and a half ago, and although the arrangement was supported by much fining and imprisonment, I do not find that it is quite successful, even yet.

His Sowship, having that uncommonly high opinion of himself as a king, had a very low opinion of Parliament as a power that audaciously wanted to control him. When he called his first Parliament after he had been king a year, he accordingly thought he would take pretty high ground with them, and told them that he commanded them 'as an absolute king.' The Parliament thought those strong words, and saw the necessity of upholding their authority. His Sowship had three children: Prince Henry, Prince Charles, and the Princess Elizabeth. It would have been well for one of these, and we shall too soon see which, if he had learnt a little wisdom concerning Parliaments from his father's obstinacy.

Now, the people still labouring under their old dread of the Catholic religion, this Parliament revived and strengthened the severe laws against it. And this so angered Robert Catesby, a restless Catholic gentleman of an old family, that he formed one of the most desperate and terrible designs ever conceived in the mind of man; no less a scheme than the Gunpowder Plot.

His object was, when the King, lords, and commons, should be assembled at the next opening of Parliament, to blow them up, one and all, with a great mine of gunpowder. The first person to whom he confided this horrible idea was Thomas Winter, a Worcestershire gentleman who had served in the army abroad, and had been secretly employed in Catholic projects. While Winter was yet undecided, and when he had gone over to the Netherlands, to learn from the Spanish Ambassador there whether there was any hope of Catholics being relieved through the intercession of the King of Spain with his Sowship, he found at Ostend a tall, dark, daring man, whom he had known when they were both soldiers abroad, and whose name was Guido—or Guy—Fawkes. Resolved to join the plot, he proposed it to this man, knowing him to be the man for any desperate deed, and they two came back to England together. Here, they admitted two other conspirators; Thomas Percy, related to the Earl of Northumberland, and John Wright, his brother-in-law. All these met together in a solitary house in the open fields which were then near Clement's Inn, now a closely blocked-up part of London; and when they had all taken a great oath of secrecy, Catesby told the rest what his plan was. They then went up-stairs into a garret, and received the Sacrament from Father Gerard, a Jesuit, who is said not to have known actually of the Gunpowder Plot, but who, I think, must have had his suspicions that there was something desperate afoot.

Percy was a Gentleman Pensioner, and as he had occasional duties to perform about the Court, then kept at Whitehall, there would be nothing suspicious in his living at Westminster. So, having looked well about him, and having found a house to let, the back of which joined the Parliament House, he hired it of a person named Ferris, for the purpose of undermining the wall. Having got possession of this house, the conspirators hired another on the Lambeth side of the Thames, which they used as a storehouse for wood, gunpowder, and other combustible matters. These were to be removed at night (and afterwards were removed), bit by bit, to the house at Westminster; and, that there might be some trusty person to keep watch over the Lambeth stores, they admitted another conspirator, by name Robert Kay, a very poor Catholic gentleman.

All these arrangements had been made some months, and it was a dark, wintry, December night, when the conspirators, who had been in the meantime dispersed to avoid observation, met in the house at Westminster, and began to dig. They had laid in a good stock of eatables, to avoid going in and out, and they dug and dug with great ardour. But, the wall being tremendously thick, and the work very severe, they took into their plot Christopher Wright, a younger brother of John Wright, that they might have a new pair of hands to help. And Christopher Wright fell to like a fresh man, and they dug and dug by night and by day, and Fawkes stood sentinel all the time. And if any man's heart seemed to fail him at all, Fawkes said, 'Gentlemen, we have abundance of powder and shot here, and there is no fear of our being taken alive, even if discovered.' The same Fawkes, who, in the capacity of sentinel, was always prowling about, soon picked up the intelligence that the King had prorogued the Parliament again, from the seventh of February, the day first fixed upon, until the third of October. When the conspirators knew this, they agreed to separate until after the Christmas holidays, and to take no notice of each other in the meanwhile, and never to write letters to one another on any account. So, the house in Westminster was shut up again, and I suppose the neighbours thought that those strange-looking men who lived there so gloomily, and went out so seldom, were gone away to have a merry Christmas somewhere.

It was the beginning of February, sixteen hundred and five, when Catesby met his fellow-conspirators again at this Westminster house. He had now admitted three more; John Grant, a Warwickshire gentleman of a melancholy temper, who lived in a doleful house near Stratford-upon-Avon, with a frowning wall all round it, and a deep moat; Robert Winter, eldest brother of Thomas; and Catesby's own servant, Thomas Bates, who, Catesby thought, had had some suspicion of what his master was about. These three had all suffered more or less for their religion in Elizabeth's time. And now, they all began to dig again, and they dug and dug by night and by day.

They found it dismal work alone there, underground, with such a fearful secret on their minds, and so many murders before them. They were filled with wild fancies. Sometimes, they thought they heard a great bell tolling, deep down in the earth under the Parliament House; sometimes, they thought

319

they heard low voices muttering about the Gunpowder Plot; once in the morning, they really did hear a great rumbling noise over their heads, as they dug and sweated in their mine. Every man stopped and looked aghast at his neighbour, wondering what had happened, when that bold prowler, Fawkes, who had been out to look, came in and told them that it was only a dealer in coals who had occupied a cellar under the Parliament House, removing his stock in trade to some other place. Upon this, the conspirators, who with all their digging and digging had not yet dug through the tremendously thick wall, changed their plan; hired that cellar, which was directly under the House of Lords; put six-and-thirty barrels of gunpowder in it, and covered them over with fagots and coals. Then they all dispersed again till September, when the following new conspirators were admitted; Sir Edward Baynham, of Gloucestershire; Sir Everard Digby, of Rutlandshire; Ambrose Rookwood, of Suffolk; Francis Tresham, of Northamptonshire. Most of these were rich, and were to assist the plot, some with money and some with horses on which the conspirators were to ride through the country and rouse the Catholics after the Parliament should be blown into air.

Parliament being again prorogued from the third of October to the fifth of November, and the conspirators being uneasy lest their design should have been found out, Thomas Winter said he would go up into the House of Lords on the day of the prorogation, and see how matters looked. Nothing could be better. The unconscious Commissioners were walking about and talking to one another, just over the six-and-thirty barrels of gunpowder. He came back and told the rest so, and they went on with their preparations. They hired a ship, and kept it ready in the Thames, in which Fawkes was to sail for Flanders after firing with a slow match the train that was to explode the powder. A number of Catholic gentlemen not in the secret, were invited, on pretence of a hunting party, to meet Sir Everard Digby at Dunchurch on the fatal day, that they might be ready to act together. And now all was ready.

But, now, the great wickedness and danger which had been all along at the bottom of this wicked plot, began to show itself. As the fifth of November drew near, most of the conspirators, remembering that they had friends and relations who would be in the House of Lords that day, felt some natural relenting, and a wish to warn them to keep away. They were not much comforted by Catesby's declaring that in such a cause he would blow up his own son. Lord Mounteagle, Tresham's brother-in-law, was certain to be in the house; and when Tresham found that he could not prevail upon the rest to devise any means of sparing their friends, he wrote a mysterious letter to this lord and left it at his lodging in the dusk, urging him to keep away from the opening of Parliament, 'since God and man had concurred to punish the wickedness of the times.' It contained the words 'that the Parliament should receive a terrible blow, and yet should not see who hurt them.' And it added, 'the danger is past, as soon as you have burnt the letter.'

The ministers and courtiers made out that his Sowship, by a direct miracle from Heaven, found out what this letter meant. The truth is, that they were not long (as few men would be) in finding out for themselves; and it was decided to let the conspirators alone, until the very day before the opening of Parliament. That the conspirators had their fears, is certain; for, Tresham himself said before them all, that they were every one dead men; and, although even he did not take flight, there is reason to suppose that he had warned other persons besides Lord Mounteagle. However, they were all firm; and Fawkes, who was a man of iron, went down every day and night to keep watch in the cellar as usual. He was there about two in the afternoon of the fourth, when the Lord Chamberlain and Lord Mounteagle threw open the door and looked in. 'Who are you, friend?' said they. 'Why,' said Fawkes, 'I am Mr. Percy's servant, and am looking after his store of fuel here.' 'Your master has laid in a pretty good store,' they returned, and shut the door, and went away. Fawkes, upon this, posted off to the other conspirators to tell them all was quiet, and went back and shut himself up in the dark, black cellar again, where he heard the bell go twelve o'clock and usher in the fifth of November. About two hours afterwards, he slowly opened the door, and came out to look about him, in his old prowling way. He was instantly seized and bound, by a party of soldiers under Sir Thomas Knevett. He had a watch upon him, some touchwood, some tinder, some slow matches; and there was a dark lantern with a candle in it, lighted, behind the door. He had his boots and spurs on—to ride to the ship, I suppose—and it was well for the soldiers that they took him so suddenly. If they had left him but a moment's time to light a match, he certainly would have tossed it in among the powder, and blown up himself and them.

They took him to the King's bed-chamber first of all, and there the King (causing him to be held very tight, and keeping a good way off), asked him how he could have the heart to intend to destroy so many innocent people? 'Because,' said Guy Fawkes, 'desperate diseases need desperate remedies.' To a little Scotch favourite, with a face like a terrier, who asked him (with no particular wisdom) why he had collected so much gunpowder, he replied, because he had meant to blow Scotchmen back to Scotland, and it would take a deal of powder to do that. Next day he was carried to the Tower, but would make no confession. Even after being horribly tortured, he confessed nothing that the Government did not already know; though he must have been in a fearful state—as his signature, still preserved, in contrast with his natural hand-writing before he was put upon the dreadful rack, most frightfully shows. Bates, a very different man, soon said the Jesuits had had to do with the plot, and probably, under the torture, would as readily have said anything. Tresham, taken and put in the Tower too, made confessions and unmade them, and died of an illness that was heavy upon him. Rookwood, who had stationed relays of his own horses all the way to Dunchurch, did not mount to escape until the middle of the day, when the news of the plot was all over London. On the road, he came up with the two Wrights, Catesby, and Percy; and they all galloped together into Northamptonshire. Thence to Dunchurch, where they found the proposed party assembled. Finding, however, that there had been a plot, and that it had been discovered, the party disappeared in the course of the night, and left them alone with Sir Everard Digby. Away they all rode again, through Warwickshire and Worcestershire, to a house called Holbeach, on the borders of Staffordshire. They tried to raise the Catholics on their way, but were indignantly driven off by them. All this time they were hotly pursued by the sheriff of Worcester, and a fast increasing concourse of riders. At last, resolving to defend themselves at Holbeach, they shut themselves up in the house, and put some wet powder before the fire to dry. But it blew up, and Catesby was singed and blackened, and almost killed, and some of the others were sadly hurt. Still, knowing that they must die, they resolved to die there, and with only their swords in their hands appeared at the windows to be shot at by the sheriff and his assistants. Catesby said to Thomas Winter, after Thomas had been hit in the right arm which dropped powerless by his side, 'Stand by me, Tom, and we will die together!'—which they did, being shot through the body by two bullets from one gun. John Wright, and Christopher Wright, and Percy, were also shot. Rookwood and Digby were taken: the former with a broken arm and a wound in his body too.

It was the fifteenth of January, before the trial of Guy Fawkes, and such of the other conspirators as were left alive, came on. They were all found guilty, all hanged, drawn, and quartered: some, in St. Paul's Churchyard, on the top of Ludgate-hill; some, before the Parliament House. A Jesuit priest, named Henry Garnet, to whom the dreadful design was said to have been communicated, was taken and tried; and two of his servants, as well as a poor priest who was taken with him, were tortured without mercy. He himself was not tortured, but was surrounded in the Tower by tamperers and traitors, and so was made unfairly to convict himself out of his own mouth. He said, upon his trial, that he had done all he could to prevent the deed, and that he could not make public what had been told him in confession—though I am afraid he knew of the plot in other ways. He was found guilty and executed, after a manful defence, and the Catholic Church made a saint of him; some rich and powerful persons, who had had nothing to do with the project, were fined and imprisoned for it by the Star Chamber; the Catholics, in general, who had recoiled with horror from the idea of the infernal contrivance, were unjustly put under more severe laws than before; and this was the end of the Gunpowder Plot.

SECOND PART

His Sowship would pretty willingly, I think, have blown the House of Commons into the air himself; for, his dread and jealousy of it knew no bounds all through his reign. When he was hard pressed for money he was obliged to order it to meet, as he could get no money without it; and when it asked him first to abolish some of the monopolies in necessaries of life which were a great grievance to the people, and to redress other public wrongs, he flew into a rage and got rid of it again. At one time he wanted it to consent to the Union of England with Scotland, and quarrelled about that. At another time it wanted him to put down a most infamous Church abuse, called the High Commission Court, and he quarrelled with it about that. At another time it entreated him not to be quite so fond of his archbishops and bishops who made speeches in his praise too awful to be related, but to have some little consideration for the poor Puritan clergy who were persecuted for preaching in their own way, and not according to the archbishops and bishops; and they quarrelled about that. In short, what with hating the House of Commons, and pretending not to hate it; and what with now sending some of its members who opposed him, to Newgate or to the Tower, and now telling the rest that they must not presume to make speeches about the public affairs which could not possibly concern them; and what with cajoling, and bullying, and fighting, and being frightened; the House of Commons was the plague of his Sowship's existence. It was pretty firm, however, in maintaining its rights, and insisting that the Parliament should make the laws, and not the King by his own single proclamations (which he tried hard to do); and his Sowship was so often distressed for money, in consequence, that he sold every sort of title and public office as if they were merchandise, and even invented a new dignity called a Baronetcy, which anybody could buy for a thousand pounds.

These disputes with his Parliaments, and his hunting, and his drinking, and his lying in bed—for he was a great sluggard—occupied his Sowship pretty well. The rest of his time he chiefly passed in hugging and slobbering his favourites. The first of these was Sir Philip Herbert, who had no knowledge whatever, except of dogs, and horses, and hunting, but whom he soon made Earl of Montgomery. The next, and a much more famous one, was Robert Carr, or Ker (for it is not certain which was his right name), who came from the Border country, and whom he soon made Viscount Rochester, and afterwards, Earl of Somerset. The way in which his Sowship doted on this handsome young man, is even more odious to think of, than the way in which the really great men of England condescended to bow down before him. The favourite's great friend was a certain Sir Thomas Overbury, who wrote his love-letters for him, and assisted him in the duties of his many high places, which his own ignorance prevented him from discharging. But this same Sir Thomas having just manhood enough to dissuade the favourite from a wicked marriage with the beautiful Countess of Essex, who was to get a divorce from her husband for the purpose, the said Countess, in her rage, got Sir Thomas put into the Tower, and there poisoned him. Then the favourite and this bad woman were publicly married by the King's pet bishop, with as much to-do and rejoicing, as if he had been the best man, and she the best woman, upon the face of the earth.

But, after a longer sunshine than might have been expected—of seven years or so, that is to say—another handsome young man started up and eclipsed the Earl of Somerset. This was George Villiers, the youngest son of a Leicestershire gentleman: who came to Court with all the Paris fashions on him, and could dance as well as the best mountebank that ever was seen. He soon danced himself into the good graces of his Sowship, and danced the other favourite out of favour. Then, it was all at once discovered that the Earl and Countess of Somerset had not deserved all those great promotions and mighty rejoicings, and they were separately tried for the murder of Sir Thomas Overbury, and for other crimes. But, the King was so afraid of his late favourite's publicly telling some disgraceful things he knew of him— which he darkly threatened to do—that he was even examined with two men standing, one on either side of him, each with a cloak in his hand, ready to throw it over his head and stop his mouth if he should break out with what he had it in his power to tell. So, a very lame affair was purposely made of the trial, and his punishment was an allowance of four thousand pounds a year in retirement, while the Countess was pardoned, and allowed to pass into retirement too. They hated one another by this time, and lived to revile and torment each other some years.

While these events were in progress, and while his Sowship was making such an exhibition of himself, from day to day and from year to year, as is not often seen in any sty, three remarkable deaths took place in England. The first was that of the Minister, Robert Cecil, Earl of Salisbury, who was past sixty, and had never been strong, being deformed from his birth. He said at last that he had no wish to live; and no Minister need have had, with his experience of the meanness and wickedness of those disgraceful times.

The second was that of the Lady Arabella Stuart, who alarmed his Sowship mightily, by privately marrying William Seymour, son of Lord Beauchamp, who was a descendant of King Henry the Seventh, and who, his Sowship thought, might consequently increase and strengthen any claim she might one day set up to the throne. She was separated from her husband (who was put in the Tower) and thrust into a boat to be confined at Durham. She escaped in a man's dress to get away in a French ship from Gravesend to France, but unhappily missed her husband, who had escaped too, and was soon taken. She went raving mad in the miserable Tower, and died there after four years. The last, and the most important of these three deaths, was that of Prince Henry, the heir to the throne, in the nineteenth year of his age. He was a promising young prince, and greatly liked; a quiet, well-conducted youth, of whom two very good things are known: first, that his father was jealous of him; secondly, that he was the friend of Sir Walter Raleigh, languishing through all those years in the Tower, and often said that no man but his father would keep such a bird in such a cage. On the occasion of the preparations for the marriage of his sister the Princess Elizabeth with a foreign prince (and an unhappy marriage it turned out), he came from Richmond, where he had been very ill, to greet his new brother-in-law, at the palace at Whitehall. There he played a great game at tennis, in his shirt, though it was very cold weather, and was seized with an alarming illness, and died within a fortnight of a putrid fever. For this young prince Sir Walter Raleigh wrote, in his prison in the Tower, the beginning of a History of the World: a wonderful instance how little his Sowship could do to confine a great man's mind, however long he might imprison his body.

And this mention of Sir Walter Raleigh, who had many faults, but who never showed so many merits as in trouble and adversity, may bring me at once to the end of his sad story. After an imprisonment in the Tower of twelve long years, he proposed to resume those old sea voyages of his, and to go to South America in search of gold. His Sowship, divided between his wish to be on good terms with the Spaniards through whose territory Sir Walter must pass (he had long had an idea of marrying Prince Henry to a Spanish Princess), and his avaricious eagerness to get hold of the gold, did not know what to do. But, in the end, he set Sir Walter free, taking securities for his return; and Sir

Walter fitted out an expedition at his own coast and, on the twenty-eighth of March, one thousand six hundred and seventeen, sailed away in command of one of its ships, which he ominously called the Destiny. The expedition failed; the common men, not finding the gold they had expected, mutinied; a quarrel broke out between Sir Walter and the Spaniards, who hated him for old successes of his against them; and he took and burnt a little town called Saint Thomas. For this he was denounced to his Sowship by the Spanish Ambassador as a pirate; and returning almost broken-hearted, with his hopes and fortunes shattered, his company of friends dispersed, and his brave son (who had been one of them) killed, he was taken—through the treachery of Sir Lewis Stukely, his near relation, a scoundrel and a Vice-Admiral—and was once again immured in his prison-home of so many years.

His Sowship being mightily disappointed in not getting any gold, Sir Walter Raleigh was tried as unfairly, and with as many lies and evasions as the judges and law officers and every other authority in Church and State habitually practised under such a King. After a great deal of prevarication on all parts but his own, it was declared that he must die under his former sentence, now fifteen years old. So, on the twenty-eighth of October, one thousand six hundred and eighteen, he was shut up in the Gate House at Westminster to pass his late night on earth, and there he took leave of his good and faithful lady who was worthy to have lived in better days. At eight o'clock next morning, after a cheerful breakfast, and a pipe, and a cup of good wine, he was taken to Old Palace Yard in Westminster, where the scaffold was set up, and where so many people of high degree were assembled to see him die, that it was a matter of some difficulty to get him through the crowd. He behaved most nobly, but if anything lay heavy on his mind, it was that Earl of Essex, whose head he had seen roll off; and he solemnly said that he had had no hand in bringing him to the block, and that he had shed tears for him when he died. As the morning was very cold, the Sheriff said, would he come down to a fire for a little space, and warm himself? But Sir Walter thanked him, and said no, he would rather it were done at once, for he was ill of fever and ague, and in another quarter of an hour his shaking fit would come upon him if he were still alive, and his enemies might then suppose that he trembled for fear. With that, he kneeled and made a very beautiful and Christian prayer. Before he laid his head upon the block he felt the edge of the axe, and said, with a smile upon his face, that it was a sharp medicine, but would cure the worst disease. When he was bent down ready for death, he said to the executioner, finding that he hesitated, 'What dost thou fear? Strike, man!' So, the axe came down and struck his head off, in the sixty-sixth year of his age.

The new favourite got on fast. He was made a viscount, he was made Duke of Buckingham, he was made a marquis, he was made Master of the Horse, he was made Lord High Admiral—and the Chief Commander of the gallant English forces that had dispersed the Spanish Armada, was displaced to make room for him. He had the whole kingdom at his disposal, and his mother sold all the profits and honours of the State, as if she had kept a shop. He blazed all over with diamonds and other precious stones, from his hatband and his earrings to his shoes. Yet he was an ignorant presumptuous, swaggering compound of knave and fool, with nothing but his beauty and his dancing to recommend him. This is the gentleman who called himself his Majesty's dog and slave, and called his Majesty Your Sowship. His Sowship called him Steenie; it is supposed, because that was a nickname for Stephen, and because St. Stephen was generally represented in pictures as a handsome saint.

His Sowship was driven sometimes to his wits'-end by his trimming between the general dislike of the Catholic religion at home, and his desire to wheedle and flatter it abroad, as his only means of getting a rich princess for his son's wife: a part of whose fortune he might cram into his greasy pockets. Prince Charles—or as his Sowship called him, Baby Charles—being now Prince of Wales, the old project of a marriage with the Spanish King's daughter had been revived for him; and as she could not marry a Protestant without leave from the Pope, his Sowship himself secretly and meanly wrote to his Infallibility, asking for it. The negotiation for this Spanish marriage takes up a larger space in great books, than you can imagine, but the upshot of it all is, that when it had been held off by the Spanish Court for a long time, Baby Charles and Steenie set off in disguise as Mr. Thomas Smith and Mr. John Smith, to see the Spanish Princess; that Baby Charles pretended to be desperately in love with her, and jumped off walls to look at her, and made a considerable fool of himself in a good many ways; that she was called Princess of Wales and that the whole Spanish Court believed Baby Charles to be all but dying for her sake, as he expressly told them he was; that Baby Charles and Steenie came back to England, and were received with as much rapture as if they had been a blessing to it; that Baby Charles had actually fallen in love with Henrietta Maria, the French King's sister, whom he had seen in Paris; that he thought it a wonderfully fine and princely thing to have deceived the Spaniards, all through; and that he openly said, with a chuckle, as soon as he was safe and sound at home again, that the Spaniards were great fools to have believed him.

Like most dishonest men, the Prince and the favourite complained that the people whom they had deluded were dishonest. They made such misrepresentations of the treachery of the Spaniards in this business of the Spanish match, that the English nation became eager for a war with them. Although the gravest Spaniards laughed at the idea of his Sowship in a warlike attitude, the Parliament granted money for the beginning of hostilities, and the treaties with Spain were publicly declared to be at an end. The Spanish ambassador in London—probably with the help of the fallen favourite, the Earl of Somerset—being unable to obtain speech with his Sowship, slipped a paper into his hand, declaring that he was a prisoner in his own house, and was entirely governed by Buckingham and his creatures. The first effect of this letter was that his Sowship began to cry and whine, and took Baby Charles away from Steenie, and went down to Windsor, gabbling all sorts of nonsense. The end of it was that his Sowship hugged his dog and slave, and said he was quite satisfied.

He had given the Prince and the favourite almost unlimited power to settle anything with the Pope as to the Spanish marriage; and he now, with a view to the French one, signed a treaty that all Roman Catholics in England should exercise their religion freely, and should never be required to take any oath contrary thereto. In return for this, and for other concessions much less to be defended, Henrietta Maria was to become the Prince's wife, and was to bring him a fortune of eight hundred thousand crowns.

His Sowship's eyes were getting red with eagerly looking for the money, when the end of a gluttonous life came upon him; and, after a fortnight's illness, on Sunday the twenty-seventh of March, one thousand six hundred and twenty-five, he died. He had reigned twenty-two years, and was fifty-nine years old. I know of nothing more abominable in history than the adulation that was lavished on this King, and the vice and corruption that such a barefaced habit of lying produced in his court. It is much to be doubted whether one man of honour, and not utterly self-disgraced, kept his place near James the First. Lord Bacon, that able and wise philosopher, as the First Judge in the Kingdom in this reign, became a public spectacle of dishonesty and corruption; and in his base flattery of his Sowship, and in his crawling servility to his dog and slave, disgraced himself even more. But, a creature like his Sowship set upon a throne is like the Plague, and everybody receives infection from him.

CHAPTER XXXIII—ENGLAND UNDER CHARLES THE FIRST

Baby Charles became King Charles the First, in the twenty-fifth year of his age. Unlike his father, he was usually amiable in his private character, and grave and dignified in his bearing; but, like his father, he had monstrously exaggerated notions of the rights of a king, and was evasive, and not to be trusted. If his word could have been relied upon, his history might have had a different end.

His first care was to send over that insolent upstart, Buckingham, to bring Henrietta Maria from Paris to be his Queen; upon which occasion Buckingham—with his usual audacity—made love to the young Queen of Austria, and was very indignant indeed with Cardinal Richelieu, the French Minister, for thwarting his intentions. The English people were very well disposed to like their new Queen, and to receive her with great favour when she came among them as a stranger. But, she held the Protestant religion in great dislike, and brought over a crowd of unpleasant priests, who made her do some very ridiculous things, and forced themselves upon the public notice in many disagreeable ways. Hence, the people soon came to dislike her, and she soon came to dislike them; and she did so much all through this reign in setting the King (who was dotingly fond of her) against his subjects, that it would have been better for him if she had never been born.

Now, you are to understand that King Charles the First—of his own determination to be a high and mighty King not to be called to account by anybody, and urged on by his Queen besides—deliberately set himself to put his Parliament down and to put himself up. You are also to understand, that even in pursuit of this wrong idea (enough in itself to have ruined any king) he never took a straight course, but always took a crooked one.

He was bent upon war with Spain, though neither the House of Commons nor the people were quite clear as to the justice of that war, now that they began to think a little more about the story of the Spanish match. But the King rushed into it hotly, raised money by illegal means to meet its expenses, and encountered a miserable failure at Cadiz, in the very first year of his reign. An expedition to Cadiz had been made in the hope of plunder, but as it was not successful, it was necessary to get a grant of money from the Parliament; and when they met, in no very complying humour, the King told them, 'to make haste to let him have it, or it would be the worse for themselves.' Not put in a more complying humour by this, they impeached the King's favourite, the Duke of Buckingham, as the cause (which he undoubtedly was) of many great public grievances and wrongs. The King, to save him, dissolved the Parliament without getting the money he wanted; and when the Lords implored him to consider and grant a little delay, he replied, 'No, not one minute.' He then began to raise money for himself by the following means among others.

He levied certain duties called tonnage and poundage which had not been granted by the Parliament, and could lawfully be levied by no other power; he called upon the seaport towns to furnish, and to pay all the cost for three months of, a fleet of armed ships; and he required the people to unite in lending him large sums of money, the repayment of which was very doubtful. If the poor people refused, they were pressed as soldiers or sailors; if the gentry refused, they were sent to prison. Five gentlemen, named Sir Thomas Darnel, John Corbet, Walter Earl, John Heveningham, and Everard Hampden, for refusing were taken up by a warrant of the King's privy council, and were sent to prison without any cause but the King's pleasure being stated for their imprisonment. Then the question came to be solemnly tried, whether this was not a violation of Magna Charta, and an encroachment by the King on the highest rights of the English people. His lawyers contended No, because to encroach upon the rights of the English people would be to do wrong, and the King could do no wrong. The accommodating judges decided in favour of this wicked nonsense; and here was a fatal division between the King and the people.

For all this, it became necessary to call another Parliament. The people, sensible of the danger in which their liberties were, chose for it those who were best known for their determined opposition to the King; but still the King, quite blinded by his determination to carry everything before him, addressed them when they met, in a contemptuous manner, and just told them in so many words that he had only called them together because he wanted money. The Parliament, strong enough and resolute enough to know that they would lower his tone, cared little for what he said, and laid before him one of the great documents of history, which is called the Petition of Right, requiring that the free men of England should no longer be called upon to lend the King money, and should no longer be pressed or imprisoned for refusing to do so; further, that the free men of England should no longer be seized by the King's special mandate or warrant, it being contrary to their rights and liberties and the laws of their country. At first the King returned an answer to this petition, in which he tried to shirk it altogether; but, the House of Commons then showing their determination to go on with the impeachment of Buckingham, the King in alarm returned an answer, giving his consent to all that was required of him. He not only afterwards departed from his word and honour on these points, over and over again, but, at this very time, he did the mean and dissembling act of publishing his first answer and not his second—merely that the people might suppose that the Parliament had not got the better of him.

That pestilent Buckingham, to gratify his own wounded vanity, had by this time involved the country in war with France, as well as with Spain. For such miserable causes and such miserable creatures are wars sometimes made! But he was destined to do little more mischief in this world. One morning, as he was going out of his house to his carriage, he turned to speak to a certain Colonel Fryer who was with him; and he was violently stabbed with a knife, which the murderer left sticking in his heart. This happened in his hall. He had had angry words up-stairs, just before, with some French gentlemen, who were immediately suspected by his servants, and had a close escape from being set upon and killed. In the midst of the noise, the real murderer, who had gone to the kitchen and might easily have got away, drew his sword and cried out, 'I am the man!' His name was John Felton, a Protestant and a retired officer in the army. He said he had had no personal ill-will to the Duke, but had killed him as a curse to the country. He had aimed his blow well, for Buckingham had only had time to cry out, 'Villain!' and then he drew out the knife, fell against a table, and died.

The council made a mighty business of examining John Felton about this murder, though it was a plain case enough, one would think. He had come seventy miles to do it, he told them, and he did it for the reason he had declared; if they put him upon the rack, as that noble Marquis of Dorset whom he saw before him, had the goodness to threaten, he gave that marquis warning, that he would accuse him as his accomplice! The King was unpleasantly anxious to have him racked, nevertheless; but as the judges now found out that torture was contrary to the law of England—it is a pity they did not make the discovery a little sooner—John Felton was simply executed for the murder he had done. A murder it undoubtedly was, and not in the least to be defended: though he had freed England from one of the most profligate, contemptible, and base court favourites to whom it has ever yielded.

A very different man now arose. This was Sir Thomas Wentworth, a Yorkshire gentleman, who had sat in Parliament for a long time, and who had favoured arbitrary and haughty principles, but who had gone over to the people's side on receiving offence from Buckingham. The King, much wanting such a man—for, besides being naturally favourable to the King's cause, he had great abilities—made him first a Baron, and then a Viscount, and gave him high employment, and won him most completely.

A Parliament, however, was still in existence, and was not to be won. On the twentieth of January, one thousand six hundred and twenty-nine, Sir John Eliot, a great man who had been active in the Petition of Right, brought forward other strong resolutions against the King's chief instruments, and called upon the Speaker to put them to the vote. To this the Speaker answered, 'he was commanded otherwise by the King,' and got up to leave the chair— which, according to the rules of the House of Commons would have obliged it to adjourn without doing anything more—when two members, named Mr. Hollis and Mr. Valentine, held him down. A scene of great confusion arose among the members; and while many swords were drawn and flashing about, the King, who was kept informed of all that was going on, told the captain of his guard to go down to the House and force the doors. The resolutions were by that time, however, voted, and the House adjourned. Sir John Eliot and those two members who had held the Speaker down, were quickly summoned before the council. As they claimed it to be their privilege not to answer out of Parliament for anything they had said in it, they were committed to the Tower. The King then went down and dissolved the Parliament, in a speech wherein he made mention of these gentlemen as 'Vipers'—which did not do him much good that ever I have heard of.

As they refused to gain their liberty by saying they were sorry for what they had done, the King, always remarkably unforgiving, never overlooked their offence. When they demanded to be brought up before the court of King's Bench, he even resorted to the meanness of having them moved about from prison to prison, so that the writs issued for that purpose should not legally find them. At last they came before the court and were sentenced to heavy fines, and to be imprisoned during the King's pleasure. When Sir John Eliot's health had quite given way, and he so longed for change of air and scene as to petition for his release, the King sent back the answer (worthy of his Sowship himself) that the petition was not humble enough. When he sent another petition by his young son, in which he pathetically offered to go back to prison when his health was restored, if he might be released for its recovery, the King still disregarded it. When he died in the Tower, and his children petitioned to be allowed to take his body down to Cornwall, there to lay it among the ashes of his forefathers, the King returned for answer, 'Let Sir John Eliot's body be buried in the church of that parish where he died.' All this was like a very little King indeed, I think.

And now, for twelve long years, steadily pursuing his design of setting himself up and putting the people down, the King called no Parliament; but ruled without one. If twelve thousand volumes were written in his praise (as a good many have been) it would still remain a fact, impossible to be denied, that for twelve years King Charles the First reigned in England unlawfully and despotically, seized upon his subjects' goods and money at his pleasure, and punished according to his unbridled will all who ventured to oppose him. It is a fashion with some people to think that this King's career was cut short; but I must say myself that I think he ran a pretty long one.

William Laud, Archbishop of Canterbury, was the King's right-hand man in the religious part of the putting down of the people's liberties. Laud, who was a sincere man, of large learning but small sense—for the two things sometimes go together in very different quantities—though a Protestant, held opinions so near those of the Catholics, that the Pope wanted to make a Cardinal of him, if he would have accepted that favour. He looked upon vows, robes, lighted candles, images, and so forth, as amazingly important in religious ceremonies; and he brought in an immensity of bowing and candle-snuffing. He also regarded archbishops and bishops as a sort of miraculous persons, and was inveterate in the last degree against any who thought otherwise. Accordingly, he offered up thanks to Heaven, and was in a state of much pious pleasure, when a Scotch clergyman, named Leighton, was pilloried, whipped, branded in the cheek, and had one of his ears cut off and one of his nostrils slit, for calling bishops trumpery and the inventions of men. He originated on a Sunday morning the prosecution of William Prynne, a barrister who was of similar opinions, and who was fined a thousand pounds; who was pilloried; who had his ears cut off on two occasions—one ear at a time—and who was imprisoned for life. He highly approved of the punishment of Doctor Bastwick, a physician; who was also fined a thousand pounds; and who afterwards had his ears cut off, and was imprisoned for life. These were gentle methods of persuasion, some will tell you: I think, they were rather calculated to be alarming to the people.

In the money part of the putting down of the people's liberties, the King was equally gentle, as some will tell you: as I think, equally alarming. He levied those duties of tonnage and poundage, and increased them as he thought fit. He granted monopolies to companies of merchants on their paying him for them, notwithstanding the great complaints that had, for years and years, been made on the subject of monopolies. He fined the people for disobeying proclamations issued by his Sowship in direct violation of law. He revived the detested Forest laws, and took private property to himself as his forest right. Above all, he determined to have what was called Ship Money; that is to say, money for the support of the fleet—not only from the seaports, but from all the counties of England: having found out that, in some ancient time or other, all the counties paid it. The grievance of this ship money being somewhat too strong, John Chambers, a citizen of London, refused to pay his part of it. For this the Lord Mayor ordered John Chambers to prison, and for that John Chambers brought a suit against the Lord Mayor. Lord Say, also, behaved like a real nobleman, and declared he would not pay. But, the sturdiest and best opponent of the ship money was John Hampden, a gentleman of Buckinghamshire, who had sat among the 'vipers' in the House of Commons when there was such a thing, and who had been the bosom friend of Sir John Eliot. This case was tried before the twelve judges in the Court of Exchequer, and again the King's lawyers said it was impossible that ship money could be wrong, because the King could do no wrong, however hard he tried—and he really did try very hard during these twelve years. Seven of the judges said that was quite true, and Mr. Hampden was bound to pay: five of the judges said that was quite false, and Mr. Hampden was not bound to pay. So, the King triumphed (as he thought), by making Hampden the most popular man in England; where matters were getting to that height now, that many honest Englishmen could not endure their country, and sailed away across the seas to found a colony in Massachusetts Bay in America. It is said that Hampden himself and his relation Oliver Cromwell were going with a company of such voyagers, and were actually on board ship, when they were stopped by a proclamation, prohibiting sea captains to carry out such passengers without the royal license. But O! it would have been well for the King if he had let them go! This was the state of England. If Laud had been a madman just broke loose, he could not have done more mischief than he did in Scotland. In his endeavours (in which he was seconded by the King, then in person in that part of his dominions) to force his own ideas of bishops, and his own religious forms and ceremonies upon the Scotch, he roused that nation to a perfect frenzy. They formed a solemn league, which they called The Covenant, for the preservation of their own religious forms; they rose in arms throughout the whole country; they summoned all their men to prayers and sermons twice a day by beat of drum; they sang psalms, in which they compared their enemies to all the evil spirits that ever were heard of; and they solemnly vowed to smite them with the sword. At first the King tried force, then treaty, then a Scottish Parliament which did not answer at all. Then he tried the Earl of Strafford, formerly Sir Thomas Wentworth; who, as Lord Wentworth, had been governing Ireland. He, too, had carried it with a very high hand there, though to the benefit and prosperity of that country.

Strafford and Laud were for conquering the Scottish people by force of arms. Other lords who were taken into council, recommended that a Parliament should at last be called; to which the King unwillingly consented. So, on the thirteenth of April, one thousand six hundred and forty, that then strange sight, a Parliament, was seen at Westminster. It is called the Short Parliament, for it lasted a very little while. While the members were all looking at one another, doubtful who would dare to speak, Mr. Pym arose and set forth all that the King had done unlawfully during the past twelve years, and what was the position to which England was reduced. This great example set, other members took courage and spoke the truth freely, though with great patience and moderation. The King, a little frightened, sent to say that if they would grant him a certain sum on certain terms, no more ship money should be raised. They debated the matter for two days; and then, as they would not give him all he asked without promise or inquiry, he dissolved them.

But they knew very well that he must have a Parliament now; and he began to make that discovery too, though rather late in the day. Wherefore, on the twenty-fourth of September, being then at York with an army collected against the Scottish people, but his own men sullen and discontented like the rest of the nation, the King told the great council of the Lords, whom he had called to meet him there, that he would summon another Parliament to assemble on the third of November. The soldiers of the Covenant had now forced their way into England and had taken possession of the northern counties, where the coals are got. As it would never do to be without coals, and as the King's troops could make no head against the Covenanters so full of gloomy zeal, a truce was made, and a treaty with Scotland was taken into consideration. Meanwhile the northern counties paid the Covenanters to leave the coals alone, and keep quiet.

We have now disposed of the Short Parliament. We have next to see what memorable things were done by the Long one.

SECOND PART

The Long Parliament assembled on the third of November, one thousand six hundred and forty-one. That day week the Earl of Strafford arrived from York, very sensible that the spirited and determined men who formed that Parliament were no friends towards him, who had not only deserted the cause of the people, but who had on all occasions opposed himself to their liberties. The King told him, for his comfort, that the Parliament 'should not hurt one hair of his head.' But, on the very next day Mr. Pym, in the House of Commons, and with great solemnity, impeached the Earl of Strafford as a traitor. He was immediately taken into custody and fell from his proud height.

It was the twenty-second of March before he was brought to trial in Westminster Hall; where, although he was very ill and suffered great pain, he defended himself with such ability and majesty, that it was doubtful whether he would not get the best of it. But on the thirteenth day of the trial, Pym produced in the House of Commons a copy of some notes of a council, found by young Sir Harry Vane in a red velvet cabinet belonging to his father (Secretary Vane, who sat at the council-table with the Earl), in which Strafford had distinctly told the King that he was free from all rules and obligations of government, and might do with his people whatever he liked; and in which he had added—'You have an army in Ireland that you may employ to reduce this kingdom to obedience.' It was not clear whether by the words 'this kingdom,' he had really meant England or Scotland; but the Parliament contended that he meant England, and this was treason. At the same sitting of the House of Commons it was resolved to bring in a bill of attainder declaring the treason to have been committed: in preference to proceeding with the trial by impeachment, which would have required the treason to be proved.

So, a bill was brought in at once, was carried through the House of Commons by a large majority, and was sent up to the House of Lords. While it was still uncertain whether the House of Lords would pass it and the King consent to it, Pym disclosed to the House of Commons that the King and Queen had both been plotting with the officers of the army to bring up the soldiers and control the Parliament, and also to introduce two hundred soldiers into the Tower of London to effect the Earl's escape. The plotting with the army was revealed by one George Goring, the son of a lord of that name: a bad fellow who was one of the original plotters, and turned traitor. The King had actually given his warrant for the admission of the two hundred men into the Tower, and they would have got in too, but for the refusal of the governor—a sturdy Scotchman of the name of Balfour—to admit them. These matters being made public, great numbers of people began to riot outside the Houses of Parliament, and to cry out for the execution of the Earl of Strafford, as one of the King's chief instruments against them. The bill passed the House of Lords while the people were in this state of agitation, and was laid before the King for his assent, together with another bill declaring that the Parliament then assembled should not be dissolved or adjourned without their own consent. The King—not unwilling to save a faithful servant, though he had no great attachment for him—was in some doubt what to do; but he gave his consent to both bills, although he in his heart believed that the bill against the Earl of Strafford was unlawful and unjust. The Earl had written to him, telling him that he was willing to die for his sake. But he had not expected that his royal master would take him at his word quite so readily; for, when he heard his doom, he laid his hand upon his heart, and said, 'Put not your trust in Princes!'

The King, who never could be straightforward and plain, through one single day or through one single sheet of paper, wrote a letter to the Lords, and sent it by the young Prince of Wales, entreating them to prevail with the Commons that 'that unfortunate man should fulfil the natural course of his life in a close imprisonment.' In a postscript to the very same letter, he added, 'If he must die, it were charity to reprieve him till Saturday.' If there had been any doubt of his fate, this weakness and meanness would have settled it. The very next day, which was the twelfth of May, he was brought out to be beheaded on Tower Hill.

Archbishop Laud, who had been so fond of having people's ears cropped off and their noses slit, was now confined in the Tower too; and when the Earl went by his window to his death, he was there, at his request, to give him his blessing. They had been great friends in the King's cause, and the Earl had written to him in the days of their power that he thought it would be an admirable thing to have Mr. Hampden publicly whipped for refusing to pay the ship money. However, those high and mighty doings were over now, and the Earl went his way to death with dignity and heroism. The governor wished him to get into a coach at the Tower gate, for fear the people should tear him to pieces; but he said it was all one to him whether he died by the axe or by the people's hands. So, he walked, with a firm tread and a stately look, and sometimes pulled off his hat to them as he passed along. They were profoundly quiet. He made a speech on the scaffold from some notes he had prepared (the paper was found lying there after his head was struck off), and one blow of the axe killed him, in the forty-ninth year of his age.

This bold and daring act, the Parliament accompanied by other famous measures, all originating (as even this did) in the King's having so grossly and so long abused his power. The name of Delinquents was applied to all sheriffs and other officers who had been concerned in raising the ship money, or any other money, from the people, in an unlawful manner; the Hampden judgment was reversed; the judges who had decided against Hampden were called upon to give large securities that they would take such consequences as Parliament might impose upon them; and one was arrested as he sat in High Court, and carried off to prison. Laud was impeached; the unfortunate victims whose ears had been cropped and whose noses had been slit, were brought out of prison in triumph; and a bill was passed declaring that a Parliament should be called every third year, and that if the King and the King's officers did not call it, the people should assemble of themselves and summon it, as of their own right and power. Great illuminations and rejoicings took place over all these things, and the country was wildly excited. That the Parliament took advantage of this excitement and stirred them up by every means, there is no doubt; but you are always to remember those twelve long years, during which the King had tried so hard whether he really could do any wrong or not.

All this time there was a great religious outcry against the right of the Bishops to sit in Parliament; to which the Scottish people particularly objected.

The English were divided on this subject, and, partly on this account and partly because they had had foolish expectations that the Parliament would be able to take off nearly all the taxes, numbers of them sometimes wavered and inclined towards the King.

I believe myself, that if, at this or almost any other period of his life, the King could have been trusted by any man not out of his senses, he might have saved himself and kept his throne. But, on the English army being disbanded, he plotted with the officers again, as he had done before, and established the fact beyond all doubt by putting his signature of approval to a petition against the Parliamentary leaders, which was drawn up by certain officers. When the Scottish army was disbanded, he went to Edinburgh in four days—which was going very fast at that time—to plot again, and so darkly too, that it is difficult to decide what his whole object was. Some suppose that he wanted to gain over the Scottish Parliament, as he did in fact gain over, by presents and favours, many Scottish lords and men of power. Some think that he went to get proofs against the Parliamentary leaders in England of their having treasonably invited the Scottish people to come and help them. With whatever object he went to Scotland, he did little good by going. At the instigation of the Earl of Montrose, a desperate man who was then in prison for plotting, he tried to kidnap three Scottish lords who escaped. A committee of the Parliament at home, who had followed to watch him, writing an account of this Incident, as it was called, to the Parliament, the Parliament made a fresh stir about it; were, or feigned to be, much alarmed for themselves; and wrote to the Earl of Essex, the commander-in-chief, for a guard to protect them.

It is not absolutely proved that the King plotted in Ireland besides, but it is very probable that he did, and that the Queen did, and that he had some wild hope of gaining the Irish people over to his side by favouring a rise among them. Whether or no, they did rise in a most brutal and savage rebellion; in which, encouraged by their priests, they committed such atrocities upon numbers of the English, of both sexes and of all ages, as nobody could believe, but for their being related on oath by eye-witnesses. Whether one hundred thousand or two hundred thousand Protestants were murdered in this outbreak, is uncertain; but, that it was as ruthless and barbarous an outbreak as ever was known among any savage people, is certain.

The King came home from Scotland, determined to make a great struggle for his lost power. He believed that, through his presents and favours, Scotland would take no part against him; and the Lord Mayor of London received him with such a magnificent dinner that he thought he must have become popular again in England. It would take a good many Lord Mayors, however, to make a people, and the King soon found himself mistaken.

Not so soon, though, but that there was a great opposition in the Parliament to a celebrated paper put forth by Pym and Hampden and the rest, called 'The Remonstrance,' which set forth all the illegal acts that the King had ever done, but politely laid the blame of them on his bad advisers. Even when it was passed and presented to him, the King still thought himself strong enough to discharge Balfour from his command in the Tower, and to put in his place a man of bad character; to whom the Commons instantly objected, and whom he was obliged to abandon. At this time, the old outcry about the Bishops became louder than ever, and the old Archbishop of York was so near being murdered as he went down to the House of Lords—being laid hold of by the mob and violently knocked about, in return for very foolishly scolding a shrill boy who was yelping out 'No Bishops!'—that he sent for all the Bishops who were in town, and proposed to them to sign a declaration that, as they could no longer without danger to their lives attend their duty in Parliament, they protested against the lawfulness of everything done in their absence. This they asked the King to send to the House of Lords, which he did. Then the House of Commons impeached the whole party of Bishops and sent them off to the Tower:

Taking no warning from this; but encouraged by there being a moderate party in the Parliament who objected to these strong measures, the King, on the third of January, one thousand six hundred and forty-two, took the rashest step that ever was taken by mortal man.

Of his own accord and without advice, he sent the Attorney-General to the House of Lords, to accuse of treason certain members of Parliament who as popular leaders were the most obnoxious to him; Lord Kimbolton, Sir Arthur Haselrig, Denzil Hollis, John Pym (they used to call him King Pym, he possessed such power and looked so big), John Hampden, and William Strode. The houses of those members he caused to be entered, and their papers to be sealed up. At the same time, he sent a messenger to the House of Commons demanding to have the five gentlemen who were members of that House immediately produced. To this the House replied that they should appear as soon as there was any legal charge against them, and immediately adjourned.

Next day, the House of Commons send into the City to let the Lord Mayor know that their privileges are invaded by the King, and that there is no safety for anybody or anything. Then, when the five members are gone out of the way, down comes the King himself, with all his guard and from two to three hundred gentlemen and soldiers, of whom the greater part were armed. These he leaves in the hall; and then, with his nephew at his side, goes into the House, takes off his hat, and walks up to the Speaker's chair. The Speaker leaves it, the King stands in front of it, looks about him steadily for a little while, and says he has come for those five members. No one speaks, and then he calls John Pym by name. No one speaks, and then he calls Denzil Hollis by name. No one speaks, and then he asks the Speaker of the House where those five members are? The Speaker, answering on his knee, nobly replies that he is the servant of that House, and that he has neither eyes to see, nor tongue to speak, anything but what the House commands him. Upon this, the King, beaten from that time evermore, replies that he will seek them himself, for they have committed treason; and goes out, with his hat in his hand, amid some audible murmurs from the members.

No words can describe the hurry that arose out of doors when all this was known. The five members had gone for safety to a house in Coleman-street, in the City, where they were guarded all night; and indeed the whole city watched in arms like an army. At ten o'clock in the morning, the King, already frightened at what he had done, came to the Guildhall, with only half a dozen lords, and made a speech to the people, hoping they would not shelter those whom he accused of treason. Next day, he issued a proclamation for the apprehension of the five members; but the Parliament minded it so little that they made great arrangements for having them brought down to Westminster in great state, five days afterwards. The King was so alarmed now at his own imprudence, if not for his own safety, that he left his palace at Whitehall, and went away with his Queen and children to Hampton Court.

It was the eleventh of May, when the five members were carried in state and triumph to Westminster. They were taken by water. The river could not be seen for the boats on it; and the five members were hemmed in by barges full of men and great guns, ready to protect them, at any cost. Along the Strand a large body of the train-bands of London, under their commander, Skippon, marched to be ready to assist the little fleet. Beyond them, came a crowd who choked the streets, roaring incessantly about the Bishops and the Papists, and crying out contemptuously as they passed Whitehall, 'What has become of the King?' With this great noise outside the House of Commons, and with great silence within, Mr. Pym rose and informed the House of the great kindness with which they had been received in the City. Upon that, the House called the sheriffs in and thanked them, and requested the train-bands, under their commander Skippon, to guard the House of Commons every day. Then, came four thousand men on horseback out of Buckinghamshire, offering their services as a guard too, and bearing a petition to the King, complaining of the injury that had been done to Mr. Hampden, who was their county man and much beloved and honoured.

When the King set off for Hampton Court, the gentlemen and soldiers who had been with him followed him out of town as far as Kingston-upon-Thames; next day, Lord Digby came to them from the King at Hampton Court, in his coach and six, to inform them that the King accepted their protection. This, the Parliament said, was making war against the kingdom, and Lord Digby fled abroad. The Parliament then immediately applied themselves to getting hold of the military power of the country, well knowing that the King was already trying hard to use it against them, and that he had secretly sent the Earl of Newcastle to Hull, to secure a valuable magazine of arms and gunpowder that was there. In those times, every county had its own magazines of arms and powder, for its own train-bands or militia; so, the Parliament brought in a bill claiming the right (which up to this time had belonged to the King) of appointing the Lord Lieutenants of counties, who commanded these train-bands; also, of having all the forts, castles, and garrisons in the kingdom, put into the hands of such governors as they, the Parliament, could confide in. It also passed a law depriving the Bishops of their votes. The King gave his assent to that bill, but would not abandon the right of appointing the Lord Lieutenants, though he said he was willing to appoint such as might be suggested to him by the Parliament. When the Earl of Pembroke asked him whether he would not give way on that question for a time, he said, 'By God! not for one hour!' and upon this he and the Parliament went to war.

His young daughter was betrothed to the Prince of Orange. On pretence of taking her to the country of her future husband, the Queen was already got safely away to Holland, there to pawn the Crown jewels for money to raise an army on the King's side. The Lord Admiral being sick, the House of Commons now named the Earl of Warwick to hold his place for a year. The King named another gentleman; the House of Commons took its own way, and the Earl of Warwick became Lord Admiral without the King's consent. The Parliament sent orders down to Hull to have that magazine removed to London; the King went down to Hull to take it himself. The citizens would not admit him into the town, and the governor would not admit him into the castle. The Parliament resolved that whatever the two Houses passed, and the King would not consent to, should be called an Ordinance, and should be as much a law as if he did consent to it. The King protested against this, and gave notice that these ordinances were not to be obeyed. The King, attended by the majority of the House of Peers, and by many members of the House of Commons, established himself at York. The Chancellor went to him with the Great Seal, and the Parliament made a new Great Seal. The Queen sent over a ship full of arms and ammunition, and the King issued letters to borrow money at high interest. The Parliament raised twenty regiments of foot and seventy-five troops of horse; and the people willingly aided them with their money, plate, jewellery, and trinkets—the married women even with their wedding-rings. Every member of Parliament who could raise a troop or a regiment in his own part of the country, dressed it according to his taste and in his own colours, and commanded it. Foremost among them all, Oliver Cromwell raised a troop of horse—thoroughly in earnest and thoroughly well armed—who were, perhaps, the best soldiers that ever were seen.

In some of their proceedings, this famous Parliament passed the bounds of previous law and custom, yielded to and favoured riotous assemblages of the people, and acted tyrannically in imprisoning some who differed from the popular leaders. But again, you are always to remember that the twelve years during which the King had had his own wilful way, had gone before; and that nothing could make the times what they might, could, would, or should have been, if those twelve years had never rolled away.

THIRD PART

I shall not try to relate the particulars of the great civil war between King Charles the First and the Long Parliament, which lasted nearly four years, and a full account of which would fill many large books. It was a sad thing that Englishmen should once more be fighting against Englishmen on English ground; but, it is some consolation to know that on both sides there was great humanity, forbearance, and honour. The soldiers of the Parliament were far more remarkable for these good qualities than the soldiers of the King (many of whom fought for mere pay without much caring for the cause); but those of the nobility and gentry who were on the King's side were so brave, and so faithful to him, that their conduct cannot but command our highest admiration. Among them were great numbers of Catholics, who took the royal side because the Queen was so strongly of their persuasion.

The King might have distinguished some of these gallant spirits, if he had been as generous a spirit himself, by giving them the command of his army. Instead of that, however, true to his old high notions of royalty, he entrusted it to his two nephews, Prince Rupert and Prince Maurice, who were of royal blood and came over from abroad to help him. It might have been better for him if they had stayed away; since Prince Rupert was an impetuous, hot-headed fellow, whose only idea was to dash into battle at all times and seasons, and lay about him.

The general-in-chief of the Parliamentary army was the Earl of Essex, a gentleman of honour and an excellent soldier. A little while before the war broke out, there had been some rioting at Westminster between certain officious law students and noisy soldiers, and the shopkeepers and their apprentices, and the general people in the streets. At that time the King's friends called the crowd, Roundheads, because the apprentices wore short hair; the crowd, in return, called their opponents Cavaliers, meaning that they were a blustering set, who pretended to be very military. These two words now began to be used to distinguish the two sides in the civil war. The Royalists also called the Parliamentary men Rebels and Rogues, while the Parliamentary men called them Malignants, and spoke of themselves as the Godly, the Honest, and so forth.

The war broke out at Portsmouth, where that double traitor Goring had again gone over to the King and was besieged by the Parliamentary troops. Upon this, the King proclaimed the Earl of Essex and the officers serving under him, traitors, and called upon his loyal subjects to meet him in arms at Nottingham on the twenty-fifth of August. But his loyal subjects came about him in scanty numbers, and it was a windy, gloomy day, and the Royal Standard got blown down, and the whole affair was very melancholy. The chief engagements after this, took place in the vale of the Red Horse near Banbury, at Brentford, at Devizes, at Chalgrave Field (where Mr. Hampden was so sorely wounded while fighting at the head of his men, that he died within a week), at Newbury (in which battle Lord Falkland, one of the best noblemen on the King's side, was killed), at Leicester, at Naseby, at Winchester, at Marston Moor near York, at Newcastle, and in many other parts of England and Scotland. These battles were attended with various successes. At one time, the King was victorious; at another time, the Parliament. But almost all the great and busy towns were against the King; and when it was considered necessary to fortify London, all ranks of people, from labouring men and women, up to lords and ladies, worked hard together with heartiness and good will. The most distinguished leaders on the Parliamentary side were Hampden, Sir Thomas Fairfax, and, above all, Oliver Cromwell, and his son-in-law Ireton.

During the whole of this war, the people, to whom it was very expensive and irksome, and to whom it was made the more distressing by almost every family being divided—some of its members attaching themselves to one side and some to the other—were over and over again most anxious for peace. So were some of the best men in each cause. Accordingly, treaties of peace were discussed between commissioners from the Parliament and the King; at York, at Oxford (where the King held a little Parliament of his own), and at Uxbridge. But they came to nothing. In all these negotiations, and in all his difficulties, the King showed himself at his best. He was courageous, cool, self-possessed, and clever; but, the old taint of his character was always in him, and he was never for one single moment to be trusted. Lord Clarendon, the historian, one of his highest admirers, supposes that he had unhappily promised the Queen never to make peace without her consent, and that this must often be taken as his excuse. He never kept his word from night to morning. He signed a cessation of hostilities with the blood-stained Irish rebels for a sum of money, and invited the Irish regiments over, to help him against the Parliament. In the battle of Naseby, his cabinet was seized and was found to contain a correspondence with the Queen, in which he expressly told her that he had deceived the Parliament—a mongrel Parliament, he called it now, as an improvement on his old term of vipers—in pretending to recognise it and to treat with it; and from which it further appeared that he had long been in secret treaty with the Duke of Lorraine for a foreign army of ten thousand men. Disappointed in this, he sent a most devoted friend of his, the Earl of Glamorgan, to Ireland, to conclude a secret treaty with the Catholic powers, to send him an Irish army of ten thousand men; in return for which he was to bestow great favours on the Catholic religion. And, when this treaty was discovered in the carriage of a fighting Irish Archbishop who was killed in one of the many skirmishes of those days, he basely denied and deserted his attached friend, the Earl, on his being charged with high treason; and—even worse than this—had left blanks in the secret instructions he gave him with his own kingly hand, expressly that he might thus save himself.

At last, on the twenty-seventh day of April, one thousand six hundred and forty-six, the King found himself in the city of Oxford, so surrounded by the Parliamentary army who were closing in upon him on all sides that he felt that if he would escape he must delay no longer. So, that night, having altered the cut of his hair and beard, he was dressed up as a servant and put upon a horse with a cloak strapped behind him, and rode out of the town behind one of his own faithful followers, with a clergyman of that country who knew the road well, for a guide. He rode towards London as far as Harrow, and then altered his plans and resolved, it would seem, to go to the Scottish camp. The Scottish men had been invited over to help the Parliamentary army, and had a large force then in England. The King was so desperately intriguing in everything he did, that it is doubtful what he exactly meant by this step. He took it, anyhow, and delivered himself up to the Earl of Leven, the Scottish general-in-chief, who treated him as an honourable prisoner. Negotiations between the Parliament on the one hand and the Scottish authorities on the other, as to what should be done with him, lasted until the following February. Then, when the King had refused to the Parliament the concession of that old militia point for twenty years, and had refused to Scotland the recognition of its Solemn League and Covenant, Scotland got a handsome sum for its army and its help, and the King into the bargain. He was taken, by certain Parliamentary commissioners appointed to receive him, to one of his own houses, called Holmby House, near Althorpe, in Northamptonshire.

While the Civil War was still in progress, John Pym died, and was buried with great honour in Westminster Abbey—not with greater honour than he deserved, for the liberties of Englishmen owe a mighty debt to Pym and Hampden. The war was but newly over when the Earl of Essex died, of an illness brought on by his having overheated himself in a stag hunt in Windsor Forest. He, too, was buried in Westminster Abbey, with great state. I wish it were not necessary to add that Archbishop Laud died upon the scaffold when the war was not yet done. His trial lasted in all nearly a year, and, it being doubtful even then whether the charges brought against him amounted to treason, the odious old contrivance of the worst kings was resorted to, and a bill of attainder was brought in against him. He was a violently prejudiced and mischievous person; had had strong ear-cropping and nose-splitting propensities, as you know; and had done a world of harm. But he died peaceably, and like a brave old man.

350

FOURTH PART

When the Parliament had got the King into their hands, they became very anxious to get rid of their army, in which Oliver Cromwell had begun to acquire great power; not only because of his courage and high abilities, but because he professed to be very sincere in the Scottish sort of Puritan religion that was then exceedingly popular among the soldiers. They were as much opposed to the Bishops as to the Pope himself; and the very privates, drummers, and trumpeters, had such an inconvenient habit of starting up and preaching long-winded discourses, that I would not have belonged to that army on any account.

So, the Parliament, being far from sure but that the army might begin to preach and fight against them now it had nothing else to do, proposed to disband the greater part of it, to send another part to serve in Ireland against the rebels, and to keep only a small force in England. But, the army would not consent to be broken up, except upon its own conditions; and, when the Parliament showed an intention of compelling it, it acted for itself in an unexpected manner. A certain cornet, of the name of Joice, arrived at Holmby House one night, attended by four hundred horsemen, went into the King's room with his hat in one hand and a pistol in the other, and told the King that he had come to take him away. The King was willing enough to go, and only stipulated that he should be publicly required to do so next morning. Next morning, accordingly, he appeared on the top of the steps of the house, and asked Comet Joice before his men and the guard set there by the Parliament, what authority he had for taking him away? To this Cornet Joice replied, 'The authority of the army.' 'Have you a written commission?' said the King. Joice, pointing to his four hundred men on horseback, replied, 'That is my commission.' 'Well,' said the King, smiling, as if he were pleased, 'I never before read such a commission; but it is written in fair and legible characters. This is a company of as handsome proper gentlemen as I have seen a long while.' He was asked where he would like to live, and he said at Newmarket. So, to Newmarket he and Cornet Joice and the four hundred horsemen rode; the King remarking, in the same smiling way, that he could ride as far at a spell as Cornet Joice, or any man there.

The King quite believed, I think, that the army were his friends. He said as much to Fairfax when that general, Oliver Cromwell, and Ireton, went to persuade him to return to the custody of the Parliament. He preferred to remain as he was, and resolved to remain as he was. And when the army moved nearer and nearer London to frighten the Parliament into yielding to their demands, they took the King with them. It was a deplorable thing that England should be at the mercy of a great body of soldiers with arms in their hands; but the King certainly favoured them at this important time of his life, as compared with the more lawful power that tried to control him. It must be added, however, that they treated him, as yet, more respectfully and kindly than the Parliament had done. They allowed him to be attended by his own servants, to be splendidly entertained at various houses, and to see his children—at Cavesham House, near Reading—for two days. Whereas, the Parliament had been rather hard with him, and had only allowed him to ride out and play at bowls.

It is much to be believed that if the King could have been trusted, even at this time, he might have been saved. Even Oliver Cromwell expressly said that he did believe that no man could enjoy his possessions in peace, unless the King had his rights. He was not unfriendly towards the King; he had been present when he received his children, and had been much affected by the pitiable nature of the scene; he saw the King often; he frequently walked and talked with him in the long galleries and pleasant gardens of the Palace at Hampton Court, whither he was now removed; and in all this risked something of his influence with the army. But, the King was in secret hopes of help from the Scottish people; and the moment he was encouraged to join them he began to be cool to his new friends, the army, and to tell the officers that they could not possibly do without him. At the very time, too, when he was promising to make Cromwell and Ireton noblemen, if they would help him up to his old height, he was writing to the Queen that he meant to hang them. They both afterwards declared that they had been privately informed that such a letter would be found, on a certain evening, sewed up in a saddle which would be taken to the Blue Boar in Holborn to be sent to Dover; and that they went there, disguised as common soldiers, and sat drinking in the inn-yard until a man came with the saddle, which they ripped up with their knives, and therein found the letter. I see little reason to doubt the story. It is certain that Oliver Cromwell told one of the King's most faithful followers that the King could not be trusted, and that he would not be answerable if anything amiss were to happen to him. Still, even after that, he kept a promise he had made to the King, by letting him know that there was a plot with a certain portion of the army to seize him. I believe that, in fact, he sincerely wanted the King to escape abroad, and so to be got rid of without more trouble or danger. That Oliver himself had work enough with the army is pretty plain; for some of the troops were so mutinous against him, and against those who acted with him at this time, that he found it necessary to have one man shot at the head of his regiment to overawe the rest.

The King, when he received Oliver's warning, made his escape from Hampton Court; after some indecision and uncertainty, he went to Carisbrooke Castle in the Isle of Wight. At first, he was pretty free there; but, even there, he carried on a pretended treaty with the Parliament, while he was really treating with commissioners from Scotland to send an army into England to take his part. When he broke off this treaty with the Parliament (having settled with Scotland) and was treated as a prisoner, his treatment was not changed too soon, for he had plotted to escape that very night to a ship sent by the Queen, which was lying off the island.

He was doomed to be disappointed in his hopes from Scotland. The agreement he had made with the Scottish Commissioners was not favourable enough to the religion of that country to please the Scottish clergy; and they preached against it. The consequence was, that the army raised in Scotland and sent over, was too small to do much; and that, although it was helped by a rising of the Royalists in England and by good soldiers from Ireland, it could make no head against the Parliamentary army under such men as Cromwell and Fairfax. The King's eldest son, the Prince of Wales, came over from Holland with nineteen ships (a part of the English fleet having gone over to him) to help his father; but nothing came of his voyage, and he was fain to return. The most remarkable event of this second civil war was the cruel execution by the Parliamentary General, of Sir Charles Lucas and Sir George Lisle, two grand Royalist generals, who had bravely defended

Colchester under every disadvantage of famine and distress for nearly three months. When Sir Charles Lucas was shot, Sir George Lisle kissed his body, and said to the soldiers who were to shoot him, 'Come nearer, and make sure of me.' 'I warrant you, Sir George,' said one of the soldiers, 'we shall hit you.' 'Ay?' he returned with a smile, 'but I have been nearer to you, my friends, many a time, and you have missed me.'

The Parliament, after being fearfully bullied by the army—who demanded to have seven members whom they disliked given up to them—had voted that they would have nothing more to do with the King. On the conclusion, however, of this second civil war (which did not last more than six months), they appointed commissioners to treat with him. The King, then so far released again as to be allowed to live in a private house at Newport in the Isle of Wight, managed his own part of the negotiation with a sense that was admired by all who saw him, and gave up, in the end, all that was asked of him—even yielding (which he had steadily refused, so far) to the temporary abolition of the bishops, and the transfer of their church land to the Crown. Still, with his old fatal vice upon him, when his best friends joined the commissioners in beseeching him to yield all those points as the only means of saving himself from the army, he was plotting to escape from the island; he was holding correspondence with his friends and the Catholics in Ireland, though declaring that he was not; and he was writing, with his own hand, that in what he yielded he meant nothing but to get time to escape.

Matters were at this pass when the army, resolved to defy the Parliament, marched up to London. The Parliament, not afraid of them now, and boldly led by Hollis, voted that the King's concessions were sufficient ground for settling the peace of the kingdom. Upon that, Colonel Rich and Colonel Pride went down to the House of Commons with a regiment of horse soldiers and a regiment of foot; and Colonel Pride, standing in the lobby with a list of the members who were obnoxious to the army in his hand, had them pointed out to him as they came through, and took them all into custody. This proceeding was afterwards called by the people, for a joke, Pride's Purge. Cromwell was in the North, at the head of his men, at the time, but when he came home, approved of what had been done.

What with imprisoning some members and causing others to stay away, the army had now reduced the House of Commons to some fifty or so. These soon voted that it was treason in a king to make war against his parliament and his people, and sent an ordinance up to the House of Lords for the King's being tried as a traitor. The House of Lords, then sixteen in number, to a man rejected it. Thereupon, the Commons made an ordinance of their own, that they were the supreme government of the country, and would bring the King to trial.

The King had been taken for security to a place called Hurst Castle: a lonely house on a rock in the sea, connected with the coast of Hampshire by a rough road two miles long at low water. Thence, he was ordered to be removed to Windsor; thence, after being but rudely used there, and having none but soldiers to wait upon him at table, he was brought up to St. James's Palace in London, and told that his trial was appointed for next day.

On Saturday, the twentieth of January, one thousand six hundred and forty-nine, this memorable trial began. The House of Commons had settled that one hundred and thirty-five persons should form the Court, and these were taken from the House itself, from among the officers of the army, and from among the lawyers and citizens. John Bradshaw, serjeant-at-law, was appointed president. The place was Westminster Hall. At the upper end, in a red velvet chair, sat the president, with his hat (lined with plates of iron for his protection) on his head. The rest of the Court sat on side benches, also wearing their hats. The King's seat was covered with velvet, like that of the president, and was opposite to it. He was brought from St. James's to Whitehall, and from Whitehall he came by water to his trial.

When he came in, he looked round very steadily on the Court, and on the great number of spectators, and then sat down: presently he got up and looked round again. On the indictment 'against Charles Stuart, for high treason,' being read, he smiled several times, and he denied the authority of the Court, saying that there could be no parliament without a House of Lords, and that he saw no House of Lords there. Also, that the King ought to be there, and that he saw no King in the King's right place. Bradshaw replied, that the Court was satisfied with its authority, and that its authority was God's authority and the kingdom's. He then adjourned the Court to the following Monday. On that day, the trial was resumed, and went on all the week. When the Saturday came, as the King passed forward to his place in the Hall, some soldiers and others cried for 'justice!' and execution on him. That day, too, Bradshaw, like an angry Sultan, wore a red robe, instead of the black robe he had worn before. The King was sentenced to death that day. As he went out, one solitary soldier said, 'God bless you, Sir!' For this, his officer struck him. The King said he thought the punishment exceeded the offence. The silver head of his walking-stick had fallen off while he leaned upon it, at one time of the trial. The accident seemed to disturb him, as if he thought it ominous of the falling of his own head; and he admitted as much, now it was all over.

Being taken back to Whitehall, he sent to the House of Commons, saying that as the time of his execution might be nigh, he wished he might be allowed to see his darling children. It was granted. On the Monday he was taken back to St. James's; and his two children then in England, the Princess Elizabeth thirteen years old, and the Duke Of Gloucester nine years old, were brought to take leave of him, from Sion House, near Brentford. It was a sad and touching scene, when he kissed and fondled those poor children, and made a little present of two diamond seals to the Princess, and gave them tender messages to their mother (who little deserved them, for she had a lover of her own whom she married soon afterwards), and told them that he died 'for the laws and liberties of the land.' I am bound to say that I don't think he did, but I dare say he believed so.

There were ambassadors from Holland that day, to intercede for the unhappy King, whom you and I both wish the Parliament had spared; but they got no answer. The Scottish Commissioners interceded too; so did the Prince of Wales, by a letter in which he offered as the next heir to the throne, to accept any conditions from the Parliament; so did the Queen, by letter likewise.

Notwithstanding all, the warrant for the execution was this day signed. There is a story that as Oliver Cromwell went to the table with the pen in his hand to put his signature to it, he drew his pen across the face of one of the commissioners, who was standing near, and marked it with ink. That commissioner had not signed his own name yet, and the story adds that when he came to do it he marked Cromwell's face with ink in the same way.

The King slept well, untroubled by the knowledge that it was his last night on earth, and rose on the thirtieth of January, two hours before day, and dressed himself carefully. He put on two shirts lest he should tremble with the cold, and had his hair very carefully combed. The warrant had been directed to three officers of the army, Colonel Hacker, Colonel Hunks, and Colonel Phayer. At ten o'clock, the first of these came to the door and said it was time to go to Whitehall. The King, who had always been a quick walker, walked at his usual speed through the Park, and called out to the guard, with his accustomed voice of command, 'March on apace!' When he came to Whitehall, he was taken to his own bedroom, where a breakfast was set forth. As he had taken the Sacrament, he would eat nothing more; but, at about the time when the church bells struck twelve at noon (for he had to wait, through the scaffold not being ready), he took the advice of the good Bishop Juxon who was with him, and ate a little bread and drank a glass of claret. Soon after he had taken this refreshment, Colonel Hacker came to the chamber with the warrant in his hand, and called for Charles Stuart.

And then, through the long gallery of Whitehall Palace, which he had often seen light and gay and merry and crowded, in very different times, the fallen King passed along, until he came to the centre window of the Banqueting House, through which he emerged upon the scaffold, which was hung with black. He looked at the two executioners, who were dressed in black and masked; he looked at the troops of soldiers on horseback and on foot, and all looked up at him in silence; he looked at the vast array of spectators, filling up the view beyond, and turning all their faces upon him; he looked at his old Palace of St. James's; and he looked at the block. He seemed a little troubled to find that it was so low, and asked, 'if there were no place higher?' Then, to those upon the scaffold, he said, 'that it was the Parliament who had begun the war, and not he; but he hoped they might be guiltless too, as ill instruments had gone between them. In one respect,' he said, 'he suffered justly; and that was because he had permitted an unjust sentence to be executed on another.' In this he referred to the Earl of Strafford.

He was not at all afraid to die; but he was anxious to die easily. When some one touched the axe while he was speaking, he broke off and called out, 'Take heed of the axe! take heed of the axe!' He also said to Colonel Hacker, 'Take care that they do not put me to pain.' He told the executioner, 'I shall say but very short prayers, and then thrust out my hands'—as the sign to strike.

He put his hair up, under a white satin cap which the bishop had carried, and said, 'I have a good cause and a gracious God on my side.' The bishop told him that he had but one stage more to travel in this weary world, and that, though it was a turbulent and troublesome stage, it was a short one, and would carry him a great way—all the way from earth to Heaven. The King's last word, as he gave his cloak and the George—the decoration from his breast—to the bishop, was, 'Remember!' He then kneeled down, laid his head on the block, spread out his hands, and was instantly killed. One universal groan broke from the crowd; and the soldiers, who had sat on their horses and stood in their ranks immovable as statues, were of a sudden all in motion, clearing the streets.

Thus, in the forty-ninth year of his age, falling at the same time of his career as Strafford had fallen in his, perished Charles the First. With all my sorrow for him, I cannot agree with him that he died 'the martyr of the people;' for the people had been martyrs to him, and to his ideas of a King's rights, long before. Indeed, I am afraid that he was but a bad judge of martyrs; for he had called that infamous Duke of Buckingham 'the Martyr of his Sovereign.'

CHAPTER XXXIV—ENGLAND UNDER OLIVER CROMWELL

Before sunset on the memorable day on which King Charles the First was executed, the House of Commons passed an act declaring it treason in any one to proclaim the Prince of Wales—or anybody else—King of England. Soon afterwards, it declared that the House of Lords was useless and dangerous, and ought to be abolished; and directed that the late King's statue should be taken down from the Royal Exchange in the City and other public places. Having laid hold of some famous Royalists who had escaped from prison, and having beheaded the Duke Of Hamilton, Lord Holland, and Lord Capel, in Palace Yard (all of whom died very courageously), they then appointed a Council of State to govern the country. It consisted of forty-one members, of whom five were peers. Bradshaw was made president. The House of Commons also re-admitted members who had opposed the King's death, and made up its numbers to about a hundred and fifty.

But, it still had an army of more than forty thousand men to deal with, and a very hard task it was to manage them. Before the King's execution, the army had appointed some of its officers to remonstrate between them and the Parliament; and now the common soldiers began to take that office upon themselves. The regiments under orders for Ireland mutinied; one troop of horse in the city of London seized their own flag, and refused to obey orders. For this, the ringleader was shot: which did not mend the matter, for, both his comrades and the people made a public funeral for him, and accompanied the body to the grave with sound of trumpets and with a gloomy procession of persons carrying bundles of rosemary steeped in blood. Oliver was the only man to deal with such difficulties as these, and he soon cut them short by bursting at midnight into the town of Burford, near Salisbury, where the mutineers were sheltered, taking four hundred of them prisoners, and shooting a number of them by sentence of court-martial. The soldiers soon found, as all men did, that Oliver was not a man to be trifled with. And there was an end of the mutiny.

The Scottish Parliament did not know Oliver yet; so, on hearing of the King's execution, it proclaimed the Prince of Wales King Charles the Second, on condition of his respecting the Solemn League and Covenant. Charles was abroad at that time, and so was Montrose, from whose help he had hopes enough to keep him holding on and off with commissioners from Scotland, just as his father might have done. These hopes were soon at an end; for, Montrose, having raised a few hundred exiles in Germany, and landed with them in Scotland, found that the people there, instead of joining him, deserted the country at his approach. He was soon taken prisoner and carried to Edinburgh. There he was received with every possible insult, and carried to prison in a cart, his officers going two and two before him. He was sentenced by the Parliament to be hanged on a gallows thirty feet high, to have his head set on a spike in Edinburgh, and his limbs distributed in other places, according to the old barbarous manner. He said he had always acted under the Royal orders, and only wished he had limbs enough to be distributed through Christendom, that it might be the more widely known how loyal he had been. He went to the scaffold in a bright and brilliant dress, and made a bold end at thirty-eight years of age. The breath was scarcely out of his body when Charles abandoned his memory, and denied that he had ever given him orders to rise in his behalf. O the family failing was strong in that Charles then!

Oliver had been appointed by the Parliament to command the army in Ireland, where he took a terrible vengeance for the sanguinary rebellion, and made tremendous havoc, particularly in the siege of Drogheda, where no quarter was given, and where he found at least a thousand of the inhabitants shut up together in the great church: every one of whom was killed by his soldiers, usually known as Oliver's Ironsides. There were numbers of friars and priests among them, and Oliver gruffly wrote home in his despatch that these were 'knocked on the head' like the rest.

But, Charles having got over to Scotland where the men of the Solemn League and Covenant led him a prodigiously dull life and made him very weary with long sermons and grim Sundays, the Parliament called the redoubtable Oliver home to knock the Scottish men on the head for setting up that Prince. Oliver left his son-in-law, Ireton, as general in Ireland in his stead (he died there afterwards), and he imitated the example of his father-in-law with such good will that he brought the country to subjection, and laid it at the feet of the Parliament. In the end, they passed an act for the settlement of Ireland, generally pardoning all the common people, but exempting from this grace such of the wealthier sort as had been concerned in the rebellion, or in any killing of Protestants, or who refused to lay down their arms. Great numbers of Irish were got out of the country to serve under Catholic powers abroad, and a quantity of land was declared to have been forfeited by past offences, and was given to people who had lent money to the Parliament early in the war. These were sweeping measures; but, if Oliver Cromwell had had his own way fully, and had stayed in Ireland, he would have done more yet.

However, as I have said, the Parliament wanted Oliver for Scotland; so, home Oliver came, and was made Commander of all the Forces of the Commonwealth of England, and in three days away he went with sixteen thousand soldiers to fight the Scottish men. Now, the Scottish men, being then—as you will generally find them now—mighty cautious, reflected that the troops they had were not used to war like the Ironsides, and would be beaten in an open fight. Therefore they said, 'If we live quiet in our trenches in Edinburgh here, and if all the farmers come into the town and desert the country, the Ironsides will be driven out by iron hunger and be forced to go away.' This was, no doubt, the wisest plan; but as the Scottish clergy would interfere with what they knew nothing about, and would perpetually preach long sermons exhorting the soldiers to come out and fight, the soldiers got it in their heads that they absolutely must come out and fight. Accordingly, in an evil hour for themselves, they came out of their safe position. Oliver fell upon them instantly, and killed three thousand, and took ten thousand prisoners.

To gratify the Scottish Parliament, and preserve their favour, Charles had signed a declaration they laid before him, reproaching the memory of his father and mother, and representing himself as a most religious Prince, to whom the Solemn League and Covenant was as dear as life. He meant no sort of truth in this, and soon afterwards galloped away on horseback to join some tiresome Highland friends, who were always flourishing dirks and broadswords. He was overtaken and induced to return; but this attempt, which was called 'The Start,' did him just so much service, that they did not preach quite such long sermons at him afterwards as they had done before.

On the first of January, one thousand six hundred and fifty-one, the Scottish people crowned him at Scone. He immediately took the chief command of an army of twenty thousand men, and marched to Stirling. His hopes were heightened, I dare say, by the redoubtable Oliver being ill of an ague; but Oliver scrambled out of bed in no time, and went to work with such energy that he got behind the Royalist army and cut it off from all communication with Scotland. There was nothing for it then, but to go on to England; so it went on as far as Worcester, where the mayor and some of the gentry proclaimed King Charles the Second straightway. His proclamation, however, was of little use to him, for very few Royalists appeared; and, on the very same day, two people were publicly beheaded on Tower Hill for espousing his cause. Up came Oliver to Worcester too, at double quick speed, and he and his Ironsides so laid about them in the great battle which was fought there, that they completely beat the Scottish men, and destroyed the Royalist army; though the Scottish men fought so gallantly that it took five hours to do.

The escape of Charles after this battle of Worcester did him good service long afterwards, for it induced many of the generous English people to take a romantic interest in him, and to think much better of him than he ever deserved. He fled in the night, with not more than sixty followers, to the house of a Catholic lady in Staffordshire. There, for his greater safety, the whole sixty left him. He cropped his hair, stained his face and hands brown as if they were sunburnt, put on the clothes of a labouring countryman, and went out in the morning with his axe in his hand, accompanied by four wood-cutters who were brothers, and another man who was their brother-in-law. These good fellows made a bed for him under a tree, as the weather was very bad; and the wife of one of them brought him food to eat; and the old mother of the four brothers came and fell down on her knees before him in the wood, and thanked God that her sons were engaged in saving his life. At night, he came out of the forest and went on to another house which was near the river

Severn, with the intention of passing into Wales; but the place swarmed with soldiers, and the bridges were guarded, and all the boats were made fast. So, after lying in a hayloft covered over with hay, for some time, he came out of his place, attended by Colonel Careless, a Catholic gentleman who had met him there, and with whom he lay hid, all next day, up in the shady branches of a fine old oak. It was lucky for the King that it was September-time, and that the leaves had not begun to fall, since he and the Colonel, perched up in this tree, could catch glimpses of the soldiers riding about below, and could hear the crash in the wood as they went about beating the boughs.

After this, he walked and walked until his feet were all blistered; and, having been concealed all one day in a house which was searched by the troopers while he was there, went with Lord Wilmot, another of his good friends, to a place called Bentley, where one Miss Lane, a Protestant lady, had obtained a pass to be allowed to ride through the guards to see a relation of hers near Bristol. Disguised as a servant, he rode in the saddle before this young lady to the house of Sir John Winter, while Lord Wilmot rode there boldly, like a plain country gentleman, with dogs at his heels. It happened that Sir John Winter's butler had been servant in Richmond Palace, and knew Charles the moment he set eyes upon him; but, the butler was faithful and kept the secret. As no ship could be found to carry him abroad, it was planned that he should go—still travelling with Miss Lane as her servant—to another house, at Trent near Sherborne in Dorsetshire; and then Miss Lane and her cousin, Mr. Lascelles, who had gone on horseback beside her all the way, went home. I hope Miss Lane was going to marry that cousin, for I am sure she must have been a brave, kind girl. If I had been that cousin, I should certainly have loved Miss Lane.

When Charles, lonely for the loss of Miss Lane, was safe at Trent, a ship was hired at Lyme, the master of which engaged to take two gentlemen to France. In the evening of the same day, the King—now riding as servant before another young lady—set off for a public-house at a place called Charmouth, where the captain of the vessel was to take him on board. But, the captain's wife, being afraid of her husband getting into trouble, locked him up and would not let him sail. Then they went away to Bridport; and, coming to the inn there, found the stable-yard full of soldiers who were on the look-out for Charles, and who talked about him while they drank. He had such presence of mind, that he led the horses of his party through the yard as any other servant might have done, and said, 'Come out of the way, you soldiers; let us have room to pass here!' As he went along, he met a half-tipsy ostler, who rubbed his eyes and said to him, 'Why, I was formerly servant to Mr. Potter at Exeter, and surely I have sometimes seen you there, young man?' He certainly had, for Charles had lodged there. His ready answer was, 'Ah, I did live with him once; but I have no time to talk now. We'll have a pot of beer together when I come back.'

From this dangerous place he returned to Trent, and lay there concealed several days. Then he escaped to Heale, near Salisbury; where, in the house of a widow lady, he was hidden five days, until the master of a collier lying off Shoreham in Sussex, undertook to convey a 'gentleman' to France. On the night of the fifteenth of October, accompanied by two colonels and a merchant, the King rode to Brighton, then a little fishing village, to give the captain of the ship a supper before going on board; but, so many people knew him, that this captain knew him too, and not only he, but the landlord and landlady also. Before he went away, the landlord came behind his chair, kissed his hand, and said he hoped to live to be a lord and to see his wife a lady; at which Charles laughed. They had had a good supper by this time, and plenty of smoking and drinking, at which the King was a first-rate hand; so, the captain assured him that he would stand by him, and he did. It was agreed that the captain should pretend to sail to Deal, and that Charles should address the sailors and say he was a gentleman in debt who was running away from his creditors, and that he hoped they would join him in persuading the captain to put him ashore in France. As the King acted his part very well indeed, and gave the sailors twenty shillings to drink, they begged the captain to do what such a worthy gentleman asked. He pretended to yield to their entreaties, and the King got safe to Normandy.

Ireland being now subdued, and Scotland kept quiet by plenty of forts and soldiers put there by Oliver, the Parliament would have gone on quietly enough, as far as fighting with any foreign enemy went, but for getting into trouble with the Dutch, who in the spring of the year one thousand six hundred and fifty-one sent a fleet into the Downs under their Admiral Van Tromp, to call upon the bold English Admiral Blake (who was there with half as many ships as the Dutch) to strike his flag. Blake fired a raging broadside instead, and beat off Van Tromp; who, in the autumn, came back again with seventy ships, and challenged the bold Blake—who still was only half as strong—to fight him. Blake fought him all day; but, finding that the Dutch were too many for him, got quietly off at night. What does Van Tromp upon this, but goes cruising and boasting about the Channel, between the North Foreland and the Isle of Wight, with a great Dutch broom tied to his masthead, as a sign that he could and would sweep the English of the sea! Within three months, Blake lowered his tone though, and his broom too; for, he and two other bold commanders, Dean and Monk, fought him three whole days, took twenty-three of his ships, shivered his broom to pieces, and settled his business.

Things were no sooner quiet again, than the army began to complain to the Parliament that they were not governing the nation properly, and to hint that they thought they could do it better themselves. Oliver, who had now made up his mind to be the head of the state, or nothing at all, supported them in this, and called a meeting of officers and his own Parliamentary friends, at his lodgings in Whitehall, to consider the best way of getting rid of the Parliament. It had now lasted just as many years as the King's unbridled power had lasted, before it came into existence. The end of the deliberation was, that Oliver went down to the House in his usual plain black dress, with his usual grey worsted stockings, but with an unusual party of soldiers behind him. These last he left in the lobby, and then went in and sat down. Presently he got up, made the Parliament a speech, told them that the Lord had done with them, stamped his foot and said, 'You are no Parliament. Bring them in! Bring them in!' At this signal the door flew open, and the soldiers appeared. 'This is not honest,' said Sir Harry Vane, one of the members. 'Sir Harry Vane!' cried Cromwell; 'O, Sir Harry Vane! The Lord deliver me from Sir Harry Vane!' Then he pointed out members one by one, and said this man was a drunkard, and that man a dissipated fellow, and that man a liar, and so on. Then he caused the Speaker to be walked out of his chair, told the guard to clear the House, called the mace upon the table—which is a sign that the House is sitting—'a fool's bauble,' and said, 'here, carry it away!' Being obeyed in all these orders, he quietly locked the door, put the key in his pocket, walked back to Whitehall again, and told his friends, who were still assembled there, what he had done.

They formed a new Council of State after this extraordinary proceeding, and got a new Parliament together in their own way: which Oliver himself opened in a sort of sermon, and which he said was the beginning of a perfect heaven upon earth. In this Parliament there sat a well-known leather-seller, who had taken the singular name of Praise God Barebones, and from whom it was called, for a joke, Barebones's Parliament, though its general name was the Little Parliament. As it soon appeared that it was not going to put Oliver in the first place, it turned out to be not at all like the beginning of heaven upon earth, and Oliver said it really was not to be borne with. So he cleared off that Parliament in much the same way as he had disposed of the other; and then the council of officers decided that he must be made the supreme authority of the kingdom, under the title of the Lord Protector of the Commonwealth.

So, on the sixteenth of December, one thousand six hundred and fifty-three, a great procession was formed at Oliver's door, and he came out in a black velvet suit and a big pair of boots, and got into his coach and went down to Westminster, attended by the judges, and the lord mayor, and the aldermen, and all the other great and wonderful personages of the country. There, in the Court of Chancery, he publicly accepted the office of Lord Protector. Then he was sworn, and the City sword was handed to him, and the seal was handed to him, and all the other things were handed to him which are usually handed to Kings and Queens on state occasions. When Oliver had handed them all back, he was quite made and completely finished off as Lord Protector; and several of the Ironsides preached about it at great length, all the evening.

SECOND PART

Oliver Cromwell—whom the people long called Old Noll—in accepting the office of Protector, had bound himself by a certain paper which was handed to him, called 'the Instrument,' to summon a Parliament, consisting of between four and five hundred members, in the election of which neither the Royalists nor the Catholics were to have any share. He had also pledged himself that this Parliament should not be dissolved without its own consent until it had sat five months.

When this Parliament met, Oliver made a speech to them of three hours long, very wisely advising them what to do for the credit and happiness of the country. To keep down the more violent members, he required them to sign a recognition of what they were forbidden by 'the Instrument' to do; which was, chiefly, to take the power from one single person at the head of the state or to command the army. Then he dismissed them to go to work. With his usual vigour and resolution he went to work himself with some frantic preachers—who were rather overdoing their sermons in calling him a villain and a tyrant—by shutting up their chapels, and sending a few of them off to prison.

There was not at that time, in England or anywhere else, a man so able to govern the country as Oliver Cromwell. Although he ruled with a strong hand, and levied a very heavy tax on the Royalists (but not until they had plotted against his life), he ruled wisely, and as the times required. He caused England to be so respected abroad, that I wish some lords and gentlemen who have governed it under kings and queens in later days would have taken a leaf out of Oliver Cromwell's book. He sent bold Admiral Blake to the Mediterranean Sea, to make the Duke of Tuscany pay sixty thousand pounds for injuries he had done to British subjects, and spoliation he had committed on English merchants. He further despatched him and his fleet to Algiers, Tunis, and Tripoli, to have every English ship and every English man delivered up to him that had been taken by pirates in those parts. All this was gloriously done; and it began to be thoroughly well known, all over the world, that England was governed by a man in earnest, who would not allow the English name to be insulted or slighted anywhere.

These were not all his foreign triumphs. He sent a fleet to sea against the Dutch; and the two powers, each with one hundred ships upon its side, met in the English Channel off the North Foreland, where the fight lasted all day long. Dean was killed in this fight; but Monk, who commanded in the same ship with him, threw his cloak over his body, that the sailors might not know of his death, and be disheartened. Nor were they. The English broadsides so exceedingly astonished the Dutch that they sheered off at last, though the redoubtable Van Tromp fired upon them with his own guns for deserting their flag. Soon afterwards, the two fleets engaged again, off the coast of Holland. There, the valiant Van Tromp was shot through the heart, and the Dutch gave in, and peace was made.

Further than this, Oliver resolved not to bear the domineering and bigoted conduct of Spain, which country not only claimed a right to all the gold and silver that could be found in South America, and treated the ships of all other countries who visited those regions, as pirates, but put English subjects into the horrible Spanish prisons of the Inquisition. So, Oliver told the Spanish ambassador that English ships must be free to go wherever they would, and that English merchants must not be thrown into those same dungeons, no, not for the pleasure of all the priests in Spain. To this, the Spanish ambassador replied that the gold and silver country, and the Holy Inquisition, were his King's two eyes, neither of which he could submit to have put out. Very well, said Oliver, then he was afraid he (Oliver) must damage those two eyes directly.

So, another fleet was despatched under two commanders, Penn and Venables, for Hispaniola; where, however, the Spaniards got the better of the fight. Consequently, the fleet came home again, after taking Jamaica on the way. Oliver, indignant with the two commanders who had not done what bold Admiral Blake would have done, clapped them both into prison, declared war against Spain, and made a treaty with France, in virtue of which it was to shelter the King and his brother the Duke of York no longer. Then, he sent a fleet abroad under bold Admiral Blake, which brought the King of Portugal to his senses—just to keep its hand in—and then engaged a Spanish fleet, sunk four great ships, and took two more, laden with silver to the value of two millions of pounds: which dazzling prize was brought from Portsmouth to London in waggons, with the populace of all the towns and villages through which the waggons passed, shouting with all their might.

After this victory, bold Admiral Blake sailed away to the port of Santa Cruz to cut off the Spanish treasure-ships coming from Mexico. There, he found them, ten in number, with seven others to take care of them, and a big castle, and seven batteries, all roaring and blazing away at him with great guns. Blake cared no more for great guns than for pop-guns—no more for their hot iron balls than for snow-balls. He dashed into the harbour, captured and burnt every one of the ships, and came sailing out again triumphantly, with the victorious English flag flying at his masthead. This was the last triumph of this great commander, who had sailed and fought until he was quite worn out. He died, as his successful ship was coming into Plymouth Harbour amidst the joyful acclamations of the people, and was buried in state in Westminster Abbey. Not to lie there, long.

Over and above all this, Oliver found that the Vaudois, or Protestant people of the valleys of Lucerne, were insolently treated by the Catholic powers, and were even put to death for their religion, in an audacious and bloody manner. Instantly, he informed those powers that this was a thing which Protestant England would not allow; and he speedily carried his point, through the might of his great name, and established their right to worship God in peace after their own harmless manner.

Lastly, his English army won such admiration in fighting with the French against the Spaniards, that, after they had assaulted the town of Dunkirk together, the French King in person gave it up to the English, that it might be a token to them of their might and valour.

There were plots enough against Oliver among the frantic religionists (who called themselves Fifth Monarchy Men), and among the disappointed Republicans. He had a difficult game to play, for the Royalists were always ready to side with either party against him. The 'King over the water,' too, as Charles was called, had no scruples about plotting with any one against his life; although there is reason to suppose that he would willingly have married one of his daughters, if Oliver would have had such a son-in-law. There was a certain Colonel Saxby of the army, once a great supporter of Oliver's but now turned against him, who was a grievous trouble to him through all this part of his career; and who came and went between the discontented in England

and Spain, and Charles who put himself in alliance with Spain on being thrown off by France. This man died in prison at last; but not until there had been very serious plots between the Royalists and Republicans, and an actual rising of them in England, when they burst into the city of Salisbury, on a Sunday night, seized the judges who were going to hold the assizes there next day, and would have hanged them but for the merciful objections of the more temperate of their number. Oliver was so vigorous and shrewd that he soon put this revolt down, as he did most other conspiracies; and it was well for one of its chief managers—that same Lord Wilmot who had assisted in Charles's flight, and was now Earl of Rochester—that he made his escape. Oliver seemed to have eyes and ears everywhere, and secured such sources of information as his enemies little dreamed of. There was a chosen body of six persons, called the Sealed Knot, who were in the closest and most secret confidence of Charles. One of the foremost of these very men, a Sir Richard Willis, reported to Oliver everything that passed among them, and had two hundred a year for it.

Miles Syndarcomb, also of the old army, was another conspirator against the Protector. He and a man named Cecil, bribed one of his Life Guards to let them have good notice when he was going out—intending to shoot him from a window. But, owing either to his caution or his good fortune, they could never get an aim at him. Disappointed in this design, they got into the chapel in Whitehall, with a basketful of combustibles, which were to explode by means of a slow match in six hours; then, in the noise and confusion of the fire, they hoped to kill Oliver. But, the Life Guardsman himself disclosed this plot; and they were seized, and Miles died (or killed himself in prison) a little while before he was ordered for execution. A few such plotters Oliver caused to be beheaded, a few more to be hanged, and many more, including those who rose in arms against him, to be sent as slaves to the West Indies. If he were rigid, he was impartial too, in asserting the laws of England. When a Portuguese nobleman, the brother of the Portuguese ambassador, killed a London citizen in mistake for another man with whom he had had a quarrel, Oliver caused him to be tried before a jury of Englishmen and foreigners, and had him executed in spite of the entreaties of all the ambassadors in London.

One of Oliver's own friends, the Duke of Oldenburgh, in sending him a present of six fine coach-horses, was very near doing more to please the Royalists than all the plotters put together. One day, Oliver went with his coach, drawn by these six horses, into Hyde Park, to dine with his secretary and some of his other gentlemen under the trees there. After dinner, being merry, he took it into his head to put his friends inside and to drive them home: a postillion riding one of the foremost horses, as the custom was. On account of Oliver's being too free with the whip, the six fine horses went off at a gallop, the postillion got thrown, and Oliver fell upon the coach-pole and narrowly escaped being shot by his own pistol, which got entangled with his clothes in the harness, and went off. He was dragged some distance by the foot, until his foot came out of the shoe, and then he came safely to the ground under the broad body of the coach, and was very little the worse. The gentlemen inside were only bruised, and the discontented people of all parties were much disappointed.

The rest of the history of the Protectorate of Oliver Cromwell is a history of his Parliaments. His first one not pleasing him at all, he waited until the five months were out, and then dissolved it. The next was better suited to his views; and from that he desired to get—if he could with safety to himself—the title of King. He had had this in his mind some time: whether because he thought that the English people, being more used to the title, were more likely to obey it; or whether because he really wished to be a king himself, and to leave the succession to that title in his family, is far from clear. He was already as high, in England and in all the world, as he would ever be, and I doubt if he cared for the mere name. However, a paper, called the 'Humble Petition and Advice,' was presented to him by the House of Commons, praying him to take a high title and to appoint his successor. That he would have taken the title of King there is no doubt, but for the strong opposition of the army. This induced him to forbear, and to assent only to the other points of the petition. Upon which occasion there was another grand show in Westminster Hall, when the Speaker of the House of Commons formally invested him with a purple robe lined with ermine, and presented him with a splendidly bound Bible, and put a golden sceptre in his hand. The next time the Parliament met, he called a House of Lords of sixty members, as the petition gave him power to do; but as that Parliament did not please him either, and would not proceed to the business of the country, he jumped into a coach one morning, took six Guards with him, and sent them to the right-about. I wish this had been a warning to Parliaments to avoid long speeches, and do more work.

It was the month of August, one thousand six hundred and fifty-eight, when Oliver Cromwell's favourite daughter, Elizabeth Claypole (who had lately lost her youngest son), lay very ill, and his mind was greatly troubled, because he loved her dearly. Another of his daughters was married to Lord Falconberg, another to the grandson of the Earl of Warwick, and he had made his son Richard one of the Members of the Upper House. He was very kind and loving to them all, being a good father and a good husband; but he loved this daughter the best of the family, and went down to Hampton Court to see her, and could hardly be induced to stir from her sick room until she died. Although his religion had been of a gloomy kind, his disposition had been always cheerful. He had been fond of music in his home, and had kept open table once a week for all officers of the army not below the rank of captain, and had always preserved in his house a quiet, sensible dignity. He encouraged men of genius and learning, and loved to have them about him. Milton was one of his great friends. He was good humoured too, with the nobility, whose dresses and manners were very different from his; and to show them what good information he had, he would sometimes jokingly tell them when they were his guests, where they had last drunk the health of the 'King over the water,' and would recommend them to be more private (if they could) another time. But he had lived in busy times, had borne the weight of heavy State affairs, and had often gone in fear of his life. He was ill of the gout and ague; and when the death of his beloved child came upon him in addition, he sank, never to raise his head again. He told his physicians on the twenty-fourth of August that the Lord had assured him that he was not to die in that illness, and that he would certainly get better. This was only his sick fancy, for on the third of September, which was the anniversary of the great battle of Worcester, and the day of the year which he called his fortunate day, he died, in the sixtieth year of his age. He had been delirious, and had lain insensible some hours, but he had been overheard to murmur a very good prayer the day before. The whole country lamented his death. If you want to know the real worth of Oliver Cromwell, and his real services to his country, you can hardly do better than compare England under him, with England under Charles the Second.

He had appointed his son Richard to succeed him, and after there had been, at Somerset House in the Strand, a lying in state more splendid than sensible—as all such vanities after death are, I think—Richard became Lord Protector. He was an amiable country gentleman, but had none of his father's great genius, and was quite unfit for such a post in such a storm of parties. Richard's Protectorate, which only lasted a year and a half, is a history of quarrels between the officers of the army and the Parliament, and between the officers among themselves; and of a growing discontent among the people, who had far too many long sermons and far too few amusements, and wanted a change. At last, General Monk got the army well into his own hands, and then in pursuance of a secret plan he seems to have entertained from the time of Oliver's death, declared for the King's cause. He did not do this openly; but, in his place in the House of Commons, as one of the members for Devonshire, strongly advocated the proposals of one Sir John Greenville, who came to the House with a letter from Charles, dated from Breda, and with whom he had previously been in secret communication. There had been plots and counterplots, and a recall of the last members of the Long Parliament, and an end of the Long Parliament, and risings of the Royalists that were made too soon; and most men being tired out, and there being no one to head the country now great Oliver was dead, it was readily agreed to welcome Charles Stuart. Some of the wiser and better members said—what was most true—that in the letter from Breda, he gave no real promise to govern well, and that it would be best to make him pledge himself beforehand as to what he should be bound to do for the benefit of the kingdom. Monk said, however, it would be all right when he came, and he could not come too soon.

So, everybody found out all in a moment that the country must be prosperous and happy, having another Stuart to condescend to reign over it; and there was a prodigious firing off of guns, lighting of bonfires, ringing of bells, and throwing up of caps. The people drank the King's health by thousands in the open streets, and everybody rejoiced. Down came the Arms of the Commonwealth, up went the Royal Arms instead, and out came the public money. Fifty thousand pounds for the King, ten thousand pounds for his brother the Duke of York, five thousand pounds for his brother the Duke of Gloucester. Prayers for these gracious Stuarts were put up in all the churches; commissioners were sent to Holland (which suddenly found out that Charles was a great man, and that it loved him) to invite the King home; Monk and the Kentish grandees went to Dover, to kneel down before him as he landed. He kissed and embraced Monk, made him ride in the coach with himself and his brothers, came on to London amid wonderful shoutings, and passed through the army at Blackheath on the twenty-ninth of May (his birthday), in the year one thousand six hundred and sixty. Greeted by splendid dinners under tents, by flags and tapestry streaming from all the houses, by delighted crowds in all the streets, by troops of noblemen and gentlemen in rich dresses, by City companies, train-bands, drummers, trumpeters, the great Lord Mayor, and the majestic Aldermen, the King went on to Whitehall. On entering it, he commemorated his Restoration with the joke that it really would seem to have been his own fault that he had not come long ago, since everybody told him that he had always wished for him with all his heart.

CHAPTER XXXV—ENGLAND UNDER CHARLES THE SECOND, CALLED THE MERRY MONARCH

There never were such profligate times in England as under Charles the Second. Whenever you see his portrait, with his swarthy, ill-looking face and great nose, you may fancy him in his Court at Whitehall, surrounded by some of the very worst vagabonds in the kingdom (though they were lords and ladies), drinking, gambling, indulging in vicious conversation, and committing every kind of profligate excess. It has been a fashion to call Charles the Second 'The Merry Monarch.' Let me try to give you a general idea of some of the merry things that were done, in the merry days when this merry gentleman sat upon his merry throne, in merry England.

The first merry proceeding was—of course—to declare that he was one of the greatest, the wisest, and the noblest kings that ever shone, like the blessed sun itself, on this benighted earth. The next merry and pleasant piece of business was, for the Parliament, in the humblest manner, to give him one million two hundred thousand pounds a year, and to settle upon him for life that old disputed tonnage and poundage which had been so bravely fought for. Then, General Monk being made Earl of Albemarle, and a few other Royalists similarly rewarded, the law went to work to see what was to be done to those persons (they were called Regicides) who had been concerned in making a martyr of the late King. Ten of these were merrily executed; that is to say, six of the judges, one of the council, Colonel Hacker and another officer who had commanded the Guards, and Hugh Peters, a preacher who had preached against the martyr with all his heart. These executions were so extremely merry, that every horrible circumstance which Cromwell had abandoned was revived with appalling cruelty. The hearts of the sufferers were torn out of their living bodies; their bowels were burned before their faces; the executioner cut jokes to the next victim, as he rubbed his filthy hands together, that were reeking with the blood of the last; and the heads of the dead were drawn on sledges with the living to the place of suffering. Still, even so merry a monarch could not force one of these dying men to say that he was sorry for what he had done. Nay, the most memorable thing said among them was, that if the thing were to do again they would do it.

Sir Harry Vane, who had furnished the evidence against Strafford, and was one of the most staunch of the Republicans, was also tried, found guilty, and ordered for execution. When he came upon the scaffold on Tower Hill, after conducting his own defence with great power, his notes of what he had meant to say to the people were torn away from him, and the drums and trumpets were ordered to sound lustily and drown his voice; for, the people had been so much impressed by what the Regicides had calmly said with their last breath, that it was the custom now, to have the drums and trumpets always under the scaffold, ready to strike up. Vane said no more than this: 'It is a bad cause which cannot bear the words of a dying man:' and bravely died.

These merry scenes were succeeded by another, perhaps even merrier. On the anniversary of the late King's death, the bodies of Oliver Cromwell, Ireton, and Bradshaw, were torn out of their graves in Westminster Abbey, dragged to Tyburn, hanged there on a gallows all day long, and then beheaded. Imagine the head of Oliver Cromwell set upon a pole to be stared at by a brutal crowd, not one of whom would have dared to look the living Oliver in the face for half a moment! Think, after you have read this reign, what England was under Oliver Cromwell who was torn out of his grave, and what it was under this merry monarch who sold it, like a merry Judas, over and over again.

Of course, the remains of Oliver's wife and daughter were not to be spared either, though they had been most excellent women. The base clergy of that time gave up their bodies, which had been buried in the Abbey, and—to the eternal disgrace of England—they were thrown into a pit, together with the mouldering bones of Pym and of the brave and bold old Admiral Blake.

The clergy acted this disgraceful part because they hoped to get the nonconformists, or dissenters, thoroughly put down in this reign, and to have but one prayer-book and one service for all kinds of people, no matter what their private opinions were. This was pretty well, I think, for a Protestant

Church, which had displaced the Romish Church because people had a right to their own opinions in religious matters. However, they carried it with a high hand, and a prayer-book was agreed upon, in which the extremest opinions of Archbishop Laud were not forgotten. An Act was passed, too, preventing any dissenter from holding any office under any corporation. So, the regular clergy in their triumph were soon as merry as the King. The army being by this time disbanded, and the King crowned, everything was to go on easily for evermore.

I must say a word here about the King's family. He had not been long upon the throne when his brother the Duke of Gloucester, and his sister the Princess of Orange, died within a few months of each other, of small-pox. His remaining sister, the Princess Henrietta, married the Duke of Orleans, the brother of Louis the Fourteenth, King of France. His brother James, Duke of York, was made High Admiral, and by-and-by became a Catholic. He was a gloomy, sullen, bilious sort of man, with a remarkable partiality for the ugliest women in the country. He married, under very discreditable circumstances, Anne Hyde, the daughter of Lord Clarendon, then the King's principal Minister—not at all a delicate minister either, but doing much of the dirty work of a very dirty palace. It became important now that the King himself should be married; and divers foreign Monarchs, not very particular about the character of their son-in-law, proposed their daughters to him. The King of Portugal offered his daughter, Catherine of Braganza, and fifty thousand pounds: in addition to which, the French King, who was favourable to that match, offered a loan of another fifty thousand. The King of Spain, on the other hand, offered any one out of a dozen of Princesses, and other hopes of gain. But the ready money carried the day, and Catherine came over in state to her merry marriage.

The whole Court was a great flaunting crowd of debauched men and shameless women; and Catherine's merry husband insulted and outraged her in every possible way, until she consented to receive those worthless creatures as her very good friends, and to degrade herself by their companionship. A Mrs. Palmer, whom the King made Lady Castlemaine, and afterwards Duchess of Cleveland, was one of the most powerful of the bad women about the Court, and had great influence with the King nearly all through his reign. Another merry lady named Moll Davies, a dancer at the theatre, was afterwards her rival. So was Nell Gwyn, first an orange girl and then an actress, who really had good in her, and of whom one of the worst things I know is, that actually she does seem to have been fond of the King. The first Duke of St. Albans was this orange girl's child. In like manner the son of a merry waiting-lady, whom the King created Duchess Of Portsmouth, became the Duke of Richmond. Upon the whole it is not so bad a thing to be a commoner.

The Merry Monarch was so exceedingly merry among these merry ladies, and some equally merry (and equally infamous) lords and gentlemen, that he soon got through his hundred thousand pounds, and then, by way of raising a little pocket-money, made a merry bargain. He sold Dunkirk to the French King for five millions of livres. When I think of the dignity to which Oliver Cromwell raised England in the eyes of foreign powers, and when I think of the manner in which he gained for England this very Dunkirk, I am much inclined to consider that if the Merry Monarch had been made to follow his father for this action, he would have received his just deserts.

Though he was like his father in none of that father's greater qualities, he was like him in being worthy of no trust. When he sent that letter to the Parliament, from Breda, he did expressly promise that all sincere religious opinions should be respected. Yet he was no sooner firm in his power than he consented to one of the worst Acts of Parliament ever passed. Under this law, every minister who should not give his solemn assent to the Prayer-Book by a certain day, was declared to be a minister no longer, and to be deprived of his church. The consequence of this was that some two thousand honest men were taken from their congregations, and reduced to dire poverty and distress. It was followed by another outrageous law, called the Conventicle Act, by which any person above the age of sixteen who was present at any religious service not according to the Prayer-Book, was to be imprisoned three months for the first offence, six for the second, and to be transported for the third. This Act alone filled the prisons, which were then most dreadful dungeons, to overflowing.

The Covenanters in Scotland had already fared no better. A base Parliament, usually known as the Drunken Parliament, in consequence of its principal members being seldom sober, had been got together to make laws against the Covenanters, and to force all men to be of one mind in religious matters. The Marquis of Argyle, relying on the King's honour, had given himself up to him; but, he was wealthy, and his enemies wanted his wealth. He was tried for treason, on the evidence of some private letters in which he had expressed opinions—as well he might—more favourable to the government of the late Lord Protector than of the present merry and religious King. He was executed, as were two men of mark among the Covenanters; and Sharp, a traitor who had once been the friend of the Presbyterians and betrayed them, was made Archbishop of St. Andrew's, to teach the Scotch how to like bishops.

Things being in this merry state at home, the Merry Monarch undertook a war with the Dutch; principally because they interfered with an African company, established with the two objects of buying gold-dust and slaves, of which the Duke of York was a leading member. After some preliminary hostilities, the said Duke sailed to the coast of Holland with a fleet of ninety-eight vessels of war, and four fire-ships. This engaged with the Dutch fleet, of no fewer than one hundred and thirteen ships. In the great battle between the two forces, the Dutch lost eighteen ships, four admirals, and seven thousand men. But, the English on shore were in no mood of exultation when they heard the news.

For, this was the year and the time of the Great Plague in London. During the winter of one thousand six hundred and sixty-four it had been whispered about, that some few people had died here and there of the disease called the Plague, in some of the unwholesome suburbs around London. News was not published at that time as it is now, and some people believed these rumours, and some disbelieved them, and they were soon forgotten. But, in the month of May, one thousand six hundred and sixty-five, it began to be said all over the town that the disease had burst out with great violence in St. Giles's, and that the people were dying in great numbers. This soon turned out to be awfully true. The roads out of London were choked up by people endeavouring to escape from the infected city, and large sums were paid for any kind of conveyance. The disease soon spread so fast, that it was necessary to shut up the houses in which sick people were, and to cut them off from communication with the living. Every one of these houses was marked on the outside of the door with a red cross, and the words, Lord, have mercy upon us! The streets were all deserted, grass grew in the public ways, and there was a dreadful silence in the air. When night came on, dismal rumblings used to be heard, and these were the wheels of the death-carts, attended by men with veiled faces and holding cloths to their mouths, who rang doleful bells and cried in a loud and solemn voice, 'Bring out your dead!' The corpses put into these carts were buried by torchlight in great pits; no service being performed over them; all men being afraid to stay for a moment on the brink of the ghastly graves. In the general fear, children ran away from their parents, and parents from their children. Some who were taken ill, died alone, and without any help. Some were stabbed or strangled by hired nurses who robbed them of all their money, and stole the very beds on which they lay. Some went mad, dropped from the windows, ran through the streets, and in their pain and frenzy flung themselves into the river.

These were not all the horrors of the time. The wicked and dissolute, in wild desperation, sat in the taverns singing roaring songs, and were stricken as they drank, and went out and died. The fearful and superstitious persuaded themselves that they saw supernatural sights—burning swords in the sky, gigantic arms and darts. Others pretended that at nights vast crowds of ghosts walked round and round the dismal pits. One madman, naked, and carrying a brazier full of burning coals upon his head, stalked through the streets, crying out that he was a Prophet, commissioned to denounce the vengeance of the Lord on wicked London. Another always went to and fro, exclaiming, 'Yet forty days, and London shall be destroyed!' A third awoke the echoes in the dismal streets, by night and by day, and made the blood of the sick run cold, by calling out incessantly, in a deep hoarse voice, 'O, the great and dreadful God!'

Through the months of July and August and September, the Great Plague raged more and more. Great fires were lighted in the streets, in the hope of stopping the infection; but there was a plague of rain too, and it beat the fires out. At last, the winds which usually arise at that time of the year which is called the equinox, when day and night are of equal length all over the world, began to blow, and to purify the wretched town. The deaths began to decrease, the red crosses slowly to disappear, the fugitives to return, the shops to open, pale frightened faces to be seen in the streets. The Plague had been in every part of England, but in close and unwholesome London it had killed one hundred thousand people.

All this time, the Merry Monarch was as merry as ever, and as worthless as ever. All this time, the debauched lords and gentlemen and the shameless ladies danced and gamed and drank, and loved and hated one another, according to their merry ways.

So little humanity did the government learn from the late affliction, that one of the first things the Parliament did when it met at Oxford (being as yet afraid to come to London), was to make a law, called the Five Mile Act, expressly directed against those poor ministers who, in the time of the Plague, had manfully come back to comfort the unhappy people. This infamous law, by forbidding them to teach in any school, or to come within five miles of any city, town, or village, doomed them to starvation and death.

The fleet had been at sea, and healthy. The King of France was now in alliance with the Dutch, though his navy was chiefly employed in looking on while the English and Dutch fought. The Dutch gained one victory; and the English gained another and a greater; and Prince Rupert, one of the English admirals, was out in the Channel one windy night, looking for the French Admiral, with the intention of giving him something more to do than he had had yet, when the gale increased to a storm, and blew him into Saint Helen's. That night was the third of September, one thousand six hundred and sixty-six, and that wind fanned the Great Fire of London.

It broke out at a baker's shop near London Bridge, on the spot on which the Monument now stands as a remembrance of those raging flames. It spread and spread, and burned and burned, for three days. The nights were lighter than the days; in the daytime there was an immense cloud of smoke, and in the night-time there was a great tower of fire mounting up into the sky, which lighted the whole country landscape for ten miles round. Showers of hot ashes rose into the air and fell on distant places; flying sparks carried the conflagration to great distances, and kindled it in twenty new spots at a time; church steeples fell down with tremendous crashes; houses crumbled into cinders by the hundred and the thousand. The summer had been intensely hot and dry, the streets were very narrow, and the houses mostly built of wood and plaster. Nothing could stop the tremendous fire, but the want of more houses to burn; nor did it stop until the whole way from the Tower to Temple Bar was a desert, composed of the ashes of thirteen thousand houses and eighty-nine churches.

This was a terrible visitation at the time, and occasioned great loss and suffering to the two hundred thousand burnt-out people, who were obliged to lie in the fields under the open night sky, or in hastily-made huts of mud and straw, while the lanes and roads were rendered impassable by carts which had broken down as they tried to save their goods. But the Fire was a great blessing to the City afterwards, for it arose from its ruins very much improved—built more regularly, more widely, more cleanly and carefully, and therefore much more healthily. It might be far more healthy than it is, but there are some people in it still—even now, at this time, nearly two hundred years later—so selfish, so pig-headed, and so ignorant, that I doubt if even another Great Fire would warm them up to do their duty.

The Catholics were accused of having wilfully set London in flames; one poor Frenchman, who had been mad for years, even accused himself of having with his own hand fired the first house. There is no reasonable doubt, however, that the fire was accidental. An inscription on the Monument long attributed it to the Catholics; but it is removed now, and was always a malicious and stupid untruth.

SECOND PART

That the Merry Monarch might be very merry indeed, in the merry times when his people were suffering under pestilence and fire, he drank and gambled and flung away among his favourites the money which the Parliament had voted for the war. The consequence of this was that the stout-hearted

English sailors were merrily starving of want, and dying in the streets; while the Dutch, under their admirals De Witt and De Ruyter, came into the River Thames, and up the River Medway as far as Upnor, burned the guard-ships, silenced the weak batteries, and did what they would to the English coast for six whole weeks. Most of the English ships that could have prevented them had neither powder nor shot on board; in this merry reign, public officers made themselves as merry as the King did with the public money; and when it was entrusted to them to spend in national defences or preparations, they put it into their own pockets with the merriest grace in the world.

Lord Clarendon had, by this time, run as long a course as is usually allotted to the unscrupulous ministers of bad kings. He was impeached by his political opponents, but unsuccessfully. The King then commanded him to withdraw from England and retire to France, which he did, after defending himself in writing. He was no great loss at home, and died abroad some seven years afterwards.

There then came into power a ministry called the Cabal Ministry, because it was composed of Lord Clifford, the Earl of Arlington, the Duke of Buckingham (a great rascal, and the King's most powerful favourite), Lord Ashley, and the Duke of Lauderdale, c. a. b. a. l. As the French were making conquests in Flanders, the first Cabal proceeding was to make a treaty with the Dutch, for uniting with Spain to oppose the French. It was no sooner made than the Merry Monarch, who always wanted to get money without being accountable to a Parliament for his expenditure, apologised to the King of France for having had anything to do with it, and concluded a secret treaty with him, making himself his infamous pensioner to the amount of two millions of livres down, and three millions more a year; and engaging to desert that very Spain, to make war against those very Dutch, and to declare himself a Catholic when a convenient time should arrive. This religious king had lately been crying to his Catholic brother on the subject of his strong desire to be a Catholic; and now he merrily concluded this treasonable conspiracy against the country he governed, by undertaking to become one as soon as he safely could. For all of which, though he had had ten merry heads instead of one, he richly deserved to lose them by the headsman's axe.

As his one merry head might have been far from safe, if these things had been known, they were kept very quiet, and war was declared by France and England against the Dutch. But, a very uncommon man, afterwards most important to English history and to the religion and liberty of this land, arose among them, and for many long years defeated the whole projects of France. This was William of Nassau, Prince of Orange, son of the last Prince of Orange of the same name, who married the daughter of Charles the First of England. He was a young man at this time, only just of age; but he was brave, cool, intrepid, and wise. His father had been so detested that, upon his death, the Dutch had abolished the authority to which this son would have otherwise succeeded (Stadtholder it was called), and placed the chief power in the hands of John de Witt, who educated this young prince. Now, the Prince became very popular, and John de Witt's brother Cornelius was sentenced to banishment on a false accusation of conspiring to kill him. John went to the prison where he was, to take him away to exile, in his coach; and a great mob who collected on the occasion, then and there cruelly murdered both the brothers. This left the government in the hands of the Prince, who was really the choice of the nation; and from this time he exercised it with the greatest vigour, against the whole power of France, under its famous generals Condé and Turenne, and in support of the Protestant religion. It was full seven years before this war ended in a treaty of peace made at Nimeguen, and its details would occupy a very considerable space. It is enough to say that William of Orange established a famous character with the whole world; and that the Merry Monarch, adding to and improving on his former baseness, bound himself to do everything the King of France liked, and nothing the King of France did not like, for a pension of one hundred thousand pounds a year, which was afterwards doubled. Besides this, the King of France, by means of his corrupt ambassador—who wrote accounts of his proceedings in England, which are not always to be believed, I think—bought our English members of Parliament, as he wanted them. So, in point of fact, during a considerable portion of this merry reign, the King of France was the real King of this country.

But there was a better time to come, and it was to come (though his royal uncle little thought so) through that very William, Prince of Orange.

He came over to England, saw Mary, the elder daughter of the Duke of York, and married her. We shall see by-and-by what came of that marriage, and why it is never to be forgotten.

This daughter was a Protestant, but her mother died a Catholic. She and her sister Anne, also a Protestant, were the only survivors of eight children. Anne afterwards married George, Prince of Denmark, brother to the King of that country.

Lest you should do the Merry Monarch the injustice of supposing that he was even good humoured (except when he had everything his own way), or that he was high spirited and honourable, I will mention here what was done to a member of the House of Commons, Sir John Coventry. He made a remark in a debate about taxing the theatres, which gave the King offence. The King agreed with his illegitimate son, who had been born abroad, and whom he had made Duke of Monmouth, to take the following merry vengeance. To waylay him at night, fifteen armed men to one, and to slit his nose with a penknife. Like master, like man. The King's favourite, the Duke of Buckingham, was strongly suspected of setting on an assassin to murder the Duke of Ormond as he was returning home from a dinner; and that Duke's spirited son, Lord Ossory, was so persuaded of his guilt, that he said to him at Court, even as he stood beside the King, 'My lord, I know very well that you are at the bottom of this late attempt upon my father. But I give you warning, if he ever come to a violent end, his blood shall be upon you, and wherever I meet you I will pistol you! I will do so, though I find you standing behind the King's chair; and I tell you this in his Majesty's presence, that you may be quite sure of my doing what I threaten.' Those were merry times indeed.

There was a fellow named Blood, who was seized for making, with two companions, an audacious attempt to steal the crown, the globe, and sceptre, from the place where the jewels were kept in the Tower. This robber, who was a swaggering ruffian, being taken, declared that he was the man who had endeavoured to kill the Duke of Ormond, and that he had meant to kill the King too, but was overawed by the majesty of his appearance, when he might otherwise have done it, as he was bathing at Battersea. The King being but an ill-looking fellow, I don't believe a word of this. Whether he was flattered, or whether he knew that Buckingham had really set Blood on to murder the Duke, is uncertain. But it is quite certain that he pardoned this thief, gave him an estate of five hundred a year in Ireland (which had had the honour of giving him birth), and presented him at Court to the debauched lords and the shameless ladies, who made a great deal of him—as I have no doubt they would have made of the Devil himself, if the King had introduced him.

Infamously pensioned as he was, the King still wanted money, and consequently was obliged to call Parliaments. In these, the great object of the Protestants was to thwart the Catholic Duke of York, who married a second time; his new wife being a young lady only fifteen years old, the Catholic sister of the Duke of Modena. In this they were seconded by the Protestant Dissenters, though to their own disadvantage: since, to exclude Catholics from power, they were even willing to exclude themselves. The King's object was to pretend to be a Protestant, while he was really a Catholic; to swear to the bishops that he was devoutly attached to the English Church, while he knew he had bargained it away to the King of France; and by cheating and deceiving them, and all who were attached to royalty, to become despotic and be powerful enough to confess what a rascal he was. Meantime, the King of France, knowing his merry pensioner well, intrigued with the King's opponents in Parliament, as well as with the King and his friends.

The fears that the country had of the Catholic religion being restored, if the Duke of York should come to the throne, and the low cunning of the King in pretending to share their alarms, led to some very terrible results. A certain Dr. Tonge, a dull clergyman in the City, fell into the hands of a certain Titus Oates, a most infamous character, who pretended to have acquired among the Jesuits abroad a knowledge of a great plot for the murder of the King, and the re-establishment if the Catholic religion. Titus Oates, being produced by this unlucky Dr. Tonge and solemnly examined before the council, contradicted himself in a thousand ways, told the most ridiculous and improbable stories, and implicated Coleman, the Secretary of the Duchess of York. Now, although what he charged against Coleman was not true, and although you and I know very well that the real dangerous Catholic plot was that one with the King of France of which the Merry Monarch was himself the head, there happened to be found among Coleman's papers, some letters, in which he did praise the days of Bloody Queen Mary, and abuse the Protestant religion. This was great good fortune for Titus, as it seemed to confirm him; but better still was in store. Sir Edmundbury Godfrey, the magistrate who had first examined him, being unexpectedly found dead near Primrose Hill, was confidently believed to have been killed by the Catholics. I think there is no doubt that he had been melancholy mad, and that he killed himself; but he had a great Protestant funeral, and Titus was called the Saver of the Nation, and received a pension of twelve hundred pounds a year.

As soon as Oates's wickedness had met with this success, up started another villain, named William Bedloe, who, attracted by a reward of five hundred pounds offered for the apprehension of the murderers of Godfrey, came forward and charged two Jesuits and some other persons with having committed it at the Queen's desire. Oates, going into partnership with this new informer, had the audacity to accuse the poor Queen herself of high treason. Then appeared a third informer, as bad as either of the two, and accused a Catholic banker named Stayley of having said that the King was the greatest rogue in the world (which would not have been far from the truth), and that he would kill him with his own hand. This banker, being at once tried and executed, Coleman and two others were tried and executed. Then, a miserable wretch named Prance, a Catholic silversmith, being accused by Bedloe, was tortured into confessing that he had taken part in Godfrey's murder, and into accusing three other men of having committed it. Then, five Jesuits were accused by Oates, Bedloe, and Prance together, and were all found guilty, and executed on the same kind of contradictory and absurd evidence. The Queen's physician and three monks were next put on their trial; but Oates and Bedloe had for the time gone far enough and these four were acquitted. The public mind, however, was so full of a Catholic plot, and so strong against the Duke of York, that James consented to obey a written order from his brother, and to go with his family to Brussels, provided that his rights should never be sacrificed in his absence to the Duke of Monmouth. The House of Commons, not satisfied with this as the King hoped, passed a bill to exclude the Duke from ever succeeding to the throne. In return, the

King dissolved the Parliament. He had deserted his old favourite, the Duke of Buckingham, who was now in the opposition.

To give any sufficient idea of the miseries of Scotland in this merry reign, would occupy a hundred pages. Because the people would not have bishops, and were resolved to stand by their solemn League and Covenant, such cruelties were inflicted upon them as make the blood run cold. Ferocious dragoons galloped through the country to punish the peasants for deserting the churches; sons were hanged up at their fathers' doors for refusing to disclose where their fathers were concealed; wives were tortured to death for not betraying their husbands; people were taken out of their fields and gardens, and shot on the public roads without trial; lighted matches were tied to the fingers of prisoners, and a most horrible torment called the Boot was invented, and constantly applied, which ground and mashed the victims' legs with iron wedges. Witnesses were tortured as well as prisoners. All the prisons were full; all the gibbets were heavy with bodies; murder and plunder devastated the whole country. In spite of all, the Covenanters were by no means to be dragged into the churches, and persisted in worshipping God as they thought right. A body of ferocious Highlanders, turned upon them from the mountains of their own country, had no greater effect than the English dragoons under Grahame of Claverhouse, the most cruel and rapacious of all their enemies, whose name will ever be cursed through the length and breadth of Scotland. Archbishop Sharp had ever aided and abetted all these outrages. But he fell at last; for, when the injuries of the Scottish people were at their height, he was seen, in his coach-and-six coming across a moor, by a body of men, headed by one John Balfour, who were waiting for another of their oppressors. Upon this they cried out that Heaven had delivered him into their hands, and killed him with many wounds. If ever a man deserved such a death, I think Archbishop Sharp did.

It made a great noise directly, and the Merry Monarch—strongly suspected of having goaded the Scottish people on, that he might have an excuse for a greater army than the Parliament were willing to give him—sent down his son, the Duke of Monmouth, as commander-in-chief, with instructions to attack the Scottish rebels, or Whigs as they were called, whenever he came up with them. Marching with ten thousand men from Edinburgh, he found them, in number four or five thousand, drawn up at Bothwell Bridge, by the Clyde. They were soon dispersed; and Monmouth showed a more humane character towards them, than he had shown towards that Member of Parliament whose nose he had caused to be slit with a penknife. But the Duke of Lauderdale was their bitter foe, and sent Claverhouse to finish them.

As the Duke of York became more and more unpopular, the Duke of Monmouth became more and more popular. It would have been decent in the latter not to have voted in favour of the renewed bill for the exclusion of James from the throne; but he did so, much to the King's amusement, who used to sit in the House of Lords by the fire, hearing the debates, which he said were as good as a play. The House of Commons passed the bill by a large majority, and it was carried up to the House of Lords by Lord Russell, one of the best of the leaders on the Protestant side. It was rejected there, chiefly because the bishops helped the King to get rid of it; and the fear of Catholic plots revived again. There had been another got up, by a fellow out of Newgate, named Dangerfield, which is more famous than it deserves to be, under the name of the Meal-Tub Plot. This jail-bird having been got out of Newgate by a Mrs. Cellier, a Catholic nurse, had turned Catholic himself, and pretended that he knew of a plot among the Presbyterians against the King's life. This was very pleasant to the Duke of York, who hated the Presbyterians, who returned the compliment. He gave Dangerfield twenty guineas, and sent him to the King his brother. But Dangerfield, breaking down altogether in his charge, and being sent back to Newgate, almost astonished the Duke out of his five senses by suddenly swearing that the Catholic nurse had put that false design into his head, and that what he really knew about, was, a Catholic plot against the King; the evidence of which would be found in some papers, concealed in a meal-tub in Mrs. Cellier's house. There they were, of course—for he had put them there himself—and so the tub gave the name to the plot. But, the nurse was acquitted on her trial, and it came to nothing.

Lord Ashley, of the Cabal, was now Lord Shaftesbury, and was strong against the succession of the Duke of York. The House of Commons, aggravated to the utmost extent, as we may well suppose, by suspicions of the King's conspiracy with the King of France, made a desperate point of the exclusion, still, and were bitter against the Catholics generally. So unjustly bitter were they, I grieve to say, that they impeached the venerable Lord Stafford, a Catholic nobleman seventy years old, of a design to kill the King. The witnesses were that atrocious Oates and two other birds of the same feather. He was found guilty, on evidence quite as foolish as it was false, and was beheaded on Tower Hill. The people were opposed to him when he first appeared upon the scaffold; but, when he had addressed them and shown them how innocent he was and how wickedly he was sent there, their better nature was aroused, and they said, 'We believe you, my Lord. God bless you, my Lord!'

The House of Commons refused to let the King have any money until he should consent to the Exclusion Bill; but, as he could get it and did get it from his master the King of France, he could afford to hold them very cheap. He called a Parliament at Oxford, to which he went down with a great show of being armed and protected as if he were in danger of his life, and to which the opposition members also went armed and protected, alleging that they were in fear of the Papists, who were numerous among the King's guards. However, they went on with the Exclusion Bill, and were so earnest upon it that they would have carried it again, if the King had not popped his crown and state robes into a sedan-chair, bundled himself into it along with them, hurried down to the chamber where the House of Lords met, and dissolved the Parliament. After which he scampered home, and the members of Parliament scampered home too, as fast as their legs could carry them.

The Duke of York, then residing in Scotland, had, under the law which excluded Catholics from public trust, no right whatever to public employment. Nevertheless, he was openly employed as the King's representative in Scotland, and there gratified his sullen and cruel nature to his heart's content by directing the dreadful cruelties against the Covenanters. There were two ministers named Cargill and Cameron who had escaped from the battle of Bothwell Bridge, and who returned to Scotland, and raised the miserable but still brave and unsubdued Covenanters afresh, under the name of Cameronians. As Cameron publicly posted a declaration that the King was a forsworn tyrant, no mercy was shown to his unhappy followers after he was slain in battle. The Duke of York, who was particularly fond of the Boot and derived great pleasure from having it applied, offered their lives to some of these people, if they would cry on the scaffold 'God save the King!' But their relations, friends, and countrymen, had been so barbarously tortured and murdered in this merry reign, that they preferred to die, and did die. The Duke then obtained his merry brother's permission to hold a Parliament in Scotland, which first, with most shameless deceit, confirmed the laws for securing the Protestant religion against Popery, and then declared that nothing must or should prevent the succession of the Popish Duke. After this double-faced beginning, it established an oath which no human being could understand, but which everybody was to take, as a proof that his religion was the lawful religion. The Earl of Argyle, taking it with the explanation that he did not consider it to prevent him from favouring any alteration either in the Church or State which was not inconsistent with the Protestant religion or with his loyalty, was tried for high treason before a Scottish jury of which the Marquis of Montrose was foreman, and was found guilty. He escaped the scaffold, for that time, by getting away, in the disguise of a page, in the train of his daughter, Lady Sophia Lindsay. It was absolutely proposed, by certain members of the Scottish Council, that this lady should be whipped through the streets of Edinburgh. But this was too much even for the Duke, who had the manliness then (he had very little at most times) to remark that Englishmen were not accustomed to treat ladies in that manner. In those merry times nothing could equal the brutal servility of the Scottish fawners, but the conduct of similar degraded beings in England.

After the settlement of these little affairs, the Duke returned to England, and soon resumed his place at the Council, and his office of High Admiral— all this by his brother's favour, and in open defiance of the law. It would have been no loss to the country, if he had been drowned when his ship, in going to Scotland to fetch his family, struck on a sand-bank, and was lost with two hundred souls on board. But he escaped in a boat with some friends; and the sailors were so brave and unselfish, that, when they saw him rowing away, they gave three cheers, while they themselves were going down for ever.

The Merry Monarch, having got rid of his Parliament, went to work

to make himself despotic, with all speed. Having had the villainy to order
the execution of Oliver Plunket, Bishop of Armagh, falsely accused of a plot
to establish Popery in that country by means of a French army—the very
thing this royal traitor was himself trying to do at home—and having tried
to ruin Lord Shaftesbury, and failed—he turned his hand to controlling the
corporations all over the country; because, if he could only do that, he could
get what juries he chose, to bring in perjured verdicts, and could get what
members he chose returned to Parliament. These merry times produced,
and made Chief Justice of the Court of King's Bench, a drunken ruffian of
the name of Jeffreys; a red-faced, swollen, bloated, horrible creature, with
a bullying, roaring voice, and a more savage nature perhaps than was ever
lodged in any human breast. This monster was the Merry Monarch's especial
favourite, and he testified his admiration of him by giving him a ring from
his own finger, which the people used to call Judge Jeffreys's Bloodstone.
Him the King employed to go about and bully the corporations, beginning
with London; or, as Jeffreys himself elegantly called it, 'to give them a lick
with the rough side of his tongue.' And he did it so thoroughly, that they
soon became the basest and most sycophantic bodies in the kingdom—except
the University of Oxford, which, in that respect, was quite pre-eminent and
unapproachable.

Lord Shaftesbury (who died soon after the King's failure against him),
Lord William Russell, the Duke of Monmouth, Lord Howard, Lord Jersey,
Algernon Sidney, John Hampden (grandson of the great Hampden), and some
others, used to hold a council together after the dissolution of the Parliament,
arranging what it might be necessary to do, if the King carried his Popish plot
to the utmost height. Lord Shaftesbury having been much the most violent
of this party, brought two violent men into their secrets—Rumsey, who had
been a soldier in the Republican army; and West, a lawyer. These two knew
an old officer of Cromwell's, called Rumbold, who had married a maltster's
widow, and so had come into possession of a solitary dwelling called the Rye
House, near Hoddesdon, in Hertfordshire. Rumbold said to them what a
capital place this house of his would be from which to shoot at the King,
who often passed there going to and fro from Newmarket. They liked the
idea, and entertained it. But, one of their body gave information; and they,

together with Shepherd a wine merchant, Lord Russell, Algernon Sidney, Lord Essex, Lord Howard, and Hampden, were all arrested.

Lord Russell might have easily escaped, but scorned to do so, being innocent of any wrong; Lord Essex might have easily escaped, but scorned to do so, lest his flight should prejudice Lord Russell. But it weighed upon his mind that he had brought into their council, Lord Howard—who now turned a miserable traitor—against a great dislike Lord Russell had always had of him. He could not bear the reflection, and destroyed himself before Lord Russell was brought to trial at the Old Bailey.

He knew very well that he had nothing to hope, having always been manful in the Protestant cause against the two false brothers, the one on the throne, and the other standing next to it. He had a wife, one of the noblest and best of women, who acted as his secretary on his trial, who comforted him in his prison, who supped with him on the night before he died, and whose love and virtue and devotion have made her name imperishable. Of course, he was found guilty, and was sentenced to be beheaded in Lincoln's Inn-fields, not many yards from his own house. When he had parted from his children on the evening before his death, his wife still stayed with him until ten o'clock at night; and when their final separation in this world was over, and he had kissed her many times, he still sat for a long while in his prison, talking of her goodness. Hearing the rain fall fast at that time, he calmly said, 'Such a rain to-morrow will spoil a great show, which is a dull thing on a rainy day.' At midnight he went to bed, and slept till four; even when his servant called him, he fell asleep again while his clothes were being made ready. He rode to the scaffold in his own carriage, attended by two famous clergymen, Tillotson and Burnet, and sang a psalm to himself very softly, as he went along. He was as quiet and as steady as if he had been going out for an ordinary ride. After saying that he was surprised to see so great a crowd, he laid down his head upon the block, as if upon the pillow of his bed, and had it struck off at the second blow. His noble wife was busy for him even then; for that true-hearted lady printed and widely circulated his last words, of which he had given her a copy. They made the blood of all the honest men in England boil.

The University of Oxford distinguished itself on the very same day by pretending to believe that the accusation against Lord Russell was true, and by calling the King, in a written paper, the Breath of their Nostrils and the Anointed of the Lord. This paper the Parliament afterwards caused to be burned by the common hangman; which I am sorry for, as I wish it had been framed and glazed and hung up in some public place, as a monument of baseness for the scorn of mankind.

Next, came the trial of Algernon Sidney, at which Jeffreys presided, like a great crimson toad, sweltering and swelling with rage. 'I pray God, Mr. Sidney,' said this Chief Justice of a merry reign, after passing sentence, 'to work in you a temper fit to go to the other world, for I see you are not fit for this.' 'My lord,' said the prisoner, composedly holding out his arm, 'feel my pulse, and see if I be disordered. I thank Heaven I never was in better temper than I am now.' Algernon Sidney was executed on Tower Hill, on the seventh of December, one thousand six hundred and eighty-three. He died a hero, and died, in his own words, 'For that good old cause in which he had been engaged from his youth, and for which God had so often and so wonderfully declared himself.'

The Duke of Monmouth had been making his uncle, the Duke of York, very jealous, by going about the country in a royal sort of way, playing at the people's games, becoming godfather to their children, and even touching for the King's evil, or stroking the faces of the sick to cure them—though, for the matter of that, I should say he did them about as much good as any crowned king could have done. His father had got him to write a letter, confessing his having had a part in the conspiracy, for which Lord Russell had been beheaded; but he was ever a weak man, and as soon as he had written it, he was ashamed of it and got it back again. For this, he was banished to the Netherlands; but he soon returned and had an interview with his father, unknown to his uncle. It would seem that he was coming into the Merry Monarch's favour again, and that the Duke of York was sliding out of it, when Death appeared to the merry galleries at Whitehall, and astonished the debauched lords and gentlemen, and the shameless ladies, very considerably.

On Monday, the second of February, one thousand six hundred and eighty-five, the merry pensioner and servant of the King of France fell down in a fit of apoplexy. By the Wednesday his case was hopeless, and on the Thursday he was told so. As he made a difficulty about taking the sacrament from the Protestant Bishop of Bath, the Duke of York got all who were present away from the bed, and asked his brother, in a whisper, if he should send for a Catholic priest? The King replied, 'For God's sake, brother, do!' The Duke smuggled in, up the back stairs, disguised in a wig and gown, a priest named Huddleston, who had saved the King's life after the battle of Worcester: telling him that this worthy man in the wig had once saved his body, and was now come to save his soul.

The Merry Monarch lived through that night, and died before noon on the next day, which was Friday, the sixth. Two of the last things he said were of a human sort, and your remembrance will give him the full benefit of them. When the Queen sent to say she was too unwell to attend him and to ask his pardon, he said, 'Alas! poor woman, she beg my pardon! I beg hers with all my heart. Take back that answer to her.' And he also said, in reference to Nell Gwyn, 'Do not let poor Nelly starve.'

He died in the fifty-fifth year of his age, and the twenty-fifth of his reign.

CHAPTER XXXVI—ENGLAND UNDER JAMES THE SECOND

King James the Second was a man so very disagreeable, that even the best of historians has favoured his brother Charles, as becoming, by comparison, quite a pleasant character. The one object of his short reign was to re-establish the Catholic religion in England; and this he doggedly pursued with such a stupid obstinacy, that his career very soon came to a close.

The first thing he did, was, to assure his council that he would make it his endeavour to preserve the Government, both in Church and State, as it was by law established; and that he would always take care to defend and support the Church. Great public acclamations were raised over this fair speech, and a great deal was said, from the pulpits and elsewhere, about the word of a King which was never broken, by credulous people who little supposed that he had formed a secret council for Catholic affairs, of which a mischievous Jesuit, called Father Petre, was one of the chief members. With tears of joy in his eyes, he received, as the beginning of his pension from the King of France, five hundred thousand livres; yet, with a mixture of meanness and arrogance that belonged to his contemptible character, he was always jealous of making some show of being independent of the King of France, while he pocketed his money. As—notwithstanding his publishing two papers in favour of Popery (and not likely to do it much service, I should think) written by the King, his brother, and found in his strong-box; and his open display of himself attending mass—the Parliament was very obsequious, and granted him a large sum of money, he began his reign with a belief that he could do what he pleased, and with a determination to do it.

Before we proceed to its principal events, let us dispose of Titus Oates. He was tried for perjury, a fortnight after the coronation, and besides being very heavily fined, was sentenced to stand twice in the pillory, to be whipped from Aldgate to Newgate one day, and from Newgate to Tyburn two days afterwards, and to stand in the pillory five times a year as long as he lived. This fearful sentence was actually inflicted on the rascal. Being unable to stand after his first flogging, he was dragged on a sledge from Newgate to Tyburn, and flogged as he was drawn along. He was so strong a villain that he did not die under the torture, but lived to be afterwards pardoned and rewarded, though not to be ever believed in any more. Dangerfield, the only other one of that crew left alive, was not so fortunate. He was almost killed by a whipping from Newgate to Tyburn, and, as if that were not punishment enough, a ferocious barrister of Gray's Inn gave him a poke in the eye with his cane, which caused his death; for which the ferocious barrister was deservedly tried and executed.

As soon as James was on the throne, Argyle and Monmouth went from Brussels to Rotterdam, and attended a meeting of Scottish exiles held there, to concert measures for a rising in England. It was agreed that Argyle should effect a landing in Scotland, and Monmouth in England; and that two Englishmen should be sent with Argyle to be in his confidence, and two Scotchmen with the Duke of Monmouth.

Argyle was the first to act upon this contract. But, two of his men being taken prisoners at the Orkney Islands, the Government became aware of his intention, and was able to act against him with such vigour as to prevent his raising more than two or three thousand Highlanders, although he sent a fiery cross, by trusty messengers, from clan to clan and from glen to glen, as the custom then was when those wild people were to be excited by their chiefs. As he was moving towards Glasgow with his small force, he was betrayed by some of his followers, taken, and carried, with his hands tied behind his back, to his old prison in Edinburgh Castle. James ordered him to be executed, on his old shamefully unjust sentence, within three days; and he appears to have been anxious that his legs should have been pounded with his old favourite the boot. However, the boot was not applied; he was simply beheaded, and his head was set upon the top of Edinburgh Jail. One of those Englishmen who had been assigned to him was that old soldier Rumbold, the master of the Rye House. He was sorely wounded, and within a week after Argyle had suffered with great courage, was brought up for trial, lest he should die and disappoint the King. He, too, was executed, after defending himself with great spirit, and saying that he did not believe that God had made the greater part of mankind to carry saddles on their backs and bridles in their mouths, and to be ridden by a few, booted and spurred for the purpose—in which I thoroughly agree with Rumbold.

The Duke of Monmouth, partly through being detained and partly through idling his time away, was five or six weeks behind his friend when he landed at Lyme, in Dorset: having at his right hand an unlucky nobleman called Lord Grey of Werk, who of himself would have ruined a far more promising expedition. He immediately set up his standard in the market-place, and proclaimed the King a tyrant, and a Popish usurper, and I know not what else; charging him, not only with what he had done, which was bad enough, but with what neither he nor anybody else had done, such as setting fire to London, and poisoning the late King. Raising some four thousand men by these means, he marched on to Taunton, where there were many Protestant dissenters who were strongly opposed to the Catholics. Here, both the rich and poor turned out to receive him, ladies waved a welcome to him from all the windows as he passed along the streets, flowers were strewn in his way, and every compliment and honour that could be devised was showered upon him. Among the rest, twenty young ladies came forward, in their best clothes, and in their brightest beauty, and gave him a Bible ornamented with their own fair hands, together with other presents.

Encouraged by this homage, he proclaimed himself King, and went on to Bridgewater. But, here the Government troops, under the Earl of Feversham, were close at hand; and he was so dispirited at finding that he made but few powerful friends after all, that it was a question whether he should disband his army and endeavour to escape. It was resolved, at the instance of that unlucky Lord Grey, to make a night attack on the King's army, as it lay encamped on the edge of a morass called Sedgemoor. The horsemen were commanded by the same unlucky lord, who was not a brave man. He gave up the battle almost at the first obstacle—which was a deep drain; and although the poor countrymen, who had turned out for Monmouth, fought bravely with scythes, poles, pitchforks, and such poor weapons as they had, they were soon dispersed by the trained soldiers, and fled in all directions. When the Duke of Monmouth himself fled, was not known in the confusion;

but the unlucky Lord Grey was taken early next day, and then another of the party was taken, who confessed that he had parted from the Duke only four hours before. Strict search being made, he was found disguised as a peasant, hidden in a ditch under fern and nettles, with a few peas in his pocket which he had gathered in the fields to eat. The only other articles he had upon him were a few papers and little books: one of the latter being a strange jumble, in his own writing, of charms, songs, recipes, and prayers. He was completely broken. He wrote a miserable letter to the King, beseeching and entreating to be allowed to see him. When he was taken to London, and conveyed bound into the King's presence, he crawled to him on his knees, and made a most degrading exhibition. As James never forgave or relented towards anybody, he was not likely to soften towards the issuer of the Lyme proclamation, so he told the suppliant to prepare for death.

On the fifteenth of July, one thousand six hundred and eighty-five, this unfortunate favourite of the people was brought out to die on Tower Hill. The crowd was immense, and the tops of all the houses were covered with gazers. He had seen his wife, the daughter of the Duke of Buccleuch, in the Tower, and had talked much of a lady whom he loved far better—the Lady Harriet Wentworth—who was one of the last persons he remembered in this life. Before laying down his head upon the block he felt the edge of the axe, and told the executioner that he feared it was not sharp enough, and that the axe was not heavy enough. On the executioner replying that it was of the proper kind, the Duke said, 'I pray you have a care, and do not use me so awkwardly as you used my Lord Russell.' The executioner, made nervous by this, and trembling, struck once and merely gashed him in the neck. Upon this, the Duke of Monmouth raised his head and looked the man reproachfully in the face. Then he struck twice, and then thrice, and then threw down the axe, and cried out in a voice of horror that he could not finish that work. The sheriffs, however, threatening him with what should be done to himself if he did not, he took it up again and struck a fourth time and a fifth time. Then the wretched head at last fell off, and James, Duke of Monmouth, was dead, in the thirty-sixth year of his age. He was a showy, graceful man, with many popular qualities, and had found much favour in the open hearts of the English.

The atrocities, committed by the Government, which followed this Monmouth rebellion, form the blackest and most lamentable page in English history. The poor peasants, having been dispersed with great loss, and their leaders having been taken, one would think that the implacable King might have been satisfied. But no; he let loose upon them, among other intolerable monsters, a Colonel Kirk, who had served against the Moors, and whose soldiers—called by the people Kirk's lambs, because they bore a lamb upon their flag, as the emblem of Christianity—were worthy of their leader. The atrocities committed by these demons in human shape are far too horrible to be related here. It is enough to say, that besides most ruthlessly murdering and robbing them, and ruining them by making them buy their pardons at the price of all they possessed, it was one of Kirk's favourite amusements, as he and his officers sat drinking after dinner, and toasting the King, to have batches of prisoners hanged outside the windows for the company's diversion; and that when their feet quivered in the convulsions of death, he used to swear that they should have music to their dancing, and would order the drums to beat and the trumpets to play. The detestable King informed him, as an acknowledgment of these services, that he was 'very well satisfied with his proceedings.' But the King's great delight was in the proceedings of Jeffreys, now a peer, who went down into the west, with four other judges, to try persons accused of having had any share in the rebellion. The King pleasantly called this 'Jeffreys's campaign.' The people down in that part of the country remember it to this day as The Bloody Assize.

It began at Winchester, where a poor deaf old lady, Mrs. Alicia Lisle, the widow of one of the judges of Charles the First (who had been murdered abroad by some Royalist assassins), was charged with having given shelter in her house to two fugitives from Sedgemoor. Three times the jury refused to find her guilty, until Jeffreys bullied and frightened them into that false verdict. When he had extorted it from them, he said, 'Gentlemen, if I had been one of you, and she had been my own mother, I would have found her guilty;'—as I dare say he would. He sentenced her to be burned alive, that very afternoon. The clergy of the cathedral and some others interfered in her favour, and she was beheaded within a week. As a high mark of his approbation, the King made Jeffreys Lord Chancellor; and he then went on to Dorchester, to Exeter, to Taunton, and to Wells. It is astonishing, when we read of the enormous injustice and barbarity of this beast, to know that no one struck him dead on the judgment-seat. It was enough for any man or woman to be accused by an enemy, before Jeffreys, to be found guilty of high treason. One man who pleaded not guilty, he ordered to be taken out of court upon the instant, and hanged; and this so terrified the prisoners in general that they mostly pleaded guilty at once. At Dorchester alone, in the course of a few days, Jeffreys hanged eighty people; besides whipping, transporting, imprisoning, and selling as slaves, great numbers. He executed, in all, two hundred and fifty, or three hundred.

These executions took place, among the neighbours and friends of the sentenced, in thirty-six towns and villages. Their bodies were mangled, steeped in caldrons of boiling pitch and tar, and hung up by the roadsides, in the streets, over the very churches. The sight and smell of heads and limbs, the hissing and bubbling of the infernal caldrons, and the tears and terrors of the people, were dreadful beyond all description. One rustic, who was forced to steep the remains in the black pot, was ever afterwards called 'Tom Boilman.' The hangman has ever since been called Jack Ketch, because a man of that name went hanging and hanging, all day long, in the train of Jeffreys. You will hear much of the horrors of the great French Revolution. Many and terrible they were, there is no doubt; but I know of nothing worse, done by the maddened people of France in that awful time, than was done by the highest judge in England, with the express approval of the King of England, in The Bloody Assize.

Nor was even this all. Jeffreys was as fond of money for himself as of misery for others, and he sold pardons wholesale to fill his pockets. The King ordered, at one time, a thousand prisoners to be given to certain of his favourites, in order that they might bargain with them for their pardons. The young ladies of Taunton who had presented the Bible, were bestowed upon the maids of honour at court; and those precious ladies made very hard bargains with them indeed. When The Bloody Assize was at its most dismal height, the King was diverting himself with horse-races in the very place where Mrs. Lisle had been executed. When Jeffreys had done his worst, and came home again, he was particularly complimented in the Royal Gazette; and when the King heard that through drunkenness and raging he was very ill, his odious Majesty remarked that such another man could not easily be found in England. Besides all this, a former sheriff of London, named Cornish, was hanged within sight of his own house, after an abominably conducted trial, for having had a share in the Rye House Plot, on evidence given by Rumsey, which that villain was obliged to confess was directly opposed to the evidence he had given on the trial of Lord Russell. And on the very same day, a worthy widow, named Elizabeth Gaunt, was burned alive at Tyburn, for having sheltered a wretch who himself gave evidence against her. She settled the fuel about herself with her own hands, so that the flames should reach her quickly: and nobly said, with her last breath, that she had obeyed the sacred command of God, to give refuge to the outcast, and not to betray the wanderer.

After all this hanging, beheading, burning, boiling, mutilating, exposing, robbing, transporting, and selling into slavery, of his unhappy subjects, the King not unnaturally thought that he could do whatever he would. So, he went to work to change the religion of the country with all possible speed; and what he did was this.

He first of all tried to get rid of what was called the Test Act—which prevented the Catholics from holding public employments—by his own power of dispensing with the penalties. He tried it in one case, and, eleven of the twelve judges deciding in his favour, he exercised it in three others, being those of three dignitaries of University College, Oxford, who had become Papists, and whom he kept in their places and sanctioned. He revived the hated Ecclesiastical Commission, to get rid of Compton, Bishop of London, who manfully opposed him. He solicited the Pope to favour England with an ambassador, which the Pope (who was a sensible man then) rather unwillingly did. He flourished Father Petre before the eyes of the people on all possible occasions. He favoured the establishment of convents in several parts of London. He was delighted to have the streets, and even the court itself, filled with Monks and Friars in the habits of their orders. He constantly endeavoured to make Catholics of the Protestants about him. He held private interviews, which he called 'closetings,' with those Members of

Parliament who held offices, to persuade them to consent to the design he had in view. When they did not consent, they were removed, or resigned of themselves, and their places were given to Catholics. He displaced Protestant officers from the army, by every means in his power, and got Catholics into their places too. He tried the same thing with the corporations, and also (though not so successfully) with the Lord Lieutenants of counties. To terrify the people into the endurance of all these measures, he kept an army of fifteen thousand men encamped on Hounslow Heath, where mass was openly performed in the General's tent, and where priests went among the soldiers endeavouring to persuade them to become Catholics. For circulating a paper among those men advising them to be true to their religion, a Protestant clergyman, named Johnson, the chaplain of the late Lord Russell, was actually sentenced to stand three times in the pillory, and was actually whipped from Newgate to Tyburn. He dismissed his own brother-in-law from his Council because he was a Protestant, and made a Privy Councillor of the before-mentioned Father Petre. He handed Ireland over to Richard Talbot, Earl of Tyrconnell, a worthless, dissolute knave, who played the same game there for his master, and who played the deeper game for himself of one day putting it under the protection of the French King. In going to these extremities, every man of sense and judgment among the Catholics, from the Pope to a porter, knew that the King was a mere bigoted fool, who would undo himself and the cause he sought to advance; but he was deaf to all reason, and, happily for England ever afterwards, went tumbling off his throne in his own blind way.

A spirit began to arise in the country, which the besotted blunderer little expected. He first found it out in the University of Cambridge. Having made a Catholic a dean at Oxford without any opposition, he tried to make a monk a master of arts at Cambridge: which attempt the University resisted, and defeated him. He then went back to his favourite Oxford. On the death of the President of Magdalen College, he commanded that there should be elected to succeed him, one Mr. Anthony Farmer, whose only recommendation was, that he was of the King's religion. The University plucked up courage at last, and refused. The King substituted another man, and it still refused, resolving to stand by its own election of a Mr. Hough. The dull tyrant, upon this, punished Mr. Hough, and five-and-twenty more, by causing them to be expelled and declared incapable of holding any church preferment; then he proceeded to what he supposed to be his highest step, but to what was, in fact, his last plunge head-foremost in his tumble off his throne.

He had issued a declaration that there should be no religious tests or penal laws, in order to let in the Catholics more easily; but the Protestant dissenters, unmindful of themselves, had gallantly joined the regular church in opposing it tooth and nail. The King and Father Petre now resolved to have this read, on a certain Sunday, in all the churches, and to order it to be circulated for that purpose by the bishops. The latter took counsel with the Archbishop of Canterbury, who was in disgrace; and they resolved that the declaration should not be read, and that they would petition the King against it. The Archbishop himself wrote out the petition, and six bishops went into the King's bedchamber the same night to present it, to his infinite astonishment. Next day was the Sunday fixed for the reading, and it was only read by two hundred clergymen out of ten thousand. The King resolved against all advice to prosecute the bishops in the Court of King's Bench, and within three weeks they were summoned before the Privy Council, and committed to the Tower. As the six bishops were taken to that dismal place, by water, the people who were assembled in immense numbers fell upon their knees, and wept for them, and prayed for them. When they got to the Tower, the officers and soldiers on guard besought them for their blessing. While they were confined there, the soldiers every day drank to their release with loud shouts. When they were brought up to the Court of King's Bench for their trial, which the Attorney-General said was for the high offence of censuring the Government, and giving their opinion about affairs of state, they were attended by similar multitudes, and surrounded by a throng of noblemen and gentlemen. When the jury went out at seven o'clock at night to consider of their verdict, everybody (except the King) knew that they would rather starve than yield to the King's brewer, who was one of them, and wanted a verdict for his customer. When they came into court next morning, after resisting the brewer all night, and gave a verdict of not guilty, such a shout rose up in Westminster Hall as it had never heard before; and it was passed on among the people away to Temple Bar, and away again to the Tower. It did not pass only to the east, but passed to the west too, until it reached the camp at Hounslow, where the fifteen thousand soldiers took it up and echoed it. And still, when the dull King, who was then with Lord Feversham, heard the mighty roar, asked in alarm what it was, and was told that it was 'nothing but the acquittal of the bishops,' he said, in his dogged way, 'Call you that nothing? It is so much the worse for them.'

Between the petition and the trial, the Queen had given birth to a son, which Father Petre rather thought was owing to Saint Winifred. But I doubt if Saint Winifred had much to do with it as the King's friend, inasmuch as the entirely new prospect of a Catholic successor (for both the King's daughters were Protestants) determined the Earls of Shrewsbury, Danby, and Devonshire, Lord Lumley, the Bishop of London, Admiral Russell, and Colonel Sidney, to invite the Prince of Orange over to England. The Royal Mole, seeing his danger at last, made, in his fright, many great concessions, besides raising an army of forty thousand men; but the Prince of Orange was not a man for James the Second to cope with. His preparations were extraordinarily vigorous, and his mind was resolved.

For a fortnight after the Prince was ready to sail for England, a great wind from the west prevented the departure of his fleet. Even when the wind lulled, and it did sail, it was dispersed by a storm, and was obliged to put back to refit. At last, on the first of November, one thousand six hundred and eighty-eight, the Protestant east wind, as it was long called, began to blow; and on the third, the people of Dover and the people of Calais saw a fleet twenty miles long sailing gallantly by, between the two places. On Monday, the fifth, it anchored at Torbay in Devonshire, and the Prince, with a splendid retinue of officers and men, marched into Exeter. But the people in that western part of the country had suffered so much in The Bloody Assize, that they had lost heart. Few people joined him; and he began to think of returning, and publishing the invitation he had received from those lords, as his justification for having come at all. At this crisis, some of the gentry joined him; the Royal army began to falter; an engagement was signed, by which all who set their hand to it declared that they would support one another in defence of the laws and liberties of the three Kingdoms, of the Protestant religion, and of the Prince of Orange. From that time, the cause received no check; the greatest towns in England began, one after another, to declare for the Prince; and he knew that it was all safe with him when the University of Oxford offered to melt down its plate, if he wanted any money.

By this time the King was running about in a pitiable way, touching people for the King's evil in one place, reviewing his troops in another, and bleeding from the nose in a third. The young Prince was sent to Portsmouth, Father Petre went off like a shot to France, and there was a general and swift dispersal of all the priests and friars. One after another, the King's most important officers and friends deserted him and went over to the Prince. In the night, his daughter Anne fled from Whitehall Palace; and the Bishop of London, who had once been a soldier, rode before her with a drawn sword in his hand, and pistols at his saddle. 'God help me,' cried the miserable King: 'my very children have forsaken me!' In his wildness, after debating with such lords as were in London, whether he should or should not call a Parliament, and after naming three of them to negotiate with the Prince, he resolved to fly to France. He had the little Prince of Wales brought back from Portsmouth; and the child and the Queen crossed the river to Lambeth in an open boat, on a miserable wet night, and got safely away. This was on the night of the ninth of December.

At one o'clock on the morning of the eleventh, the King, who had, in the meantime, received a letter from the Prince of Orange, stating his objects, got out of bed, told Lord Northumberland who lay in his room not to open the door until the usual hour in the morning, and went down the back stairs (the same, I suppose, by which the priest in the wig and gown had come up to his brother) and crossed the river in a small boat: sinking the great seal of England by the way. Horses having been provided, he rode, accompanied by Sir Edward Hales, to Feversham, where he embarked in a Custom House Hoy. The master of this Hoy, wanting more ballast, ran into the Isle of Sheppy to get it, where the fishermen and smugglers crowded about the boat, and informed the King of their suspicions that he was a 'hatchet-faced Jesuit.' As they took his money and would not let him go, he told them who he was, and that the Prince of Orange wanted to take his life; and he began to scream for a boat—and then to cry, because he had lost a piece of wood on his ride which he called a fragment of Our Saviour's cross. He put himself into the hands of the Lord Lieutenant of the county, and his detention was made known to the Prince of Orange at Windsor—who, only wanting to get rid of him, and not caring where he went, so that he went away, was very much disconcerted that they did not let him go. However, there was nothing for it but to have him brought back, with some state in the way of Life Guards, to Whitehall. And as soon as he got there, in his infatuation, he heard mass, and set a Jesuit to say grace at his public dinner.

The people had been thrown into the strangest state of confusion by his flight, and had taken it into their heads that the Irish part of the army were going to murder the Protestants. Therefore, they set the bells a ringing, and lighted watch-fires, and burned Catholic Chapels, and looked about in all directions for Father Petre and the Jesuits, while the Pope's ambassador was running away in the dress of a footman. They found no Jesuits; but a man, who had once been a frightened witness before Jeffreys in court, saw a swollen, drunken face looking through a window down at Wapping, which he well remembered. The face was in a sailor's dress, but he knew it to be the face of that accursed judge, and he seized him. The people, to their lasting honour, did not tear him to pieces. After knocking him about a little, they took him, in the basest agonies of terror, to the Lord Mayor, who sent him, at his own shrieking petition, to the Tower for safety. There, he died.

Their bewilderment continuing, the people now lighted bonfires and made rejoicings, as if they had any reason to be glad to have the King back again. But, his stay was very short, for the English guards were removed from Whitehall, Dutch guards were marched up to it, and he was told by one of his late ministers that the Prince would enter London, next day, and he had better go to Ham. He said, Ham was a cold, damp place, and he would rather go to Rochester. He thought himself very cunning in this, as he meant to escape from Rochester to France. The Prince of Orange and his friends knew that, perfectly well, and desired nothing more. So, he went to Gravesend, in his royal barge, attended by certain lords, and watched by Dutch troops, and pitied by the generous people, who were far more forgiving than he had ever been, when they saw him in his humiliation. On the night of the twenty-third of December, not even then understanding that everybody wanted to get rid of him, he went out, absurdly, through his Rochester garden, down to the Medway, and got away to France, where he rejoined the Queen.

There had been a council in his absence, of the lords, and the authorities of London. When the Prince came, on the day after the King's departure, he summoned the Lords to meet him, and soon afterwards, all those who had served in any of the Parliaments of King Charles the Second. It was finally resolved by these authorities that the throne was vacant by the conduct of King James the Second; that it was inconsistent with the safety and welfare of this Protestant kingdom, to be governed by a Popish prince; that the Prince and Princess of Orange should be King and Queen during their lives and the life of the survivor of them; and that their children should succeed them, if they had any. That if they had none, the Princess Anne and her children should succeed; that if she had none, the heirs of the Prince of Orange should succeed.

On the thirteenth of January, one thousand six hundred and eighty-nine, the Prince and Princess, sitting on a throne in Whitehall, bound themselves to these conditions. The Protestant religion was established in England, and England's great and glorious Revolution was complete.

CHAPTER XXXVII

I have now arrived at the close of my little history. The events which succeeded the famous Revolution of one thousand six hundred and eighty-eight, would neither be easily related nor easily understood in such a book as this.

William and Mary reigned together, five years. After the death of his good wife, William occupied the throne, alone, for seven years longer. During his reign, on the sixteenth of September, one thousand seven hundred and one, the poor weak creature who had once been James the Second of England, died in France. In the meantime he had done his utmost (which was not much) to cause William to be assassinated, and to regain his lost dominions. James's son was declared, by the French King, the rightful King of England; and was called in France The Chevalier Saint George, and in England The Pretender. Some infatuated people in England, and particularly in Scotland, took up the Pretender's cause from time to time—as if the country had not had Stuarts enough!—and many lives were sacrificed, and much misery was occasioned. King William died on Sunday, the seventh of March, one thousand seven hundred and two, of the consequences of an accident occasioned by his horse stumbling with him. He was always a brave, patriotic Prince, and a man of remarkable abilities. His manner was cold, and he made but few friends; but he had truly loved his queen. When he was dead, a lock of her hair, in a ring, was found tied with a black ribbon round his left arm.

He was succeeded by the Princess Anne, a popular Queen, who reigned twelve years. In her reign, in the month of May, one thousand seven hundred and seven, the Union between England and Scotland was effected, and the two countries were incorporated under the name of Great Britain. Then, from the year one thousand seven hundred and fourteen to the year one thousand, eight hundred and thirty, reigned the four Georges.

It was in the reign of George the Second, one thousand seven hundred and forty-five, that the Pretender did his last mischief, and made his last appearance. Being an old man by that time, he and the Jacobites—as his friends were called—put forward his son, Charles Edward, known as the young Chevalier. The Highlanders of Scotland, an extremely troublesome and wrong-headed race on the subject of the Stuarts, espoused his cause, and he joined them, and there was a Scottish rebellion to make him king, in which many gallant and devoted gentlemen lost their lives. It was a hard matter for Charles Edward to escape abroad again, with a high price on his head; but the Scottish people were extraordinarily faithful to him, and, after undergoing many romantic adventures, not unlike those of Charles the Second, he escaped to France. A number of charming stories and delightful songs arose out of the Jacobite feelings, and belong to the Jacobite times. Otherwise I think the Stuarts were a public nuisance altogether.

It was in the reign of George the Third that England lost North America, by persisting in taxing her without her own consent. That immense country, made independent under Washington, and left to itself, became the United States; one of the greatest nations of the earth. In these times in which I write, it is honourably remarkable for protecting its subjects, wherever they may travel, with a dignity and a determination which is a model for England. Between you and me, England has rather lost ground in this respect since the days of Oliver Cromwell.

The Union of Great Britain with Ireland—which had been getting on very ill by itself—took place in the reign of George the Third, on the second of July, one thousand seven hundred and ninety-eight.

William the Fourth succeeded George the Fourth, in the year one thousand eight hundred and thirty, and reigned seven years. Queen Victoria, his niece, the only child of the Duke of Kent, the fourth son of George the Third, came to the throne on the twentieth of June, one thousand eight hundred and thirty-seven. She was married to Prince Albert of Saxe Gotha on the tenth of February, one thousand eight hundred and forty. She is very good, and much beloved. So I end, like the crier, with

God Save the Queen!

REPRINTED PIECES

THE LONG VOYAGE

When the wind is blowing and the sleet or rain is driving against the dark windows, I love to sit by the fire, thinking of what I have read in books of voyage and travel. Such books have had a strong fascination for my mind from my earliest childhood; and I wonder it should have come to pass that I never have been round the world, never have been shipwrecked, ice-environed, tomahawked, or eaten.

Sitting on my ruddy hearth in the twilight of New Year's Eve, I find incidents of travel rise around me from all the latitudes and longitudes of the globe. They observe no order or sequence, but appear and vanish as they will—'come like shadows, so depart.' Columbus, alone upon the sea with his disaffected crew, looks over the waste of waters from his high station on the poop of his ship, and sees the first uncertain glimmer of the light, 'rising and falling with the waves, like a torch in the bark of some fisherman,' which is the shining star of a new world. Bruce is caged in Abyssinia, surrounded by the gory horrors which shall often startle him out of his sleep at home when years have passed away. Franklin, come to the end of his unhappy overland journey—would that it had been his last!—lies perishing of hunger with his brave companions: each emaciated figure stretched upon its miserable bed without the power to rise: all, dividing the weary days between their prayers, their remembrances of the dear ones at home, and conversation on the pleasures of eating; the last-named topic being ever present to them, likewise, in their dreams. All the African travellers, wayworn, solitary and sad, submit themselves again to drunken, murderous, man-selling despots, of the lowest order of humanity; and Mungo Park, fainting under a tree and succoured by a woman, gratefully remembers how his Good Samaritan has always come to him in woman's shape, the wide world over.

A shadow on the wall in which my mind's eye can discern some traces of a rocky sea-coast, recalls to me a fearful story of travel derived from that unpromising narrator of such stories, a parliamentary blue-book. A convict is its chief figure, and this man escapes with other prisoners from a penal settlement. It is an island, and they seize a boat, and get to the main land. Their way is by a rugged and precipitous sea-shore, and they have no earthly hope of ultimate escape, for the party of soldiers despatched by an easier course to cut them off, must inevitably arrive at their distant bourne long before them, and retake them if by any hazard they survive the horrors of the way. Famine, as they all must have foreseen, besets them early in their course. Some of the party die and are eaten; some are murdered by the rest and eaten. This one awful creature eats his fill, and sustains his strength, and lives on to be recaptured and taken back. The unrelateable experiences through which he has passed have been so tremendous, that he is not hanged as he might be, but goes back to his old chained-gang work. A little time, and he tempts one other prisoner away, seizes another boat, and flies once more—necessarily in the old hopeless direction, for he can take no other. He is soon cut off, and met by the pursuing party face to face, upon the beach. He is alone. In his former journey he acquired an inappeasable relish for his dreadful food. He urged the new man away, expressly to kill him and eat him. In the pockets on one side of his coarse convict-dress, are portions of the man's body, on which he is regaling; in the pockets on the other side is an untouched store of salted pork (stolen before he left the island) for which he has no appetite. He is taken back, and he is hanged. But I shall never see that sea-beach on the wall or in the fire, without him, solitary monster, eating as he prowls along, while the sea rages and rises at him.

Captain Bligh (a worse man to be entrusted with arbitrary power there could scarcely be) is handed over the side of the Bounty, and turned adrift on the wide ocean in an open boat, by order of Fletcher Christian, one of his officers, at this very minute. Another flash of my fire, and 'Thursday October Christian,' five-and-twenty years of age, son of the dead and gone Fletcher by a savage mother, leaps aboard His Majesty's ship Briton, hove-to off Pitcairn's Island; says his simple grace before eating, in good English; and knows that a pretty little animal on board is called a dog, because in his childhood he

414

had heard of such strange creatures from his father and the other mutineers, grown grey under the shade of the bread-fruit trees, speaking of their lost country far away.

See the Halsewell, East Indiaman outward bound, driving madly on a January night towards the rocks near Seacombe, on the island of Purbeck! The captain's two dear daughters are aboard, and five other ladies. The ship has been driving many hours, has seven feet water in her hold, and her mainmast has been cut away. The description of her loss, familiar to me from my early boyhood, seems to be read aloud as she rushes to her destiny.

'About two in the morning of Friday the sixth of January, the ship still driving, and approaching very fast to the shore, Mr. Henry Meriton, the second mate, went again into the cuddy, where the captain then was. Another conversation taking place, Captain Pierce expressed extreme anxiety for the preservation of his beloved daughters, and earnestly asked the officer if he could devise any method of saving them. On his answering with great concern, that he feared it would be impossible, but that their only chance would be to wait for morning, the captain lifted up his hands in silent and distressful ejaculation.

'At this dreadful moment, the ship struck, with such violence as to dash the heads of those standing in the cuddy against the deck above them, and the shock was accompanied by a shriek of horror that burst at one instant from every quarter of the ship.

'Many of the seamen, who had been remarkably inattentive and remiss in their duty during great part of the storm, now poured upon deck, where no exertions of the officers could keep them, while their assistance might have been useful. They had actually skulked in their hammocks, leaving the working of the pumps and other necessary labours to the officers of the ship, and the soldiers, who had made uncommon exertions. Roused by a sense of their danger, the same seamen, at this moment, in frantic exclamations, demanded of heaven and their fellow-sufferers that succour which their own efforts, timely made, might possibly have procured.

'The ship continued to beat on the rocks; and soon bilging, fell with her broadside towards the shore. When she struck, a number of the men climbed up the ensign-staff, under an apprehension of her immediately going to pieces.

'Mr. Meriton, at this crisis, offered to these unhappy beings the best advice which could be given; he recommended that all should come to the side of the ship lying lowest on the rocks, and singly to take the opportunities which might then offer, of escaping to the shore.

'Having thus provided, to the utmost of his power, for the safety of the desponding crew, he returned to the round-house, where, by this time, all the passengers and most of the officers had assembled. The latter were employed in offering consolation to the unfortunate ladies; and, with unparalleled magnanimity, suffering their compassion for the fair and amiable companions of their misfortunes to prevail over the sense of their own danger.

'In this charitable work of comfort, Mr. Meriton now joined, by assurances of his opinion, that, the ship would hold together till the morning, when all would be safe. Captain Pierce, observing one of the young gentlemen loud in his exclamations of terror, and frequently cry that the ship was parting, cheerfully bid him be quiet, remarking that though the ship should go to pieces, he would not, but would be safe enough.

'It is difficult to convey a correct idea of the scene of this deplorable catastrophe, without describing the place where it happened. The Haleswell struck on the rocks at a part of the shore where the cliff is of vast height, and rises almost perpendicular from its base. But at this particular spot, the foot of the cliff is excavated into a cavern of ten or twelve yards in depth, and of breadth equal to the length of a large ship. The sides of the cavern are so nearly upright, as to be of extremely difficult access; and the bottom is strewed with sharp and uneven rocks, which seem, by some convulsion of the earth, to have been detached from its roof.

'The ship lay with her broadside opposite to the mouth of this cavern, with her whole length stretched almost from side to side of it. But when she struck, it was too dark for the unfortunate persons on board to discover the real magnitude of the danger, and the extreme horror of such a situation.

'In addition to the company already in the round-house, they had admitted three black women and two soldiers' wives; who, with the husband of one of them, had been allowed to come in, though the seamen, who had tumultuously demanded entrance to get the lights, had been opposed and kept out by Mr. Rogers and Mr. Brimer, the third and fifth mates. The numbers there were, therefore, now increased to near fifty. Captain Pierce sat on a chair, a cot, or some other moveable, with a daughter on each side, whom he alternately pressed to his affectionate breast. The rest of the melancholy assembly were seated on the deck, which was strewed with musical instruments, and the wreck of furniture and other articles.

'Here also Mr. Meriton, after having cut several wax-candles in pieces, and stuck them up in various parts of the round-house, and lighted up all the glass lanthorns he could find, took his seat, intending to wait the approach of dawn; and then assist the partners of his dangers to escape. But, observing that the poor ladies appeared parched and exhausted, he brought a basket of oranges and prevailed on some of them to refresh themselves by sucking a little of the juice. At this time they were all tolerably composed, except Miss Mansel, who was in hysteric fits on the floor of the deck of the round-house.

'But on Mr. Meriton's return to the company, he perceived a considerable alteration in the appearance of the ship; the sides were visibly giving way; the deck seemed to be lifting, and he discovered other strong indications that she could not hold much longer together. On this account, he attempted to go forward to look out, but immediately saw that the ship had separated in the middle, and that the forepart having changed its position, lay rather further out towards the sea. In such an emergency, when the next moment might plunge him into eternity, he determined to seize the present opportunity, and follow the example of the crew and the soldiers, who were now quitting the ship in numbers, and making their way to the shore, though quite ignorant of its nature and description.

'Among other expedients, the ensign-staff had been unshipped, and attempted to be laid between the ship's side and some of the rocks, but without success, for it snapped asunder before it reached them. However, by the light of a lanthorn, which a seaman handed through the skylight of the round-house to the deck, Mr. Meriton discovered a spar which appeared to be laid from the ship's side to the rocks, and on this spar he resolved to attempt his escape.

'Accordingly, lying down upon it, he thrust himself forward; however, he soon found that it had no communication with the rock; he reached the end of it, and then slipped off, receiving a very violent bruise in his fall, and before he could recover his legs, he was washed off by the surge. He now supported himself by swimming, until a returning wave dashed him against the back part of the cavern. Here he laid hold of a small projection in the rock, but was so much benumbed that he was on the point of quitting it, when a seaman, who had already gained a footing, extended his hand, and assisted him until he could secure himself a little on the rock; from which he clambered on a shelf still higher, and out of the reach of the surf.

'Mr. Rogers, the third mate, remained with the captain and the unfortunate ladies and their companions nearly twenty minutes after Mr. Meriton had quitted the ship. Soon after the latter left the round-house, the captain asked what was become of him, to which Mr. Rogers replied, that he was gone on deck to see what could be done. After this, a heavy sea breaking over the ship, the ladies exclaimed, "Oh, poor Meriton! he is drowned; had he stayed with us he would have been safe!" and they all, particularly Miss Mary Pierce, expressed great concern at the apprehension of his loss.

'The sea was now breaking in at the fore part of the ship, and reached as far as the mainmast. Captain Pierce gave Mr. Rogers a nod, and they took a lamp and went together into the stern-gallery, where, after viewing the rocks for some time, Captain Pierce asked Mr. Rogers if he thought there was any possibility of saving the girls; to which he replied, he feared there was none; for they could only discover the black face of the perpendicular rock, and not the cavern which afforded shelter to those who escaped. They then returned to the round-house, where Mr. Rogers hung up the lamp, and Captain Pierce sat down between his two daughters.

'The sea continuing to break in very fast, Mr. Macmanus, a midshipman, and Mr. Schutz, a passenger, asked Mr. Rogers what they could do to escape.

"Follow me," he replied, and they all went into the stern-gallery, and from thence to the upper-quarter-gallery on the poop. While there, a very heavy sea fell on board, and the round-house gave way; Mr. Rogers heard the ladies shriek at intervals, as if the water reached them; the noise of the sea at other times drowning their voices.

'Mr. Brimer had followed him to the poop, where they remained together about five minutes, when on the breaking of this heavy sea, they jointly seized a hen-coop. The same wave which proved fatal to some of those below, carried him and his companion to the rock, on which they were violently dashed and miserably bruised.

'Here on the rock were twenty-seven men; but it now being low water, and as they were convinced that on the flowing of the tide all must be washed off, many attempted to get to the back or the sides of the cavern, beyond the reach of the returning sea. Scarcely more than six, besides Mr. Rogers and Mr. Brimer, succeeded.

'Mr. Rogers, on gaining this station, was so nearly exhausted, that had his exertions been protracted only a few minutes longer, he must have sunk under them. He was now prevented from joining Mr. Meriton, by at least twenty men between them, none of whom could move, without the imminent peril of his life.

'They found that a very considerable number of the crew, seamen and soldiers, and some petty officers, were in the same situation as themselves, though many who had reached the rocks below, perished in attempting to ascend. They could yet discern some part of the ship, and in their dreary station solaced themselves with the hopes of its remaining entire until day-break; for, in the midst of their own distress, the sufferings of the females on board affected them with the most poignant anguish; and every sea that broke inspired them with terror for their safety.

'But, alas, their apprehensions were too soon realised! Within a very few minutes of the time that Mr. Rogers gained the rock, an universal shriek, which long vibrated in their ears, in which the voice of female distress was lamentably distinguished, announced the dreadful catastrophe. In a few moments all was hushed, except the roaring of the winds and the dashing of the waves; the wreck was buried in the deep, and not an atom of it was ever afterwards seen.'

The most beautiful and affecting incident I know, associated with a shipwreck, succeeds this dismal story for a winter night. The Grosvenor, East Indiaman, homeward bound, goes ashore on the coast of Caffraria. It is resolved that the officers, passengers, and crew, in number one hundred and thirty-five souls, shall endeavour to penetrate on foot, across trackless deserts, infested by wild beasts and cruel savages, to the Dutch settlements at the Cape of Good Hope. With this forlorn object before them, they finally separate into two parties—never more to meet on earth.

There is a solitary child among the passengers—a little boy of seven years old who has no relation there; and when the first party is moving away he cries after some member of it who has been kind to him. The crying of a child might be supposed to be a little thing to men in such great extremity; but it touches them, and he is immediately taken into that detachment.

From which time forth, this child is sublimely made a sacred charge. He is pushed, on a little raft, across broad rivers by the swimming sailors; they carry him by turns through the deep sand and long grass (he patiently walking at all other times); they share with him such putrid fish as they find to eat; they lie down and wait for him when the rough carpenter, who becomes his especial friend, lags behind. Beset by lions and tigers, by savages, by thirst, by hunger, by death in a crowd of ghastly shapes, they never—O Father of all mankind, thy name be blessed for it!—forget this child. The captain stops exhausted, and his faithful coxswain goes back and is seen to sit down by his side, and neither of the two shall be any more beheld until the great last day; but, as the rest go on for their lives, they take the child with them. The carpenter dies of poisonous berries eaten in starvation; and the steward, succeeding to the command of the party, succeeds to the sacred guardianship of the child.

God knows all he does for the poor baby; how he cheerfully carries him in his arms when he himself is weak and ill; how he feeds him when he himself is griped with want; how he folds his ragged jacket round him, lays his little worn face with a woman's tenderness upon his sunburnt breast, soothes him in his sufferings, sings to him as he limps along, unmindful of his own parched and bleeding feet. Divided for a few days from the rest, they dig a grave in the sand and bury their good friend the cooper—these two companions alone in the wilderness—and then the time comes when they both are ill, and beg their wretched partners in despair, reduced and few in number now, to wait by them one day. They wait by them one day, they wait by them two days. On the morning of the third, they move very softly about, in making their preparations for the resumption of their journey; for, the child is sleeping by the fire, and it is agreed with one consent that he shall not be disturbed until the last moment. The moment comes, the fire is dying—and the child is dead.

His faithful friend, the steward, lingers but a little while behind him. His grief is great, he staggers on for a few days, lies down in the desert, and dies. But he shall be re-united in his immortal spirit—who can doubt it!—with the child, when he and the poor carpenter shall be raised up with the words, 'Inasmuch as ye have done it unto the least of these, ye have done it unto Me.'

As I recall the dispersal and disappearance of nearly all the participators in this once famous shipwreck (a mere handful being recovered at last), and the legends that were long afterwards revived from time to time among the English officers at the Cape, of a white woman with an infant, said to have been seen weeping outside a savage hut far in the interior, who was whisperingly associated with the remembrance of the missing ladies saved from the wrecked vessel, and who was often sought but never found, thoughts of another kind of travel came into my mind.

Thoughts of a voyager unexpectedly summoned from home, who travelled a vast distance, and could never return. Thoughts of this unhappy wayfarer in the depths of his sorrow, in the bitterness of his anguish, in the helplessness of his self-reproach, in the desperation of his desire to set right what he had left wrong, and do what he had left undone.

For, there were many, many things he had neglected. Little matters while he was at home and surrounded by them, but things of mighty moment when he was at an immeasurable distance. There were many many blessings that he had inadequately felt, there were many trivial injuries that he had not forgiven, there was love that he had but poorly returned, there was friendship that he had too lightly prized: there were a million kind words that he might have spoken, a million kind looks that he might have given, uncountable slight easy deeds in which he might have been most truly great and good. O for a day (he would exclaim), for but one day to make amends! But the sun never shone upon that happy day, and out of his remote captivity he never came.

Why does this traveller's fate obscure, on New Year's Eve, the other histories of travellers with which my mind was filled but now, and cast a solemn shadow over me! Must I one day make his journey? Even so. Who shall say, that I may not then be tortured by such late regrets: that I may not then look from my exile on my empty place and undone work? I stand upon a sea-shore, where the waves are years. They break and fall, and I may little heed them; but, with every wave the sea is rising, and I know that it will float me on this traveller's voyage at last.

THE BEGGING-LETTER WRITER

The amount of money he annually diverts from wholesome and useful purposes in the United Kingdom, would be a set-off against the Window Tax. He is one of the most shameless frauds and impositions of this time. In his idleness, his mendacity, and the immeasurable harm he does to the deserving,—dirtying the stream of true benevolence, and muddling the brains of foolish justices, with inability to distinguish between the base coin of distress, and the true currency we have always among us,—he is more worthy of Norfolk Island than three-fourths of the worst characters who are sent there. Under any rational system, he would have been sent there long ago.

I, the writer of this paper, have been, for some time, a chosen receiver of Begging Letters. For fourteen years, my house has been made as regular a Receiving House for such communications as any one of the great branch Post-Offices is for general correspondence. I ought to know something of the Begging-Letter Writer. He has besieged my door at all hours of the day and night; he has fought my servant; he has lain in ambush for me, going out and coming in; he has followed me out of town into the country; he has appeared at provincial hotels, where I have been staying for only a few hours; he has written to me from immense distances, when I have been out of England. He has fallen sick; he has died and been buried; he has come to life again, and again departed from this transitory scene: he has been his own son, his own mother, his own baby, his idiot brother, his uncle, his aunt, his aged grandfather. He has wanted a greatcoat, to go to India in; a pound to set him up in life for ever; a pair of boots to take him to the coast of China; a hat to get him into a permanent situation under Government. He has frequently been exactly seven-and-sixpence short of independence. He has had such openings at Liverpool—posts of great trust and confidence in merchants' houses, which nothing but seven-and-sixpence was wanting to him to secure—that I wonder he is not Mayor of that flourishing town at the present moment.

The natural phenomena of which he has been the victim, are of a most astounding nature. He has had two children who have never grown up; who have never had anything to cover them at night; who have been continually driving him mad, by asking in vain for food; who have never come out of fevers and measles (which, I suppose, has accounted for his fuming his letters with tobacco smoke, as a disinfectant); who have never changed in the least degree through fourteen long revolving years. As to his wife, what that suffering woman has undergone, nobody knows. She has always been in an interesting situation through the same long period, and has never been confined yet. His devotion to her has been unceasing. He has never cared for himself; he could have perished—he would rather, in short—but was it not his Christian duty as a man, a husband, and a father,—to write begging letters when he looked at her? (He has usually remarked that he would call in the evening for an answer to this question.)

He has been the sport of the strangest misfortunes. What his brother has done to him would have broken anybody else's heart. His brother went into business with him, and ran away with the money; his brother got him to be security for an immense sum and left him to pay it; his brother would have given him employment to the tune of hundreds a-year, if he would have consented to write letters on a Sunday; his brother enunciated principles incompatible with his religious views, and he could not (in consequence) permit his brother to provide for him. His landlord has never shown a spark of human feeling. When he put in that execution I don't know, but he has never taken it out. The broker's man has grown grey in possession. They will have to bury him some day.

He has been attached to every conceivable pursuit. He has been in the army, in the navy, in the church, in the law; connected with the press, the fine arts, public institutions, every description and grade of business. He has been brought up as a gentleman; he has been at every college in Oxford and Cambridge; he can quote Latin in his letters (but generally misspells some minor English word); he can tell you what Shakespeare says about begging, better than you know it. It is to be observed, that in the midst of his afflictions he always reads the newspapers; and rounds off his appeal with some allusion, that may be supposed to be in my way, to the popular subject of the hour.

His life presents a series of inconsistencies. Sometimes he has never written such a letter before. He blushes with shame. That is the first time; that shall be the last. Don't answer it, and let it be understood that, then, he will kill himself quietly. Sometimes (and more frequently) he has written a few such letters. Then he encloses the answers, with an intimation that they are of inestimable value to him, and a request that they may be carefully returned. He is fond of enclosing something—verses, letters, pawnbrokers' duplicates, anything to necessitate an answer. He is very severe upon 'the pampered minion of fortune,' who refused him the half-sovereign referred to in the enclosure number two—but he knows me better.

He writes in a variety of styles; sometimes in low spirits; sometimes quite jocosely. When he is in low spirits he writes down-hill and repeats words—these little indications being expressive of the perturbation of his mind. When he is more vivacious, he is frank with me; he is quite the agreeable rattle. I know what human nature is,—who better? Well! He had a little money once, and he ran through it—as many men have done before him. He finds his old friends turn away from him now—many men have done that before him too! Shall he tell me why he writes to me? Because he has no kind of claim upon me. He puts it on that ground plainly; and begs to ask for the loan (as I know human nature) of two sovereigns, to be repaid next Tuesday six weeks, before twelve at noon.

Sometimes, when he is sure that I have found him out, and that there is no chance of money, he writes to inform me that I have got rid of him at last. He has enlisted into the Company's service, and is off directly—but he wants a cheese. He is informed by the serjeant that it is essential to his prospects in the regiment that he should take out a single Gloucester cheese, weighing from twelve to fifteen pounds. Eight or nine shillings would buy it. He does not ask for money, after what has passed; but if he calls at nine, to-morrow morning may he hope to find a cheese? And is there anything he can do to show his gratitude in Bengal?

Once he wrote me rather a special letter, proposing relief in kind. He had got into a little trouble by leaving parcels of mud done up in brown paper, at people's houses, on pretence of being a Railway-Porter, in which character he received carriage money. This sportive fancy he expiated in the House of Correction. Not long after his release, and on a Sunday morning, he called with a letter (having first dusted himself all over), in which he gave me to understand that, being resolved to earn an honest livelihood, he had been travelling about the country with a cart of crockery. That he had been doing pretty well until the day before, when his horse had dropped down dead near Chatham, in Kent. That this had reduced him to the unpleasant necessity of getting into the shafts himself, and drawing the cart of crockery to London—a somewhat exhausting pull of thirty miles. That he did not venture to ask again for money; but that if I would have the goodness to leave him out a donkey, he would call for the animal before breakfast!

At another time my friend (I am describing actual experiences) introduced himself as a literary gentleman in the last extremity of distress. He had had a play accepted at a certain Theatre—which was really open; its representation was delayed by the indisposition of a leading actor—who was really ill; and he and his were in a state of absolute starvation. If he made his necessities known to the Manager of the Theatre, he put it to me to say what kind of treatment he might expect? Well! we got over that difficulty to our mutual satisfaction. A little while afterwards he was in some other strait. I think Mrs. Southcote, his wife, was in extremity—and we adjusted that point too. A little while afterwards he had taken a new house, and was going headlong to ruin for want of a water-butt. I had my misgivings about the water-butt, and did not reply to that epistle. But a little while afterwards, I had reason to feel penitent for my neglect. He wrote me a few broken-hearted lines, informing me that the dear partner of his sorrows died in his arms last night at nine o'clock!

I despatched a trusty messenger to comfort the bereaved mourner and his poor children; but the messenger went so soon, that the play was not ready to be played out; my friend was not at home, and his wife was in a most delightful state of health. He was taken up by the Mendicity Society (informally it afterwards appeared), and I presented myself at a London Police-

Office with my testimony against him. The Magistrate was wonderfully struck by his educational acquirements, deeply impressed by the excellence of his letters, exceedingly sorry to see a man of his attainments there, complimented him highly on his powers of composition, and was quite charmed to have the agreeable duty of discharging him. A collection was made for the 'poor fellow,' as he was called in the reports, and I left the court with a comfortable sense of being universally regarded as a sort of monster. Next day comes to me a friend of mine, the governor of a large prison. 'Why did you ever go to the Police-Office against that man,' says he, 'without coming to me first? I know all about him and his frauds. He lodged in the house of one of my warders, at the very time when he first wrote to you; and then he was eating spring-lamb at eighteen-pence a pound, and early asparagus at I don't know how much a bundle!' On that very same day, and in that very same hour, my injured gentleman wrote a solemn address to me, demanding to know what compensation I proposed to make him for his having passed the night in a 'loathsome dungeon.' And next morning an Irish gentleman, a member of the same fraternity, who had read the case, and was very well persuaded I should be chary of going to that Police-Office again, positively refused to leave my door for less than a sovereign, and, resolved to besiege me into compliance, literally 'sat down' before it for ten mortal hours. The garrison being well provisioned, I remained within the walls; and he raised the siege at midnight with a prodigious alarum on the bell.

The Begging-Letter Writer often has an extensive circle of acquaintance. Whole pages of the 'Court Guide' are ready to be references for him. Noblemen and gentlemen write to say there never was such a man for probity and virtue. They have known him time out of mind, and there is nothing they wouldn't do for him. Somehow, they don't give him that one pound ten he stands in need of; but perhaps it is not enough—they want to do more, and his modesty will not allow it. It is to be remarked of his trade that it is a very fascinating one. He never leaves it; and those who are near to him become smitten with a love of it, too, and sooner or later set up for themselves. He employs a messenger—man, woman, or child. That messenger is certain ultimately to become an independent Begging-Letter Writer. His sons and daughters succeed to his calling, and write begging-letters when he is no more. He throws off the infection of begging-letter writing, like the contagion of disease. What Sydney Smith so happily called 'the dangerous luxury of dishonesty' is more tempting, and more catching, it would seem, in this instance than in any other.

He always belongs to a Corresponding-Society of Begging-Letter Writers. Any one who will, may ascertain this fact. Give money to-day in recognition of a begging-letter,—no matter how unlike a common begging-letter,—and for the next fortnight you will have a rush of such communications. Steadily refuse to give; and the begging-letters become Angels' visits, until the Society is from some cause or other in a dull way of business, and may as well try you as anybody else. It is of little use inquiring into the Begging-Letter Writer's circumstances. He may be sometimes accidentally found out, as in the case already mentioned (though that was not the first inquiry made); but apparent misery is always a part of his trade, and real misery very often is, in the intervals of spring-lamb and early asparagus. It is naturally an incident of his dissipated and dishonest life.

That the calling is a successful one, and that large sums of money are gained by it, must be evident to anybody who reads the Police Reports of such cases. But, prosecutions are of rare occurrence, relatively to the extent to which the trade is carried on. The cause of this is to be found (as no one knows better than the Begging-Letter Writer, for it is a part of his speculation) in the aversion people feel to exhibit themselves as having been imposed upon, or as having weakly gratified their consciences with a lazy, flimsy substitute for the noblest of all virtues. There is a man at large, at the moment when this paper is preparing for the press (on the 29th of April, 1850), and never once taken up yet, who, within these twelvemonths, has been probably the most audacious and the most successful swindler that even this trade has ever known. There has been something singularly base in this fellow's proceedings; it has been his business to write to all sorts and conditions of people, in the names of persons of high reputation and unblemished honour, professing to be in distress—the general admiration and respect for whom has ensured a ready and generous reply.

Now, in the hope that the results of the real experience of a real person

428

may do something more to induce reflection on this subject than any abstract treatise—and with a personal knowledge of the extent to which the Begging-Letter Trade has been carried on for some time, and has been for some time constantly increasing—the writer of this paper entreats the attention of his readers to a few concluding words. His experience is a type of the experience of many; some on a smaller, some on an infinitely larger scale. All may judge of the soundness or unsoundness of his conclusions from it.

Long doubtful of the efficacy of such assistance in any case whatever, and able to recall but one, within his whole individual knowledge, in which he had the least after-reason to suppose that any good was done by it, he was led, last autumn, into some serious considerations. The begging-letters flying about by every post, made it perfectly manifest that a set of lazy vagabonds were interposed between the general desire to do something to relieve the sickness and misery under which the poor were suffering, and the suffering poor themselves. That many who sought to do some little to repair the social wrongs, inflicted in the way of preventible sickness and death upon the poor, were strengthening those wrongs, however innocently, by wasting money on pestilent knaves cumbering society. That imagination,—soberly following one of these knaves into his life of punishment in jail, and comparing it with the life of one of these poor in a cholera-stricken alley, or one of the children of one of these poor, soothed in its dying hour by the late lamented Mr. Drouet,—contemplated a grim farce, impossible to be presented very much longer before God or man. That the crowning miracle of all the miracles summed up in the New Testament, after the miracle of the blind seeing, and the lame walking, and the restoration of the dead to life, was the miracle that the poor had the Gospel preached to them. That while the poor were unnaturally and unnecessarily cut off by the thousand, in the prematurity of their age, or in the rottenness of their youth—for of flower or blossom such youth has none—the Gospel was NOT preached to them, saving in hollow and unmeaning voices. That of all wrongs, this was the first mighty wrong the Pestilence warned us to set right. And that no Post-Office Order to any amount, given to a Begging-Letter Writer for the quieting of an uneasy breast, would be presentable on the Last Great Day as anything towards it.

The poor never write these letters. Nothing could be more unlike their habits. The writers are public robbers; and we who support them are parties to their depredations. They trade upon every circumstance within their knowledge that affects us, public or private, joyful or sorrowful; they pervert the lessons of our lives; they change what ought to be our strength and virtue into weakness, and encouragement of vice. There is a plain remedy, and it is in our own hands. We must resolve, at any sacrifice of feeling, to be deaf to such appeals, and crush the trade.

There are degrees in murder. Life must be held sacred among us in more ways than one—sacred, not merely from the murderous weapon, or the subtle poison, or the cruel blow, but sacred from preventible diseases, distortions, and pains. That is the first great end we have to set against this miserable imposition. Physical life respected, moral life comes next. What will not content a Begging-Letter Writer for a week, would educate a score of children for a year. Let us give all we can; let us give more than ever. Let us do all we can; let us do more than ever. But let us give, and do, with a high purpose; not to endow the scum of the earth, to its own greater corruption, with the offals of our duty.

A CHILD'S DREAM OF A STAR

There was once a child, and he strolled about a good deal, and thought of a number of things. He had a sister, who was a child too, and his constant companion. These two used to wonder all day long. They wondered at the beauty of the flowers; they wondered at the height and blueness of the sky; they wondered at the depth of the bright water; they wondered at the goodness and the power of God who made the lovely world.

They used to say to one another, sometimes, Supposing all the children upon earth were to die, would the flowers, and the water, and the sky be sorry? They believed they would be sorry. For, said they, the buds are the children of the flowers, and the little playful streams that gambol down the hill-sides are the children of the water; and the smallest bright specks playing at hide and seek in the sky all night, must surely be the children of the stars; and they would all be grieved to see their playmates, the children of men, no more.

There was one clear shining star that used to come out in the sky before the rest, near the church spire, above the graves. It was larger and more beautiful, they thought, than all the others, and every night they watched for it, standing hand in hand at a window. Whoever saw it first cried out, 'I see the star!' And often they cried out both together, knowing so well when it would rise, and where. So they grew to be such friends with it, that, before lying down in their beds, they always looked out once again, to bid it good night; and when they were turning round to sleep, they used to say, 'God bless the star!'

But while she was still very young, oh, very, very young, the sister drooped, and came to be so weak that she could no longer stand in the window at night; and then the child looked sadly out by himself, and when he saw the star, turned round and said to the patient pale face on the bed, 'I see the star!' and then a smile would come upon the face, and a little weak voice used to say, 'God bless my brother and the star!'

And so the time came all too soon! when the child looked out alone, and when there was no face on the bed; and when there was a little grave among the graves, not there before; and when the star made long rays down towards him, as he saw it through his tears.

Now, these rays were so bright, and they seemed to make such a shining way from earth to Heaven, that when the child went to his solitary bed, he dreamed about the star; and dreamed that, lying where he was, he saw a train of people taken up that sparkling road by angels. And the star, opening, showed him a great world of light, where many more such angels waited to receive them.

All these angels, who were waiting, turned their beaming eyes upon the people who were carried up into the star; and some came out from the long rows in which they stood, and fell upon the people's necks, and kissed them tenderly, and went away with them down avenues of light, and were so happy in their company, that lying in his bed he wept for joy.

But, there were many angels who did not go with them, and among them one he knew. The patient face that once had lain upon the bed was glorified and radiant, but his heart found out his sister among all the host.

His sister's angel lingered near the entrance of the star, and said to the leader among those who had brought the people thither:

'Is my brother come?'

And he said 'No.'

She was turning hopefully away, when the child stretched out his arms, and cried, 'O, sister, I am here! Take me!' and then she turned her beaming eyes upon him, and it was night; and the star was shining into the room, making long rays down towards him as he saw it through his tears.

From that hour forth, the child looked out upon the star as on the home he was to go to, when his time should come; and he thought that he did not belong to the earth alone, but to the star too, because of his sister's angel gone before.

There was a baby born to be a brother to the child; and while he was so little that he never yet had spoken word, he stretched his tiny form out on his bed, and died.

Again the child dreamed of the open star, and of the company of angels, and the train of people, and the rows of angels with their beaming eyes all turned upon those people's faces.

Said his sister's angel to the leader:

'Is my brother come?'

And he said, 'Not that one, but another.'

As the child beheld his brother's angel in her arms, he cried, 'O, sister, I am here! Take me!' And she turned and smiled upon him, and the star was shining.

He grew to be a young man, and was busy at his books when an old servant came to him and said:

'Thy mother is no more. I bring her blessing on her darling son!'

Again at night he saw the star, and all that former company. Said his sister's angel to the leader.

'Is my brother come?'

And he said, 'Thy mother!'

A mighty cry of joy went forth through all the star, because the mother was re-united to her two children. And he stretched out his arms and cried, 'O, mother, sister, and brother, I am here! Take me!' And they answered him, 'Not yet,' and the star was shining.

He grew to be a man, whose hair was turning grey, and he was sitting in his chair by the fireside, heavy with grief, and with his face bedewed with tears, when the star opened once again.

Said his sister's angel to the leader: 'Is my brother come?'

And he said, 'Nay, but his maiden daughter.'

And the man who had been the child saw his daughter, newly lost to him, a celestial creature among those three, and he said, 'My daughter's head is on my sister's bosom, and her arm is around my mother's neck, and at her feet there is the baby of old time, and I can bear the parting from her, God be praised!'

And the star was shining.

Thus the child came to be an old man, and his once smooth face was wrinkled, and his steps were slow and feeble, and his back was bent. And one night as he lay upon his bed, his children standing round, he cried, as he had cried so long ago:

'I see the star!'

They whispered one another, 'He is dying.'

And he said, 'I am. My age is falling from me like a garment, and I move towards the star as a child. And O, my Father, now I thank thee that it has so often opened, to receive those dear ones who await me!'

And the star was shining; and it shines upon his grave.

OUR ENGLISH WATERING-PLACE

In the Autumn-time of the year, when the great metropolis is so much hotter, so much noisier, so much more dusty or so much more water-carted, so much more crowded, so much more disturbing and distracting in all respects, than it usually is, a quiet sea-beach becomes indeed a blessed spot. Half awake and half asleep, this idle morning in our sunny window on the edge of a chalk-cliff in the old-fashioned watering-place to which we are a faithful resorter, we feel a lazy inclination to sketch its picture.

The place seems to respond. Sky, sea, beach, and village, lie as still before us as if they were sitting for the picture. It is dead low-water. A ripple plays among the ripening corn upon the cliff, as if it were faintly trying from recollection to imitate the sea; and the world of butterflies hovering over the crop of radish-seed are as restless in their little way as the gulls are in their larger manner when the wind blows. But the ocean lies winking in the sunlight like a drowsy lion—its glassy waters scarcely curve upon the shore—the fishing-boats in the tiny harbour are all stranded in the mud—our two colliers (our watering-place has a maritime trade employing that amount of shipping) have not an inch of water within a quarter of a mile of them, and turn, exhausted, on their sides, like faint fish of an antediluvian species. Rusty cables and chains, ropes and rings, undermost parts of posts and piles and confused timber-defences against the waves, lie strewn about, in a brown litter of tangled sea-weed and fallen cliff which looks as if a family of giants had been making tea here for ages, and had observed an untidy custom of throwing their tea-leaves on the shore.

In truth, our watering-place itself has been left somewhat high and dry by the tide of years. Concerned as we are for its honour, we must reluctantly admit that the time when this pretty little semicircular sweep of houses, tapering off at the end of the wooden pier into a point in the sea, was a gay place, and when the lighthouse overlooking it shone at daybreak on company dispersing from public balls, is but dimly traditional now. There is a bleak chamber in our watering-place which is yet called the Assembly 'Rooms,' and understood to be available on hire for balls or concerts; and, some few seasons since, an ancient little gentleman came down and stayed at the hotel, who said that he had danced there, in bygone ages, with the Honourable Miss Peepy, well known to have been the Beauty of her day and the cruel occasion of innumerable duels. But he was so old and shrivelled, and so very rheumatic in the legs, that it demanded more imagination than our watering-place can usually muster, to believe him; therefore, except the Master of the 'Rooms' (who to this hour wears knee-breeches, and who confirmed the statement with tears in his eyes), nobody did believe in the little lame old gentleman, or even in the Honourable Miss Peepy, long deceased.

As to subscription balls in the Assembly Rooms of our watering-place now, red-hot cannon balls are less improbable. Sometimes, a misguided wanderer of a Ventriloquist, or an Infant Phenomenon, or a juggler, or somebody with an Orrery that is several stars behind the time, takes the place for a night, and issues bills with the name of his last town lined out, and the name of ours ignominiously written in, but you may be sure this never happens twice to the same unfortunate person. On such occasions the discoloured old Billiard Table that is seldom played at (unless the ghost of the Honourable Miss Peepy plays at pool with other ghosts) is pushed into a corner, and benches are solemnly constituted into front seats, back seats, and reserved seats—which are much the same after you have paid—and a few dull candles are lighted—wind permitting—and the performer and the scanty audience play out a short match which shall make the other most low-spirited—which is usually a drawn game. After that, the performer instantly departs with maledictory expressions, and is never heard of more.

But the most wonderful feature of our Assembly Rooms, is, that an annual sale of 'Fancy and other China,' is announced here with mysterious constancy and perseverance. Where the china comes from, where it goes to, why it is annually put up to auction when nobody ever thinks of bidding for it, how it comes to pass that it is always the same china, whether it would not have been cheaper, with the sea at hand, to have thrown it away, say in eighteen hundred and thirty, are standing enigmas. Every year the bills come out, every year the Master of the Rooms gets into a little pulpit on a table, and offers it for sale, every year nobody buys it, every year it is put away somewhere till next year, when it appears again as if the whole thing were a new idea. We have a faint remembrance of an unearthly collection of clocks, purporting to be the work of Parisian and Genevese artists—chiefly bilious-faced clocks, supported on sickly white crutches, with their pendulums dangling like lame legs—to which a similar course of events occurred for several years, until they seemed to lapse away, of mere imbecility.

Attached to our Assembly Rooms is a library. There is a wheel of fortune in it, but it is rusty and dusty, and never turns. A large doll, with moveable eyes, was put up to be raffled for, by five-and-twenty members at two shillings, seven years ago this autumn, and the list is not full yet. We are rather sanguine, now, that the raffle will come off next year. We think so, because we only want nine members, and should only want eight, but for number two having grown up since her name was entered, and withdrawn it when she was married. Down the street, there is a toy-ship of considerable burden, in the same condition. Two of the boys who were entered for that raffle have gone to India in real ships, since; and one was shot, and died in the arms of his sister's lover, by whom he sent his last words home.

This is the library for the Minerva Press. If you want that kind of reading, come to our watering-place. The leaves of the romances, reduced to a condition very like curl-paper, are thickly studded with notes in pencil: sometimes complimentary, sometimes jocose. Some of these commentators, like commentators in a more extensive way, quarrel with one another. One young gentleman who sarcastically writes 'O!!!' after every sentimental passage, is pursued through his literary career by another, who writes 'Insulting Beast!' Miss Julia Mills has read the whole collection of these books. She has left marginal notes on the pages, as 'Is not this truly touching? J. M.' 'How thrilling! J. M.' 'Entranced here by the Magician's potent spell. J. M.' She has also italicised her favourite traits in the description of the hero, as 'his hair, which was dark and wavy, clustered in rich profusion around a marble brow, whose lofty paleness bespoke the intellect within.' It reminds her of another hero. She adds, 'How like B. L. Can this be mere coincidence? J.

M.'

You would hardly guess which is the main street of our watering-place, but you may know it by its being always stopped up with donkey-chaises. Whenever you come here, and see harnessed donkeys eating clover out of barrows drawn completely across a narrow thoroughfare, you may be quite sure you are in our High Street. Our Police you may know by his uniform, likewise by his never on any account interfering with anybody—especially the tramps and vagabonds. In our fancy shops we have a capital collection of damaged goods, among which the flies of countless summers 'have been roaming.' We are great in obsolete seals, and in faded pin-cushions, and in rickety camp-stools, and in exploded cutlery, and in miniature vessels, and in stunted little telescopes, and in objects made of shells that pretend not to be shells. Diminutive spades, barrows, and baskets, are our principal articles of commerce; but even they don't look quite new somehow. They always seem to have been offered and refused somewhere else, before they came down to our watering-place.

Yet, it must not be supposed that our watering-place is an empty place, deserted by all visitors except a few staunch persons of approved fidelity. On the contrary, the chances are that if you came down here in August or September, you wouldn't find a house to lay your head in. As to finding either house or lodging of which you could reduce the terms, you could scarcely engage in a more hopeless pursuit. For all this, you are to observe that every season is the worst season ever known, and that the householding population of our watering-place are ruined regularly every autumn. They are like the farmers, in regard that it is surprising how much ruin they will bear. We have an excellent hotel—capital baths, warm, cold, and shower—first-rate bathing-machines—and as good butchers, bakers, and grocers, as heart could desire. They all do business, it is to be presumed, from motives of philanthropy—but it is quite certain that they are all being ruined. Their interest in strangers, and their politeness under ruin, bespeak their amiable nature. You would say so, if you only saw the baker helping a new comer to find suitable apartments.

So far from being at a discount as to company, we are in fact what would be popularly called rather a nobby place. Some tip-top 'Nobbs' come down occasionally—even Dukes and Duchesses. We have known such carriages to blaze among the donkey-chaises, as made beholders wink. Attendant on these equipages come resplendent creatures in plush and powder, who are sure to be stricken disgusted with the indifferent accommodation of our watering-place, and who, of an evening (particularly when it rains), may be seen very much out of drawing, in rooms far too small for their fine figures, looking discontentedly out of little back windows into bye-streets. The lords and ladies get on well enough and quite good-humouredly: but if you want to see the gorgeous phenomena who wait upon them at a perfect non-plus, you should come and look at the resplendent creatures with little back parlours for servants' halls, and turn-up bedsteads to sleep in, at our watering-place. You have no idea how they take it to heart.

We have a pier—a queer old wooden pier, fortunately without the slightest pretensions to architecture, and very picturesque in consequence. Boats are hauled up upon it, ropes are coiled all over it; lobster-pots, nets, masts, oars, spars, sails, ballast, and rickety capstans, make a perfect labyrinth of it. For ever hovering about this pier, with their hands in their pockets, or leaning over the rough bulwark it opposes to the sea, gazing through telescopes which they carry about in the same profound receptacles, are the Boatmen of our watering-place. Looking at them, you would say that surely these must be the laziest boatmen in the world. They lounge about, in obstinate and inflexible pantaloons that are apparently made of wood, the whole season through. Whether talking together about the shipping in the Channel, or gruffly unbending over mugs of beer at the public-house, you would consider them the slowest of men. The chances are a thousand to one that you might stay here for ten seasons, and never see a boatman in a hurry. A certain expression about his loose hands, when they are not in his pockets, as if he were carrying a considerable lump of iron in each, without any inconvenience, suggests strength, but he never seems to use it. He has the appearance of perpetually strolling—running is too inappropriate a word to be thought of—to seed. The only subject on which he seems to feel any approach to enthusiasm, is pitch. He pitches everything he can lay hold of,—the pier, the palings, his boat, his house,—when there is nothing else left he turns to and even pitches his hat, or his rough-weather clothing. Do not judge him by deceitful appearances. These are among the bravest and most skilful mariners that exist. Let a gale arise and swell into a storm, let a sea run that might appal the stoutest heart that ever beat, let the Light-boat on these dangerous sands throw up a rocket in the night, or let them hear through the angry roar the signal-guns of a ship in distress, and these men spring up into activity so dauntless, so valiant, and heroic, that the world cannot surpass it. Cavillers may object that they chiefly live upon the salvage of valuable cargoes. So they do, and God knows it is no great living that they get out of the deadly risks they run. But put that hope of gain aside. Let these rough fellows be asked, in any storm, who volunteers for the life-boat to save some perishing souls, as poor and empty-handed as themselves, whose lives the perfection of human reason does not rate at the value of a farthing each; and that boat will be manned, as surely and as cheerfully, as if a thousand pounds were told down on the weather-beaten pier. For this, and for the recollection of their comrades whom we have known, whom the raging sea has engulfed before their children's eyes in such brave efforts, whom the secret sand has buried, we hold the boatmen of our watering-place in our love and honour, and are tender of the fame they well deserve.

So many children are brought down to our watering-place that, when they are not out of doors, as they usually are in fine weather, it is wonderful where they are put: the whole village seeming much too small to hold them under cover. In the afternoons, you see no end of salt and sandy little boots drying on upper window-sills. At bathing-time in the morning, the little bay re-echoes with every shrill variety of shriek and splash—after which, if the weather be at all fresh, the sands teem with small blue mottled legs. The sands are the children's great resort. They cluster there, like ants: so busy burying their particular friends, and making castles with infinite labour which the next tide overthrows, that it is curious to consider how their play, to the music of the sea, foreshadows the realities of their after lives.

It is curious, too, to observe a natural ease of approach that there seems to be between the children and the boatmen. They mutually make acquaintance, and take individual likings, without any help. You will come upon one of those slow heavy fellows sitting down patiently mending a little ship for a mite of a boy, whom he could crush to death by throwing his lightest pair of trousers on him. You will be sensible of the oddest contrast between the smooth little creature, and the rough man who seems to be carved out of hard-grained wood—between the delicate hand expectantly held out, and the immense thumb and finger that can hardly feel the rigging of thread they mend—between the small voice and the gruff growl—and yet there is a natural propriety in the companionship: always to be noted in confidence between a child and a person who has any merit of reality and genuineness: which is admirably pleasant.

We have a preventive station at our watering-place, and much the same thing may be observed—in a lesser degree, because of their official character—of the coast blockade; a steady, trusty, well-conditioned, well-conducted set of men, with no misgiving about looking you full in the face, and with a quiet thorough-going way of passing along to their duty at night, carrying huge sou'-wester clothing in reserve, that is fraught with all good prepossession. They are handy fellows—neat about their houses—industrious at gardening—would get on with their wives, one thinks, in a desert island—and people it, too, soon.

As to the naval officer of the station, with his hearty fresh face, and his blue eye that has pierced all kinds of weather, it warms our hearts when he comes into church on a Sunday, with that bright mixture of blue coat, buff waistcoat, black neck-kerchief, and gold epaulette, that is associated in the minds of all Englishmen with brave, unpretending, cordial, national service. We like to look at him in his Sunday state; and if we were First Lord (really possessing the indispensable qualification for the office of knowing nothing whatever about the sea), we would give him a ship to-morrow.

We have a church, by-the-by, of course—a hideous temple of flint, like a great petrified haystack. Our chief clerical dignitary, who, to his honour, has done much for education both in time and money, and has established excellent schools, is a sound, shrewd, healthy gentleman, who has got into little occasional difficulties with the neighbouring farmers, but has had a pestilent trick of being right. Under a new regulation, he has yielded the

441

church of our watering-place to another clergyman. Upon the whole we get on in church well. We are a little bilious sometimes, about these days of fraternisation, and about nations arriving at a new and more unprejudiced knowledge of each other (which our Christianity don't quite approve), but it soon goes off, and then we get on very well.

There are two dissenting chapels, besides, in our small watering-place; being in about the proportion of a hundred and twenty guns to a yacht. But the dissension that has torn us lately, has not been a religious one. It has arisen on the novel question of Gas. Our watering-place has been convulsed by the agitation, Gas or No Gas. It was never reasoned why No Gas, but there was a great No Gas party. Broadsides were printed and stuck about—a startling circumstance in our watering-place. The No Gas party rested content with chalking 'No Gas!' and 'Down with Gas!' and other such angry war-whoops, on the few back gates and scraps of wall which the limits of our watering-place afford; but the Gas party printed and posted bills, wherein they took the high ground of proclaiming against the No Gas party, that it was said Let there be light and there was light; and that not to have light (that is gas-light) in our watering-place, was to contravene the great decree. Whether by these thunderbolts or not, the No Gas party were defeated; and in this present season we have had our handful of shops illuminated for the first time. Such of the No Gas party, however, as have got shops, remain in opposition and burn tallow—exhibiting in their windows the very picture of the sulkiness that punishes itself, and a new illustration of the old adage about cutting off your nose to be revenged on your face, in cutting off their gas to be revenged on their business.

Other population than we have indicated, our watering-place has none. There are a few old used-up boatmen who creep about in the sunlight with the help of sticks, and there is a poor imbecile shoemaker who wanders his lonely life away among the rocks, as if he were looking for his reason—which he will never find. Sojourners in neighbouring watering-places come occasionally in flys to stare at us, and drive away again as if they thought us very dull; Italian boys come, Punch comes, the Fantoccini come, the Tumblers come, the Ethiopians come; Glee-singers come at night, and hum and vibrate (not always melodiously) under our windows. But they all go soon, and leave us to ourselves again. We once had a travelling Circus and Wombwell's Menagerie at the same time. They both know better than ever to try it again; and the Menagerie had nearly razed us from the face of the earth in getting the elephant away—his caravan was so large, and the watering-place so small. We have a fine sea, wholesome for all people; profitable for the body, profitable for the mind. The poet's words are sometimes on its awful lips:

And the stately ships go on

To their haven under the hill;

But O for the touch of a vanish'd hand.

And the sound of a voice that is still!

Break, break, break,

At the foot of thy crags, O sea!

But the tender grace of a day that is dead

Will never come back to me.

Yet it is not always so, for the speech of the sea is various, and wants not abundant resource of cheerfulness, hope, and lusty encouragement. And since I have been idling at the window here, the tide has risen. The boats are dancing on the bubbling water; the colliers are afloat again; the white-bordered waves rush in; the children

Do chase the ebbing Neptune, and do fly him

When he comes back;

the radiant sails are gliding past the shore, and shining on the far horizon; all the sea is sparkling, heaving, swelling up with life and beauty, this bright morning.

OUR FRENCH WATERING-PLACE

Having earned, by many years of fidelity, the right to be sometimes inconstant to our English watering-place, we have dallied for two or three seasons with a French watering-place: once solely known to us as a town with a very long street, beginning with an abattoir and ending with a steam-boat, which it seemed our fate to behold only at daybreak on winter mornings, when (in the days before continental railroads), just sufficiently awake to know that we were most uncomfortably asleep, it was our destiny always to clatter through it, in the coupé of the diligence from Paris, with a sea of mud behind us, and a sea of tumbling waves before. In relation to which latter monster, our mind's eye now recalls a worthy Frenchman in a seal-skin cap with a braided hood over it, once our travelling companion in the coupé aforesaid, who, waking up with a pale and crumpled visage, and looking ruefully out at the grim row of breakers enjoying themselves fanatically on an instrument of torture called 'the Bar,' inquired of us whether we were ever sick at sea? Both to prepare his mind for the abject creature we were presently to become, and also to afford him consolation, we replied, 'Sir, your servant is always sick when it is possible to be so.' He returned, altogether uncheered by the bright example, 'Ah, Heaven, but I am always sick, even when it is impossible to be so.'

The means of communication between the French capital and our French watering-place are wholly changed since those days; but, the Channel remains unbridged as yet, and the old floundering and knocking about go on there. It must be confessed that saving in reasonable (and therefore rare) sea-weather, the act of arrival at our French watering-place from England is difficult to be achieved with dignity. Several little circumstances combine to render the visitor an object of humiliation. In the first place, the steamer no sooner touches the port, than all the passengers fall into captivity: being boarded by an overpowering force of Custom-house officers, and marched into a gloomy dungeon. In the second place, the road to this dungeon is fenced off with ropes breast-high, and outside those ropes all the English in the place who have lately been sea-sick and are now well, assemble in their best clothes to enjoy the degradation of their dilapidated fellow-creatures. 'Oh, my gracious! how ill this one has been!' 'Here's a damp one coming next!' 'Here's a pale one!' 'Oh! Ain't he green in the face, this next one!' Even we ourself (not deficient in natural dignity) have a lively remembrance of staggering up this detested lane one September day in a gale of wind, when we were received like an irresistible comic actor, with a burst of laughter and applause, occasioned by the extreme imbecility of our legs.

We were coming to the third place. In the third place, the captives, being shut up in the gloomy dungeon, are strained, two or three at a time, into an inner cell, to be examined as to passports; and across the doorway of communication, stands a military creature making a bar of his arm. Two ideas are generally present to the British mind during these ceremonies; first, that it is necessary to make for the cell with violent struggles, as if it were a life-boat and the dungeon a ship going down; secondly, that the military creature's arm is a national affront, which the government at home ought instantly to 'take up.' The British mind and body becoming heated by these fantasies, delirious answers are made to inquiries, and extravagant actions performed. Thus, Johnson persists in giving Johnson as his baptismal name, and substituting for his ancestral designation the national 'Dam!' Neither can he by any means be brought to recognise the distinction between a portmanteau-key and a passport, but will obstinately persevere in tendering the one when asked for the other. This brings him to the fourth place, in a state of mere idiotcy; and when he is, in the fourth place, cast out at a little door into a howling wilderness of touters, he becomes a lunatic with wild eyes and floating hair until rescued and soothed. If friendless and unrescued, he is generally put into a railway omnibus and taken to Paris.

But, our French watering-place, when it is once got into, is a very enjoyable place. It has a varied and beautiful country around it, and many characteristic and agreeable things within it. To be sure, it might have fewer bad smells and less decaying refuse, and it might be better drained, and much cleaner in many parts, and therefore infinitely more healthy. Still, it is a bright, airy, pleasant, cheerful town; and if you were to walk down either of its three well-paved main streets, towards five o'clock in the afternoon, when delicate odours of cookery fill the air, and its hotel windows (it is full of hotels) give glimpses of long tables set out for dinner, and made to look sumptuous by the aid of napkins folded fan-wise, you would rightly judge it to be an uncommonly good town to eat and drink in.

We have an old walled town, rich in cool public wells of water, on the top of a hill within and above the present business-town; and if it were some hundreds of miles further from England, instead of being, on a clear day, within sight of the grass growing in the crevices of the chalk-cliffs of Dover, you would long ago have been bored to death about that town. It is more picturesque and quaint than half the innocent places which tourists, following their leader like sheep, have made impostors of. To say nothing of its houses with grave courtyards, its queer by-corners, and its many-windowed streets white and quiet in the sunlight, there is an ancient belfry in it that would have been in all the Annuals and Albums, going and gone, these hundred years if it had but been more expensive to get at. Happily it has escaped so well, being only in our French watering-place, that you may like it of your own accord in a natural manner, without being required to go into convulsions about it. We regard it as one of the later blessings of our life, that Bilkins, the only authority on Taste, never took any notice that we can find out, of our French watering-place. Bilkins never wrote about it, never pointed out anything to be seen in it, never measured anything in it, always left it alone. For which relief, Heaven bless the town and the memory of the immortal Bilkins likewise!

There is a charming walk, arched and shaded by trees, on the old walls that form the four sides of this High Town, whence you get glimpses of the streets below, and changing views of the other town and of the river, and of the hills and of the sea. It is made more agreeable and peculiar by some of the solemn houses that are rooted in the deep streets below, bursting into a fresher existence a-top, and having doors and windows, and even gardens, on these ramparts. A child going in at the courtyard gate of one of these houses, climbing up the many stairs, and coming out at the fourth-floor window, might conceive himself another Jack, alighting on enchanted ground from another bean-stalk. It is a place wonderfully populous in children; English children, with governesses reading novels as they walk down the shady lanes of trees, or nursemaids interchanging gossip on the seats; French children with their smiling bonnes in snow-white caps, and themselves—if little boys—in straw head-gear like bee-hives, work-baskets and church hassocks. Three years ago, there were three weazen old men, one bearing a frayed red ribbon in his threadbare button-hole, always to be found walking together among these children, before dinner-time. If they walked for an appetite, they doubtless lived en pension—were contracted for—otherwise their poverty would have made it a rash action. They were stooping, blear-eyed, dull old men, slip-shod and shabby, in long-skirted short-waisted coats and meagre trousers, and yet with a ghost of gentility hovering in their company. They spoke little to each other, and looked as if they might have been politically discontented if they had had vitality enough. Once, we overheard red-ribbon feebly complain to the other two that somebody, or something, was 'a Robber;' and then they all three set their mouths so that they would have ground their teeth if they had had any. The ensuing winter gathered red-ribbon unto the great company of faded ribbons, and next year the remaining two were there—getting themselves entangled with hoops and dolls—familiar mysteries to the children—probably in the eyes of most of them, harmless creatures who had never been like children, and whom children could never be like. Another winter came, and another old man went, and so, this present year, the last of the triumvirate, left off walking—it was no good, now—and sat by himself on a little solitary bench, with the hoops and the dolls as lively as ever all about him.

In the Place d'Armes of this town, a little decayed market is held, which seems to slip through the old gateway, like water, and go rippling down the hill, to mingle with the murmuring market in the lower town, and get lost in its movement and bustle. It is very agreeable on an idle summer morning to pursue this market-stream from the hill-top. It begins, dozingly and dully, with a few sacks of corn; starts into a surprising collection of boots and shoes; goes brawling down the hill in a diversified channel of old cordage, old iron, old crockery, old clothes, civil and military, old rags, new cotton goods, flaming prints of saints, little looking-glasses, and incalculable lengths of tape; dives

447

into a backway, keeping out of sight for a little while, as streams will, or only sparkling for a moment in the shape of a market drinking-shop; and suddenly reappears behind the great church, shooting itself into a bright confusion of white-capped women and blue-bloused men, poultry, vegetables, fruits, flowers, pots, pans, praying-chairs, soldiers, country butter, umbrellas and other sun-shades, girl-porters waiting to be hired with baskets at their backs, and one weazen little old man in a cocked hat, wearing a cuirass of drinking-glasses and carrying on his shoulder a crimson temple fluttering with flags, like a glorified pavior's rammer without the handle, who rings a little bell in all parts of the scene, and cries his cooling drink Hola, Hola, Ho-o-o! in a shrill cracked voice that somehow makes itself heard, above all the chaffering and vending hum. Early in the afternoon, the whole course of the stream is dry. The praying-chairs are put back in the church, the umbrellas are folded up, the unsold goods are carried away, the stalls and stands disappear, the square is swept, the hackney coaches lounge there to be hired, and on all the country roads (if you walk about, as much as we do) you will see the peasant women, always neatly and comfortably dressed, riding home, with the pleasantest saddle-furniture of clean milk-pails, bright butter-kegs, and the like, on the jolliest little donkeys in the world.

We have another market in our French watering-place—that is to say, a few wooden hutches in the open street, down by the Port—devoted to fish. Our fishing-boats are famous everywhere; and our fishing people, though they love lively colours, and the taste is neutral (see Bilkins), are among the most picturesque people we ever encountered. They have not only a quarter of their own in the town itself, but they occupy whole villages of their own on the neighbouring cliffs. Their churches and chapels are their own; they consort with one another, they intermarry among themselves, their customs are their own, and their costume is their own and never changes. As soon as one of their boys can walk, he is provided with a long bright red nightcap; and one of their men would as soon think of going afloat without his head, as without that indispensable appendage to it. Then, they wear the noblest boots, with the hugest tops—flapping and bulging over anyhow; above which, they encase themselves in such wonderful overalls and petticoat trousers, made to all appearance of tarry old sails, so additionally stiffened with pitch and salt, that the wearers have a walk of their own, and go straddling and swinging about among the boats and barrels and nets and rigging, a sight to see. Then, their younger women, by dint of going down to the sea barefoot, to fling their baskets into the boats as they come in with the tide, and bespeak the first fruits of the haul with propitiatory promises to love and marry that dear fisherman who shall fill that basket like an Angel, have the finest legs ever carved by Nature in the brightest mahogany, and they walk like Juno. Their eyes, too, are so lustrous that their long gold ear-rings turn dull beside those brilliant neighbours; and when they are dressed, what with these beauties, and their fine fresh faces, and their many petticoats—striped petticoats, red petticoats, blue petticoats, always clean and smart, and never too long—and their home-made stockings, mulberry-coloured, blue, brown, purple, lilac—which the older women, taking care of the Dutch-looking children, sit in all sorts of places knitting, knitting, knitting from morning to night—and what with their little saucy bright blue jackets, knitted too, and fitting close to their handsome figures; and what with the natural grace with which they wear the commonest cap, or fold the commonest handkerchief round their luxuriant hair—we say, in a word and out of breath, that taking all these premises into our consideration, it has never been a matter of the least surprise to us that we have never once met, in the cornfields, on the dusty roads, by the breezy windmills, on the plots of short sweet grass overhanging the sea—anywhere—a young fisherman and fisherwoman of our French watering-place together, but the arm of that fisherman has invariably been, as a matter of course and without any absurd attempt to disguise so plain a necessity, round the neck or waist of that fisherwoman. And we have had no doubt whatever, standing looking at their uphill streets, house rising above house, and terrace above terrace, and bright garments here and there lying sunning on rough stone parapets, that the pleasant mist on all such objects, caused by their being seen through the brown nets hung across on poles to dry, is, in the eyes of every true young fisherman, a mist of love and beauty, setting off the goddess of his heart.

Moreover, it is to be observed that these are an industrious people, and a domestic people, and an honest people. And though we are aware that at the bidding of Bilkins it is our duty to fall down and worship the Neapolitans, we make bold very much to prefer the fishing people of our French watering-place—especially since our last visit to Naples within these twelvemonths, when we found only four conditions of men remaining in the whole city: to wit, lazzaroni, priests, spies, and soldiers, and all of them beggars; the paternal government having banished all its subjects except the rascals.

But we can never henceforth separate our French watering-place from our own landlord of two summers, M. Loyal Devasseur, citizen and town-councillor. Permit us to have the pleasure of presenting M. Loyal Devasseur.

His own family name is simply Loyal; but, as he is married, and as in that part of France a husband always adds to his own name the family name of his wife, he writes himself Loyal Devasseur. He owns a compact little estate of some twenty or thirty acres on a lofty hill-side, and on it he has built two country houses, which he lets furnished. They are by many degrees the best houses that are so let near our French watering-place; we have had the honour of living in both, and can testify. The entrance-hall of the first we inhabited was ornamented with a plan of the estate, representing it as about twice the size of Ireland; insomuch that when we were yet new to the property (M. Loyal always speaks of it as 'La propriété') we went three miles straight on end in search of the bridge of Austerlitz—which we afterwards found to be immediately outside the window. The Château of the Old Guard, in another part of the grounds, and, according to the plan, about two leagues from the little dining-room, we sought in vain for a week, until, happening one evening to sit upon a bench in the forest (forest in the plan), a few yards from the house-door, we observed at our feet, in the ignominious circumstances of being upside down and greenly rotten, the Old Guard himself: that is to say, the painted effigy of a member of that distinguished corps, seven feet high, and in the act of carrying arms, who had had the misfortune to be blown down in the previous winter. It will be perceived that M. Loyal is a staunch admirer of the great Napoleon. He is an old soldier himself—captain of the National Guard, with a handsome gold vase on his chimney-piece presented to him by his company—and his respect for the memory of the illustrious general is enthusiastic. Medallions of him, portraits of him, busts of him, pictures of him, are thickly sprinkled all over the property. During the first

450

month of our occupation, it was our affliction to be constantly knocking down Napoleon: if we touched a shelf in a dark corner, he toppled over with a crash; and every door we opened, shook him to the soul. Yet M. Loyal is not a man of mere castles in the air, or, as he would say, in Spain. He has a specially practical, contriving, clever, skilful eye and hand. His houses are delightful. He unites French elegance and English comfort, in a happy manner quite his own. He has an extraordinary genius for making tasteful little bedrooms in angles of his roofs, which an Englishman would as soon think of turning to any account as he would think of cultivating the Desert. We have ourself reposed deliciously in an elegant chamber of M. Loyal's construction, with our head as nearly in the kitchen chimney-pot as we can conceive it likely for the head of any gentleman, not by profession a Sweep, to be. And, into whatsoever strange nook M. Loyal's genius penetrates, it, in that nook, infallibly constructs a cupboard and a row of pegs. In either of our houses, we could have put away the knapsacks and hung up the hats of the whole regiment of Guides.

Aforetime, M. Loyal was a tradesman in the town. You can transact business with no present tradesman in the town, and give your card 'chez M. Loyal,' but a brighter face shines upon you directly. We doubt if there is, ever was, or ever will be, a man so universally pleasant in the minds of people as M. Loyal is in the minds of the citizens of our French watering-place. They rub their hands and laugh when they speak of him. Ah, but he is such a good child, such a brave boy, such a generous spirit, that Monsieur Loyal! It is the honest truth. M. Loyal's nature is the nature of a gentleman. He cultivates his ground with his own hands (assisted by one little labourer, who falls into a fit now and then); and he digs and delves from morn to eve in prodigious perspirations—'works always,' as he says—but, cover him with dust, mud, weeds, water, any stains you will, you never can cover the gentleman in M. Loyal. A portly, upright, broad-shouldered, brown-faced man, whose soldierly bearing gives him the appearance of being taller than he is, look into the bright eye of M. Loyal, standing before you in his working-blouse and cap, not particularly well shaved, and, it may be, very earthy, and you shall discern in M. Loyal a gentleman whose true politeness is ingrain, and confirmation of whose word by his bond you would blush to think of.

Not without reason is M. Loyal when he tells that story, in his own vivacious way, of his travelling to Fulham, near London, to buy all these hundreds and hundreds of trees you now see upon the Property, then a bare, bleak hill; and of his sojourning in Fulham three months; and of his jovial evenings with the market-gardeners; and of the crowning banquet before his departure, when the market-gardeners rose as one man, clinked their glasses all together (as the custom at Fulham is), and cried, 'Vive Loyal!'

M. Loyal has an agreeable wife, but no family; and he loves to drill the children of his tenants, or run races with them, or do anything with them, or for them, that is good-natured. He is of a highly convivial temperament, and his hospitality is unbounded. Billet a soldier on him, and he is delighted. Five-and-thirty soldiers had M. Loyal billeted on him this present summer, and they all got fat and red-faced in two days. It became a legend among the troops that whosoever got billeted on M. Loyal rolled in clover; and so it fell out that the fortunate man who drew the billet 'M. Loyal Devasseur' always leaped into the air, though in heavy marching order. M. Loyal cannot bear to admit anything that might seem by any implication to disparage the military profession. We hinted to him once, that we were conscious of a remote doubt arising in our mind, whether a sou a day for pocket-money, tobacco, stockings, drink, washing, and social pleasures in general, left a very large margin for a soldier's enjoyment. Pardon! said Monsieur Loyal, rather wincing. It was not a fortune, but—à la bonne heure—it was better than it used to be! What, we asked him on another occasion, were all those neighbouring peasants, each living with his family in one room, and each having a soldier (perhaps two) billeted on him every other night, required to provide for those soldiers? 'Faith!' said M. Loyal, reluctantly; a bed, monsieur, and fire to cook with, and a candle. And they share their supper with those soldiers. It is not possible that they could eat alone.'—'And what allowance do they get for this?' said we. Monsieur Loyal drew himself up taller, took a step back, laid his hand upon his breast, and said, with majesty, as speaking for himself and all France, 'Monsieur, it is a contribution to the State!'

It is never going to rain, according to M. Loyal. When it is impossible to deny that it is now raining in torrents, he says it will be fine—charming—

magnificent—to-morrow. It is never hot on the Property, he contends. Likewise it is never cold. The flowers, he says, come out, delighting to grow there; it is like Paradise this morning; it is like the Garden of Eden. He is a little fanciful in his language: smilingly observing of Madame Loyal, when she is absent at vespers, that she is 'gone to her salvation'—allée à son salut. He has a great enjoyment of tobacco, but nothing would induce him to continue smoking face to face with a lady. His short black pipe immediately goes into his breast pocket, scorches his blouse, and nearly sets him on fire. In the Town Council and on occasions of ceremony, he appears in a full suit of black, with a waistcoat of magnificent breadth across the chest, and a shirt-collar of fabulous proportions. Good M. Loyal! Under blouse or waistcoat, he carries one of the gentlest hearts that beat in a nation teeming with gentle people. He has had losses, and has been at his best under them. Not only the loss of his way by night in the Fulham times—when a bad subject of an Englishman, under pretence of seeing him home, took him into all the night public-houses, drank 'arfanarf' in every one at his expense, and finally fled, leaving him shipwrecked at Cleefeeway, which we apprehend to be Ratcliffe Highway—but heavier losses than that. Long ago a family of children and a mother were left in one of his houses without money, a whole year. M. Loyal—anything but as rich as we wish he had been—had not the heart to say 'you must go;' so they stayed on and stayed on, and paying-tenants who would have come in couldn't come in, and at last they managed to get helped home across the water; and M. Loyal kissed the whole group, and said, 'Adieu, my poor infants!' and sat down in their deserted salon and smoked his pipe of peace.—'The rent, M. Loyal?' 'Eh! well! The rent!' M. Loyal shakes his head. 'Le bon Dieu,' says M. Loyal presently, 'will recompense me,' and he laughs and smokes his pipe of peace. May he smoke it on the Property, and not be recompensed, these fifty years!

There are public amusements in our French watering-place, or it would not be French. They are very popular, and very cheap. The sea-bathing—which may rank as the most favoured daylight entertainment, inasmuch as the French visitors bathe all day long, and seldom appear to think of remaining less than an hour at a time in the water—is astoundingly cheap. Omnibuses convey you, if you please, from a convenient part of the town to the beach and back again; you have a clean and comfortable bathing-machine, dress, linen, and all appliances; and the charge for the whole is half-a-franc, or fivepence. On the pier, there is usually a guitar, which seems presumptuously enough to set its tinkling against the deep hoarseness of the sea, and there is always some boy or woman who sings, without any voice, little songs without any tune: the strain we have most frequently heard being an appeal to 'the sportsman' not to bag that choicest of game, the swallow. For bathing purposes, we have also a subscription establishment with an esplanade, where people lounge about with telescopes, and seem to get a good deal of weariness for their money; and we have also an association of individual machine proprietors combined against this formidable rival. M. Féroce, our own particular friend in the bathing line, is one of these. How he ever came by his name we cannot imagine. He is as gentle and polite a man as M. Loyal Devasseur himself; immensely stout withal; and of a beaming aspect. M. Féroce has saved so many people from drowning, and has been decorated with so many medals in consequence, that his stoutness seems a special dispensation of Providence to enable him to wear them; if his girth were the girth of an ordinary man, he could never hang them on, all at once. It is only on very great occasions that M. Féroce displays his shining honours. At other times they lie by, with rolls of manuscript testifying to the causes of their presentation, in a huge glass case in the red-sofa'd salon of his private residence on the beach, where M. Féroce also keeps his family pictures, his portraits of himself as he appears both in bathing life and in private life, his little boats that rock by clockwork, and his other ornamental possessions.

Then, we have a commodious and gay Theatre—or had, for it is burned down now—where the opera was always preceded by a vaudeville, in which (as usual) everybody, down to the little old man with the large hat and the little cane and tassel, who always played either my Uncle or my Papa, suddenly broke out of the dialogue into the mildest vocal snatches, to the great perplexity of unaccustomed strangers from Great Britain, who never could make out when they were singing and when they were talking— and indeed it was pretty much the same. But, the caterers in the way of entertainment to whom we are most beholden, are the Society of Welldoing, who are active all the summer, and give the proceeds of their good works to the poor. Some of the most agreeable fêtes they contrive, are announced as 'Dedicated to the children;' and the taste with which they turn a small public enclosure into an elegant garden beautifully illuminated; and the thorough-going heartiness and energy with which they personally direct the childish pleasures; are supremely delightful. For fivepence a head, we have on these occasions donkey races with English 'Jokeis,' and other rustic sports; lotteries for toys; roundabouts, dancing on the grass to the music of an admirable band, fire-balloons and fireworks. Further, almost every week all through the summer—never mind, now, on what day of the week—there is a fête in some adjoining village (called in that part of the country a Ducasse), where the people—really the people—dance on the green turf in the open air, round a little orchestra, that seems itself to dance, there is such an airy motion of flags and streamers all about it. And we do not suppose that between the Torrid Zone and the North Pole there are to be found male dancers with such astonishingly loose legs, furnished with so many joints in wrong places, utterly unknown to Professor Owen, as those who here disport themselves. Sometimes, the fête appertains to a particular trade; you will see among the cheerful young women at the joint Ducasse of the milliners and tailors, a wholesome knowledge of the art of making common and cheap things uncommon and pretty, by good sense and good taste, that is a practical lesson to any rank of society in a whole island we could mention. The oddest feature of these agreeable scenes is the everlasting Roundabout (we preserve an English word wherever we can, as we are writing the English language), on the wooden horses of which machine grown-up people of all ages are wound round and round with the utmost solemnity, while the proprietor's wife grinds an organ, capable of only one tune, in the centre.

As to the boarding-houses of our French watering-place, they are Legion, and would require a distinct treatise. It is not without a sentiment of national pride that we believe them to contain more bores from the shores of Albion than all the clubs in London. As you walk timidly in their neighbourhood, the very neckcloths and hats of your elderly compatriots cry to you from the stones of the streets, 'We are Bores—avoid us!' We have never overheard at street corners such lunatic scraps of political and social discussion as among these dear countrymen of ours. They believe everything that is impossible and nothing that is true. They carry rumours, and ask questions, and make corrections and improvements on one another, staggering to the human intellect. And they are for ever rushing into the English library, propounding such incomprehensible paradoxes to the fair mistress of that establishment, that we beg to recommend her to her Majesty's gracious consideration as a fit object for a pension.

The English form a considerable part of the population of our French watering-place, and are deservedly addressed and respected in many ways. Some of the surface-addresses to them are odd enough, as when a laundress puts a placard outside her house announcing her possession of that curious British instrument, a 'Mingle;' or when a tavern-keeper provides accommodation for the celebrated English game of 'Nokemdon.' But, to us, it is not the least pleasant feature of our French watering-place that a long and constant fusion of the two great nations there, has taught each to like the other, and to learn from the other, and to rise superior to the absurd prejudices that have lingered among the weak and ignorant in both countries equally.

Drumming and trumpeting of course go on for ever in our French watering-place. Flag-flying is at a premium, too; but, we cheerfully avow that we consider a flag a very pretty object, and that we take such outward signs of innocent liveliness to our heart of hearts. The people, in the town and in the country, are a busy people who work hard; they are sober, temperate, good-humoured, light-hearted, and generally remarkable for their engaging manners. Few just men, not immoderately bilious, could see them in their recreations without very much respecting the character that is so easily, so harmlessly, and so simply, pleased.

BILL-STICKING

If I had an enemy whom I hated—which Heaven forbid!—and if I knew of something which sat heavy on his conscience, I think I would introduce that something into a Posting-Bill, and place a large impression in the hands of an active sticker. I can scarcely imagine a more terrible revenge. I should haunt him, by this means, night and day. I do not mean to say that I would publish his secret, in red letters two feet high, for all the town to read: I would darkly refer to it. It should be between him, and me, and the Posting-Bill. Say, for example, that, at a certain period of his life, my enemy had surreptitiously possessed himself of a key. I would then embark my capital in the lock business, and conduct that business on the advertising principle. In all my placards and advertisements, I would throw up the line Secret Keys. Thus, if my enemy passed an uninhabited house, he would see his conscience glaring down on him from the parapets, and peeping up at him from the cellars. If he took a dead wall in his walk, it would be alive with reproaches. If he sought refuge in an omnibus, the panels thereof would become Belshazzar's palace to him. If he took boat, in a wild endeavour to escape, he would see the fatal words lurking under the arches of the bridges over the Thames. If he walked the streets with downcast eyes, he would recoil from the very stones of the pavement, made eloquent by lamp-black lithograph. If he drove or rode, his way would be blocked up by enormous vans, each proclaiming the same words over and over again from its whole extent of surface. Until, having gradually grown thinner and paler, and having at last totally rejected food, he would miserably perish, and I should be revenged. This conclusion I should, no doubt, celebrate by laughing a hoarse laugh in three syllables, and folding my arms tight upon my chest agreeably to most of the examples of glutted animosity that I have had an opportunity of observing in connexion with the Drama—which, by-the-by, as involving a good deal of noise, appears to me to be occasionally confounded with the Drummer.

The foregoing reflections presented themselves to my mind, the other day, as I contemplated (being newly come to London from the East Riding of Yorkshire, on a house-hunting expedition for next May), an old warehouse which rotting paste and rotting paper had brought down to the condition of an old cheese. It would have been impossible to say, on the most conscientious survey, how much of its front was brick and mortar, and how much decaying and decayed plaster. It was so thickly encrusted with fragments of bills, that no ship's keel after a long voyage could be half so foul. All traces of the broken windows were billed out, the doors were billed across, the water-spout was billed over. The building was shored up to prevent its tumbling into the street; and the very beams erected against it were less wood than paste and paper, they had been so continually posted and reposted. The forlorn dregs of old posters so encumbered this wreck, that there was no hold for new posters, and the stickers had abandoned the place in despair, except one enterprising man who had hoisted the last masquerade to a clear spot near the level of the stack of chimneys where it waved and drooped like a shattered flag. Below the rusty cellar-grating, crumpled remnants of old bills torn down, rotted away in wasting heaps of fallen leaves. Here and there, some of the thick rind of the house had peeled off in strips, and fluttered heavily down, littering the street; but, still, below these rents and gashes, layers of decomposing posters showed themselves, as if they were interminable. I thought the building could never even be pulled down, but in one adhesive heap of rottenness and poster. As to getting in—I don't believe that if the Sleeping Beauty and her Court had been so billed up, the young Prince could have done it.

Knowing all the posters that were yet legible, intimately, and pondering on their ubiquitous nature, I was led into the reflections with which I began this paper, by considering what an awful thing it would be, ever to have wronged—say M. Jullien for example—and to have his avenging name in characters of fire incessantly before my eyes. Or to have injured Madame Tussaud, and undergo a similar retribution. Has any man a self-reproachful thought associated with pills, or ointment? What an avenging spirit to that man is Professor Holloway! Have I sinned in oil? Cabburn pursues me. Have I a dark remembrance associated with any gentlemanly garments, bespoke or ready made? Moses and Son are on my track. Did I ever aim a blow at a defenceless fellow-creature's head? That head eternally being measured for a wig, or that worse head which was bald before it used the balsam, and hirsute afterwards—enforcing the benevolent moral, 'Better to be bald as a Dutch cheese than come to this,'—undoes me. Have I no sore places in my mind which Mechi touches—which Nicoll probes—which no registered article whatever lacerates? Does no discordant note within me thrill responsive to mysterious watchwords, as 'Revalenta Arabica,' or 'Number One St. Paul's Churchyard'? Then may I enjoy life, and be happy.

Lifting up my eyes, as I was musing to this effect, I beheld advancing towards me (I was then on Cornhill, near to the Royal Exchange), a solemn procession of three advertising vans, of first-class dimensions, each drawn by a very little horse. As the cavalcade approached, I was at a loss to reconcile the careless deportment of the drivers of these vehicles, with the terrific announcements they conducted through the city, which being a summary of the contents of a Sunday newspaper, were of the most thrilling kind. Robbery, fire, murder, and the ruin of the United Kingdom—each discharged in a line by itself, like a separate broad-side of red-hot shot—were among the least of the warnings addressed to an unthinking people. Yet, the Ministers of Fate who drove the awful cars, leaned forward with their arms upon their knees in a state of extreme lassitude, for want of any subject of interest. The first man, whose hair I might naturally have expected to see standing on end, scratched his head—one of the smoothest I ever beheld—with profound indifference. The second whistled. The third yawned.

Pausing to dwell upon this apathy, it appeared to me, as the fatal cars came by me, that I descried in the second car, through the portal in which the charioteer was seated, a figure stretched upon the floor. At the same time, I thought I smelt tobacco. The latter impression passed quickly from me; the former remained. Curious to know whether this prostrate figure was the one impressible man of the whole capital who had been stricken insensible by the terrors revealed to him, and whose form had been placed in the car by the charioteer, from motives of humanity, I followed the procession. It turned into Leadenhall-market, and halted at a public-house. Each driver dismounted. I then distinctly heard, proceeding from the second car, where I had dimly seen the prostrate form, the words:

'And a pipe!'

The driver entering the public-house with his fellows, apparently for purposes of refreshment, I could not refrain from mounting on the shaft of the second vehicle, and looking in at the portal. I then beheld, reclining on his back upon the floor, on a kind of mattress or divan, a little man in a shooting-coat. The exclamation 'Dear me' which irresistibly escaped my lips caused him to sit upright, and survey me. I found him to be a good-looking little man of about fifty, with a shining face, a tight head, a bright eye, a moist wink, a quick speech, and a ready air. He had something of a sporting way with him.

He looked at me, and I looked at him, until the driver displaced me by handing in a pint of beer, a pipe, and what I understand is called 'a screw' of tobacco—an object which has the appearance of a curl-paper taken off the barmaid's head, with the curl in it.

'I beg your pardon,' said I, when the removed person of the driver again admitted of my presenting my face at the portal. 'But—excuse my curiosity, which I inherit from my mother—do you live here?'

'That's good, too!' returned the little man, composedly laying aside a pipe he had smoked out, and filling the pipe just brought to him.

'Oh, you don't live here then?' said I.

He shook his head, as he calmly lighted his pipe by means of a German tinder-box, and replied, 'This is my carriage. When things are flat, I take a ride sometimes, and enjoy myself. I am the inventor of these wans.'

His pipe was now alight. He drank his beer all at once, and he smoked and he smiled at me.

'It was a great idea!' said I.

'Not so bad,' returned the little man, with the modesty of merit.

'Might I be permitted to inscribe your name upon the tablets of my memory?' I asked.

'There's not much odds in the name,' returned the little man, '—no

460

name particular—I am the King of the Bill-Stickers.'

'Good gracious!' said I.

The monarch informed me, with a smile, that he had never been crowned or installed with any public ceremonies, but that he was peaceably acknowledged as King of the Bill-Stickers in right of being the oldest and most respected member of 'the old school of bill-sticking.' He likewise gave me to understand that there was a Lord Mayor of the Bill-Stickers, whose genius was chiefly exercised within the limits of the city. He made some allusion, also, to an inferior potentate, called 'Turkey-legs;' but I did not understand that this gentleman was invested with much power. I rather inferred that he derived his title from some peculiarity of gait, and that it was of an honorary character.

'My father,' pursued the King of the Bill-Stickers, 'was Engineer, Beadle, and Bill-Sticker to the parish of St. Andrew's, Holborn, in the year one thousand seven hundred and eighty. My father stuck bills at the time of the riots of London.'

'You must be acquainted with the whole subject of bill-sticking, from that time to the present!' said I.

'Pretty well so,' was the answer.

'Excuse me,' said I; 'but I am a sort of collector—'

"Not Income-tax?' cried His Majesty, hastily removing his pipe from his lips.

'No, no,' said I.

'Water-rate?' said His Majesty.

'No, no,' I returned.

'Gas? Assessed? Sewers?' said His Majesty.

'You misunderstand me,' I replied, soothingly. 'Not that sort of collector at all: a collector of facts.'

'Oh, if it's only facts,' cried the King of the Bill-Stickers, recovering his good-humour, and banishing the great mistrust that had suddenly fallen upon him, 'come in and welcome! If it had been income, or winders, I think I should have pitched you out of the wan, upon my soul!'

Readily complying with the invitation, I squeezed myself in at the small aperture. His Majesty, graciously handing me a little three-legged stool on which I took my seat in a corner, inquired if I smoked.

'I do;—that is, I can,' I answered.

'Pipe and a screw!' said His Majesty to the attendant charioteer. 'Do you prefer a dry smoke, or do you moisten it?'

As unmitigated tobacco produces most disturbing effects upon my system (indeed, if I had perfect moral courage, I doubt if I should smoke at all, under any circumstances), I advocated moisture, and begged the Sovereign of the Bill-Stickers to name his usual liquor, and to concede to me the privilege of paying for it. After some delicate reluctance on his part, we were provided, through the instrumentality of the attendant charioteer, with a can of cold rum-and-water, flavoured with sugar and lemon. We were also furnished with a tumbler, and I was provided with a pipe. His Majesty, then observing that we might combine business with conversation, gave the word for the car to proceed; and, to my great delight, we jogged away at a foot pace.

I say to my great delight, because I am very fond of novelty, and it was a new sensation to be jolting through the tumult of the city in that secluded Temple, partly open to the sky, surrounded by the roar without, and seeing nothing but the clouds. Occasionally, blows from whips fell heavily on the Temple's walls, when by stopping up the road longer than usual, we irritated carters and coachmen to madness; but they fell harmless upon us within and disturbed not the serenity of our peaceful retreat. As I looked upward, I felt, I should imagine, like the Astronomer Royal. I was enchanted by the contrast between the freezing nature of our external mission on the blood of the populace, and the perfect composure reigning within those sacred precincts: where His Majesty, reclining easily on his left arm, smoked his pipe and drank his rum-and-water from his own side of the tumbler, which stood impartially between us. As I looked down from the clouds and caught his royal eye, he understood my reflections. 'I have an idea,' he observed, with an upward glance, 'of training scarlet runners across in the season,—making a arbour of it,—and sometimes taking tea in the same, according to the song.'

I nodded approval.

'And here you repose and think?' said I.

'And think,' said he, 'of posters—walls—and hoardings.'

We were both silent, contemplating the vastness of the subject. I remembered a surprising fancy of dear Thomas Hood's, and wondered whether this monarch ever sighed to repair to the great wall of China, and stick bills all over it.

'And so,' said he, rousing himself, 'it's facts as you collect?'

'Facts,' said I.

'The facts of bill-sticking,' pursued His Majesty, in a benignant manner, 'as known to myself, air as following. When my father was Engineer, Beadle, and Bill-Sticker to the parish of St. Andrew's, Holborn, he employed women to post bills for him. He employed women to post bills at the time of the riots of London. He died at the age of seventy-five year, and was buried by the murdered Eliza Grimwood, over in the Waterloo Road.'

As this was somewhat in the nature of a royal speech, I listened with deference and silently. His Majesty, taking a scroll from his pocket, proceeded, with great distinctness, to pour out the following flood of information:—

'"The bills being at that period mostly proclamations and declarations, and which were only a demy size, the manner of posting the bills (as they did not use brushes) was by means of a piece of wood which they called a 'dabber.' Thus things continued till such time as the State Lottery was passed, and then the printers began to print larger bills, and men were employed instead of women, as the State Lottery Commissioners then began to send men all over England to post bills, and would keep them out for six or eight months at a time, and they were called by the London bill-stickers 'trampers,' their wages at the time being ten shillings per day, besides expenses. They used sometimes to be stationed in large towns for five or six months together, distributing the schemes to all the houses in the town. And then there were more caricature wood-block engravings for posting-bills than there are at the present time, the principal printers, at that time, of posting-bills being Messrs. Evans and Ruffy, of Budge Row; Thoroughgood and Whiting, of the present day; and Messrs. Gye and Balne, Gracechurch Street, City. The largest bills printed at that period were a two-sheet double crown; and when they commenced printing four-sheet bills, two bill-stickers would work together. They had no settled wages per week, but had a fixed price for their work, and the London bill-stickers, during a lottery week, have been known to earn, each, eight or nine pounds per week, till the day of drawing; likewise the men who carried boards in the street used to have one pound per week, and the bill-stickers at that time would not allow any one to wilfully cover or destroy their bills, as they had a society amongst themselves, and very frequently dined together at some public-house where they used to go of an evening to have their work delivered out untoe 'em.'"

All this His Majesty delivered in a gallant manner; posting it, as it were, before me, in a great proclamation. I took advantage of the pause he now made, to inquire what a 'two-sheet double crown' might express?

'A two-sheet double crown,' replied the King, 'is a bill thirty-nine inches wide by thirty inches high.'

'Is it possible,' said I, my mind reverting to the gigantic admonitions we were then displaying to the multitude—which were as infants to some of the posting-bills on the rotten old warehouse—'that some few years ago the largest bill was no larger than that?'

'The fact,' returned the King, 'is undoubtedly so.' Here he instantly rushed again into the scroll.

'"Since the abolishing of the State Lottery all that good feeling has gone, and nothing but jealousy exists, through the rivalry of each other. Several bill-sticking companies have started, but have failed. The first party that started a company was twelve year ago; but what was left of the old school and their dependants joined together and opposed them. And for some time we were quiet again, till a printer of Hatton Garden formed a company by hiring the sides of houses; but he was not supported by the public, and he left his wooden frames fixed up for rent. The last company that started, took advantage of the New Police Act, and hired of Messrs. Grissell and Peto the hoarding of Trafalgar Square, and established a bill-sticking office in Cursitor Street, Chancery Lane, and engaged some of the new bill-stickers to do their work, and for a time got the half of all our work, and with such spirit did they carry on their opposition towards us, that they used to give us in charge before the magistrate, and get us fined; but they found it so expensive, that they could not keep it up, for they were always employing a lot of ruffians from the Seven Dials to come and fight us; and on one occasion the old bill-stickers went to Trafalgar Square to attempt to post bills, when they were given in custody by the watchman in their employ, and fined at Queen Square five pounds, as they would not allow any of us to speak in the office; but when they were gone, we had an interview with the magistrate, who mitigated the fine to fifteen shillings. During the time the men were waiting for the fine, this company started off to a public-house that we were in the habit of using, and waited for us coming back, where a fighting scene took place that beggars description. Shortly after this, the principal one day came and shook hands with us, and acknowledged that he had broken up the company, and that he himself had lost five hundred pound in trying to overthrow us. We then took possession of the hoarding in Trafalgar Square; but Messrs. Grissell and Peto would not allow us to post our bills on the said hoarding without paying them—and from first to last we paid upwards of two hundred pounds for that hoarding, and likewise the hoarding of the Reform Club-house, Pall Mall.'"

His Majesty, being now completely out of breath, laid down his scroll (which he appeared to have finished), puffed at his pipe, and took some rum-and-water. I embraced the opportunity of asking how many divisions the art and mystery of bill-sticking comprised? He replied, three—auctioneers' bill-sticking, theatrical bill-sticking, general bill-sticking.

'The auctioneers' porters,' said the King, 'who do their bill-sticking, are mostly respectable and intelligent, and generally well paid for their work, whether in town or country. The price paid by the principal auctioneers for country work is nine shillings per day; that is, seven shillings for day's work, one shilling for lodging, and one for paste. Town work is five shillings a day, including paste.'

'Town work must be rather hot work,' said I, 'if there be many of those fighting scenes that beggar description, among the bill-stickers?'

'Well,' replied the King, 'I an't a stranger, I assure you, to black eyes; a bill-sticker ought to know how to handle his fists a bit. As to that row I have mentioned, that grew out of competition, conducted in an uncompromising spirit. Besides a man in a horse-and-shay continually following us about, the company had a watchman on duty, night and day, to prevent us sticking bills upon the hoarding in Trafalgar Square. We went there, early one morning, to stick bills and to black-wash their bills if we were interfered with. We were interfered with, and I gave the word for laying on the wash. It was laid on—pretty brisk—and we were all taken to Queen Square: but they couldn't fine me. I knew that,'—with a bright smile—'I'd only give directions—I was only the General.' Charmed with this monarch's affability, I inquired if he had ever hired a hoarding himself.

'Hired a large one,' he replied, 'opposite the Lyceum Theatre, when the buildings was there. Paid thirty pound for it; let out places on it, and called it "The External Paper-Hanging Station." But it didn't answer. Ah!' said His Majesty thoughtfully, as he filled the glass, 'Bill-stickers have a deal to contend with. The bill-sticking clause was got into the Police Act by a member of Parliament that employed me at his election. The clause is pretty stiff respecting where bills go; but he didn't mind where his bills went. It was all right enough, so long as they was his bills!'

Fearful that I observed a shadow of misanthropy on the King's cheerful face, I asked whose ingenious invention that was, which I greatly admired, of sticking bills under the arches of the bridges.

'Mine!' said His Majesty. 'I was the first that ever stuck a bill under a bridge! Imitators soon rose up, of course.—When don't they? But they stuck 'em at low-water, and the tide came and swept the bills clean away. I knew that!' The King laughed.

'What may be the name of that instrument, like an immense fishing-rod,' I inquired, 'with which bills are posted on high places?'

'The joints,' returned His Majesty. 'Now, we use the joints where formerly we used ladders—as they do still in country places. Once, when Madame' (Vestris, understood) 'was playing in Liverpool, another bill-sticker and me were at it together on the wall outside the Clarence Dock—me with the joints—him on a ladder. Lord! I had my bill up, right over his head, yards above him, ladder and all, while he was crawling to his work. The people going in and out of the docks, stood and laughed!—It's about thirty years since the joints come in.'

'Are there any bill-stickers who can't read?' I took the liberty of inquiring.

'Some,' said the King. 'But they know which is the right side up'ards of their work. They keep it as it's given out to 'em. I have seen a bill or so stuck wrong side up'ards. But it's very rare.'

Our discourse sustained some interruption at this point, by the procession of cars occasioning a stoppage of about three-quarters of a mile in length, as nearly as I could judge. His Majesty, however, entreating me not to be discomposed by the contingent uproar, smoked with great placidity, and surveyed the firmament.

When we were again in motion, I begged to be informed what was the largest poster His Majesty had ever seen. The King replied, 'A thirty-six sheet poster.' I gathered, also, that there were about a hundred and fifty bill-stickers in London, and that His Majesty considered an average hand equal to the posting of one hundred bills (single sheets) in a day. The King was of opinion, that, although posters had much increased in size, they had not increased in number; as the abolition of the State Lotteries had occasioned a great falling off, especially in the country. Over and above which change, I bethought myself that the custom of advertising in newspapers had greatly increased. The completion of many London improvements, as Trafalgar Square (I particularly observed the singularity of His Majesty's calling that an improvement), the Royal Exchange, &c., had of late years reduced the number of advantageous posting-places. Bill-Stickers at present rather confine themselves to districts, than to particular descriptions of work. One man would strike over Whitechapel, another would take round Houndsditch, Shoreditch, and the City Road; one (the King said) would stick to the Surrey side; another would make a beat of the West-end.

His Majesty remarked, with some approach to severity, on the neglect of delicacy and taste, gradually introduced into the trade by the new school: a profligate and inferior race of impostors who took jobs at almost any price, to the detriment of the old school, and the confusion of their own misguided employers. He considered that the trade was overdone with competition, and observed speaking of his subjects, 'There are too many of 'em.' He believed, still, that things were a little better than they had been; adducing, as a proof, the fact that particular posting places were now reserved, by common consent, for particular posters; those places, however, must be regularly occupied by those posters, or, they lapsed and fell into other hands. It was of no use giving a man a Drury Lane bill this week and not next. Where was it to go? He was of opinion that going to the expense of putting up your own board on which your sticker could display your own bills, was the only complete way of posting yourself at the present time; but, even to effect this, on payment of a shilling a week to the keepers of steamboat piers and other such places, you must be able, besides, to give orders for theatres and public exhibitions, or you would be sure to be cut out by somebody. His Majesty regarded the passion for orders, as one of the most unappeasable appetites of human nature. If there were a building, or if there were repairs, going on, anywhere, you could generally stand something and make it right with the foreman of the works; but, orders would be expected from you, and the man who could give the most orders was the man who would come off best. There was this other objectionable point, in orders, that workmen sold them for drink, and often sold them to persons who were likewise troubled with the weakness of thirst: which led (His Majesty said) to the presentation of your orders at Theatre doors, by individuals who were 'too shakery' to derive intellectual profit from the entertainments, and who brought a scandal on you. Finally, His Majesty said that you could hardly put too little in a poster; what you wanted, was, two or three good catch-lines for the eye to rest on—then, leave it alone—and there you were!

These are the minutes of my conversation with His Majesty, as I noted them down shortly afterwards. I am not aware that I have been betrayed into any alteration or suppression. The manner of the King was frank in the extreme; and he seemed to me to avoid, at once that slight tendency to repetition which may have been observed in the conversation of His Majesty King George the Third, and—that slight under-current of egotism which the curious observer may perhaps detect in the conversation of Napoleon Bonaparte.

I must do the King the justice to say that it was I, and not he, who closed the dialogue. At this juncture, I became the subject of a remarkable optical delusion; the legs of my stool appeared to me to double up; the car to spin round and round with great violence; and a mist to arise between myself and His Majesty. In addition to these sensations, I felt extremely unwell. I refer these unpleasant effects, either to the paste with which the posters were affixed to the van: which may have contained some small portion of arsenic; or, to the printer's ink, which may have contained some equally deleterious ingredient. Of this, I cannot be sure. I am only sure that I was not affected, either by the smoke, or the rum-and-water. I was assisted out of the vehicle, in a state of mind which I have only experienced in two other places—I allude to the Pier at Dover, and to the corresponding portion of the town of Calais—and sat upon a door-step until I recovered. The procession had then disappeared. I have since looked anxiously for the King in several other cars, but I have not yet had the happiness of seeing His Majesty.

'BIRTHS. MRS. MEEK, OF A SON

My name is Meek. I am, in fact, Mr. Meek. That son is mine and Mrs. Meek's. When I saw the announcement in the Times, I dropped the paper. I had put it in, myself, and paid for it, but it looked so noble that it overpowered me.

As soon as I could compose my feelings, I took the paper up to Mrs. Meek's bedside. 'Maria Jane,' said I (I allude to Mrs. Meek), 'you are now a public character.' We read the review of our child, several times, with feelings of the strongest emotion; and I sent the boy who cleans the boots and shoes, to the office for fifteen copies. No reduction was made on taking that quantity.

It is scarcely necessary for me to say, that our child had been expected. In fact, it had been expected, with comparative confidence, for some months. Mrs. Meek's mother, who resides with us—of the name of Bigby—had made every preparation for its admission to our circle.

I hope and believe I am a quiet man. I will go farther. I know I am a quiet man. My constitution is tremulous, my voice was never loud, and, in point of stature, I have been from infancy, small. I have the greatest respect for Maria Jane's Mama. She is a most remarkable woman. I honour Maria Jane's Mama. In my opinion she would storm a town, single-handed, with a hearth-broom, and carry it. I have never known her to yield any point whatever, to mortal man. She is calculated to terrify the stoutest heart.

Still—but I will not anticipate.

The first intimation I had, of any preparations being in progress, on the part of Maria Jane's Mama, was one afternoon, several months ago. I came home earlier than usual from the office, and, proceeding into the dining-room, found an obstruction behind the door, which prevented it from opening freely. It was an obstruction of a soft nature. On looking in, I found it to be a female.

The female in question stood in the corner behind the door, consuming

Sherry Wine. From the nutty smell of that beverage pervading the apartment, I have no doubt she was consuming a second glassful. She wore a black bonnet of large dimensions, and was copious in figure. The expression of her countenance was severe and discontented. The words to which she gave utterance on seeing me, were these, 'Oh, git along with you, Sir, if you please; me and Mrs. Bigby don't want no male parties here!'

That female was Mrs. Prodgit.

I immediately withdrew, of course. I was rather hurt, but I made no remark. Whether it was that I showed a lowness of spirits after dinner, in consequence of feeling that I seemed to intrude, I cannot say. But, Maria Jane's Mama said to me on her retiring for the night: in a low distinct voice, and with a look of reproach that completely subdued me: 'George Meek, Mrs. Prodgit is your wife's nurse!'

I bear no ill-will towards Mrs. Prodgit. Is it likely that I, writing this with tears in my eyes, should be capable of deliberate animosity towards a female, so essential to the welfare of Maria Jane? I am willing to admit that Fate may have been to blame, and not Mrs. Prodgit; but, it is undeniably true, that the latter female brought desolation and devastation into my lowly dwelling.

We were happy after her first appearance; we were sometimes exceedingly so. But, whenever the parlour door was opened, and 'Mrs. Prodgit!' announced (and she was very often announced), misery ensued. I could not bear Mrs. Prodgit's look. I felt that I was far from wanted, and had no business to exist in Mrs. Prodgit's presence. Between Maria Jane's Mama, and Mrs. Prodgit, there was a dreadful, secret, understanding—a dark mystery and conspiracy, pointing me out as a being to be shunned. I appeared to have done something that was evil. Whenever Mrs. Prodgit called, after dinner, I retired to my dressing-room—where the temperature is very low indeed, in the wintry time of the year—and sat looking at my frosty breath as it rose before me, and at my rack of boots; a serviceable article of furniture, but never, in my opinion, an exhilarating object. The length of the councils that were held with Mrs. Prodgit, under these circumstances, I will not attempt to describe. I will merely remark, that Mrs. Prodgit always consumed Sherry Wine while the deliberations were in progress; that they always ended in Maria Jane's being in wretched spirits on the sofa; and that Maria Jane's Mama always received me, when I was recalled, with a look of desolate triumph that too plainly said, 'Now, George Meek! You see my child, Maria Jane, a ruin, and I hope you are satisfied!'

I pass, generally, over the period that intervened between the day when Mrs. Prodgit entered her protest against male parties, and the ever-memorable midnight when I brought her to my unobtrusive home in a cab, with an extremely large box on the roof, and a bundle, a bandbox, and a basket, between the driver's legs. I have no objection to Mrs. Prodgit (aided and abetted by Mrs. Bigby, who I never can forget is the parent of Maria Jane) taking entire possession of my unassuming establishment. In the recesses of my own breast, the thought may linger that a man in possession cannot be so dreadful as a woman, and that woman Mrs. Prodgit; but, I ought to bear a good deal, and I hope I can, and do. Huffing and snubbing, prey upon my feelings; but, I can bear them without complaint. They may tell in the long run; I may be hustled about, from post to pillar, beyond my strength; nevertheless, I wish to avoid giving rise to words in the family.

The voice of Nature, however, cries aloud in behalf of Augustus George, my infant son. It is for him that I wish to utter a few plaintive household words. I am not at all angry; I am mild—but miserable.

I wish to know why, when my child, Augustus George, was expected in our circle, a provision of pins was made, as if the little stranger were a criminal who was to be put to the torture immediately, on his arrival, instead of a holy babe? I wish to know why haste was made to stick those pins all over his innocent form, in every direction? I wish to be informed why light and air are excluded from Augustus George, like poisons? Why, I ask, is my unoffending infant so hedged into a basket-bedstead, with dimity and calico, with miniature sheets and blankets, that I can only hear him snuffle (and no wonder!) deep down under the pink hood of a little bathing-machine, and can never peruse even so much of his lineaments as his nose?

Was I expected to be the father of a French Roll, that the brushes of

All Nations were laid in, to rasp Augustus George? Am I to be told that his sensitive skin was ever intended by Nature to have rashes brought out upon it, by the premature and incessant use of those formidable little instruments?

Is my son a Nutmeg, that he is to be grated on the stiff edges of sharp frills? Am I the parent of a Muslin boy, that his yielding surface is to be crimped and small plaited? Or is my child composed of Paper or of Linen, that impressions of the finer getting-up art, practised by the laundress, are to be printed off, all over his soft arms and legs, as I constantly observe them? The starch enters his soul; who can wonder that he cries?

Was Augustus George intended to have limbs, or to be born a Torso? I presume that limbs were the intention, as they are the usual practice. Then, why are my poor child's limbs fettered and tied up? Am I to be told that there is any analogy between Augustus George Meek and Jack Sheppard?

Analyse Castor Oil at any Institution of Chemistry that may be agreed upon, and inform me what resemblance, in taste, it bears to that natural provision which it is at once the pride and duty of Maria Jane to administer to Augustus George! Yet, I charge Mrs. Prodgit (aided and abetted by Mrs. Bigby) with systematically forcing Castor Oil on my innocent son, from the first hour of his birth. When that medicine, in its efficient action, causes internal disturbance to Augustus George, I charge Mrs. Prodgit (aided and abetted by Mrs. Bigby) with insanely and inconsistently administering opium to allay the storm she has raised! What is the meaning of this?

If the days of Egyptian Mummies are past, how dare Mrs. Prodgit require, for the use of my son, an amount of flannel and linen that would carpet my humble roof? Do I wonder that she requires it? No! This morning, within an hour, I beheld this agonising sight. I beheld my son—Augustus George—in Mrs. Prodgit's hands, and on Mrs. Prodgit's knee, being dressed. He was at the moment, comparatively speaking, in a state of nature; having nothing on, but an extremely short shirt, remarkably disproportionate to the length of his usual outer garments. Trailing from Mrs. Prodgit's lap, on the floor, was a long narrow roller or bandage—I should say of several yards in extent. In this, I SAW Mrs. Prodgit tightly roll the body of my unoffending infant, turning him over and over, now presenting his unconscious face upwards, now the back of his bald head, until the unnatural feat was accomplished, and the bandage secured by a pin, which I have every reason to believe entered the body of my only child. In this tourniquet, he passes the present phase of his existence. Can I know it, and smile!

I fear I have been betrayed into expressing myself warmly, but I feel deeply. Not for myself; for Augustus George. I dare not interfere. Will any one? Will any publication? Any doctor? Any parent? Any body? I do not complain that Mrs. Prodgit (aided and abetted by Mrs. Bigby) entirely alienates Maria Jane's affections from me, and interposes an impassable barrier between us. I do not complain of being made of no account. I do not want to be of any account. But, Augustus George is a production of Nature (I cannot think otherwise), and I claim that he should be treated with some remote reference to Nature. In my opinion, Mrs. Prodgit is, from first to last, a convention and a superstition. Are all the faculty afraid of Mrs. Prodgit? If not, why don't they take her in hand and improve her?

P.S. Maria Jane's Mama boasts of her own knowledge of the subject, and says she brought up seven children besides Maria Jane. But how do I know that she might not have brought them up much better? Maria Jane herself is far from strong, and is subject to headaches, and nervous indigestion. Besides which, I learn from the statistical tables that one child in five dies within the first year of its life; and one child in three, within the fifth. That don't look as if we could never improve in these particulars, I think!

P.P.S. Augustus George is in convulsions.

LYING AWAKE

'My uncle lay with his eyes half closed, and his nightcap drawn almost down to his nose. His fancy was already wandering, and began to mingle up the present scene with the crater of Vesuvius, the French Opera, the Coliseum at Rome, Dolly's Chop-house in London, and all the farrago of noted places with which the brain of a traveller is crammed; in a word, he was just falling asleep.'

Thus, that delightful writer, Washington Irving, in his Tales of a Traveller. But, it happened to me the other night to be lying: not with my eyes half closed, but with my eyes wide open; not with my nightcap drawn almost down to my nose, for on sanitary principles I never wear a nightcap: but with my hair pitchforked and touzled all over the pillow; not just falling asleep by any means, but glaringly, persistently, and obstinately, broad awake. Perhaps, with no scientific intention or invention, I was illustrating the theory of the Duality of the Brain; perhaps one part of my brain, being wakeful, sat up to watch the other part which was sleepy. Be that as it may, something in me was as desirous to go to sleep as it possibly could be, but something else in me would not go to sleep, and was as obstinate as George the Third.

Thinking of George the Third—for I devote this paper to my train of thoughts as I lay awake: most people lying awake sometimes, and having some interest in the subject—put me in mind of Benjamin Franklin, and so Benjamin Franklin's paper on the art of procuring pleasant dreams, which would seem necessarily to include the art of going to sleep, came into my head. Now, as I often used to read that paper when I was a very small boy, and as I recollect everything I read then as perfectly as I forget everything I read now, I quoted 'Get out of bed, beat up and turn your pillow, shake the bed-clothes well with at least twenty shakes, then throw the bed open and leave it to cool; in the meanwhile, continuing undrest, walk about your chamber. When you begin to feel the cold air unpleasant, then return to your bed, and you will soon fall asleep, and your sleep will be sweet and pleasant.'

Not a bit of it! I performed the whole ceremony, and if it were possible for me to be more saucer-eyed than I was before, that was the only result that came of it.

Except Niagara. The two quotations from Washington Irving and Benjamin Franklin may have put it in my head by an American association of ideas; but there I was, and the Horse-shoe Fall was thundering and tumbling in my eyes and ears, and the very rainbows that I left upon the spray when I really did last look upon it, were beautiful to see. The night-light being quite as plain, however, and sleep seeming to be many thousand miles further off than Niagara, I made up my mind to think a little about Sleep; which I no sooner did than I whirled off in spite of myself to Drury Lane Theatre, and there saw a great actor and dear friend of mine (whom I had been thinking of in the day) playing Macbeth, and heard him apostrophising 'the death of each day's life,' as I have heard him many a time, in the days that are gone.

But, Sleep. I will think about Sleep. I am determined to think (this is the way I went on) about Sleep. I must hold the word Sleep, tight and fast, or I shall be off at a tangent in half a second. I feel myself unaccountably straying, already, into Clare Market. Sleep. It would be curious, as illustrating the equality of sleep, to inquire how many of its phenomena are common to all classes, to all degrees of wealth and poverty, to every grade of education and ignorance. Here, for example, is her Majesty Queen Victoria in her palace, this present blessed night, and here is Winking Charley, a sturdy vagrant, in one of her Majesty's jails. Her Majesty has fallen, many thousands of times, from that same Tower, which I claim a right to tumble off now and then. So has Winking Charley. Her Majesty in her sleep has opened or prorogued Parliament, or has held a Drawing Room, attired in some very scanty dress, the deficiencies and improprieties of which have caused her great uneasiness. I, in my degree, have suffered unspeakable agitation of mind from taking the chair at a public dinner at the London Tavern in my night-clothes, which not all the courtesy of my kind friend and host Mr. Bathe could persuade me were quite adapted to the occasion. Winking Charley has been repeatedly tried in a worse condition. Her Majesty is no stranger to a vault or firmament, of a sort of floorcloth, with an indistinct pattern distantly resembling eyes, which occasionally obtrudes itself on her repose. Neither am I. Neither is Winking Charley. It is quite common to all three of us to skim along with airy strides a little above the ground; also to hold, with the deepest interest, dialogues with various people, all represented by ourselves; and to be at our wit's end to know what they are going to tell us; and to be indescribably astonished by the secrets they disclose. It is probable that we have all three committed murders and hidden bodies. It is pretty certain that we have all desperately wanted to cry out, and have had no voice; that we have all gone to the play and not been able to get in; that we have all dreamed much more of our youth than of our later lives; that—I have lost it! The thread's broken.

And up I go. I, lying here with the night-light before me, up I go, for no reason on earth that I can find out, and drawn by no links that are visible to me, up the Great Saint Bernard! I have lived in Switzerland, and rambled among the mountains; but, why I should go there now, and why up the Great Saint Bernard in preference to any other mountain, I have no idea. As I lie here broad awake, and with every sense so sharpened that I can distinctly hear distant noises inaudible to me at another time, I make that journey, as I really did, on the same summer day, with the same happy party—ah! two since dead, I grieve to think—and there is the same track, with the same black wooden arms to point the way, and there are the same storm-refuges here and there; and there is the same snow falling at the top, and there are the same frosty mists, and there is the same intensely cold convent with its ménagerie smell, and the same breed of dogs fast dying out, and the same breed of jolly young monks whom I mourn to know as humbugs, and the same convent parlour with its piano and the sitting round the fire, and the same supper, and the same lone night in a cell, and the same bright fresh morning when going out into the highly rarefied air was like a plunge into an icy bath. Now, see here what comes along; and why does this thing stalk into my mind on the top of a Swiss mountain!

It is a figure that I once saw, just after dark, chalked upon a door in a little back lane near a country church—my first church. How young a child I may have been at the time I don't know, but it horrified me so intensely—in connexion with the churchyard, I suppose, for it smokes a pipe, and has a big hat with each of its ears sticking out in a horizontal line under the brim, and is not in itself more oppressive than a mouth from ear to ear, a pair of goggle eyes, and hands like two bunches of carrots, five in each, can make it—that it is still vaguely alarming to me to recall (as I have often done before, lying awake) the running home, the looking behind, the horror, of its following me; though whether disconnected from the door, or door and all, I can't say, and perhaps never could. It lays a disagreeable train. I must resolve to think of something on the voluntary principle.

The balloon ascents of this last season. They will do to think about, while I lie awake, as well as anything else. I must hold them tight though, for I feel them sliding away, and in their stead are the Mannings, husband and wife, hanging on the top of Horse-monger Lane Jail. In connexion with which dismal spectacle, I recall this curious fantasy of the mind. That, having beheld that execution, and having left those two forms dangling on the top of the entrance gateway—the man's, a limp, loose suit of clothes as if the man had gone out of them; the woman's, a fine shape, so elaborately corseted and artfully dressed, that it was quite unchanged in its trim appearance as it slowly swung from side to side—I never could, by my uttermost efforts, for some weeks, present the outside of that prison to myself (which the terrible impression I had received continually obliged me to do) without presenting it with the two figures still hanging in the morning air. Until, strolling past the gloomy place one night, when the street was deserted and quiet, and actually seeing that the bodies were not there, my fancy was persuaded, as it were, to take them down and bury them within the precincts of the jail, where they have lain ever since.

The balloon ascents of last season. Let me reckon them up. There were the horse, the bull, the parachute,—and the tumbler hanging on—chiefly by his toes, I believe—below the car. Very wrong, indeed, and decidedly to be stopped. But, in connexion with these and similar dangerous exhibitions, it strikes me that that portion of the public whom they entertain, is unjustly reproached. Their pleasure is in the difficulty overcome. They are a public of great faith, and are quite confident that the gentleman will not fall off the horse, or the lady off the bull or out of the parachute, and that the tumbler has a firm hold with his toes. They do not go to see the adventurer vanquished, but triumphant. There is no parallel in public combats between men and beasts, because nobody can answer for the particular beast—unless it were always the same beast, in which case it would be a mere stage-show, which the same public would go in the same state of mind to see, entirely believing in the brute being beforehand safely subdued by the man. That they are not accustomed to calculate hazards and dangers with any nicety, we may know from their rash exposure of themselves in overcrowded steamboats, and unsafe conveyances and places of all kinds. And I cannot help thinking that instead of railing, and attributing savage motives to a people naturally well disposed and humane, it is better to teach them, and lead them argumentatively and reasonably—for they are very reasonable, if you will discuss a matter with them—to more considerate and wise conclusions.

This is a disagreeable intrusion! Here is a man with his throat cut, dashing towards me as I lie awake! A recollection of an old story of a kinsman of mine, who, going home one foggy winter night to Hampstead, when London was much smaller and the road lonesome, suddenly encountered such a figure rushing past him, and presently two keepers from a madhouse in pursuit. A very unpleasant creature indeed, to come into my mind unbidden, as I lie awake.

—The balloon ascents of last season. I must return to the balloons. Why did the bleeding man start out of them? Never mind; if I inquire, he will be back again. The balloons. This particular public have inherently a great pleasure in the contemplation of physical difficulties overcome; mainly, as I take it, because the lives of a large majority of them are exceedingly monotonous and real, and further, are a struggle against continual difficulties, and further still, because anything in the form of accidental injury, or any kind of illness or disability is so very serious in their own sphere. I will explain this seeming paradox of mine. Take the case of a Christmas Pantomime. Surely nobody supposes that the young mother in the pit who falls into fits of laughter when the baby is boiled or sat upon, would be at all diverted by such an occurrence off the stage. Nor is the decent workman in the gallery, who is transported beyond the ignorant present by the delight with which he sees

479

a stout gentleman pushed out of a two pair of stairs window, to be slandered by the suspicion that he would be in the least entertained by such a spectacle in any street in London, Paris, or New York. It always appears to me that the secret of this enjoyment lies in the temporary superiority to the common hazards and mischances of life; in seeing casualties, attended when they really occur with bodily and mental suffering, tears, and poverty, happen through a very rough sort of poetry without the least harm being done to any one—the pretence of distress in a pantomime being so broadly humorous as to be no pretence at all. Much as in the comic fiction I can understand the mother with a very vulnerable baby at home, greatly relishing the invulnerable baby on the stage, so in the Cremorne reality I can understand the mason who is always liable to fall off a scaffold in his working jacket and to be carried to the hospital, having an infinite admiration of the radiant personage in spangles who goes into the clouds upon a bull, or upside down, and who, he takes it for granted—not reflecting upon the thing—has, by uncommon skill and dexterity, conquered such mischances as those to which he and his acquaintance are continually exposed.

I wish the Morgue in Paris would not come here as I lie awake, with its ghastly beds, and the swollen saturated clothes hanging up, and the water dripping, dripping all day long, upon that other swollen saturated something in the corner, like a heap of crushed over-ripe figs that I have seen in Italy! And this detestable Morgue comes back again at the head of a procession of forgotten ghost stories. This will never do. I must think of something else as I lie awake; or, like that sagacious animal in the United States who recognised the colonel who was such a dead shot, I am a gone 'Coon. What shall I think of? The late brutal assaults. Very good subject. The late brutal assaults.

(Though whether, supposing I should see, here before me as I lie awake, the awful phantom described in one of those ghost stories, who, with a head-dress of shroud, was always seen looking in through a certain glass door at a certain dead hour—whether, in such a case it would be the least consolation to me to know on philosophical grounds that it was merely my imagination, is a question I can't help asking myself by the way.)

The late brutal assaults. I strongly question the expediency of advocating the revival of whipping for those crimes. It is a natural and generous impulse to be indignant at the perpetration of inconceivable brutality, but I doubt the whipping panacea gravely. Not in the least regard or pity for the criminal, whom I hold in far lower estimation than a mad wolf, but in consideration for the general tone and feeling, which is very much improved since the whipping times. It is bad for a people to be familiarised with such punishments. When the whip went out of Bridewell, and ceased to be flourished at the carts tail and at the whipping-post, it began to fade out of madhouses, and workhouses, and schools and families, and to give place to a better system everywhere, than cruel driving. It would be hasty, because a few brutes may be inadequately punished, to revive, in any aspect, what, in so many aspects, society is hardly yet happily rid of. The whip is a very contagious kind of thing, and difficult to confine within one set of bounds. Utterly abolish punishment by fine—a barbarous device, quite as much out of date as wager by battle, but particularly connected in the vulgar mind with this class of offence—at least quadruple the term of imprisonment for aggravated assaults—and above all let us, in such cases, have no Pet Prisoning, vain glorifying, strong soup, and roasted meats, but hard work, and one unchanging and uncompromising dietary of bread and water, well or ill; and we shall do much better than by going down into the dark to grope for the whip among the rusty fragments of the rack, and the branding iron, and the chains and gibbet from the public roads, and the weights that pressed men to death in the cells of Newgate.

I had proceeded thus far, when I found I had been lying awake so long that the very dead began to wake too, and to crowd into my thoughts most sorrowfully. Therefore, I resolved to lie awake no more, but to get up and go out for a night walk—which resolution was an acceptable relief to me, as I dare say it may prove now to a great many more.

THE GHOST OF ART

I AM a bachelor, residing in rather a dreary set of chambers in the Temple. They are situated in a square court of high houses, which would be a complete well, but for the want of water and the absence of a bucket. I live at the top of the house, among the tiles and sparrows. Like the little man in the nursery-story, I live by myself, and all the bread and cheese I get—which is not much—I put upon a shelf. I need scarcely add, perhaps, that I am in love, and that the father of my charming Julia objects to our union.

I mention these little particulars as I might deliver a letter of introduction. The reader is now acquainted with me, and perhaps will condescend to listen to my narrative.

I am naturally of a dreamy turn of mind; and my abundant leisure—for I am called to the Bar—coupled with much lonely listening to the twittering of sparrows, and the pattering of rain, has encouraged that disposition. In my 'top set' I hear the wind howl on a winter night, when the man on the ground floor believes it is perfectly still weather. The dim lamps with which our Honourable Society (supposed to be as yet unconscious of the new discovery called Gas) make the horrors of the staircase visible, deepen the gloom which generally settles on my soul when I go home at night.

I am in the Law, but not of it. I can't exactly make out what it means. I sit in Westminster Hall sometimes (in character) from ten to four; and when I go out of Court, I don't know whether I am standing on my wig or my boots.

It appears to me (I mention this in confidence) as if there were too much talk and too much law—as if some grains of truth were started overboard into a tempestuous sea of chaff.

All this may make me mystical. Still, I am confident that what I am going to describe myself as having seen and heard, I actually did see and hear.

It is necessary that I should observe that I have a great delight in pictures. I am no painter myself, but I have studied pictures and written about them. I have seen all the most famous pictures in the world; my education and reading have been sufficiently general to possess me beforehand with a knowledge of most of the subjects to which a Painter is likely to have recourse; and, although I might be in some doubt as to the rightful fashion of the scabbard of King Lear's sword, for instance, I think I should know King Lear tolerably well, if I happened to meet with him.

I go to all the Modern Exhibitions every season, and of course I revere the Royal Academy. I stand by its forty Academical articles almost as firmly as I stand by the thirty-nine Articles of the Church of England. I am convinced that in neither case could there be, by any rightful possibility, one article more or less.

It is now exactly three years—three years ago, this very month—since I went from Westminster to the Temple, one Thursday afternoon, in a cheap steamboat. The sky was black, when I imprudently walked on board. It began to thunder and lighten immediately afterwards, and the rain poured down in torrents. The deck seeming to smoke with the wet, I went below; but so many passengers were there, smoking too, that I came up again, and buttoning my pea-coat, and standing in the shadow of the paddle-box, stood as upright as I could, and made the best of it.

It was at this moment that I first beheld the terrible Being, who is the subject of my present recollections.

Standing against the funnel, apparently with the intention of drying himself by the heat as fast as he got wet, was a shabby man in threadbare black, and with his hands in his pockets, who fascinated me from the memorable instant when I caught his eye.

Where had I caught that eye before? Who was he? Why did I connect him, all at once, with the Vicar of Wakefield, Alfred the Great, Gil Blas, Charles the Second, Joseph and his Brethren, the Fairy Queen, Tom Jones, the Decameron of Boccaccio, Tam O'Shanter, the Marriage of the Doge of Venice with the Adriatic, and the Great Plague of London? Why, when he bent one leg, and placed one hand upon the back of the seat near him, did my mind associate him wildly with the words, 'Number one hundred and forty-two, Portrait of a gentleman'? Could it be that I was going mad?

I looked at him again, and now I could have taken my affidavit that he belonged to the Vicar of Wakefield's family. Whether he was the Vicar, or Moses, or Mr. Burchill, or the Squire, or a conglomeration of all four, I knew not; but I was impelled to seize him by the throat, and charge him with being, in some fell way, connected with the Primrose blood. He looked up at the rain, and then—oh Heaven!—he became Saint John. He folded his arms, resigning himself to the weather, and I was frantically inclined to address him as the Spectator, and firmly demand to know what he had done with Sir Roger de Coverley.

The frightful suspicion that I was becoming deranged, returned upon me with redoubled force. Meantime, this awful stranger, inexplicably linked to my distress, stood drying himself at the funnel; and ever, as the steam rose from his clothes, diffusing a mist around him, I saw through the ghostly medium all the people I have mentioned, and a score more, sacred and profane.

I am conscious of a dreadful inclination that stole upon me, as it thundered and lightened, to grapple with this man, or demon, and plunge him over the side. But, I constrained myself—I know not how—to speak to him, and in a pause of the storm, I crossed the deck, and said:

'What are you?'

He replied, hoarsely, 'A Model.'

'A what?' said I.

'A Model,' he replied. 'I sets to the profession for a bob a-hour.' (All through this narrative I give his own words, which are indelibly imprinted on my memory.)

The relief which this disclosure gave me, the exquisite delight of the restoration of my confidence in my own sanity, I cannot describe. I should have fallen on his neck, but for the consciousness of being observed by the man at the wheel.

'You then,' said I, shaking him so warmly by the hand, that I wrung the rain out of his coat-cuff, 'are the gentleman whom I have so frequently contemplated, in connection with a high-backed chair with a red cushion, and a table with twisted legs.'

'I am that Model,' he rejoined moodily, 'and I wish I was anything else.'

'Say not so,' I returned. 'I have seen you in the society of many beautiful young women;' as in truth I had, and always (I now remember) in the act of making the most of his legs.

'No doubt,' said he. 'And you've seen me along with warses of flowers, and any number of table-kivers, and antique cabinets, and warious gammon.'

'Sir?' said I.

'And warious gammon,' he repeated, in a louder voice. 'You might have seen me in armour, too, if you had looked sharp. Blessed if I ha'n't stood in half the suits of armour as ever came out of Pratt's shop: and sat, for weeks together, a-eating nothing, out of half the gold and silver dishes as has ever been lent for the purpose out of Storrses, and Mortimerses, or Garrardses, and Davenportseseses.'

Excited, as it appeared, by a sense of injury, I thought he would never have found an end for the last word. But, at length it rolled sullenly away with the thunder.

'Pardon me,' said I, 'you are a well-favoured, well-made man, and yet— forgive me—I find, on examining my mind, that I associate you with—that my recollection indistinctly makes you, in short—excuse me—a kind of powerful monster.'

'It would be a wonder if it didn't,' he said. 'Do you know what my points are?'

'No,' said I.

'My throat and my legs,' said he. 'When I don't set for a head, I mostly sets for a throat and a pair of legs. Now, granted you was a painter, and was to work at my throat for a week together, I suppose you'd see a lot of lumps and bumps there, that would never be there at all, if you looked at me, complete, instead of only my throat. Wouldn't you?'

'Probably,' said I, surveying him.

'Why, it stands to reason,' said the Model. 'Work another week at my legs, and it'll be the same thing. You'll make 'em out as knotty and as knobby, at last, as if they was the trunks of two old trees. Then, take and stick my legs and throat on to another man's body, and you'll make a reg'lar monster. And that's the way the public gets their reg'lar monsters, every first Monday in May, when the Royal Academy Exhibition opens.'

'You are a critic,' said I, with an air of deference.

'I'm in an uncommon ill humour, if that's it,' rejoined the Model, with great indignation. 'As if it warn't bad enough for a bob a-hour, for a man to be mixing himself up with that there jolly old furniter that one 'ud think the public know'd the wery nails in by this time—or to be putting on greasy old 'ats and cloaks, and playing tambourines in the Bay o' Naples, with Wesuvius a smokin' according to pattern in the background, and the wines a bearing wonderful in the middle distance—or to be unpolitely kicking up his legs among a lot o' gals, with no reason whatever in his mind but to show 'em—as if this warn't bad enough, I'm to go and be thrown out of employment too!'

'Surely no!' said I.

'Surely yes,' said the indignant Model. 'But I'll grow one.'

The gloomy and threatening manner in which he muttered the last words, can never be effaced from my remembrance. My blood ran cold.

I asked of myself, what was it that this desperate Being was resolved to grow. My breast made no response.

I ventured to implore him to explain his meaning. With a scornful laugh, he uttered this dark prophecy:

'I'll grow one. And, mark my words, it shall haunt you!'

486

We parted in the storm, after I had forced half-a-crown on his acceptance, with a trembling hand. I conclude that something supernatural happened to the steamboat, as it bore his reeking figure down the river; but it never got into the papers.

Two years elapsed, during which I followed my profession without any vicissitudes; never holding so much as a motion, of course. At the expiration of that period, I found myself making my way home to the Temple, one night, in precisely such another storm of thunder and lightning as that by which I had been overtaken on board the steamboat—except that this storm, bursting over the town at midnight, was rendered much more awful by the darkness and the hour.

As I turned into my court, I really thought a thunderbolt would fall, and plough the pavement up. Every brick and stone in the place seemed to have an echo of its own for the thunder. The waterspouts were overcharged, and the rain came tearing down from the house-tops as if they had been mountain-tops.

Mrs. Parkins, my laundress—wife of Parkins the porter, then newly dead of a dropsy—had particular instructions to place a bedroom candle and a match under the staircase lamp on my landing, in order that I might light my candle there, whenever I came home. Mrs. Parkins invariably disregarding all instructions, they were never there. Thus it happened that on this occasion I groped my way into my sitting-room to find the candle, and came out to light it.

What were my emotions when, underneath the staircase lamp, shining with wet as if he had never been dry since our last meeting, stood the mysterious Being whom I had encountered on the steamboat in a thunderstorm, two years before! His prediction rushed upon my mind, and I turned faint.

'I said I'd do it,' he observed, in a hollow voice, 'and I have done it. May I come in?'

'Misguided creature, what have you done?' I returned.

'I'll let you know,' was his reply, 'if you'll let me in.'

Could it be murder that he had done? And had he been so successful that he wanted to do it again, at my expense?

I hesitated.

'May I come in?' said he.

I inclined my head, with as much presence of mind as I could command, and he followed me into my chambers. There, I saw that the lower part of his face was tied up, in what is commonly called a Belcher handkerchief. He slowly removed this bandage, and exposed to view a long dark beard, curling over his upper lip, twisting about the corners of his mouth, and hanging down upon his breast.

'What is this?' I exclaimed involuntarily, 'and what have you become?'

'I am the Ghost of Art!' said he.

The effect of these words, slowly uttered in the thunder-storm at midnight, was appalling in the last degree. More dead than alive, I surveyed him in silence.

'The German taste came up,' said he, 'and threw me out of bread. I am ready for the taste now.'

He made his beard a little jagged with his hands, folded his arms, and said,

'Severity!'

I shuddered. It was so severe.

He made his beard flowing on his breast, and, leaning both hands on the staff of a carpet-broom which Mrs. Parkins had left among my books, said:

'Benevolence.'

I stood transfixed. The change of sentiment was entirely in the beard. The man might have left his face alone, or had no face.

The beard did everything.

He lay down, on his back, on my table, and with that action of his head threw up his beard at the chin.

'That's death!' said he.

He got off my table and, looking up at the ceiling, cocked his beard a little awry; at the same time making it stick out before him.

'Adoration, or a vow of vengeance,' he observed.

He turned his profile to me, making his upper lip very bulky with the upper part of his beard.

'Romantic character,' said he.

He looked sideways out of his beard, as if it were an ivy-bush. 'Jealousy,' said he. He gave it an ingenious twist in the air, and informed me that he was carousing. He made it shaggy with his fingers—and it was Despair; lank—and it was avarice: tossed it all kinds of ways—and it was rage. The beard did everything.

'I am the Ghost of Art,' said he. 'Two bob a-day now, and more when it's longer! Hair's the true expression. There is no other. I said I'd grow it, and I've grown it, and it shall haunt you!'

He may have tumbled down-stairs in the dark, but he never walked down or ran down. I looked over the banisters, and I was alone with the thunder.

Need I add more of my terrific fate? It has haunted me ever since. It glares upon me from the walls of the Royal Academy, (except when Maclise subdues it to his genius,) it fills my soul with terror at the British Institution, it lures young artists on to their destruction. Go where I will, the Ghost of Art, eternally working the passions in hair, and expressing everything by beard, pursues me. The prediction is accomplished, and the victim has no rest.

OUT OF TOWN

Sitting, on a bright September morning, among my books and papers at my open window on the cliff overhanging the sea-beach, I have the sky and ocean framed before me like a beautiful picture. A beautiful picture, but with such movement in it, such changes of light upon the sails of ships and wake of steamboats, such dazzling gleams of silver far out at sea, such fresh touches on the crisp wave-tops as they break and roll towards me—a picture with such music in the billowy rush upon the shingle, the blowing of morning wind through the corn-sheaves where the farmers' waggons are busy, the singing of the larks, and the distant voices of children at play—such charms of sight and sound as all the Galleries on earth can but poorly suggest.

So dreamy is the murmur of the sea below my window, that I may have been here, for anything I know, one hundred years. Not that I have grown old, for, daily on the neighbouring downs and grassy hill-sides, I find that I can still in reason walk any distance, jump over anything, and climb up anywhere; but, that the sound of the ocean seems to have become so customary to my musings, and other realities seem so to have gone aboard ship and floated away over the horizon, that, for aught I will undertake to the contrary, I am the enchanted son of the King my father, shut up in a tower on the sea-shore, for protection against an old she-goblin who insisted on being my godmother, and who foresaw at the font—wonderful creature!—that I should get into a scrape before I was twenty-one. I remember to have been in a City (my Royal parent's dominions, I suppose), and apparently not long ago either, that was in the dreariest condition. The principal inhabitants had all been changed into old newspapers, and in that form were preserving their window-blinds from dust, and wrapping all their smaller household gods in curl-papers. I walked through gloomy streets where every house was shut up and newspapered, and where my solitary footsteps echoed on the deserted pavements. In the public rides there were no carriages, no horses, no animated existence, but a few sleepy policemen, and a few adventurous boys taking advantage of the devastation to swarm up the lamp-posts. In the

Westward streets there was no traffic; in the Westward shops, no business. The water-patterns which the 'Prentices had trickled out on the pavements early in the morning, remained uneffaced by human feet. At the corners of mews, Cochin-China fowls stalked gaunt and savage; nobody being left in the deserted city (as it appeared to me), to feed them. Public Houses, where splendid footmen swinging their legs over gorgeous hammer-cloths beside wigged coachmen were wont to regale, were silent, and the unused pewter pots shone, too bright for business, on the shelves. I beheld a Punch's Show leaning against a wall near Park Lane, as if it had fainted. It was deserted, and there were none to heed its desolation. In Belgrave Square I met the last man—an ostler—sitting on a post in a ragged red waistcoat, eating straw, and mildewing away.

If I recollect the name of the little town, on whose shore this sea is murmuring—but I am not just now, as I have premised, to be relied upon for anything—it is Pavilionstone. Within a quarter of a century, it was a little fishing town, and they do say, that the time was, when it was a little smuggling town. I have heard that it was rather famous in the hollands and brandy way, and that coevally with that reputation the lamplighter's was considered a bad life at the Assurance Offices. It was observed that if he were not particular about lighting up, he lived in peace; but that, if he made the best of the oil-lamps in the steep and narrow streets, he usually fell over the cliff at an early age. Now, gas and electricity run to the very water's edge, and the South-Eastern Railway Company screech at us in the dead of night.

But, the old little fishing and smuggling town remains, and is so tempting a place for the latter purpose, that I think of going out some night next week, in a fur cap and a pair of petticoat trousers, and running an empty tub, as a kind of archæological pursuit. Let nobody with corns come to Pavilionstone, for there are breakneck flights of ragged steps, connecting the principal streets by back-ways, which will cripple that visitor in half an hour. These are the ways by which, when I run that tub, I shall escape. I shall make a Thermopylæ of the corner of one of them, defend it with my cutlass against the coast-guard until my brave companions have sheered off, then dive into the darkness, and regain my Susan's arms. In connection with these breakneck steps I observe some wooden cottages, with tumble-down out-houses, and back-yards three feet square, adorned with garlands of dried fish, in one of which (though the General Board of Health might object) my Susan dwells.

The South-Eastern Company have brought Pavilionstone into such vogue, with their tidal trains and splendid steam-packets, that a new Pavilionstone is rising up. I am, myself, of New Pavilionstone. We are a little mortary and limey at present, but we are getting on capitally. Indeed, we were getting on so fast, at one time, that we rather overdid it, and built a street of shops, the business of which may be expected to arrive in about ten years. We are sensibly laid out in general; and with a little care and pains (by no means wanting, so far), shall become a very pretty place. We ought to be, for our situation is delightful, our air is delicious, and our breezy hills and downs, carpeted with wild thyme, and decorated with millions of wild flowers, are, on the faith of a pedestrian, perfect. In New Pavilionstone we are a little too much addicted to small windows with more bricks in them than glass, and we are not over-fanciful in the way of decorative architecture, and we get unexpected sea-views through cracks in the street doors; on the whole, however, we are very snug and comfortable, and well accommodated. But the Home Secretary (if there be such an officer) cannot too soon shut up the burial-ground of the old parish church. It is in the midst of us, and Pavilionstone will get no good of it, if it be too long left alone.

The lion of Pavilionstone is its Great Hotel. A dozen years ago, going over to Paris by South-Eastern Tidal Steamer, you used to be dropped upon the platform of the main line Pavilionstone Station (not a junction then), at eleven o'clock on a dark winter's night, in a roaring wind; and in the howling wilderness outside the station, was a short omnibus which brought you up by the forehead the instant you got in at the door; and nobody cared about you, and you were alone in the world. You bumped over infinite chalk, until you were turned out at a strange building which had just left off being a barn without having quite begun to be a house, where nobody expected your coming, or knew what to do with you when you were come, and where you were usually blown about, until you happened to be blown against the cold beef, and finally into bed. At five in the morning you were blown out of bed, and after a dreary breakfast, with crumpled company, in the midst of confusion, were hustled on board a steamboat and lay wretched on deck until you saw France lunging and surging at you with great vehemence over the bowsprit.

Now, you come down to Pavilionstone in a free and easy manner, an irresponsible agent, made over in trust to the South-Eastern Company, until you get out of the railway-carriage at high-water mark. If you are crossing by the boat at once, you have nothing to do but walk on board and be happy there if you can—I can't. If you are going to our Great Pavilionstone Hotel, the sprightliest porters under the sun, whose cheerful looks are a pleasant welcome, shoulder your luggage, drive it off in vans, bowl it away in trucks, and enjoy themselves in playing athletic games with it. If you are for public life at our great Pavilionstone Hotel, you walk into that establishment as if it were your club; and find ready for you, your news-room, dining-room, smoking-room, billiard-room, music-room, public breakfast, public dinner twice a-day (one plain, one gorgeous), hot baths and cold baths. If you want to be bored, there are plenty of bores always ready for you, and from Saturday to Monday in particular, you can be bored (if you like it) through and through. Should you want to be private at our Great Pavilionstone Hotel, say but the word, look at the list of charges, choose your floor, name your figure—there you are, established in your castle, by the day, week, month, or year, innocent of all comers or goers, unless you have my fancy for walking early in the morning down the groves of boots and shoes, which so regularly flourish at all the chamber-doors before breakfast, that it seems to me as if nobody ever got up or took them in. Are you going across the Alps, and would you like to air your Italian at our Great Pavilionstone Hotel? Talk to the Manager—always conversational, accomplished, and polite. Do you want to be aided, abetted, comforted, or advised, at our Great Pavilionstone Hotel? Send for the good landlord, and he is your friend. Should you, or any one belonging to you, ever be taken ill at our Great Pavilionstone Hotel, you will not soon forget him or his kind wife. And when you pay your bill at our Great Pavilionstone Hotel, you will not be put out of humour by anything you find in it.

A thoroughly good inn, in the days of coaching and posting, was a noble place. But no such inn would have been equal to the reception of four or five hundred people, all of them wet through, and half of them dead sick, every day in the year. This is where we shine, in our Pavilionstone Hotel. Again—who, coming and going, pitching and tossing, boating and training, hurrying in, and flying out, could ever have calculated the fees to be paid at an old-fashioned house? In our Pavilionstone Hotel vocabulary, there is no such word as fee. Everything is done for you; every service is provided at a fixed and reasonable charge; all the prices are hung up in all the rooms; and you can make out your own bill beforehand, as well as the book-keeper.

In the case of your being a pictorial artist, desirous of studying at small expense the physiognomies and beards of different nations, come, on receipt of this, to Pavilionstone. You shall find all the nations of the earth, and all the styles of shaving and not shaving, hair cutting and hair letting alone, for ever flowing through our hotel. Couriers you shall see by hundreds; fat leathern bags for five-franc pieces, closing with violent snaps, like discharges of fire-arms, by thousands; more luggage in a morning than, fifty years ago, all Europe saw in a week. Looking at trains, steamboats, sick travellers, and luggage, is our great Pavilionstone recreation. We are not strong in other public amusements. We have a Literary and Scientific Institution, and we have a Working Men's Institution—may it hold many gipsy holidays in summer fields, with the kettle boiling, the band of music playing, and the people dancing; and may I be on the hill-side, looking on with pleasure at a wholesome sight too rare in England!—and we have two or three churches, and more chapels than I have yet added up. But public amusements are scarce with us. If a poor theatrical manager comes with his company to give us, in a loft, Mary Bax, or the Murder on the Sand Hills, we don't care much for him—starve him out, in fact. We take more kindly to wax-work, especially if it moves; in which case it keeps much clearer of the second commandment than when it is still. Cooke's Circus (Mr. Cooke is my friend, and always leaves a good name behind him) gives us only a night in passing through. Nor does the travelling menagerie think us worth a longer visit. It gave us a look-in the other day, bringing with it the residentiary van with the stained glass windows, which Her Majesty kept ready-made at Windsor Castle, until she found a suitable opportunity of submitting it for the proprietor's acceptance. I brought away five wonderments from this exhibition. I have wondered ever since, Whether the beasts ever do get used to those small places of confinement; Whether the monkeys have that very horrible flavour in their free state; Whether wild animals have a natural ear for time and tune, and therefore every four-footed creature began to howl in despair when the band began to play; What the giraffe does with his neck when his cart is shut up; and, Whether the elephant feels ashamed of himself when he is brought out of his den to stand on his head in the presence of the whole Collection.

We are a tidal harbour at Pavilionstone, as indeed I have implied already in my mention of tidal trains. At low water, we are a heap of mud, with an empty channel in it where a couple of men in big boots always shovel and scoop: with what exact object, I am unable to say. At that time, all the stranded fishing-boats turn over on their sides, as if they were dead marine monsters; the colliers and other shipping stick disconsolate in the mud; the steamers look as if their white chimneys would never smoke more, and their red paddles never turn again; the green sea-slime and weed upon the rough stones at the entrance, seem records of obsolete high tides never more to flow; the flagstaff-halyards droop; the very little wooden lighthouse shrinks in the idle glare of the sun. And here I may observe of the very little wooden lighthouse, that when it is lighted at night,—red and green,—it looks so like a medical man's, that several distracted husbands have at various times been found, on occasions of premature domestic anxiety, going round and round it, trying to find the Nightbell.

But, the moment the tide begins to make, the Pavilionstone Harbour begins to revive. It feels the breeze of the rising water before the water comes, and begins to flutter and stir. When the little shallow waves creep in, barely overlapping one another, the vanes at the mastheads wake, and become agitated. As the tide rises, the fishing-boats get into good spirits and dance, the flagstaff hoists a bright red flag, the steamboat smokes, cranes creak, horses and carriages dangle in the air, stray passengers and luggage appear. Now, the shipping is afloat, and comes up buoyantly, to look at the wharf. Now, the carts that have come down for coals, load away as hard as they can load. Now, the steamer smokes immensely, and occasionally blows at the paddle-boxes like a vaporous whale-greatly disturbing nervous loungers. Now, both the tide and the breeze have risen, and you are holding your hat on (if you want to see how the ladies hold their hats on, with a stay, passing over the broad brim and down the nose, come to Pavilionstone). Now, everything in the harbour splashes, dashes, and bobs. Now, the Down Tidal Train is telegraphed, and you know (without knowing how you know), that two hundred and eighty-seven people are coming. Now, the fishing-boats that have been out, sail in at the top of the tide. Now, the bell goes, and the locomotive hisses and shrieks, and the train comes gliding in, and the two hundred and eighty-seven come scuffling out. Now, there is not only a tide of water, but a tide of people, and a tide of luggage—all tumbling and flowing and bouncing about together. Now, after infinite bustle, the steamer steams out, and we (on the Pier) are all delighted when she rolls as if she would roll her funnel out, and all are disappointed when she don't. Now, the other steamer is coming in, and the Custom House prepares, and the wharf-labourers assemble, and the hawsers are made ready, and the Hotel Porters come rattling down with van and truck, eager to begin more Olympic games with more luggage. And this is the way in which we go on, down at Pavilionstone, every tide. And, if you want to live a life of luggage, or to see it lived, or to breathe sweet air which will send you to sleep at a moment's notice at any period of the day or night, or to disport yourself upon or in the sea, or to scamper about Kent, or to come out of town for the enjoyment of all or any of these pleasures, come to Pavilionstone.

OUT OF THE SEASON

It fell to my lot, this last bleak Spring, to find myself in a watering-place out of the Season. A vicious north-east squall blew me into it from foreign parts, and I tarried in it alone for three days, resolved to be exceedingly busy.

On the first day, I began business by looking for two hours at the sea, and staring the Foreign Militia out of countenance. Having disposed of these important engagements, I sat down at one of the two windows of my room, intent on doing something desperate in the way of literary composition, and writing a chapter of unheard-of excellence—with which the present essay has no connexion.

It is a remarkable quality in a watering-place out of the season, that everything in it, will and must be looked at. I had no previous suspicion of this fatal truth but, the moment I sat down to write, I began to perceive it. I had scarcely fallen into my most promising attitude, and dipped my pen in the ink, when I found the clock upon the pier—a red-faced clock with a white rim—importuning me in a highly vexatious manner to consult my watch, and see how I was off for Greenwich time. Having no intention of making a voyage or taking an observation, I had not the least need of Greenwich time, and could have put up with watering-place time as a sufficiently accurate article. The pier-clock, however, persisting, I felt it necessary to lay down my pen, compare my watch with him, and fall into a grave solicitude about half-seconds. I had taken up my pen again, and was about to commence that valuable chapter, when a Custom-house cutter under the window requested that I would hold a naval review of her, immediately.

It was impossible, under the circumstances, for any mental resolution, merely human, to dismiss the Custom-house cutter, because the shadow of her topmast fell upon my paper, and the vane played on the masterly blank chapter. I was therefore under the necessity of going to the other window; sitting astride of the chair there, like Napoleon bivouacking in the print; and inspecting the cutter as she lay, all that day, in the way of my chapter, O!

She was rigged to carry a quantity of canvas, but her hull was so very small that four giants aboard of her (three men and a boy) who were vigilantly scraping at her, all together, inspired me with a terror lest they should scrape her away. A fifth giant, who appeared to consider himself 'below'—as indeed he was, from the waist downwards—meditated, in such close proximity with the little gusty chimney-pipe, that he seemed to be smoking it. Several boys looked on from the wharf, and, when the gigantic attention appeared to be fully occupied, one or other of these would furtively swing himself in mid-air over the Custom-house cutter, by means of a line pendant from her rigging, like a young spirit of the storm. Presently, a sixth hand brought down two little water-casks; presently afterwards, a truck came, and delivered a hamper. I was now under an obligation to consider that the cutter was going on a cruise, and to wonder where she was going, and when she was going, and why she was going, and at what date she might be expected back, and who commanded her? With these pressing questions I was fully occupied when the Packet, making ready to go across, and blowing off her spare steam, roared, 'Look at me!'

It became a positive duty to look at the Packet preparing to go across; aboard of which, the people newly come down by the rail-road were hurrying in a great fluster. The crew had got their tarry overalls on—and one knew what that meant—not to mention the white basins, ranged in neat little piles of a dozen each, behind the door of the after-cabin. One lady as I looked, one resigning and far-seeing woman, took her basin from the store of crockery, as she might have taken a refreshment-ticket, laid herself down on deck with that utensil at her ear, muffled her feet in one shawl, solemnly covered her countenance after the antique manner with another, and on the completion of these preparations appeared by the strength of her volition to become insensible. The mail-bags (O that I myself had the sea-legs of a mail-bag!) were tumbled aboard; the Packet left off roaring, warped out, and made at the white line upon the bar. One dip, one roll, one break of the sea over her bows, and Moore's Almanack or the sage Raphael could not have told me more of the state of things aboard, than I knew.

The famous chapter was all but begun now, and would have been quite begun, but for the wind. It was blowing stiffly from the east, and it rumbled in the chimney and shook the house. That was not much; but, looking out into the wind's grey eye for inspiration, I laid down my pen again to make the remark to myself, how emphatically everything by the sea declares that it has a great concern in the state of the wind. The trees blown all one way; the defences of the harbour reared highest and strongest against the raging point; the shingle flung up on the beach from the same direction; the number of arrows pointed at the common enemy; the sea tumbling in and rushing towards them as if it were inflamed by the sight. This put it in my head that I really ought to go out and take a walk in the wind; so, I gave up the magnificent chapter for that day, entirely persuading myself that I was under a moral obligation to have a blow.

I had a good one, and that on the high road—the very high road—on the top of the cliffs, where I met the stage-coach with all the outsides holding their hats on and themselves too, and overtook a flock of sheep with the wool about their necks blown into such great ruffs that they looked like fleecy owls. The wind played upon the lighthouse as if it were a great whistle, the spray was driven over the sea in a cloud of haze, the ships rolled and pitched heavily, and at intervals long slants and flaws of light made mountain-steeps of communication between the ocean and the sky. A walk of ten miles brought me to a seaside town without a cliff, which, like the town I had come from, was out of the season too. Half of the houses were shut up; half of the other half were to let; the town might have done as much business as it was doing then, if it had been at the bottom of the sea. Nobody seemed to flourish save the attorney; his clerk's pen was going in the bow-window of his wooden house; his brass door-plate alone was free from salt, and had been polished up that morning. On the beach, among the rough buggers and capstans, groups of storm-beaten boatmen, like a sort of marine monsters, watched under the lee of those objects, or stood leaning forward against the wind, looking out through battered spy-glasses. The parlour bell in the Admiral Benbow had grown so flat with being out of the season, that neither could I hear it ring when I pulled the handle for lunch, nor could the young woman in black stockings and strong shoes, who acted as waiter out of the season, until it had been tinkled three times.

Admiral Benbow's cheese was out of the season, but his home-made bread was good, and his beer was perfect. Deluded by some earlier spring day which had been warm and sunny, the Admiral had cleared the firing out of his parlour stove, and had put some flower-pots in—which was amiable and hopeful in the Admiral, but not judicious: the room being, at that present visiting, transcendantly cold. I therefore took the liberty of peeping out across a little stone passage into the Admiral's kitchen, and, seeing a high settle with its back towards me drawn out in front of the Admiral's kitchen fire, I strolled in, bread and cheese in hand, munching and looking about. One landsman and two boatmen were seated on the settle, smoking pipes and drinking beer out of thick pint crockery mugs—mugs peculiar to such places, with parti-coloured rings round them, and ornaments between the rings like frayed-out roots. The landsman was relating his experience, as yet only three nights old, of a fearful running-down case in the Channel, and therein presented to my imagination a sound of music that it will not soon forget.

'At that identical moment of time,' said he (he was a prosy man by nature, who rose with his subject), 'the night being light and calm, but with a grey mist upon the water that didn't seem to spread for more than two or three mile, I was walking up and down the wooden causeway next the pier, off where it happened, along with a friend of mine, which his name is Mr. Clocker. Mr. Clocker is a grocer over yonder.' (From the direction in which he pointed the bowl of his pipe, I might have judged Mr. Clocker to be a merman, established in the grocery trade in five-and-twenty fathoms of water.) 'We were smoking our pipes, and walking up and down the causeway, talking of one thing and talking of another. We were quite alone there, except that a few hovellers' (the Kentish name for 'long-shore boatmen like his companions) 'were hanging about their lugs, waiting while the tide made, as hovellers will.' (One of the two boatmen, thoughtfully regarding me, shut up one eye; this I understood to mean: first, that he took me into the conversation: secondly, that he confirmed the proposition: thirdly, that he announced himself as a hoveller.) 'All of a sudden Mr. Clocker and me stood rooted to the spot, by hearing a sound come through the stillness, right over the sea, like a great sorrowful flute or Æolian harp. We didn't in the least know what it was, and judge of our surprise when we saw the hovellers, to a man, leap into the boats and tear about to hoist sail and get off, as if they had every one of 'em gone, in a moment, raving mad! But they knew it was the cry of distress from the sinking emigrant ship.'

When I got back to my watering-place out of the season, and had done my twenty miles in good style, I found that the celebrated Black Mesmerist intended favouring the public that evening in the Hall of the Muses, which he had engaged for the purpose. After a good dinner, seated by the fire in an easy chair, I began to waver in a design I had formed of waiting on the Black Mesmerist, and to incline towards the expediency of remaining where I was. Indeed a point of gallantry was involved in my doing so, inasmuch as I had not left France alone, but had come from the prisons of St. Pélagie with my distinguished and unfortunate friend Madame Roland (in two volumes which I bought for two francs each, at the book-stall in the Place de la Concorde, Paris, at the corner of the Rue Royale). Deciding to pass the evening tête-à-tête with Madame Roland, I derived, as I always do, great pleasure from that spiritual woman's society, and the charms of her brave soul and engaging conversation. I must confess that if she had only some more faults, only a few more passionate failings of any kind, I might love her better; but I am content to believe that the deficiency is in me, and not in her. We spent some sadly interesting hours together on this occasion, and she told me again of her cruel discharge from the Abbaye, and of her being re-arrested before her free feet had sprung lightly up half-a-dozen steps of her own staircase, and carried off to the prison which she only left for the guillotine.

Madame Roland and I took leave of one another before mid-night, and I went to bed full of vast intentions for next day, in connexion with the unparalleled chapter. To hear the foreign mail-steamers coming in at dawn of day, and to know that I was not aboard or obliged to get up, was very comfortable; so, I rose for the chapter in great force.

I had advanced so far as to sit down at my window again on my second morning, and to write the first half-line of the chapter and strike it out, not liking it, when my conscience reproached me with not having surveyed the watering-place out of the season, after all, yesterday, but with having gone straight out of it at the rate of four miles and a half an hour. Obviously the best amends that I could make for this remissness was to go and look at it without another moment's delay. So—altogether as a matter of duty—I gave up the magnificent chapter for another day, and sauntered out with my hands in my pockets.

All the houses and lodgings ever let to visitors, were to let that morning. It seemed to have snowed bills with To Let upon them. This put me upon thinking what the owners of all those apartments did, out of the season; how they employed their time, and occupied their minds. They could not be always going to the Methodist chapels, of which I passed one every other minute. They must have some other recreation. Whether they pretended to take one another's lodgings, and opened one another's tea-caddies in fun? Whether they cut slices off their own beef and mutton, and made believe that it belonged to somebody else? Whether they played little dramas of life, as children do, and said, 'I ought to come and look at your apartments, and you ought to ask two guineas a-week too much, and then I ought to say I must have the rest of the day to think of it, and then you ought to say that another lady and gentleman with no children in family had made an offer very close to your own terms, and you had passed your word to give them a positive answer in half an hour, and indeed were just going to take the bill down when you heard the knock, and then I ought to take them, you know?' Twenty such speculations engaged my thoughts. Then, after passing, still clinging to the walls, defaced rags of the bills of last year's Circus, I came to a back field near a timber-yard where the Circus itself had been, and where there was yet a sort of monkish tonsure on the grass, indicating the spot where the young lady had gone round upon her pet steed Firefly in her daring flight. Turning into the town again, I came among the shops, and they were emphatically out of the season. The chemist had no boxes of ginger-beer powders, no beautifying sea-side soaps and washes, no attractive scents; nothing but his great goggle-eyed red bottles, looking as if the winds of winter and the drift of the salt-sea had inflamed them. The grocers' hot pickles, Harvey's Sauce, Doctor Kitchener's Zest, Anchovy Paste, Dundee Marmalade, and the whole stock of luxurious helps to appetite, were hybernating somewhere underground. The china-shop had no trifles from anywhere. The Bazaar had given in altogether, and presented a notice on the shutters that this establishment would re-open

at Whitsuntide, and that the proprietor in the meantime might be heard of
at Wild Lodge, East Cliff. At the Sea-bathing Establishment, a row of neat
little wooden houses seven or eight feet high, I saw the proprietor in bed in
the shower-bath. As to the bathing-machines, they were (how they got there,
is not for me to say) at the top of a hill at least a mile and a half off. The
library, which I had never seen otherwise than wide open, was tight shut; and
two peevish bald old gentlemen seemed to be hermetically sealed up inside,
eternally reading the paper. That wonderful mystery, the music-shop, carried
it off as usual (except that it had more cabinet pianos in stock), as if season
or no season were all one to it. It made the same prodigious display of bright
brazen wind-instruments, horribly twisted, worth, as I should conceive, some
thousands of pounds, and which it is utterly impossible that anybody in any
season can ever play or want to play. It had five triangles in the window,
six pairs of castanets, and three harps; likewise every polka with a coloured
frontispiece that ever was published; from the original one where a smooth
male and female Pole of high rank are coming at the observer with their arms
a-kimbo, to the Ratcatcher's Daughter. Astonishing establishment, amazing
enigma! Three other shops were pretty much out of the season, what they
were used to be in it. First, the shop where they sell the sailors' watches, which
had still the old collection of enormous timekeepers, apparently designed to
break a fall from the masthead: with places to wind them up, like fire-plugs.
Secondly, the shop where they sell the sailors' clothing, which displayed
the old sou'-westers, and the old oily suits, and the old pea-jackets, and the
old one sea-chest, with its handles like a pair of rope ear-rings. Thirdly,
the unchangeable shop for the sale of literature that has been left behind.
Here, Dr. Faustus was still going down to very red and yellow perdition,
under the superintendence of three green personages of a scaly humour, with
excrescential serpents growing out of their blade-bones. Here, the Golden
Dreamer, and the Norwood Fortune Teller, were still on sale at sixpence each,
with instructions for making the dumb cake, and reading destinies in teacups, and with a picture of a young woman with a high waist lying on a sofa
in an attitude so uncomfortable as almost to account for her dreaming at one
and the same time of a conflagration, a shipwreck, an earthquake, a skeleton,
a church-porch, lightning, funerals performed, and a young man in a bright

blue coat and canary pantaloons. Here, were Little Warblers and Fairburn's Comic Songsters. Here, too, were ballads on the old ballad paper and in the old confusion of types; with an old man in a cocked hat, and an arm-chair, for the illustration to Will Watch the bold Smuggler; and the Friar of Orders Grey, represented by a little girl in a hoop, with a ship in the distance. All these as of yore, when they were infinite delights to me!

It took me so long fully to relish these many enjoyments, that I had not more than an hour before bedtime to devote to Madame Roland. We got on admirably together on the subject of her convent education, and I rose next morning with the full conviction that the day for the great chapter was at last arrived.

It had fallen calm, however, in the night, and as I sat at breakfast I blushed to remember that I had not yet been on the Downs. I a walker, and not yet on the Downs! Really, on so quiet and bright a morning this must be set right. As an essential part of the Whole Duty of Man, therefore, I left the chapter to itself—for the present—and went on the Downs. They were wonderfully green and beautiful, and gave me a good deal to do. When I had done with the free air and the view, I had to go down into the valley and look after the hops (which I know nothing about), and to be equally solicitous as to the cherry orchards. Then I took it on myself to cross-examine a tramping family in black (mother alleged, I have no doubt by herself in person, to have died last week), and to accompany eighteenpence which produced a great effect, with moral admonitions which produced none at all. Finally, it was late in the afternoon before I got back to the unprecedented chapter, and then I determined that it was out of the season, as the place was, and put it away.

I went at night to the benefit of Mrs. B. Wedgington at the Theatre, who had placarded the town with the admonition, 'Don't forget it!' I made the house, according to my calculation, four and ninepence to begin with, and it may have warmed up, in the course of the evening, to half a sovereign. There was nothing to offend any one,—the good Mr. Baines of Leeds excepted. Mrs. B. Wedgington sang to a grand piano. Mr. B. Wedgington did the like, and also took off his coat, tucked up his trousers, and danced in clogs. Master B. Wedgington, aged ten months, was nursed by a shivering young person in the boxes, and the eye of Mrs. B. Wedgington wandered that way more than once. Peace be with all the Wedgingtons from A. to Z. May they find themselves in the Season somewhere!

A POOR MAN'S TALE OF A PATENT

I AM not used to writing for print. What working-man, that never labours less (some Mondays, and Christmas Time and Easter Time excepted) than twelve or fourteen hours a day, is? But I have been asked to put down, plain, what I have got to say; and so I take pen-and-ink, and do it to the best of my power, hoping defects will find excuse.

I was born nigh London, but have worked in a shop at Birmingham (what you would call Manufactories, we call Shops), almost ever since I was out of my time. I served my apprenticeship at Deptford, nigh where I was born, and I am a smith by trade. My name is John. I have been called 'Old John' ever since I was nineteen year of age, on account of not having much hair. I am fifty-six year of age at the present time, and I don't find myself with more hair, nor yet with less, to signify, than at nineteen year of age aforesaid.

I have been married five and thirty year, come next April. I was married on All Fools' Day. Let them laugh that will. I won a good wife that day, and it was as sensible a day to me as ever I had.

We have had a matter of ten children, six whereof are living. My eldest son is engineer in the Italian steam-packet 'Mezzo Giorno, plying between Marseilles and Naples, and calling at Genoa, Leghorn, and Civita Vecchia.' He was a good workman. He invented a many useful little things that brought him in—nothing. I have two sons doing well at Sydney, New South Wales— single, when last heard from. One of my sons (James) went wild and for a soldier, where he was shot in India, living six weeks in hospital with a musket-ball lodged in his shoulder-blade, which he wrote with his own hand. He was the best looking. One of my two daughters (Mary) is comfortable in her circumstances, but water on the chest. The other (Charlotte), her husband run away from her in the basest manner, and she and her three children live with us. The youngest, six year old, has a turn for mechanics.

I am not a Chartist, and I never was. I don't mean to say but what I see a good many public points to complain of, still I don't think that's the way to set them right. If I did think so, I should be a Chartist. But I don't think so, and I am not a Chartist. I read the paper, and hear discussion, at what we call 'a parlour,' in Birmingham, and I know many good men and workmen who are Chartists. Note. Not Physical force.

It won't be took as boastful in me, if I make the remark (for I can't put down what I have got to say, without putting that down before going any further), that I have always been of an ingenious turn. I once got twenty pound by a screw, and it's in use now. I have been twenty year, off and on, completing an Invention and perfecting it. I perfected of it, last Christmas Eve at ten o'clock at night. Me and my wife stood and let some tears fall over the Model, when it was done and I brought her in to take a look at it.

A friend of mine, by the name of William Butcher, is a Chartist. Moderate. He is a good speaker. He is very animated. I have often heard him deliver that what is, at every turn, in the way of us working-men, is, that too many places have been made, in the course of time, to provide for people that never ought to have been provided for; and that we have to obey forms and to pay fees to support those places when we shouldn't ought. 'True,' (delivers William Butcher), 'all the public has to do this, but it falls heaviest on the working-man, because he has least to spare; and likewise because impediments shouldn't be put in his way, when he wants redress of wrong or furtherance of right.' Note. I have wrote down those words from William Butcher's own mouth. W. B. delivering them fresh for the aforesaid purpose.

Now, to my Model again. There it was, perfected of, on Christmas Eve, gone nigh a year, at ten o'clock at night. All the money I could spare I had laid out upon the Model; and when times was bad, or my daughter Charlotte's children sickly, or both, it had stood still, months at a spell. I had pulled it to pieces, and made it over again with improvements, I don't know how often. There it stood, at last, a perfected Model as aforesaid.

William Butcher and me had a long talk, Christmas Day, respecting of the Model. William is very sensible. But sometimes cranky. William said, 'What will you do with it, John?' I said, 'Patent it.' William said, 'How patent it, John?' I said, 'By taking out a Patent.' William then delivered that the law of Patent was a cruel wrong. William said, 'John, if you make your invention public, before you get a Patent, any one may rob you of the fruits of your hard work. You are put in a cleft stick, John. Either you must drive a bargain very much against yourself, by getting a party to come forward beforehand with the great expenses of the Patent; or, you must be put about, from post to pillar, among so many parties, trying to make a better bargain for yourself, and showing your invention, that your invention will be took from you over your head.' I said, 'William Butcher, are you cranky? You are sometimes cranky.' William said, 'No, John, I tell you the truth;' which he then delivered more at length. I said to W. B. I would Patent the invention myself.

My wife's brother, George Bury of West Bromwich (his wife unfortunately took to drinking, made away with everything, and seventeen times committed to Birmingham Jail before happy release in every point of view), left my wife, his sister, when he died, a legacy of one hundred and twenty-eight pound ten, Bank of England Stocks. Me and my wife never broke into that money yet. Note. We might come to be old and past our work. We now agreed to Patent the invention. We said we would make a hole in it—I mean in the aforesaid money—and Patent the invention. William Butcher wrote me a letter to Thomas Joy, in London. T. J. is a carpenter, six foot four in height, and plays quoits well. He lives in Chelsea, London, by the church. I got leave from the shop, to be took on again when I come back. I am a good workman. Not a Teetotaller; but never drunk. When the Christmas holidays were over, I went up to London by the Parliamentary Train, and hired a lodging for a week with Thomas Joy. He is married. He has one son gone to sea.

Thomas Joy delivered (from a book he had) that the first step to be took, in Patenting the invention, was to prepare a petition unto Queen Victoria. William Butcher had delivered similar, and drawn it up. Note. William is a ready writer. A declaration before a Master in Chancery was to be added to it. That, we likewise drew up. After a deal of trouble I found out a Master, in Southampton Buildings, Chancery Lane, nigh Temple Bar, where I made the declaration, and paid eighteen-pence. I was told to take the declaration and petition to the Home Office, in Whitehall, where I left it to be signed by the Home Secretary (after I had found the office out), and where I paid two pound, two, and sixpence. In six days he signed it, and I was told to take it to the Attorney-General's chambers, and leave it there for a report. I did so, and paid four pound, four. Note. Nobody all through, ever thankful for their money, but all uncivil.

My lodging at Thomas Joy's was now hired for another week, whereof five days were gone. The Attorney-General made what they called a Report-of-course (my invention being, as William Butcher had delivered before starting, unopposed), and I was sent back with it to the Home Office. They made a Copy of it, which was called a Warrant. For this warrant, I paid seven pound, thirteen, and six. It was sent to the Queen, to sign. The Queen sent it back, signed. The Home Secretary signed it again. The gentleman throwed it at me when I called, and said, 'Now take it to the Patent Office in Lincoln's Inn.' I was then in my third week at Thomas Joy's living very sparing, on account of fees. I found myself losing heart.

At the Patent Office in Lincoln's Inn, they made 'a draft of the Queen's bill,' of my invention, and a 'docket of the bill.' I paid five pound, ten, and six, for this. They 'engrossed two copies of the bill; one for the Signet Office, and one for the Privy-Seal Office.' I paid one pound, seven, and six, for this. Stamp duty over and above, three pound. The Engrossing Clerk of the same office engrossed the Queen's bill for signature. I paid him one pound, one. Stamp-duty, again, one pound, ten. I was next to take the Queen's bill to the Attorney-General again, and get it signed again. I took it, and paid five pound more. I fetched it away, and took it to the Home Secretary again. He sent it to the Queen again. She signed it again. I paid seven pound, thirteen, and six, more, for this. I had been over a month at Thomas Joy's. I was quite wore out, patience and pocket.

Thomas Joy delivered all this, as it went on, to William Butcher. William Butcher delivered it again to three Birmingham Parlours, from which it got to all the other Parlours, and was took, as I have been told since, right through all the shops in the North of England. Note. William Butcher delivered, at his Parlour, in a speech, that it was a Patent way of making Chartists.

But I hadn't nigh done yet. The Queen's bill was to be took to the Signet Office in Somerset House, Strand—where the stamp shop is. The Clerk of the Signet made 'a Signet bill for the Lord Keeper of the Privy Seal.' I paid him four pound, seven. The Clerk of the Lord Keeper of the Privy Seal made 'a Privy-Seal bill for the Lord Chancellor.' I paid him, four pound, two. The Privy-Seal bill was handed over to the Clerk of the Patents, who engrossed the aforesaid. I paid him five pound, seventeen, and eight; at the same time, I paid Stamp-duty for the Patent, in one lump, thirty pound. I next paid for 'boxes for the Patent,' nine and sixpence. Note. Thomas Joy would have made the same at a profit for eighteen-pence. I next paid 'fees to the Deputy, the Lord Chancellor's Purse-bearer,' two pound, two. I next paid 'fees to the Clerk of the Hanapar,' seven pound, thirteen. I next paid 'fees to the Deputy Clerk of the Hanaper,' ten shillings. I next paid, to the Lord Chancellor again, one pound, eleven, and six. Last of all, I paid 'fees to the Deputy Sealer, and Deputy Chaff-wax,' ten shillings and sixpence. I had lodged at Thomas Joy's over six weeks, and the unopposed Patent for my invention, for England only, had cost me ninety-six pound, seven, and eightpence. If I had taken it out for the United Kingdom, it would have cost me more than three hundred pound.

Now, teaching had not come up but very limited when I was young. So much the worse for me you'll say. I say the same. William Butcher is twenty year younger than me. He knows a hundred year more. If William Butcher had wanted to Patent an invention, he might have been sharper than myself when hustled backwards and forwards among all those offices, though I doubt if so patient. Note. William being sometimes cranky, and consider porters, messengers, and clerks.

Thereby I say nothing of my being tired of my life, while I was Patenting my invention. But I put this: Is it reasonable to make a man feel as if, in inventing an ingenious improvement meant to do good, he had done something wrong? How else can a man feel, when he is met by such difficulties at every turn? All inventors taking out a Patent MUST feel so. And look at the expense. How hard on me, and how hard on the country if there's any merit in me (and my invention is took up now, I am thankful to say, and doing well), to put me to all that expense before I can move a finger! Make the addition yourself, and it'll come to ninety-six pound, seven, and eightpence. No more, and no less.

What can I say against William Butcher, about places? Look at the Home Secretary, the Attorney-General, the Patent Office, the Engrossing Clerk, the Lord Chancellor, the Privy Seal, the Clerk of the Patents, the Lord Chancellor's Purse-bearer, the Clerk of the Hanaper, the Deputy Clerk of the Hanaper, the Deputy Sealer, and the Deputy Chaff-wax. No man in England could get a Patent for an Indian-rubber band, or an iron-hoop, without feeing all of them. Some of them, over and over again. I went through thirty-five stages. I began with the Queen upon the Throne. I ended with the Deputy Chaff-wax. Note. I should like to see the Deputy Chaff-wax. Is it a man, or what is it?

What I had to tell, I have told. I have wrote it down. I hope it's plain. Not so much in the handwriting (though nothing to boast of there), as in the sense of it. I will now conclude with Thomas Joy. Thomas said to me, when we parted, 'John, if the laws of this country were as honest as they ought to be, you would have come to London—registered an exact description and drawing of your invention—paid half-a-crown or so for doing of it—and therein and thereby have got your Patent.'

My opinion is the same as Thomas Joy. Further. In William Butcher's delivering 'that the whole gang of Hanapers and Chaff-waxes must be done away with, and that England has been chaffed and waxed sufficient,' I agree.

THE NOBLE SAVAGE

To come to the point at once, I beg to say that I have not the least belief in the Noble Savage. I consider him a prodigious nuisance, and an enormous superstition. His calling rum fire-water, and me a pale face, wholly fail to reconcile me to him. I don't care what he calls me. I call him a savage, and I call a savage a something highly desirable to be civilised off the face of the earth. I think a mere gent (which I take to be the lowest form of civilisation) better than a howling, whistling, clucking, stamping, jumping, tearing savage. It is all one to me, whether he sticks a fish-bone through his visage, or bits of trees through the lobes of his ears, or bird's feathers in his head; whether he flattens his hair between two boards, or spreads his nose over the breadth of his face, or drags his lower lip down by great weights, or blackens his teeth, or knocks them out, or paints one cheek red and the other blue, or tattoos himself, or oils himself, or rubs his body with fat, or crimps it with knives. Yielding to whichsoever of these agreeable eccentricities, he is a savage—cruel, false, thievish, murderous; addicted more or less to grease, entrails, and beastly customs; a wild animal with the questionable gift of boasting; a conceited, tiresome, bloodthirsty, monotonous humbug.

Yet it is extraordinary to observe how some people will talk about him, as they talk about the good old times; how they will regret his disappearance, in the course of this world's development, from such and such lands where his absence is a blessed relief and an indispensable preparation for the sowing of the very first seeds of any influence that can exalt humanity; how, even with the evidence of himself before them, they will either be determined to believe, or will suffer themselves to be persuaded into believing, that he is something which their five senses tell them he is not.

There was Mr. Catlin, some few years ago, with his Ojibbeway Indians. Mr. Catlin was an energetic, earnest man, who had lived among more tribes of Indians than I need reckon up here, and who had written a picturesque and glowing book about them. With his party of Indians squatting and spitting on the table before him, or dancing their miserable jigs after their own dreary manner, he called, in all good faith, upon his civilised audience to take notice of their symmetry and grace, their perfect limbs, and the exquisite expression of their pantomime; and his civilised audience, in all good faith, complied and admired. Whereas, as mere animals, they were wretched creatures, very low in the scale and very poorly formed; and as men and women possessing any power of truthful dramatic expression by means of action, they were no better than the chorus at an Italian Opera in England—and would have been worse if such a thing were possible.

Mine are no new views of the noble savage. The greatest writers on natural history found him out long ago. Buffon knew what he was, and showed why he is the sulky tyrant that he is to his women, and how it happens (Heaven be praised!) that his race is spare in numbers. For evidence of the quality of his moral nature, pass himself for a moment and refer to his 'faithful dog.' Has he ever improved a dog, or attached a dog, since his nobility first ran wild in woods, and was brought down (at a very long shot) by Pope? Or does the animal that is the friend of man, always degenerate in his low society?

It is not the miserable nature of the noble savage that is the new thing; it is the whimpering over him with maudlin admiration, and the affecting to regret him, and the drawing of any comparison of advantage between the blemishes of civilisation and the tenor of his swinish life. There may have been a change now and then in those diseased absurdities, but there is none in him.

Think of the Bushmen. Think of the two men and the two women who have been exhibited about England for some years. Are the majority of persons—who remember the horrid little leader of that party in his festering bundle of hides, with his filth and his antipathy to water, and his straddled legs, and his odious eyes shaded by his brutal hand, and his cry of 'Qu-u-u-u-aaa!' (Bosjesman for something desperately insulting I have no doubt)— conscious of an affectionate yearning towards that noble savage, or is it idiosyncratic in me to abhor, detest, abominate, and abjure him? I have no reserve on this subject, and will frankly state that, setting aside that stage of the entertainment when he counterfeited the death of some creature he had shot, by laying his head on his hand and shaking his left leg—at which time

I think it would have been justifiable homicide to slay him—I have never seen that group sleeping, smoking, and expectorating round their brazier, but I have sincerely desired that something might happen to the charcoal smouldering therein, which would cause the immediate suffocation of the whole of the noble strangers.

There is at present a party of Zulu Kaffirs exhibiting at the St. George's Gallery, Hyde Park Corner, London. These noble savages are represented in a most agreeable manner; they are seen in an elegant theatre, fitted with appropriate scenery of great beauty, and they are described in a very sensible and unpretending lecture, delivered with a modesty which is quite a pattern to all similar exponents. Though extremely ugly, they are much better shaped than such of their predecessors as I have referred to; and they are rather picturesque to the eye, though far from odoriferous to the nose. What a visitor left to his own interpretings and imaginings might suppose these noblemen to be about, when they give vent to that pantomimic expression which is quite settled to be the natural gift of the noble savage, I cannot possibly conceive; for it is so much too luminous for my personal civilisation that it conveys no idea to my mind beyond a general stamping, ramping, and raving, remarkable (as everything in savage life is) for its dire uniformity. But let us—with the interpreter's assistance, of which I for one stand so much in need—see what the noble savage does in Zulu Kaffirland.

The noble savage sets a king to reign over him, to whom he submits his life and limbs without a murmur or question, and whose whole life is passed chin deep in a lake of blood; but who, after killing incessantly, is in his turn killed by his relations and friends, the moment a grey hair appears on his head. All the noble savage's wars with his fellow-savages (and he takes no pleasure in anything else) are wars of extermination—which is the best thing I know of him, and the most comfortable to my mind when I look at him. He has no moral feelings of any kind, sort, or description; and his 'mission' may be summed up as simply diabolical.

The ceremonies with which he faintly diversifies his life are, of course, of a kindred nature. If he wants a wife he appears before the kennel of the gentleman whom he has selected for his father-in-law, attended by a party of male friends of a very strong flavour, who screech and whistle and stamp an offer of so many cows for the young lady's hand. The chosen father-in-law—also supported by a high-flavoured party of male friends—screeches, whistles, and yells (being seated on the ground, he can't stamp) that there never was such a daughter in the market as his daughter, and that he must have six more cows. The son-in-law and his select circle of backers screech, whistle, stamp, and yell in reply, that they will give three more cows. The father-in-law (an old deluder, overpaid at the beginning) accepts four, and rises to bind the bargain. The whole party, the young lady included, then falling into epileptic convulsions, and screeching, whistling, stamping, and yelling together—and nobody taking any notice of the young lady (whose charms are not to be thought of without a shudder)—the noble savage is considered married, and his friends make demoniacal leaps at him by way of congratulation.

When the noble savage finds himself a little unwell, and mentions the circumstance to his friends, it is immediately perceived that he is under the influence of witchcraft. A learned personage, called an Imyanger or Witch Doctor, is immediately sent for to Nooker the Umtargartie, or smell out the witch. The male inhabitants of the kraal being seated on the ground, the learned doctor, got up like a grizzly bear, appears, and administers a dance of a most terrific nature, during the exhibition of which remedy he incessantly gnashes his teeth, and howls:—'I am the original physician to Nooker the Umtargartie. Yow yow yow! No connexion with any other establishment. Till till till! All other Umtargarties are feigned Umtargarties, Boroo Boroo! but I perceive here a genuine and real Umtargartie, Hoosh Hoosh Hoosh! in whose blood I, the original Imyanger and Nookerer, Blizzerum Boo! will wash these bear's claws of mine. O yow yow yow!' All this time the learned physician is looking out among the attentive faces for some unfortunate man who owes him a cow, or who has given him any small offence, or against whom, without offence, he has conceived a spite. Him he never fails to Nooker as the Umtargartie, and he is instantly killed. In the absence of such an individual, the usual practice is to Nooker the quietest and most gentlemanly person in company. But the nookering is invariably followed on the spot by the butchering.

Some of the noble savages in whom Mr. Catlin was so strongly interested, and the diminution of whose numbers, by rum and smallpox, greatly affected

515

him, had a custom not unlike this, though much more appalling and disgusting in its odious details.

The women being at work in the fields, hoeing the Indian corn, and the noble savage being asleep in the shade, the chief has sometimes the condescension to come forth, and lighten the labour by looking at it. On these occasions, he seats himself in his own savage chair, and is attended by his shield-bearer: who holds over his head a shield of cowhide—in shape like an immense mussel shell—fearfully and wonderfully, after the manner of a theatrical supernumerary. But lest the great man should forget his greatness in the contemplation of the humble works of agriculture, there suddenly rushes in a poet, retained for the purpose, called a Praiser. This literary gentleman wears a leopard's head over his own, and a dress of tigers' tails; he has the appearance of having come express on his hind legs from the Zoological Gardens; and he incontinently strikes up the chief's praises, plunging and tearing all the while. There is a frantic wickedness in this brute's manner of worrying the air, and gnashing out, 'O what a delightful chief he is! O what a delicious quantity of blood he sheds! O how majestically he laps it up! O how charmingly cruel he is! O how he tears the flesh of his enemies and crunches the bones! O how like the tiger and the leopard and the wolf and the bear he is! O, row row row row, how fond I am of him!' which might tempt the Society of Friends to charge at a hand-gallop into the Swartz-Kop location and exterminate the whole kraal.

When war is afoot among the noble savages—which is always—the chief holds a council to ascertain whether it is the opinion of his brothers and friends in general that the enemy shall be exterminated. On this occasion, after the performance of an Umsebeuza, or war song,—which is exactly like all the other songs,—the chief makes a speech to his brothers and friends, arranged in single file. No particular order is observed during the delivery of this address, but every gentleman who finds himself excited by the subject, instead of crying 'Hear, hear!' as is the custom with us, darts from the rank and tramples out the life, or crushes the skull, or mashes the face, or scoops out the eyes, or breaks the limbs, or performs a whirlwind of atrocities on the body, of an imaginary enemy. Several gentlemen becoming thus excited at once, and pounding away without the least regard to the orator, that illustrious person is rather in the position of an orator in an Irish House of Commons. But, several of these scenes of savage life bear a strong generic resemblance to an Irish election, and I think would be extremely well received and understood at Cork.

In all these ceremonies the noble savage holds forth to the utmost possible extent about himself; from which (to turn him to some civilised account) we may learn, I think, that as egotism is one of the most offensive and contemptible littlenesses a civilised man can exhibit, so it is really incompatible with the interchange of ideas; inasmuch as if we all talked about ourselves we should soon have no listeners, and must be all yelling and screeching at once on our own separate accounts: making society hideous. It is my opinion that if we retained in us anything of the noble savage, we could not get rid of it too soon. But the fact is clearly otherwise. Upon the wife and dowry question, substituting coin for cows, we have assuredly nothing of the Zulu Kaffir left. The endurance of despotism is one great distinguishing mark of a savage always. The improving world has quite got the better of that too. In like manner, Paris is a civilised city, and the Théâtre Français a highly civilised theatre; and we shall never hear, and never have heard in these later days (of course) of the Praiser there. No, no, civilised poets have better work to do. As to Nookering Umtargarties, there are no pretended Umtargarties in Europe, and no European powers to Nooker them; that would be mere spydom, subordination, small malice, superstition, and false pretence. And as to private Umtargarties, are we not in the year eighteen hundred and fifty-three, with spirits rapping at our doors?

To conclude as I began. My position is, that if we have anything to learn from the Noble Savage, it is what to avoid. His virtues are a fable; his happiness is a delusion; his nobility, nonsense.

We have no greater justification for being cruel to the miserable object, than for being cruel to a William Shakespeare or an Isaac Newton; but he passes away before an immeasurably better and higher power than ever ran wild in any earthly woods, and the world will be all the better when his place knows him no more.

A FLIGHT

When Don Diego de—I forget his name—the inventor of the last new Flying Machines, price so many francs for ladies, so many more for gentlemen—when Don Diego, by permission of Deputy Chaff-wax and his noble band, shall have taken out a Patent for the Queen's dominions, and shall have opened a commodious Warehouse in an airy situation; and when all persons of any gentility will keep at least a pair of wings, and be seen skimming about in every direction; I shall take a flight to Paris (as I soar round the world) in a cheap and independent manner. At present, my reliance is on the South-Eastern Railway Company, in whose Express Train here I sit, at eight of the clock on a very hot morning, under the very hot roof of the Terminus at London Bridge, in danger of being 'forced' like a cucumber or a melon, or a pine-apple. And talking of pine-apples, I suppose there never were so many pine-apples in a Train as there appear to be in this Train.

Whew! The hot-house air is faint with pine-apples. Every French citizen or citizeness is carrying pine-apples home. The compact little Enchantress in the corner of my carriage (French actress, to whom I yielded up my heart under the auspices of that brave child, 'Meat-chell,' at the St. James's Theatre the night before last) has a pine-apple in her lap. Compact Enchantress's friend, confidante, mother, mystery, Heaven knows what, has two pine-apples in her lap, and a bundle of them under the seat. Tobacco-smoky Frenchman in Algerine wrapper, with peaked hood behind, who might be Abd-el-Kader dyed rifle-green, and who seems to be dressed entirely in dirt and braid, carries pine-apples in a covered basket. Tall, grave, melancholy Frenchman, with black Vandyke beard, and hair close-cropped, with expansive chest to waistcoat, and compressive waist to coat: saturnine as to his pantaloons, calm as to his feminine boots, precious as to his jewellery, smooth and white as to his linen: dark-eyed, high-foreheaded, hawk-nosed—got up, one thinks, like Lucifer or Mephistopheles, or Zamiel, transformed into a highly genteel Parisian—has the green end of a pine-apple sticking out of his neat valise.

Whew! If I were to be kept here long, under this forcing-frame, I wonder what would become of me—whether I should be forced into a giant, or should sprout or blow into some other phenomenon! Compact Enchantress is not ruffled by the heat—she is always composed, always compact. O look at her little ribbons, frills, and edges, at her shawl, at her gloves, at her hair, at her bracelets, at her bonnet, at everything about her! How is it accomplished? What does she do to be so neat? How is it that every trifle she wears belongs to her, and cannot choose but be a part of her? And even Mystery, look at her! A model. Mystery is not young, not pretty, though still of an average candle-light passability; but she does such miracles in her own behalf, that, one of these days, when she dies, they'll be amazed to find an old woman in her bed, distantly like her. She was an actress once, I shouldn't wonder, and had a Mystery attendant on herself. Perhaps, Compact Enchantress will live to be a Mystery, and to wait with a shawl at the side-scenes, and to sit opposite to Mademoiselle in railway carriages, and smile and talk subserviently, as Mystery does now. That's hard to believe!

Two Englishmen, and now our carriage is full. First Englishman, in the monied interest—flushed, highly respectable—Stock Exchange, perhaps—City, certainly. Faculties of second Englishman entirely absorbed in hurry. Plunges into the carriage, blind. Calls out of window concerning his luggage, deaf. Suffocates himself under pillows of great-coats, for no reason, and in a demented manner. Will receive no assurance from any porter whatsoever. Is stout and hot, and wipes his head, and makes himself hotter by breathing so hard. Is totally incredulous respecting assurance of Collected Guard, that 'there's no hurry.' No hurry! And a flight to Paris in eleven hours!

It is all one to me in this drowsy corner, hurry or no hurry. Until Don Diego shall send home my wings, my flight is with the South-Eastern Company. I can fly with the South-Eastern, more lazily, at all events, than in the upper air. I have but to sit here thinking as idly as I please, and be whisked away. I am not accountable to anybody for the idleness of my thoughts in such an idle summer flight; my flight is provided for by the South-Eastern and is no business of mine.

The bell! With all my heart. It does not require me to do so much as even to flap my wings. Something snorts for me, something shrieks for me, something proclaims to everything else that it had better keep out of my way,—and away I go.

Ah! The fresh air is pleasant after the forcing-frame, though it does blow over these interminable streets, and scatter the smoke of this vast wilderness of chimneys. Here we are—no, I mean there we were, for it has darted far into the rear—in Bermondsey where the tanners live. Flash! The distant shipping in the Thames is gone. Whirr! The little streets of new brick and red tile, with here and there a flagstaff growing like a tall weed out of the scarlet beans, and, everywhere, plenty of open sewer and ditch for the promotion of the public health, have been fired off in a volley. Whizz! Dust-heaps, market-gardens, and waste grounds. Rattle! New Cross Station. Shock! There we were at Croydon. Bur-r-r-r! The tunnel.

I wonder why it is that when I shut my eyes in a tunnel I begin to feel as if I were going at an Express pace the other way. I am clearly going back to London now. Compact Enchantress must have forgotten something, and reversed the engine. No! After long darkness, pale fitful streaks of light appear. I am still flying on for Folkestone. The streaks grow stronger—become continuous—become the ghost of the day—become the living day—became I mean—the tunnel is miles and miles away, and here I fly through sunlight, all among the harvest and the Kentish hops.

There is a dreamy pleasure in this flying. I wonder where it was, and when it was, that we exploded, blew into space somehow, a Parliamentary Train, with a crowd of heads and faces looking at us out of cages, and some hats waving. Monied Interest says it was at Reigate Station. Expounds to Mystery how Reigate Station is so many miles from London, which Mystery again develops to Compact Enchantress. There might be neither a Reigate nor a London for me, as I fly away among the Kentish hops and harvest. What do I care?

Bang! We have let another Station off, and fly away regardless. Everything is flying. The hop-gardens turn gracefully towards me, presenting regular avenues of hops in rapid flight, then whirl away. So do the pools and rushes, haystacks, sheep, clover in full bloom delicious to the sight and smell, corn-sheaves, cherry-orchards, apple-orchards, reapers, gleaners, hedges, gates, fields that taper off into little angular corners, cottages, gardens, now and then a church. Bang, bang! A double-barrelled Station! Now a wood, now a bridge, now a landscape, now a cutting, now a—Bang! a single-barrelled Station—there was a cricket-match somewhere with two white tents, and then four flying cows, then turnips—now the wires of the electric telegraph are all alive, and spin, and blurr their edges, and go up and down, and make the intervals between each other most irregular: contracting and expanding in the strangest manner. Now we slacken. With a screwing, and a grinding, and a smell of water thrown on ashes, now we stop!

Demented Traveller, who has been for two or three minutes watchful, clutches his great-coats, plunges at the door, rattles it, cries 'Hi!' eager to embark on board of impossible packets, far inland. Collected Guard appears. 'Are you for Tunbridge, sir?' 'Tunbridge? No. Paris.' 'Plenty of time, sir. No hurry. Five minutes here, sir, for refreshment.' I am so blest (anticipating Zamiel, by half a second) as to procure a glass of water for Compact Enchantress.

Who would suppose we had been flying at such a rate, and shall take wing again directly? Refreshment-room full, platform full, porter with watering-pot deliberately cooling a hot wheel, another porter with equal deliberation helping the rest of the wheels bountifully to ice cream. Monied Interest and I re-entering the carriage first, and being there alone, he intimates to me that the French are 'no go' as a Nation. I ask why? He says, that Reign of Terror of theirs was quite enough. I ventured to inquire whether he remembers anything that preceded said Reign of Terror? He says not particularly. 'Because,' I remark, 'the harvest that is reaped, has sometimes been sown.' Monied Interest repeats, as quite enough for him, that the French are revolutionary,—'and always at it.'

Bell. Compact Enchantress, helped in by Zamiel (whom the stars confound!), gives us her charming little side-box look, and smites me to the core. Mystery eating sponge-cake. Pine-apple atmosphere faintly tinged with suspicions of sherry. Demented Traveller flits past the carriage, looking for it. Is blind with agitation, and can't see it. Seems singled out by Destiny to be the only unhappy creature in the flight, who has any cause to hurry himself. Is nearly left behind. Is seized by Collected Guard after the Train is in motion, and bundled in. Still, has lingering suspicions that there must be a boat in the neighbourhood, and will look wildly out of window for it.

Flight resumed. Corn-sheaves, hop-gardens, reapers, gleaners, apple-orchards, cherry-orchards, Stations single and double-barrelled, Ashford. Compact Enchantress (constantly talking to Mystery, in an exquisite manner) gives a little scream; a sound that seems to come from high up in her precious little head; from behind her bright little eyebrows. 'Great Heaven, my pine-apple! My Angel! It is lost!' Mystery is desolated. A search made. It is not lost. Zamiel finds it. I curse him (flying) in the Persian manner. May his face be turned upside down, and jackasses sit upon his uncle's grave!

Now fresher air, now glimpses of unenclosed Down-land with flapping crows flying over it whom we soon outfly, now the Sea, now Folkestone at a quarter after ten. 'Tickets ready, gentlemen!' Demented dashes at the door. 'For Paris, sir? No hurry.'

Not the least. We are dropped slowly down to the Port, and sidle to and fro (the whole Train) before the insensible Royal George Hotel, for some ten minutes. The Royal George takes no more heed of us than its namesake under water at Spithead, or under earth at Windsor, does. The Royal George's dog lies winking and blinking at us, without taking the trouble to sit up; and the Royal George's 'wedding party' at the open window (who seem, I must say, rather tired of bliss) don't bestow a solitary glance upon us, flying thus to Paris in eleven hours. The first gentleman in Folkestone is evidently used up, on this subject.

Meanwhile, Demented chafes. Conceives that every man's hand is against him, and exerting itself to prevent his getting to Paris. Refuses consolation. Rattles door. Sees smoke on the horizon, and 'knows' it's the boat gone without him. Monied Interest resentfully explains that he is going to Paris too. Demented signifies, that if Monied Interest chooses to be left behind, he don't.

'Refreshments in the Waiting-Room, ladies and gentlemen. No hurry, ladies and gentlemen, for Paris. No hurry whatever!'

Twenty minutes' pause, by Folkestone clock, for looking at Enchantress while she eats a sandwich, and at Mystery while she eats of everything there that is eatable, from pork-pie, sausage, jam, and gooseberries, to lumps of sugar. All this time, there is a very waterfall of luggage, with a spray of dust, tumbling slantwise from the pier into the steamboat. All this time, Demented (who has no business with it) watches it with starting eyes, fiercely requiring to be shown his luggage. When it at last concludes the cataract, he rushes hotly to refresh—is shouted after, pursued, jostled, brought back, pitched into the departing steamer upside down, and caught by mariners disgracefully.

A lovely harvest-day, a cloudless sky, a tranquil sea. The piston-rods of the engines so regularly coming up from below, to look (as well they may) at the bright weather, and so regularly almost knocking their iron heads against the cross beam of the skylight, and never doing it! Another Parisian actress is on board, attended by another Mystery. Compact Enchantress greets her sister artist—Oh, the Compact One's pretty teeth!—and Mystery greets Mystery. My Mystery soon ceases to be conversational—is taken poorly, in a word, having lunched too miscellaneously—and goes below. The remaining Mystery then smiles upon the sister artists (who, I am afraid, wouldn't greatly mind stabbing each other), and is upon the whole ravished.

And now I find that all the French people on board begin to grow, and all the English people to shrink. The French are nearing home, and shaking off a disadvantage, whereas we are shaking it on. Zamiel is the same man, and Abd-el-Kader is the same man, but each seems to come into possession of an indescribable confidence that departs from us—from Monied Interest, for instance, and from me. Just what they gain, we lose. Certain British 'Gents' about the steersman, intellectually nurtured at home on parody of everything and truth of nothing, become subdued, and in a manner forlorn; and when the steersman tells them (not exultingly) how he has 'been upon this station now eight year, and never see the old town of Bullum yet,' one of them, with an imbecile reliance on a reed, asks him what he considers to be the best hotel in Paris?

Now, I tread upon French ground, and am greeted by the three charming words, Liberty, Equality, Fraternity, painted up (in letters a little too thin for their height) on the Custom-house wall—also by the sight of large cocked hats, without which demonstrative head-gear nothing of a public nature can be done upon this soil. All the rabid Hotel population of Boulogne howl and shriek outside a distant barrier, frantic to get at us. Demented, by some unlucky means peculiar to himself, is delivered over to their fury, and is presently seen struggling in a whirlpool of Touters—is somehow understood to be going to Paris—is, with infinite noise, rescued by two cocked hats, and brought into Custom-house bondage with the rest of us.

Here, I resign the active duties of life to an eager being, of preternatural sharpness, with a shelving forehead and a shabby snuff-coloured coat, who (from the wharf) brought me down with his eye before the boat came into port. He darts upon my luggage, on the floor where all the luggage is strewn like a wreck at the bottom of the great deep; gets it proclaimed and weighed as the property of 'Monsieur a traveller unknown;' pays certain francs for it, to a certain functionary behind a Pigeon Hole, like a pay-box at a Theatre (the arrangements in general are on a wholesale scale, half military and half theatrical); and I suppose I shall find it when I come to Paris—he says I shall. I know nothing about it, except that I pay him his small fee, and pocket the ticket he gives me, and sit upon a counter, involved in the general distraction.

Railway station. 'Lunch or dinner, ladies and gentlemen. Plenty of time for Paris. Plenty of time!' Large hall, long counter, long strips of dining-table, bottles of wine, plates of meat, roast chickens, little loaves of bread, basins of soup, little caraffes of brandy, cakes, and fruit. Comfortably restored from these resources, I begin to fly again.

I saw Zamiel (before I took wing) presented to Compact Enchantress and Sister Artist, by an officer in uniform, with a waist like a wasp's, and pantaloons like two balloons. They all got into the next carriage together, accompanied by the two Mysteries. They laughed. I am alone in the carriage (for I don't consider Demented anybody) and alone in the world.

Fields, windmills, low grounds, pollard-trees, windmills, fields, fortifications, Abbeville, soldiering and drumming. I wonder where England is, and when I was there last—about two years ago, I should say. Flying in and out among these trenches and batteries, skimming the clattering drawbridges, looking down into the stagnant ditches, I become a prisoner of state, escaping. I am confined with a comrade in a fortress. Our room is in an upper story. We have tried to get up the chimney, but there's an iron grating across it, imbedded in the masonry. After months of labour, we have worked the grating loose with the poker, and can lift it up. We have also made a hook, and twisted our rugs and blankets into ropes. Our plan is, to go up the chimney, hook our ropes to the top, descend hand over hand upon the roof of the guard-house far below, shake the hook loose, watch the opportunity of the sentinels pacing away, hook again, drop into the ditch, swim across it, creep into the shelter of the wood. The time is come—a wild and stormy night. We are up the chimney, we are on the guard-house roof, we are swimming in the murky ditch, when lo! 'Qui v'là?' a bugle, the alarm, a crash! What is it? Death? No, Amiens.

More fortifications, more soldiering and drumming, more basins of soup, more little loaves of bread, more bottles of wine, more caraffes of brandy, more time for refreshment. Everything good, and everything ready. Bright, unsubstantial-looking, scenic sort of station. People waiting. Houses, uniforms, beards, moustaches, some sabots, plenty of neat women, and a few old-visaged children. Unless it be a delusion born of my giddy flight, the grown-up people and the children seem to change places in France. In general, the boys and girls are little old men and women, and the men and women lively boys and girls.

Bugle, shriek, flight resumed. Monied Interest has come into my carriage. Says the manner of refreshing is 'not bad,' but considers it French. Admits great dexterity and politeness in the attendants. Thinks a decimal currency may have something to do with their despatch in settling accounts, and don't know but what it's sensible and convenient. Adds, however, as a general protest, that they're a revolutionary people—and always at it.

Ramparts, canals, cathedral, river, soldiering and drumming, open country, river, earthenware manufactures, Creil. Again ten minutes. Not even Demented in a hurry. Station, a drawing-room with a verandah: like a planter's house. Monied Interest considers it a band-box, and not made to last. Little round tables in it, at one of which the Sister Artists and attendant Mysteries are established with Wasp and Zamiel, as if they were going to stay a week.

Anon, with no more trouble than before, I am flying again, and lazily wondering as I fly. What has the South-Eastern done with all the horrible little villages we used to pass through, in the Diligence? What have they done with all the summer dust, with all the winter mud, with all the dreary avenues of little trees, with all the ramshackle postyards, with all the beggars (who used to turn out at night with bits of lighted candle, to look in at the coach windows), with all the long-tailed horses who were always biting one another, with all the big postilions in jack-boots—with all the mouldy cafés that we used to stop at, where a long mildewed table-cloth, set forth with jovial bottles of vinegar and oil, and with a Siamese arrangement of pepper and salt, was never wanting? Where are the grass-grown little towns, the wonderful little market-places all unconscious of markets, the shops that nobody kept, the streets that nobody trod, the churches that nobody went to, the bells that nobody rang, the tumble-down old buildings plastered with many-coloured bills that nobody read? Where are the two-and-twenty weary hours of long, long day and night journey, sure to be either insupportably hot or insupportably cold? Where are the pains in my bones, where are the fidgets in my legs, where is the Frenchman with the nightcap who never would have the little coupé-window down, and who always fell upon me when he went to sleep, and always slept all night snoring onions?

A voice breaks in with 'Paris! Here we are!'

I have overflown myself, perhaps, but I can't believe it. I feel as if I were enchanted or bewitched. It is barely eight o'clock yet—it is nothing like half-past—when I have had my luggage examined at that briskest of Custom-houses attached to the station, and am rattling over the pavement in a hackney-cabriolet.

Surely, not the pavement of Paris? Yes, I think it is, too. I don't know any other place where there are all these high houses, all these haggard-looking wine shops, all these billiard tables, all these stocking-makers with flat red or yellow legs of wood for signboard, all these fuel shops with stacks of billets painted outside, and real billets sawing in the gutter, all these dirty corners of streets, all these cabinet pictures over dark doorways representing discreet matrons nursing babies. And yet this morning—I'll think of it in a warm-bath.

Very like a small room that I remember in the Chinese baths upon the Boulevard, certainly; and, though I see it through the steam, I think that I might swear to that peculiar hot-linen basket, like a large wicker hour-glass. When can it have been that I left home? When was it that I paid 'through to Paris' at London Bridge, and discharged myself of all responsibility, except the preservation of a voucher ruled into three divisions, of which the first was snipped off at Folkestone, the second aboard the boat, and the third taken at my journey's end? It seems to have been ages ago. Calculation is useless. I will go out for a walk.

The crowds in the streets, the lights in the shops and balconies, the elegance, variety, and beauty of their decorations, the number of the theatres, the brilliant cafés with their windows thrown up high and their vivacious groups at little tables on the pavement, the light and glitter of the houses turned as it were inside out, soon convince me that it is no dream; that I am in Paris, howsoever I got there. I stroll down to the sparkling Palais Royal, up the Rue de Rivoli, to the Place Vendôme. As I glance into a print-shop window, Monied Interest, my late travelling companion, comes upon me, laughing with the highest relish of disdain. 'Here's a people!' he says, pointing to Napoleon in the window and Napoleon on the column. 'Only one idea all over Paris! A monomania!' Humph! I THINK I have seen Napoleon's match? There was a statue, when I came away, at Hyde Park Corner, and another in the City, and a print or two in the shops.

I walk up to the Barrière de l'Etoile, sufficiently dazed by my flight to have a pleasant doubt of the reality of everything about me; of the lively crowd, the overhanging trees, the performing dogs, the hobby-horses, the beautiful perspectives of shining lamps: the hundred and one enclosures, where the singing is, in gleaming orchestras of azure and gold, and where a star-eyed Houri comes round with a box for voluntary offerings. So, I pass to my hotel, enchanted; sup, enchanted; go to bed, enchanted; pushing back this morning (if it really were this morning) into the remoteness of time, blessing the South-Eastern Company for realising the Arabian Nights in these prose days, murmuring, as I wing my idle flight into the land of dreams, 'No hurry, ladies and gentlemen, going to Paris in eleven hours. It is so well done, that there really is no hurry!'

THE DETECTIVE POLICE

We are not by any means devout believers in the old Bow Street Police. To say the truth, we think there was a vast amount of humbug about those worthies. Apart from many of them being men of very indifferent character, and far too much in the habit of consorting with thieves and the like, they never lost a public occasion of jobbing and trading in mystery and making the most of themselves. Continually puffed besides by incompetent magistrates anxious to conceal their own deficiencies, and hand-in-glove with the penny-a-liners of that time, they became a sort of superstition. Although as a Preventive Police they were utterly ineffective, and as a Detective Police were very loose and uncertain in their operations, they remain with some people a superstition to the present day.

On the other hand, the Detective Force organised since the establishment of the existing Police, is so well chosen and trained, proceeds so systematically and quietly, does its business in such a workmanlike manner, and is always so calmly and steadily engaged in the service of the public, that the public really do not know enough of it, to know a tithe of its usefulness. Impressed with this conviction, and interested in the men themselves, we represented to the authorities at Scotland Yard, that we should be glad, if there were no official objection, to have some talk with the Detectives. A most obliging and ready permission being given, a certain evening was appointed with a certain Inspector for a social conference between ourselves and the Detectives, at The Household Words Office in Wellington Street, Strand, London. In consequence of which appointment the party 'came off,' which we are about to describe. And we beg to repeat that, avoiding such topics as it might for obvious reasons be injurious to the public, or disagreeable to respectable individuals, to touch upon in print, our description is as exact as we can make it.

The reader will have the goodness to imagine the Sanctum Sanctorum of Household Words. Anything that best suits the reader's fancy, will best represent that magnificent chamber. We merely stipulate for a round table in the middle, with some glasses and cigars arranged upon it; and the editorial sofa elegantly hemmed in between that stately piece of furniture and the wall.

It is a sultry evening at dusk. The stones of Wellington Street are hot and gritty, and the watermen and hackney-coachmen at the Theatre opposite, are much flushed and aggravated. Carriages are constantly setting down the people who have come to Fairy-Land; and there is a mighty shouting and bellowing every now and then, deafening us for the moment, through the open windows.

Just at dusk, Inspectors Wield and Stalker are announced; but we do not undertake to warrant the orthography of any of the names here mentioned. Inspector Wield presents Inspector Stalker. Inspector Wield is a middle-aged man of a portly presence, with a large, moist, knowing eye, a husky voice, and a habit of emphasising his conversation by the aid of a corpulent fore-finger, which is constantly in juxtaposition with his eyes or nose. Inspector Stalker is a shrewd, hard-headed Scotchman—in appearance not at all unlike a very acute, thoroughly-trained schoolmaster, from the Normal Establishment at Glasgow. Inspector Wield one might have known, perhaps, for what he is— Inspector Stalker, never.

The ceremonies of reception over, Inspectors Wield and Stalker observe that they have brought some sergeants with them. The sergeants are presented—five in number, Sergeant Dornton, Sergeant Witchem, Sergeant Mith, Sergeant Fendall, and Sergeant Straw. We have the whole Detective Force from Scotland Yard, with one exception. They sit down in a semi-circle (the two Inspectors at the two ends) at a little distance from the round table, facing the editorial sofa. Every man of them, in a glance, immediately takes an inventory of the furniture and an accurate sketch of the editorial presence. The Editor feels that any gentleman in company could take him up, if need should be, without the smallest hesitation, twenty years hence.

The whole party are in plain clothes. Sergeant Dornton about fifty years of age, with a ruddy face and a high sunburnt forehead, has the air of one who has been a Sergeant in the army—he might have sat to Wilkie for the Soldier in the Reading of the Will. He is famous for steadily pursuing the inductive process, and, from small beginnings, working on from clue to clue until he bags his man. Sergeant Witchem, shorter and thicker-set, and marked with the small-pox, has something of a reserved and thoughtful air, as if he were engaged in deep arithmetical calculations. He is renowned for his acquaintance with the swell mob. Sergeant Mith, a smooth-faced man with a fresh bright complexion, and a strange air of simplicity, is a dab at housebreakers. Sergeant Fendall, a light-haired, well-spoken, polite person, is a prodigious hand at pursuing private inquiries of a delicate nature. Straw, a little wiry Sergeant of meek demeanour and strong sense, would knock at a door and ask a series of questions in any mild character you choose to prescribe to him, from a charity-boy upwards, and seem as innocent as an infant. They are, one and all, respectable-looking men; of perfectly good deportment and unusual intelligence; with nothing lounging or slinking in their manners; with an air of keen observation and quick perception when addressed; and generally presenting in their faces, traces more or less marked of habitually leading lives of strong mental excitement. They have all good eyes; and they all can, and they all do, look full at whomsoever they speak to.

We light the cigars, and hand round the glasses (which are very temperately used indeed), and the conversation begins by a modest amateur reference on the Editorial part to the swell mob. Inspector Wield immediately removes his cigar from his lips, waves his right hand, and says, 'Regarding the swell mob, sir, I can't do better than call upon Sergeant Witchem. Because the reason why? I'll tell you. Sergeant Witchem is better acquainted with the swell mob than any officer in London.'

Our heart leaping up when we beheld this rainbow in the sky, we turn to Sergeant Witchem, who very concisely, and in well-chosen language, goes into the subject forthwith. Meantime, the whole of his brother officers are closely interested in attending to what he says, and observing its effect. Presently they begin to strike in, one or two together, when an opportunity offers, and the conversation becomes general. But these brother officers only come in to the assistance of each other—not to the contradiction—and a more amicable brotherhood there could not be. From the swell mob, we diverge to the kindred topics of cracksmen, fences, public-house dancers, area-sneaks, designing young people who go out 'gonophing,' and other 'schools.' It is observable throughout these revelations, that Inspector Stalker, the Scotchman, is always exact and statistical, and that when any question of figures arises, everybody as by one consent pauses, and looks to him.

When we have exhausted the various schools of Art—during which discussion the whole body have remained profoundly attentive, except when some unusual noise at the Theatre over the way has induced some gentleman to glance inquiringly towards the window in that direction, behind his next neighbour's back—we burrow for information on such points as the following. Whether there really are any highway robberies in London, or whether some circumstances not convenient to be mentioned by the aggrieved party, usually precede the robberies complained of, under that head, which quite change their character? Certainly the latter, almost always. Whether in the case of robberies in houses, where servants are necessarily exposed to doubt, innocence under suspicion ever becomes so like guilt in appearance, that a good officer need be cautious how he judges it? Undoubtedly. Nothing is so common or deceptive as such appearances at first. Whether in a place of public amusement, a thief knows an officer, and an officer knows a thief—supposing them, beforehand, strangers to each other—because each recognises in the other, under all disguise, an inattention to what is going on, and a purpose that is not the purpose of being entertained? Yes. That's the way exactly. Whether it is reasonable or ridiculous to trust to the alleged experiences of thieves as narrated by themselves, in prisons, or penitentiaries, or anywhere? In general, nothing more absurd. Lying is their habit and their trade; and they would rather lie—even if they hadn't an interest in it, and didn't want to make themselves agreeable—than tell the truth.

From these topics, we glide into a review of the most celebrated and horrible of the great crimes that have been committed within the last fifteen or twenty years. The men engaged in the discovery of almost all of them, and in the pursuit or apprehension of the murderers, are here, down to the very last instance. One of our guests gave chase to and boarded the emigrant ship, in which the murderess last hanged in London was supposed to have embarked.

We learn from him that his errand was not announced to the passengers, who may have no idea of it to this hour. That he went below, with the captain, lamp in hand—it being dark, and the whole steerage abed and sea-sick—and engaged the Mrs. Manning who was on board, in a conversation about her luggage, until she was, with no small pains, induced to raise her head, and turn her face towards the light. Satisfied that she was not the object of his search, he quietly re-embarked in the Government steamer along-side, and steamed home again with the intelligence.

When we have exhausted these subjects, too, which occupy a considerable time in the discussion, two or three leave their chairs, whisper Sergeant Witchem, and resume their seat. Sergeant Witchem, leaning forward a little, and placing a hand on each of his legs, then modestly speaks as follows:

'My brother-officers wish me to relate a little account of my taking Tally-ho Thompson. A man oughtn't to tell what he has done himself; but still, as nobody was with me, and, consequently, as nobody but myself can tell it, I'll do it in the best way I can, if it should meet your approval.'

We assure Sergeant Witchem that he will oblige us very much, and we all compose ourselves to listen with great interest and attention.

'Tally-ho Thompson,' says Sergeant Witchem, after merely wetting his lips with his brandy-and-water, 'Tally-ho Thompson was a famous horse-stealer, couper, and magsman. Thompson, in conjunction with a pal that occasionally worked with him, gammoned a countryman out of a good round sum of money, under pretence of getting him a situation—the regular old dodge—and was afterwards in the "Hue and Cry" for a horse—a horse that he stole down in Hertfordshire. I had to look after Thompson, and I applied myself, of course, in the first instance, to discovering where he was. Now, Thompson's wife lived, along with a little daughter, at Chelsea. Knowing that Thompson was somewhere in the country, I watched the house—especially at post-time in the morning—thinking Thompson was pretty likely to write to her. Sure enough, one morning the postman comes up, and delivers a letter at Mrs. Thompson's door. Little girl opens the door, and takes it in. We're not always sure of postmen, though the people at the post-offices are always very obliging. A postman may help us, or he may not,—just as it happens. However, I go across the road, and I say to the postman, after he has left the letter, "Good morning! how are you?" "How are you?" says he. "You've just delivered a letter for Mrs. Thompson." "Yes, I have." "You didn't happen to remark what the post-mark was, perhaps?" "No," says he, "I didn't." "Come," says I, "I'll be plain with you. I'm in a small way of business, and I have given Thompson credit, and I can't afford to lose what he owes me. I know he's got money, and I know he's in the country, and if you could tell me what the post-mark was, I should be very much obliged to you, and you'd do a service to a tradesman in a small way of business that can't afford a loss." "Well," he said, "I do assure you that I did not observe what the post-mark was; all I know is, that there was money in the letter—I should say a sovereign." This was enough for me, because of course I knew that Thompson having sent his wife money, it was probable she'd write to Thompson, by return of post, to acknowledge the receipt. So I said "Thankee" to the postman, and I kept on the watch. In the afternoon I saw the little girl come out. Of course I followed her. She went into a stationer's shop, and I needn't say to you that I looked in at the window. She bought some writing-paper and envelopes, and a pen. I think to myself, "That'll do!"—watch her home again—and don't go away, you may be sure, knowing that Mrs. Thompson was writing her letter to Tally-ho, and that the letter would be posted presently. In about an hour or so, out came the little girl again, with the letter in her hand. I went up, and said something to the child, whatever it might have been; but I couldn't see the direction of the letter, because she held it with the seal upwards. However, I observed that on the back of the letter there was what we call a kiss—a drop of wax by the side of the seal—and again, you understand, that was enough for me. I saw her post the letter, waited till she was gone, then went into the shop, and asked to see the Master. When he came out, I told him, "Now, I'm an Officer in the Detective Force; there's a letter with a kiss been posted here just now, for a man that I'm in search of; and what I have to ask of you, is, that you will let me look at the direction of that letter." He was very civil—took a lot of letters from the box in the window—shook 'em out on the counter with the faces downwards—and there among 'em was the identical letter with the kiss. It was directed, Mr. Thomas Pigeon, Post Office, B—, to be left till called for. Down I went to B— (a hundred and twenty miles or so) that night. Early next morning I went to the Post Office; saw the gentleman in charge of that department; told him who I was; and that my object was to see, and track, the party that should come for the letter for Mr. Thomas Pigeon. He was very polite, and said, "You shall have every assistance we can give you; you can wait inside the office; and we'll take care to let you know when anybody comes for the letter." Well, I waited there three days, and began to think that nobody ever would come. At last the clerk whispered to me, "Here! Detective! Somebody's come for the letter!" "Keep him a minute," said I, and I ran round to the outside of the office. There I saw a young chap with the appearance of an Ostler, holding a horse by the bridle—stretching the bridle across the pavement, while he waited at the Post Office Window for the letter. I began to pat the horse, and that; and I said to the boy, "Why, this is Mr. Jones's Mare!" "No. It an't." "No?" said I. "She's very like Mr. Jones's Mare!" "She an't Mr. Jones's Mare, anyhow," says he. "It's Mr. So and So's, of the Warwick Arms." And up he jumped, and off he went—letter and all. I got a cab, followed on the box, and was so quick after him that I came into the stable-yard of the Warwick Arms, by one gate, just as he came in by another. I went into the bar, where there was a young woman serving, and called for a glass of brandy-and-water. He came in directly, and handed her the letter. She casually looked at it, without saying anything, and stuck it up behind the glass over the chimney-piece. What was to be done next?

'I turned it over in my mind while I drank my brandy-and-water (looking pretty sharp at the letter the while), but I couldn't see my way out of it at all. I tried to get lodgings in the house, but there had been a horse-fair, or something of that sort, and it was full. I was obliged to put up somewhere else, but I came backwards and forwards to the bar for a couple of days, and there was the letter always behind the glass. At last I thought I'd write a letter to Mr. Pigeon myself, and see what that would do. So I wrote one, and posted it, but I purposely addressed it, Mr. John Pigeon, instead of Mr. Thomas Pigeon, to see what that would do. In the morning (a very wet morning it was) I watched the postman down the street, and cut into the bar, just before he reached the Warwick Arms. In he came presently with my letter. "Is there a Mr. John Pigeon staying here?" "No!—stop a bit though," says the barmaid; and she took down the letter behind the glass. "No," says she, "it's Thomas, and he is not staying here. Would you do me a favour, and post this for me, as it is so wet?" The postman said Yes; she folded it in another envelope, directed it, and gave it him. He put it in his hat, and away he went.

'I had no difficulty in finding out the direction of that letter. It was addressed Mr. Thomas Pigeon, Post Office, R——, Northamptonshire, to be left till called for. Off I started directly for R——; I said the same at the Post Office there, as I had said at B——; and again I waited three days before anybody came. At last another chap on horseback came. "Any letters for Mr. Thomas Pigeon?" "Where do you come from?" "New Inn, near R——." He got the letter, and away he went at a canter.

'I made my inquiries about the New Inn, near R——, and hearing it was a solitary sort of house, a little in the horse line, about a couple of miles from the station, I thought I'd go and have a look at it. I found it what it had been described, and sauntered in, to look about me. The landlady was in the bar, and I was trying to get into conversation with her; asked her how business was, and spoke about the wet weather, and so on; when I saw, through an open door, three men sitting by the fire in a sort of parlour, or kitchen; and one of those men, according to the description I had of him, was Tally-ho Thompson!

'I went and sat down among 'em, and tried to make things agreeable; but they were very shy—wouldn't talk at all—looked at me, and at one another, in a way quite the reverse of sociable. I reckoned 'em up, and finding that they were all three bigger men than me, and considering that their looks were ugly—that it was a lonely place—railroad station two miles off—and night coming on—thought I couldn't do better than have a drop of brandy-and-water to keep my courage up. So I called for my brandy-and-water; and as I was sitting drinking it by the fire, Thompson got up and went out.

'Now the difficulty of it was, that I wasn't sure it was Thompson, because I had never set eyes on him before; and what I had wanted was to be quite certain of him. However, there was nothing for it now, but to follow, and put a bold face upon it. I found him talking, outside in the yard, with the landlady. It turned out afterwards that he was wanted by a Northampton officer for something else, and that, knowing that officer to be pock-marked (as I am myself), he mistook me for him. As I have observed, I found him talking to the landlady, outside. I put my hand upon his shoulder—this way—and said, "Tally-ho Thompson, it's no use. I know you. I'm an officer from London, and I take you into custody for felony!" "That be d-d!" says Tally-ho Thompson.

'We went back into the house, and the two friends began to cut up rough, and their looks didn't please me at all, I assure you. "Let the man go. What are you going to do with him?" "I'll tell you what I'm going to do with him. I'm going to take him to London to-night, as sure as I'm alive. I'm not alone here, whatever you may think. You mind your own business, and keep yourselves to yourselves. It'll be better for you, for I know you both very well." I'd never seen or heard of 'em in all my life, but my bouncing cowed 'em a bit, and they kept off, while Thompson was making ready to go. I thought to myself, however, that they might be coming after me on the dark road, to rescue Thompson; so I said to the landlady, "What men have you got in the house, Missis?" "We haven't got no men here," she says, sulkily. "You have got an ostler, I suppose?" "Yes, we've got an ostler." "Let me see him." Presently he came, and a shaggy-headed young fellow he was. "Now attend to me, young man," says I; "I'm a Detective Officer from London. This man's name is Thompson. I have taken him into custody for felony. I am going to take him to the railroad station. I call upon you in the Queen's name to assist me; and mind you, my friend, you'll get yourself into more trouble than you know of, if you don't!" You never saw a person open his eyes so wide. "Now, Thompson, come along!" says I. But when I took out the handcuffs, Thompson cries, "No! None of that! I won't stand them! I'll go along with you quiet, but I won't bear none of that!" "Tally-ho Thompson," I said, "I'm willing to behave as a man to you, if you are willing to behave as a man to me. Give me your word that you'll come peaceably along, and I don't want to handcuff you." "I will," says Thompson, "but I'll have a glass of brandy first." "I don't care if I've another," said I. "We'll have two more, Missis," said the friends, "and confound you, Constable, you'll give your man a drop, won't you?" I was agreeable to that, so we had it all round, and then my man and I took Tally-ho Thompson safe to the railroad, and I carried him to London that night. He was afterwards acquitted, on account of a defect in the evidence; and I understand he always praises me up to the skies, and says I'm one of the best of men.'

This story coming to a termination amidst general applause, Inspector Wield, after a little grave smoking, fixes his eye on his host, and thus delivers himself:

'It wasn't a bad plant that of mine, on Fikey, the man accused of forging the Sou'-Western Railway debentures—it was only t'other day—because the reason why? I'll tell you.

'I had information that Fikey and his brother kept a factory over yonder there,'—indicating any region on the Surrey side of the river—'where he bought second-hand carriages; so after I'd tried in vain to get hold of him by other means, I wrote him a letter in an assumed name, saying that I'd got a horse and shay to dispose of, and would drive down next day that he might view the lot, and make an offer—very reasonable it was, I said—a reg'lar bargain. Straw and me then went off to a friend of mine that's in the livery and job business, and hired a turn-out for the day, a precious smart turn-out it was—quite a slap-up thing! Down we drove, accordingly, with a friend (who's not in the Force himself); and leaving my friend in the shay near a public-house, to take care of the horse, we went to the factory, which was some little way off. In the factory, there was a number of strong fellows at work, and after reckoning 'em up, it was clear to me that it wouldn't do to try it on there. They were too many for us. We must get our man out of doors. "Mr. Fikey at home?" "No, he ain't." "Expected home soon?" "Why, no, not soon." "Ah! Is his brother here?" "I'm his brother." "Oh! well, this is an ill-conwenience, this is. I wrote him a letter yesterday, saying I'd got a little turn-out to dispose of, and I've took the trouble to bring the turn-out down a' purpose, and now he ain't in the way." "No, he ain't in the way. You couldn't make it convenient to call again, could you?" "Why, no, I couldn't. I want to sell; that's the fact; and I can't put it off. Could you find him anywheres?" At first he said No, he couldn't, and then he wasn't sure about it, and then he'd

538

go and try. So at last he went up-stairs, where there was a sort of loft, and presently down comes my man himself in his shirt-sleeves.

'"Well," he says, "this seems to be rayther a pressing matter of yours." "Yes," I says, "it is rayther a pressing matter, and you'll find it a bargain—dirt cheap." "I ain't in partickler want of a bargain just now," he says, "but where is it?" "Why," I says, "the turn-out's just outside. Come and look at it." He hasn't any suspicions, and away we go. And the first thing that happens is, that the horse runs away with my friend (who knows no more of driving than a child) when he takes a little trot along the road to show his paces. You never saw such a game in your life!

'When the bolt is over, and the turn-out has come to a standstill again, Fikey walks round and round it as grave as a judge—me too. "There, sir!" I says. "There's a neat thing!" "It ain't a bad style of thing," he says. "I believe you," says I. "And there's a horse!"—for I saw him looking at it. "Rising eight!" I says, rubbing his fore-legs. (Bless you, there ain't a man in the world knows less of horses than I do, but I'd heard my friend at the Livery Stables say he was eight year old, so I says, as knowing as possible, "Rising eight.") "Rising eight, is he?" says he. "Rising eight," says I. "Well," he says, "what do you want for it?" "Why, the first and last figure for the whole concern is five-and-twenty pound!" "That's very cheap!" he says, looking at me. "Ain't it?" I says. "I told you it was a bargain! Now, without any higgling and haggling about it, what I want is to sell, and that's my price. Further, I'll make it easy to you, and take half the money down, and you can do a bit of stiff [415] for the balance."

"Well," he says again, "that's very cheap." "I believe you," says I; "get in and try it, and you'll buy it. Come! take a trial!"

'Ecod, he gets in, and we get in, and we drive along the road, to show him to one of the railway clerks that was hid in the public-house window to identify him. But the clerk was bothered, and didn't know whether it was him, or wasn't—because the reason why? I'll tell you,—on account of his having shaved his whiskers. "It's a clever little horse," he says, "and trots well; and the shay runs light." "Not a doubt about it," I says. "And now, Mr. Fikey,

I may as well make it all right, without wasting any more of your time. The fact is, I'm Inspector Wield, and you're my prisoner." "You don't mean that?" he says. "I do, indeed." "Then burn my body," says Fikey, "if this ain't too bad!"

'Perhaps you never saw a man so knocked over with surprise. "I hope you'll let me have my coat?" he says. "By all means." "Well, then, let's drive to the factory." "Why, not exactly that, I think," said I; "I've been there, once before, to-day. Suppose we send for it." He saw it was no go, so he sent for it, and put it on, and we drove him up to London, comfortable.'

This reminiscence is in the height of its success, when a general proposal is made to the fresh-complexioned, smooth-faced officer, with the strange air of simplicity, to tell the 'Butcher's Story.'

The fresh-complexioned, smooth-faced officer, with the strange air of simplicity, began with a rustic smile, and in a soft, wheedling tone of voice, to relate the Butcher's Story, thus:

'It's just about six years ago, now, since information was given at Scotland Yard of there being extensive robberies of lawns and silks going on, at some wholesale houses in the City. Directions were given for the business being looked into; and Straw, and Fendall, and me, we were all in it.'

'When you received your instructions,' said we, 'you went away, and held a sort of Cabinet Council together!'

The smooth-faced officer coaxingly replied, 'Ye-es. Just so. We turned it over among ourselves a good deal. It appeared, when we went into it, that the goods were sold by the receivers extraordinarily cheap—much cheaper than they could have been if they had been honestly come by. The receivers were in the trade, and kept capital shops—establishments of the first respectability— one of 'em at the West End, one down in Westminster. After a lot of watching and inquiry, and this and that among ourselves, we found that the job was managed, and the purchases of the stolen goods made, at a little public-house near Smithfield, down by Saint Bartholomew's; where the Warehouse Porters, who were the thieves, took 'em for that purpose, don't you see? and made appointments to meet the people that went between themselves and the receivers. This public-house was principally used by journeymen butchers from the country, out of place, and in want of situations; so, what did we do, but—ha, ha, ha!—we agreed that I should be dressed up like a butcher myself, and go and live there!'

Never, surely, was a faculty of observation better brought to bear upon a purpose, than that which picked out this officer for the part. Nothing in all creation could have suited him better. Even while he spoke, he became a greasy, sleepy, shy, good-natured, chuckle-headed, unsuspicious, and confiding young butcher. His very hair seemed to have suet in it, as he made it smooth upon his head, and his fresh complexion to be lubricated by large quantities of animal food.

'—So I—ha, ha, ha!' (always with the confiding snigger of the foolish young butcher) 'so I dressed myself in the regular way, made up a little bundle of clothes, and went to the public-house, and asked if I could have a lodging there? They says, "yes, you can have a lodging here," and I got a bedroom, and settled myself down in the tap. There was a number of people about the place, and coming backwards and forwards to the house; and first one says, and then another says, "Are you from the country, young man?" "Yes," I says, "I am. I'm come out of Northamptonshire, and I'm quite lonely here, for I don't know London at all, and it's such a mighty big town." "It is a big town," they says. "Oh, it's a very big town!" I says. "Really and truly I never was in such a town. It quite confuses of me!" and all that, you know.

'When some of the journeymen Butchers that used the house, found that I wanted a place, they says, "Oh, we'll get you a place!" And they actually took me to a sight of places, in Newgate Market, Newport Market, Clare, Carnaby—I don't know where all. But the wages was—ha, ha, ha!—was not sufficient, and I never could suit myself, don't you see? Some of the queer frequenters of the house were a little suspicious of me at first, and I was obliged to be very cautious indeed how I communicated with Straw or Fendall. Sometimes, when I went out, pretending to stop and look into the shop windows, and just casting my eye round, I used to see some of 'em following me; but, being perhaps better accustomed than they thought for, to that sort of thing, I used to lead 'em on as far as I thought necessary or convenient—sometimes a long way—and then turn sharp round, and meet 'em, and say, "Oh, dear, how glad I am to come upon you so fortunate! This London's such a place, I'm blowed if I ain't lost again!" And then we'd go back all together, to the public-house, and—ha, ha, ha! and smoke our pipes, don't you see?

'They were very attentive to me, I am sure. It was a common thing, while I was living there, for some of 'em to take me out, and show me London. They showed me the Prisons—showed me Newgate—and when they showed me Newgate, I stops at the place where the Porters pitch their loads, and says, "Oh dear, is this where they hang the men? Oh Lor!" "That!" they says, "what a simple cove he is! That ain't it!" And then, they pointed out which was it, and I says "Lor!" and they says, "Now you'll know it agen, won't you?" And I said I thought I should if I tried hard—and I assure you I kept a sharp look out for the City Police when we were out in this way, for if any of 'em had happened to know me, and had spoke to me, it would have been all up in a minute. However, by good luck such a thing never happened, and all went on quiet: though the difficulties I had in communicating with my brother officers were quite extraordinary.

'The stolen goods that were brought to the public-house by the Warehouse Porters, were always disposed of in a back parlour. For a long time, I never could get into this parlour, or see what was done there. As I sat smoking my pipe, like an innocent young chap, by the tap-room fire, I'd hear some of the parties to the robbery, as they came in and out, say softly to the landlord, "Who's that? What does he do here?" "Bless your soul," says the landlord, "he's only a"—ha, ha, ha!—"he's only a green young fellow from the country, as is looking for a butcher's sitiwation. Don't mind him!" So, in course of time, they were so convinced of my being green, and got to be so accustomed to me, that I was as free of the parlour as any of 'em, and I have seen as much as Seventy Pounds' Worth of fine lawn sold there, in one night, that was stolen from a warehouse in Friday Street. After the sale the buyers always stood treat—hot supper, or dinner, or what not—and they'd say on those occasions, "Come on, Butcher! Put your best leg foremost, young 'un, and walk into it!" Which I used to do—and hear, at table, all manner of particulars that it was very important for us Detectives to know.

'This went on for ten weeks. I lived in the public-house all the time, and never was out of the Butcher's dress—except in bed. At last, when I had followed seven of the thieves, and set 'em to rights—that's an expression of ours, don't you see, by which I mean to say that I traced 'em, and found out where the robberies were done, and all about 'em—Straw, and Fendall, and I, gave one another the office, and at a time agreed upon, a descent was made upon the public-house, and the apprehensions effected. One of the first things the officers did, was to collar me—for the parties to the robbery weren't to suppose yet, that I was anything but a Butcher—on which the landlord cries out, "Don't take him," he says, "whatever you do! He's only a poor young chap from the country, and butter wouldn't melt in his mouth!" However, they—ha, ha, ha!—they took me, and pretended to search my bedroom, where nothing was found but an old fiddle belonging to the landlord, that had got there somehow or another. But, it entirely changed the landlord's opinion, for when it was produced, he says, "My fiddle! The Butcher's a purloiner! I give him into custody for the robbery of a musical instrument!"

'The man that had stolen the goods in Friday Street was not taken yet. He had told me, in confidence, that he had his suspicions there was something wrong (on account of the City Police having captured one of the party), and that he was going to make himself scarce. I asked him, "Where do you mean to go, Mr. Shepherdson?" "Why, Butcher," says he, "the Setting Moon, in the Commercial Road, is a snug house, and I shall bang out there for a time. I shall call myself Simpson, which appears to me to be a modest sort of a name. Perhaps you'll give us a look in, Butcher?" "Well," says I, "I think I will give you a call"—which I fully intended, don't you see, because, of course, he was to be taken! I went over to the Setting Moon next day, with a brother officer, and asked at the bar for Simpson. They pointed out his room, up-stairs. As we were going up, he looks down over the banister, and calls out, "Halloa, Butcher! is that you?" "Yes, it's me. How do you find yourself?" "Bobbish," he says; "but who's that with you?" "It's only a young man, that's a friend of mine," I says. "Come along, then," says he; "any friend of the Butcher's is as welcome as the Butcher!" So, I made my friend acquainted with him, and we took him into custody.

'You have no idea, sir, what a sight it was, in Court, when they first knew that I wasn't a Butcher, after all! I wasn't produced at the first examination, when there was a remand; but I was at the second. And when I stepped into the box, in full police uniform, and the whole party saw how they had been done, actually a groan of horror and dismay proceeded from 'em in the dock!

'At the Old Bailey, when their trials came on, Mr. Clarkson was engaged for the defence, and he couldn't make out how it was, about the Butcher. He thought, all along, it was a real Butcher. When the counsel for the prosecution said, "I will now call before you, gentlemen, the Police-officer," meaning myself, Mr. Clarkson says, "Why Police-officer? Why more Police-officers? I don't want Police. We have had a great deal too much of the Police. I want the Butcher!" However, sir, he had the Butcher and the Police-officer, both in one. Out of seven prisoners committed for trial, five were found guilty, and some of 'em were transported. The respectable firm at the West End got a term of imprisonment; and that's the Butcher's Story!'

The story done, the chuckle-headed Butcher again resolved himself into the smooth-faced Detective. But, he was so extremely tickled by their having taken him about, when he was that Dragon in disguise, to show him London, that he could not help reverting to that point in his narrative; and gently repeating with the Butcher snigger, "'Oh, dear,' I says, 'is that where they hang the men? Oh, Lor!' 'That!' says they. 'What a simple cove he is!'"

It being now late, and the party very modest in their fear of being too diffuse, there were some tokens of separation; when Sergeant Dornton, the soldierly-looking man, said, looking round him with a smile:

'Before we break up, sir, perhaps you might have some amusement in hearing of the Adventures of a Carpet Bag. They are very short; and, I think, curious.'

We welcomed the Carpet Bag, as cordially as Mr. Shepherdson welcomed the false Butcher at the Setting Moon. Sergeant Dornton proceeded.

'In 1847, I was despatched to Chatham, in search of one Mesheck, a Jew. He had been carrying on, pretty heavily, in the bill-stealing way, getting acceptances from young men of good connexions (in the army chiefly), on pretence of discount, and bolting with the same.

'Mesheck was off, before I got to Chatham. All I could learn about him was, that he had gone, probably to London, and had with him—a Carpet Bag.

'I came back to town, by the last train from Blackwall, and made inquiries concerning a Jew passenger with—a Carpet Bag.

'The office was shut up, it being the last train. There were only two or three porters left. Looking after a Jew with a Carpet Bag, on the Blackwall Railway, which was then the high road to a great Military Depôt, was worse than looking after a needle in a hayrick. But it happened that one of these porters had carried, for a certain Jew, to a certain public-house, a certain—Carpet Bag.

'I went to the public-house, but the Jew had only left his luggage there for a few hours, and had called for it in a cab, and taken it away. I put such questions there, and to the porter, as I thought prudent, and got at this description of—the Carpet Bag.

'It was a bag which had, on one side of it, worked in worsted, a green parrot on a stand. A green parrot on a stand was the means by which to identify that—Carpet Bag.

'I traced Mesheck, by means of this green parrot on a stand, to Cheltenham, to Birmingham, to Liverpool, to the Atlantic Ocean. At Liverpool he was too many for me. He had gone to the United States, and I gave up all thoughts of Mesheck, and likewise of his—Carpet Bag.

'Many months afterwards—near a year afterwards—there was a bank in Ireland robbed of seven thousand pounds, by a person of the name of Doctor Dundey, who escaped to America; from which country some of the stolen notes came home. He was supposed to have bought a farm in New Jersey. Under proper management, that estate could be seized and sold, for the benefit of the parties he had defrauded. I was sent off to America for this purpose.

'I landed at Boston. I went on to New York. I found that he had lately changed New York paper-money for New Jersey paper money, and had banked cash in New Brunswick. To take this Doctor Dundey, it was necessary to entrap him into the State of New York, which required a deal of artifice and trouble. At one time, he couldn't be drawn into an appointment. At another time, he appointed to come to meet me, and a New York officer, on a pretext I made; and then his children had the measles. At last he came, per steamboat, and I took him, and lodged him in a New York prison called the Tombs; which I dare say you know, sir?'

Editorial acknowledgment to that effect.

'I went to the Tombs, on the morning after his capture, to attend the examination before the magistrate. I was passing through the magistrate's private room, when, happening to look round me to take notice of the place, as we generally have a habit of doing, I clapped my eyes, in one corner, on a—Carpet Bag.

'What did I see upon that Carpet Bag, if you'll believe me, but a green parrot on a stand, as large as life!

'"That Carpet Bag, with the representation of a green parrot on a stand," said I, "belongs to an English Jew, named Aaron Mesheck, and to no other man, alive or dead!"

'I give you my word the New York Police Officers were doubled up with surprise.

'"How did you ever come to know that?" said they.

'"I think I ought to know that green parrot by this time," said I; "for I have had as pretty a dance after that bird, at home, as ever I had, in all my life!"'

'And was it Mesheck's?' we submissively inquired.

'Was it, sir? Of course it was! He was in custody for another offence, in that very identical Tombs, at that very identical time. And, more than that! Some memoranda, relating to the fraud for which I had vainly endeavoured to take him, were found to be, at that moment, lying in that very same individual—Carpet Bag!'

Such are the curious coincidences and such is the peculiar ability, always sharpening and being improved by practice, and always adapting itself to every variety of circumstances, and opposing itself to every new device that perverted ingenuity can invent, for which this important social branch of the public service is remarkable! For ever on the watch, with their wits stretched to the utmost, these officers have, from day to day and year to year, to set themselves against every novelty of trickery and dexterity that the combined imaginations of all the lawless rascals in England can devise, and to keep pace with every such invention that comes out. In the Courts of Justice, the materials of thousands of such stories as we have narrated—often elevated into the marvellous and romantic, by the circumstances of the case—are dryly compressed into the set phrase, 'in consequence of information I received, I did so and so.' Suspicion was to be directed, by careful inference and deduction, upon the right person; the right person was to be taken, wherever he had gone, or whatever he was doing to avoid detection: he is taken; there he is at the bar; that is enough. From information I, the officer, received, I did it; and, according to the custom in these cases, I say no more.

These games of chess, played with live pieces, are played before small audiences, and are chronicled nowhere. The interest of the game supports the player. Its results are enough for justice. To compare great things with small, suppose Leverrier or Adams informing the public that from information he had received he had discovered a new planet; or Columbus informing the public of his day that from information he had received he had discovered a new continent; so the Detectives inform it that they have discovered a new fraud or an old offender, and the process is unknown.

Thus, at midnight, closed the proceedings of our curious and interesting party. But one other circumstance finally wound up the evening, after our Detective guests had left us. One of the sharpest among them, and the officer best acquainted with the Swell Mob, had his pocket picked, going home!

THREE 'DETECTIVE' ANECDOTES

I.—THE PAIR OF GLOVES

'It's a singler story, sir,' said Inspector Wield, of the Detective Police, who, in company with Sergeants Dornton and Mith, paid us another twilight visit, one July evening; 'and I've been thinking you might like to know it.

'It's concerning the murder of the young woman, Eliza Grimwood, some years ago, over in the Waterloo Road. She was commonly called The Countess, because of her handsome appearance and her proud way of carrying of herself; and when I saw the poor Countess (I had known her well to speak to), lying dead, with her throat cut, on the floor of her bedroom, you'll believe me that a variety of reflections calculated to make a man rather low in his spirits, came into my head.

'That's neither here nor there. I went to the house the morning after the murder, and examined the body, and made a general observation of the bedroom where it was. Turning down the pillow of the bed with my hand, I found, underneath it, a pair of gloves. A pair of gentleman's dress gloves, very dirty; and inside the lining, the letters Tr, and a cross.

'Well, sir, I took them gloves away, and I showed 'em to the magistrate, over at Union Hall, before whom the case was. He says, "Wield," he says, "there's no doubt this is a discovery that may lead to something very important; and what you have got to do, Wield, is, to find out the owner of these gloves."

'I was of the same opinion, of course, and I went at it immediately. I looked at the gloves pretty narrowly, and it was my opinion that they had been cleaned. There was a smell of sulphur and rosin about 'em, you know, which cleaned gloves usually have, more or less. I took 'em over to a friend of mine at Kennington, who was in that line, and I put it to him. "What do you say now? Have these gloves been cleaned?" "These gloves have been cleaned," says he. "Have you any idea who cleaned them?" says I. "Not at all," says he; "I've a very distinct idea who didn't clean 'em, and that's myself. But I'll tell you what, Wield, there ain't above eight or nine reg'lar glove-cleaners in London,"—there were not, at that time, it seems—"and I think I can give you their addresses, and you may find out, by that means, who did clean 'em." Accordingly, he gave me the directions, and I went here, and I went there, and I looked up this man, and I looked up that man; but, though they all agreed that the gloves had been cleaned, I couldn't find the man, woman, or child, that had cleaned that aforesaid pair of gloves.

'What with this person not being at home, and that person being expected home in the afternoon, and so forth, the inquiry took me three days. On the evening of the third day, coming over Waterloo Bridge from the Surrey side of the river, quite beat, and very much vexed and disappointed, I thought I'd have a shilling's worth of entertainment at the Lyceum Theatre to freshen myself up. So I went into the Pit, at half-price, and I sat myself down next to a very quiet, modest sort of young man. Seeing I was a stranger (which I thought it just as well to appear to be) he told me the names of the actors on the stage, and we got into conversation. When the play was over, we came out together, and I said, "We've been very companionable and agreeable, and perhaps you wouldn't object to a drain?" "Well, you're very good," says he; "I shouldn't object to a drain." Accordingly, we went to a public-house, near the Theatre, sat ourselves down in a quiet room up-stairs on the first floor, and called for a pint of half-and-half, apiece, and a pipe.

'Well, sir, we put our pipes aboard, and we drank our half-and-half, and sat a-talking, very sociably, when the young man says, "You must excuse me stopping very long," he says, "because I'm forced to go home in good time. I must be at work all night." "At work all night?" says I. "You ain't a baker?" "No," he says, laughing, "I ain't a baker." "I thought not," says I, "you haven't the looks of a baker." "No," says he, "I'm a glove-cleaner."

'I never was more astonished in my life, than when I heard them words come out of his lips. "You're a glove-cleaner, are you?" says I. "Yes," he says, "I am." "Then, perhaps," says I, taking the gloves out of my pocket, "you can tell me who cleaned this pair of gloves? It's a rum story," I says. "I was dining over at Lambeth, the other day, at a free-and-easy—quite promiscuous—with a public company—when some gentleman, he left these gloves behind him! Another gentleman and me, you see, we laid a wager of a sovereign, that I wouldn't find out who they belonged to. I've spent as much as seven shillings already, in trying to discover; but, if you could help me, I'd stand another seven and welcome. You see there's Tr and a cross, inside." "I see," he says. "Bless you, I know these gloves very well! I've seen dozens of pairs belonging to the same party." "No?" says I. "Yes," says he. "Then you know who cleaned 'em?" says I. "Rather so," says he. "My father cleaned 'em."

'"Where does your father live?" says I. "Just round the corner," says the young man, "near Exeter Street, here. He'll tell you who they belong to, directly." "Would you come round with me now?" says I. "Certainly," says he, "but you needn't tell my father that you found me at the play, you know, because he mightn't like it." "All right!" We went round to the place, and there we found an old man in a white apron, with two or three daughters, all rubbing and cleaning away at lots of gloves, in a front parlour. "Oh, Father!" says the young man, "here's a person been and made a bet about the ownership of a pair of gloves, and I've told him you can settle it." "Good evening, sir," says I to the old gentleman. "Here's the gloves your son speaks of. Letters Tr, you see, and a cross." "Oh yes," he says, "I know these gloves very well; I've cleaned dozens of pairs of 'em. They belong to Mr. Trinkle, the great upholsterer in Cheapside." "Did you get 'em from Mr. Trinkle, direct," says I, "if you'll excuse my asking the question?" "No," says he; "Mr. Trinkle always sends 'em to Mr. Phibbs's, the haberdasher's, opposite his shop, and the haberdasher sends 'em to me." "Perhaps you wouldn't object to a drain?" says I. "Not in the least!" says he. So I took the old gentleman out, and had a little more talk with him and his son, over a glass, and we parted excellent friends.

'This was late on a Saturday night. First thing on the Monday morning, I went to the haberdasher's shop, opposite Mr. Trinkle's, the great upholsterer's in Cheapside. "Mr. Phibbs in the way?" "My name is Phibbs." "Oh! I believe you sent this pair of gloves to be cleaned?" "Yes, I did, for young Mr. Trinkle over the way. There he is in the shop!" "Oh! that's him in the shop, is it? Him in the green coat?" "The same individual." "Well, Mr. Phibbs, this is an unpleasant affair; but the fact is, I am Inspector Wield of the Detective Police, and I found these gloves under the pillow of the young woman that was murdered the other day, over in the Waterloo Road!" "Good Heaven!" says he. "He's a most respectable young man, and if his father was to hear of it, it would be the ruin of him!" "I'm very sorry for it," says I, "but I must take him into custody." "Good Heaven!" says Mr. Phibbs, again; "can nothing be done?" "Nothing," says I. "Will you allow me to call him over here," says he, "that his father may not see it done?" "I don't object to that," says I; "but unfortunately, Mr. Phibbs, I can't allow of any communication between you. If any was attempted, I should have to interfere directly. Perhaps you'll beckon him over here?" Mr. Phibbs went to the door and beckoned, and the young fellow came across the street directly; a smart, brisk young fellow.

"'Good morning, sir," says I. "Good morning, sir," says he. "Would you allow me to inquire, sir," says I, "if you ever had any acquaintance with a party of the name of Grimwood?" "Grimwood! Grimwood!" says he. "No!" "You know the Waterloo Road?" "Oh! of course I know the Waterloo Road!" "Happen to have heard of a young woman being murdered there?" "Yes, I read it in the paper, and very sorry I was to read it." "Here's a pair of gloves belonging to you, that I found under her pillow the morning afterwards!"

'He was in a dreadful state, sir; a dreadful state I "Mr. Wield," he says, "upon my solemn oath I never was there. I never so much as saw her, to my knowledge, in my life!" "I am very sorry," says I. "To tell you the truth; I don't think you are the murderer, but I must take you to Union Hall in a cab. However, I think it's a case of that sort, that, at present, at all events, the magistrate will hear it in private."

'A private examination took place, and then it came out that this young man was acquainted with a cousin of the unfortunate Eliza Grimwood, and that, calling to see this cousin a day or two before the murder, he left these gloves upon the table. Who should come in, shortly afterwards, but Eliza Grimwood! "Whose gloves are these?" she says, taking 'em up. "Those are Mr. Trinkle's gloves," says her cousin. "Oh!" says she, "they are very dirty, and of no use to him, I am sure. I shall take 'em away for my girl to clean

551

the stoves with." And she put 'em in her pocket. The girl had used 'em to clean the stoves, and, I have no doubt, had left 'em lying on the bedroom mantelpiece, or on the drawers, or somewhere; and her mistress, looking round to see that the room was tidy, had caught 'em up and put 'em under the pillow where I found 'em.

That's the story, sir.'

II.—THE ARTFUL TOUCH

'One of the most beautiful things that ever was done, perhaps,' said Inspector Wield, emphasising the adjective, as preparing us to expect dexterity or ingenuity rather than strong interest, 'was a move of Sergeant Witchem's. It was a lovely idea!

'Witchem and me were down at Epsom one Derby Day, waiting at the station for the Swell Mob. As I mentioned, when we were talking about these things before, we are ready at the station when there's races, or an Agricultural Show, or a Chancellor sworn in for an university, or Jenny Lind, or anything of that sort; and as the Swell Mob come down, we send 'em back again by the next train. But some of the Swell Mob, on the occasion of this Derby that I refer to, so far kidded us as to hire a horse and shay; start away from London by Whitechapel, and miles round; come into Epsom from the opposite direction; and go to work, right and left, on the course, while we were waiting for 'em at the Rail. That, however, ain't the point of what I'm going to tell you.

'While Witchem and me were waiting at the station, there comes up one Mr. Tatt; a gentleman formerly in the public line, quite an amateur Detective in his way, and very much respected. "Halloa, Charley Wield," he says. "What are you doing here? On the look out for some of your old friends?" "Yes, the old move, Mr. Tatt." "Come along," he says, "you and Witchem, and have a glass of sherry." "We can't stir from the place," says I, "till the next train comes in; but after that, we will with pleasure." Mr. Tatt waits, and the train comes in, and then Witchem and me go off with him to the Hotel. Mr. Tatt he's got up quite regardless of expense, for the occasion;

and in his shirt-front there's a beautiful diamond prop, cost him fifteen or twenty pound—a very handsome pin indeed. We drink our sherry at the bar, and have had our three or four glasses, when Witchem cries suddenly, "Look out, Mr. Wield! stand fast!" and a dash is made into the place by the Swell Mob—four of 'em—that have come down as I tell you, and in a moment Mr. Tatt's prop is gone! Witchem, he cuts 'em off at the door, I lay about me as hard as I can, Mr. Tatt shows fight like a good 'un, and there we are, all down together, heads and heels, knocking about on the floor of the bar—perhaps you never see such a scene of confusion! However, we stick to our men (Mr. Tatt being as good as any officer), and we take 'em all, and carry 'em off to the station.' The station's full of people, who have been took on the course; and it's a precious piece of work to get 'em secured. However, we do it at last, and we search 'em; but nothing's found upon 'em, and they're locked up; and a pretty state of heat we are in by that time, I assure you!

'I was very blank over it, myself, to think that the prop had been passed away; and I said to Witchem, when we had set 'em to rights, and were cooling ourselves along with Mr. Tatt, "we don't take much by this move, anyway, for nothing's found upon 'em, and it's only the braggadocia, [426] after all." "What do you mean, Mr. Wield?" says Witchem. "Here's the diamond pin!" and in the palm of his hand there it was, safe and sound! "Why, in the name of wonder," says me and Mr. Tatt, in astonishment, "how did you come by that?" "I'll tell you how I come by it," says he. "I saw which of 'em took it; and when we were all down on the floor together, knocking about, I just gave him a little touch on the back of his hand, as I knew his pal would; and he thought it WAS his pal; and gave it me!" It was beautiful, beau-ti-ful!

'Even that was hardly the best of the case, for that chap was tried at the Quarter Sessions at Guildford. You know what Quarter Sessions are, sir. Well, if you'll believe me, while them slow justices were looking over the Acts of Parliament, to see what they could do to him, I'm blowed if he didn't cut out of the dock before their faces! He cut out of the dock, sir, then and there; swam across a river; and got up into a tree to dry himself. In the tree he was took—an old woman having seen him climb up—and Witchem's artful touch transported him!'

III.—THE SOFA

'What young men will do, sometimes, to ruin themselves and break their friends' hearts,' said Sergeant Dornton, 'it's surprising! I had a case at Saint Blank's Hospital which was of this sort. A bad case, indeed, with a bad end!

'The Secretary, and the House-Surgeon, and the Treasurer, of Saint Blank's Hospital, came to Scotland Yard to give information of numerous robberies having been committed on the students. The students could leave nothing in the pockets of their great-coats, while the great-coats were hanging at the hospital, but it was almost certain to be stolen. Property of various descriptions was constantly being lost; and the gentlemen were naturally uneasy about it, and anxious, for the credit of the institution, that the thief or thieves should be discovered. The case was entrusted to me, and I went to the hospital.

'"Now, gentlemen," said I, after we had talked it over; "I understand this property is usually lost from one room."

'Yes, they said. It was.

'"I should wish, if you please," said I, "to see the room."

'It was a good-sized bare room down-stairs, with a few tables and forms in it, and a row of pegs, all round, for hats and coats.

'"Next, gentlemen," said I, "do you suspect anybody?"

'Yes, they said. They did suspect somebody. They were sorry to say, they suspected one of the porters.

'"I should like," said I, "to have that man pointed out to me, and to have a little time to look after him."

'He was pointed out, and I looked after him, and then I went back to the hospital, and said, "Now, gentlemen, it's not the porter. He's, unfortunately for himself, a little too fond of drink, but he's nothing worse. My suspicion is, that these robberies are committed by one of the students; and if you'll put me a sofa into that room where the pegs are—as there's no closet—I think I shall be able to detect the thief. I wish the sofa, if you please, to be covered with chintz, or something of that sort, so that I may lie on my chest, underneath it, without being seen."

'The sofa was provided, and next day at eleven o'clock, before any of the students came, I went there, with those gentlemen, to get underneath it. It turned out to be one of those old-fashioned sofas with a great cross-beam at the bottom, that would have broken my back in no time if I could ever have got below it. We had quite a job to break all this away in the time; however, I fell to work, and they fell to work, and we broke it out, and made a clear place for me. I got under the sofa, lay down on my chest, took out my knife, and made a convenient hole in the chintz to look through. It was then settled between me and the gentlemen that when the students were all up in the wards, one of the gentlemen should come in, and hang up a great-coat on one of the pegs. And that that great-coat should have, in one of the pockets, a pocket-book containing marked money.

'After I had been there some time, the students began to drop into the room, by ones, and twos, and threes, and to talk about all sorts of things, little thinking there was anybody under the sofa—and then to go up-stairs. At last there came in one who remained until he was alone in the room by himself. A tallish, good-looking young man of one or two and twenty, with a light whisker. He went to a particular hat-peg, took off a good hat that was hanging there, tried it on, hung his own hat in its place, and hung that hat on another peg, nearly opposite to me. I then felt quite certain that he was the thief, and would come back by-and-by.

'When they were all up-stairs, the gentleman came in with the great-coat. I showed him where to hang it, so that I might have a good view of it; and he went away; and I lay under the sofa on my chest, for a couple of hours or so, waiting.

'At last, the same young man came down. He walked across the room, whistling—stopped and listened—took another walk and whistled—stopped again, and listened—then began to go regularly round the pegs, feeling in the pockets of all the coats. When he came to the great-coat, and felt the pocket-book, he was so eager and so hurried that he broke the strap in tearing it open. As he began to put the money in his pocket, I crawled out from under the sofa, and his eyes met mine.

'My face, as you may perceive, is brown now, but it was pale at that time, my health not being good; and looked as long as a horse's. Besides which, there was a great draught of air from the door, underneath the sofa, and I had tied a handkerchief round my head; so what I looked like, altogether, I don't know. He turned blue—literally blue—when he saw me crawling out, and I couldn't feel surprised at it.

'"I am an officer of the Detective Police," said I, "and have been lying here, since you first came in this morning. I regret, for the sake of yourself and your friends, that you should have done what you have; but this case is complete. You have the pocket-book in your hand and the money upon you; and I must take you into custody!"

'It was impossible to make out any case in his behalf, and on his trial he pleaded guilty. How or when he got the means I don't know; but while he was awaiting his sentence, he poisoned himself in Newgate.'

We inquired of this officer, on the conclusion of the foregoing anecdote, whether the time appeared long, or short, when he lay in that constrained position under the sofa?

'Why, you see, sir,' he replied, 'if he hadn't come in, the first time, and I had not been quite sure he was the thief, and would return, the time would have seemed long. But, as it was, I being dead certain of my man, the time seemed pretty short.'

ON DUTY WITH INSPECTOR FIELD

How goes the night? Saint Giles's clock is striking nine. The weather is dull and wet, and the long lines of street lamps are blurred, as if we saw them through tears. A damp wind blows and rakes the pieman's fire out, when he opens the door of his little furnace, carrying away an eddy of sparks.

Saint Giles's clock strikes nine. We are punctual. Where is Inspector Field? Assistant Commissioner of Police is already here, enwrapped in oil-skin cloak, and standing in the shadow of Saint Giles's steeple. Detective Sergeant, weary of speaking French all day to foreigners unpacking at the Great Exhibition, is already here. Where is Inspector Field?

Inspector Field is, to-night, the guardian genius of the British Museum. He is bringing his shrewd eye to bear on every corner of its solitary galleries, before he reports 'all right.' Suspicious of the Elgin marbles, and not to be done by cat-faced Egyptian giants with their hands upon their knees, Inspector Field, sagacious, vigilant, lamp in hand, throwing monstrous shadows on the walls and ceilings, passes through the spacious rooms. If a mummy trembled in an atom of its dusty covering, Inspector Field would say, 'Come out of that, Tom Green. I know you!' If the smallest 'Gonoph' about town were crouching at the bottom of a classic bath, Inspector Field would nose him with a finer scent than the ogre's, when adventurous Jack lay trembling in his kitchen copper. But all is quiet, and Inspector Field goes warily on, making little outward show of attending to anything in particular, just recognising the Ichthyosaurus as a familiar acquaintance, and wondering, perhaps, how the detectives did it in the days before the Flood.

Will Inspector Field be long about this work? He may be half-an-hour longer. He sends his compliments by Police Constable, and proposes that we meet at St. Giles's Station House, across the road. Good. It were as well to stand by the fire, there, as in the shadow of Saint Giles's steeple.

Anything doing here to-night? Not much. We are very quiet. A lost boy, extremely calm and small, sitting by the fire, whom we now confide to a constable to take home, for the child says that if you show him Newgate Street, he can show you where he lives—a raving drunken woman in the cells, who has screeched her voice away, and has hardly power enough left to declare, even with the passionate help of her feet and arms, that she is the daughter of a British officer, and, strike her blind and dead, but she'll write a letter to the Queen! but who is soothed with a drink of water—in another cell, a quiet woman with a child at her breast, for begging—in another, her husband in a smock-frock, with a basket of watercresses—in another, a pickpocket—in another, a meek tremulous old pauper man who has been out for a holiday 'and has took but a little drop, but it has overcome him after so many months in the house'—and that's all as yet. Presently, a sensation at the Station House door. Mr. Field, gentlemen!

Inspector Field comes in, wiping his forehead, for he is of a burly figure, and has come fast from the ores and metals of the deep mines of the earth, and from the Parrot Gods of the South Sea Islands, and from the birds and beetles of the tropics, and from the Arts of Greece and Rome, and from the Sculptures of Nineveh, and from the traces of an elder world, when these were not. Is Rogers ready? Rogers is ready, strapped and great-coated, with a flaming eye in the middle of his waist, like a deformed Cyclops. Lead on, Rogers, to Rats' Castle!

How many people may there be in London, who, if we had brought them deviously and blindfold, to this street, fifty paces from the Station House, and within call of Saint Giles's church, would know it for a not remote part of the city in which their lives are passed? How many, who amidst this compound of sickening smells, these heaps of filth, these tumbling houses, with all their vile contents, animate, and inanimate, slimily overflowing into the black road, would believe that they breathe this air? How much Red Tape may there be, that could look round on the faces which now hem us in—for our appearance here has caused a rush from all points to a common centre—the lowering foreheads, the sallow cheeks, the brutal eyes, the matted hair, the infected, vermin-haunted heaps of rags—and say, 'I have thought of this. I have not dismissed the thing. I have neither blustered it away, nor frozen it away, nor tied it up and put it away, nor smoothly said pooh, pooh! to it when it has been shown to me?'

This is not what Rogers wants to know, however. What Rogers wants to know, is, whether you will clear the way here, some of you, or whether you won't; because if you don't do it right on end, he'll lock you up! 'What! You are there, are you, Bob Miles? You haven't had enough of it yet, haven't you? You want three months more, do you? Come away from that gentleman! What are you creeping round there for?'

'What am I a doing, thinn, Mr. Rogers?' says Bob Miles, appearing, villainous, at the end of a lane of light, made by the lantern.

'I'll let you know pretty quick, if you don't hook it. Will you hook it?'

A sycophantic murmur rises from the crowd. 'Hook it, Bob, when Mr. Rogers and Mr. Field tells you! Why don't you hook it, when you are told to?'

The most importunate of the voices strikes familiarly on Mr. Rogers's ear. He suddenly turns his lantern on the owner.

'What! You are there, are you, Mister Click? You hook it too—come!'

'What for?' says Mr. Click, discomfited.

'You hook it, will you!' says Mr. Rogers with stern emphasis.

Both Click and Miles do 'hook it,' without another word, or, in plainer English, sneak away.

'Close up there, my men!' says Inspector Field to two constables on duty who have followed. 'Keep together, gentlemen; we are going down here. Heads!'

Saint Giles's church strikes half-past ten. We stoop low, and creep down a precipitous flight of steps into a dark close cellar. There is a fire. There is a long deal table. There are benches. The cellar is full of company, chiefly very young men in various conditions of dirt and raggedness. Some are eating supper. There are no girls or women present. Welcome to Rats' Castle, gentlemen, and to this company of noted thieves!

'Well, my lads! How are you, my lads? What have you been doing to-day? Here's some company come to see you, my lads!—There's a plate of beefsteak, sir, for the supper of a fine young man! And there's a mouth for a steak, sir! Why, I should be too proud of such a mouth as that, if I had it myself! Stand up and show it, sir! Take off your cap. There's a fine young man for a nice little party, sir! An't he?'

Inspector Field is the bustling speaker. Inspector Field's eye is the roving eye that searches every corner of the cellar as he talks. Inspector Field's hand is the well-known hand that has collared half the people here, and motioned their brothers, sisters, fathers, mothers, male and female friends, inexorably to New South Wales. Yet Inspector Field stands in this den, the Sultan of the place. Every thief here cowers before him, like a schoolboy before his schoolmaster. All watch him, all answer when addressed, all laugh at his jokes, all seek to propitiate him. This cellar company alone—to say nothing of the crowd surrounding the entrance from the street above, and making the steps shine with eyes—is strong enough to murder us all, and willing enough to do it; but, let Inspector Field have a mind to pick out one thief here, and take him; let him produce that ghostly truncheon from his pocket, and say, with his business-air, 'My lad, I want you!' and all Rats' Castle shall be stricken with paralysis, and not a finger move against him, as he fits the handcuffs on!

Where's the Earl of Warwick?—Here he is, Mr. Field! Here's the Earl of Warwick, Mr. Field!—O there you are, my Lord. Come for'ard. There's a chest, sir, not to have a clean shirt on. An't it? Take your hat off, my Lord. Why, I should be ashamed if I was you—and an Earl, too—to show myself to a gentleman with my hat on!—The Earl of Warwick laughs and uncovers. All the company laugh. One pickpocket, especially, laughs with great enthusiasm. O what a jolly game it is, when Mr. Field comes down—and don't want nobody!

So, you are here, too, are you, you tall, grey, soldierly-looking, grave man, standing by the fire?—Yes, sir. Good evening, Mr. Field!—Let us see. You lived servant to a nobleman once?—Yes, Mr. Field.—And what is it you do now; I forget?—Well, Mr. Field, I job about as well as I can. I left my employment on account of delicate health. The family is still kind to me. Mr. Wix of Piccadilly is also very kind to me when I am hard up. Likewise Mr. Nix of Oxford Street. I get a trifle from them occasionally, and rub on as well as I can, Mr. Field. Mr. Field's eye rolls enjoyingly, for this man is a notorious begging-letter writer.—Good night, my lads!—Good night, Mr. Field, and thank'ee, sir!

Clear the street here, half a thousand of you! Cut it, Mrs. Stalker—none of that—we don't want you! Rogers of the flaming eye, lead on to the tramps' lodging-house!

A dream of baleful faces attends to the door. Now, stand back all of you! In the rear Detective Sergeant plants himself, composedly whistling, with his strong right arm across the narrow passage. Mrs. Stalker, I am something'd that need not be written here, if you won't get yourself into trouble, in about half a minute, if I see that face of yours again!

Saint Giles's church clock, striking eleven, hums through our hand from the dilapidated door of a dark outhouse as we open it, and are stricken back by the pestilent breath that issues from within. Rogers to the front with the light, and let us look!

Ten, twenty, thirty—who can count them! Men, women, children, for the most part naked, heaped upon the floor like maggots in a cheese! Ho! In that dark corner yonder! Does anybody lie there? Me sir, Irish me, a widder, with six children. And yonder? Me sir, Irish me, with me wife and eight poor babes. And to the left there? Me sir, Irish me, along with two more Irish boys as is me friends. And to the right there? Me sir and the Murphy fam'ly, numbering five blessed souls. And what's this, coiling, now, about my foot? Another Irish me, pitifully in want of shaving, whom I have awakened from sleep—and across my other foot lies his wife—and by the shoes of Inspector Field lie their three eldest—and their three youngest are at present squeezed between the open door and the wall. And why is there no one on that little mat before the sullen fire? Because O'Donovan, with his wife and daughter, is not come in from selling Lucifers! Nor on the bit of sacking in the nearest corner? Bad luck! Because that Irish family is late to-night, a-cadging in the

561

streets!

They are all awake now, the children excepted, and most of them sit up, to stare. Wheresoever Mr. Rogers turns the flaming eye, there is a spectral figure rising, unshrouded, from a grave of rags. Who is the landlord here?—I am, Mr. Field! says a bundle of ribs and parchment against the wall, scratching itself.—Will you spend this money fairly, in the morning, to buy coffee for 'em all?—Yes, sir, I will!—O he'll do it, sir, he'll do it fair. He's honest! cry the spectres. And with thanks and Good Night sink into their graves again.

Thus, we make our New Oxford Streets, and our other new streets, never heeding, never asking, where the wretches whom we clear out, crowd. With such scenes at our doors, with all the plagues of Egypt tied up with bits of cobweb in kennels so near our homes, we timorously make our Nuisance Bills and Boards of Health, nonentities, and think to keep away the Wolves of Crime and Filth, by our electioneering ducking to little vestrymen and our gentlemanly handling of Red Tape!

Intelligence of the coffee-money has got abroad. The yard is full, and Rogers of the flaming eye is beleaguered with entreaties to show other Lodging Houses. Mine next! Mine! Mine! Rogers, military, obdurate, stiff-necked, immovable, replies not, but leads away; all falling back before him. Inspector Field follows. Detective Sergeant, with his barrier of arm across the little passage, deliberately waits to close the procession. He sees behind him, without any effort, and exceedingly disturbs one individual far in the rear by coolly calling out, 'It won't do, Mr. Michael! Don't try it!'

After council holden in the street, we enter other lodging-houses, public-houses, many lairs and holes; all noisome and offensive; none so filthy and so crowded as where Irish are. In one, The Ethiopian party are expected home presently—were in Oxford Street when last heard of—shall be fetched, for our delight, within ten minutes. In another, one of the two or three Professors who drew Napoleon Buonaparte and a couple of mackerel, on the pavement and then let the work of art out to a speculator, is refreshing after his labours. In another, the vested interest of the profitable nuisance has been in one family for a hundred years, and the landlord drives in comfortably from the country to his snug little stew in town. In all, Inspector Field is received with warmth. Coiners and smashers droop before him; pickpockets defer to him; the gentle sex (not very gentle here) smile upon him. Half-drunken hags check themselves in the midst of pots of beer, or pints of gin, to drink to Mr. Field, and pressingly to ask the honour of his finishing the draught. One beldame in rusty black has such admiration for him, that she runs a whole street's length to shake him by the hand; tumbling into a heap of mud by the way, and still pressing her attentions when her very form has ceased to be distinguishable through it. Before the power of the law, the power of superior sense—for common thieves are fools beside these men—and the power of a perfect mastery of their character, the garrison of Rats' Castle and the adjacent Fortresses make but a skulking show indeed when reviewed by Inspector Field.

Saint Giles's clock says it will be midnight in half-an-hour, and Inspector Field says we must hurry to the Old Mint in the Borough. The cab-driver is low-spirited, and has a solemn sense of his responsibility. Now, what's your fare, my lad?—O you know, Inspector Field, what's the good of asking me!

Say, Parker, strapped and great-coated, and waiting in dim Borough doorway by appointment, to replace the trusty Rogers whom we left deep in Saint Giles's, are you ready? Ready, Inspector Field, and at a motion of my wrist behold my flaming eye.

This narrow street, sir, is the chief part of the Old Mint, full of low lodging-houses, as you see by the transparent canvas-lamps and blinds, announcing beds for travellers! But it is greatly changed, friend Field, from my former knowledge of it; it is infinitely quieter and more subdued than when I was here last, some seven years ago? O yes! Inspector Haynes, a first-rate man, is on this station now and plays the Devil with them!

Well, my lads! How are you to-night, my lads? Playing cards here, eh? Who wins?—Why, Mr. Field, I, the sulky gentleman with the damp flat side-curls, rubbing my bleared eye with the end of my neckerchief which is like a dirty eel-skin, am losing just at present, but I suppose I must take my pipe out of my mouth, and be submissive to you—I hope I see you well,

563

Mr. Field?—Aye, all right, my lad. Deputy, who have you got up-stairs? Be pleased to show the rooms!

Why Deputy, Inspector Field can't say. He only knows that the man who takes care of the beds and lodgers is always called so. Steady, O Deputy, with the flaring candle in the blacking-bottle, for this is a slushy back-yard, and the wooden staircase outside the house creaks and has holes in it.

Again, in these confined intolerable rooms, burrowed out like the holes of rats or the nests of insect-vermin, but fuller of intolerable smells, are crowds of sleepers, each on his foul truckle-bed coiled up beneath a rug. Holloa here! Come! Let us see you! Show your face! Pilot Parker goes from bed to bed and turns their slumbering heads towards us, as a salesman might turn sheep. Some wake up with an execration and a threat.—What! who spoke? O! If it's the accursed glaring eye that fixes me, go where I will, I am helpless. Here! I sit up to be looked at. Is it me you want? Not you, lie down again! and I lie down, with a woful growl.

Whenever the turning lane of light becomes stationary for a moment, some sleeper appears at the end of it, submits himself to be scrutinised, and fades away into the darkness.

There should be strange dreams here, Deputy. They sleep sound enough, says Deputy, taking the candle out of the blacking-bottle, snuffing it with his fingers, throwing the snuff into the bottle, and corking it up with the candle; that's all I know. What is the inscription, Deputy, on all the discoloured sheets? A precaution against loss of linen. Deputy turns down the rug of an unoccupied bed and discloses it. Stop Thief!

To lie at night, wrapped in the legend of my slinking life; to take the cry that pursues me, waking, to my breast in sleep; to have it staring at me, and clamouring for me, as soon as consciousness returns; to have it for my first-foot on New-Year's day, my Valentine, my Birthday salute, my Christmas greeting, my parting with the old year. Stop Thief!

And to know that I must be stopped, come what will. To know that I am no match for this individual energy and keenness, or this organised and steady system! Come across the street, here, and, entering by a little shop and yard, examine these intricate passages and doors, contrived for escape, flapping and counter-flapping, like the lids of the conjurer's boxes. But what avail they? Who gets in by a nod, and shows their secret working to us? Inspector Field.

Don't forget the old Farm House, Parker! Parker is not the man to forget it. We are going there, now. It is the old Manor-House of these parts, and stood in the country once. Then, perhaps, there was something, which was not the beastly street, to see from the shattered low fronts of the overhanging wooden houses we are passing under—shut up now, pasted over with bills about the literature and drama of the Mint, and mouldering away. This long paved yard was a paddock or a garden once, or a court in front of the Farm House. Perchance, with a dovecot in the centre, and fowls peeking about—with fair elm trees, then, where discoloured chimney-stacks and gables are now—noisy, then, with rooks which have yielded to a different sort of rookery. It's likelier than not, Inspector Field thinks, as we turn into the common kitchen, which is in the yard, and many paces from the house.

Well, my lads and lasses, how are you all? Where's Blackey, who has stood near London Bridge these five-and-twenty years, with a painted skin to represent disease?—Here he is, Mr. Field!—How are you, Blackey?—Jolly, sa! Not playing the fiddle to-night, Blackey?—Not a night, sa! A sharp, smiling youth, the wit of the kitchen, interposes. He an't musical to-night, sir. I've been giving him a moral lecture; I've been talking to him about his latter end, you see. A good many of these are my pupils, sir. This here young man (smoothing down the hair of one near him, reading a Sunday paper) is a pupil of mine. I'm a teaching of him to read, sir. He's a promising cove, sir. He's a smith, he is, and gets his living by the sweat of the brow, sir. So do I, myself, sir. This young woman is my sister, Mr. Field. She's getting on very well too. I've a deal of trouble with 'em, sir, but I'm richly rewarded, now I see 'em all a doing so well, and growing up so creditable. That's a great comfort, that is, an't it, sir?—In the midst of the kitchen (the whole kitchen is in ecstasies with this impromptu 'chaff') sits a young, modest, gentle-looking creature, with a beautiful child in her lap. She seems to belong to the company, but is so strangely unlike it. She has such a pretty, quiet face and voice, and is so proud to hear the child admired—thinks you would hardly believe that he is only nine months old! Is she as bad as the rest, I wonder? Inspectorial experience does not engender a belief contrariwise, but prompts the answer, Not a ha'porth of difference!

There is a piano going in the old Farm House as we approach. It stops. Landlady appears. Has no objections, Mr. Field, to gentlemen being brought, but wishes it were at earlier hours, the lodgers complaining of ill-conwenience. Inspector Field is polite and soothing—knows his woman and the sex. Deputy (a girl in this case) shows the way up a heavy, broad old staircase, kept very clean, into clean rooms where many sleepers are, and where painted panels of an older time look strangely on the truckle beds. The sight of whitewash and the smell of soap—two things we seem by this time to have parted from in infancy—make the old Farm House a phenomenon, and connect themselves with the so curiously misplaced picture of the pretty mother and child long after we have left it,—long after we have left, besides, the neighbouring nook with something of a rustic flavour in it yet, where once, beneath a low wooden colonnade still standing as of yore, the eminent Jack Sheppard condescended to regale himself, and where, now, two old bachelor brothers in broad hats (who are whispered in the Mint to have made a compact long ago that if either should ever marry, he must forfeit his share of the joint property) still keep a sequestered tavern, and sit o' nights smoking pipes in the bar, among ancient bottles and glasses, as our eyes behold them.

How goes the night now? Saint George of Southwark answers with twelve blows upon his bell. Parker, good night, for Williams is already waiting over in the region of Ratcliffe Highway, to show the houses where the sailors dance.

I should like to know where Inspector Field was born. In Ratcliffe Highway, I would have answered with confidence, but for his being equally at home wherever we go. He does not trouble his head as I do, about the river at night. He does not care for its creeping, black and silent, on our right there, rushing through sluice-gates, lapping at piles and posts and iron rings, hiding strange things in its mud, running away with suicides and accidentally drowned bodies faster than midnight funeral should, and acquiring such various experience between its cradle and its grave. It has no mystery for him. Is there not the Thames Police!

Accordingly, Williams leads the way. We are a little late, for some of the houses are already closing. No matter. You show us plenty. All the landlords know Inspector Field. All pass him, freely and good-humouredly, wheresoever he wants to go. So thoroughly are all these houses open to him and our local guide, that, granting that sailors must be entertained in their own way—as I suppose they must, and have a right to be—I hardly know how such places could be better regulated. Not that I call the company very select, or the dancing very graceful—even so graceful as that of the German Sugar Bakers, whose assembly, by the Minories, we stopped to visit—but there is watchful maintenance of order in every house, and swift expulsion where need is. Even in the midst of drunkenness, both of the lethargic kind and the lively, there is sharp landlord supervision, and pockets are in less peril than out of doors. These houses show, singularly, how much of the picturesque and romantic there truly is in the sailor, requiring to be especially addressed. All the songs (sung in a hailstorm of halfpence, which are pitched at the singer without the least tenderness for the time or tune—mostly from great rolls of copper carried for the purpose—and which he occasionally dodges like shot as they fly near his head) are of the sentimental sea sort. All the rooms are decorated with nautical subjects. Wrecks, engagements, ships on fire, ships passing lighthouses on iron-bound coasts, ships blowing up, ships going down, ships running ashore, men lying out upon the main-yard in a gale of wind, sailors and ships in every variety of peril, constitute the illustrations of fact. Nothing can be done in the fanciful way, without a thumping boy upon a scaly dolphin.

How goes the night now? Past one. Black and Green are waiting in Whitechapel to unveil the mysteries of Wentworth Street. Williams, the best of friends must part. Adieu!

Are not Black and Green ready at the appointed place? O yes! They glide out of shadow as we stop. Imperturbable Black opens the cab-door; Imperturbable Green takes a mental note of the driver. Both Green and

Black then open each his flaming eye, and marshal us the way that we are going.

The lodging-house we want is hidden in a maze of streets and courts. It is fast shut. We knock at the door, and stand hushed looking up for a light at one or other of the begrimed old lattice windows in its ugly front, when another constable comes up—supposes that we want 'to see the school.' Detective Sergeant meanwhile has got over a rail, opened a gate, dropped down an area, overcome some other little obstacles, and tapped at a window. Now returns. The landlord will send a deputy immediately.

Deputy is heard to stumble out of bed. Deputy lights a candle, draws back a bolt or two, and appears at the door. Deputy is a shivering shirt and trousers by no means clean, a yawning face, a shock head much confused externally and internally. We want to look for some one. You may go up with the light, and take 'em all, if you like, says Deputy, resigning it, and sitting down upon a bench in the kitchen with his ten fingers sleepily twisting in his hair.

Halloa here! Now then! Show yourselves. That'll do. It's not you. Don't disturb yourself any more! So on, through a labyrinth of airless rooms, each man responding, like a wild beast, to the keeper who has tamed him, and who goes into his cage. What, you haven't found him, then? says Deputy, when we came down. A woman mysteriously sitting up all night in the dark by the smouldering ashes of the kitchen fire, says it's only tramps and cadgers here; it's gonophs over the way. A man mysteriously walking about the kitchen all night in the dark, bids her hold her tongue. We come out. Deputy fastens the door and goes to bed again.

Black and Green, you know Bark, lodging-house keeper and receiver of stolen goods?—O yes, Inspector Field.—Go to Bark's next.

Bark sleeps in an inner wooden hutch, near his street door. As we parley on the step with Bark's Deputy, Bark growls in his bed. We enter, and Bark flies out of bed. Bark is a red villain and a wrathful, with a sanguine throat that looks very much as if it were expressly made for hanging, as he stretches it out, in pale defiance, over the half-door of his hutch. Bark's parts of speech are of an awful sort—principally adjectives. I won't, says Bark, have no adjective police and adjective strangers in my adjective premises! I won't, by adjective and substantive! Give me my trousers, and I'll send the whole adjective police to adjective and substantive! Give me, says Bark, my adjective trousers! I'll put an adjective knife in the whole bileing of 'em. I'll punch their adjective heads. I'll rip up their adjective substantives. Give me my adjective trousers! says Bark, and I'll spile the bileing of 'em!

Now, Bark, what's the use of this? Here's Black and Green, Detective Sergeant, and Inspector Field. You know we will come in.—I know you won't! says Bark. Somebody give me my adjective trousers! Bark's trousers seem difficult to find. He calls for them as Hercules might for his club. Give me my adjective trousers! says Bark, and I'll spile the bileing of 'em!

Inspector Field holds that it's all one whether Bark likes the visit or don't like it. He, Inspector Field, is an Inspector of the Detective Police, Detective Sergeant is Detective Sergeant, Black and Green are constables in uniform. Don't you be a fool, Bark, or you know it will be the worse for you.—I don't care, says Bark. Give me my adjective trousers!

At two o'clock in the morning, we descend into Bark's low kitchen, leaving Bark to foam at the mouth above, and Imperturbable Black and Green to look at him. Bark's kitchen is crammed full of thieves, holding a conversazione there by lamp-light. It is by far the most dangerous assembly we have seen yet. Stimulated by the ravings of Bark, above, their looks are sullen, but not a man speaks. We ascend again. Bark has got his trousers, and is in a state of madness in the passage with his back against a door that shuts off the upper staircase. We observe, in other respects, a ferocious individuality in Bark. Instead of 'Stop Thief!' on his linen, he prints 'Stolen from Bark's!'

Now, Bark, we are going up-stairs!—No, you ain't!—You refuse admission to the Police, do you, Bark?—Yes, I do! I refuse it to all the adjective police, and to all the adjective substantives. If the adjective coves in the kitchen was men, they'd come up now, and do for you! Shut me that there door! says Bark, and suddenly we are enclosed in the passage. They'd come up and do for you! cries Bark, and waits. Not a sound in the kitchen! They'd come up and do for you! cries Bark again, and waits. Not a sound in the kitchen! We are shut up, half-a-dozen of us, in Bark's house in the innermost recesses of the worst part of London, in the dead of the night—the house is crammed with notorious robbers and ruffians—and not a man stirs. No, Bark. They know the weight of the law, and they know Inspector Field and Co. too well.

We leave bully Bark to subside at leisure out of his passion and his trousers, and, I dare say, to be inconveniently reminded of this little brush before long. Black and Green do ordinary duty here, and look serious.

As to White, who waits on Holborn Hill to show the courts that are eaten out of Rotten Gray's Inn, Lane, where other lodging-houses are, and where (in one blind alley) the Thieves' Kitchen and Seminary for the teaching of the art to children is, the night has so worn away, being now

almost at odds with morning, which is which,

that they are quiet, and no light shines through the chinks in the shutters. As undistinctive Death will come here, one day, sleep comes now. The wicked cease from troubling sometimes, even in this life.

DOWN WITH THE TIDE

A VERY dark night it was, and bitter cold; the east wind blowing bleak, and bringing with it stinging particles from marsh, and moor, and fen—from the Great Desert and Old Egypt, may be. Some of the component parts of the sharp-edged vapour that came flying up the Thames at London might be mummy-dust, dry atoms from the Temple at Jerusalem, camels' foot-prints, crocodiles' hatching-places, loosened grains of expression from the visages of blunt-nosed sphynxes, waifs and strays from caravans of turbaned merchants, vegetation from jungles, frozen snow from the Himalayas. O! It was very, very dark upon the Thames, and it was bitter, bitter cold.

'And yet,' said the voice within the great pea-coat at my side, 'you'll have seen a good many rivers, too, I dare say?'

'Truly,' said I, 'when I come to think of it, not a few. From the Niagara, downward to the mountain rivers of Italy, which are like the national spirit— very tame, or chafing suddenly and bursting bounds, only to dwindle away again. The Moselle, and the Rhine, and the Rhone; and the Seine, and the Saone; and the St. Lawrence, Mississippi, and Ohio; and the Tiber, the Po, and the Arno; and the—'

Peacoat coughing as if he had had enough of that, I said no more. I could have carried the catalogue on to a teasing length, though, if I had been in the cruel mind.

'And after all,' said he, 'this looks so dismal?'

'So awful,' I returned, 'at night. The Seine at Paris is very gloomy too, at such a time, and is probably the scene of far more crime and greater wickedness; but this river looks so broad and vast, so murky and silent, seems such an image of death in the midst of the great city's life, that—'

That Peacoat coughed again. He could not stand my holding forth.

We were in a four-oared Thames Police Galley, lying on our oars in the deep shadow of Southwark Bridge—under the corner arch on the Surrey side—having come down with the tide from Vauxhall. We were fain to hold on pretty tight, though close in shore, for the river was swollen and the tide running down very strong. We were watching certain water-rats of human growth, and lay in the deep shade as quiet as mice; our light hidden and our scraps of conversation carried on in whispers. Above us, the massive iron girders of the arch were faintly visible, and below us its ponderous shadow seemed to sink down to the bottom of the stream.

We had been lying here some half an hour. With our backs to the wind, it is true; but the wind being in a determined temper blew straight through us, and would not take the trouble to go round. I would have boarded a fireship to get into action, and mildly suggested as much to my friend Pea.

'No doubt,' says he as patiently as possible; 'but shore-going tactics wouldn't do with us. River-thieves can always get rid of stolen property in a moment by dropping it overboard. We want to take them with the property, so we lurk about and come out upon 'em sharp. If they see us or hear us, over it goes.'

Pea's wisdom being indisputable, there was nothing for it but to sit there and be blown through, for another half-hour. The water-rats thinking it wise to abscond at the end of that time without commission of felony, we shot out, disappointed, with the tide.

'Grim they look, don't they?' said Pea, seeing me glance over my shoulder at the lights upon the bridge, and downward at their long crooked reflections in the river.

'Very,' said I, 'and make one think with a shudder of Suicides. What a night for a dreadful leap from that parapet!'

'Aye, but Waterloo's the favourite bridge for making holes in the water from,' returned Pea. 'By the bye—avast pulling, lads!—would you like to speak to Waterloo on the subject?'

My face confessing a surprised desire to have some friendly conversation with Waterloo Bridge, and my friend Pea being the most obliging of men, we put about, pulled out of the force of the stream, and in place of going at great speed with the tide, began to strive against it, close in shore again. Every colour but black seemed to have departed from the world. The air was black, the water was black, the barges and hulks were black, the piles were black, the buildings were black, the shadows were only a deeper shade of black upon a black ground. Here and there, a coal fire in an iron cresset blazed upon a wharf; but, one knew that it too had been black a little while ago, and would be black again soon. Uncomfortable rushes of water suggestive of gurgling and drowning, ghostly rattlings of iron chains, dismal clankings of discordant engines, formed the music that accompanied the dip of our oars and their rattling in the rowlocks. Even the noises had a black sound to me—as the trumpet sounded red to the blind man.

Our dexterous boat's crew made nothing of the tide, and pulled us gallantly up to Waterloo Bridge. Here Pea and I disembarked, passed under the black stone archway, and climbed the steep stone steps. Within a few feet of their summit, Pea presented me to Waterloo (or an eminent toll-taker representing that structure), muffled up to the eyes in a thick shawl, and amply great-coated and fur-capped.

Waterloo received us with cordiality, and observed of the night that it was 'a Searcher.' He had been originally called the Strand Bridge, he informed us, but had received his present name at the suggestion of the proprietors, when Parliament had resolved to vote three hundred thousand pound for the erection of a monument in honour of the victory. Parliament took the hint (said Waterloo, with the least flavour of misanthropy) and saved the money. Of course the late Duke of Wellington was the first passenger, and of course he paid his penny, and of course a noble lord preserved it evermore. The treadle and index at the toll-house (a most ingenious contrivance for rendering fraud impossible), were invented by Mr. Lethbridge, then property-man at Drury Lane Theatre.

Was it suicide, we wanted to know about? said Waterloo. Ha! Well, he had seen a good deal of that work, he did assure us. He had prevented some. Why, one day a woman, poorish looking, came in between the hatch, slapped down a penny, and wanted to go on without the change! Waterloo suspected this, and says to his mate, 'give an eye to the gate,' and bolted after her. She had got to the third seat between the piers, and was on the parapet just a going over, when he caught her and gave her in charge. At the police office next morning, she said it was along of trouble and a bad husband.

'Likely enough,' observed Waterloo to Pea and myself, as he adjusted his chin in his shawl. 'There's a deal of trouble about, you see—and bad husbands too!'

Another time, a young woman at twelve o'clock in the open day, got through, darted along; and, before Waterloo could come near her, jumped upon the parapet, and shot herself over sideways. Alarm given, watermen put off, lucky escape.—Clothes buoyed her up.

'This is where it is,' said Waterloo. 'If people jump off straight forwards from the middle of the parapet of the bays of the bridge, they are seldom killed by drowning, but are smashed, poor things; that's what they are; they dash themselves upon the buttress of the bridge. But you jump off,' said Waterloo to me, putting his fore-finger in a button-hole of my great-coat; 'you jump off from the side of the bay, and you'll tumble, true, into the stream under the arch. What you have got to do, is to mind how you jump in! There was poor Tom Steele from Dublin. Didn't dive! Bless you, didn't dive at all! Fell down so flat into the water, that he broke his breast-bone, and lived two days!'

I asked Waterloo if there were a favourite side of his bridge for this dreadful purpose? He reflected, and thought yes, there was. He should say the Surrey side.

Three decent-looking men went through one day, soberly and quietly, and went on abreast for about a dozen yards: when the middle one, he sung out, all of a sudden, 'Here goes, Jack!' and was over in a minute.

Body found? Well. Waterloo didn't rightly recollect about that. They were compositors, they were.

He considered it astonishing how quick people were! Why, there was a cab came up one Boxing-night, with a young woman in it, who looked, according to Waterloo's opinion of her, a little the worse for liquor; very handsome she was too—very handsome. She stopped the cab at the gate, and said she'd pay the cabman then, which she did, though there was a little hankering about the fare, because at first she didn't seem quite to know where she wanted to be drove to. However, she paid the man, and the toll too, and looking Waterloo in the face (he thought she knew him, don't you see!) said, 'I'll finish it somehow!' Well, the cab went off, leaving Waterloo a little doubtful in his mind, and while it was going on at full speed the young woman jumped out, never fell, hardly staggered, ran along the bridge pavement a little way, passing several people, and jumped over from the second opening. At the inquest it was giv' in evidence that she had been quarrelling at the Hero of Waterloo, and it was brought in jealousy. (One of the results of Waterloo's experience was, that there was a deal of jealousy about.)

'Do we ever get madmen?' said Waterloo, in answer to an inquiry of mine. 'Well, we do get madmen. Yes, we have had one or two; escaped from 'Sylums, I suppose. One hadn't a halfpenny; and because I wouldn't let him through, he went back a little way, stooped down, took a run, and butted at the hatch like a ram. He smashed his hat rarely, but his head didn't seem no worse—in my opinion on account of his being wrong in it afore. Sometimes people haven't got a halfpenny. If they are really tired and poor we give 'em one and let 'em through. Other people will leave things—pocket-handkerchiefs mostly. I have taken cravats and gloves, pocket-knives, tooth-picks, studs, shirt-pins, rings (generally from young gents, early in the morning), but handkerchiefs is the general thing.'

'Regular customers?' said Waterloo. 'Lord, yes! We have regular customers. One, such a worn-out, used-up old file as you can scarcely picter, comes from the Surrey side as regular as ten o'clock at night comes; and goes over, I think, to some flash house on the Middlesex side. He comes back, he does, as reg'lar as the clock strikes three in the morning, and then can hardly drag one of his old legs after the other. He always turns down the water-stairs, comes up again, and then goes on down the Waterloo Road. He always does the same thing, and never varies a minute. Does it every night—even Sundays.'

I asked Waterloo if he had given his mind to the possibility of this particular customer going down the water-stairs at three o'clock some morning, and never coming up again? He didn't think that of him, he replied. In fact, it was Waterloo's opinion, founded on his observation of that file, that he know'd a trick worth two of it.

'There's another queer old customer,' said Waterloo, 'comes over, as punctual as the almanack, at eleven o'clock on the sixth of January, at eleven o'clock on the fifth of April, at eleven o'clock on the sixth of July, at eleven o'clock on the tenth of October. Drives a shaggy little, rough pony, in a sort of a rattle-trap arm-chair sort of a thing. White hair he has, and white whiskers, and muffles himself up with all manner of shawls. He comes back again the same afternoon, and we never see more of him for three months. He is a captain in the navy—retired—wery old—wery odd—and served with Lord Nelson. He is particular about drawing his pension at Somerset House afore the clock strikes twelve every quarter. I have heerd say that he thinks it wouldn't be according to the Act of Parliament, if he didn't draw it afore twelve.'

Having related these anecdotes in a natural manner, which was the best warranty in the world for their genuine nature, our friend Waterloo was sinking deep into his shawl again, as having exhausted his communicative powers and taken in enough east wind, when my other friend Pea in a moment brought him to the surface by asking whether he had not been occasionally the subject of assault and battery in the execution of his duty? Waterloo recovering his spirits, instantly dashed into a new branch of his subject. We learnt how 'both these teeth'—here he pointed to the places where two front teeth were not—were knocked out by an ugly customer who one night made a dash at him (Waterloo) while his (the ugly customer's) pal and coadjutor made a dash at the toll-taking apron where the money-pockets were; how Waterloo, letting the teeth go (to Blazes, he observed indefinitely), grappled with the apron-seizer, permitting the ugly one to run away; and how he saved the bank, and captured his man, and consigned him to fine and imprisonment. Also how, on another night, 'a Cove' laid hold of Waterloo, then presiding at the horse-gate of his bridge, and threw him unceremoniously over his knee, having first cut his head open with his whip. How Waterloo 'got right,' and started after the Cove all down the Waterloo Road, through Stamford Street, and round to the foot of Blackfriars Bridge, where the Cove 'cut into' a public-house. How Waterloo cut in too; but how an aider and abettor of the Cove's, who happened to be taking a promiscuous drain at the bar, stopped Waterloo; and the Cove cut out again, ran across the road down Holland Street, and where not, and into a beer-shop. How Waterloo breaking away from his detainer was close upon the Cove's heels, attended by no end of people, who, seeing him running with the blood streaming down his face, thought something worse was 'up,' and roared Fire! and Murder! on the hopeful chance of the matter in hand being one or both. How the Cove was ignominiously taken, in a shed where he had run to hide, and how at the Police Court they at first wanted to make a sessions job of it; but eventually Waterloo was allowed to be 'spoke to,' and the Cove made it square with Waterloo by paying his doctor's bill (W. was laid up for a week) and giving him 'Three, ten.' Likewise we learnt what we had faintly suspected before, that your sporting amateur on the Derby day, albeit a captain, can be—'if he be,' as Captain Bobadil observes, 'so generously minded'—anything but a man of honour and a gentleman; not sufficiently gratifying his nice sense of humour by the witty scattering of flour and rotten eggs on obtuse civilians, but requiring the further excitement of 'bilking the toll,' and 'Pitching into' Waterloo, and 'cutting him about the head with his whip;' finally being, when called upon to answer for the assault, what Waterloo described as 'Minus,' or, as I humbly conceived it, not to be found. Likewise did Waterloo inform us, in reply to my inquiries, admiringly and deferentially preferred through my friend Pea, that the takings at the Bridge had more than doubled in amount, since the reduction of the toll one half. And being asked if the aforesaid takings included much bad money, Waterloo responded, with a look far deeper than the deepest part of the river, he should think not!—and so retired into his shawl for the rest of the night.

Then did Pea and I once more embark in our four-oared galley, and glide swiftly down the river with the tide. And while the shrewd East rasped and notched us, as with jagged razors, did my friend Pea impart to me confidences of interest relating to the Thames Police; we, between whiles, finding 'duty boats' hanging in dark corners under banks, like weeds—our own was a 'supervision boat'—and they, as they reported 'all right!' flashing their hidden light on us, and we flashing ours on them. These duty boats had one sitter in each: an Inspector: and were rowed 'Ran-dan,' which—for the information of those who never graduated, as I was once proud to do, under a fireman-waterman and winner of Kean's Prize Wherry: who, in the course of his tuition, took hundreds of gallons of rum and egg (at my expense) at the various houses of note above and below bridge; not by any means because he liked it, but to cure a weakness in his liver, for which the faculty had particularly recommended it—may be explained as rowed by three men, two pulling an oar each, and one a pair of sculls.

Thus, floating down our black highway, sullenly frowned upon by the knitted brows of Blackfriars, Southwark, and London, each in his lowering turn, I was shown by my friend Pea that there are, in the Thames Police Force, whose district extends from Battersea to Barking Creek, ninety-eight men, eight duty boats, and two supervision boats; and that these go about so silently, and lie in wait in such dark places, and so seem to be nowhere, and so may be anywhere, that they have gradually become a police of prevention, keeping the river almost clear of any great crimes, even while the increased vigilance on shore has made it much harder than of yore to live by 'thieving' in the streets. And as to the various kinds of water-thieves, said my friend Pea, there were the Tier-rangers, who silently dropped alongside the tiers of shipping in the Pool, by night, and who, going to the companion-head, listened for two snores—snore number one, the skipper's; snore number two, the mate's—mates and skippers always snoring great guns, and being dead sure to be hard at it if they had turned in and were asleep. Hearing the double fire, down went the Rangers into the skippers' cabins; groped for the skippers' inexpressibles, which it was the custom of those gentlemen to shake off, watch, money, braces, boots, and all together, on the floor; and therewith made off as silently as might be. Then there were the Lumpers, or labourers employed to unload vessels. They wore loose canvas jackets with a broad hem in the bottom, turned inside, so as to form a large circular pocket in which they could conceal, like clowns in pantomimes, packages of surprising sizes. A great deal of property was stolen in this manner (Pea confided to me) from steamers; first, because steamers carry a larger number of small packages than other ships; next, because of the extreme rapidity with which they are obliged to be unladen for their return voyages. The Lumpers dispose of their booty easily to marine store dealers, and the only remedy to be suggested is that marine store shops should be licensed, and thus brought under the eye of the police as rigidly as public-houses. Lumpers also smuggle goods ashore for the crews of vessels. The smuggling of tobacco is so considerable, that it is well worth the while of the sellers of smuggled tobacco to use hydraulic presses, to squeeze a single pound into a package small enough to be contained in an ordinary pocket. Next, said my friend Pea, there were the Truckers—less thieves than smugglers, whose business it was to land more considerable parcels of goods than the Lumpers could manage. They sometimes sold articles of grocery and so forth, to the crews, in order to cloak their real calling, and get aboard without suspicion. Many of them had boats of their own, and made money. Besides these, there were the Dredgermen, who, under pretence of dredging up coals and such like from the bottom of the river, hung about barges and other undecked craft, and when they saw an opportunity, threw any property they could lay their hands on overboard: in order slyly to dredge it up when the vessel was gone. Sometimes, they dexterously used their dredges to whip away anything that might lie within reach. Some of them were mighty neat at this, and the accomplishment was called dry dredging. Then, there was a vast deal of property, such as copper nails, sheathing, hardwood, &c., habitually brought away by shipwrights and other workmen from their employers' yards, and disposed of to marine store dealers, many of whom escaped detection through hard swearing, and their extraordinary artful ways of accounting for the possession of stolen property. Likewise, there were special-pleading practitioners, for whom barges 'drifted away of their own selves'—they having no hand in it, except first cutting them loose, and afterwards plundering them—innocents, meaning no harm, who had the misfortune to observe those foundlings wandering about the Thames.

We were now going in and out, with little noise and great nicety, among the tiers of shipping, whose many hulls, lying close together, rose out of the water like black streets. Here and there, a Scotch, an Irish, or a foreign steamer, getting up her steam as the tide made, looked, with her great chimney and high sides, like a quiet factory among the common buildings. Now, the streets opened into clearer spaces, now contracted into alleys; but the tiers were so like houses, in the dark, that I could almost have believed myself in the narrower bye-ways of Venice. Everything was wonderfully still; for, it wanted full three hours of flood, and nothing seemed awake but a dog here and there.

So we took no Tier-rangers captive, nor any Lumpers, nor Truckers, nor Dredgermen, nor other evil-disposed person or persons; but went ashore at Wapping, where the old Thames Police office is now a station-house, and where the old Court, with its cabin windows looking on the river, is a quaint charge room: with nothing worse in it usually than a stuffed cat in a glass case, and a portrait, pleasant to behold, of a rare old Thames Police officer, Mr. Superintendent Evans, now succeeded by his son. We looked over the charge books, admirably kept, and found the prevention so good that there were not five hundred entries (including drunken and disorderly) in a whole year. Then, we looked into the store-room; where there was an oakum smell, and a nautical seasoning of dreadnought clothing, rope yarn, boat-hooks, sculls and oars, spare stretchers, rudders, pistols, cutlasses, and the like. Then, into the cell, aired high up in the wooden wall through an opening like a kitchen plate-rack: wherein there was a drunken man, not at all warm, and very wishful to know if it were morning yet. Then, into a better sort of watch and ward room, where there was a squadron of stone bottles drawn up, ready to be filled with hot water and applied to any unfortunate creature who might be brought in apparently drowned. Finally, we shook hands with our worthy friend Pea, and ran all the way to Tower Hill, under strong Police suspicion occasionally, before we got warm.

A WALK IN A WORKHOUSE

On a certain Sunday, I formed one of the congregation assembled in the chapel of a large metropolitan Workhouse. With the exception of the clergyman and clerk, and a very few officials, there were none but paupers present. The children sat in the galleries; the women in the body of the chapel, and in one of the side aisles; the men in the remaining aisle. The service was decorously performed, though the sermon might have been much better adapted to the comprehension and to the circumstances of the hearers. The usual supplications were offered, with more than the usual significancy in such a place, for the fatherless children and widows, for all sick persons and young children, for all that were desolate and oppressed, for the comforting and helping of the weak-hearted, for the raising-up of them that had fallen; for all that were in danger, necessity, and tribulation. The prayers of the congregation were desired 'for several persons in the various wards dangerously ill;' and others who were recovering returned their thanks to Heaven.

Among this congregation, were some evil-looking young women, and beetle-browed young men; but not many—perhaps that kind of characters kept away. Generally, the faces (those of the children excepted) were depressed and subdued, and wanted colour. Aged people were there, in every variety. Mumbling, blear-eyed, spectacled, stupid, deaf, lame; vacantly winking in the gleams of sun that now and then crept in through the open doors, from the paved yard; shading their listening ears, or blinking eyes, with their withered hands; poring over their books, leering at nothing, going to sleep, crouching and drooping in corners. There were weird old women, all skeleton within, all bonnet and cloak without, continually wiping their eyes with dirty dusters of pocket-handkerchiefs; and there were ugly old crones, both male and female, with a ghastly kind of contentment upon them which was not at all comforting to see. Upon the whole, it was the dragon, Pauperism, in a very weak and impotent condition; toothless, fangless, drawing his breath heavily enough, and hardly worth chaining up.

When the service was over, I walked with the humane and conscientious gentleman whose duty it was to take that walk, that Sunday morning, through the little world of poverty enclosed within the workhouse walls. It was inhabited by a population of some fifteen hundred or two thousand paupers, ranging from the infant newly born or not yet come into the pauper world, to the old man dying on his bed.

In a room opening from a squalid yard, where a number of listless women were lounging to and fro, trying to get warm in the ineffectual sunshine of the tardy May morning—in the 'Itch Ward,' not to compromise the truth—a woman such as Hogarth has often drawn, was hurriedly getting on her gown before a dusty fire. She was the nurse, or wardswoman, of that insalubrious department—herself a pauper—flabby, raw-boned, untidy—unpromising and coarse of aspect as need be. But, on being spoken to about the patients whom she had in charge, she turned round, with her shabby gown half on, half off, and fell a crying with all her might. Not for show, not querulously, not in any mawkish sentiment, but in the deep grief and affliction of her heart; turning away her dishevelled head: sobbing most bitterly, wringing her hands, and letting fall abundance of great tears, that choked her utterance. What was the matter with the nurse of the itch-ward? Oh, 'the dropped child' was dead! Oh, the child that was found in the street, and she had brought up ever since, had died an hour ago, and see where the little creature lay, beneath this cloth! The dear, the pretty dear!

The dropped child seemed too small and poor a thing for Death to be in earnest with, but Death had taken it; and already its diminutive form was neatly washed, composed, and stretched as if in sleep upon a box. I thought I heard a voice from Heaven saying, It shall be well for thee, O nurse of the itch-ward, when some less gentle pauper does those offices to thy cold form, that such as the dropped child are the angels who behold my Father's face!

In another room, were several ugly old women crouching, witch-like, round a hearth, and chattering and nodding, after the manner of the monkeys. 'All well here? And enough to eat?' A general chattering and chuckling; at last an answer from a volunteer. 'Oh yes, gentleman! Bless you, gentleman! Lord bless the Parish of St. So-and-So! It feed the hungry, sir, and give drink to the thusty, and it warm them which is cold, so it do, and good luck to the parish of St. So-and-So, and thankee, gentleman!' Elsewhere, a party of pauper nurses were at dinner. 'How do you get on?' 'Oh pretty well, sir! We works hard, and we lives hard—like the sodgers!'

In another room, a kind of purgatory or place of transition, six or eight noisy madwomen were gathered together, under the superintendence of one sane attendant. Among them was a girl of two or three and twenty, very prettily dressed, of most respectable appearance and good manners, who had been brought in from the house where she had lived as domestic servant (having, I suppose, no friends), on account of being subject to epileptic fits, and requiring to be removed under the influence of a very bad one. She was by no means of the same stuff, or the same breeding, or the same experience, or in the same state of mind, as those by whom she was surrounded; and she pathetically complained that the daily association and the nightly noise made her worse, and was driving her mad—which was perfectly evident. The case was noted for inquiry and redress, but she said she had already been there for some weeks.

If this girl had stolen her mistress's watch, I do not hesitate to say she would have been infinitely better off. We have come to this absurd, this dangerous, this monstrous pass, that the dishonest felon is, in respect of cleanliness, order, diet, and accommodation, better provided for, and taken care of, than the honest pauper.

And this conveys no special imputation on the workhouse of the parish of St. So-and-So, where, on the contrary, I saw many things to commend. It was very agreeable, recollecting that most infamous and atrocious enormity committed at Tooting—an enormity which, a hundred years hence, will still be vividly remembered in the bye-ways of English life, and which has done more to engender a gloomy discontent and suspicion among many thousands of the people than all the Chartist leaders could have done in all their lives—to find the pauper children in this workhouse looking robust and well, and apparently the objects of very great care. In the Infant School—a large, light, airy room at the top of the building—the little creatures, being at dinner, and eating their potatoes heartily, were not cowed by the presence of strange visitors, but stretched out their small hands to be shaken, with a very pleasant confidence. And it was comfortable to see two mangy pauper rocking-horses rampant in a corner. In the girls' school, where the dinner was also in progress, everything bore a cheerful and healthy aspect. The meal was over, in the boys' school, by the time of our arrival there, and the room was not yet quite rearranged; but the boys were roaming unrestrained about a large and airy yard, as any other schoolboys might have done. Some of them had been drawing large ships upon the schoolroom wall; and if they had a mast with shrouds and stays set up for practice (as they have in the Middlesex House of Correction), it would be so much the better. At present, if a boy should feel a strong impulse upon him to learn the art of going aloft, he could only gratify it, I presume, as the men and women paupers gratify their aspirations after better board and lodging, by smashing as many workhouse windows as possible, and being promoted to prison.

In one place, the Newgate of the Workhouse, a company of boys and youths were locked up in a yard alone; their day-room being a kind of kennel where the casual poor used formerly to be littered down at night. Divers of them had been there some long time. 'Are they never going away?' was the natural inquiry. 'Most of them are crippled, in some form or other,' said the Wardsman, 'and not fit for anything.' They slunk about, like dispirited wolves or hyænas; and made a pounce at their food when it was served out, much as those animals do. The big-headed idiot shuffling his feet along the pavement, in the sunlight outside, was a more agreeable object everyway.

Groves of babies in arms; groves of mothers and other sick women in bed; groves of lunatics; jungles of men in stone-paved down-stairs day-rooms, waiting for their dinners; longer and longer groves of old people, in up-stairs Infirmary wards, wearing out life, God knows how—this was the scenery through which the walk lay, for two hours. In some of these latter chambers, there were pictures stuck against the wall, and a neat display of crockery and pewter on a kind of sideboard; now and then it was a treat to see a plant or two; in almost every ward there was a cat.

In all of these Long Walks of aged and infirm, some old people were bedridden, and had been for a long time; some were sitting on their beds half-naked; some dying in their beds; some out of bed, and sitting at a table near the fire. A sullen or lethargic indifference to what was asked, a blunted sensibility to everything but warmth and food, a moody absence of complaint as being of no use, a dogged silence and resentful desire to be left alone again, I thought were generally apparent. On our walking into the midst of one of these dreary perspectives of old men, nearly the following little dialogue took place, the nurse not being immediately at hand:

'All well here?'

No answer. An old man in a Scotch cap sitting among others on a form at the table, eating out of a tin porringer, pushes back his cap a little to look at us, claps it down on his forehead again with the palm of his hand, and goes on eating.

'All well here?' (repeated).

No answer. Another old man sitting on his bed, paralytically peeling a boiled potato, lifts his head and stares.

'Enough to eat?'

No answer. Another old man, in bed, turns himself and coughs.

'How are you to-day?' To the last old man.

That old man says nothing; but another old man, a tall old man of very good address, speaking with perfect correctness, comes forward from somewhere, and volunteers an answer. The reply almost always proceeds from a volunteer, and not from the person looked at or spoken to.

'We are very old, sir,' in a mild, distinct voice. 'We can't expect to be well, most of us.'

'Are you comfortable?'

'I have no complaint to make, sir.' With a half shake of his head, a half shrug of his shoulders, and a kind of apologetic smile.

'Enough to eat?'

'Why, sir, I have but a poor appetite,' with the same air as before; 'and

585

yet I get through my allowance very easily.'

'But,' showing a porringer with a Sunday dinner in it; 'here is a portion of mutton, and three potatoes. You can't starve on that?'

'Oh dear no, sir,' with the same apologetic air. 'Not starve.'

'What do you want?'

'We have very little bread, sir. It's an exceedingly small quantity of bread.'

The nurse, who is now rubbing her hands at the questioner's elbow, interferes with, 'It ain't much raly, sir. You see they've only six ounces a day, and when they've took their breakfast, there can only be a little left for night, sir.'

Another old man, hitherto invisible, rises out of his bed-clothes, as out of a grave, and looks on.

'You have tea at night?' The questioner is still addressing the well-spoken old man.

'Yes, sir, we have tea at night.'

'And you save what bread you can from the morning, to eat with it?'

'Yes, sir—if we can save any.'

'And you want more to eat with it?'

'Yes, sir.' With a very anxious face.

The questioner, in the kindness of his heart, appears a little discomposed, and changes the subject.

'What has become of the old man who used to lie in that bed in the corner?'

The nurse don't remember what old man is referred to. There has been such a many old men. The well-spoken old man is doubtful. The spectral old man who has come to life in bed, says, 'Billy Stevens.' Another old man who has previously had his head in the fireplace, pipes out,

'Charley Walters.'

Something like a feeble interest is awakened. I suppose Charley Walters had conversation in him.

'He's dead,' says the piping old man.

Another old man, with one eye screwed up, hastily displaces the piping old man, and says.

'Yes! Charley Walters died in that bed, and—and—'

'Billy Stevens,' persists the spectral old man.

'No, no! and Johnny Rogers died in that bed, and—and—they're both on 'em dead—and Sam'l Bowyer;' this seems very extraordinary to him; 'he went out!'

With this he subsides, and all the old men (having had quite enough of it) subside, and the spectral old man goes into his grave again, and takes the shade of Billy Stevens with him.

As we turn to go out at the door, another previously invisible old man, a hoarse old man in a flannel gown, is standing there, as if he had just come up through the floor.

'I beg your pardon, sir, could I take the liberty of saying a word?'

'Yes; what is it?'

'I am greatly better in my health, sir; but what I want, to get me quite round,' with his hand on his throat, 'is a little fresh air, sir. It has always done my complaint so much good, sir. The regular leave for going out, comes round so seldom, that if the gentlemen, next Friday, would give me leave to go out walking, now and then—for only an hour or so, sir!—'

Who could wonder, looking through those weary vistas of bed and infirmity, that it should do him good to meet with some other scenes, and assure himself that there was something else on earth? Who could help wondering why the old men lived on as they did; what grasp they had on life; what crumbs of interest or occupation they could pick up from its bare board; whether Charley Walters had ever described to them the days when he kept company with some old pauper woman in the bud, or Billy Stevens ever told them of the time when he was a dweller in the far-off foreign land called Home!

The morsel of burnt child, lying in another room, so patiently, in bed, wrapped in lint, and looking steadfastly at us with his bright quiet eyes when we spoke to him kindly, looked as if the knowledge of these things, and of all the tender things there are to think about, might have been in his mind—as if he thought, with us, that there was a fellow-feeling in the pauper nurses which appeared to make them more kind to their charges than the race of common nurses in the hospitals—as if he mused upon the Future of some older children lying around him in the same place, and thought it best, perhaps, all things considered, that he should die—as if he knew, without fear, of those many coffins, made and unmade, piled up in the store below—and of his unknown friend, 'the dropped child,' calm upon the box-lid covered with a cloth. But there was something wistful and appealing, too, in his tiny face, as if, in the midst of all the hard necessities and incongruities he pondered on, he pleaded, in behalf of the helpless and the aged poor, for a little more liberty—and a little more bread.

PRINCE BULL. A FAIRY TALE

Once upon a time, and of course it was in the Golden Age, and I hope you may know when that was, for I am sure I don't, though I have tried hard to find out, there lived in a rich and fertile country, a powerful Prince whose name was Bull. He had gone through a great deal of fighting, in his time, about all sorts of things, including nothing; but, had gradually settled down to be a steady, peaceable, good-natured, corpulent, rather sleepy Prince.

This Puissant Prince was married to a lovely Princess whose name was Fair Freedom. She had brought him a large fortune, and had borne him an immense number of children, and had set them to spinning, and farming, and engineering, and soldiering, and sailoring, and doctoring, and lawyering, and preaching, and all kinds of trades. The coffers of Prince Bull were full of treasure, his cellars were crammed with delicious wines from all parts of the world, the richest gold and silver plate that ever was seen adorned his sideboards, his sons were strong, his daughters were handsome, and in short you might have supposed that if there ever lived upon earth a fortunate and happy Prince, the name of that Prince, take him for all in all, was assuredly Prince Bull.

But, appearances, as we all know, are not always to be trusted—far from it; and if they had led you to this conclusion respecting Prince Bull, they would have led you wrong as they often have led me.

For, this good Prince had two sharp thorns in his pillow, two hard knobs in his crown, two heavy loads on his mind, two unbridled nightmares in his sleep, two rocks ahead in his course. He could not by any means get servants to suit him, and he had a tyrannical old godmother, whose name was Tape.

She was a Fairy, this Tape, and was a bright red all over. She was disgustingly prim and formal, and could never bend herself a hair's breadth this way or that way, out of her naturally crooked shape. But, she was very potent in her wicked art. She could stop the fastest thing in the world, change the strongest thing into the weakest, and the most useful into the most useless. To do this she had only to put her cold hand upon it, and repeat her own name, Tape. Then it withered away.

At the Court of Prince Bull—at least I don't mean literally at his court, because he was a very genteel Prince, and readily yielded to his godmother when she always reserved that for his hereditary Lords and Ladies—in the dominions of Prince Bull, among the great mass of the community who were called in the language of that polite country the Mobs and the Snobs, were a number of very ingenious men, who were always busy with some invention or other, for promoting the prosperity of the Prince's subjects, and augmenting the Prince's power. But, whenever they submitted their models for the Prince's approval, his godmother stepped forward, laid her hand upon them, and said 'Tape.' Hence it came to pass, that when any particularly good discovery was made, the discoverer usually carried it off to some other Prince, in foreign parts, who had no old godmother who said Tape. This was not on the whole an advantageous state of things for Prince Bull, to the best of my understanding.

The worst of it was, that Prince Bull had in course of years lapsed into such a state of subjection to this unlucky godmother, that he never made any serious effort to rid himself of her tyranny. I have said this was the worst of it, but there I was wrong, because there is a worse consequence still, behind. The Prince's numerous family became so downright sick and tired of Tape, that when they should have helped the Prince out of the difficulties into which that evil creature led him, they fell into a dangerous habit of moodily keeping away from him in an impassive and indifferent manner, as though they had quite forgotten that no harm could happen to the Prince their father, without its inevitably affecting themselves.

Such was the aspect of affairs at the court of Prince Bull, when this great Prince found it necessary to go to war with Prince Bear. He had been for some time very doubtful of his servants, who, besides being indolent and addicted to enriching their families at his expense, domineered over him dreadfully; threatening to discharge themselves if they were found the least fault with, pretending that they had done a wonderful amount of work when they had done nothing, making the most unmeaning speeches that ever were heard in the Prince's name, and uniformly showing themselves to be very inefficient indeed. Though, that some of them had excellent characters from previous situations is not to be denied. Well; Prince Bull called his servants together, and said to them one and all, 'Send out my army against Prince Bear. Clothe it, arm it, feed it, provide it with all necessaries and contingencies, and I will pay the piper! Do your duty by my brave troops,' said the Prince, 'and do it well, and I will pour my treasure out like water, to defray the cost. Who ever heard ME complain of money well laid out!' Which indeed he had reason for saying, inasmuch as he was well known to be a truly generous and munificent Prince.

When the servants heard those words, they sent out the army against Prince Bear, and they set the army tailors to work, and the army provision merchants, and the makers of guns both great and small, and the gunpowder makers, and the makers of ball, shell, and shot; and they bought up all manner of stores and ships, without troubling their heads about the price, and appeared to be so busy that the good Prince rubbed his hands, and (using a favourite expression of his), said, 'It's all right!' But, while they were thus employed, the Prince's godmother, who was a great favourite with those servants, looked in upon them continually all day long, and whenever she popped in her head at the door said, How do you do, my children? What are you doing here?' 'Official business, godmother.' 'Oho!' says this wicked Fairy. '—Tape!' And then the business all went wrong, whatever it was, and the servants' heads became so addled and muddled that they thought they were doing wonders.

Now, this was very bad conduct on the part of the vicious old nuisance, and she ought to have been strangled, even if she had stopped here; but, she didn't stop here, as you shall learn. For, a number of the Prince's subjects, being very fond of the Prince's army who were the bravest of men, assembled together and provided all manner of eatables and drinkables, and books to read, and clothes to wear, and tobacco to smoke, and candies to burn, and nailed them up in great packing-cases, and put them aboard a great many ships, to be carried out to that brave army in the cold and inclement country

591

where they were fighting Prince Bear. Then, up comes this wicked Fairy as the ships were weighing anchor, and says, 'How do you do, my children? What are you doing here?'—'We are going with all these comforts to the army, godmother.'—'Oho!' says she. 'A pleasant voyage, my darlings.—Tape!' And from that time forth, those enchanting ships went sailing, against wind and tide and rhyme and reason, round and round the world, and whenever they touched at any port were ordered off immediately, and could never deliver their cargoes anywhere.

This, again, was very bad conduct on the part of the vicious old nuisance, and she ought to have been strangled for it if she had done nothing worse; but, she did something worse still, as you shall learn. For, she got astride of an official broomstick, and muttered as a spell these two sentences, 'On Her Majesty's service,' and 'I have the honour to be, sir, your most obedient servant,' and presently alighted in the cold and inclement country where the army of Prince Bull were encamped to fight the army of Prince Bear. On the sea-shore of that country, she found piled together, a number of houses for the army to live in, and a quantity of provisions for the army to live upon, and a quantity of clothes for the army to wear: while, sitting in the mud gazing at them, were a group of officers as red to look at as the wicked old woman herself. So, she said to one of them, 'Who are you, my darling, and how do you do?'—'I am the Quartermaster General's Department, godmother, and I am pretty well.' Then she said to another, 'Who are you, my darling, and how do you do?'—'I am the Commissariat Department, godmother, and I am pretty well! Then she said to another, 'Who are you, my darling, and how do you do?'—'I am the Head of the Medical Department, godmother, and I am pretty well.' Then, she said to some gentlemen scented with lavender, who kept themselves at a great distance from the rest, 'And who are you, my pretty pets, and how do you do?' And they answered, 'We-aw-are-the-aw-Staff-aw-Department, godmother, and we are very well indeed.'—'I am delighted to see you all, my beauties,' says this wicked old Fairy, '—Tape!' Upon that, the houses, clothes, and provisions, all mouldered away; and the soldiers who were sound, fell sick; and the soldiers who were sick, died miserably: and the noble army of Prince Bull perished.

When the dismal news of his great loss was carried to the Prince, he suspected his godmother very much indeed; but, he knew that his servants must have kept company with the malicious beldame, and must have given way to her, and therefore he resolved to turn those servants out of their places. So, he called to him a Roebuck who had the gift of speech, and he said, 'Good Roebuck, tell them they must go.' So, the good Roebuck delivered his message, so like a man that you might have supposed him to be nothing but a man, and they were turned out—but, not without warning, for that they had had a long time.

And now comes the most extraordinary part of the history of this Prince. When he had turned out those servants, of course he wanted others. What was his astonishment to find that in all his dominions, which contained no less than twenty-seven millions of people, there were not above five-and-twenty servants altogether! They were so lofty about it, too, that instead of discussing whether they should hire themselves as servants to Prince Bull, they turned things topsy-turvy, and considered whether as a favour they should hire Prince Bull to be their master! While they were arguing this point among themselves quite at their leisure, the wicked old red Fairy was incessantly going up and down, knocking at the doors of twelve of the oldest of the five-and-twenty, who were the oldest inhabitants in all that country, and whose united ages amounted to one thousand, saying, 'Will you hire Prince Bull for your master?—Will you hire Prince Bull for your master?' To which one answered, 'I will if next door will;' and another, 'I won't if over the way does;' and another, 'I can't if he, she, or they, might, could, would, or should.' And all this time Prince Bull's affairs were going to rack and ruin.

At last, Prince Bull in the height of his perplexity assumed a thoughtful face, as if he were struck by an entirely new idea. The wicked old Fairy, seeing this, was at his elbow directly, and said, 'How do you do, my Prince, and what are you thinking of?'—'I am thinking, godmother,' says he, 'that among all the seven-and-twenty millions of my subjects who have never been in service, there are men of intellect and business who have made me very famous both among my friends and enemies.'—'Aye, truly?' says the Fairy.—'Aye, truly,' says the Prince.—'And what then?' says the Fairy.—'Why, then,' says he, 'since the regular old class of servants do so ill, are so hard to get, and carry it with so high a hand, perhaps I might try to make good servants of some of these.' The words had no sooner passed his lips than she returned, chuckling, 'You think so, do you? Indeed, my Prince?—Tape!' Thereupon he directly forgot what he was thinking of, and cried out lamentably to the old servants, 'O, do come and hire your poor old master! Pray do! On any terms!'

And this, for the present, finishes the story of Prince Bull. I wish I could wind it up by saying that he lived happy ever afterwards, but I cannot in my conscience do so; for, with Tape at his elbow, and his estranged children fatally repelled by her from coming near him, I do not, to tell you the plain truth, believe in the possibility of such an end to it.

A PLATED ARTICLE

Putting up for the night in one of the chiefest towns of Staffordshire, I find it to be by no means a lively town. In fact, it is as dull and dead a town as any one could desire not to see. It seems as if its whole population might be imprisoned in its Railway Station. The Refreshment Room at that Station is a vortex of dissipation compared with the extinct town-inn, the Dodo, in the dull High Street.

Why High Street? Why not rather Low Street, Flat Street, Low-Spirited Street, Used-up Street? Where are the people who belong to the High Street? Can they all be dispersed over the face of the country, seeking the unfortunate Strolling Manager who decamped from the mouldy little Theatre last week, in the beginning of his season (as his play-bills testify), repentantly resolved to bring him back, and feed him, and be entertained? Or, can they all be gathered to their fathers in the two old churchyards near to the High Street—retirement into which churchyards appears to be a mere ceremony, there is so very little life outside their confines, and such small discernible difference between being buried alive in the town, and buried dead in the town tombs? Over the way, opposite to the staring blank bow windows of the Dodo, are a little ironmonger's shop, a little tailor's shop (with a picture of the Fashions in the small window and a bandy-legged baby on the pavement staring at it)—a watchmakers shop, where all the clocks and watches must be stopped, I am sure, for they could never have the courage to go, with the town in general, and the Dodo in particular, looking at them. Shade of Miss Linwood, erst of Leicester Square, London, thou art welcome here, and thy retreat is fitly chosen! I myself was one of the last visitors to that awful storehouse of thy life's work, where an anchorite old man and woman took my shilling with a solemn wonder, and conducting me to a gloomy sepulchre of needlework dropping to pieces with dust and age and shrouded in twilight at high noon, left me there, chilled, frightened, and alone. And now, in ghostly letters on all the dead walls of this dead town, I read thy honoured name, and find that thy Last Supper, worked in Berlin Wool, invites inspection as a powerful excitement!

Where are the people who are bidden with so much cry to this feast of little wool? Where are they? Who are they? They are not the bandy-legged baby studying the fashions in the tailor's window. They are not the two earthy ploughmen lounging outside the saddler's shop, in the stiff square where the Town Hall stands, like a brick and mortar private on parade. They are not the landlady of the Dodo in the empty bar, whose eye had trouble in it and no welcome, when I asked for dinner. They are not the turnkeys of the Town Jail, looking out of the gateway in their uniforms, as if they had locked up all the balance (as my American friends would say) of the inhabitants, and could now rest a little. They are not the two dusty millers in the white mill down by the river, where the great water-wheel goes heavily round and round, like the monotonous days and nights in this forgotten place. Then who are they, for there is no one else? No; this deponent maketh oath and saith that there is no one else, save and except the waiter at the Dodo, now laying the cloth. I have paced the streets, and stared at the houses, and am come back to the blank bow window of the Dodo; and the town clocks strike seven, and the reluctant echoes seem to cry, 'Don't wake us!' and the bandy-legged baby has gone home to bed.

If the Dodo were only a gregarious bird—if he had only some confused idea of making a comfortable nest—I could hope to get through the hours between this and bed-time, without being consumed by devouring melancholy. But, the Dodo's habits are all wrong. It provides me with a trackless desert of sitting-room, with a chair for every day in the year, a table for every month, and a waste of sideboard where a lonely China vase pines in a corner for its mate long departed, and will never make a match with the candlestick in the opposite corner if it live till Doomsday. The Dodo has nothing in the larder. Even now, I behold the Boots returning with my sole in a piece of paper; and with that portion of my dinner, the Boots, perceiving me at the blank bow window, slaps his leg as he comes across the road, pretending it is something else. The Dodo excludes the outer air. When I mount up to my bedroom, a smell of closeness and flue gets lazily up my nose like sleepy snuff. The loose little bits of carpet writhe under my tread, and take wormy shapes. I don't know the ridiculous man in the looking-glass, beyond having met him once or twice in a dish-cover—and I can never shave him to-morrow morning! The Dodo is narrow-minded as to towels; expects me to wash on a freemason's apron without the trimming: when I asked for soap, gives me a stony-hearted something white, with no more lather in it than the Elgin marbles. The Dodo has seen better days, and possesses interminable stables at the back—silent, grass-grown, broken-windowed, horseless.

This mournful bird can fry a sole, however, which is much. Can cook a steak, too, which is more. I wonder where it gets its Sherry? If I were to send my pint of wine to some famous chemist to be analysed, what would it turn out to be made of? It tastes of pepper, sugar, bitter-almonds, vinegar, warm knives, any flat drinks, and a little brandy. Would it unman a Spanish exile by reminding him of his native land at all? I think not. If there really be any townspeople out of the churchyards, and if a caravan of them ever do dine, with a bottle of wine per man, in this desert of the Dodo, it must make good for the doctor next day!

Where was the waiter born? How did he come here? Has he any hope of getting away from here? Does he ever receive a letter, or take a ride upon the railway, or see anything but the Dodo? Perhaps he has seen the Berlin Wool. He appears to have a silent sorrow on him, and it may be that. He clears the table; draws the dingy curtains of the great bow window, which so unwillingly consent to meet, that they must be pinned together; leaves me by the fire with my pint decanter, and a little thin funnel-shaped wine-glass, and a plate of pale biscuits—in themselves engendering desperation.

No book, no newspaper! I left the Arabian Nights in the railway carriage, and have nothing to read but Bradshaw, and 'that way madness lies.' Remembering what prisoners and ship-wrecked mariners have done to exercise their minds in solitude, I repeat the multiplication table, the pence table, and the shilling table: which are all the tables I happen to know. What if I write something? The Dodo keeps no pens but steel pens; and those I always stick through the paper, and can turn to no other account.

What am I to do? Even if I could have the bandy-legged baby knocked up and brought here, I could offer him nothing but sherry, and that would be the death of him. He would never hold up his head again if he touched it. I can't go to bed, because I have conceived a mortal hatred for my bedroom; and I can't go away, because there is no train for my place of destination until morning. To burn the biscuits will be but a fleeting joy; still it is a temporary relief, and here they go on the fire! Shall I break the plate? First let me look at the back, and see who made it. Copeland.

Copeland! Stop a moment. Was it yesterday I visited Copeland's works, and saw them making plates? In the confusion of travelling about, it might be yesterday or it might be yesterday month; but I think it was yesterday. I appeal to the plate. The plate says, decidedly, yesterday. I find the plate, as I look at it, growing into a companion.

Don't you remember (says the plate) how you steamed away, yesterday morning, in the bright sun and the east wind, along the valley of the sparkling Trent? Don't you recollect how many kilns you flew past, looking like the bowls of gigantic tobacco-pipes, cut short off from the stem and turned upside down? And the fires—and the smoke—and the roads made with bits of crockery, as if all the plates and dishes in the civilised world had been Macadamised, expressly for the laming of all the horses? Of course I do!

And don't you remember (says the plate) how you alighted at Stoke—a picturesque heap of houses, kilns, smoke, wharfs, canals, and river, lying (as was most appropriate) in a basin—and how, after climbing up the sides of the basin to look at the prospect, you trundled down again at a walking-match pace, and straight proceeded to my father's, Copeland's, where the whole of my family, high and low, rich and poor, are turned out upon the world from our nursery and seminary, covering some fourteen acres of ground? And don't you remember what we spring from:—heaps of lumps of clay, partially prepared and cleaned in Devonshire and Dorsetshire, whence said clay principally comes—and hills of flint, without which we should want our ringing sound, and should never be musical? And as to the flint, don't you recollect that it is first burnt in kilns, and is then laid under the four iron feet of a demon slave, subject to violent stamping fits, who, when they come on, stamps away insanely with his four iron legs, and would crush all the flint in the Isle of Thanet to powder, without leaving off? And as to the clay, don't you recollect how it is put into mills or teazers, and is sliced, and dug, and cut at, by endless knives, clogged and sticky, but persistent—and is pressed out of that machine through a square trough, whose form it takes—and is cut off in square lumps and thrown into a vat, and there mixed with water, and beaten to a pulp by paddle-wheels—and is then run into a rough house, all rugged beams and ladders splashed with white,—superintended by Grindoff the Miller in his working clothes, all splashed with white,—where it passes through no end of machinery-moved sieves all splashed with white, arranged in an ascending scale of fineness (some so fine, that three hundred silk threads cross each other in a single square inch of their surface), and all in a violent state of ague with their teeth for ever chattering, and their bodies for ever shivering! And as to the flint again, isn't it mashed and mollified and troubled and soothed, exactly as rags are in a paper-mill, until it is reduced to a pap so fine that it contains no atom of 'grit' perceptible to the nicest taste? And as to the flint and the clay together, are they not, after all this, mixed in the proportion of five of clay to one of flint, and isn't the compound—known as 'slip'—run into oblong troughs, where its superfluous moisture may evaporate; and finally, isn't it slapped and banged and beaten and patted and kneaded and wedged and knocked about like butter, until it becomes a beautiful grey dough, ready for the potter's use?

In regard of the potter, popularly so called (says the plate), you don't mean to say you have forgotten that a workman called a Thrower is the man under whose hand this grey dough takes the shapes of the simpler household vessels as quickly as the eye can follow? You don't mean to say you cannot call him up before you, sitting, with his attendant woman, at his potter's wheel—a disc about the size of a dinner-plate, revolving on two drums slowly or quickly as he wills—who made you a complete breakfast-set for a bachelor, as a good-humoured little off-hand joke? You remember how he took up as much dough as he wanted, and, throwing it on his wheel, in a moment fashioned it into a teacup—caught up more clay and made a saucer—a larger dab and whirled it into a teapot—winked at a smaller dab and converted it into the lid of the teapot, accurately fitting by the measurement of his eye alone—coaxed a middle-sized dab for two seconds, broke it, turned it over at the rim, and made a milkpot—laughed, and turned out a slop-basin—coughed, and provided for the sugar? Neither, I think, are you oblivious of the newer mode of making various articles, but especially basins, according to which improvement a mould revolves instead of a disc? For you must remember (says the plate) how you saw the mould of a little basin spinning round and round, and how the workmen smoothed and pressed a handful of dough upon it, and how with an instrument called a profile (a piece of wood, representing the profile of a basin's foot) he cleverly scraped and carved the ring which makes the base of any such basin, and then took the basin off the lathe like a doughy skull-cap to be dried, and afterwards (in what is called a green state) to be put into a second lathe, there to be finished and burnished with a steel burnisher? And as to moulding in general (says the plate), it can't be necessary for me to remind you that all ornamental articles, and indeed all articles not quite circular, are made in moulds. For you must remember how you saw the vegetable dishes, for example, being made in moulds; and how the handles of teacups, and the spouts of teapots, and the feet of tureens, and so forth, are all made in little separate moulds, and are each stuck on to the body corporate, of which it is destined to form a part, with a stuff called 'slag,' as quickly as you can recollect it. Further, you learnt—you know you did—in the same visit, how the beautiful sculptures in the delicate new material called Parian, are all constructed in moulds; how, into that material, animal bones are ground up, because the phosphate of lime contained in bones makes it translucent; how everything is moulded, before going into the fire, one-fourth larger than it is intended to come out of the fire, because it shrinks in that proportion in the intense heat; how, when a figure shrinks unequally, it is spoiled—emerging from the furnace a misshapen birth; a big head and a little body, or a little head and a big body, or a Quasimodo with long arms and short legs, or a Miss Biffin with neither legs nor arms worth mentioning.

And as to the Kilns, in which the firing takes place, and in which some of the more precious articles are burnt repeatedly, in various stages of their process towards completion,—as to the Kilns (says the plate, warming with the recollection), if you don't remember THEM with a horrible interest, what did you ever go to Copeland's for? When you stood inside of one of those

600

inverted bowls of a Pre-Adamite tobacco-pipe, looking up at the blue sky through the open top far off, as you might have looked up from a well, sunk under the centre of the pavement of the Pantheon at Rome, had you the least idea where you were? And when you found yourself surrounded, in that dome-shaped cavern, by innumerable columns of an unearthly order of architecture, supporting nothing, and squeezed close together as if a Pre-Adamite Samson had taken a vast Hall in his arms and crushed it into the smallest possible space, had you the least idea what they were? No (says the plate), of course not! And when you found that each of those pillars was a pile of ingeniously made vessels of coarse clay—called Saggers—looking, when separate, like raised-pies for the table of the mighty Giant Blunderbore, and now all full of various articles of pottery ranged in them in baking order, the bottom of each vessel serving for the cover of the one below, and the whole Kiln rapidly filling with these, tier upon tier, until the last workman should have barely room to crawl out, before the closing of the jagged aperture in the wall and the kindling of the gradual fire; did you not stand amazed to think that all the year round these dread chambers are heating, white hot—and cooling—and filling—and emptying—and being bricked up—and broken open—humanly speaking, for ever and ever? To be sure you did! And standing in one of those Kilns nearly full, and seeing a free crow shoot across the aperture a-top, and learning how the fire would wax hotter and hotter by slow degrees, and would cool similarly through a space of from forty to sixty hours, did no remembrance of the days when human clay was burnt oppress you? Yes. I think so! I suspect that some fancy of a fiery haze and a shortening breath, and a growing heat, and a gasping prayer; and a figure in black interposing between you and the sky (as figures in black are very apt to do), and looking down, before it grew too hot to look and live, upon the Heretic in his edifying agony—I say I suspect (says the plate) that some such fancy was pretty strong upon you when you went out into the air, and blessed God for the bright spring day and the degenerate times!

After that, I needn't remind you what a relief it was to see the simplest process of ornamenting this 'biscuit' (as it is called when baked) with brown circles and blue trees—converting it into the common crockery-ware that is exported to Africa, and used in cottages at home. For (says the plate) I am well persuaded that you bear in mind how those particular jugs and mugs were once more set upon a lathe and put in motion; and how a man blew the brown colour (having a strong natural affinity with the material in that condition) on them from a blowpipe as they twirled; and how his daughter, with a common brush, dropped blotches of blue upon them in the right places; and how, tilting the blotches upside down, she made them run into rude images of trees, and there an end.

And didn't you see (says the plate) planted upon my own brother that astounding blue willow, with knobbed and gnarled trunk, and foliage of blue ostrich feathers, which gives our family the title of 'willow pattern'? And didn't you observe, transferred upon him at the same time, that blue bridge which spans nothing, growing out from the roots of the willow; and the three blue Chinese going over it into a blue temple, which has a fine crop of blue bushes sprouting out of the roof; and a blue boat sailing above them, the mast of which is burglariously sticking itself into the foundations of a blue villa, suspended sky-high, surmounted by a lump of blue rock, sky-higher, and a couple of billing blue birds, sky-highest—together with the rest of that amusing blue landscape, which has, in deference to our revered ancestors of the Cerulean Empire, and in defiance of every known law of perspective, adorned millions of our family ever since the days of platters? Didn't you inspect the copper-plate on which my pattern was deeply engraved? Didn't you perceive an impression of it taken in cobalt colour at a cylindrical press, upon a leaf of thin paper, streaming from a plunge-bath of soap and water? Wasn't the paper impression daintily spread, by a light-fingered damsel (you know you admired her!), over the surface of the plate, and the back of the paper rubbed prodigiously hard—with a long tight roll of flannel, tied up like a round of hung beef—without so much as ruffling the paper, wet as it was? Then (says the plate), was not the paper washed away with a sponge, and didn't there appear, set off upon the plate, this identical piece of Pre-Raphaelite blue distemper which you now behold? Not to be denied! I had seen all this—and more. I had been shown, at Copeland's, patterns of beautiful design, in faultless perspective, which are causing the ugly old willow to wither out of public favour; and which, being quite as cheap, insinuate good wholesome natural art into the humblest households. When Mr. and Mrs. Sprat have satisfied their material tastes by that equal division of fat and lean which has made their ménage immortal; and have, after the elegant tradition, 'licked the platter clean,' they can—thanks to modern artists in clay—feast their intellectual tastes upon excellent delineations of natural objects.

This reflection prompts me to transfer my attention from the blue plate to the forlorn but cheerfully painted vase on the sideboard. And surely (says the plate) you have not forgotten how the outlines of such groups of flowers as you see there, are printed, just as I was printed, and are afterwards shaded and filled in with metallic colours by women and girls? As to the aristocracy of our order, made of the finer clay-porcelain peers and peeresses;—the slabs, and panels, and table-tops, and tazze; the endless nobility and gentry of dessert, breakfast, and tea services; the gemmed perfume bottles, and scarlet and gold salvers; you saw that they were painted by artists, with metallic colours laid on with camel-hair pencils, and afterwards burnt in.

And talking of burning in (says the plate), didn't you find that every subject, from the willow pattern to the landscape after Turner—having been framed upon clay or porcelain biscuit—has to be glazed? Of course, you saw the glaze—composed of various vitreous materials—laid over every article; and of course you witnessed the close imprisonment of each piece in saggers upon the separate system rigidly enforced by means of fine-pointed earthenware stilts placed between the articles to prevent the slightest communication or contact. We had in my time—and I suppose it is the same now—fourteen hours' firing to fix the glaze and to make it 'run' all over us equally, so as to put a good shiny and unscratchable surface upon us. Doubtless, you observed that one sort of glaze—called printing-body—is burnt into the better sort of ware before it is printed. Upon this you saw some of the finest steel engravings transferred, to be fixed by an after glazing—didn't you? Why, of course you did!

Of course I did. I had seen and enjoyed everything that the plate recalled to me, and had beheld with admiration how the rotatory motion which keeps this ball of ours in its place in the great scheme, with all its busy mites upon it, was necessary throughout the process, and could only be dispensed with in the fire. So, listening to the plate's reminders, and musing upon them, I got through the evening after all, and went to bed. I made but one sleep of it—for which I have no doubt I am also indebted to the plate—and left the lonely Dodo in the morning, quite at peace with it, before the bandy-legged baby was up.

OUR HONOURABLE FRIEND

We are delighted to find that he has got in! Our honourable friend is triumphantly returned to serve in the next Parliament. He is the honourable member for Verbosity—the best represented place in England.

Our honourable friend has issued an address of congratulation to the Electors, which is worthy of that noble constituency, and is a very pretty piece of composition. In electing him, he says, they have covered themselves with glory, and England has been true to herself. (In his preliminary address he had remarked, in a poetical quotation of great rarity, that nought could make us rue, if England to herself did prove but true.)

Our honourable friend delivers a prediction, in the same document, that the feeble minions of a faction will never hold up their heads any more; and that the finger of scorn will point at them in their dejected state, through countless ages of time. Further, that the hireling tools that would destroy the sacred bulwarks of our nationality are unworthy of the name of Englishman; and that so long as the sea shall roll around our ocean-girded isle, so long his motto shall be, No surrender. Certain dogged persons of low principles and no intellect, have disputed whether anybody knows who the minions are, or what the faction is, or which are the hireling tools and which the sacred bulwarks, or what it is that is never to be surrendered, and if not, why not? But, our honourable friend the member for Verbosity knows all about it.

Our honourable friend has sat in several parliaments, and given bushels of votes. He is a man of that profundity in the matter of vote-giving, that you never know what he means. When he seems to be voting pure white, he may be in reality voting jet black. When he says Yes, it is just as likely as not—or rather more so—that he means No. This is the statesmanship of our honourable friend. It is in this, that he differs from mere unparliamentary men. You may not know what he meant then, or what he means now; but, our honourable friend knows, and did from the first know, both what he meant then, and what he means now; and when he said he didn't mean it then, he did in fact say, that he means it now. And if you mean to say that you did not then, and do not now, know what he did mean then, or does mean now, our honourable friend will be glad to receive an explicit declaration from you whether you are prepared to destroy the sacred bulwarks of our nationality.

Our honourable friend, the member for Verbosity, has this great attribute, that he always means something, and always means the same thing. When he came down to that House and mournfully boasted in his place, as an individual member of the assembled Commons of this great and happy country, that he could lay his hand upon his heart, and solemnly declare that no consideration on earth should induce him, at any time or under any circumstances, to go as far north as Berwick-upon-Tweed; and when he nevertheless, next year, did go to Berwick-upon-Tweed, and even beyond it, to Edinburgh; he had one single meaning, one and indivisible. And God forbid (our honourable friend says) that he should waste another argument upon the man who professes that he cannot understand it! 'I do NOT, gentlemen,' said our honourable friend, with indignant emphasis and amid great cheering, on one such public occasion. 'I do NOT, gentlemen, I am free to confess, envy the feelings of that man whose mind is so constituted as that he can hold such language to me, and yet lay his head upon his pillow, claiming to be a native of that land,

Whose march is o'er the mountain-wave,

Whose home is on the deep!

(Vehement cheering, and man expelled.)

When our honourable friend issued his preliminary address to the constituent body of Verbosity on the occasion of one particular glorious triumph, it was supposed by some of his enemies, that even he would be placed in a situation of difficulty by the following comparatively trifling conjunction of circumstances. The dozen noblemen and gentlemen whom our honourable friend supported, had 'come in,' expressly to do a certain thing. Now, four of the dozen said, at a certain place, that they didn't mean to do that thing, and had never meant to do it; another four of the dozen said, at another certain place, that they did mean to do that thing, and had always meant to do it; two of the remaining four said, at two other certain places, that they meant to do half of that thing (but differed about which half), and to do a variety of nameless wonders instead of the other half; and one of the remaining two declared that the thing itself was dead and buried, while the other as strenuously protested that it was alive and kicking. It was admitted that the parliamentary genius of our honourable friend would be quite able to reconcile such small discrepancies as these; but, there remained the additional difficulty that each of the twelve made entirely different statements at different places, and that all the twelve called everything visible and invisible, sacred and profane, to witness, that they were a perfectly impregnable phalanx of unanimity. This, it was apprehended, would be a stumbling-block to our honourable friend.

The difficulty came before our honourable friend, in this way. He went down to Verbosity to meet his free and independent constituents, and to render an account (as he informed them in the local papers) of the trust they had confided to his hands—that trust which it was one of the proudest privileges of an Englishman to possess—that trust which it was the proudest privilege of an Englishman to hold. It may be mentioned as a proof of the great general interest attaching to the contest, that a Lunatic whom nobody employed or knew, went down to Verbosity with several thousand pounds in gold, determined to give the whole away—which he actually did; and that all the publicans opened their houses for nothing. Likewise, several fighting men, and a patriotic group of burglars sportively armed with life-preservers, proceeded (in barouches and very drunk) to the scene of action at their own expense; these children of nature having conceived a warm attachment to our honourable friend, and intending, in their artless manner, to testify it by knocking the voters in the opposite interest on the head.

Our honourable friend being come into the presence of his constituents, and having professed with great suavity that he was delighted to see his good friend Tipkisson there, in his working-dress—his good friend Tipkisson being an inveterate saddler, who always opposes him, and for whom he has a mortal hatred—made them a brisk, ginger-beery sort of speech, in which

607

he showed them how the dozen noblemen and gentlemen had (in exactly ten days from their coming in) exercised a surprisingly beneficial effect on the whole financial condition of Europe, had altered the state of the exports and imports for the current half-year, had prevented the drain of gold, had made all that matter right about the glut of the raw material, and had restored all sorts of balances with which the superseded noblemen and gentlemen had played the deuce—and all this, with wheat at so much a quarter, gold at so much an ounce, and the Bank of England discounting good bills at so much per cent.! He might be asked, he observed in a peroration of great power, what were his principles? His principles were what they always had been. His principles were written in the countenances of the lion and unicorn; were stamped indelibly upon the royal shield which those grand animals supported, and upon the free words of fire which that shield bore. His principles were, Britannia and her sea-king trident! His principles were, commercial prosperity co-existently with perfect and profound agricultural contentment; but short of this he would never stop. His principles were, these,—with the addition of his colours nailed to the mast, every man's heart in the right place, every man's eye open, every man's hand ready, every man's mind on the alert. His principles were these, concurrently with a general revision of something—speaking generally—and a possible readjustment of something else, not to be mentioned more particularly. His principles, to sum up all in a word, were, Hearths and Altars, Labour and Capital, Crown and Sceptre, Elephant and Castle. And now, if his good friend Tipkisson required any further explanation from him, he (our honourable friend) was there, willing and ready to give it.

Tipkisson, who all this time had stood conspicuous in the crowd, with his arms folded and his eyes intently fastened on our honourable friend: Tipkisson, who throughout our honourable friend's address had not relaxed a muscle of his visage, but had stood there, wholly unaffected by the torrent of eloquence: an object of contempt and scorn to mankind (by which we mean, of course, to the supporters of our honourable friend); Tipkisson now said that he was a plain man (Cries of 'You are indeed!'), and that what he wanted to know was, what our honourable friend and the dozen noblemen and gentlemen were driving at?

Our honourable friend immediately replied, 'At the illimitable perspective.'

It was considered by the whole assembly that this happy statement of our honourable friend's political views ought, immediately, to have settled Tipkisson's business and covered him with confusion; but, that implacable person, regardless of the execrations that were heaped upon him from all sides (by which we mean, of course, from our honourable friend's side), persisted in retaining an unmoved countenance, and obstinately retorted that if our honourable friend meant that, he wished to know what that meant?

It was in repelling this most objectionable and indecent opposition, that our honourable friend displayed his highest qualifications for the representation of Verbosity. His warmest supporters present, and those who were best acquainted with his generalship, supposed that the moment was come when he would fall back upon the sacred bulwarks of our nationality. No such thing. He replied thus: 'My good friend Tipkisson, gentlemen, wishes to know what I mean when he asks me what we are driving at, and when I candidly tell him, at the illimitable perspective, he wishes (if I understand him) to know what I mean?'—'I do!' says Tipkisson, amid cries of 'Shame' and 'Down with him.' 'Gentlemen,' says our honourable friend, 'I will indulge my good friend Tipkisson, by telling him, both what I mean and what I don't mean. (Cheers and cries of 'Give it him!') Be it known to him then, and to all whom it may concern, that I do mean altars, hearths, and homes, and that I don't mean mosques and Mohammedanism!' The effect of this home-thrust was terrific. Tipkisson (who is a Baptist) was hooted down and hustled out, and has ever since been regarded as a Turkish Renegade who contemplates an early pilgrimage to Mecca. Nor was he the only discomfited man. The charge, while it stuck to him, was magically transferred to our honourable friend's opponent, who was represented in an immense variety of placards as a firm believer in Mahomet; and the men of Verbosity were asked to choose between our honourable friend and the Bible, and our honourable friend's opponent and the Koran. They decided for our honourable friend, and rallied round the illimitable perspective.

It has been claimed for our honourable friend, with much appearance of reason, that he was the first to bend sacred matters to electioneering tactics. However this may be, the fine precedent was undoubtedly set in a Verbosity election: and it is certain that our honourable friend (who was a disciple of Brahma in his youth, and was a Buddhist when we had the honour of travelling with him a few years ago) always professes in public more anxiety than the whole Bench of Bishops, regarding the theological and doxological opinions of every man, woman, and child, in the United Kingdom.

As we began by saying that our honourable friend has got in again at this last election, and that we are delighted to find that he has got in, so we will conclude. Our honourable friend cannot come in for Verbosity too often. It is a good sign; it is a great example. It is to men like our honourable friend, and to contests like those from which he comes triumphant, that we are mainly indebted for that ready interest in politics, that fresh enthusiasm in the discharge of the duties of citizenship, that ardent desire to rush to the poll, at present so manifest throughout England. When the contest lies (as it sometimes does) between two such men as our honourable friend, it stimulates the finest emotions of our nature, and awakens the highest admiration of which our heads and hearts are capable.

It is not too much to predict that our honourable friend will be always at his post in the ensuing session. Whatever the question be, or whatever the form of its discussion; address to the crown, election petition, expenditure of the public money, extension of the public suffrage, education, crime; in the whole house, in committee of the whole house, in select committee; in every parliamentary discussion of every subject, everywhere: the Honourable Member for Verbosity will most certainly be found.

OUR SCHOOL

We went to look at it, only this last Midsummer, and found that the Railway had cut it up root and branch. A great trunk-line had swallowed the playground, sliced away the schoolroom, and pared off the corner of the house: which, thus curtailed of its proportions, presented itself, in a green stage of stucco, profilewise towards the road, like a forlorn flat-iron without a handle, standing on end.

It seems as if our schools were doomed to be the sport of change. We have faint recollections of a Preparatory Day-School, which we have sought in vain, and which must have been pulled down to make a new street, ages ago. We have dim impressions, scarcely amounting to a belief, that it was over a dyer's shop. We know that you went up steps to it; that you frequently grazed your knees in doing so; that you generally got your leg over the scraper, in trying to scrape the mud off a very unsteady little shoe. The mistress of the Establishment holds no place in our memory; but, rampant on one eternal door-mat, in an eternal entry long and narrow, is a puffy pug-dog, with a personal animosity towards us, who triumphs over Time. The bark of that baleful Pug, a certain radiating way he had of snapping at our undefended legs, the ghastly grinning of his moist black muzzle and white teeth, and the insolence of his crisp tail curled like a pastoral crook, all live and flourish. From an otherwise unaccountable association of him with a fiddle, we conclude that he was of French extraction, and his name Fidèle. He belonged to some female, chiefly inhabiting a back-parlour, whose life appears to us to have been consumed in sniffing, and in wearing a brown beaver bonnet. For her, he would sit up and balance cake upon his nose, and not eat it until twenty had been counted. To the best of our belief we were once called in to witness this performance; when, unable, even in his milder moments, to endure our presence, he instantly made at us, cake and all.

Why a something in mourning, called 'Miss Frost,' should still connect itself with our preparatory school, we are unable to say. We retain no impression of the beauty of Miss Frost—if she were beautiful; or of the mental fascinations of Miss Frost—if she were accomplished; yet her name and her black dress hold an enduring place in our remembrance. An equally impersonal boy, whose name has long since shaped itself unalterably into 'Master Mawls,' is not to be dislodged from our brain. Retaining no vindictive feeling towards Mawls—no feeling whatever, indeed—we infer that neither he nor we can have loved Miss Frost. Our first impression of Death and Burial is associated with this formless pair. We all three nestled awfully in a corner one wintry day, when the wind was blowing shrill, with Miss Frost's pinafore over our heads; and Miss Frost told us in a whisper about somebody being 'screwed down.' It is the only distinct recollection we preserve of these impalpable creatures, except a suspicion that the manners of Master Mawls were susceptible of much improvement. Generally speaking, we may observe that whenever we see a child intently occupied with its nose, to the exclusion of all other subjects of interest, our mind reverts, in a flash, to Master Mawls.

But, the School that was Our School before the Railroad came and overthrew it, was quite another sort of place. We were old enough to be put into Virgil when we went there, and to get Prizes for a variety of polishing on which the rust has long accumulated. It was a School of some celebrity in its neighbourhood—nobody could have said why—and we had the honour to attain and hold the eminent position of first boy. The master was supposed among us to know nothing, and one of the ushers was supposed to know everything. We are still inclined to think the first-named supposition perfectly correct.

We have a general idea that its subject had been in the leather trade, and had bought us—meaning Our School—of another proprietor who was immensely learned. Whether this belief had any real foundation, we are not likely ever to know now. The only branches of education with which he showed the least acquaintance, were, ruling and corporally punishing. He was always ruling ciphering-books with a bloated mahogany ruler, or smiting the palms of offenders with the same diabolical instrument, or viciously drawing a pair of pantaloons tight with one of his large hands, and caning the wearer with the other. We have no doubt whatever that this occupation was the principal solace of his existence.

A profound respect for money pervaded Our School, which was, of course, derived from its Chief. We remember an idiotic goggle-eyed boy, with a big head and half-crowns without end, who suddenly appeared as a parlour-boarder, and was rumoured to have come by sea from some mysterious part of the earth where his parents rolled in gold. He was usually called 'Mr.' by the Chief, and was said to feed in the parlour on steaks and gravy; likewise to drink currant wine. And he openly stated that if rolls and coffee were ever denied him at breakfast, he would write home to that unknown part of the globe from which he had come, and cause himself to be recalled to the regions of gold. He was put into no form or class, but learnt alone, as little as he liked—and he liked very little—and there was a belief among us that this was because he was too wealthy to be 'taken down.' His special treatment, and our vague association of him with the sea, and with storms, and sharks, and Coral Reefs occasioned the wildest legends to be circulated as his history. A tragedy in blank verse was written on the subject—if our memory does not deceive us, by the hand that now chronicles these recollections—in which his father figured as a Pirate, and was shot for a voluminous catalogue of atrocities: first imparting to his wife the secret of the cave in which his wealth was stored, and from which his only son's half-crowns now issued. Dumbledon (the boy's name) was represented as 'yet unborn' when his brave father met his fate; and the despair and grief of Mrs. Dumbledon at that calamity was movingly shadowed forth as having weakened the parlour-boarder's mind. This production was received with great favour, and was twice performed with closed doors in the dining-room. But, it got wind, and was seized as libellous, and brought the unlucky poet into severe affliction. Some two years afterwards, all of a sudden one day, Dumbledon vanished. It was whispered that the Chief himself had taken him down to the Docks, and re-shipped him for the Spanish Main; but nothing certain was ever known about his disappearance. At this hour, we cannot thoroughly disconnect him from California.

Our School was rather famous for mysterious pupils. There was another—a heavy young man, with a large double-cased silver watch, and a fat knife the handle of which was a perfect tool-box—who unaccountably appeared one day at a special desk of his own, erected close to that of the Chief, with whom he held familiar converse. He lived in the parlour, and went out for his walks, and never took the least notice of us—even of us, the first boy—unless to give us a deprecatory kick, or grimly to take our hat off and throw it away, when he encountered us out of doors, which unpleasant ceremony he always performed as he passed—not even condescending to stop for the purpose. Some of us believed that the classical attainments of this phenomenon were terrific, but that his penmanship and arithmetic were defective, and he had come there to mend them; others, that he was going to set up a school, and had paid the Chief 'twenty-five pound down,' for leave to see Our School at work. The gloomier spirits even said that he was going to buy us; against which contingency, conspiracies were set on foot for a general defection and running away. However, he never did that. After staying for a quarter, during which period, though closely observed, he was never seen to do anything but make pens out of quills, write small hand in a secret portfolio, and punch the point of the sharpest blade in his knife into his desk all over it, he too disappeared, and his place knew him no more.

There was another boy, a fair, meek boy, with a delicate complexion and rich curling hair, who, we found out, or thought we found out (we have no idea now, and probably had none then, on what grounds, but it was confidentially revealed from mouth to mouth), was the son of a Viscount who had deserted his lovely mother. It was understood that if he had his rights, he would be worth twenty thousand a year. And that if his mother ever met his father, she would shoot him with a silver pistol, which she carried, always loaded to the muzzle, for that purpose. He was a very suggestive topic. So was a young Mulatto, who was always believed (though very amiable) to have a dagger about him somewhere. But, we think they were both outshone, upon the whole, by another boy who claimed to have been born on the twenty-ninth of February, and to have only one birthday in five years. We suspect this to have been a fiction—but he lived upon it all the time he was at Our School.

The principal currency of Our School was slate pencil. It had some inexplicable value, that was never ascertained, never reduced to a standard.

614

To have a great hoard of it was somehow to be rich. We used to bestow it in charity, and confer it as a precious boon upon our chosen friends. When the holidays were coming, contributions were solicited for certain boys whose relatives were in India, and who were appealed for under the generic name of 'Holiday-stoppers,'—appropriate marks of remembrance that should enliven and cheer them in their homeless state. Personally, we always contributed these tokens of sympathy in the form of slate pencil, and always felt that it would be a comfort and a treasure to them.

Our School was remarkable for white mice. Red-polls, linnets, and even canaries, were kept in desks, drawers, hat-boxes, and other strange refuges for birds; but white mice were the favourite stock. The boys trained the mice, much better than the masters trained the boys. We recall one white mouse, who lived in the cover of a Latin dictionary, who ran up ladders, drew Roman chariots, shouldered muskets, turned wheels, and even made a very creditable appearance on the stage as the Dog of Montargis. He might have achieved greater things, but for having the misfortune to mistake his way in a triumphal procession to the Capitol, when he fell into a deep inkstand, and was dyed black and drowned. The mice were the occasion of some most ingenious engineering, in the construction of their houses and instruments of performance. The famous one belonged to a company of proprietors, some of whom have since made Railroads, Engines, and Telegraphs; the chairman has erected mills and bridges in New Zealand.

The usher at Our School, who was considered to know everything as opposed to the Chief, who was considered to know nothing, was a bony, gentle-faced, clerical-looking young man in rusty black. It was whispered that he was sweet upon one of Maxby's sisters (Maxby lived close by, and was a day pupil), and further that he 'favoured Maxby.' As we remember, he taught Italian to Maxby's sisters on half-holidays. He once went to the play with them, and wore a white waistcoat and a rose: which was considered among us equivalent to a declaration. We were of opinion on that occasion, that to the last moment he expected Maxby's father to ask him to dinner at five o'clock, and therefore neglected his own dinner at half-past one, and finally got none. We exaggerated in our imaginations the extent to which he punished Maxby's father's cold meat at supper; and we agreed to believe that he was elevated with wine and water when he came home. But, we all liked him; for he had a good knowledge of boys, and would have made it a much better school if he had had more power. He was writing master, mathematical master, English master, made out the bills, mended the pens, and did all sorts of things. He divided the little boys with the Latin master (they were smuggled through their rudimentary books, at odd times when there was nothing else to do), and he always called at parents' houses to inquire after sick boys, because he had gentlemanly manners. He was rather musical, and on some remote quarter-day had bought an old trombone; but a bit of it was lost, and it made the most extraordinary sounds when he sometimes tried to play it of an evening. His holidays never began (on account of the bills) until long after ours; but, in the summer vacations he used to take pedestrian excursions with a knapsack; and at Christmas time, he went to see his father at Chipping Norton, who we all said (on no authority) was a dairy-fed pork-butcher. Poor fellow! He was very low all day on Maxby's sister's wedding-day, and afterwards was thought to favour Maxby more than ever, though he had been expected to spite him. He has been dead these twenty years. Poor fellow!

Our remembrance of Our School, presents the Latin master as a colourless doubled-up near-sighted man with a crutch, who was always cold, and always putting onions into his ears for deafness, and always disclosing ends of flannel under all his garments, and almost always applying a ball of pocket-handkerchief to some part of his face with a screwing action round and round. He was a very good scholar, and took great pains where he saw intelligence and a desire to learn: otherwise, perhaps not. Our memory presents him (unless teased into a passion) with as little energy as colour—as having been worried and tormented into monotonous feebleness—as having had the best part of his life ground out of him in a Mill of boys. We remember with terror how he fell asleep one sultry afternoon with the little smuggled class before him, and awoke not when the footstep of the Chief fell heavy on the floor; how the Chief aroused him, in the midst of a dread silence, and said, 'Mr. Blinkins, are you ill, sir?' how he blushingly replied, 'Sir, rather so;' how the Chief retorted with severity, 'Mr. Blinkins, this is

616

no place to be ill in' (which was very, very true), and walked back solemn as the ghost in Hamlet, until, catching a wandering eye, he called that boy for inattention, and happily expressed his feelings towards the Latin master through the medium of a substitute.

There was a fat little dancing-master who used to come in a gig, and taught the more advanced among us hornpipes (as an accomplishment in great social demand in after life); and there was a brisk little French master who used to come in the sunniest weather, with a handleless umbrella, and to whom the Chief was always polite, because (as we believed), if the Chief offended him, he would instantly address the Chief in French, and for ever confound him before the boys with his inability to understand or reply.

There was besides, a serving man, whose name was Phil. Our retrospective glance presents Phil as a shipwrecked carpenter, cast away upon the desert island of a school, and carrying into practice an ingenious inkling of many trades. He mended whatever was broken, and made whatever was wanted. He was general glazier, among other things, and mended all the broken windows—at the prime cost (as was darkly rumoured among us) of ninepence, for every square charged three-and-six to parents. We had a high opinion of his mechanical genius, and generally held that the Chief 'knew something bad of him,' and on pain of divulgence enforced Phil to be his bondsman. We particularly remember that Phil had a sovereign contempt for learning: which engenders in us a respect for his sagacity, as it implies his accurate observation of the relative positions of the Chief and the ushers. He was an impenetrable man, who waited at table between whiles, and throughout 'the half' kept the boxes in severe custody. He was morose, even to the Chief, and never smiled, except at breaking-up, when, in acknowledgment of the toast, 'Success to Phil! Hooray!' he would slowly carve a grin out of his wooden face, where it would remain until we were all gone. Nevertheless, one time when we had the scarlet fever in the school, Phil nursed all the sick boys of his own accord, and was like a mother to them.

There was another school not far off, and of course Our School could have nothing to say to that school. It is mostly the way with schools, whether of boys or men. Well! the railway has swallowed up ours, and the locomotives now run smoothly over its ashes.

So fades and languishes, grows dim and dies,

All that this world is proud of,

- and is not proud of, too. It had little reason to be proud of Our School, and has done much better since in that way, and will do far better yet.

OUR VESTRY

We have the glorious privilege of being always in hot water if we like. We are a shareholder in a Great Parochial British Joint Stock Bank of Balderdash. We have a Vestry in our borough, and can vote for a vestryman—might even be a vestryman, mayhap, if we were inspired by a lofty and noble ambition. Which we are not.

Our Vestry is a deliberative assembly of the utmost dignity and importance. Like the Senate of ancient Rome, its awful gravity overpowers (or ought to overpower) barbarian visitors. It sits in the Capitol (we mean in the capital building erected for it), chiefly on Saturdays, and shakes the earth to its centre with the echoes of its thundering eloquence, in a Sunday paper.

To get into this Vestry in the eminent capacity of Vestryman, gigantic efforts are made, and Herculean exertions used. It is made manifest to the dullest capacity at every election, that if we reject Snozzle we are done for, and that if we fail to bring in Blunderbooze at the top of the poll, we are unworthy of the dearest rights of Britons. Flaming placards are rife on all the dead walls in the borough, public-houses hang out banners, hackney-cabs burst into full-grown flowers of type, and everybody is, or should be, in a paroxysm of anxiety.

At these momentous crises of the national fate, we are much assisted in our deliberations by two eminent volunteers; one of whom subscribes himself A Fellow Parishioner, the other, A Rate-Payer. Who they are, or what they are, or where they are, nobody knows; but, whatever one asserts, the other contradicts. They are both voluminous writers, indicting more epistles than Lord Chesterfield in a single week; and the greater part of their feelings are too big for utterance in anything less than capital letters. They require the additional aid of whole rows of notes of admiration, like balloons, to point their generous indignation; and they sometimes communicate a crushing severity to stars. As thus:

MEN OF MOONEYMOUNT.

Is it, or is it not, a * * * to saddle the parish with a debt of £2,745 6s. 9d., yet claim to be a RIGID ECONOMIST?

Is it, or is it not, a * * * to state as a fact what is proved to be both a moral and a PHYSICAL IMPOSSIBILITY?

Is it, or is it not, a * * * to call £2,745 6s. 9d. nothing; and nothing, something?

Do you, or do you not want a * * * TO REPRESENT YOU IN THE VESTRY?

Your consideration of these questions is recommended to you by

A Fellow Parishioner.

It was to this important public document that one of our first orators, Mr. Magg (of Little Winkling Street), adverted, when he opened the great debate of the fourteenth of November by saying, 'Sir, I hold in my hand an anonymous slander'—and when the interruption, with which he was at that point assailed by the opposite faction, gave rise to that memorable discussion on a point of order which will ever be remembered with interest by constitutional assemblies. In the animated debate to which we refer, no fewer than thirty-seven gentlemen, many of them of great eminence, including Mr. Wigsby (of Chumbledon Square), were seen upon their legs at one time; and it was on the same great occasion that Dogginson—regarded in our Vestry as 'a regular John Bull:' we believe, in consequence of his having always made up his mind on every subject without knowing anything about it— informed another gentleman of similar principles on the opposite side, that if he 'cheek'd him,' he would resort to the extreme measure of knocking his blessed head off.

This was a great occasion. But, our Vestry shines habitually. In asserting its own pre-eminence, for instance, it is very strong. On the least provocation, or on none, it will be clamorous to know whether it is to be 'dictated to,' or 'trampled on,' or 'ridden over rough-shod.' Its great watchword is

Self-government. That is to say, supposing our Vestry to favour any little harmless disorder like Typhus Fever, and supposing the Government of the country to be, by any accident, in such ridiculous hands, as that any of its authorities should consider it a duty to object to Typhus Fever—obviously an unconstitutional objection—then, our Vestry cuts in with a terrible manifesto about Self-government, and claims its independent right to have as much Typhus Fever as pleases itself. Some absurd and dangerous persons have represented, on the other hand, that though our Vestry may be able to 'beat the bounds' of its own parish, it may not be able to beat the bounds of its own diseases; which (say they) spread over the whole land, in an ever expanding circle of waste, and misery, and death, and widowhood, and orphanage, and desolation. But, our Vestry makes short work of any such fellows as these.

It was our Vestry—pink of Vestries as it is—that in support of its favourite principle took the celebrated ground of denying the existence of the last pestilence that raged in England, when the pestilence was raging at the Vestry doors. Dogginson said it was plums; Mr. Wigsby (of Chumbledon Square) said it was oysters; Mr. Magg (of Little Winkling Street) said, amid great cheering, it was the newspapers. The noble indignation of our Vestry with that un-English institution the Board of Health, under those circumstances, yields one of the finest passages in its history. It wouldn't hear of rescue. Like Mr. Joseph Miller's Frenchman, it would be drowned and nobody should save it. Transported beyond grammar by its kindled ire, it spoke in unknown tongues, and vented unintelligible bellowings, more like an ancient oracle than the modern oracle it is admitted on all hands to be. Rare exigencies produce rare things; and even our Vestry, new hatched to the woful time, came forth a greater goose than ever.

But this, again, was a special occasion. Our Vestry, at more ordinary periods, demands its meed of praise.

Our Vestry is eminently parliamentary. Playing at Parliament is its favourite game. It is even regarded by some of its members as a chapel of ease to the House of Commons: a Little Go to be passed first. It has its strangers' gallery, and its reported debates (see the Sunday paper before mentioned), and our Vestrymen are in and out of order, and on and off their legs, and above all are transcendently quarrelsome, after the pattern of the real original.

Our Vestry being assembled, Mr. Magg never begs to trouble Mr. Wigsby with a simple inquiry. He knows better than that. Seeing the honourable gentleman, associated in their minds with Chumbledon Square, in his place, he wishes to ask that honourable gentleman what the intentions of himself, and those with whom he acts, may be, on the subject of the paving of the district known as Piggleum Buildings? Mr. Wigsby replies (with his eye on next Sunday's paper) that in reference to the question which has been put to him by the honourable gentleman opposite, he must take leave to say, that if that honourable gentleman had had the courtesy to give him notice of that question, he (Mr. Wigsby) would have consulted with his colleagues in reference to the advisability, in the present state of the discussions on the new paving-rate, of answering that question. But, as the honourable gentleman has NOT had the courtesy to give him notice of that question (great cheering from the Wigsby interest), he must decline to give the honourable gentleman the satisfaction he requires. Mr. Magg, instantly rising to retort, is received with loud cries of 'Spoke!' from the Wigsby interest, and with cheers from the Magg side of the house. Moreover, five gentlemen rise to order, and one of them, in revenge for being taken no notice of, petrifies the assembly by moving that this Vestry do now adjourn; but, is persuaded to withdraw that awful proposal, in consideration of its tremendous consequences if persevered in. Mr. Magg, for the purpose of being heard, then begs to move, that you, sir, do now pass to the order of the day; and takes that opportunity of saying, that if an honourable gentleman whom he has in his eye, and will not demean himself by more particularly naming (oh, oh, and cheers), supposes that he is to be put down by clamour, that honourable gentleman—however supported he may be, through thick and thin, by a Fellow Parishioner, with whom he is well acquainted (cheers and counter-cheers, Mr. Magg being invariably backed by the Rate-Payer)—will find himself mistaken. Upon this, twenty members of our Vestry speak in succession concerning what the two great men have meant, until it appears, after an hour and twenty minutes, that neither of them meant anything. Then our Vestry begins business.

We have said that, after the pattern of the real original, our Vestry in playing at Parliament is transcendently quarrelsome. It enjoys a personal altercation above all things. Perhaps the most redoubtable case of this kind we have ever had—though we have had so many that it is difficult to decide— was that on which the last extreme solemnities passed between Mr. Tiddypot (of Gumption House) and Captain Banger (of Wilderness Walk).

In an adjourned debate on the question whether water could be regarded in the light of a necessary of life; respecting which there were great differences of opinion, and many shades of sentiment; Mr. Tiddypot, in a powerful burst of eloquence against that hypothesis, frequently made use of the expression that such and such a rumour had 'reached his ears.' Captain Banger, following him, and holding that, for purposes of ablution and refreshment, a pint of water per diem was necessary for every adult of the lower classes, and half a pint for every child, cast ridicule upon his address in a sparkling speech, and concluded by saying that instead of those rumours having reached the ears of the honourable gentleman, he rather thought the honourable gentleman's ears must have reached the rumours, in consequence of their well-known length. Mr. Tiddypot immediately rose, looked the honourable and gallant gentleman full in the face, and left the Vestry.

The excitement, at this moment painfully intense, was heightened to an acute degree when Captain Banger rose, and also left the Vestry. After a few moments of profound silence—one of those breathless pauses never to be forgotten—Mr. Chib (of Tucket's Terrace, and the father of the Vestry) rose. He said that words and looks had passed in that assembly, replete with consequences which every feeling mind must deplore. Time pressed. The sword was drawn, and while he spoke the scabbard might be thrown away. He moved that those honourable gentlemen who had left the Vestry be recalled, and required to pledge themselves upon their honour that this affair should go no farther. The motion being by a general union of parties unanimously agreed to (for everybody wanted to have the belligerents there, instead of out of sight: which was no fun at all), Mr. Magg was deputed to recover Captain Banger, and Mr. Chib himself to go in search of Mr. Tiddypot. The Captain was found in a conspicuous position, surveying the passing omnibuses from the top step of the front-door immediately adjoining the beadle's box; Mr.

Tiddypot made a desperate attempt at resistance, but was overpowered by Mr. Chib (a remarkably hale old gentleman of eighty-two), and brought back in safety.

Mr. Tiddypot and the Captain being restored to their places, and glaring on each other, were called upon by the chair to abandon all homicidal intentions, and give the Vestry an assurance that they did so. Mr. Tiddypot remained profoundly silent. The Captain likewise remained profoundly silent, saying that he was observed by those around him to fold his arms like Napoleon Buonaparte, and to snort in his breathing—actions but too expressive of gunpowder.

The most intense emotion now prevailed. Several members clustered in remonstrance round the Captain, and several round Mr. Tiddypot; but, both were obdurate. Mr. Chib then presented himself amid tremendous cheering, and said, that not to shrink from the discharge of his painful duty, he must now move that both honourable gentlemen be taken into custody by the beadle, and conveyed to the nearest police-office, there to be held to bail. The union of parties still continuing, the motion was seconded by Mr. Wigsby— on all usual occasions Mr. Chib's opponent—and rapturously carried with only one dissentient voice. This was Dogginson's, who said from his place 'Let 'em fight it out with fistes;' but whose coarse remark was received as it merited.

The beadle now advanced along the floor of the Vestry, and beckoned with his cocked hat to both members. Every breath was suspended. To say that a pin might have been heard to fall, would be feebly to express the all-absorbing interest and silence. Suddenly, enthusiastic cheering broke out from every side of the Vestry. Captain Banger had risen—being, in fact, pulled up by a friend on either side, and poked up by a friend behind.

The Captain said, in a deep determined voice, that he had every respect for that Vestry and every respect for that chair; that he also respected the honourable gentleman of Gumpton House; but, that he respected his honour more. Hereupon the Captain sat down, leaving the whole Vestry much affected. Mr. Tiddypot instantly rose, and was received with the same encouragement. He likewise said—and the exquisite art of this orator communicated to the observation an air of freshness and novelty—that he too had every respect for that Vestry; that he too had every respect for that chair. That he too respected the honourable and gallant gentleman of Wilderness Walk; but, that he too respected his honour more. 'Hows'ever,' added the distinguished Vestryman, 'if the honourable and gallant gentleman's honour is never more doubted and damaged than it is by me, he's all right.' Captain Banger immediately started up again, and said that after those observations, involving as they did ample concession to his honour without compromising the honour of the honourable gentleman, he would be wanting in honour as well as in generosity, if he did not at once repudiate all intention of wounding the honour of the honourable gentleman, or saying anything dishonourable to his honourable feelings. These observations were repeatedly interrupted by bursts of cheers. Mr. Tiddypot retorted that he well knew the spirit of honour by which the honourable and gallant gentleman was so honourably animated, and that he accepted an honourable explanation, offered in a way that did him honour; but, he trusted that the Vestry would consider that his (Mr. Tiddypot's) honour had imperatively demanded of him that painful course which he had felt it due to his honour to adopt. The Captain and Mr. Tiddypot then touched their hats to one another across the Vestry, a great many times, and it is thought that these proceedings (reported to the extent of several columns in next Sunday's paper) will bring them in as church-wardens next year.

All this was strictly after the pattern of the real original, and so are the whole of our Vestry's proceedings. In all their debates, they are laudably imitative of the windy and wordy slang of the real original, and of nothing that is better in it. They have head-strong party animosities, without any reference to the merits of questions; they tack a surprising amount of debate to a very little business; they set more store by forms than they do by substances:—all very like the real original! It has been doubted in our borough, whether our Vestry is of any utility; but our own conclusion is, that it is of the use to the Borough that a diminishing mirror is to a painter, as enabling it to perceive in a small focus of absurdity all the surface defects of the real original.

OUR BORE

It is unnecessary to say that we keep a bore. Everybody does. But, the bore whom we have the pleasure and honour of enumerating among our particular friends, is such a generic bore, and has so many traits (as it appears to us) in common with the great bore family, that we are tempted to make him the subject of the present notes. May he be generally accepted!

Our bore is admitted on all hands to be a good-hearted man. He may put fifty people out of temper, but he keeps his own. He preserves a sickly solid smile upon his face, when other faces are ruffled by the perfection he has attained in his art, and has an equable voice which never travels out of one key or rises above one pitch. His manner is a manner of tranquil interest. None of his opinions are startling. Among his deepest-rooted convictions, it may be mentioned that he considers the air of England damp, and holds that our lively neighbours—he always calls the French our lively neighbours—have the advantage of us in that particular. Nevertheless he is unable to forget that John Bull is John Bull all the world over, and that England with all her faults is England still.

Our bore has travelled. He could not possibly be a complete bore without having travelled. He rarely speaks of his travels without introducing, sometimes on his own plan of construction, morsels of the language of the country—which he always translates. You cannot name to him any little remote town in France, Italy, Germany, or Switzerland but he knows it well; stayed there a fortnight under peculiar circumstances. And talking of that little place, perhaps you know a statue over an old fountain, up a little court, which is the second—no, the third—stay—yes, the third turning on the right, after you come out of the Post-house, going up the hill towards the market? You don't know that statue? Nor that fountain? You surprise him! They are not usually seen by travellers (most extraordinary, he has never yet met with a single traveller who knew them, except one German, the most intelligent man he ever met in his life!) but he thought that YOU would have been the man to find them out. And then he describes them, in a circumstantial lecture half an hour long, generally delivered behind a door which is constantly being opened from the other side; and implores you, if you ever revisit that place, now do go and look at that statue and fountain!

Our bore, in a similar manner, being in Italy, made a discovery of a dreadful picture, which has been the terror of a large portion of the civilized world ever since. We have seen the liveliest men paralysed by it, across a broad dining-table. He was lounging among the mountains, sir, basking in the mellow influences of the climate, when he came to una piccola chiesa—a little church—or perhaps it would be more correct to say una piccolissima cappella—the smallest chapel you can possibly imagine—and walked in. There was nobody inside but a cieco—a blind man—saying his prayers, and a vecchio padre—old friar-rattling a money-box. But, above the head of that friar, and immediately to the right of the altar as you enter—to the right of the altar? No. To the left of the altar as you enter—or say near the centre—there hung a painting (subject, Virgin and Child) so divine in its expression, so pure and yet so warm and rich in its tone, so fresh in its touch, at once so glowing in its colour and so statuesque in its repose, that our bore cried out in ecstasy, 'That's the finest picture in Italy!' And so it is, sir. There is no doubt of it. It is astonishing that that picture is so little known. Even the painter is uncertain. He afterwards took Blumb, of the Royal Academy (it is to be observed that our bore takes none but eminent people to see sights, and that none but eminent people take our bore), and you never saw a man so affected in your life as Blumb was. He cried like a child! And then our bore begins his description in detail—for all this is introductory—and strangles his hearers with the folds of the purple drapery.

By an equally fortunate conjunction of accidental circumstances, it happened that when our bore was in Switzerland, he discovered a Valley, of that superb character, that Chamouni is not to be mentioned in the same breath with it. This is how it was, sir. He was travelling on a mule—had been in the saddle some days—when, as he and the guide, Pierre Blanquo: whom you may know, perhaps?—our bore is sorry you don't, because he's the only guide deserving of the name—as he and Pierre were descending, towards evening, among those everlasting snows, to the little village of La Croix, our bore observed a mountain track turning off sharply to the right. At first he was uncertain whether it was a track at all, and in fact, he said to Pierre, 'Qu'est que c'est donc, mon ami?—What is that, my friend? 'Où, monsieur?' said Pierre—'Where, sir?' 'Là!—there!' said our bore. 'Monsieur, ce n'est rien de tout—sir, it's nothing at all,' said Pierre. 'Allons!—Make haste. Il va neiget—it's going to snow!' But, our bore was not to be done in that way, and he firmly replied, 'I wish to go in that direction—je veux y aller. I am bent upon it—je suis déterminé. En avant!—go ahead!' In consequence of which firmness on our bore's part, they proceeded, sir, during two hours of evening, and three of moonlight (they waited in a cavern till the moon was up), along the slenderest track, overhanging perpendicularly the most awful gulfs, until they arrived, by a winding descent, in a valley that possibly, and he may say probably, was never visited by any stranger before. What a valley! Mountains piled on mountains, avalanches stemmed by pine forests; waterfalls, chalets, mountain-torrents, wooden bridges, every conceivable picture of Swiss scenery! The whole village turned out to receive our bore. The peasant girls kissed him, the men shook hands with him, one old lady of benevolent appearance wept upon his breast. He was conducted, in a primitive triumph, to the little inn: where he was taken ill next morning, and lay for six weeks, attended by the amiable hostess (the same benevolent old lady who had wept over night) and her charming daughter, Fanchette. It is nothing to say that they were attentive to him; they doted on him. They called him in their simple way, l'Ange Anglais—the English Angel. When our bore left the valley, there was not a dry eye in the place; some of the people attended him for miles. He begs and entreats of you as a personal favour, that if you ever go to Switzerland again (you have mentioned that your last visit was your twenty-third), you will go to that valley, and see Swiss scenery for the first time. And if you want really to know the pastoral people of Switzerland, and to understand them, mention, in that valley, our bore's name!

Our bore has a crushing brother in the East, who, somehow or other, was admitted to smoke pipes with Mehemet Ali, and instantly became an authority on the whole range of Eastern matters, from Haroun Alraschid to the present Sultan. He is in the habit of expressing mysterious opinions on this wide range of subjects, but on questions of foreign policy more particularly, to our bore, in letters; and our bore is continually sending bits of these letters to the newspapers (which they never insert), and carrying other bits about in his pocket-book. It is even whispered that he has been seen at the Foreign Office, receiving great consideration from the messengers, and having his card promptly borne into the sanctuary of the temple. The havoc committed in society by this Eastern brother is beyond belief. Our bore is always ready with him. We have known our bore to fall upon an intelligent young sojourner in the wilderness, in the first sentence of a narrative, and beat all confidence out of him with one blow of his brother. He became omniscient, as to foreign policy, in the smoking of those pipes with Mehemet Ali. The balance of power in Europe, the machinations of the Jesuits, the gentle and humanising influence of Austria, the position and prospects of that hero of the noble soul who is worshipped by happy France, are all easy reading to our bore's brother. And our bore is so provokingly self-denying about him! 'I don't pretend to more than a very general knowledge of these subjects myself,' says he, after enervating the intellects of several strong men, 'but these are my brother's opinions, and I believe he is known to be well-informed.'

The commonest incidents and places would appear to have been made special, expressly for our bore. Ask him whether he ever chanced to walk, between seven and eight in the morning, down St. James's Street, London, and he will tell you, never in his life but once. But, it's curious that that once was in eighteen thirty; and that as our bore was walking down the street you have just mentioned, at the hour you have just mentioned—half-past seven—or twenty minutes to eight. No! Let him be correct!—exactly a quarter before eight by the palace clock—he met a fresh-coloured, grey-haired, good-humoured looking gentleman, with a brown umbrella, who, as he passed him, touched his hat and said, 'Fine morning, sir, fine morning!'—William the Fourth!

Ask our bore whether he has seen Mr. Barry's new Houses of Parliament, and he will reply that he has not yet inspected them minutely, but, that you remind him that it was his singular fortune to be the last man to see the old Houses of Parliament before the fire broke out. It happened in this way. Poor John Spine, the celebrated novelist, had taken him over to South Lambeth to read to him the last few chapters of what was certainly his best book—as our bore told him at the time, adding, 'Now, my dear John, touch it, and you'll spoil it!'—and our bore was going back to the club by way of Millbank and Parliament Street, when he stopped to think of Canning, and look at the Houses of Parliament. Now, you know far more of the philosophy of Mind than our bore does, and are much better able to explain to him than he is to explain to you why or wherefore, at that particular time, the thought of fire should come into his head. But, it did. It did. He thought, What a national calamity if an edifice connected with so many associations should be consumed by fire! At that time there was not a single soul in the street but himself. All was quiet, dark, and solitary. After contemplating the building for a minute—or, say a minute and a half, not more—our bore proceeded on his way, mechanically repeating, What a national calamity if such an edifice, connected with such associations, should be destroyed by—A man coming towards him in a violent state of agitation completed the sentence, with the exclamation, Fire! Our bore looked round, and the whole structure was in a blaze.

In harmony and union with these experiences, our bore never went anywhere in a steamboat but he made either the best or the worst voyage ever known on that station. Either he overheard the captain say to himself, with his hands clasped, 'We are all lost!' or the captain openly declared to him that he had never made such a run before, and never should be able to do it again. Our bore was in that express train on that railway, when they made (unknown to the passengers) the experiment of going at the rate of a hundred to miles an hour. Our bore remarked on that occasion to the other people in the carriage, 'This is too fast, but sit still!' He was at the Norwich musical festival when the extraordinary echo for which science has been wholly unable to account, was heard for the first and last time. He and the bishop heard it at the same moment, and caught each other's eye. He was present at that illumination of St. Peter's, of which the Pope is known to have remarked, as he looked at it out of his window in the Vatican, 'O Cielo! Questa cosa non sara fatta, mai ancora, come questa—O Heaven! this thing will never be done again, like this!' He has seen every lion he ever saw, under some remarkably propitious circumstances. He knows there is no fancy in it, because in every case the showman mentioned the fact at the time, and congratulated him upon it.

At one period of his life, our bore had an illness. It was an illness of a dangerous character for society at large. Innocently remark that you are very well, or that somebody else is very well; and our bore, with a preface that one never knows what a blessing health is until one has lost it, is reminded of that illness, and drags you through the whole of its symptoms, progress, and treatment. Innocently remark that you are not well, or that somebody else is not well, and the same inevitable result ensues. You will learn how our bore felt a tightness about here, sir, for which he couldn't account, accompanied with a constant sensation as if he were being stabbed—or, rather, jobbed—that expresses it more correctly—jobbed—with a blunt knife. Well, sir! This went on, until sparks began to flit before his eyes, water-wheels to turn round in his head, and hammers to beat incessantly, thump, thump, thump, all down his back—along the whole of the spinal vertebræ. Our bore, when his sensations had come to this, thought it a duty he owed to himself to take advice, and he said, Now, whom shall I consult? He naturally thought of Callow, at that time one of the most eminent physicians in London, and he went to Callow. Callow said, 'Liver!' and prescribed rhubarb and calomel, low diet, and moderate exercise. Our bore went on with this treatment, getting worse every day, until he lost confidence in Callow, and went to Moon, whom half the town was then mad about. Moon was interested in the case; to do him justice he was very much interested in the case; and he said, 'Kidneys!' He altered the whole treatment, sir—gave strong acids, cupped, and blistered. This went on, our bore still getting worse every day, until he openly told Moon it would be a satisfaction to him if he would have a consultation with Clatter. The moment Clatter saw our bore, he said, 'Accumulation of fat about the heart!' Snugglewood, who was called in with him, differed, and said, 'Brain!' But, what they all agreed upon was, to lay our bore upon his back, to shave his head, to leech him, to administer enormous quantities of medicine, and to keep him low; so that he was reduced to a mere shadow, you wouldn't have known him, and nobody considered it possible that he could ever recover. This was his condition, sir, when he heard of Jilkins—at that period in a very small practice, and living in the upper part of a house in Great Portland Street; but still, you understand, with a rising reputation among the few people to whom he was known. Being in that condition in which a drowning man catches at a straw, our bore sent for Jilkins. Jilkins came. Our bore liked his eye, and said, 'Mr. Jilkins, I have a presentiment that you will do me good.' Jilkins's reply was characteristic of the man. It was, 'Sir, I mean to do you good.' This confirmed our bore's opinion of his eye, and they went into the case together—went completely into it. Jilkins then got up, walked across the room, came back, and sat down. His words were these. 'You have been humbugged. This is a case of indigestion, occasioned by deficiency of power in the Stomach. Take a mutton chop in half-an-hour, with a glass of the finest old sherry that can be got for money. Take two mutton chops to-morrow, and two glasses of the finest old sherry. Next day, I'll come again.' In a week our bore was on his legs, and Jilkins's success dates from that period!

Our bore is great in secret information. He happens to know many things that nobody else knows. He can generally tell you where the split is in the Ministry; he knows a great deal about the Queen; and has little anecdotes to relate of the royal nursery. He gives you the judge's private opinion of Sludge the murderer, and his thoughts when he tried him. He happens to know what such a man got by such a transaction, and it was fifteen thousand five hundred pounds, and his income is twelve thousand a year. Our bore is also great in mystery. He believes, with an exasperating appearance of profound meaning, that you saw Parkins last Sunday?—Yes, you did.—Did he say anything particular?—No, nothing particular.—Our bore is surprised at that.—Why?—Nothing. Only he understood that Parkins had come to tell you something.—What about?—Well! our bore is not at liberty to mention what about. But, he believes you will hear that from Parkins himself, soon, and he hopes it may not surprise you as it did him. Perhaps, however, you never heard about Parkins's wife's sister?—No.—Ah! says our bore, that explains it!

Our bore is also great in argument. He infinitely enjoys a long humdrum, drowsy interchange of words of dispute about nothing. He considers that it

632

strengthens the mind, consequently, he 'don't see that,' very often. Or, he would be glad to know what you mean by that. Or, he doubts that. Or, he has always understood exactly the reverse of that. Or, he can't admit that. Or, he begs to deny that. Or, surely you don't mean that. And so on. He once advised us; offered us a piece of advice, after the fact, totally impracticable and wholly impossible of acceptance, because it supposed the fact, then eternally disposed of, to be yet in abeyance. It was a dozen years ago, and to this hour our bore benevolently wishes, in a mild voice, on certain regular occasions, that we had thought better of his opinion.

The instinct with which our bore finds out another bore, and closes with him, is amazing. We have seen him pick his man out of fifty men, in a couple of minutes. They love to go (which they do naturally) into a slow argument on a previously exhausted subject, and to contradict each other, and to wear the hearers out, without impairing their own perennial freshness as bores. It improves the good understanding between them, and they get together afterwards, and bore each other amicably. Whenever we see our bore behind a door with another bore, we know that when he comes forth, he will praise the other bore as one of the most intelligent men he ever met. And this bringing us to the close of what we had to say about our bore, we are anxious to have it understood that he never bestowed this praise on us.

A MONUMENT OF FRENCH FOLLY

It was profoundly observed by a witty member of the Court of Common Council, in Council assembled in the City of London, in the year of our Lord one thousand eight hundred and fifty, that the French are a frog-eating people, who wear wooden shoes.

We are credibly informed, in reference to the nation whom this choice spirit so happily disposed of, that the caricatures and stage representations which were current in England some half a century ago, exactly depict their present condition. For example, we understand that every Frenchman, without exception, wears a pigtail and curl-papers. That he is extremely sallow, thin, long-faced, and lantern-jawed. That the calves of his legs are invariably undeveloped; that his legs fail at the knees, and that his shoulders are always higher than his ears. We are likewise assured that he rarely tastes any food but soup maigre, and an onion; that he always says, 'By Gar! Aha! Vat you tell me, sare?' at the end of every sentence he utters; and that the true generic name of his race is the Mounseers, or the Parly-voos. If he be not a dancing-master, or a barber, he must be a cook; since no other trades but those three are congenial to the tastes of the people, or permitted by the Institutions of the country. He is a slave, of course. The ladies of France (who are also slaves) invariably have their heads tied up in Belcher handkerchiefs, wear long earrings, carry tambourines, and beguile the weariness of their yoke by singing in head voices through their noses—principally to barrel-organs.

It may be generally summed up, of this inferior people, that they have no idea of anything.

Of a great Institution like Smithfield, they are unable to form the least conception. A Beast Market in the heart of Paris would be regarded an impossible nuisance. Nor have they any notion of slaughter-houses in the midst of a city. One of these benighted frog-eaters would scarcely understand your meaning, if you told him of the existence of such a British bulwark.

It is agreeable, and perhaps pardonable, to indulge in a little self-complacency when our right to it is thoroughly established. At the present time, to be rendered memorable by a final attack on that good old market which is the (rotten) apple of the Corporation's eye, let us compare ourselves, to our national delight and pride as to these two subjects of slaughter-house and beast-market, with the outlandish foreigner.

The blessings of Smithfield are too well understood to need recapitulation; all who run (away from mad bulls and pursuing oxen) may read. Any market-day they may be beheld in glorious action. Possibly the merits of our slaughter-houses are not yet quite so generally appreciated.

Slaughter-houses, in the large towns of England, are always (with the exception of one or two enterprising towns) most numerous in the most densely crowded places, where there is the least circulation of air. They are often underground, in cellars; they are sometimes in close back yards; sometimes (as in Spitalfields) in the very shops where the meat is sold. Occasionally, under good private management, they are ventilated and clean. For the most part, they are unventilated and dirty; and, to the reeking walls, putrid fat and other offensive animal matter clings with a tenacious hold. The busiest slaughter-houses in London are in the neighbourhood of Smithfield, in Newgate Market, in Whitechapel, in Newport Market, in Leadenhall Market, in Clare Market. All these places are surrounded by houses of a poor description, swarming with inhabitants. Some of them are close to the worst burial-grounds in London. When the slaughter-house is below the ground, it is a common practice to throw the sheep down areas, neck and crop—which is exciting, but not at all cruel. When it is on the level surface, it is often extremely difficult of approach. Then, the beasts have to be worried, and goaded, and pronged, and tail-twisted, for a long time before they can be got in—which is entirely owing to their natural obstinacy. When it is not difficult of approach, but is in a foul condition, what they see and scent makes them still more reluctant to enter—which is their natural obstinacy again. When they do get in at last, after no trouble and suffering to speak of (for, there is nothing in the previous journey into the heart of London, the night's endurance in Smithfield, the struggle out again, among the crowded multitude, the coaches, carts, waggons, omnibuses, gigs, chaises, phaetons, cabs, trucks, dogs, boys, whoopings, roarings, and ten thousand other distractions), they are represented to be in a most unfit state to be killed, according to microscopic examinations made of their fevered blood by one of the most distinguished physiologists in the world, Professor Owen—but that's humbug. When they are killed, at last, their reeking carcases are hung in impure air, to become, as the same Professor will explain to you, less nutritious and more unwholesome—but he is only an uncommon counsellor, so don't mind him. In half a quarter of a mile's length of Whitechapel, at one time, there shall be six hundred newly slaughtered oxen hanging up, and seven hundred sheep—but, the more the merrier—proof of prosperity. Hard by Snow Hill and Warwick Lane, you shall see the little children, inured to sights of brutality from their birth, trotting along the alleys, mingled with troops of horribly busy pigs, up to their ankles in blood—but it makes the young rascals hardy. Into the imperfect sewers of this overgrown city, you shall have the immense mass of corruption, engendered by these practices, lazily thrown out of sight, to rise, in poisonous gases, into your house at night, when your sleeping children will most readily absorb them, and to find its languid way, at last, into the river that you drink—but, the French are a frog-eating people who wear wooden shoes, and it's O the roast beef of England, my boy, the jolly old English roast beef.

It is quite a mistake—a newfangled notion altogether—to suppose that there is any natural antagonism between putrefaction and health. They know better than that, in the Common Council. You may talk about Nature, in her wisdom, always warning man through his sense of smell, when he draws near to something dangerous; but, that won't go down in the City. Nature very often don't mean anything. Mrs. Quickly says that prunes are ill for a green wound; but whosoever says that putrid animal substances are ill for a green wound, or for robust vigour, or for anything or for anybody, is a humanity-monger and a humbug. Britons never, never, never, &c., therefore. And prosperity to cattle-driving, cattle-slaughtering, bone-crushing, blood-boiling, trotter-scraping, tripe-dressing, paunch-cleaning, gut-spinning, hide-preparing, tallow-melting, and other salubrious proceedings, in the midst of hospitals, churchyards, workhouses, schools, infirmaries, refuges, dwellings, provision-shops nurseries, sick-beds, every stage and baiting-place in the journey from birth to death!

These uncommon counsellors, your Professor Owens and fellows, will contend that to tolerate these things in a civilised city, is to reduce it to a worse condition than Bruce found to prevail in Abyssinia. For there (say they) the jackals and wild dogs came at night to devour the offal; whereas, here there are no such natural scavengers, and quite as savage customs. Further, they will demonstrate that nothing in Nature is intended to be wasted, and that besides the waste which such abuses occasion in the articles of health and life—main sources of the riches of any community—they lead to a prodigious waste of changing matters, which might, with proper preparation, and under scientific direction, be safely applied to the increase of the fertility of the land. Thus (they argue) does Nature ever avenge infractions of her beneficent laws, and so surely as Man is determined to warp any of her blessings into curses, shall they become curses, and shall he suffer heavily. But, this is cant. Just as it is cant of the worst description to say to the London Corporation, 'How can you exhibit to the people so plain a spectacle of dishonest equivocation, as to claim the right of holding a market in the midst of the great city, for one of your vested privileges, when you know that when your last market holding charter was granted to you by King Charles the First, Smithfield stood in the Suburbs of London, and is in that very charter so described in those five words?'—which is certainly true, but has nothing to do with the question.

Now to the comparison, in these particulars of civilisation, between the capital of England, and the capital of that frog-eating and wooden-shoe wearing country, which the illustrious Common Councilman so sarcastically settled.

In Paris, there is no Cattle Market. Cows and calves are sold within the city, but, the Cattle Markets are at Poissy, about thirteen miles off, on a line of railway; and at Sceaux, about five miles off. The Poissy market is held every Thursday; the Sceaux market, every Monday. In Paris, there are no slaughter-houses, in our acceptation of the term. There are five public Abattoirs—within the walls, though in the suburbs—and in these all the slaughtering for the city must be performed. They are managed by a Syndicat or Guild of Butchers, who confer with the Minister of the Interior on all matters affecting the trade, and who are consulted when any new regulations are contemplated for its government. They are, likewise, under the vigilant superintendence of the police. Every butcher must be licensed: which proves him at once to be a slave, for we don't license butchers in England—we only license apothecaries, attorneys, post-masters, publicans, hawkers, retailers of tobacco, snuff, pepper, and vinegar—and one or two other little trades, not worth mentioning. Every arrangement in connexion with the slaughtering and sale of meat, is matter of strict police regulation. (Slavery again, though we certainly have a general sort of Police Act here.)

But, in order that the reader may understand what a monument of folly these frog-eaters have raised in their abattoirs and cattle-markets, and may compare it with what common counselling has done for us all these years, and would still do but for the innovating spirit of the times, here follows a short account of a recent visit to these places:

It was as sharp a February morning as you would desire to feel at your fingers' ends when I turned out—tumbling over a chiffonier with his little basket and rake, who was picking up the bits of coloured paper that had been swept out, over-night, from a Bon-Bon shop—to take the Butchers' Train to Poissy. A cold, dim light just touched the high roofs of the Tuileries which have seen such changes, such distracted crowds, such riot and bloodshed; and they looked as calm, and as old, all covered with white frost, as the very Pyramids. There was not light enough, yet, to strike upon the towers of Notre Dame across the water; but I thought of the dark pavement of the old Cathedral as just beginning to be streaked with grey; and of the lamps in the 'House of God,' the Hospital close to it, burning low and being quenched; and of the keeper of the Morgue going about with a fading lantern, busy in the arrangement of his terrible waxwork for another sunny day.

The sun was up, and shining merrily when the butchers and I, announcing our departure with an engine shriek to sleepy Paris, rattled away for the Cattle Market. Across the country, over the Seine, among a forest of scrubby trees—the hoar frost lying cold in shady places, and glittering in the light—and here we are—at Poissy! Out leap the butchers, who have been chattering all the way like madmen, and off they straggle for the Cattle Market (still chattering, of course, incessantly), in hats and caps of all shapes, in coats and blouses, in calf-skins, cow-skins, horse-skins, furs, shaggy mantles, hairy coats, sacking, baize, oil-skin, anything you please that will keep a man and a butcher warm, upon a frosty morning.

Many a French town have I seen, between this spot of ground and Strasburg or Marseilles, that might sit for your picture, little Poissy! Barring the details of your old church, I know you well, albeit we make acquaintance, now, for the first time. I know your narrow, straggling, winding streets, with a kennel in the midst, and lamps slung across. I know your picturesque street-corners, winding up-hill Heaven knows why or where! I know your tradesmen's inscriptions, in letters not quite fat enough; your barbers' brazen basins dangling over little shops; your Cafés and Estaminets, with cloudy bottles of stale syrup in the windows, and pictures of crossed billiard cues outside. I know this identical grey horse with his tail rolled up in a knot like the 'back hair' of an untidy woman, who won't be shod, and who makes himself heraldic by clattering across the street on his hind-legs, while twenty voices shriek and growl at him as a Brigand, an accursed Robber, and an everlastingly-doomed Pig. I know your sparkling town-fountain, too, my Poissy, and am glad to see it near a cattle-market, gushing so freshly, under the auspices of a gallant little sublimated Frenchman wrought in metal, perched upon the top. Through all the land of France I know this unswept room at The Glory, with its peculiar smell of beans and coffee, where the butchers crowd about the stove, drinking the thinnest of wine from the smallest of tumblers; where the thickest of coffee-cups mingle with the longest of loaves, and the weakest of lump sugar; where Madame at the counter easily acknowledges the homage of all entering and departing butchers; where the billiard-table is covered up in the midst like a great bird-cake—but the bird may sing by-and-by!

A bell! The Calf Market! Polite departure of butchers. Hasty payment and departure on the part of amateur Visitor. Madame reproaches Ma'amselle for too fine a susceptibility in reference to the devotion of a Butcher in a bear-skin. Monsieur, the landlord of The Glory, counts a double handful of sous, without an unobliterated inscription, or an undamaged crowned head, among them.

There is little noise without, abundant space, and no confusion. The open area devoted to the market is divided into three portions: the Calf Market, the Cattle Market, the Sheep Market. Calves at eight, cattle at ten, sheep at mid-day. All is very clean.

The Calf Market is a raised platform of stone, some three or four feet high, open on all sides, with a lofty overspreading roof, supported on stone columns, which give it the appearance of a sort of vineyard from Northern Italy. Here, on the raised pavement, lie innumerable calves, all bound hind-legs and fore-legs together, and all trembling violently—perhaps with cold, perhaps with fear, perhaps with pain; for, this mode of tying, which seems to be an absolute superstition with the peasantry, can hardly fail to cause great suffering. Here, they lie, patiently in rows, among the straw, with their stolid faces and inexpressive eyes, superintended by men and women, boys and girls; here they are inspected by our friends, the butchers, bargained for, and bought. Plenty of time; plenty of room; plenty of good humour. 'Monsieur Francois in the bear-skin, how do you do, my friend? You come from Paris by train? The fresh air does you good. If you are in want of three or four fine calves this market morning, my angel, I, Madame Doche, shall be happy to deal with you. Behold these calves, Monsieur Francois! Great Heaven, you are doubtful! Well, sir, walk round and look about you. If you find better for the money, buy them. If not, come to me!' Monsieur Francois goes his way leisurely, and keeps a wary eye upon the stock. No other butcher jostles Monsieur Francois; Monsieur Francois jostles no other butcher. Nobody is flustered and aggravated. Nobody is savage. In the midst of the country blue frocks and red handkerchiefs, and the butchers' coats, shaggy, furry, and hairy: of calf-skin, cow-skin, horse-skin, and bear-skin: towers a cocked hat and a blue cloak. Slavery! For our Police wear great-coats and glazed hats.

But now the bartering is over, and the calves are sold. 'Ho! Gregoire, Antoine, Jean, Louis! Bring up the carts, my children! Quick, brave infants! Hola! Hi!'

The carts, well littered with straw, are backed up to the edge of the raised pavement, and various hot infants carry calves upon their heads, and dexterously pitch them in, while other hot infants, standing in the carts, arrange the calves, and pack them carefully in straw. Here is a promising young calf, not sold, whom Madame Doche unbinds. Pardon me, Madame Doche, but I fear this mode of tying the four legs of a quadruped together, though strictly à la mode, is not quite right. You observe, Madame Doche, that the cord leaves deep indentations in the skin, and that the animal is so cramped at first as not to know, or even remotely suspect that he is unbound, until you are so obliging as to kick him, in your delicate little way, and pull his tail like a bell-rope. Then, he staggers to his knees, not being able to stand, and stumbles about like a drunken calf, or the horse at Franconi's, whom you may have seen, Madame Doche, who is supposed to have been mortally wounded in battle. But, what is this rubbing against me, as I apostrophise Madame Doche? It is another heated infant with a calf upon his head. 'Pardon, Monsieur, but will you have the politeness to allow me to pass?' 'Ah, sir, willingly. I am vexed to obstruct the way.' On he staggers, calf and all, and makes no allusion whatever either to my eyes or limbs.

Now, the carts are all full. More straw, my Antoine, to shake over these top rows; then, off we will clatter, rumble, jolt, and rattle, a long row of us, out of the first town-gate, and out at the second town-gate, and past the empty sentry-box, and the little thin square bandbox of a guardhouse, where nobody seems to live: and away for Paris, by the paved road, lying, a straight, straight line, in the long, long avenue of trees. We can neither choose our road, nor our pace, for that is all prescribed to us. The public convenience demands that our carts should get to Paris by such a route, and no other (Napoleon had leisure to find that out, while he had a little war with the world upon his hands), and woe betide us if we infringe orders.

Drovers of oxen stand in the Cattle Market, tied to iron bars fixed into posts of granite. Other droves advance slowly down the long avenue, past the second town-gate, and the first town-gate, and the sentry-box, and the bandbox, thawing the morning with their smoky breath as they come along. Plenty of room; plenty of time. Neither man nor beast is driven out of his wits by coaches, carts, waggons, omnibuses, gigs, chaises, phaetons, cabs, trucks, boys, whoopings, roarings, and multitudes. No tail-twisting is necessary—no iron pronging is necessary. There are no iron prongs here. The market for cattle is held as quietly as the market for calves. In due time, off the cattle go to Paris; the drovers can no more choose their road, nor their time, nor the numbers they shall drive, than they can choose their hour for dying in the course of nature.

Sheep next. The sheep-pens are up here, past the Branch Bank of Paris established for the convenience of the butchers, and behind the two pretty fountains they are making in the Market. My name is Bull: yet I think I should like to see as good twin fountains—not to say in Smithfield, but in England anywhere. Plenty of room; plenty of time. And here are sheep-dogs, sensible as ever, but with a certain French air about them—not without a suspicion of dominoes—with a kind of flavour of moustache and beard—demonstrative dogs, shaggy and loose where an English dog would be tight and close—not so troubled with business calculations as our English drovers' dogs, who have always got their sheep upon their minds, and think about their work, even resting, as you may see by their faces; but, dashing, showy, rather unreliable dogs: who might worry me instead of their legitimate charges if they saw occasion—and might see it somewhat suddenly.

The market for sheep passes off like the other two; and away they go, by their allotted road to Paris. My way being the Railway, I make the best of it at twenty miles an hour; whirling through the now high-lighted landscape; thinking that the inexperienced green buds will be wishing, before long, they had not been tempted to come out so soon; and wondering who lives in this or that château, all window and lattice, and what the family may have for breakfast this sharp morning.

After the Market comes the Abattoir. What abattoir shall I visit first? Montmartre is the largest. So I will go there.

The abattoirs are all within the walls of Paris, with an eye to the receipt of the octroi duty; but, they stand in open places in the suburbs, removed from the press and bustle of the city. They are managed by the Syndicat or Guild of Butchers, under the inspection of the Police. Certain smaller items of the revenue derived from them are in part retained by the Guild for the payment of their expenses, and in part devoted by it to charitable purposes in connexion with the trade. They cost six hundred and eighty thousand pounds; and they return to the city of Paris an interest on that outlay, amounting to nearly six and a-half per cent.

Here, in a sufficiently dismantled space is the Abattoir of Montmartre, covering nearly nine acres of ground, surrounded by a high wall, and looking from the outside like a cavalry barrack. At the iron gates is a small functionary in a large cocked hat. 'Monsieur desires to see the abattoir? Most certainly.' State being inconvenient in private transactions, and Monsieur being already aware of the cocked hat, the functionary puts it into a little official bureau which it almost fills, and accompanies me in the modest attire—as to his head—of ordinary life.

Many of the animals from Poissy have come here. On the arrival of each drove, it was turned into yonder ample space, where each butcher who had bought, selected his own purchases. Some, we see now, in these long perspectives of stalls with a high over-hanging roof of wood and open tiles rising above the walls. While they rest here, before being slaughtered, they are required to be fed and watered, and the stalls must be kept clean. A stated amount of fodder must always be ready in the loft above; and the supervision is of the strictest kind. The same regulations apply to sheep and calves; for which, portions of these perspectives are strongly railed off. All the buildings are of the strongest and most solid description.

After traversing these lairs, through which, besides the upper provision for ventilation just mentioned, there may be a thorough current of air from opposite windows in the side walls, and from doors at either end, we traverse the broad, paved, court-yard until we come to the slaughter-houses. They are all exactly alike, and adjoin each other, to the number of eight or nine together, in blocks of solid building. Let us walk into the first.

It is firmly built and paved with stone. It is well lighted, thoroughly aired, and lavishly provided with fresh water. It has two doors opposite each other; the first, the door by which I entered from the main yard; the second, which is opposite, opening on another smaller yard, where the sheep and calves are killed on benches. The pavement of that yard, I see, slopes downward to a gutter, for its being more easily cleansed. The slaughter-house is fifteen feet high, sixteen feet and a-half wide, and thirty-three feet long. It is fitted with a powerful windlass, by which one man at the handle can bring the head of an ox down to the ground to receive the blow from the pole-axe that is to fell him—with the means of raising the carcass and keeping it suspended during the after-operation of dressing—and with hooks on which carcasses can hang, when completely prepared, without touching the walls. Upon the pavement of this first stone chamber, lies an ox scarcely dead. If I except the blood draining from him, into a little stone well in a corner of the pavement, the place is free from offence as the Place de la Concorde. It is infinitely purer and cleaner, I know, my friend the functionary, than the Cathedral of Notre Dame. Ha, ha! Monsieur is pleasant, but, truly, there is reason, too, in what he says.

I look into another of these slaughter-houses. 'Pray enter,' says a gentleman in bloody boots. 'This is a calf I have killed this morning. Having a little time upon my hands, I have cut and punctured this lace pattern in the coats of his stomach. It is pretty enough. I did it to divert myself.'—'It is beautiful, Monsieur, the slaughterer!' He tells me I have the gentility to say so.

I look into rows of slaughter-houses. In many, retail dealers, who have come here for the purpose, are making bargains for meat. There is killing enough, certainly, to satiate an unused eye; and there are steaming carcasses enough, to suggest the expediency of a fowl and salad for dinner; but, everywhere, there is an orderly, clean, well-systematised routine of work in progress—horrible work at the best, if you please; but, so much the greater reason why it should be made the best of. I don't know (I think I have observed, my name is Bull) that a Parisian of the lowest order is particularly delicate, or that his nature is remarkable for an infinitesimal infusion of ferocity; but, I do know, my potent, grave, and common counselling Signors, that he is forced, when at this work, to submit himself to a thoroughly good system, and to make an Englishman very heartily ashamed of you.

Here, within the walls of the same abattoir, in other roomy and commodious buildings, are a place for converting the fat into tallow and packing it for market—a place for cleansing and scalding calves' heads and sheep's feet—a place for preparing tripe—stables and coach-houses for the butchers—innumerable conveniences, aiding in the diminution of offensiveness to its lowest possible point, and the raising of cleanliness and supervision to their highest. Hence, all the meat that goes out of the gate is sent away in clean covered carts. And if every trade connected with the slaughtering of animals were obliged by law to be carried on in the same place, I doubt, my friend, now reinstated in the cocked hat (whose civility these two francs imperfectly acknowledge, but appear munificently to repay), whether there could be better regulations than those which are carried out at the Abattoir of Montmartre. Adieu, my friend, for I am away to the other side of Paris, to the Abattoir of Grenelle! And there I find exactly the same thing on a smaller scale, with the addition of a magnificent Artesian well, and a different sort of conductor, in the person of a neat little woman with neat little eyes, and a neat little voice, who picks her neat little way among the bullocks in a very neat little pair of shoes and stockings.

Such is the Monument of French Folly which a foreigneering people have erected, in a national hatred and antipathy for common counselling wisdom. That wisdom, assembled in the City of London, having distinctly refused, after a debate of three days long, and by a majority of nearly seven to one, to associate itself with any Metropolitan Cattle Market unless it be held in the midst of the City, it follows that we shall lose the inestimable advantages of common counselling protection, and be thrown, for a market, on our own wretched resources. In all human probability we shall thus come, at last, to erect a monument of folly very like this French monument. If that be done, the consequences are obvious. The leather trade will be ruined, by the introduction of American timber, to be manufactured into shoes for the fallen English; the Lord Mayor will be required, by the popular voice, to live entirely on frogs; and both these changes will (how, is not at present quite clear, but certainly somehow or other) fall on that unhappy landed interest which is always being killed, yet is always found to be alive—and kicking.

FOOTNOTES

[415] Give a bill

[426] Three months' imprisonment as reputed thieves.

About Author

Dickens's literary success began with the 1836 serial publication of The Pickwick Papers. Within a few years he had become an international literary celebrity, famous for his humour, satire, and keen observation of character and society. His novels, most published in monthly or weekly instalments, pioneered the serial publication of narrative fiction, which became the dominant Victorian mode for novel publication. Cliffhanger endings in his serial publications kept readers in suspense. The instalment format allowed Dickens to evaluate his audience's reaction, and he often modified his plot and character development based on such feedback. For example, when his wife's chiropodist expressed distress at the way Miss Mowcher in David Copperfield seemed to reflect her disabilities, Dickens improved the character with positive features. His plots were carefully constructed, and he often wove elements from topical events into his narratives. Masses of the illiterate poor chipped in ha'pennies to have each new monthly episode read to them, opening up and inspiring a new class of readers.

Dickens was regarded as the literary colossus of his age. His 1843 novella, A Christmas Carol, remains popular and continues to inspire adaptations in every artistic genre. Oliver Twist and Great Expectations are also frequently adapted, and, like many of his novels, evoke images of early Victorian London. His 1859 novel, A Tale of Two Cities, set in London and Paris, is his best-known work of historical fiction. Dickens has been praised by fellow writers—from Leo Tolstoy to George Orwell, G. K. Chesterton and Tom Wolfe—for his realism, comedy, prose style, unique characterisations, and social criticism. On the other hand, Oscar Wilde, Henry James, and Virginia Woolf complained of a lack of psychological depth, loose writing, and a vein of sentimentalism. The term Dickensian is used to describe something that is reminiscent of Dickens and his writings, such as poor social conditions or comically repulsive characters.

Early years

Charles John Huffam Dickens was born on 7 February 1812, at 1 Mile End Terrace (now 393 Commercial Road), Landport in Portsea Island (Portsmouth), the second of eight children of Elizabeth Dickens (née Barrow; 1789–1863) and John Dickens (1785–1851). His father was a clerk in the Navy Pay Office and was temporarily stationed in the district. He asked Christopher Huffam, rigger to His Majesty's Navy, gentleman, and head of an established firm, to act as godfather to Charles. Huffam is thought to be the inspiration for Paul Dombey, the owner of a shipping company in Dickens's novel Dombey and Son (1848).

In January 1815, John Dickens was called back to London, and the family moved to Norfolk Street, Fitzrovia. When Charles was four, they relocated to Sheerness, and thence to Chatham, Kent, where he spent his formative years until the age of 11. His early life seems to have been idyllic, though he thought himself a "very small and not-over-particularly-taken-care-of boy".

Charles spent time outdoors, but also read voraciously, including the picaresque novels of Tobias Smollett and Henry Fielding, as well as Robinson Crusoe and Gil Blas. He read and reread The Arabian Nights and the Collected Farces of Elizabeth Inchbald. He retained poignant memories of childhood, helped by an excellent memory of people and events, which he used in his writing. His father's brief work as a clerk in the Navy Pay Office afforded him a few years of private education, first at a dame school, and then at a school run by William Giles, a dissenter, in Chatham.

This period came to an end in June 1822, when John Dickens was recalled to Navy Pay Office headquarters at Somerset House, and the family (except for Charles, who stayed behind to finish his final term of work) moved to Camden Town in London. The family had left Kent amidst rapidly mounting debts, and, living beyond his means, John Dickens was forced by his creditors into the Marshalsea debtors' prison in Southwark, London in 1824. His wife and youngest children joined him there, as was the practice at the time. Charles, then 12 years old, boarded with Elizabeth Roylance, a family friend, at 112 College Place, Camden Town. Roylance was "a reduced [impoverished] old lady, long known to our family", whom Dickens later immortalised, "with a few alterations and embellishments", as "Mrs Pipchin" in Dombey and Son. Later, he lived in a back-attic in the house of an agent for the Insolvent Court, Archibald Russell, "a fat, good-natured, kind old gentleman... with a quiet old wife" and lame son, in Lant Street in Southwark. They provided the inspiration for the Garlands in The Old Curiosity Shop.

On Sundays—with his sister Frances, free from her studies at the Royal Academy of Music—he spent the day at the Marshalsea. Dickens later used the prison as a setting in Little Dorrit. To pay for his board and to help his family, Dickens was forced to leave school and work ten-hour days at Warren's Blacking Warehouse, on Hungerford Stairs, near the present Charing Cross railway station, where he earned six shillings a week pasting labels on pots of boot blacking. The strenuous and often harsh working conditions made a lasting impression on Dickens and later influenced his fiction and essays, becoming the foundation of his interest in the reform of socio-economic and labour conditions, the rigours of which he believed were unfairly borne by the poor. He later wrote that he wondered "how I could have been so easily cast away at such an age". As he recalled to John Forster (from The Life of Charles Dickens):

The blacking-warehouse was the last house on the left-hand side of the way, at old Hungerford Stairs. It was a crazy, tumble-down old house, abutting of course on the river, and literally overrun with rats. Its wainscoted rooms, and its rotten floors and staircase, and the old grey rats swarming down in the cellars, and the sound of their squeaking and scuffling coming up the stairs at all times, and the dirt and decay of the place, rise up visibly before me, as if I were there again. The counting-house was on the first floor, looking over the coal-barges and the river. There was a recess in it, in which I was to sit and work. My work was to cover the pots of paste-blacking; first with a piece of oil-paper, and then with a piece of blue paper; to tie them round with a string; and then to clip the paper close and neat, all round, until it looked as smart as a pot of ointment from an apothecary's shop. When a certain number of grosses of pots had attained this pitch of perfection, I was to paste on each a printed label, and then go on again with more pots. Two or three other boys were kept at similar duty down-stairs on similar wages. One of them came up, in a ragged apron and a paper cap, on the first Monday morning, to show me the trick of using the string and tying the knot. His name was Bob Fagin; and I took the liberty of using his name, long afterwards, in Oliver Twist.

When the warehouse was moved to Chandos Street in the smart, busy district of Covent Garden the boys worked in a room in which the window gave onto the street and little audiences gathered and watched them at work—in Dickens biographer Simon Callow's estimation, the public display was "a new refinement added to his misery".

A few months after his imprisonment, John Dickens's mother, Elizabeth Dickens, died and bequeathed him £450. On the expectation of this legacy, Dickens was released from prison. Under the Insolvent Debtors Act, Dickens arranged for payment of his creditors, and he and his family left Marshalsea, for the home of Mrs Roylance.

Charles's mother, Elizabeth Dickens, did not immediately support his removal from the boot-blacking warehouse. This influenced Dickens's view that a father should rule the family, and a mother find her proper sphere inside the home: "I never afterwards forgot, I never shall forget, I never can forget, that my mother was warm for my being sent back". His mother's failure to request his return was a factor in his dissatisfied attitude towards women.

Righteous indignation stemming from his own situation and the conditions under which working-class people lived became major themes of his works, and it was this unhappy period in his youth to which he alluded in his favourite, and most autobiographical, novel, David Copperfield: "I had no advice, no counsel, no encouragement, no consolation, no assistance, no support, of any kind, from anyone, that I can call to mind, as I hope to go to heaven!"

Dickens was eventually sent to the Wellington House Academy in Camden Town, where he remained until March 1827, having spent about two years there. He did not consider it to be a good school: "Much of the haphazard, desultory teaching, poor discipline punctuated by the headmaster's sadistic brutality, the seedy ushers and general run-down atmosphere, are embodied in Mr Creakle's Establishment in David Copperfield."

Dickens worked at the law office of Ellis and Blackmore, attorneys, of Holborn Court, Gray's Inn, as a junior clerk from May 1827 to November 1828. He was a gifted mimic and impersonated those around him: clients, lawyers, and clerks. He went to theatres obsessively—he claimed that for at least three years he went to the theatre every single day. His favourite actor was Charles Mathews, and Dickens learnt his monopolylogues, (farces in which Mathews played every character), by heart. Then, having learned Gurney's system of shorthand in his spare time, he left to become a freelance reporter. A distant relative, Thomas Charlton, was a freelance reporter at Doctors' Commons, and Dickens was able to share his box there to report the legal proceedings for nearly four years. This education was to inform works such as Nicholas Nickleby, Dombey and Son, and especially Bleak House—whose vivid portrayal of the machinations and bureaucracy of the legal system did much to enlighten the general public and served as a vehicle for dissemination of Dickens's own views regarding, particularly, the heavy burden on the poor who were forced by circumstances to "go to law".

In 1830, Dickens met his first love, Maria Beadnell, thought to have been the model for the character Dora in David Copperfield. Maria's parents disapproved of the courtship and ended the relationship by sending her to school in Paris.

Journalism and early novels

In 1832, at age 20, Dickens was energetic and increasingly self-confident. He enjoyed mimicry and popular entertainment, lacked a clear, specific sense of what he wanted to become, and yet knew he wanted fame. Drawn to the theatre—he became an early member of the Garrick — he landed an acting audition at Covent Garden, where the manager George Bartley and the actor Charles Kemble were to see him. Dickens prepared meticulously and decided to imitate the comedian Charles Mathews, but ultimately he missed the audition because of a cold. Before another opportunity arose, he had set out on his career as a writer. In 1833, he submitted his first story, "A Dinner at Poplar Walk", to the London periodical Monthly Magazine.

William Barrow, a brother of his mother, offered him a job on The Mirror of Parliament and he worked in the House of Commons for the first time early in 1832. He rented rooms at Furnival's Inn and worked as a political journalist, reporting on Parliamentary debates, and he travelled across Britain to cover election campaigns for the Morning Chronicle. His journalism, in the form of sketches in periodicals, formed his first collection of pieces, published in 1836: Sketches by Boz—Boz being a family nickname he employed as a pseudonym for some years. Dickens apparently adopted it from the nickname "Moses", which he had given to his youngest brother Augustus Dickens, after a character in Oliver Goldsmith's The Vicar of Wakefield. When pronounced by anyone with a head cold, "Moses" became "Boses"—later shortened to Boz. Dickens's own name was considered "queer" by a contemporary critic, who wrote in 1849: "Mr Dickens, as if in revenge for his own queer name, does bestow still queerer ones upon his fictitious creations." He contributed to and edited journals throughout his literary career. In January 1835, the Morning Chronicle launched an evening edition, under the editorship of the Chronicle's music critic, George Hogarth. Hogarth invited Dickens to contribute Street Sketches and Dickens became a regular visitor to his Fulham house, excited by Hogarth's friendship with a hero of his, Walter Scott, and enjoying the company of Hogarth's three daughters—Georgina, Mary, and nineteen-year-old Catherine.

Dickens made rapid progress both professionally and socially. He began a friendship with William Harrison Ainsworth, the author of the highwayman novel Rookwood (1834), whose bachelor salon in Harrow Road had become the meeting place for a set that included Daniel Maclise, Benjamin Disraeli, Edward Bulwer-Lytton, and George Cruikshank. All these became his friends and collaborators, with the exception of Disraeli, and he met his first publisher, John Macrone, at the house. The success of Sketches by Boz led to a proposal from publishers Chapman and Hall for Dickens to supply text to match Robert Seymour's engraved illustrations in a monthly letterpress. Seymour committed suicide after the second instalment, and Dickens, who wanted to write a connected series of sketches, hired "Phiz" to provide the engravings (which were reduced from four to two per instalment) for the story. The resulting story became The Pickwick Papers, and though the first few episodes were not successful, the introduction of the Cockney character Sam Weller in the fourth episode (the first to be illustrated by Phiz) marked a sharp climb in its popularity. The final instalment sold 40,000 copies.

In November 1836, Dickens accepted the position of editor of Bentley's Miscellany, a position he held for three years, until he fell out with the owner. In 1836 as he finished the last instalments of The Pickwick Papers, he began writing the beginning instalments of Oliver Twist—writing as many as 90 pages a month—while continuing work on Bentley's and also writing four plays, the production of which he oversaw. Oliver Twist, published in 1838, became one of Dickens's better known stories, and was the first Victorian novel with a child protagonist.

On 2 April 1836, after a one-year engagement, and between episodes two and three of The Pickwick Papers, Dickens married Catherine Thomson Hogarth (1816–1879), the daughter of George Hogarth, editor of the Evening Chronicle. They were married in St. Luke's Church, Chelsea, London. After a brief honeymoon in Chalk in Kent, the couple returned to lodgings at Furnival's Inn. The first of their ten children, Charley, was born in January 1837, and a few months later the family set up home in Bloomsbury at 48 Doughty Street, London, (on which Charles had a three-year lease at £80 a year) from 25 March 1837 until December 1839. Dickens's younger brother Frederick and Catherine's 17-year-old sister Mary, moved in with them. Dickens became very attached to Mary, and she died in his arms after a brief illness in 1837. Unusually for Dickens, as a consequence of his shock, he stopped working, and he and Kate stayed at a little farm on Hampstead Heath for a fortnight. Dickens idealised Mary—the character he fashioned after her, Rose Maylie, he found he could not now kill, as he had planned, in his fiction, and, according to Ackroyd, he drew on memories of her for his later descriptions of Little Nell and Florence Dombey. His grief was so great that he was unable to meet the deadline for the June instalment of Pickwick Papers and had to cancel the Oliver Twist instalment that month as well. The time in Hampstead was the occasion for a growing bond between Dickens and John Forster to develop and Forster soon became his unofficial business manager, and the first to read his work.

His success as a novelist continued. The young Queen Victoria read both Oliver Twist and Pickwick, staying up until midnight to discuss them. Nicholas Nickleby (1838–39), The Old Curiosity Shop (1840–41) and, finally, his first historical novel, Barnaby Rudge: A Tale of the Riots of 'Eighty, as part of the Master Humphrey's Clock series (1840–41), were all published in monthly instalments before being made into books.

In the midst of all his activity during this period, there was discontent with his publishers and John Macrone was bought off, while Richard Bentley signed over all his rights in Oliver Twist. Other signs of a certain restlessness and discontent emerge—in Broadstairs he flirted with Eleanor Picken, the young fiancée of his solicitor's best friend, and one night grabbed her and ran with her down to the sea. He declared they were both to drown there in the "sad sea waves". She finally got free but afterwards kept her distance. In June 1841 he precipitously set out on a two-month tour of Scotland and then, in September 1841, telegraphed Forster that he had decided to go to America. Master Humphrey's Clock was shut down, though Dickens was still keen on the idea of the weekly magazine, a form he liked, a liking that had begun with his childhood reading of the eighteenth-century magazines Tatler and The Spectator.

Dickens was perturbed by the return to power of the Tories, whom Dickens described as "people whom, politically, I despise and abhor." He had been tempted to stand for the Liberals in Reading, but decided against it due to financial straits. He wrote three anti-Tory verse satires ("The Fine Old English Gentleman", "The Quack Doctor's Proclamation", and "Subjects for Painters") which were published in The Examiner.

First visit to the United States

On 22 January 1842, Dickens and his wife arrived in Boston, Massachusetts aboard the RMS Britannia during their first trip to the United States and Canada. At this time Georgina Hogarth, another sister of Catherine, joined the Dickens household, now living at Devonshire Terrace, Marylebone, to care for the young family they had left behind. She remained with them as housekeeper, organiser, adviser, and friend until Dickens's death in 1870. Dickens modeled the character of Agnes Wickfield after Georgina and Mary.

He described his impressions in a travelogue, American Notes for General Circulation. Dickens includes in Notes a powerful condemnation of slavery, which he had attacked as early as The Pickwick Papers, correlating the emancipation of the poor in England with the abolition of slavery abroad citing newspaper accounts of runaway slaves disfigured by their masters. In spite of the abolitionist sentiments gleaned from his trip to America, some modern commentators have pointed out inconsistencies in Dickens's views on racial inequality, for instance, he has been criticized for his subsequent acquiescence in Governor Eyre's harsh crackdown during the 1860s Morant Bay rebellion in Jamaica and his failure to join other British progressives in condemning it. From Richmond, Virginia, Dickens returned to Washington, D.C., and started a trek westward to St. Louis, Missouri. While there, he expressed a desire to see an American prairie before returning east. A group of 13 men then set out with Dickens to visit Looking Glass Prairie, a trip 30 miles into Illinois.

During his American visit, Dickens spent a month in New York City, giving lectures, raising the question of international copyright laws and the pirating of his work in America. He persuaded a group of twenty-five writers, headed by Washington Irving, to sign a petition for him to take to Congress, but the press were generally hostile to this, saying that he should be grateful for his popularity and that it was mercenary to complain about his work being pirated.

The popularity he gained caused a shift in his self-perception according to critic Kate Flint, who writes that he "found himself a cultural commodity, and its circulation had passed out his control", causing him to become interested in and delve into themes of public and personal personas in the next novels. She writes that he assumed a role of "influential commentator", publicly and in his fiction, evident in his next few books. His trip to the U.S. ended with a trip to Canada: Niagara Falls, Toronto, Kingston and Montreal where he appeared on stage in light comedies.

Soon after his return to England, Dickens began work on the first of his Christmas stories, A Christmas Carol, written in 1843, which was followed by The Chimes in 1844 and The Cricket on the Hearth in 1845. Of these, A Christmas Carol was most popular and, tapping into an old tradition, did much to promote a renewed enthusiasm for the joys of Christmas in Britain and America. The seeds for the story became planted in Dickens's mind during a trip to Manchester to witness the conditions of the manufacturing workers there. This, along with scenes he had recently witnessed at the Field Lane Ragged School, caused Dickens to resolve to "strike a sledge hammer blow" for the poor. As the idea for the story took shape and the writing began in earnest, Dickens became engrossed in the book. He later wrote that as the tale unfolded he "wept and laughed, and wept again" as he "walked about the black streets of London fifteen or twenty miles many a night when all sober folks had gone to bed."

After living briefly in Italy (1844), Dickens travelled to Switzerland (1846), where he began work on Dombey and Son (1846–48). This and David Copperfield (1849–50) mark a significant artistic break in Dickens's career as his novels became more serious in theme and more carefully planned than his early works.

At about this time, he was made aware of a large embezzlement at the firm where his brother, Augustus, worked (John Chapman & Co.). It had been carried out by Thomas Powell, a clerk, who was on friendly terms with Dickens and who had acted as mentor to Augustus when he started work. Powell was also an author and poet and knew many of the famous writers of the day. After further fraudulent activities, Powell fled to New York and published a book called The Living Authors of England with a chapter on Charles Dickens, who was not amused by what Powell had written. One item that seemed to have annoyed him was the assertion that he had based the character of Paul Dombey (Dombey and Son) on Thomas Chapman, one of the principal partners at John Chapman & Co. Dickens immediately sent a letter to Lewis Gaylord Clark, editor of the New York literary magazine The Knickerbocker, saying that Powell was a forger and thief. Clark published the letter in the New-York Tribune, and several other papers picked up on the story. Powell began proceedings to sue these publications, and Clark was arrested. Dickens, realising that he had acted in haste, contacted John Chapman & Co. to seek written confirmation of Powell's guilt. Dickens did receive a reply confirming Powell's embezzlement, but once the directors realised this information might have to be produced in court, they refused to make further disclosures. Owing to the difficulties of providing evidence in America to support his accusations, Dickens eventually made a private settlement with Powell out of court.

Philanthropy

Angela Burdett Coutts, heir to the Coutts banking fortune, approached Dickens in May 1846 about setting up a home for the redemption of fallen women of the working class. Coutts envisioned a home that would replace the punitive regimes of existing institutions with a reformative environment conducive to education and proficiency in domestic household chores. After initially resisting, Dickens eventually founded the home, named "Urania Cottage", in the Lime Grove section of Shepherds Bush, which he managed for ten years, setting the house rules, reviewing the accounts and interviewing prospective residents. Emigration and marriage were central to Dickens's agenda for the women on leaving Urania Cottage, from which it is estimated that about 100 women graduated between 1847 and 1859.

Death

On 8 June 1870, Dickens suffered another stroke at his home after a full day's work on Edwin Drood. He never regained consciousness, and the next day, five years to the day after the Staplehurst rail crash, he died at Gads Hill Place. Biographer Claire Tomalin has suggested Dickens was actually in Peckham when he suffered the stroke, and his mistress Ellen Ternan and her maids had him taken back to Gad's Hill so the public would not know the truth about their relationship. Contrary to his wish to be buried at Rochester Cathedral "in an inexpensive, unostentatious, and strictly private manner", he was laid to rest in the Poets' Corner of Westminster Abbey. A printed epitaph circulated at the time of the funeral reads:

To the Memory of Charles Dickens (England's most popular author) who died at his residence, Higham, near Rochester, Kent, 9 June 1870, aged 58 years. He was a sympathiser with the poor, the suffering, and the oppressed; and by his death, one of England's greatest writers is lost to the world.

His last words were: "On the ground", in response to his sister-in-law Georgina's request that he lie down. On Sunday, 19 June 1870, five days after Dickens was buried in the Abbey, Dean Arthur Penrhyn Stanley delivered a memorial elegy, lauding "the genial and loving humorist whom we now mourn", for showing by his own example "that even in dealing with the darkest scenes and the most degraded characters, genius could still be clean, and mirth could be innocent". Pointing to the fresh flowers that adorned the novelist's grave, Stanley assured those present that "the spot would thenceforth be a sacred one with both the New World and the Old, as that of the representative of literature, not of this island only, but of all who speak our English tongue."

In his will, drafted more than a year before his death, Dickens left the care of his £80,000 estate to his longtime colleague John Forster and his "best and truest friend" Georgina Hogarth who, along with Dickens's two sons, also received a tax-free sum of £8,000 (about £800,000 in present terms). Although Dickens and his wife had been separated for several years at the time of his death, he provided her with an annual income of £600 and made her similar allowances in his will. He also bequeathed £19 19s to each servant in his employment at the time of his death. (Source: Wikipedia)

9 789353 859107